COLD IS THE GRAVE
&
THE SUMMER THAT
NEVER WAS

Peter Robinson grew up in Yorkshire, and now lives in Canada.

His critically acclaimed Inspector Banks series has won numerous awards in Britain, the United States, Canada and Europe.

PETER
ROBINSON

COLD IS THE GRAVE

&

THE SUMMER THAT
NEVER WAS

PAN BOOKS

Cold is the Grave first published 2001 by Macmillan.
First published in paperback by Pan Books 2001.
The Summer That Never Was first published 2003 by Macmillan.
First published in paperback by Pan Books 2004.

This omnibus first published 2005 by Pan Books
an imprint of Pan Macmillan Ltd
Pan Macmillan, 20 New Wharf Road, London N1 9RR
Basingstoke and Oxford
Associated companies throughout the world
www.panmacmillan.com

ISBN 0 330 44377 1

1 3 5 7 9 8 6 4 2

A CIP catalogue record for this book is available from
the British Library.

Printed and bound in Great Britain by
Mackays of Chatham plc, Chatham, Kent

COLD IS THE GRAVE

For Sheila

ACKNOWLEDGEMENTS

First, many thanks to those who read and commented on the manuscript throughout its development: in particular, Sheila Halladay, Dominick Abel, Patricia Lande Grader, Beverley Cousins, Erika Schmid and Mary Adachi. Also, many thanks to Robert Barnard for his inimitably valuable and entertaining comments.

While I frequently tweak police procedure for dramatic purposes, any accuracy I may display in this area is entirely due to my conversations with Area Commander Phil Gormley, Detective Inspector Alan Young and Detective Inspector Claire Stevens, all of Thames Valley Police, and Detective Sergeant Keith Wright, of Nottingham CID. Any mistakes are my own.

The wind it doth blow hard
And the cold rain down doth rain
And cold, cold is the grave
Wherein my love is lain

Traditional folk ballad

1

'Mummy! Mummy! Come here.'

Rosalind carried on stuffing the wild mushroom, olive oil, garlic and parsley mixture between the skin and the flesh of the chicken, the way she had learned in her recent course on the art of French cuisine. 'Mummy can't come right now,' she shouted back. 'She's busy.'

'But, Mummy! You've got to come. It's our lass.'

Where on earth did he learn such common language? Rosalind wondered. Every term they forked out a fortune in fees to send him to the best school Yorkshire had to offer, and still he ended up sounding like some vulgar tyke. Perhaps if they lived down south again, the situation would improve. 'Benjamin,' she called back, 'I told you. Mummy's busy. Daddy has an important dinner tonight and Mummy has to prepare.'

Rosalind didn't mind cooking – in fact, she had taken several courses and quite enjoyed them – but just for a moment, as she spoke, she wished she had been able to say that 'cook' was preparing the meal and that she was busy deciding what to wear. But they had no cook, only a cleaning lady who came in once a week. It wasn't that they couldn't afford it, but simply that her husband drew the line at such extravagance. Honestly, Rosalind sometimes thought, anyone would imagine he was a born Yorkshireman himself instead of just living here.

'But it *is* her!' Benjamin persisted. 'It's our lass. She's got no clothes on.'

Rosalind frowned and put aside her knife. What on earth

could he be talking about? Benjamin was only eight, and she knew from experience that he had a very active imagination. She even worried that it might hold him back in life. Over-imaginative types, she had found, tend towards idleness and daydreaming; they don't get on with more profitable activities.

'Mummy, hurry up!'

Rosalind felt just the slightest tingle of apprehension, as if something were about to change for ever in her universe. Shaking off the feeling, she wiped her hands of the oily stuffing, took a quick sip of gin and tonic, then walked towards the study where Benjamin had been playing on the computer. As she did so, she heard the front door open and her husband call out that he was home. Early. She frowned. Was he checking up on her?

Ignoring him for the moment, she went to see what on earth Benjamin was talking about.

'Look,' the boy said as she walked into the room. 'It *is* our lass.' He pointed at the computer screen.

'Don't talk like that,' Rosalind said. 'I've told you before. It's common.'

Then she looked.

At first, she was simply shocked to see the screen filled with the image of a naked woman. How had Benjamin stumbled onto such a site? He wasn't even old enough to understand what he had found.

Then, as she leaned over his shoulder and peered more closely at the screen, she gasped. He was right. She was looking at a picture of her daughter, Emily, naked as the day she was born, but with considerably more curves, a tattoo and a wispy patch of blonde pubic hair between her legs. That it was her Emily, there was no mistake; the teardrop-shaped birthmark on the inside of her left thigh proved it.

Rosalind ran her hand through her hair. What was this all about? What was happening? She glanced briefly at the URL on top of the screen. She had a photographic memory, so she knew she wouldn't forget it.

'See,' said Benjamin. 'It is our lass, isn't it. What's she doing without any clothes on, Mummy?'

Then Rosalind panicked. My God, *he* mustn't see this. Emily's father. He mustn't be allowed to see it. It would destroy him. Quickly, she reached towards the mouse, but before her fingers could click on it, a deep voice behind her told her it was too late.

'What on earth's going on?' he asked mildly, putting a fatherly hand on his son's shoulder.

Then, after the briefest of silences, Rosalind heard the sharp intake of breath and knew that he had the answer.

His hand tightened and Benjamin flinched. 'Daddy, you're hurting me.'

But Chief Constable Jeremiah Riddle was oblivious to his son's pain. 'My God!' he gasped, pointing at the screen. 'Is that who I think it is?'

Detective Chief Inspector Alan Banks paused over his holdall, wondering whether he should take the leather jacket or the windcheater. There wasn't room for both. He wasn't sure how cold it would be. Probably no different from Yorkshire, he guessed. At most, perhaps a couple of degrees warmer. Still, you never could tell with November. In the end, he decided he *could* take both. He folded the windcheater and put it on top of the shirts he had already packed, then he pressed down hard on the contents before dragging the reluctant zip shut. It seemed a lot for just one weekend away from home, but it all fitted into one not-too-heavy bag. He would wear his leather jacket on the journey.

All he had to do now was choose a book and a few tapes. He probably wouldn't need them, but he didn't like to travel anywhere without something to read and something to listen to in case of delays or emergencies.

It was a lesson he had learned the hard way, having once spent four hours in the casualty department of a large London hospital on a Saturday night waiting to have six stitches sewn beside his right eye. All that time, he had held the gauze pad to staunch the bleeding and watched the endless supply of drug overdoses, attempted suicides, heart-attack victims and road accidents going in before him. That their wounds were far more serious and merited more urgent treatment than his minor cut, Banks never had a moment's doubt, but he wished to hell there had been something to read in the dingy waiting area other than a copy of the previous day's *Daily Mirror*. The person who had read it before him had even filled in the crossword. *In ink*.

But tomorrow he was going to Paris with his daughter, Tracy, for a long weekend of art galleries, museums and walks, of sumptuous dinners in small, Left Bank restaurants and idle beers at zinc-topped counters in Montmartre, looking out on the crowds passing by. They were going to take the Eurostar, which Banks had managed to book practically for free through a special newspaper offer. After all, it *was* November, and most people preferred Lanzarote to a wet weekend in Paris. He probably wouldn't need much in the way of music or books, except when he was alone in his room before bed, but he decided to err on the side of caution.

Banks carried the holdall downstairs and dug out a couple of extra batteries from the sideboard drawer. He slipped them in the side pouch, along with the Walkman itself, then picked out tapes he had made of his Cassandra Wilson, Dawn Upshaw and Lucinda Williams CDs. Three more different women's voices and styles you probably couldn't find anywhere on earth, but he liked them all, and between them they covered a wide range of moods. He cast an eye over the low bookshelf and picked out Simenon's *Maigret and the Hundred Gibbets*. He didn't usually read crime novels, but the title had caught his eye and someone had once told him that he had a lot in common with Maigret. Besides, he assumed that it was set in Paris.

When Banks had finished packing, he poured himself a couple of fingers of Laphroaig and put on Bill Evans's *Waltz for Debby* CD. Then he sat in his armchair beside the shaded reading lamp, balanced the whisky on the arm and put his feet up as 'My Foolish Heart' made its hesitant progress. A few lumps of peat burnt in the fireplace, its smell harmonizing with the smoky bite of the Islay malt on his tongue.

But too much smoke seemed to be drifting from the fireplace into the room. Banks wondered if he needed a chimney sweep, as a fire probably hadn't been lit in that grate for a long time. He had no idea how to find a sweep, nor did he even know if such an exotic creature still existed. He remembered being fascinated as a child when the chimney sweep came, and his mother covered everything in the room with old sheets. Banks was allowed to watch the strange, soot-faced man fit the extensions on his long thick brush as he pushed it up the tall chimney, but he had to leave the room before the real work began. Later, when he read about the Victorian practice of sending young boys naked up the chimneys, he always wondered about that chimney sweep, if he had ever done anything like that. In the end, he realized the man couldn't have been old enough to have been alive so long ago, no matter how ancient he had seemed to the awestruck young boy.

He decided that the chimney was fine, and it was probably just the wind blowing some smoke back down. He could hear it howling around the thick walls, rattling the loose window in the spare bedroom upstairs, spattering the panes with rain. Since there had been so much rain lately, Banks could also hear the rushing of Gratly Falls outside his cottage. They were nothing grand, only a series of shallow terraces, none more than four or five feet high, that ran diagonally through the village where the beck ran down the daleside to join the River Swain in Helmthorpe. But the music changed constantly and proved a great delight to Banks, especially when he was lying in bed having trouble getting to sleep.

Glad he didn't have to go out again that evening, Banks sat and sipped his single malt, listening to the familiar lyrical opening of 'Waltz for Debby'. His mind drifted to the problem that had been looming larger and larger ever since his last case, which had been a one-off job designed to make him fail and look like a fool.

He hadn't failed, and consequently Chief Constable Riddle, who had hated Banks from the start, was now even more pissed off at him than ever. Banks found himself back in the career doldrums, chained to his desk and with no prospect of action in the foreseeable future. It was getting to be a bore.

And he could see only one way out.

Loath as Banks was to leave Yorkshire, especially after so recently buying the cottage, he was fast coming to admit that his days here seemed numbered. Last week, after thinking long and hard, he had put in his application to the National Crime Squad, which had been designed to target organized crime. As a DCI, Banks would hardly be involved in undercover work, but he *would* be in a position to run operations and enjoy the adrenaline high when a big catch finally landed. The job would also involve travel, tracking British criminals who operated from headquarters in Holland, the Dordogne and Spain.

Banks knew he didn't have a good enough educational background for the job, lacking a degree, but he did have the experience, and he thought that might still count for something, despite Riddle. He knew he could do the 'hard sums', the language, number and management tests necessary for the job, and he thought he could count on excellent references from everyone else he had worked with in Yorkshire, including his immediate commanding officer, Detective Superintendent Gristhorpe, and the Director of Human Resources, Millicent Cummings. He only hoped that the negative report he was bound to get from Riddle would seem suspicious by its difference.

There was another reason for the change, too. Banks had thought a lot about his estranged wife, Sandra, over the past couple of months, and he had come to believe that their separation might be only temporary. A major change in his circumstances, such as a posting to the NCS, would certainly be of benefit. It would mean moving somewhere else, maybe back to London, and Sandra loved London. He felt there was a real chance to put things right now, put the silliness of the past year behind them. Banks had had his brief romance with Annie Cabbot, and Sandra hers with Sean. That Sandra was still living with Sean didn't weigh unduly on his mind. People often drifted along in relationships, lacking the courage or the initiative to go it alone. He was certain that she would come to see things differently when he presented her with his plan for the future.

When the telephone rang at nine o'clock, startling him out of Bill Evans's deft keyboard meanderings, he thought at first that it might be Tracy. He hoped she hadn't changed her mind about the weekend; he needed to talk to her about the future, to enlist her help in getting Sandra back.

It wasn't Tracy. It was Chief Constable Jeremiah 'Jimmy' Riddle, the very reason Banks had gone so far as to contemplate selling his cottage and leaving the county.

'Banks?'

Banks gritted his teeth. 'Sir?'

Riddle paused. 'I'd like to ask you a favour.'

Banks's jaw dropped. 'A favour?'

'Yes. Do you think . . . I mean, would you mind dropping by the house? It's very important. I wouldn't ask otherwise. Not on such a wretched night as this.'

Banks's mind reeled. Riddle had *never* spoken to him in such a polite manner before, with such a fragile edge to his voice. What on earth was going on? Another trick?

'It's late, sir,' Banks said. 'I'm tired, and I'm supposed to be—'

'Look, I'm asking you for a favour, man. My wife and I have had to cancel a very important dinner party at the last minute because of this. Can't you just for once put aside your bloody-mindedness and oblige me?'

That sounded more like the Jimmy Riddle of old. Banks was on the verge of telling him to fuck off when the CC's tone changed once again and threw him off balance. 'Please, Banks,' Riddle said. 'There's something I need to talk to you about. Something urgent. Don't worry. This isn't a trick. I'm not out to put one over on you. I give you my word. I honestly need your help.'

Surely even Riddle wouldn't stoop to pulling a stunt like this solely to humiliate him. Now Banks was curious, and he knew he would go. If he were the kind of man who could ignore a call so full of mystery, he had no business being a copper in the first place. He didn't want to go out into the foul night, didn't want to leave his Laphroaig, Bill Evans and the crackling peat fire, but he knew he had to. He put his glass aside, glad that he had drunk only the one small whisky all day.

'All right,' he said, reaching for the pencil and paper beside the telephone. 'But you'd better tell me where you live and give me directions. I don't believe I've ever been invited to your home before.'

Riddle lived about halfway between Eastvale and Northallerton, which meant about an hour's drive for Banks in good weather, but well over that tonight. The rain was coming down in buckets; his windscreen wipers worked overtime the whole way, and there were times when he could hardly see more than a few yards ahead. It was only two days before Bonfire Night, and the piles of wood and discarded furniture were getting soaked on the village greens.

The Riddle house was a listed building, called the Old Mill

because it had been built originally as a mill by Cistercian monks from the nearby abbey. Made of limestone, with a flagstone roof, it stood beside the mill-race, which came rushing down through the garden. The old stone barn on the other side of the house had been converted into a garage.

As Banks drove up the short gravel drive and pulled up, he noticed that there were lights showing in two of the downstairs windows, while the rest of the place was in darkness. Almost before he could knock, the door jerked open and he found himself ushered inside a dim hallway, where Riddle took his coat without ceremony and led him through to a living room bigger than Banks's entire cottage. It was all exposed beams and whitewashed walls decked with polished hunting horns and the inevitable horse brasses. A gilt-framed mirror hung above the Adam fireplace, where a fire roared, and a baby grand piano stood by the mullioned bay window.

It was very much the kind of house Banks would associate with someone pulling in a hundred grand a year or more, but for all its rusticity, and for all the heat the fire threw out, it was a curiously cold, bleak and impersonal kind of room. There were no magazines or newspapers scattered on the low glass-topped table, and no messy piles of sheet music by the piano; the woodwork gleamed as if it had been waxed just moments ago, and everything was neat, clean and orderly. Which, come to think of it, was exactly what Banks would have expected from Riddle. This effect was heightened by the silence broken only by the occasional howling of the wind outside and the rain spattering against the windows.

A woman walked into the room.

'My wife, Rosalind,' said Riddle.

Banks shook Rosalind's hand. It was soft, but her grip was firm. If this was shaping up to be a night of surprises, Rosalind Riddle was the second.

Banks had never met the chief constable's wife before – all he knew about her was that she worked with a firm of Eastvale

9

solicitors specializing in property conveyancing – and if he had ever given a passing thought to her, he might have imagined a stout, sturdy and rather characterless figure. Why, he didn't know, but that was the image that came to mind.

The woman who stood before him, however, was elegant and tall, with a model's slim figure and long shapely legs. She was casually dressed in a grey skirt and a white silk blouse, and the two buttons open at the top revealed a V of skin as pale as her complexion. She had short blonde hair – the expensive, shaggy kind of short, and the highlighted sort of blonde – a high forehead, prominent cheekbones and dark blue eyes. Her lips were fuller than one would expect in the kind of face she had, and the lipstick made them seem even more so, giving the impression of a pout.

Her expression revealed nothing, but Banks could tell from her brusque body language that she was distraught. She set her drink on the table and sat on the velvet-upholstered sofa, crossing her legs and leaning forward, one hand clasping the other in her lap. She reminded Banks of the kind of elegant, remote blondes that Alfred Hitchcock had cast in so many of his films.

Riddle asked Banks to sit down. He was still in uniform. A tall man, running to bulk but still fit, he sat opposite in an armchair, pulling at the sharp crease of his trouser leg, and leaned back. He was bald, and dark beetle brows arched over his hard, serious brown eyes.

Banks got the feeling that neither of them quite knew what to say now that he was here. You could cut the tension with a knife; something bad had happened, something delicate and painful. Banks needed a cigarette badly, but there was no way. He knew Riddle hated smoke, and the room had a sort of sweet, lavender smell that he could tell had never been sullied by cigarettes. The silence stretched on. He was beginning to feel like Philip Marlowe at the beginning of a case. Maybe he should tell them his rates and break the ice, he thought, but before he could say anything flippant, Riddle spoke.

'Banks . . . I . . . er . . . I know we've had our differences in the past, and I'm sure this request will come as much a surprise to you as it comes to me to be making it, but I need your help.'

Differences in the past? There was an understatement if ever there was one. 'Go on,' he said. 'I'm listening.'

Riddle shifted in his chair and plucked at his creases. His wife reached forward and picked up her drink. The ring of moisture it left on the glass surface was the only thing that marred the room's sterile perfection.

'It's a personal matter,' Riddle went on. 'Very personal. And unofficial. Before we go any farther, Banks, I want your absolute assurance that what I have to say won't be repeated outside these four walls. Can you give me that?'

Banks nodded.

'I'm sorry,' Rosalind said, standing up. 'You must think me a terrible hostess. You've come all this way, and I haven't even offered you a drink. Will you have something, Mr Banks? A small whisky perhaps?'

'The man's driving,' said Riddle.

'Surely just the one?'

Banks held his hand up. 'No, thank you,' he said. What he really wanted was a cup of tea, but more than that, he wanted to get this all over with and go home. If he could do without a cigarette for a while, he could do without a drink, too. He wished one of them would get to the point.

'It's about our daughter,' Rosalind Riddle began, hands wriggling on her lap. 'She left home when she was sixteen.'

'She ran away, Ros,' said Riddle, his voice tight with anger. 'Let's not fool ourselves about what happened.'

'How long ago was that?' Banks asked.

Riddle answered him. 'Six months.'

'I'm sorry to hear it,' said Banks, 'but I'm not sure what—'

'Our son, Benjamin, was playing on the computer earlier this evening,' Rosalind chipped in. 'By accident he stumbled across some pictures on one of those sex sites.'

Banks knew that inadvertently accessing a porno site was easily enough done. Look for 'Spice Girls' on some of those search engines and you might end up at 'Spicy Girls'.

'Some of the pictures . . .' Rosalind went on. 'Well, they were of Emily, our daughter. Benjamin's only eight. He doesn't really know what any of it means. We put him to bed and told him not to say anything.'

'Are you certain it was your daughter?' Banks asked. 'Some of those photos can be doctored, you know. Heads and bodies rearranged.'

'It was her,' Rosalind answered. 'Believe me. There's a distinctive birthmark.'

'I'm sure this is all very upsetting,' Banks said. 'And you have my sympathies. But what do you want me to do?'

'I want you to find her,' Riddle said.

'Why haven't you tried yourself?'

Riddle looked at his wife. The gaze that passed between them spoke volumes of discord and recrimination. 'I have,' said Riddle. 'But I had nothing to go on. I couldn't go through official channels. I mean, it wasn't even as if there was a *crime*. She was perfectly within her legal rights. And the fewer people who knew about what happened, the better.'

'You're worried about your reputation?'

Riddle's voice rose. 'I know what you think, Banks, but these things *are* important. If only you realized that, you might have made something better of yourself.'

'More important than your daughter's well-being?'

'Valuing reputation doesn't mean that either my husband or I care any the less about our daughter, Mr Banks,' said Rosalind. 'As her mother, I resent that implication.'

'Then I apologize.'

Riddle spoke again. 'Look, what I'm saying, Banks, is that

before tonight I didn't think I had any real cause to worry about her – Emily's an intelligent and resourceful girl, if a bit too headstrong and rebellious – but now I think I do have something tangible to be concerned about. And this isn't *all* about ambition and reputation, no matter what you think.'

'So why didn't you try to find her yourself?'

'Be realistic, Banks. For a start, I can't be seen going off on some sort of private chase.'

'And I can?'

'You're not in the public eye as much as I am. People might recognize me. I can cover for you up here, if that's what you're worried about. I *am* chief constable, after all. And I'll also cover all reasonable expenses. I don't expect you to be out of pocket over this. But you'll be on your own. You can't use police resources or anything like that. I want to keep this private. A family matter.'

'You mean your career's important and mine's expendable?'

'You might try looking at it in a slightly different light. It's not that there's nothing in it for you.'

'Oh?'

'Look at it this way. If you succeed, you'll have earned my gratitude. Whatever you think of me, I'm a man of honour, a man of my word, and I promise you that whatever happens, your career in Eastvale can only benefit if you do as I ask.'

'And the other reason?'

Riddle sighed. 'I'm afraid that if she found out it was *me* looking for her, then she'd give me the slip. She blames me for all her problems. She made that clear in the months before she left. I want you to go about this discreetly, Banks. Try to get to her before she knows anyone's looking. I'm not asking you to kidnap her or anything like that. Just find her, talk to her, make sure she's all right, tell her we'd be happy to see her again and talk things over.'

'And persuade her to stop posing on Internet sex sites?'

Riddle paled. 'If you can.'

'Have you any idea where she went? Has she been in touch?'

'We had a postcard a couple of weeks after she'd left,' Rosalind answered. 'She said she was doing fine and that we weren't to worry about her. Or bother looking for her.'

'Where was it postmarked?'

'London.'

'That's all?'

'Apart from a card for Benjamin on his birthday, yes.'

'Did she say anything else on the postcard?'

'Just that she had a job,' Rosalind went on. 'So we wouldn't have to worry about her living on the streets or anything like that. Not that Emily *would* live on the streets. She was always a very high-maintenance girl.'

'Ros!'

'Well, it's true. And you—'

'Was there any specific reason she left?' Banks cut in. 'Anything that sparked her leaving? A row or something?'

'Nothing specific,' Riddle said. 'It was cumulative. She just didn't come home from school.'

'School?'

Rosalind answered. 'A couple of years ago we sent her to a very expensive and highly reputable all-girls' boarding school outside Warwick. At the end of last term, the beginning of summer, instead of returning home, she ran off to London.'

'By herself?'

'As far as we know.'

'Did she usually come home for the holidays?'

'Yes.'

'What stopped her this time? Were you having any problems with her?'

Riddle picked up the thread again. 'When she was last home, for the spring holidays, there were the usual arguments over staying out late, drinking in pubs, hanging around with the wrong crowd, that sort of thing. But nothing out of the ordinary. She's a very bright girl. She was doing well at school, academically, but it bored her. It all seemed too easy. Especially languages. She has a way with words. Of course, we wanted her to stay on and do her A levels, go to university, but she didn't want to. She wanted to get out on her own. We gave her everything, Banks. She had her own horse, piano lessons, trips to America with the school, skiing holidays in Austria, a good education. We were very proud of Emily. We gave her everything she ever wanted.'

Except perhaps what she needed most, thought Banks: *you*. To reach the dizzying heights of chief constable, especially by the age of forty-five, as Riddle had done, you needed to be driven, ruthless and ambitious. You also needed to be able to move around a lot, which can have a devastating effect on young children who sometimes find it hard to make friends. Add to that the hours spent on the job and on special courses, and Riddle had probably hardly set foot in the family home from one day to the next.

Banks was hardly one to take the moral high ground in raising children, he had to admit to himself. Even to reach the rank of DCI, he had been an absent father far more often than was good for Brian and Tracy. As it happened, both of them had turned out fine, on the whole, but he knew that was more a matter of good luck than good parenting on his part. Much of the task had fallen to Sandra, and she hadn't always burdened him with the children's problems. Perhaps Banks hadn't sacrificed his family to ambition the way he suspected Riddle had, but he had certainly sacrificed a lot for the sake of being a good *detective*.

'Are there any friends from around here she might have confided in?' he asked. 'Anyone who might have stayed in touch with her?'

Rosalind shook her head. 'I don't think so,' she said. 'Emily is very . . . self-sufficient. She had plenty of friends, but none that close, I don't think. It came of moving around a lot. When she moves on, she burns her bridges. And she hadn't actually spent much time in this area.'

'You mentioned "the wrong crowd". Was there a boy-friend?'

'Nobody serious.'

'His name could still be a help.'

Rosalind glanced at her husband, who said, 'Banks, I've told you I don't want this to be official. If you start looking up Emily's old boyfriends and asking questions around these parts, how long do you think the affair's going to remain under wraps? I told you, she's run off to London. *That*'s where you'll find her.'

Banks sighed. It looked as if this were going to be an investigation carried out with his hands tied. 'Does she know anyone in London, then?' he asked. 'Anyone she might go to for help?'

Riddle shook his head. 'It's been years since I was on the Met. She was only a little girl when we left.'

'I know this might be difficult for you,' Banks said, 'but do you think I might have a look at this website?'

'Ros?'

Rosalind Riddle scowled at her husband and said, 'Follow me.'

Banks followed her under a beam so low that he had to duck into a book-lined study. A tangerine iMac sat on a desk by the window. Wind rattled the glass beyond the heavy curtains, and every once in a while it sounded as if someone sloshed a bucket of water over the windows. Rosalind sat down and flexed her fingers, but before she hit any keys or clicked the mouse, she turned in her chair and looked up at Banks. He couldn't read the expression on her face.

'You don't approve of us, do you?' she said.

'*Us?*'

'Our kind. People who have ... oh, wealth, success, ambition.'

'I can't say I pay you much mind, really.'

'Ah, but you do. That's just where you're wrong.' Her eyes narrowed. 'You're envious. You've got a chip on your shoulder the size of that sideboard over there. You think you're better than us – purer, somehow – don't you?'

'Mrs Riddle,' said Banks, with a sigh, 'I don't need this kind of crap. I've driven all the way out here on a miserable night when I'd far rather be at home listening to music and reading a good book. So if we're going to do this, let's just get on with it, shall we, or shall I just go home and go to bed?'

She studied him coolly. 'Hit a nerve, did I?'

'Mrs Riddle, what do you want from me?'

'He's thinking of going into politics, you know.'

'So I've heard.'

'Any hint of a family scandal would ruin everything we've worked so hard for all these years.'

'I imagine it probably would. It's best to get into office first, *then* have the scandal.'

'That's cynical.'

'But true. Read the papers.'

'He says you have a tendency to make waves.'

'I like to get at the truth of things. Sometimes that means rocking a few boats. The more expensive the boat, the more noise it seems to make when it rocks.'

Rosalind smiled. 'I wish we could all afford to be so high-minded. This job will require the utmost discretion.'

'I'll bear that in mind. *If* I decide to take it on.' Banks held her stare until she blinked and swivelled her chair back to face the screen.

'I just thought we'd get that clear before you get to look at nude pictures of my daughter,' she said without looking at him.

He watched over her shoulder as she started to work at the keyboard and mouse. Finally, a black screen with a series of thumbnail-sized photographs appeared. Rosalind clicked on

17

one of them and another screen, with five more images, began to load. At the top of the screen, the script announced that the model's name was Louisa Gamine, and that she was an eighteen-year-old biology student. Looking at the pictures, Banks could believe it.

'Why Louisa Gamine?' he asked.

'I've no idea. Louisa's her middle name. Louise, actually. Emily Louise Riddle. I suppose she thinks Louisa sounds more exotic. Maybe when she left she decided she needed a new identity?'

Banks understood that. When he was younger he had always regretted that his parents hadn't given him a middle name. So much so that he made one up for himself: Davy, after Davy Crockett, one of his heroes at the time. That lasted a couple of months, then he finally accepted his own name.

Rosalind clicked on one of the images, and it began to fill the screen, loading from top to bottom. Banks was looking at an amateur photograph, taken in a bedroom with poor lighting, which showed a pretty young girl sitting naked and cross-legged on a pale blue duvet. The smile on her face looked a little forced, and her eyes didn't seem quite focused.

The resemblance between Louisa and her mother was astonishing. They both had the same long-legged grace, the same pale, almost translucent complexion, the same generous mouth. The only real difference, apart from their ages, was that Louisa's blonde hair hung over her shoulders. Otherwise, Banks felt he could easily have been looking at a photograph of Rosalind taken maybe twenty-five years ago, and that embarrassed him. He noticed a discoloration the shape of a teardrop on the inside of Louisa's left thigh: the birthmark. She also had a small ring of some sort in her navel, and below it, what looked like a black tattoo of a spider. Banks thought of Annie Cabbot's rose tattoo above her left breast, how long it was since he had last seen it, and how he would probably never see it again, especially if he managed to get back together with Sandra.

The other photos were much the same, all taken in the same location, with the same poor lighting. Only the poses were different. Her new surname was certainly apt, Banks thought, as there was definitely something of the *gamine* about her, a young girl with mischievous charm. There was something else that nagged him about the surname she had chosen, too, but he couldn't think what it was at the moment. If he put it to the back of his mind, it would probably come eventually. Those things usually did.

Banks examined the pictures more closely, aware of Rosalind's subtle perfume as he leaned over her shoulder. He could make out a few details of the room – the corner of a pop-star poster, a row of books – but they were all too blurred to be of any use.

'Seen enough?' asked Rosalind, tilting her head towards him and hinting that perhaps he was lingering too long, enjoying himself too much.

'She looks as if she knows what she's doing,' said Banks.

Rosalind paused, then said, 'Emily's been sexually active since she was fourteen. At least, as far as we know. She was thirteen when she started becoming . . . wayward, so it might have been earlier. That's partly why we sent her away to school in the first place.'

'That's not unusual,' said Banks, thinking with alarm of Tracy. He was sure she hadn't been quite that young, but it was hardly something he could ask her about. He didn't even know whether she was active now, come to think of it, and he didn't think he wanted to know. Tracy was nineteen, so she had a few years on Emily, but she was still Banks's little girl. 'Do you think the school helped?' he asked.

'Obviously not. She didn't come back, did she?'

'Have you spoken with the principal, or with any of her classmates?'

'No. Jerry's too worried about indiscretion.'

'Of course. Print that one.' Banks pointed to a photograph

where Louisa sat on the edge of the bed staring expressionlessly into the camera, wearing a red T-shirt and nothing else. 'Head and shoulders will do. We can trim off the bottom part.'

Rosalind looked over her shoulder at him, and he thought he could sense a little gratitude in her expression. At least she didn't seem so openly hostile as she had earlier. 'You'll do it?' she asked. 'You'll try to find Emily?'

'I'll try.'

'You don't need to make her come home. She won't want to come. I can guarantee you that.'

'You don't sound as if you want her to.'

Rosalind frowned, then said, 'Perhaps you're right. I did suggest to Jerry that we simply let her go her own way. She's old enough, and certainly she's smart enough to take care of herself. And she's a troublemaker. I know she's my daughter, and I don't mean to sound uncaring, but . . . Well, you can see for yourself what's happened after only six months, can't you? That tattoo, those pictures . . . She never considers anyone else's feelings. I can just imagine what chaos life would be like here if we had all her problems to deal with as well.'

'As well?'

'Nothing. It doesn't matter.'

'Is there anything else you think I should know?'

'I don't know what you mean.'

'Anything you're not telling me.'

'No. Why should there be?'

But there was, Banks sensed by the way Rosalind glanced away from him as she spoke. There may have been family problems that neither she nor her husband wanted to discuss. And maybe they were right not to. Perhaps he should hold his curiosity in check for once and not rip open cans of worms the way he usually did. Just find the girl, he told himself, make sure she isn't in any danger, and leave the rest well alone. Lord knows, the last thing he wanted to do was get caught up in the Riddle family dysfunctions.

He scribbled down as much information as he could get from the website, which was run by an organization called GlamourPuss Ltd based in Soho. It shouldn't be too difficult to track them down, he thought, and they should be able to point him towards Emily, or Louisa, as she now preferred to be called. He just hoped she wasn't on the game, as so many teenagers who appeared on porno websites were. She didn't sound like the type who would turn to prostitution for gain, but it sounded as if she might try anything for kicks. He would have to cross that bridge when, and if, he got to it.

Rosalind printed the photo, took some scissors from the desk drawer and trimmed it from the navel ring down before she handed it to him. Banks followed her back into the living room, where Riddle sat staring into space. 'All done?' he asked.

Banks nodded. He didn't bother sitting. 'Tell me something,' he said. 'Why me? You know damn well how things stand between us.'

Riddle seemed to flinch slightly, and Banks was surprised at the venom in his own voice. Then Riddle paused and looked him in the eye. 'Two reasons,' he said. 'First, because you're the best detective in the county. I'm not saying I approve of your methods or your attitude, but you get results. And in an unorthodox business like this, well, let's just say that some of your maverick qualities might actually be of real value for a change.'

Even being damned with faint praise by Jimmy Riddle was a new experience for Banks. 'And second?' he asked.

'You've got a teenage daughter yourself, haven't you? Tracy's her name. Am I right?'

'Yes.'

Riddle spread his hands, palms out. 'Then you know what I'm getting at. I think you can imagine something of how I feel.'

And to his surprise, Banks could. 'I can't start till next week,' he said.

Riddle leaned forward. 'You've nothing pressing on right now.'

'I was planning a weekend away with Tracy. In Paris.'

'Please start now. Tomorrow. In the morning. I need to know.' There was a sense of desperation in Riddle's voice that Banks had never heard from him before.

'Why so urgent?'

Riddle stared into the huge fireplace, as if addressing his words to the flames. 'I'm afraid for her, Banks. She's so young and vulnerable. I want her back. At the very least I need to know how she is, what she's doing. Imagine how you'd feel if it happened to you. Imagine what you'd do if it was *your* daughter in trouble.'

Damn it, thought Banks, seeing his weekend in Paris with Tracy start to slip beyond his grasp. *Daughters.* Who'd have them? Nothing but trouble. But Riddle had touched a nerve all right. Now there was no getting away from it, no declining; Banks knew he *had* to head off to London to find Emily Louise Riddle.

'Oh, Dad! You *can't* mean it! You woke me up in the middle of the night to tell me we can't go to Paris after all?'

'I'm sorry, love. We'll just have to postpone it for a while.'

'I don't *believe* this. I've been looking forward to this weekend for *ages*.'

'Me, too, sweetheart. What can I say?'

'And you won't even tell me why?'

'I can't. I promised.'

'You promised *me* a weekend in Paris. It was easy enough to break *that* one.'

Touché. 'I know. I'm sorry.'

'Don't you trust me to keep my mouth shut?'

'Of course I do. It's not that.'

'What, then?'

'I just can't tell you yet. That's all. Maybe next week, if things work out.'

'Oh, don't bother.' Tracy fell into one of her sulky silences for a while, the way her mother did, then said, 'It's not dangerous, is it?'

'Of course not. It's a private matter. I'm helping out a—' Banks almost said 'friend' but managed to stop himself in time. 'I'm helping someone out. Someone in trouble. Believe me, love, if you knew the details, you'd see it's the right thing to do. Look, when it's over, I'll make it up to you. I promise.'

'Heard that before. Been there. Got the T-shirt.'

'Give me a little leeway here, Tracy. This isn't easy for me, you know. It's not just you who's upset. I was looking forward to Paris, too.'

'Okay, I know. I'm sorry. But what about the tickets? The hotel?'

'The hotel's easily cancelled. I'll see if I can get the tickets changed.'

'You'll be lucky.' She paused again. 'Wait a minute! I've just had an idea.'

'What?'

'Well, I know *you* can't go, but there's no reason I shouldn't go, is there?'

'Not that I know of. Except, would you really want to be in Paris all by yourself? And it's not safe, especially for a young woman alone.'

Tracy laughed. 'I can take care of myself, Dad. I'm a big girl now.'

Yes, Banks thought, all of nineteen. 'I'm sure you can,' he said. 'But I'd be worried.'

'You're *always* worried. It's what fathers do best for their daughters: worry about them. Besides, I wasn't necessarily thinking of going by myself.'

'What do you mean?'

'I'll bet Damon would like to go. He doesn't have any lectures tomorrow, either. I could ask him.'

'Wait a minute,' said Banks. 'Damon? Who on earth is Damon?'

'My boyfriend. I bet he'd jump at the chance of a weekend in Paris with me.'

I'll bet he would, Banks thought, with that sinking feeling. This wasn't going at all the way he had expected it to. He had expected recriminations, yes, anger, yes, but this . . .? 'I'm not so sure that's a good idea,' he said weakly.

'Of course it is. You know it is. We'd save money, too.'

'How?'

'Well, you'll only have to cancel one of the hotel rooms, for a start.'

'Tracy!'

She laughed. 'Oh, Dad. Parents are so silly, you know. If kids want to sleep together it doesn't have to be in a foreign city at night. They can do it in the student residence in the daytime, you know.'

Banks swallowed. Now he had an answer to a question he had avoided asking. In for a penny, in for a pound. 'Are you and Damon . . . I mean . . .?'

'Don't worry. I'm a very careful girl. Now, the only problem is getting the tickets to us before tomorrow morning. I don't suppose you'd like to drive over tonight, would you?'

'No. I wouldn't,' said Banks. Then he weakened. After all, she was right; there was no reason to spoil her weekend just because his own was spoiled, Damon notwithstanding. 'But as a matter of fact, I have to go down to London tomorrow anyway, so I can go that far on the train with you.' And check Damon out, too, while I'm at it, he thought. 'I'll give you the tickets then.'

'That's great!'

Banks felt depressed; Tracy sounded far more thrilled at going off with Damon than with him. But she would; she was young. 'I'll see you in the morning,' he said. 'At the station. Same time as we arranged.'

'Cool, Dad. Thanks a lot.'

When he hung up the telephone, Banks fell back into his armchair and reached for his cigarettes. He had to go to London, of that there was no doubt. In the first place, he had promised, and in the second, there was something Riddle didn't know. Tracy herself had almost run away from home once, around her thirteenth birthday, and the thought of what might have happened if she had gone through with it haunted him.

It had happened just before they left London for Eastvale. Tracy had been upset for days about leaving her friends behind, and one night, when Banks actually happened to be home, he heard a noise downstairs. Going to investigate, he found Tracy at the door with a suitcase in her hand. In the end, he managed to persuade her to stay without forcing her, but it had been touch and go. One part of their bargain was that he had agreed not to tell her mother, and he never had. Sandra had slept through the whole thing. Remembering that night, he could imagine something of how the Riddles must feel.

Even so, was this what he got for doing his enemy a favour? He got to go hunting for a runaway teen while his own daughter got a dirty weekend in Paris with her boyfriend. Where was the justice in that? he asked. All the answer he got was the howling of the wind and the relentless music of the water flowing over Gratly Falls.

2

On Friday afternoon, Banks was walking along Old Compton Street in the chilly November sunshine, having travelled down to London with Tracy and Damon that morning. After a grunted 'Hi' Damon had hardly spoken a word. The train was almost full, and the three of them couldn't sit together, which seemed a relief to Tracy and Damon. Banks had to sit half the carriage away next to a fresh-faced young businessman wearing too much aftershave and playing FreeCell on his laptop computer.

Most of the journey he spent listening to Lucinda Williams's *Car Wheels on a Gravel Road* and reading *The Big Sleep*, which he had substituted for *Maigret and the Hundred Gibbets* when he realized he wasn't going to Paris. He had seen the Bogart film version a few weeks ago and enjoyed it so much it had made him want to read the book. Besides, Raymond Chandler seemed more suitable reading for the kind of job he was doing: *Banks, P.I.*

Shortly before King's Cross, his thoughts had returned to Tracy's boyfriend.

Banks wasn't at all certain what to think of Damon. The grunt was no more than he would have expected from any of his daughter's friends, and he didn't read anything into it, except perhaps that the lad was a bit embarrassed at coming face to face with the father of the girl he was sleeping with. Even the thought of that made Banks's chest tighten, though he told himself not to get upset, not to interfere. The last thing he wanted to do was alienate his daughter, especially as he was hoping to get back together with her mother. It wouldn't do any good, anyway. Tracy had her own life to lead now, and she was no fool. He hoped.

He had left the young lovers at King's Cross and first gone to check in at the small Bloomsbury hotel he had telephoned the previous evening. Called simply Hotel Fifty-Five, after the street number, it was the place he favoured whenever he visited London: quiet, discreet, well located and relatively inexpensive. Riddle might have said he would pay any expenses, but Banks wouldn't want to see the CC's face if he got a bill from the Dorchester.

The morning's rain had dispersed during the journey, and the day had turned out windy and cool under the kind of piercingly clear blue sky you only get in November. Maybe the bonfires would dry out in time for Guy Fawkes' Night after all, Banks thought, as he zipped his leather jacket a bit higher. He tapped his briefcase against his thigh to the rhythm of some hip-hop music that drifted out of a sex shop.

Banks had strong feelings and memories associated with Soho ever since he used to walk the beat or drive the panda cars there out of Vine Street station, after it had been reopened in the early seventies. Certainly the area had been cleaned up since then, but Soho could never be *really* clean. Cleanliness wasn't in its nature.

He loved the whiff of villainy he got whenever he walked Old Compton Street or Dean Street, where a fiddle had been simply a hair's breadth away from a legitimate business deal. He remembered the cold dawns at Berwick Street Market, a cigarette and mug of hot sweet tea in his hands, chatting with Sam, whose old brown collie Fetchit used to sit under the stall all day and watch the world go by with sad eyes. As the other stallholders set up their displays – fruit, crockery, knives and forks, knickers and socks, watches, egg slicers, you name it – Sam used to give Banks a running commentary on what was hot and what wasn't. Probably dead now, along with Fetchit. They'd been old enough back then, when Banks was new to the job.

Not that Soho was ever without its dark side. Banks had found his first murder victim there in an alley off Frith Street: a seventeen-year-old prostitute who had been stabbed and mutilated, her breasts cut off and several of her inner organs removed. 'Homage to Jack the Ripper', as the newspaper headlines had screamed. Banks had been sick on the spot, and he still had nightmares about the long minutes he had spent alone with the disembowelled body just before dawn in a garbage-strewn Soho alley.

As with all the dead in his life, he had put a name to her: Dawn Wadley. Being junior at the time, Banks was given the job of telling her parents. He would never forget the choking smell of urine, rotten meat and unwashed nappies in the cramped flat on the tenth floor of an East End tower block, or Dawn's washed-out junkie mother, apparently unconcerned about the fate of the daughter she gave up on years ago. To her, Dawn's murder was just another in the endless succession of life's cruel blows, as if it had happened solely in order to do her down.

Banks turned into Wardour Street. Soho had changed, like the rest of the city. The old bookshops and video booths were still around, as was the Raymond Revuebar, but cheap sex was definitely on the wane. In its place came a younger crowd, many of them gay, who chatted on their mobiles while sipping cappuccinos at chic outdoor cafés. Young men with shaved heads and earrings flirted on street corners with clean-cut boys from Palmer's Green or Sudbury Hill. Gay bars had sprung up all over the place, and the party never stopped.

Banks checked the address for GlamourPuss Ltd he had got from the first place he tried: the phone book. Sometimes things really are that easy.

From the outside, it looked like any number of other businesses operating in Soho. The building was run-down, paint flaking from the doors, the lino on the creaky corridors cracked and worn, but inside, through the second set of doors, it was all high-tech glam and potted plants, and he could still smell the fresh paint on the walls.

'Can I help you, sir?'

To Banks's surprise, there was a female receptionist sitting behind a chest-high semicircle of black Plexiglas. Written on it, in florid pink script scattered with some sort of glitter, at about waist height, was the logo 'GlamourPuss Ltd: Erotica and More!' Banks had the idea, somehow, that women – right-thinking women, anyway – didn't want anything to do with the porn business, that they wanted, in fact, to outlaw it if they could. Maybe this was a wrong-thinking woman? Or was she the respectable face of porn? If so, it was about nineteen, with short henna hair, a ghostly complexion and a stud through its left nostril. A little badge over her flat chest read 'Tamara: Client Interface Officer'. Banks's mind boggled. *Can we interface, Tamara?*

'I'd like to see the person in charge,' he said.

'Do you have an appointment, sir?'

'No.'

'What is the purpose of your visit?'

She was starting to sound like an immigration official, Banks thought, getting irritated. In the old days he would probably have just tweaked her nose-stud and walked right on in. Even these days he might do the same under normal circumstances, but he had to remember he was acting privately; he wasn't here officially as a policeman. 'Let's call it a business proposition,' he said.

'I see. Please take a seat for a moment, sir. I'll see if Mr Aitcheson is free.' She gestured to the orange plastic chairs behind him. An array of magazines lay spread out on the coffee table in front of them. Banks lifted a couple up. Computer stuff, mostly. Not a *Playboy* or a *Penthouse* in sight. He looked up at Tamara, who had been carrying on a hushed conversation by telephone. She smiled. 'He'll be with you in a moment, sir.' Did she think he was looking for a job or something? As what?

Banks was beginning to feel more as if he were in a dentist's waiting room than a porn emporium, and that thought didn't give him any comfort. Clearly, things had changed a lot since he had walked the Soho beat; enough to make him feel like an old fogey when he was only in his mid-forties. In the old days, at least you knew where you were: people like GlamourPuss Ltd, as befitted their name and business, used to operate out of seedy offices in seedy basements; they didn't run Internet websites; they didn't have client interface officers; and they certainly didn't come out from under their stones to meet strangers offering vague business propositions the way this young man was doing right now, smiling, hand outstretched, wearing a suit, no less.

'Aitcheson,' he said. 'Terry Aitcheson. And you are?'

'Banks. Alan Banks.'

'Pleased to meet you, Mr Banks. Follow me. We'll go to the office. Far more private in there.'

Banks followed him past Tamara, who gave a little wave and a nose twitch that looked painful. They crossed an open area filled with state-of-the-art computer equipment and went into a small office, which looked out over Wardour Street. There was nothing either on the desk or the walls to indicate that GlamourPuss Ltd dealt in pornography, which is what Banks thought they did.

Aitcheson sat down and clasped his hands behind the back of his neck, still smiling. Up close, he looked older than Banks had first guessed – maybe late thirties – balding, with yellowing front teeth that were rather long and lupine. A few flakes of dandruff speckled the shoulders of his suit. It was hardly fair, Banks thought, that even when you're going bald you *still* get dandruff. 'Okay, Mr Banks,' said Aitcheson, 'what can I do for you? You mentioned a business proposition.'

Banks felt a little more at home now. Smarmy smile and suit aside, he had dealt with pillocks like Aitcheson before, even if their offices weren't as pretty and they didn't bother to offer up a smug façade of decency. He took the truncated picture of Emily Riddle from his briefcase and put it on the desk, turning it so that Aitcheson could see the image the right way up. 'I'd like you to tell me where I can find this girl,' he said.

Aitcheson studied the photo. His smile faltered a moment, then returned full force as he pushed the photograph back towards Banks. 'I'm afraid we don't give out that sort of information about our models, sir. For their own protection, you understand. We get some . . . well, some rather strange people in this business, as I'm sure you can understand.'

'So she *is* one of your models?'

'I was speaking generally, sir. Even if she were, I couldn't give you the information you want.'

'Do you recognize her?'

'No.'

'What if I told you this came from a website run by your company?'

'We operate several websites, sir. They act as a major part of our interface with the public.' He smiled. 'You have to be on the web these days if you want to stay in business.'

Interface. That word again. It seemed to be a sort of buzzword around GlamourPuss Ltd. 'Are escort services part of your business?'

'We have an escort agency as one of our subsidiary companies, yes, but you can't just bring in a girl's picture from one of our websites and place an order for her. That would be tantamount to pimping on our part.'

'And you don't do that?'

'We do not.'

'What exactly *is* your business?'

'I should have thought that was obvious. Erotica in all its forms. Sex aids, videos, magazines, erotic encasement equipment and services, website design and hosting, CD-ROM, travel arrangements.'

'Erotic encasement equipment and services?'

Aitcheson smiled. 'It's a variation on bondage. Mummification's the most popular. Some people liken it to an erotic meditative state, a sort of sexual nirvana. But there are those who simply prefer to be wrapped in cling film with rose thorns pressed against their flesh. It's all a matter of taste.'

'I suppose it is,' said Banks, who was still trying to get his head around mummification. 'And travel arrangements? What travel arrangements?'

Aitcheson graced Banks with a condescending smile. 'Let's say you're gay and you want a cruise down the Nile with like-minded people. We can arrange it. Or a weekend in Amsterdam. A sex tour of Bangkok.'

'Discount vouchers for brothels? Fifty pee off your next dildo? That sort of thing?'

Aitcheson moved to stand up, his smile gone. 'I think that's about all the time I can spare you at the moment, sir.'

Banks stood up, leaned over the desk and pushed him back down into his chair. It wheeled back a couple of inches and hit the wall, taking out a small chunk of plaster.

'Just a minute!' Aitcheson said.

Banks shook his head. 'You don't understand. That picture came from *your* website. Even if you don't remember putting it up there yourself, you can find out who did and where it came from.'

'What's this got to do with you anyway? Wait a minute. Are you a copper?'

Banks paused and glanced down at the photo again. The younger version of Rosalind Riddle's features – pale skin, pouting lips, high cheekbones, blue eyes – looked up at him from under her fringe with a sort of mocking, come-hither sexuality. 'It's my daughter,' he said. 'I'm trying to find her.'

'Well, I'm sorry, but we don't run a location service for missing kids. There are organizations—'

'Pity, that,' Banks cut in. 'Her being so young, and all.'

'What do you mean?'

Banks tapped the photo. 'She can't have been more than fifteen when this was taken.'

'Look, I'm not responsible for—'

'I think you'll discover that the law says otherwise. Believe me, I've read up on it.' Banks leaned forward and rested his hands on the desk. 'Mr Aitcheson,' he said, 'here's my business proposition. There are two parts to it, actually, in case one of them alone doesn't appeal. I must admit, I'm not always certain justice is done when you bring in the police and the lawyers. Are you? I mean, you could probably beat the charges of distribution and publication of indecent photographs of minors. *Probably.* But it could be an expensive business. And I don't think you'd like the sort of *interface* it would create with your public. Do you follow? *Child pornography* is such an emotive term, isn't it?'

Aitcheson's smile had vanished completely now. 'You sure you're not a copper?' he whispered. 'Or a lawyer?'

'Me? I'm just a simple working man.'

'Two parts. You said two parts.'

'Ah, yes,' said Banks. 'As I said, I'm a simple working man, and I wouldn't want to get tangled up with the law myself. Besides, it would be bad for young Louisa, wouldn't it? All that limelight, giving evidence in court and all that. Embarrassing. Now, I work on a building site up north, and my fellow workers tend to be a conservative, even rather prudish lot when it comes to this sort of thing. It's not that they mind looking at a pair of tits on a *Playboy* centrefold or anything like that, mind you, but, believe me, I've heard them talking about child pornography, and I wouldn't want to be on the receiving end of some of the actions they propose to deal with the people who spread it, if you know what I mean.'

'Is this a threat?'

'Why not? Yes, let's call it that: a threat. Suits me. Now, you tell me what I want to know, and I won't tell the lads at the building site about GlamourPuss exploiting young Louisa. Some of them have known her since she was a little baby, you know. They're very protective. As a matter of fact, most of them will be down here next week to see Leeds play Arsenal. I'm sure they'd be happy to find the time to drop by your offices, maybe do a bit of remodelling. Does that sound like a good deal to you?'

Aitcheson swallowed and stared at Banks, who held his gaze. Finally, he brought out his smile again, a bit weaker now. 'It really *is* a threat, isn't it?'

'I thought I'd already made that clear. Do we have a deal?'

Aitcheson waved his arm. 'All right, all right. I'll see what I can do. Can you come back on Monday? We're shut over the weekend.'

'I'd rather we got it over with now.'

'It might take a while.'

'I can wait.'

Banks waited. It took all of twenty minutes, then Aitcheson came back into the office looking worried. 'I'm sorry,' he said, 'but we just don't have the information you require.'

'Come again?'

'We don't have it. The model's address. She's not on our books, not part of our . . . I mean, it was an amateur shoot. I seem to remember she was the photographer's girlfriend. He used to do some work for us now and then, and apparently he took those photos as a bit of a lark. I'm sure he didn't know the model's true age. She looks much older.'

'She's always looked older than her years,' Banks said. 'It's got a lot of boys into trouble. Well, I'm relieved to hear she's not on your books, but I don't think we're a lot further forward than when I first arrived, do you? Is there anything you can do to make amends?'

Aitcheson paused, then said, 'I shouldn't, but I can give you the photographer's name and address. Craig Newton. As I said, he used to do a spot of work for us now and then, and we've still got him on file. We just got a change of address notice from him a short while ago, as a matter of fact.'

Banks nodded. 'It'll have to do.' Aitcheson scribbled down an address for him. It was in Stony Stratford, commuter country. Banks stood up to leave. 'One more thing,' he said.

'Yes?'

'Those photos of Louisa on your website. Get rid of them.'

Aitcheson allowed himself a self-satisfied smile. 'Actually,' he said. 'I've done that already. While you were waiting.'

Banks smiled back and tapped the side of his nose with his forefinger. 'Good lad,' he said. 'You're learning.'

Back at his hotel, Banks picked up the telephone and did what he had been putting off ever since he discovered he was bound for London the previous day. Not because it was something he didn't want to do, but because he was nervous and uncertain of the outcome. And there was so much at stake.

She answered on the fourth ring. Banks's heart pounded. 'Sandra?'

'Yes. Who is this? Alan?'

'Yes.'

'What do you want? I'm in a bit of a hurry right now. I was just on my way out.'

'Off somewhere with Sean?'

'There's no need to make it sound like that. And as a matter of fact, no, I'm not. Sean's away photographing flood damage in Wales.'

Let's hope the flood water carries him away with it, Banks thought, but bit his tongue. 'I'm in town,' he said. 'In London. I was wondering if, maybe, tomorrow night you might be free for a meal. Or we could just have a drink. Lunch, even.'

'What are you doing down here? Working?'

'In a manner of speaking. Are you free?'

He could almost hear Sandra thinking across the wires. Finally, she said, 'Yes. Actually. Yes, I am. Sean won't be back until Sunday.'

'So will you have dinner with me tomorrow night?'

'Yes. All right. That's a good idea. There's a few things we have to talk about.' She named a restaurant on Camden High Street, not far from where she lived. 'Seven thirty?'

'Can you make it eight, just to be on the safe side?'

'Eight, then.'

'Fine. See you there.'

'See you.'

Sandra hung up and Banks was left with the dead line buzzing in his ear. Maybe she hadn't exactly welcomed him with open arms, but she hadn't cut him off, either. More importantly, she had agreed to see him tomorrow. And dinner was far more intimate than lunch or a quick drink in the afternoon. It was a good sign.

It was already dark by late afternoon when Banks took the train out of Euston. The Virgin InterCity sped through Hemel Hempstead so fast he could hardly read the station nameplate, then it slowed down near Berkhamsted for no reason Banks was aware of except that trains did that every now and then – something to do with leaves on the tracks, or a cow in a tunnel.

Berkhamsted was where Graham Greene came from, Banks remembered from *A Sort of Life*, which he had read a year or two ago. Greene had been one of his favourite writers ever since he first saw *The Third Man* on television back in the old Met days. After that, in his usual obsessive fashion, he collected and read everything he could get his hands on, from the 'entertainments' to the serious novels, films on video, essays and short stories.

He was particularly taken by the story of the nineteen- or twenty-year-old Greene going out to Ashbridge Park in

Berkhamsted with a loaded revolver to play Russian roulette. It was eerie now to imagine the awkward, gangly young man, destined to become one of the century's most famous writers, clicking on an empty chamber that autumn more than seventy-five years ago, not far from where the train had just stopped.

Banks had also been impressed by Greene's writings on childhood, about how we are all 'emigrants from a country we remember too little of', how important to us are the fragments we do remember clearly and how we spend our time trying to reconstruct ourselves from these.

For years, Banks hadn't dwelled much on his past, but since Sandra had left him a year ago, he had found himself returning over and over again to certain incidents; the heightened moments of joy and fear and guilt, along with the objects, sights, sounds and smells that brought them back, like Proust's madeleines, as if he were looking for clues to his future. He remembered reading that Greene, as a child, had had a number of confrontations with death, and these had helped shape his life. Banks had experienced the same thing, and he thought that in some obscure, symbolic way they partly explained why he had become a policeman.

He remembered, for example, the hot summer day when Phil Simpkins wrapped his rope around the high tree in the churchyard and spiralled down, yelling like Tarzan, right onto the spiked railings. Banks knew he would never forget the squishy thud that the body made as it hit. There had been no adults around. Banks and two others had pulled their writhing, screaming friend off the railings and stood there wondering what to do while he bled to death, soaking them in the blood that gushed from a pierced artery in his thigh. Someone later said they should have tied a tourniquet and sent for help. But they had panicked, frozen. Would Phil have lived if they hadn't? Banks thought not, but it was a possibility, and a mistake he had lived with all his life.

Then there was Jem, a neighbour in his Notting Hill days,

who had died of a heroin overdose; and Graham Marshall, a shy, quiet classmate who had gone missing and never been found. In his own way, Banks felt he was responsible for them, too. So many deaths for one so young. Sometimes Banks felt as if he had blood on his hands, that he had let so many people down.

The train stopped in Milton Keynes. Banks got off, walked up the stairs and along the overpass to the station exit.

He had never been to Milton Keynes before, though he had heard plenty of jokes about the place. One of the new towns built in the late 1960s, it was constructed on a grid system, with planned social centres, hidden pedestrian paths rather than pavements, and hundreds of roundabouts. It sounded like the sort of design that would go down well in America, but the British sneered at it. Still, at not much over half an hour by train from London, and a much cheaper place to live, it was ideal commuting territory.

As it was, it was too dark to see much of the place. The taxi seemed to circle roundabout after roundabout, all of them with numbers, like V5 and H6. Banks didn't see any pavements or people out walking. He hadn't a clue where he was.

Finally, when the taxi turned into Stony Stratford, he found himself on a typical old village high street, with ancient pubs and shop façades. For a moment, he wondered if it was all fake, just a *faux* finish to give the illusion of a real English village in the midst of all that concrete and glass modernity. It *seemed* real enough, though, and when the taxi pulled into a street of tall, narrow pre-war terraced houses, he guessed that it probably was real.

The youth who answered the door looked to be in his mid- to late twenties; he wore black jeans and a grey sweatshirt advertising an American football team. He was about Banks's height, around five foot eight or nine, with curly dark hair and finely chiselled features. His nose had a little bump at the bridge, as if it had been broken and not properly set, and he was holding something that looked like a squat vacuum flask, which he kept tipping gently from side to side. Banks recognized it as a developing tank.

Craig Newton, if that indeed was who it was, looked both puzzled and annoyed to find a stranger on his doorstep early on a Friday evening. Banks didn't look like an insurance salesman – besides, how many salesmen still called at houses in these days of direct mail and electronic advertising? He also didn't look like a religious type, or a copper.

'What are you collecting for?' Newton asked. 'I'm busy.'

'Mr Newton? Craig Newton?'

'Yes. What do you want?'

'Mind if I come in for a moment?'

'Yes, I do. Tell me what you want.'

'It's about Louisa.'

Craig Newton stepped back a couple of inches, clearly startled. 'Louisa? What about her?'

'You *do* know her, then?'

'Of course I do. If it's the same person we're talking about. Louisa. Louisa Gamine.' He pronounced it in Italian fashion, with a stress on the final e. 'What's wrong? Has something happened to Louisa?'

'Can I come in?'

He stood back and gave Banks enough room to enter. 'Yes, I'm sorry. Please.'

Banks followed him down a narrow hall into the front room. These old terrace houses weren't very wide, but they made up for it in length, with both kitchen and bathroom tacked on at the back like afterthoughts. Comfortably messy, the first thing the room told Banks was that Newton probably lived alone. A number of magazines, mostly to do with photography or movies, littered the coffee table, along with a few empty lager cans. A TV set stood at the far end. *The Simpsons* was showing. There was also a faint whiff of marijuana in the air, though Newton didn't appear stoned at all.

'Has something happened to Louisa?' he asked again. 'Is that why you're here? Are you a policeman?'

'Nothing's happened to her as far as I know,' said Banks. 'And no, I'm not a policeman. I'm looking for her.'

Craig frowned. 'Looking for Louisa? Why? I don't follow.'

'I'm her father.' The lies were starting to come rather more easily now, after just a little practice, and Banks wasn't sure how he felt about that. Something to do with the end justifying the means crossed his mind and made him feel even more uneasy. Still, it wasn't as if he hadn't told plenty of lies in the course of his work, so why worry about it now he was doing the same thing as a private citizen? All in a good cause, if it could help a teenage runaway get herself sorted *and* get Jimmy Riddle off his back for good.

Craig raised his eyebrows. 'Her *father* . . .?' Then he seemed suddenly to notice the developing tank he was shaking. 'Shit. Look, I've got to finish this off properly or it's a week's work down the drain. Come up if you like.'

Banks followed him upstairs, where Craig had turned his spare room into a makeshift darkroom. He didn't need complete darkness for this stage of the process, so a dim light glowed on the wall. With expert, economic gestures, Craig emptied the tank of developer, poured in the stop bath and shook the tank again for a while. After that, he emptied it out again and poured in the fixer.

Banks noticed a number of photographs of Emily Riddle tacked to a corkboard. Not nude shots, but professional-looking folio stuff. In some she wore a strapless black evening gown and had her hair pinned up. In another she was wearing a vest and baggy jeans, showing her bare midriff with its spider tattoo, trying to look like Kate Moss or Amber Valletta.

'These are good,' he said to Craig.

Craig glanced over at them. 'She could be a model,' he said sadly. 'She's a natural.'

The harsh chemical smells transported Banks back not to

his life with Sandra, who was a keen amateur photographer, but to his childhood, when he used to go up to the attic darkroom with his Uncle Ted and watch him processing and printing. He liked the printing best, when the blank piece of paper went in the developing tray and you could watch the image slowly forming. It seemed like magic. Every time they went to visit, he pestered his Uncle Ted to take him up. There was a safe light on the wall, too, he remembered, just enough to see by, and it gave an eerie glow in the small room. But mostly it was the sharp, chemical smells he remembered, and the way constant exposure to the chemicals made his Uncle Ted's fingernails brown, the same way nicotine stained Banks's fingers when he started smoking. He used to scrub it off with pumice stone so his mother wouldn't notice.

Then the visits to Uncle Ted's stopped abruptly and nobody ever said why. It was years before Banks thought about those days again and managed to work it out for himself. He remembered his uncle's hand on the small of his back, perhaps rubbing just a little, or the arm draped casually across his shoulders in an avuncular way. Nothing more. Never anything more. But there was some kind of scandal – not involving Banks, but someone else. Uncle Ted suddenly broke off his connection with the local youth club and no longer acted as a Boys' Brigade leader. Nothing was said, no police were involved, but he was suddenly a pariah in the community. That was how things like that were dealt with back then in that sort of close working-class community. No doubt one or two of the local fathers lay in wait one night and gave him a beating, too, but Banks heard nothing about that. Uncle Ted was simply never mentioned again, and if Banks ever asked to visit or mentioned the name, his mother's mouth formed into a tight white line – a definite warning sign to shut up or else. Eventually, he forgot Uncle Ted and moved on to discovering girls.

'Okay,' said Craig, emptying out the fixer and inserting a

hose attached to the cold water tap. 'We're all right for half an hour now.'

Banks followed him downstairs, still half-lost in memories of Uncle Ted, slowly moving to memories of Sandra and how they made love in the red glow of her darkroom once.

Back in the living room, *The Simpsons* had given way to a documentary on Hollywood narrated in a plummy, superior accent. Craig turned the TV off and they sat down opposite one another in the narrow room.

Banks reached for his cigarettes; he'd been a long time without. 'Mind if I smoke?'

'No, not at all.' Craig passed him a small ashtray from the mantelpiece. 'I don't indulge, myself, but it doesn't bother me.'

'Not cigarettes, anyway.'

Craig blushed. 'Well, a bit of weed never did anyone any harm, did it?'

'I suppose not.'

He continued to study Banks, his look wary and suspicious. 'So, you're Louisa's father,' he said. 'Funny, you don't look Italian. She said her father was Italian. Met her mother in Tuscany or somewhere like that on holiday.'

'What did she say about me?'

'Not much. Just that you were a boring, tight-arsed old fart.'

Well, Banks thought, if you will go around assuming other people's identities, you have to be prepared for the occasional unflattering remark – especially if that identity is Jimmy Riddle's. On that score, Emily Riddle probably wasn't far wrong. 'Do you know where Louisa is?' he asked.

'Haven't seen her for a couple of months,' said Craig. 'Not since I moved out here.'

Banks showed him the photo. 'This *is* the person we're talking about, isn't it?'

Craig looked at the photo and gasped. 'You've seen them, then?'

'Yes. Is it the same girl we're talking about?'

'Yeah. That's her. Louisa.'

'My daughter. What happened? The photos on the website?'

'Look, I'm sorry. It was just a lark, really. It was her as much as me. *More*, really. Though I don't expect you to believe me.'

'You took the photos?'

'Yes. We were living together at the time. Three months ago.'

'Here?'

'No. I was still in London then. Had a little flat in Dulwich.'

Emily Riddle was a fast worker, Banks thought. Only away from home three months and she was living with someone. 'How did they get on to the GlamourPuss website?'

Craig looked away, into the empty fireplace. 'I'm not proud of it,' he said. 'I used to do some work for them. I went to school with one of the blokes who run the site, Rick, and I met him in a pub when I was a bit down on my luck, just after college. I'd studied photography, got my diploma, but it was hard to get started in the business. Anyway, he offered me a bit of paying work every now and then. Models. It didn't seem that much different from life studies in college.'

It probably didn't, really, Banks thought. Sandra was a photographer, too, and Banks had seen plenty of life studies she had taken at the camera club, male *and* female. He pointed to the cropped photo of Louisa. 'You got paid for this?'

'No. Good Lord, no. This wasn't paid work. Like I said, it was a lark. A bit of fun. We were . . . well, we'd been smoking a bit of weed, if you must know. After I'd taken them, Louisa said I should put them on the web with some of the other stuff I'd done – the professional stuff. She said it would be really cool. Rick said he liked them, so we put them up in the amateurs' gallery. But that's all. I mean Louisa doesn't have any connection with the rest of the GlamourPuss business.'

Just what Aitcheson had said at the office. Maybe it was true. 'I'm glad to hear that. Are you sure?'

'Certain. She never did. The photos were just a one-off. A joke. I was trying out a new digital camera and . . . well, one thing led to another.'

'Okay,' said Banks, waving his hand. 'Let's put that behind us. I'd really like to find Louisa, just to talk to her. I'm sure you understand. Can you tell me where she is?'

'I wasn't lying. I don't know where she is. I haven't seen her in two months.'

'What happened?'

'She met another bloke.'

'And left you?'

'Like a shot.'

'Who is he?'

'I don't know his name . . . I . . .' Craig turned away again.

'Craig? Is something wrong?'

'No. Maybe. I don't know.'

'Talk to me, Craig.'

Craig stood up. 'How about a drink?'

'If it'll help loosen your tongue.'

'Lager okay?'

'Lager's fine.'

Craig brought a couple of cans from the fridge and offered one to Banks. He took it and popped the tab, watching the foam well up and subside. He took a sip and leaned back in the chair. 'I'm waiting.'

'You *sure* you're not a copper?'

'I told you. I'm Louisa's father. Why?'

'I don't know. Just something . . . Never mind. Besides, you don't really look old enough to be her father. Not like I imagined, anyway. I would've expected some bald wrinkly in a suit, to be honest. With a funny accent, waving his arms around a lot.'

'I'm flattered,' said Banks, 'but how old did you think she was?'

'Louisa? Nineteen. When I met her, that is.'

'How long ago was that?'

'About three or four months. Why?'

'Because she'd just turned sixteen, that's why.'

Craig spluttered into his beer. 'She never! I mean, for crying out loud. I wouldn't've touched . . . You've seen the photos. You're her *father*, for Christ's sake!'

'Calm down,' said Banks. 'Louisa always did look older than her age, even if she didn't always act it.'

'She had that . . . I don't know . . . she seemed young but mature, worldly and innocent at the same time. That was one of the attractive things about her. To me, anyway. She was a walking mass of contradictions. I swear, if you were me, and she told you she was nineteen, twenty-one even, you'd believe her.'

'How old are you?'

'Twenty-seven. Look, I'm sorry. I really am. About everything. But she told me she was nineteen and I believed her. What can I say? Yes, I was attracted to her. But I'm no cradle-snatcher. That wasn't it at all. Most of my girlfriends have been older than me, as a matter of fact. She just had this aura, like she knew what it was all about, but when it got right down to it she was vulnerable, too, and you felt like you wanted to protect her. It's hard to explain.'

Banks felt sad and angry, as if this really *was* his own daughter he was discussing. Stupid. 'What happened? You say you don't know where she is, that she found another boyfriend. Who?'

'I told you I don't know his name. I'd tell you if I did. I don't know who he is. All I know is the last time I saw her she was with him. They were coming out of a pub in Soho, not far from the GlamourPuss offices. I'd been there having a pint with Rick and trying to shake a bit more business out of him. I'd been taking a few candids out in the street. I was upset about her leaving me without a word, so I went up to her and tried to talk to her.'

'What happened?'

'A couple of goons attacked me.' He pointed to his nose. 'That's how I got this.' Then he pointed to his head. 'And I had to have seven stitches where my head hit the pavement.'

'Two goons?'

'That's what they looked like. Bodyguards. Minders. Nobody said a word. It all happened so quickly.'

'When did this happen?'

'About a month ago.'

'What was Louisa doing at the time?'

'She was hanging on this bloke's arm, not doing anything really. She looked high. I mean *really* high, not just like a couple of drinks and a spliff high. I heard her giggling when I went down.'

'And the man she was with? What did he look like?'

'Stone-faced. All sharp angles, like it was carved from granite. Hard eyes, too. Didn't blink. Didn't smile. Not a word. When I was on the ground, one of the goons kicked me, then they all just disappeared. Someone came out of the pub and helped me up, and that was that. I was lucky they didn't break my camera. It was a Minolta. An expensive one.'

Banks thought for a moment. He didn't like what he was hearing at all. 'Can you tell me anything more about this man?'

Craig shrugged. 'Don't know, really. I didn't get a really good look at him. Tall. Maybe about six two or three. Looked older.'

'Than who?'

'More your age than mine.'

Banks felt his stomach rumbling and realized he hadn't eaten all day, except for a slice of toast with his morning coffee.

He hadn't finished with Craig yet, though; there were still things he needed to know. 'Is there anywhere decent to eat around here?' he asked.

'Couple of good Indian places down the high street, if that's your sort of thing.'

'Fancy a meal? On me.'

Craig looked surprised. 'Sure. Why not? Just let me hang up the negs to dry. Won't be a minute.' He left the room. Banks stayed where he was, finishing his lager, and thought a bit more about darkrooms, Uncle Ted, and Sandra naked in the infrared light. Dinner. Tomorrow.

They walked down to the narrow high street. The wind had dropped, but it was a chilly evening and there weren't many people out. Banks was glad of his warm leather jacket. They passed a sign on the wall of one of the buildings that made some reference to Richard III. Historical too, then, Stony Stratford.

'It's supposed to be where he picked up the Princes in the Tower,' said Craig. 'Before they were in the Tower, like. You know, the ones he killed.'

Craig picked a relatively inexpensive Indian restaurant. It was comfortably warm inside, and the exotic smells made Banks's mouth water the minute they got in the door. When they had ordered beers and were nibbling on poppadoms in anticipation of their main courses, Banks picked up the subject of Louisa again. 'Did she ever mention this boyfriend to you before?'

'No. One day everything seemed fine, the next she packed her stuff – what little she had – and she was gone before I got home. I had a wedding to shoot that day. My first, and it was a big deal. When I got home, all I found was a note. I remember it word for word.' He closed his eyes. '"Sorry, Craig, it's just not working out. You're a sweet lad. Maybe see you around. Hugs and kisses, Louisa." That was it.'

'You had no idea at all what was going on? That she'd met someone else?'

'Not at the time, no. But the bloke's often the last to find out, isn't he?'

'Had you been arguing?'

'Yeah, but that was par for the course with Louisa.'

'You argued a lot?'

'A fair bit.'

'What about?'

'Oh, the usual stuff. She was bored. Our life lacked glamour and excitement. She wanted to go out more. She said I wasn't paying enough attention to her, that I was taking her for granted.'

'Was it true?'

'Maybe. Some of it. I was working a lot, getting paying jobs, like that wedding. I suppose I was probably spending more time in the darkroom than I was with her. And I didn't know where she was half the time. I mean, we'd only been living together a month or so. It wasn't as if we were an old married couple, or something.'

'She went out alone a lot?'

'She said she was out with her mates. Sometimes she didn't come back till two or three in the morning. Said she'd been clubbing. Well, you don't hold on to a girl like Louisa by clipping her wings, so there wasn't a lot I could do about it. It got me down a bit, though.'

'Did you know any of her friends?'

'Only Ruth. She introduced us.'

'Ruth?'

'Yeah. Ruth Walker.'

'How did she know Louisa?'

'Dunno. But Ruth's always taking in strays. Heart of gold, she's got. Do anything for you. Louisa was staying with her when we met. I've known Ruth since I was at college. She was doing a computer course at the university, and she helped me out with some digital photography software. We got to be friends. I'd see her once in a while, you know, take her down the pub or out to see a movie or a band or something – she's really into the live-music scene – and one time I went, there was Louisa, sitting on her sofa. I won't say it was love at first sight, but it was definitely *something*.'

Lust, no doubt, thought Banks. 'Were you and Ruth lovers?'

'Ruth and me? Nah. Nothing like that. We were just friends.'

The food came – Balti prawns for Craig and lamb korma for Banks, along with pilau rice, mango chutney and naan – and they paused as they shared out the dishes. The ubiquitous sitar music droned in the background.

'Okay,' said Banks after a few bites to stay the rumbling of his stomach. 'What happened next?'

'Well, Ruth got Louisa a job at the same company she worked for out Canary Wharf way. Nothing much, just fetching and carrying, really. Louisa didn't have any great job skills. But it brought in a quid or two, helped get her on her feet.'

'Did Louisa talk much about her past?'

'Only to put it down. Sounds as if you gave her a pretty rough time. Sorry, but you asked.'

'I suppose I did.' Banks tasted the lamb. It was a bit too greasy, but it would do. He soaked up some sauce with his naan.

'Anyway,' Craig went on, 'she didn't last long there. Didn't seem to take to office work at all, as a matter of fact. Or any work, for that matter.'

'Why was that?'

'I think it was mostly her attitude. Louisa thinks other people are there to work for her, not the other way around. And she's got attitude with a capital A.'

'How did she survive after that?'

'She had a few quid of her own in the bank. She never said

how much, but she never seemed to go short. Sometimes she borrowed off Ruth or me. She could go through money like nobody's business, could Louisa.'

'And the new boyfriend?'

Craig nodded. 'If he's the sort of bloke who can afford minders, then he's probably not short of a few quid, is he? Gone up in the world, she has, young Louisa.'

That's right, Banks thought. And if he's the sort of bloke who *needs* minders, then the odds are that he makes his money in a dodgy way, a way that could make him enemies who want to do him physical harm, a way that could also put Emily in jeopardy. The more Banks heard, the more worried about her he became. 'Are you sure you've got no idea who he is, where I can find them?'

'Sorry. If I knew, I'd tell you. Believe me.'

'Do you think Ruth Walker might know?'

'It's possible. She wouldn't tell me when I asked her, but I think Louisa must have told her I was obsessed with her, stalking her or something.'

'Were you?'

'Course not.'

'Then what makes you think that?'

'Just the way she looked at me. We haven't been quite the same since that whole thing with Louisa, Ruth and me. But she might tell you.'

Banks shrugged. 'It's worth a try.'

Craig gave him the address of Ruth's flat in Kennington. 'You know, I really liked Louisa,' he mused. 'Maybe I loved her . . . I don't know. She was pretty wild, and her mood swings . . . well . . . all I can say is she could make one of those divas look stable. But I liked her. Still, maybe I'm better off without her. At least I can concentrate on my work now, and I need to do that. Lord knows, she ran me ragged. But for a while there, when she'd first gone, there was a big hole in my life. I know it sounds corny, but I'd no energy, no real will to go on. The world didn't look the same. Not as bright. Not as interesting. Grey.'

Welcome to reality, thought Banks. He had come prepared to be hard on Craig Newton – after all, Craig *had* taken the nude photographs of Emily that had ended up on the GlamourPuss website for every pervert to drool over – but the lad was actually turning out to be quite likeable. If Craig was to be believed, he had genuinely thought that Emily was nineteen – and who wouldn't, going by the evidence Banks had seen and heard so far – and the web photos had simply been a foolish lark. Craig also seemed to care about Emily – he hadn't only been with her for the sex, or whatever else a sixteen-year-old girl had to offer a twenty-seven-year-old man – and that went a long way in Banks's estimation.

On the other hand, this new boyfriend sounded like trouble, and Emily Louise Riddle herself sounded like a royal pain in the arse.

'Why did you move out here?' Banks asked. 'Because of Louisa?'

'Partly. It was around that time. It's funny, but I'd mentioned getting out of London a couple of times and Louisa went all cold on me, the way she did when she wasn't getting her own way or heard something she didn't like. Anyway, I got the chance of a partnership in a small studio here with a bloke I went to college with. A straight-up, kosher business this time – portraits and weddings, mostly. No porn. I was fed up of London by then, anyway. Not just the thing with Louisa, but other things. Too expensive. Too hard to make a living. Too much competition. The hours I was putting in. You've really got to hustle hard there, and I was discovering I'm not much of a hustler at heart. I began to think I'd be better off as a bigger fish in a smaller pond.'

'And?'

He looked up from his prawns and smiled. 'It seems to be working out.' Then he paused. 'This is weird, though. I never thought I'd be sitting down having a curry with Louisa's dad, chatting in a civilized manner. I've got to say, you're not at all what I imagined.'

'So you said. A boring old fart.'

'Yeah, well, that's what *she* said. Wouldn't let her do anything, go anywhere. Kept her a virtual prisoner in the house.'

'Lock up your daughters?'

'Yeah. Did you?'

'You know what she's like. What do you think I should have done?'

'With Louisa? I used to think I knew what she was like. Now I'm not so sure. From what you say, she told me a pack of lies right from the start. How can I believe anything about her? What do you do with someone like her?'

Indeed, thought Banks, feeling just a little guilty over his deception. What *do* you do? The thing was, that the more he found himself pretending to be Louisa's father, the more he found himself slipping into the role. So much so that on the slow train back to Euston later that evening, after Craig had kindly given him a lift to the station, when he thought about what his own daughter might be up to in Paris with Damon, he wasn't sure whether he was angry at Tracy or at Emily Riddle.

And the more he thought about the situation, the more he realized that it had never been *finding* Emily Riddle that concerned him; it was what he was going to do *after* he'd found her that really bothered him.

3

Saturday morning dawned cool and overcast, but the wind was quickly tearing a few holes in the ragged clouds. 'Enough blue sky to make baby a new bonnet,' as Banks's mother would say. Banks lingered over coffee and a toasted teacake in a café on Tottenham Court Road, not far from his hotel, reading the morning papers and watching people checking out the electronics shops across the road.

He had slept well. Surprisingly so, since the hotel was the same one that he and Detective Sergeant Annie Cabbot had stayed in during his last case. Not the same room, thank God, but the same floor. Memories of her skin warm and moist against his kept him awake longer than he would have liked and made him feel vaguely guilty, but in the end he drifted into a deep and dreamless sleep, from which he awoke feeling unusually refreshed.

According to his *A to Z*, Ruth Walker lived quite close to the cramped flat off Clapham Road that Banks and Sandra had lived in for a few years in the early eighties, when the kids were little. Not exactly the 'good old days', but happy for the most part, before the job started taking too much of a toll on him. Simpler, maybe. Sandra worked part-time as a dental receptionist on Kennington Park Road, he remembered, and Banks was usually too busy out playing cops and robbers to take his wife to the theatre or help the kids with their homework.

It wasn't much more than a couple of miles from the West End, as the crow flies, and he decided the walk would do him good. He had always loved walking in cities, and London was a great place for it. He had been cheated out of Paris, so he would have to make the best of where he was. If he set off now, he realized, he would probably arrive around lunchtime. If he got Louisa's address from Ruth, he would go there in the early evening, between six and seven, which he had always found was a good time to catch people in. That should also leave him plenty of time to meet Sandra at eight in Camden Town.

A cool wind skipped off the murky river and whistled around his ears as he crossed Waterloo Bridge. He glanced back. Shafts of light lanced through the clouds and lit on the dome of St Paul's. It was odd, Banks thought, but when you visit a place you used to live in for a long time, you see it differently; you become more like a tourist in your own land. He had never noticed Big Ben, the Houses of Parliament or St Paul's in the days when he had lived there. Even now, his copper's eye was more tuned to the two shifty-looking skinheads across the road, who seemed to be following a couple of Japanese tourists, than it was to the beauty of the London architecture.

It was pushing twelve thirty when Banks got to Ruth's street just off Kennington Road. The brick terrace houses were four storeys high and so narrow they seemed pressed together like a mouthful of bad teeth. Here and there someone had added a lick of bright paint to a window frame, or put out a few potted plants in the bay window.

The name 'R. A. Walker' appeared by the third-floor bell, a dead giveaway that the occupant was a woman. Banks pressed and heard it ring way up in the distance. He waited, but nobody came. Then he tried again. Still nothing. After standing on the doorstep for a few minutes, he gave up. He hadn't wanted to phone ahead and tip her off that he was coming – finding that surprise often worked best in situations like this – so he had been prepared to wait.

Banks decided to have his lunch and call back in an hour or so. If she wasn't in then, he'd think of a new plan. He found a serviceable pub on the main street and enjoyed a pint as he finished reading the newspaper. A few regulars stood at the bar, and a younger crowd were gathered around the video machines. One man, wearing a tartan cap, kept nipping around the corner to the betting shop and coming back to tell everyone in a loud voice how much he'd lost and how the horse he'd backed belonged in the glue factory. Everyone laughed indulgently. Nobody paid Banks any mind, which was just the way he liked it. He glanced over the menu and settled finally on a chicken pie. It would have suited Annie Cabbot just fine, Banks thought as he searched in vain among peas and carrots for the meat; Annie was a vegetarian.

A short while later, he stood on Ruth Walker's doorstep again and gave her bell a long push. This time, he was rewarded by a wary voice over the intercom.

'Who is it?'

'I've come about Louisa,' Banks said. 'Louisa Gamine.'

'Louisa? What about her? She's not here.'

'I need to talk to you.'

There was a long pause – so long that Banks thought Ruth had hung up the intercom on him – then the voice said, 'Come up. Top floor.' A buzzer went off and Banks pushed the front door open.

The stairs were carpeted, though the fabric had worn thin in places and the pattern was hard to make out. A variety of cooking smells assailed Banks as he climbed the narrow staircase: a hint of curry, garlic, tomato sauce. When he got to the top, there was only one door. It opened almost immediately when he knocked, and a young woman looked at him through narrowed eyes. After she had studied him for a while, she opened the door and let him in.

The best Banks could say of Ruth Walker was that she was plain. It was a cruel and unfair description, he knew, but it was true. Ruth was the kind of girl who, in his adolescence, always went around with an attractive friend, the one you really wanted. The Ruths of this world you usually tried to palm off on *your* friend. There was nothing distinguishing about her except, perhaps, the intelligence perceptible in her disconcerting and restless grey eyes. Already she seemed to have a permanent frown etched in her forehead.

She was dressed in baggy jeans and a T-shirt commemorating an old Oasis tour. Her hair, dyed black, gelled and cut spiky, didn't suit her round face at all. Nor did the collection of rings and studs through the crescent edges of her ears. Her complexion looked dry as parchment, and she still suffered the ravages of acne.

The flat was spacious, with a high ceiling and one of those Chinese-style globe lampshades over the bulb. Bookshelves stood propped on bricks against one wall, not much on them, apart from tattered paperbacks and a few software manuals, and a computer stood on the desk under the window. A sheepskin rug covered part of the hardwood floor, and various quilts and patterned coverlets hung over the second-hand three-piece suite. It was a comfortable room. Ruth Walker, Banks had to admit, had made a nice home for herself.

'I don't usually let strangers in,' she said.

'A good policy.'

'But you mentioned Louisa. You're not one of her new friends, are you?'

'No, I'm not. You don't like them?'

'I can take them or leave them.' Ruth sniffed and reached for a packet of Embassy Regal resting on the coffee table. 'Bad habit I picked up in university. Want a cup of tea?'

'Please.' It would set them at ease, Banks thought, create the right atmosphere for the sort of informal chat he wanted. Ruth put the cigarettes down without lighting one and walked into the kitchen. She had a slight limp. Not enough to slow her down, but noticeable if you looked closely enough. Banks looked at the books: Maeve Binchy, Rosamunde Pilcher, Catherine Cookson. A few CDs lay scattered beside the stereo, but Banks hadn't heard of most of the groups, except for the Manic Street Preachers, Sheryl Crow, Beth Orton, Radiohead and P.J. Harvey. Still, Ruth probably hadn't heard of Arnold Bax or Gerald Finzi, either.

When Ruth came back with the tea and sat opposite him, she still seemed to be checking him out, probing him with those suspicious grey eyes of hers. 'Louisa,' she said, when she had finally lit her cigarette. 'What about her?'

'I'm looking for her. Do you know where she is?'

'Why?'

'Does it matter?'

'It might. You could be out to do her harm.'

'I'm not.'

'What do you want with her, then?'

Banks paused. Might as well do it again; after all, he'd got this far on a lie, and it was beginning to fit so well he almost believed it himself, even though he had never met Emily Riddle. 'I'm her father,' he said. 'I just want to talk to her.'

Ruth stared at him a moment, her eyes narrowing. 'I don't think so.' She shook her head.

'You don't think what?'

'That you're Louisa's father.'

'Why not?'

'He wouldn't come looking for her, for a start.'

'I love my daughter,' Banks said, which at least was true.

'No. You don't understand. I saw a photo. A family photo she had with the rest of her things. There's no point lying. I *know* it wasn't you.'

Banks paused, stunned as much by Emily's taking a family photo as by Ruth's immediate uncovering of his little deception. Time for a change of tack. 'Okay,' he said. 'I'm not her father. But he asked me to look for her, to try to find her and ask her if she'd talk to him.'

'Why didn't he come himself?'

'He's afraid that if she knows he's looking for her she'll make herself even more scarce.'

'He's got that one right,' said Ruth. 'Look, why should I tell you anything? Louisa left home of her own free will, and she was of legal age. She came down here to live her own life away from her parents. Why should I mess things up for her?'

'I'm not here to force her to do anything she doesn't want,' said Banks. 'She can stay down here if she likes. All her father wants is to know what she's doing, where she lives, if she's all right. And if she'll talk to him, great, if not—'

'Why should I trust you? You've already lied to me.'

'Is she in any trouble, Ruth?' Banks asked. 'Does she need help?'

'Help? Louisa? You must be joking. She's the kind who always lands on her feet, no matter what. After she's landed on her back first, that is.'

'I thought she was a friend of yours?'

'She was. Is.' Ruth made an impatient gesture. 'She just annoys me sometimes, that's all. Most people do. Don't your friends piss you off from time to time?'

'But *is* there any real reason for concern?'

'I'm sure I don't know.'

Banks sipped some tea; it tasted bitter. 'Where did you meet her?'

'Down near King's Cross. She came up to me in the street and asked me the way to the nearest youth hostel. We got talking. I could tell she'd just arrived and she wasn't quite sure what to do or where to go.' Ruth shrugged. 'I know how lonely and friendless London can be, especially when you're new to it all.'

'So you took her in?'

'I felt sorry for her.'

'And she lived with you here?'

Ruth's cheeks reddened. 'Look, I'm not a lezzy, if that's

what you're thinking. I offered her my spare room till she got on her feet. That's all. Can't a person do someone a good turn any more without it being turned into some sort of sex thing?'

'I didn't mean to suggest that,' said Banks. 'I'm sorry if it upset you.'

'Yeah . . . well. Just be careful what you go around saying to people, that's all.'

'You and Louisa *are* friends, though, you said?'

'Yeah. She stayed here for a while. I helped get her a job, but it didn't take. Then she met Craig, a bloke I knew from college, and she went off to live with him.'

Ruth spoke in a curiously dispassionate way, but Banks got the impression there was a lot beneath the surface she wasn't saying. He also got the sense that she was constantly assessing, evaluating, calculating, and that being found out in his little lie had put him somehow in thrall to her. 'I've talked to Craig Newton,' he said, 'and he told me she left him for a new boyfriend. Sounds like a nasty piece of work. Know who he is?'

'Just some bloke she met at a party.'

'Were you there? Did you meet him?'

'Yes.'

'Have you seen them since?'

'They came round here once. I think Louisa was showing him off. *He* certainly didn't seem impressed by what he saw.'

'Do you know his name?'

'Barry Clough.'

'Do you know the address?'

Ruth fumbled for another cigarette, and when she had lit it and breathed out her first lungful of smoke, she nodded. 'Yeah. They live in one of those fancy places out Little Venice way. Louisa had me over to a dinner party there once – catered, of course. I think she was trying to impress *me* that time.'

'Did it work?'

'It takes more than a big house and a couple of has-been

rock stars. And maybe a backbencher and a bent copper or two.'

Banks smiled. 'What does he do for a living?'

'Some sort of businessman. He's got connections with the music business. If you ask me, he's a drug dealer.'

'What makes you say that?'

'Fancy house. Always lots of coke around. Rock stars. Stands to reason, doesn't it?'

'Does Louisa take drugs?'

'Is the Pope Polish?'

'How long ago did they meet?'

'Bit over two months.'

'Have you seen much of her since that time?'

'Not much. You're beginning to sound like a copper, you know.'

Banks didn't like the way she was looking at him, as if she *knew.* 'I'm just worried, that's all,' he said.

'Why? She's not *your* daughter.'

Banks didn't want to explain about his own daughter, at this moment no doubt walking around Paris hand in hand with Damon, or perhaps not even bothering with the sights, deciding instead to spend the weekend in bed. 'Her father's a good mate of mine,' he said instead, the words almost sticking in his throat as he uttered them. 'I'd hate to see any harm come to her.'

'Bit late for that, isn't it? I mean, it was nearly six months ago when she first came down here. He should have put a bit more effort into finding her back then, if you ask me.' She paused, narrowed her eyes again, then said, 'I'm not sure about you. There's something you're not telling me. You weren't screwing her, were you? I wouldn't put it past her. She was no innocent from the provinces, even when she first came here. She knew what was what.'

'She's a bit young for me,' Banks said.

Ruth gave a harsh laugh. 'At your age I should think it's

often a matter of the younger the better. Why do you think they have prostitutes as young as thirteen, fourteen? 'Cos the girls like it?'

Banks felt the sting of her remark, but he couldn't think of an appropriate response. 'We're getting off track here.'

'Not if you want me to give you Louisa's address, we're not. I've got to satisfy myself you're not a pervert, not some creep, haven't I? And don't come the age bit. She could coax a ninety-year-old bishop out of his cassock, could Louisa.'

'All I can do is repeat what I've already told you. There was nothing like that. I've got a daughter her age, myself.'

'You have?'

'Yes.'

'What's her name?'

Surprised, Banks answered, 'Tracy.'

Ruth evaluated him some more. 'You don't look old enough.'

'Want to see my birth certificate?'

'No, that's not necessary. Besides, I don't suppose you actually carry it around with you, do you?'

'It was a . . . never mind,' said Banks, feeling he had had just about as much of Ruth Walker and her sharp edges as he could take. No wonder Emily had run off with Craig Newton at the first opportunity.

Ruth got up and walked to the window. 'Would you believe that sad pillock over there?' she said a few moments later, almost muttering to herself. 'He works security, on the night shift. Hasn't a clue the bloke from number fifty-three is shagging the arse off his wife every night. Dirty bastard. Maybe I should tell him?'

Before Banks could make any comment, Ruth turned sharply, arms folded, a smug smile on her face. 'All right,' she said. 'I'll tell you where they live. But you're wasting your time. She's had it with the lot of you. She won't listen to a word you've got to say.'

'It's worth a try. At least I'll find out whether she's all right, what she's up to.'

Ruth gave him a pitying look. 'Maybe you will,' she said. 'And maybe you won't.'

Shortly after six o'clock that evening, Banks got off the tube at Warwick Avenue and walked towards the address Ruth had given him. Had it been a lovely summer evening, he might have walked down the steps, lingered by the canal and admired the brightly coloured houseboats. But it had turned dark by late afternoon, as usual, and it was a chilly evening with the smell of rain in the wind.

The address turned out to be a villa-style building, square and detached within a high enclosing wall. In the wall stood an iron gate. A locked gate.

Banks could have kicked himself for not expecting something like this. If Louisa's boyfriend was the type to go around with minders, he was also the type to live in a bloody fortress. Getting to see Emily Riddle wouldn't be quite so easy as knocking on the door or ringing the bell.

At the front, two of the downstairs windows and one upstairs were lit behind dark curtains, and a light shone over the front door. Banks tried to think of the best approach. He could simply call through on the intercom and announce himself, see if that gained him admission. Alternatively, he could climb the gate and go and knock on the door. Then what? Rescue the damsel in distress? Climb to the upstairs window on her hair? Flee with her over his shoulder? As far as he knew, though, Emily Riddle wasn't in distress, nor was she held captive in a tower. In fact, she might well be having the time of her life.

He stood in front of the gate and stared through the bars, cheeks so close he could feel the cold from the iron. There was nothing else for it, really; he would have to use the intercom and just hope he could gain admittance. He obviously couldn't pass himself off as Emily's father this time, but if he said he came with an important message from her family, that ought to get him inside. It might just work.

Before he could press the buzzer, he felt a strong hand grasp the back of his neck and push his face towards the bars, so the cold iron chafed against his cheeks. 'What the fuck are you doing here?' the voice asked him.

Banks's first impulse was to kick back hard at the man's shins with his heel, or tread down sharply on his instep, then slip free, swivel around and lash out. But he had to hold himself in check, remember why he was here, who he was supposed to be. If he beat up his assailant, where would that get him? Nowhere, most likely. On the other hand, maybe this was his best way in.

'I'm looking for Louisa,' he said.

The grip loosened. Banks turned and found himself facing a man in a tight-fitting suit who looked as if he might have been one of Mike Tyson's sparring partners. Probably just as well he *hadn't* tried to fight back, he thought.

'Louisa? What do you want with Louisa?' the man said.

'I want to talk to her, that's all,' he said. 'Her father sent me.'

'Fuck a duck,' said the minder.

'I was going to ring the bell,' Banks went on. 'I was just looking to see if there were any lights on, if there was anyone home.'

'You were?'

'Yes.'

'I think you'd better come with me, mate,' the minder said, which was exactly what Banks had hoped for. 'We'll see what Mr Clough has to say about that.'

The minder slipped a credit-card-style key into the mechanism at the side of the intercom, punched in a seven-digit number which Banks was amazed he had the brains to remember, and the gate slid open on oiled hinges. The minder was holding Banks by the arm now, but only hard enough to break a few small bones, as he led him down the short path to the front door which he opened with a simple Yale key. Sometimes security, like beauty, is only skin deep.

They stood in a bright corridor, which ran all the way through to a gleaming modern kitchen at the back of the house. Several doors led off the corridor, all closed, and immediately to their right, a thickly carpeted staircase led to the upper levels. It was a hell of a lot fancier than Ruth's flat, Banks thought, and grander than anything Craig Newton could afford, too. *Always landed on her feet.* The Riddles said they had given Emily all the advantages that money could afford – the horse, piano lessons, holidays, expensive schooling – and they had certainly raised a high-maintenance daughter by the looks of this place.

Muffled music came from one of the rooms. A pop song Banks didn't recognize. As soon as the front door shut behind them, the minder called out, 'Boss?'

One of the doors opened and a tall man walked out. He wasn't fat, or even overly muscular like the minder, but he certainly looked as if he lifted a few weights at the gym once or twice a week. As Craig Newton had pointed out, his face was all angles, as if it had been carved from stone, and he was handsome, if you liked that sort of thing, rather like a younger Nick Nolte.

He was wearing a cream Armani suit over a red T-shirt, had a deep suntan and a grey ponytail about six inches long hanging over his back collar. Around his neck he wore a thick gold chain, which matched the one on his wrist and the chunky signet ring over the hairy knuckle on his right hand. Banks pegged him at early to mid-forties, which wasn't much younger than Jimmy Riddle. Or Banks himself, for that matter.

The hard glint in his eyes and the cocky confidence with which he moved showed that he was someone to watch out for. Banks had seen that look before in the eyes of hardened criminals, people to whom the world and its contents are there for the taking, and for whom any impediments are simply to be brushed aside as easily as dandruff off the collar.

'What's this?' he asked, eyes on Banks.

'Found him lurking by the gate, boss. Just standing there. Says he wants to see Louisa.'

Barry Clough raised an eyebrow, but the hardness in his eyes didn't ease a jot. 'Does he now? What might you be wanting with Louisa, little man?'

'Her father asked me to look for her,' Banks said. 'He wants me to deliver a message.'

'Private investigator?'

'Just a friend of the family.'

Clough studied Banks closely for what seemed like minutes, then a glint of humour flashed into his eyes the way a shark flashes through the water. 'No problem,' he said, ushering Banks into the room. 'A girl should stay in touch with her family, I always say, though I can't say as she's ever offered to take me home to meet Mummy and Daddy yet. I don't even know where they live.'

Banks said nothing. The minder shifted from foot to foot.

'You're lucky to find us in,' said Clough. 'Louisa and I just got back from Florida a couple of days ago. Can't stand the bloody weather here in winter. We take off as often as we can. I'll call her down for you. In the meantime, take a load off. Drink?'

'No, thanks. I won't take long.'

Clough looked at his watch. An expensive one. 'You've got twenty minutes,' he said. 'Then we've got a Bonfire Night party to go to. Sure you won't have that drink?'

'No, thanks.'

Banks sat down as Clough left the room. He heard muffled footsteps on the staircase. The minder had disappeared into the kitchen. The room Banks found himself in had that old-fashioned wainscoted look he wouldn't have expected judging by what he had seen of the bright hall and the modern kitchen at the back. Paintings hung on the walls, mostly English landscapes. A couple of them looked old and genuine. Not Constables or anything, but they probably cost a bob or two. On one wall stood a locked, barred glass case full of guns. Deactivated collector's models, Banks guessed. Nobody would be stupid enough to put real guns on display like that.

Logs crackled and spat out sparks from the large stone hearth. The music was coming from an expensive stereo set up at the far end of the room. Now he was closer to the source, Banks realized he *did* recognize it; it was an old Joy Division album. 'Heart and Soul' was playing.

He heard voices upstairs, but he couldn't make out what they were saying. At one point, a woman's voice rose almost to the point where he could hear the defiance in her tone, then, at a barked order from the man, it stopped. A few seconds later, the door opened and in she walked. He hadn't heard her come down the stairs, nor did he hear her walk across the Turkish carpet.

Craig Newton was right. Talk about a mix of innocence and experience. She could have been sixteen, which she was, but she could have been twenty-six just as easily, and in some ways she reminded Banks even more of her mother in the flesh than in the photographs he had seen: blue eyes, cherry lips. What he hadn't been able to tell from those photos, though, was that she had a smattering of freckles across her small nose and high cheekbones, and that her eyes were a much paler blue than Rosalind's. The Florida sun didn't seem to have done much for her skin, which was as pale as her mother's. Perhaps she had stayed indoors or walked around under a parasol like a Southern belle.

Rosalind was a little shorter and fuller figured than her daughter, and of course her hairstyle was different. Emily had a ragged fringe, and her fine natural-blonde hair fell straight to her shoulders and brushed against them as she moved. Tall and long-legged, she had the anorexic, thoroughbred look of a professional model. Heroin chic. She was wearing denim Capris that came halfway up her calves, and a loose cable-knit sweater. She walked barefoot, he noticed, showing off her shapely ankles and slim feet, the toenails painted crimson. For some reason, Coleridge's line from 'Christabel' flashed through Banks's mind: ' . . . her blue-veined feet unsandalled were'. It had always seemed an improbably erotic image to him, ever since he first came across the poem at school, and now he knew why.

Though Emily walked with style and self-possession, there was a list to her progress, and when he looked closely, Banks noticed a few tiny grains of white powder in the soft indentation between her nose and her upper lip. Even as he looked, her pointed pink tongue slipped out of her mouth and swept it away. She smiled at him. Her eyes were slightly unfocused and the pupils dilated, little random chips of light dancing in them like feldspar catching the sun.

'I don't believe I've had the pleasure,' she said, stretching out her hand to him. It came at the end of an impossibly long arm. Banks stood up and shook. Her cool, soft fingers grasped his loosely for a second, then disengaged. He introduced himself. Emily sat in an armchair by the fire, legs curled under her, and toyed with a loose thread at the end of one sleeve.

'So you're Banks?' she said. 'I've heard of you. Detective Chief Inspector Banks. Am I right?'

'You're right. All good, I hope?'

She smiled. 'Intriguing, at least.' Then her expression turned to one of boredom. 'What does Daddy want after all this time? Oh, Christ, what *is* this dreadfully dull music? Sometimes Barry plays the most depressing things.'

'Joy Division,' said Banks. 'He committed suicide. The lead singer.'

'I'm not bloody surprised. I'd commit suicide if I sounded like him.' She got up, shut off the CD and replaced it with Alanis Morissette's *Jagged Little Pill*. Alanis sang about all she

67

really wanted. She didn't sound a lot more cheerful than Joy Division, Banks thought, but the music was more upbeat, more modern. 'He's still an old punk at heart, is Barry. Did you know he used to be a roadie for a punk band?'

'What does he do now?' Banks asked casually.

'He's a businessman. Bit of this, bit of that. You know the sort of thing.' She laughed. It sounded like a crystal glass shattering. 'Come to think of it, I don't really know what he does. He's away a lot. He doesn't talk about it much.' She put a finger to her lips. 'It's all terribly hush-hush.'

I'll bet it is, thought Banks. As she had been speaking, he found himself trying to place her accent. He couldn't. Riddle had probably moved counties more times than he'd had hot dinners to make chief constable by his mid-forties, so Emily had ended up with a kind of characterless, nowhere accent, not especially posh, but certainly without any of the rough edges a regional bias gives. Banks knew that his own accent was hard to place too, as he had grown up in Peterborough, lived in London for more than twenty years and in North Yorkshire for about seven.

As Emily talked now, she walked around the room touching objects, occasionally picking up an ornament, such as a heavy glass paperweight with a rose design trapped inside, and putting it back, or moving it somewhere else. She ended up standing by the fireplace, elbow leaning on the mantelpiece, fist to her cheek, one hip cocked. 'Did you tell me what you'd come for?' she asked. 'I don't remember.'

'You haven't given me a chance yet.'

She put her hand to her mouth and stifled a giggle. 'Ooh, I'm sorry. That's me, that is. Talk, talk, talk.'

Banks saw an ashtray on the table with a couple of butts crushed out in it. He reached for his cigarettes, offered Emily one, which she took, and lit one for himself. Then he leaned forward a little in his armchair and said, 'I was talking to your father a couple of days ago, Emily. He's worried about you. He wants you to get in touch with him.'

'My name's Louisa. And I'm not going home.'

'Nobody said you were. But it wouldn't do you any harm to get in touch with him and let him know how you're doing, where you are, would it?'

'He'd only get angry.' She pouted, then moved away from the fireplace. 'How did you find me? I didn't tell *anyone* where I'm from. I didn't even use my real name.'

'I know,' said Banks. 'But, really: Louisa *Gamine*. You're a clever girl, you've had an expensive education. It took me a little while to work it out, but I got there in the end. *Gamine* means a girl with mischievous charm and is an anagram of enigma, which means puzzle, or, this case, Riddle. Your father said you were very good with language.'

She clapped her hands together. 'Clever man. You got it. What a brilliant detective. But that still doesn't answer my question.'

'Your little brother saw your photo on the Internet.'

Emily's jaw dropped and she fell back onto the chair. It was hard to tell, but Banks thought her reaction was genuine. 'Ben? Ben saw that?'

Banks nodded.

'Oh, shit.' She flicked her half-smoked cigarette into the fire. 'That wasn't supposed to happen.'

'I don't imagine it was.'

'And he told Mum?'

'That's right.'

'She'd never have told Dad. Not in a million years. She knows what he's like as well as I do.'

'I don't know how he found out,' said Banks, 'but he did.'

Emily laughed. 'I'd love to have seen his face.'

'No, you wouldn't.'

'And he sent you to look for me?'

'That's about it.'

'Why?'

'Why did he send me?'

'Well, I'm damn sure he wouldn't bother coming himself, but why you? He doesn't even *like* you.'

'But he knows I'm good at my job.'

'Let me guess. He's promised you he'll leave you alone if you do as he asks? Don't trust him.'

'I can't honestly say as I do, but I've got . . .'

'What?'

'Never mind. It doesn't matter.'

'Tell me what you were going to say.'

'No.' Banks didn't want to tell her about Tracy, that in an odd sort of way he was doing this for her, making up for his own absences and shortcomings as a father.

Emily sulked for a few moments, then she stood up again and paced in front of him, counting off imaginary points on her fingers. 'Let me see . . . the pictures took you to GlamourPuss . . . right? That took you to Craig . . .? But he doesn't know where I am. I told . . . Ah, Ruth! Ruth told you?'

Banks said nothing.

'Well, she would. She's a jealous cow. She'd just love to cause trouble for me, the ugly bitch, just because I've met someone like Barry and she's still stuck in her poky little flat in Kennington. Do you know . . .'

'What?'

'Nothing. Never mind.'

'What were *you* going to say?'

Emily smiled. 'No. Now it's my turn to tease. I'm not telling you.' Before Banks could frame a response, she stopped pacing and knelt in front of him, looking up into his face with her sparkling blue eyes. 'So you saw them, too, did you? The photos.'

Banks swallowed. 'Yes.'

'Did you like them? Did they excite you?'

'Not particularly.'

'Liar.' She jumped up again, a smile of triumph on her face. 'Besides, they were just a joke. A laugh. Daddy's got nothing to worry about from them. It's not as if I've taken up a career in the porno business or anything.'

'I'm glad to hear it,' said Banks.

'He's just worried about me ruining his spotless reputation, isn't he?'

'That's part of it.' Banks didn't feel he necessarily had to paint an idealized picture of Riddle, especially to his runaway daughter. She probably knew him better than anyone. 'But he did also seem genuinely concerned about you.'

'I'm sure he did.' Emily had sat down again now and seemed thoughtful. 'Chief Constable Jeremiah Riddle, champion of family values, quality time, the caring, concerned copper. "My daughter the slut" wouldn't fit at all with that image, would it?'

'It wouldn't do any harm if you just gave him a call and reassured him everything's okay, would it?' Banks said. 'And what about your mother? She's worried sick, too.'

Her eyes flashed. 'You don't know anything. What do you know about it?' She fingered the collar of her sweater and seemed to draw in on herself. 'It was like being in prison up there. You can't go here. You can't do that. You can't see him. You can't talk to her. Don't forget your piano lessons. Have you done your homework? Be in before eight o'clock. I'd no room to breathe. It was stifling me. I couldn't be free, couldn't be myself.'

'Are you now?'

'Of course I am.' She stood up again. Red patches glowed on her cheeks. 'Tell Daddy to fuck off. Tell the old man to just fuck off. Let him wonder. Let him worry. I'm not going to set his mind at rest. Because . . . you know what?'

'What?'

'Because he was never fucking there anyway. He used to make all these rules and you know what . . . he was never even there to enforce them. Mummy had to do that. And she didn't even care enough. *He was never even there to enforce his own stupid rules.* Isn't that a laugh?' She went to lean against the fireplace again. Alanis Morissette was singing about seeing right through someone, and Banks knew what she meant. Still, he'd done his job, done as he'd been asked. He could give Jimmy Riddle Emily's London address, tell him about Barry Clough. If Riddle wanted to send in the locals to check out Clough's gun collection, set the forensic accountants on his business interests and put in a call to the drugs squad, that was his business. Banks's job was over. It was up to Riddle to take it from there. He tore a page from his notebook and wrote on it: 'If you change your mind, or if there's anything else you want to tell me, any message you want me to deliver, this is where I'm staying. You can phone and leave a message if I'm not there.'

For a moment, he thought she wasn't going to take it, but she did. Then she glanced at it once, crumpled it up and threw it in the fire. The door opened and Barry Clough strode in, smile on his face. He tapped his wristwatch. 'Better get your face on, love,' he said to Emily. 'We're due at Rod's place in half an hour.' He looked at Banks, the smile gone. 'And your time's up, mate,' he said, jerking his thumb towards the front door. 'On your bike.'

4

Banks was running about five minutes late for his dinner with Sandra when he got off the tube at Camden Town. The drizzle had turned into a steady downpour now, and puddles in the gutter were smeared with the gaudy reflections of shop signs and traffic lights. Luckily, the restaurant wasn't far from the underground.

Banks turned up his jacket collar, but he was still soaked by the time he dashed into the restaurant. At first he didn't recognize the woman who smiled and waved him over to her table by the window. Though he had seen Sandra briefly just a couple of months ago, she had changed her appearance completely since then. For a start, she had had her blonde hair cut short and layered. If anything, the style emphasized her dark eyebrows more than ever, and Banks had always found Sandra's eyebrows one of her sexiest features. She was also wearing a pair of round gold-rimmed glasses, not much bigger than the 'granny glasses' that were so popular in the sixties. He had never seen her in glasses before, hadn't known she needed them. From what he could make out, her clothes looked arty, all different layers: a black shawl, a red silk scarf, a red-and-black patterned sweater.

Banks edged into the chair opposite her. He was starving. It seemed ages since that dismal chicken pie in Kennington. 'Sorry I'm a bit late,' he said, drying off his hair with a serviette. 'I'd forgotten what a pain the bloody tube can be.'

Sandra smiled. 'It's all right. Remember, I'm used to your being late.'

Banks let that one go by. He looked around. The restaurant was busy, bustling with waiters and parties coming and going. It was one of those places that Banks thought trendy in its lack of trendiness, all scratched wood tables and partitions, pork chops, steaks and mashed potatoes. But the mashed potatoes had garlic and sun-dried tomatoes in them and cost about three quid a side order.

'I've already ordered some wine,' Sandra said. 'A half-litre of the house claret. I know you prefer red. Okay with you?'

'Fine.' Banks had turned down a drink at Clough's house because he hadn't wanted to be beholden to the bastard in any way, but he wanted one now. 'You're looking good,' he said. 'You've changed. I don't mean that you didn't always look good. You know what I mean.'

Sandra laughed, blushed a little and turned away. 'Thank you,' she said.

'What's with the glasses?'

'They come with age,' she said. 'Any time after your fortieth birthday.'

'Then I'm really living on borrowed time.'

A waiter brought the wine and left it for them to pour themselves. *Pretentious in its unpretentiousness.* Sandra paused as Banks filled their glasses, then lifted hers for a toast. 'How are you, Alan?' she asked.

'Fine,' said Banks. 'Just fine. Couldn't be better.'

'Working?'

'Aren't I always?'

'I thought Jimmy Riddle had shuffled you off to the hinterlands.'

'Even Riddle needs my particular skills every now and then.' Banks sipped some wine. Perfectly quaffable. He looked around and saw it was okay to light a cigarette. 'May I cadge one?' Sandra asked.

'Of course. Still can't give them up completely?'

'Not completely. Oh, Sean doesn't like it. He keeps going on at me to stop. But I don't think one or two a month is really bad for your health.'

Good sign, that, Banks thought: Sean the nag. 'Probably not,' he said. 'I keep waiting for them to announce they were wrong all along and cigarettes are really *good* for you, and it's all the raw vegetables and fruit that do the damage.'

Sandra laughed. 'You'll have a long wait.' She clinked glasses. 'Cheers.'

'Cheers. I was out where we used to live this lunchtime. Kennington.'

'Really? Why? A sentimental journey?'

'Work.'

'It was a pretty cramped flat, as I remember. Much too small with the kids. And that dentist I worked for was a groper.'

'You never told me that.'

'There's lots of things I never told you. You usually seemed to have enough on your plate as it was.'

They studied the menu for a couple of minutes. Banks saw that he was right about the mashed potatoes. And the garlic and sun-dried tomatoes. And the price. He ordered venison sausage with braised red cabbage and garlic mashed potatoes. No sun-dried tomatoes. It seemed the perfect comfort meal for a night like this. Sandra went for steak and *frites*. Their orders given to the waiter, they smoked and drank in silence a while longer. Now he was here with her, Banks didn't know how to approach what he wanted to say. He felt curiously tongue-tied, like a teenager on his first date.

If Sandra would put this silliness with Sean aside and come back, he wanted to tell her, it was still possible that they could rebuild their relationship and move on. True, they had sold the Eastvale semi and Banks's cottage would be a bit small for two, but they could manage there for a while at least. If Banks went through with his transfer to the National Crime Squad – *if* they offered him it – then who knew where they might end up living? And with Riddle owing him now, he would be all right for a glowing recommendation.

'I saw Brian last week,' Sandra said.

'He told me when I phoned him the other evening. I wanted to drop by and see him while I was here, but he said they were off to play some gigs in Scotland.'

Sandra nodded. 'That's right. Aberdeen. He's really excited about their prospects, you know. They've already almost finished their first CD.'

'I know.' Their son Brian played in a rock band. They had just cut their first record with an indie label and were on the verge of getting a deal with a major record company. Banks had heard the band play the last time he was in London and had been knocked out by his son's singing, playing and songwriting talent, had come to see him in a whole new light, a person unto himself, not just an extension of the family. He had almost written Brian off as an idler and a layabout after he nearly failed his degree, but Brian was his own person in Banks's mind now. Independent, talented, free. The same feeling had happened with Tracy, when he had seen her with her new friends in a pub shortly after she started university. He knew he'd lost her, then – at least lost the daughter of his imagination – but in her place he had found a young woman he liked and admired, even if she was off in Paris with the monosyllabic Damon. Letting go can be painful, Banks had learned over the years, but sometimes it hurts more if you try to hold on.

'I thought you were taking Tracy to Paris this weekend.'

'She told you?'

'Of course. Why shouldn't she? I am her mother, after all.'

Banks sipped some wine. 'Something came up,' he said. 'She's gone with a friend.'

Sandra raised an eyebrow. 'Male or female?'

'Male. Bloke called Damon. Seems all right. Tracy can take care of herself.'

'I know that, Alan. It's just . . . just *difficult*, that's all.'

'What is?'

'Trying to bring up two kids this way.'

'Apart?'

'You know what I mean.'

'Even if we were still together, it would be like this. We're not bringing them up any more. They're grown up now, Sandra. They live away from home. The sooner you accept that, the better.'

'Do you think I don't know that? I'm just saying it's hard, that's all. They both seem so distant now.'

'They are. But as I said, it would be like that anyway.'

'Maybe.'

Their food arrived and they both tucked in. The sausage was good, more meat than fat for a change, and so were the garlic mashed potatoes. Sandra pronounced her positive verdict on the steak. A few minutes into the meal, she said, 'Remember when I dropped by to see you up at Gratly?'

'How could I forget?'

'I want to apologize. I'm sorry. I shouldn't have done that. Not unannounced. It was unfair of me.'

'Never mind.'

'How is she?'

'Who?'

'You know who I mean. Your pretty young girlfriend. What was her name?'

'Annie. Annie Cabbot. Detective Sergeant Annie Cabbot.'

'That's right.' Sandra smiled. 'I can't believe you tried to con me into thinking the two of you were working. Her barefoot in those tight shorts. It was plain as the nose on your face. Anyway, how is she?'

'I haven't seen much of her lately.'

'Don't tell me I scared her off?'

'Sort of.'

'Well, she can't have much staying power if she let a little thing like that scare her away.'

'I suppose not.'

'I'm sorry, Alan. Really I am. I don't want to spoil anything for you. I *want* you to find someone. I want you to be happy.'

Banks ate more food and washed it down with wine. Soon, the carafe was empty. 'Another?' he suggested.

'Fine,' said Sandra. 'I'll probably only have one glass, though. If you think you can manage the rest by yourself . . .'

'I'm not driving.' Banks ordered more wine and filled their glasses when it came.

'Was there anything . . . I mean, was there any particular reason you wanted to see me?' Sandra asked.

'Do I need a reason to have dinner with my own wife?'

Sandra flinched. 'I didn't mean you *needed* one, *I* just . . . For crying out loud, Alan, we've been separated for a year now. We've hardly spoken so much as a few words to one another in that time. And that mostly over the telephone. You can't expect me not to wonder if you've got some sort of hidden agenda.'

'I just thought it was time we buried the hatchet, that's all.'

Sandra studied him. 'Sure?'

'Yes, I'm sure.'

'All right, then. Consider it buried.' They clinked glasses again. 'How's Jenny Fuller?'

Jenny was a mutual acquaintance; she was also a clinical psychologist and Banks had sought her help on a number of cases. 'I haven't seen a lot of her. She's pretty busy now she's back teaching at York.'

'You know,' Sandra said, toying with her few remaining *frites* and looking at him sideways, 'there was a time when I thought you and Jenny . . . I mean, she's a very attractive woman.'

'It just never worked out that way,' said Banks, who had

often wondered why it hadn't, even when it seemed that both of them wanted it to. Fate, he supposed. 'She's got poor taste in men,' he said, then laughed. 'That wasn't meant to sound that way. I didn't mean to imply that I'd be a particularly good choice for her, just that she seems destined to end up with men who treat her badly, as if she's constantly reliving some sort of relationship, trying to get it right and failing every time. She can't break the cycle.' What he didn't say was that Jenny had been cool towards him ever since he stood her up on a dinner date, through no fault of his own.

'I know what you mean,' said Sandra. 'She told me once that despite everything she's done she doesn't have a lot of confidence in herself, much self-esteem. I don't know.'

They finished their meal, put their plates aside and Banks lit another cigarette. Sandra declined his offer of one. While she was in the ladies', he poured himself more wine and debated how to broach the subject that was on his mind. As she walked back across the restaurant he noticed she was wearing jeans under her various flowing layers of clothing, and her figure still looked good. His heart gave a little lurch, and another part of him stirred, unbidden.

Sandra looked at her watch after she sat down. 'I can't stay very much longer,' she said. 'I promised to meet some friends at half ten.'

'Party?'

'Mmm. Something like that.'

'You never did that up in Eastvale.'

'Things have changed since then. Besides, Eastvale closes down at nine o'clock. This is London.'

'Maybe we never should have left,' Banks said. 'It seemed like a good idea at the time. I mean, let's be honest, I was getting pretty burnt out. I thought a quieter life might bring us closer together. Shows how much I know.'

'It was nothing to do with that, Alan. It wouldn't have

mattered where we were. Even when you were there you were always somewhere else.'

'What do you mean?'

'Think about it. Most of the time you were out working; the rest of the time you were thinking about work. You just weren't at home. The damnedest thing is, you never even realized it; you thought everything was just hunky-dory.'

'It was, wasn't it? Until you met Sean.'

'Sean has nothing to do with this. Leave him out of it.'

'Nothing would suit me better.'

They fell silent. Sandra seemed restless, as if she wanted to get something off her chest before she left. 'Stay for a coffee, at least,' Banks said. 'And we'll leave Sean out of it.'

She managed a thin smile. 'All right. I'll have a cappuccino. And please don't tell me I didn't drink that in Eastvale either. You can't get a bloody cappuccino in Eastvale.'

'You can now. That new fancy coffee place opposite the community centre. It wasn't open when you left. Sells latte, too.'

'So the North's getting sophisticated, after all, is it?'

'Oh, yes. People come from miles around.'

'To sell their sheep. I remember.'

'Yorkshire never really suited you, did it?'

Sandra shook her head. 'I tried, Alan. Honestly I did. For your sake. For mine. For Brian and Tracy's. I tried. But in the end I suppose you're right. I'm a big-city girl. Take it or leave it.'

Banks filled his wineglass as Sandra's cappuccino arrived. 'I've applied for another job,' he told her finally.

She paused with the frothing cup halfway to her lips. 'You're not leaving the force?'

'No, not that.' Banks laughed. 'I suppose the force will always be with me.'

Sandra groaned.

'But I'll most likely be leaving Yorkshire. In fact there's a good chance I could be based down here. I've applied for the National Crime Squad.'

Sandra frowned and sipped some coffee. 'I read about that in the papers a while ago. Sort of an English FBI, they said. What brought all this about? I thought at least *you* were happy up to your knees in sheep droppings. Was it Jimmy Riddle?'

Banks scraped his cigarette around the rim of the ashtray. 'A lot of reasons,' he said, 'and Jimmy Riddle was a big one. I'm not so sure about that now. But maybe I've run my natural course up there, too. I'm just a bit behind you, that's all. I don't know. I think I need something new. A challenge. And maybe I'm a big-city boy at heart, too.'

Sandra laughed. 'Well, good luck. I hope you get what you want.'

'It could mean travel, too. Europe. Hunting down dangerous criminals in the Dordogne.'

'Good for you.'

Banks paused to stub out his cigarette and take another sip of wine. Here goes nothing, he thought. 'We've been apart about a year now, right?'

Sandra frowned. 'That's right.'

'It's not that long, is it, when you think about it? People give up things for a while then go back to them. Like smoking.'

'What on earth are you talking about?'

'Maybe that wasn't a good analogy. I was never much good at this sort of thing. What I'm saying is that people sometimes separate for a year or more, do other things, live in other places, then . . . you know, they get back together. Once they've got it out of their system. People can be an addiction, like cigarettes, but better for you. You find you can't give them up.'

'Back together?'

'Yes. Not like before, of course. It never could be like before. We've both changed too much for that. But better. It could be better. It might mean you coming up to Yorkshire for a little while, just until things get sorted, but I promise – and

I mean this – that even if the NCS doesn't work out, I'll get a transfer. I've still got contacts at the Met. There's bound to be something for a copper with my experience.'

'Wait a minute, Alan. Let me get this straight. You're suggesting that I come up and live with you in that tiny cottage until you can get a job down here?'

'Yes. Of course, if you don't want to, if you'd rather just wait until I get something – whatever – then I can understand that. I know it's too small for two, really. I mean, you could come for the occasional weekend. We could see each other. Have dates, like when we were first together.'

Sandra shook her head slowly.

'What? You don't like my idea?'

'Alan, you haven't heard a word I've said, have you?'

'I know things got bad. I know you had to leave. I don't blame you for that now. What I'm saying is that we can make a go of it again. It could be different this time.'

'No.'

'What do you mean?'

'No means no.'

'Okay.' Banks emptied his glass and poured some more. There wasn't much left in the second carafe by now. 'I suppose it must have been a shock coming out of the blue like that. Why don't you at least take some time to think about it? About us. I apologize for springing it on you like this. You take the opportunities where and when you find them.'

'Can't you hear what I'm saying, Alan? N. O. No. We're not moving back in together, neither up in Yorkshire nor down here in London. When I first moved out, I'll admit I didn't know what would become of us, how I would feel in a year's time.'

'And you know now?'

'Yes.'

'So? What is it?'

'I'm sorry, Alan. Jesus, you have to go and make this so

bloody difficult, don't you?' She took her glasses off and wiped her eyes with the backs of her hands.

'I don't understand.'

'Alan, we're not getting back together. Not now. Not next month. Not ever. What I want to tell you is that I want a divorce. Sean and I want to get married.'

Banks looked in the large tilted mirror and saw short black hair still wet with beads of rain which also glistened on the shoulders of his black leather jacket. Beyond the array of whisky bottles, he saw a face that was perhaps too lean and sharply angled to be called handsome, and two bright, slightly out-of-focus blue eyes looking into themselves. He saw the kind of bloke you gave a wide berth to unless you were looking for trouble.

Around him, life went on. The couple beside him argued in low, tense voices; a drunk rambled on to himself about Manchester United; noisy kids fed the machines with money, and the machines beeped and honked with gratitude. The air was dense with cigarette smoke and tinged with the smell of hops and barley. Barmen dashed about filling shouted orders, standing impatiently as the optics dispensed their miserly measures of rum or vodka. One of them, shaking drops of Rose's lime juice from a nozzled bottle into a pint of lager, muttered, 'Jesus Christ, hurry up. I could piss faster than this.'

Banks took a long swig of beer and lit another cigarette, marvelling for the umpteenth time in the last hour or so at how calm he felt. He hadn't felt this calm in ages. Certainly not in his last few months with Sandra. After she had dropped her bombshell earlier in the evening, she had dashed out of the restaurant in tears, leaving Banks alone with his wine and the bill. The whole place had seemed to fall silent as the pressure mounted in his ears, and he felt pins and needles prickle over his entire body. *Divorce. Marry Sean.* Had she really said that?

She had, he realized after he had paid up and wobbled down the rain-lashed streets of Camden Town into the first pub he saw. And now here he was at the bar, on his second pint, wondering where were the anger, the pain, the rage he was supposed to feel? He was stunned, gobsmacked, knocked for six, as anyone would be after hearing such news. But he didn't feel as if the bottom had fallen out of his world. Why?

The answer, when it came, was so simple he could have kicked himself. It was because Sandra was *right*. They weren't going to get back together. He'd been deluding himself for long enough, and reality had finally broken through. He had simply been going through the motions he thought he was supposed to go through. When it really came down it, neither of them really *wanted* to get back together. It was over. And this was one sure way of bringing about closure. Divorce. Marriage to Sean.

Sure, Banks knew, you can't write off twenty years of marriage completely, and there would always be a residue of affection, even of love and, perhaps, of pain. But – and this was the important thing – it was finally *over*. There would be no more ambiguity, no more vain hope, no more childish illusions that some external change – a new place to live, a new job – would make everything all right again. Now they could both walk away from the dead thing that was their marriage and get on with their lives.

There would be sadness, yes. They'd have regrets, perhaps a few, as the song went. They would also always be tied together by Brian and Tracy. But he realized as he looked in the pub mirror at his own reflection that if he were to be *really* honest with himself right now – and this was the moment for it – then he should be celebrating rather than drowning his sorrows. Tomorrow he would phone Sandra and tell her to go ahead with the divorce, to marry Sean, that it was fine. But tonight he would celebrate freedom. What he really felt was *relief*. The scales had fallen from his eyes. Because there was no hope, there was hope.

And so he raised the rest of his pint in celebration and

drew one or two curious looks when he toasted the face in the mirror.

Rain had smudged the neon and car lights all over the road like a finger painting as Banks walked a little unsteadily looking for the next pub. He could hear the sound of distant fireworks and see rockets flare across the sky. He didn't want to go back to the lonely hotel room just yet, didn't feel tired enough, despite what felt like a long day.

The next pub he found was less crowded, and he managed to find a seat in the corner, next to a table of pensioners well into their cups. He knew he was a bit drunk, but he also knew he was well within the limits of reason in his thoughts. And so he found himself thinking about what had transpired that day, how uneasy he felt about it all. Especially about his meeting with Emily Riddle at Barry Clough's villa. The more he thought about that, the more out of kilter everything seemed.

Emily had been high; that much was obvious. Whether she was on coke or heroin, he couldn't be certain, but the white powder on her upper lip certainly indicated one or the other. Coke, he would guess, given her jerkiness and her mood swings. She had probably been smoking marijuana, too. Craig Newton had also said she was really high when he saw her in the street, the time Clough's minders beat him up. So was she a junkie or an occasional user? Sometimes the one shaded right into the other.

Then there was Barry Clough himself: the expensive villa, the gold, the furnishings, the Armani suit, the guns. That he was a 'businessman' was all anyone would say about him, and that was a term that covered a multitude of sins. What did he really have to do with the music business? What sort of party had he met Emily at? That he was a crook of some kind, Banks had no doubt, but as to what kind of criminal activity or activities were his bent, he didn't know. How did he make his money? Drugs, perhaps. Porn? Possibly. Either way, he was bad news for Emily, no matter how much of a ball she thought she was having now, and he was even worse news for Jimmy Riddle's career prospects.

Banks hadn't felt good about walking away from Clough's house like that. Just as he hadn't felt good about not taking on the minder at the gate. Under normal circumstances, he would have gone in there with authority, with teeth, but he was acting as a private citizen, so he had to take whatever they dished out. He was also committed to acting discreetly, and who knew what damaging revelations might come out into the light of day if he upset Clough. Part of him, perhaps stimulated by the alcohol, wanted to go back there and ruffle Clough's feathers, antagonize him into making some sort of move. But he knew enough not to give in to the desire. Not tonight, at any rate.

Instead, he called upon the gods of common sense, finished his pint and hurried out into the street to find a taxi. A good night's sleep was what he needed now, and tomorrow would bring what it would.

Tomorrow came too early. It was 3.18 a.m. by the digital clock on Banks's bedside table when the telephone rang. Groaning and rubbing the sleep from his eyes, he groped for it in the dark and finally grasped the handset.

'Banks,' he grunted.

'I'm sorry to bother you at this hour, sir,' said the receptionist, 'but there's a young lady in the lobby. She seems very distraught. She says she's your daughter and she insists on seeing you.'

In Banks's half-asleep, alcohol-sodden consciousness, the only thought that came through clear was that Tracy was here and she was in trouble. Perhaps she had been talking to Sandra and was upset about the impending divorce. 'Send her up,' he said, then he got out of bed, turned on the table lamp and pulled on his clothes. His head ached and his mouth was dry. Figuring it would take Tracy a minute or so to get up to his third-floor room, he nipped into the bathroom and swallowed a few paracetamol from his travelling medicine kit, along with a couple of glasses of water. When he had done that, he filled and plugged in the little kettle and put a teabag in a cup.

By the time the soft knock came at his door, Banks was beginning to realize there was something wrong with the picture he had envisaged. Tracy knew where he would be, of course; he had given her the name of the hotel before she left for Paris with Damon. But it was still only Saturday night, or Sunday morning, so shouldn't they both still be in Paris?

When he opened the door, Emily Riddle stood there. 'Can I come in?' she said.

Banks stepped aside and locked the door behind her. Emily was wearing a black evening gown, loose-fitting, cut low over her small breasts and slit up one side to her thigh. Her bare arms were covered with goose pimples. Her blonde hair was messily piled on her head, the remains of the sophisticated style disarrayed by the wind and rain. She looked like a naughty debutante. A twenty-five-year-old naughty debutante at that. But more remarkable than all that were the tear down the right shoulder of her dress and the question mark of dried blood at the corner of her mouth. There was also a weal on her cheek that looked as if might turn into a bruise. Her eyes looked heavy, half-closed.

'I'm so tired,' she said, then she tossed her handbag on the bed and flopped into the armchair.

The kettle came to a boil and Banks made some tea. Emily took the hot cup from him and held it to herself as if she needed the heat. Her eyes opened a little more.

Suddenly, it seemed like a very small room. Banks perched on the edge of the bed. 'What is it?' he asked. 'What happened, Emily? Who did this to you?'

Emily started crying.

Banks found her a tissue from the bathroom, and she wiped her eyes with it. They were bloodshot and pink around the rims. 'I must look a sight,' she said. 'Have you got a cigarette, please?'

Banks gave her one and took one himself. After she had taken a few drags and sipped some tea, she seemed to compose herself a bit more.

'What happened?' Banks asked again. 'Did Clough do this?'

'I want to go home. Will you take me home? Please?'

'In the morning. Tell me what happened to you.'

Her eyes started to close and she leaned back in the chair with her legs stretched out and ankles crossed. Banks worried that she would slide right onto the floor, but she managed to stay put. She looked at Banks through narrowed eyes and blew some smoke out of her nose. It made her cough, which spoiled the sophisticated effect she had probably been aiming for.

'Tell me what happened,' he asked her again.

'I don't want to talk about it. I ran . . . in the rain . . . found a taxi and came here.'

'But you threw the address away.'

'I can remember things like that. I only have to look once. Like my mother.' She finished her cigarette and seemed to doze off for a moment.

'Did Clough do this to you? Was it him?'

She pretended to sleep.

'Emily?'

'Uh-huh?' she said, without opening her eyes.

'Was it Clough?'

'I don't want to go back there. I can't go back there. Will you take me home?'

'Tomorrow. I'll take you home tomorrow.'

'Can I stay here tonight?'

'Yes.' Banks stood up. 'I can get a room for you. I don't think they're full.'

'No.' Her eyes opened wide and she jerked forward so quickly she spilled tea over the front of her dress. If it scalded her, she didn't seem to feel it. 'No,' she said again. 'I don't want to be by myself. I'm scared. Let me stay here with you. Please?'

Christ Almighty, thought Banks. If anyone found out about this, his career wouldn't be worth twopence. But what else could he do? She was upset and she was scared. Something bad had happened to her. He couldn't simply abandon her.

'Okay,' he said. 'Take the bed, and I'll sleep in the chair. Come on.'

He leaned forward to help her up. She seemed listless. When she finally got out of the chair, she stumbled forward against his chest and put her arms around his neck. 'Have you got anything to smoke?' she said. 'I'm coming down. I need something to soften the edges. I think somebody put something in my drink.' He could feel her warm body touching his under the thin material of the dress, and he remembered the images he had seen of her naked. He felt ashamed of his erection and hoped she didn't notice, but as he disentangled her arms and moved away, she gave him a cock-eyed, mischievous smile and said, 'I told you before you were a liar.'

She did something with the straps of her dress, and it slipped off her shoulders over her waist to the floor. She was wearing white bikini panties and nothing more. Her nipples stood out dark and hard on her small white breasts. The black spider tattoo between her navel ring and the elastic of her panties seemed to be moving, as if it were spinning a web.

'For crying out loud,' said Banks, picking up the bedspread and swathing it around her. She giggled and fell on the bed. 'Of course you don't have anything to smoke,' she said. 'You're a copper. Detective Chief Inspector Bonks. No, he doesn't. Yes, he does. No, he doesn't.' She giggled again, then turned on her side and put her thumb in her mouth, drawing up her legs in the foetal position. 'Hold me,' she said, taking her thumb out for a moment. 'Please come and hold me.'

Banks shook his head and whispered, 'No.' There was no way he was getting in that bed with her, no matter how much she said she was in need of comfort. If he thought about it, he should probably throw her out and tear up the sheets, but he couldn't do that. Instead, he managed to pull some more blankets over her, and she offered no resistance. For a while, she seemed to be muttering and murmuring as best she could with her thumb back in her mouth, then he heard her start snoring softly.

Banks knew there would be no more sleep for him that night. In the morning, he would go to Oxford Street when the shops opened and buy her some clothes, then they would take the first train back to Eastvale. He would drive her to her father's house and there he would leave her, leave them all to sort it out. His job would be over.

But as he sat in the chair and smoked another cigarette, listening to the wind and rain rattling the window, and to Emily's ragged snoring, he couldn't help but mull the situation over. It was all wrong. He was a copper; a serious offence had been committed; the law had been broken; he should be *doing* something, not sitting in the armchair smoking as his chief constable's sixteen-year-old daughter slept in his bed practically starkers with her thumb in her mouth, to all intents and purposes nothing but a child in a woman's body.

Three fifty-two. A long wait until dawn. He glanced through the curtains and saw a flash of white moon through the grey wisps of cloud. Emily stirred, turned over, farted once and started snoring again. Banks reached for his Walkman on the table beside him and put in the Dawn Upshaw tape. Songs about sleep.

> Come, Sleep, and with
> Thy sweet deceiving
> Lock me in delight awhile.

Not much hope of that, Banks thought, not after the day he had just been through.

5

The Charlie Courage murder occurred in early December, about a month after Banks had delivered Emily Riddle to her father's house, a little battered and shop-soiled, but not too much the worse for wear. Judging by her silence on the train journey back to Yorkshire, he imagined she might lie low for a while before taking on the world again. In the meantime, Banks had been preoccupied with major changes at Eastvale Divisional Headquarters.

The county force had been reorganized from seven divisions into just three, and Eastvale was now headquarters of the large Western Division, which took in just about the entire county west of the A1 to the Lancashire border, and from the Durham border in the north to West Yorkshire in the south. There were vast areas of wilderness and moorland, including most of the Yorkshire Dales National Park, and the main occupations were tourism, agriculture and a smattering of light industry. There were no major urban areas, although there were a number of big towns such as Harrogate, Ripon, Richmond, Skipton and Eastvale itself.

There was, of course, plenty of crime, and in keeping with its new status, the Eastvale station had been extended into the adjoining building, where Vic Manson's fingerprints unit, scenes-of-crime, computer and photography departments had all set up shop. Renovations were still going on, and the place was filled with noise and dust.

While the section stations would continue to police their

areas as before – indeed, they were to be given even more autonomy – Eastvale was now to be responsible for most of the criminal investigation within the new Western Division. Nobody was sure yet how many CID officers – or Crime Management Personnel, as some now liked to call them – they would end up with, or where they would all be put, but staffing increases had already begun.

One of the first moves that Millicent Cummings, the Director of Human Resources, had made was to transfer Detective Sergeant Annie Cabbot to the new team. Millie told Banks that she thought Annie had worked well with him on their previous case, no matter what Chief Constable Riddle thought of its messy outcome, and that as Annie was going for her inspector's boards as soon as she could, the experience would be good for her.

Millie, of course, along with Riddle and everyone else, didn't know about Banks's affair with Annie, and Banks could hardly say anything now. This was a good opportunity for her to get back in the swing of things, and he certainly wasn't going to stand in her way. Annie *was* a good detective, and if she could handle working with Banks, he could at least try to accommodate her.

The county also had a new Assistant Chief Constable (Crime) in the shape of Ron McLaughlin, known jokingly as 'Red Ron' because he leaned more to New Labour than most senior policemen. ACC McLaughlin was known to be a hard but fair man, one who believed in using his officers' abilities to the best, and he was also rumoured to enjoy a wee dram of malt every now and then.

It was a misty, drizzling day – what the locals called 'mizzling' – when Riddle got the chance to make good on his promise to Banks. Over the last year or so, all serious crimes in the division that couldn't be handled by Detective Superintendent Gristhorpe, Detective Sergeant Hatchley and whichever DCs happened to be assigned to Eastvale Divisional

Headquarters at the time had been passed on to other divisions, or to the Regional Crime Squad, leaving Banks free to devote all his duty hours to paperwork and administration.

Since he had done Riddle the big favour of bringing Emily back home, since the big changes around the station, and since things had finally come to an end with Sandra, the thought of moving from his Gratly cottage and starting a new job with the NCS had begun to lose its appeal, and Banks had withdrawn his application. Eastvale was starting to seem like a good bet again, and it was where he wanted to be.

Despite the drizzle and the filthy grey sky, Banks felt in a buoyant, optimistic mood. He was reading a report on the sudden increase of car theft in rural areas, and in need of a break, so he went to stand by the window to smoke a proscribed cigarette and look down on the market square in the late afternoon.

The renovators were mercifully silent, no doubt planning their next major assault, and Banks's radio played quietly in the background: Prokofiev's Piano Concerto No. 3. The Eastvale Christmas lights, turned on in the middle of November by some third-rate television personality Banks had never heard of, made a pretty sight outside his window, hanging across Market Street and over the square like a bright lattice of jewels. Soon they'd be putting up the huge Christmas tree by the market cross, and the church choir would be out singing carols at lunchtime and early evening, collecting for charity.

Brian thought he would be busy with the band over the holidays, but Tracy had phoned the previous day and promised to spend Christmas with her father before heading down to London to see her mother on Boxing Day. Banks had never been much of a fan of Christmas – far too many holiday seasons spent working and witnessing the gaudy excess of suicides and domestic murders that peaked around that time of year had taken care of that – but this called for celebration; this year he would make an effort, buy a small tree, presents, put up some decorations, cook Christmas dinner.

Last year had been a complete wash-out. He had turned down all offers of meals, drinks and parties from friends and colleagues and spent the entire holiday alone in the Eastvale semi he had once shared with Sandra, wallowing in his own misery and keeping up his maintenance buzz with liberal tots of whisky. Brian and Tracy had both phoned, of course, and he had managed to bluff his way past any worries they might have had about him, but there was no denying it had been a grim time. This year would be different. Delia Smith had a book about cooking for Christmas, he remembered; perhaps he would go to Waterstone's and buy it before going home.

The telephone brought him back to his desk. 'Banks here.'

'Chief Inspector Banks? My name's Collaton, Detective Inspector Mike Collaton. I'm calling from Market Harborough, Leicestershire Constabulary. I just called your county head-quarters and they put me on to you.'

'What can I do for you?'

'Earlier today a motorist stopped by the roadside near here and nipped down a lane into the woods for a piss. He found a body.'

'Go on,' said Banks, tapping his pen on the desk, still wondering what the connection was.

'It's one of yours. Thought you might be interested.'

'One of my what?'

'Local villains. Bloke by the name of Charles Courage. Same as the brewery. Lived at number seventeen Cutpurse Lane, Eastvale.' He laughed. 'Sounds like it could hardly be a more appropriate address, going by his record.'

Jesus Christ, Charlie Courage! *Dutch*, as his cronies jokingly called him on account of that was about the only courage he ever exhibited. Charlie Courage had been a thorn in the side of Eastvale Division for years. In truth, he was a petty villain, a minor player, but around Eastvale he was still a big fish in a small pond. Charlie Courage had done a little bit of every-thing – except anything that involved violence or sex – from handling stolen goods to sheep-stealing, when it was worth stealing them. You had to give Charlie his due; he was a character. Two or three years ago, he used to have a stall in Eastvale market, Banks remembered, right in front of the police station, where he blithely sold videos and CDs that in all likeli-hood had 'fallen off the back of a lorry'. While questioning him about a local break-in once, Banks had even bought the Academy of Ancient Music's CD of Mozart's C Minor Mass for £3.99. A bargain at twice the price. He didn't ask where it had come from. To his credit, Charlie had also acted as police informer on a number of occasions. Rumour had it that he had been going straight lately.

'You've heard of him?' DI Collaton went on.

'I've heard of him. What happened?'

'Shot. Looks like the weapon used was a shotgun. Made a real mess, anyway.'

'Any chance it was accidental, or self-inflicted?'

'Not unless he shot himself in the chest, then got up after he was dead and hid the weapon. We can't find any sign of it.'

'Are you sure it's Charlie? What on earth was he doing all the way down there? It's not like Charlie to leave his parish.'

'I'm afraid we can't shine any light on that just yet, either. But it's definitely him. I got the ID from fingerprints. Seems he did two years once for something involving sheep. I've heard about you lot up there and your sheep. Some sort of unspeakable deed, was it?'

Banks laughed. 'Stealing them, actually. They used to be worth a bit. You might remember. As for the other, I can't say I've any idea what Charlie got up to in his spare time. Far as I know, he was single, so he could please himself. Anything more you can tell me?'

'Not much. I've checked around, and it seems he doesn't have any living relatives.'

'Sounds like Charlie. I don't think he ever did.'

'Anyway, I thought I'd ask you to have a look around his house, if you would, see if there's anything there. Save my lads some legwork. We're a bit short staffed down here.'

'Aren't we all? Sure. I'll have a look. What about his car?'

'No sign of any car. Maybe you'd like to come down here tomorrow morning, see the scene, toss a few ideas around, that sort of thing? I've a feeling that if there are any answers to be found, they're probably at your end. The post-mortem's tomorrow afternoon, by the way.'

'Okay,' said Banks. 'In the meantime I'll go have a quick poke around Charlie's place right now and see about organizing a thorough search later. If he's dead, I won't have to worry about a warrant. I'll drive down tomorrow morning.'

Banks took Collaton's directions to the Fairfield Road police station in Market Harborough, then hung up and went into the main CID office. Since the reorganization began, they had been assigned three new DCs and were promised three more. DC Gavin Rickerd was a spotty, nondescript sort of lad given to anoraks and parkas. Banks couldn't help feeling he must have been a trainspotter in a previous lifetime, if not in this one. Kevin Templeton was more flash, a bit of a jack-the-lad, but he got things done, and he was surprisingly good with people, especially kids.

The third addition was DC Winsome Jackman, who hailed from a village in the Cockpit Mountains, high above Montego Bay, Jamaica. Why she had wanted to leave there for the unpredictable summers and miserable winters of North Yorkshire was beyond Banks's ken. At least superficially. When it came right down to it, though, he imagined that a village in the Jamaican mountains was probably no place for a bright and beautiful woman like Winsome to forge ahead in a career.

Why she hadn't become a model instead of joining the police was also beyond Banks. She had the figure for it, and her face showed traces of her Maroon heritage in the high cheekbones and dark ebony colouring. She could certainly give Naomi Campbell a run for her money, and from what Banks had read about the supermodel in the papers, Winsome was a far nicer person. Some of the lads called her 'Lose Some' because of the time, back in uniform, when she had chased and caught a mugger in a shopping centre, only to have him then slip out of her grasp and escape. She took it good-naturedly and gave as good as she got. You had to when you were the only black woman in the division.

As it turned out, everyone was out of the office except Kevin Templeton and Annie, who looked up from her computer monitor as Banks entered.

'Afternoon,' she said, flashing him a quick smile. Annie had a hell of a smile. Though not much more than a twitch of the right corner of her mouth, near the small mole, accompanied by a quick blaze of light from her almond eyes, it was dazzling. Banks felt his heart lurch just a little. God, he hoped this working together wasn't going to be too difficult.

'See what you can dig up on a local villain called Charlie Courage,' he said. Then, more or less on impulse, he added, 'Fancy a ride down to Market Harborough tomorrow?' He found himself holding his breath after the words were out, almost wishing he could take them back.

'Why not?' she said, after a short pause. 'It'll make a nice break.'

'Much on?'

'Nothing the lads can't handle on their own.'

Kevin Templeton grunted from his corner.

'Okay. I'll pick you up here around nine.'

Back in his office, Banks found himself hoping that things worked out with Annie on the job. He liked working with female detectives, and he still missed his old DC, Susan Gay, with all her uncertainties and sharp edges. When he had worked with Annie before, he had come to value her near-telepathic communication skills and the way she could mix logic and intuition in her unique style of thinking. He had also cherished her touch and her laughter, but that was another matter, one he couldn't let himself dwell on any more. Or could he?

He left the office in a good mood. For the moment, Riddle had proved true to his word, and Banks finally had a case he might be able to get his teeth into. It was DI Collaton's call, of course, but Collaton had asked for help right off, which led Banks to think that he probably didn't want to spend too long away from hearth and home tracking the roots of the crime up in dreary Yorkshire, especially with Christmas being so close. Well, good for him, Banks thought. Co-operation between the forces and all that. His loss was Banks's gain.

It was after five when Banks pulled up behind a blue Metro in front of Charlie Courage's one-up-one-down. Cutpurse Lane was a cramped ragbag of terraced cottages behind the community centre. Dating from the eighteenth century for the most part, the mean little hovels had privies out back and no front gardens. During the yuppie craze for *bijou* a few years ago, a number of young couples had bought cottages on Cutpurse Lane and installed bathrooms and dormer windows.

As far as Banks knew, Charlie Courage had lived there for years. Whatever Charlie had done with his ill-gotten gains, he certainly hadn't invested it in improving his living conditions. It was a syndrome Banks had seen before in even more successful petty crooks than Charlie. He had even known one big-time criminal who must have brought in seven figures a year easily, yet still lived hardly a notch above squalor in the East End. He wondered what on earth they used the money they stole for, except in some cases to support mammoth drug habits. Did they give it to charity? Use it to buy their parents that dream house they had always yearned for? People had odd priorities. Charlie Courage, though, had not been a drug addict, was not known for his charity, and he didn't have any living relatives. A mystery, then.

First, Banks knocked on the neighbour's door, which was opened by a short, stocky man in a wrinkled fawn V-necked pullover, who looked unnervingly like Hitler, even down to the little moustache and the mad gleam in his eyes. He stood in the doorway, the sound of the television coming from the room behind him.

Banks showed his identification. 'Knightley,' the man said. 'Kenneth Knightley. Please come in out of the rain.' Banks accepted his invitation. The drizzle was the kind that immediately seemed to get right through your raincoat and your skin, all the way to your bones.

Banks followed him into a small, neat living room with rose-patterned wallpaper and a couple of framed local landscapes hanging above the tile mantelpiece. Banks recognized Gratly Falls, just outside his own cottage, and a romantic watercolour of the ruins of Devraulx Abbey, up Lyndgarth way. A fire blazed in the hearth, making the room a bit too hot and stuffy for Banks's liking. He could already smell the steam rising from his raincoat.

'It's about your neighbour, Charles Courage,' he said. 'When did you last see him?'

'I don't have much to do with him,' said Knightley. 'Except to say hello to, like. He always keeps to himself, and I've not been the most of sociable of fellows since Edie died, if truth be told.' He smiled. 'Edie didn't like him, though. Thought he was a wrong 'un. Why? What's happened?'

'I'm afraid Mr Courage is dead. It looks as if he's been murdered.'

Knightley paled. 'Murdered? Where? I mean, not . . .'

'No. Not next door. Some distance away, actually. Down Leicester way.'

'Leicester? But he never went *anywhere*. One time I did talk to him, I remember him telling me you'd never catch him going to Torremolinos or Alicante for his holidays. Yorkshire was good enough for him. Charlie didn't like foreign places or foreigners, and they began at Ripon as far as he was concerned.'

Banks smiled. 'I've met a few people like that, myself. But one way or another, he did end up in Leicestershire. Dead.'

'That's probably what killed him then. Finding himself in Leicestershire.' Knightley paused and ran his hand across his brow. 'Sorry, I shouldn't be so flippant. A man's dead, after all. I don't see how I can help you, though.'

'You said you saw him last a couple of days ago. Can you be more precise?'

'Let me think. It was early Sunday afternoon. It must have been then because I was just coming back from the Oak. I always go there on a Sunday lunchtime for a game of dominoes.'

'About what time would this be?'

'Just after two. I can't be doing with all these new hours, all-day opening and whatnot. I stick to the old times.'

'How did he seem?'

'Same as usual: a bit shifty. Said hello and that was that.'

'Shifty?'

'He always looked shifty. As if he'd just that minute done something illegal and wasn't quite sure he'd got away with it yet.'

'I know what you mean,' said Banks. Charlie Courage usually *had* just done something illegal. 'So there was nothing odd or different about his behaviour at all?'

'Nothing.'

'Was he alone?'

'Far as I could tell.'

'Coming or going?'

'Come again?'

'Was he just arriving home or leaving?'

'Oh, I see. He was going out.'

'Car?'

'Aye. He's got a blue Metro. It's usually . . . Just a minute . . .' Knightley stood up and went to the curtain, which he pulled back a few inches. 'Aye, there it is,' he said, pointing. 'Parked right outside.' Banks made a mental note to have it searched.

'Did you see or hear anyone with him in the house over the last few days?'

'No. I'm sorry I can't be much help. Like I said, there was nothing unusual at all. He went off to work, then he came home. Quiet as a mouse.'

'*Work?* Charlie?'

'Oh, aye. Didn't you know? He'd got a job as a night-watchman at that new business park down Ripon Road. Dale-view, I think it's called.'

'I know the one.'

Business park. Another to add to Banks's long list of oxy-morons, along with military intelligence. That was an interesting piece of news, anyway: Charlie Courage with a job. A nightwatchman, no less. Banks wondered if his employers knew of his past. It was worth looking into.

'Is there anything else you can help me with, Mr Knightley?'

'I don't think there is. And it's no use asking Mrs Ford on the other side. She's deaf as a post.'

'I don't suppose you have a key to Mr Courage's house, do you?' he asked.

'Key? No. Like I said, we didn't do much more than pass the time of day together out of politeness's sake.'

Banks stood up. 'I'm going to have to have a good look around the place. If there's no key, I'll have to break in somehow, so don't be alarmed if you hear a few strange noises next door.'

Knightley nodded. 'Right. Right, you are. Charlie Courage. Murdered. Bloody hell, who'd credit it?'

Banks walked around the back of the terrace block to see

if he could find an easy way into Charlie's place. A narrow cobbled alley ran past Charlie's backyard. Each house had a high wall and a tall wooden gate. Some of the walls were topped with broken glass, and some of the gates swung loose on their hinges. Banks lifted the catch and pushed at Charlie's gate. It had scratched and faded green paint and one of the rusty hinges had broken, making it grate against the flagstone path as he opened it. It wasn't much of a backyard, and most of it was taken up by a murky puddle that immediately found its way through his shoes. First, out of habit, Banks tried the doorknob.

The door opened.

Perhaps Charlie hadn't had time to lock up properly before being abducted, Banks thought, as he made his way inside the dark house. He found a light switch on the wall to his right and clicked it on. He was in the kitchen. Nothing much there except for a pile of dirty dishes waiting to be washed. They never would be now.

He walked through to the living room, which was tidy and showed no signs of a struggle. Noting the new-looking television and DVD set-up, not what you could afford on a night-watchman's salary, Banks got some idea of what Charlie had done with his money. He went upstairs.

There were two small bedrooms, a bathroom with a stained tub and a tiny WC with a ten-year-old *Playboy* magazine on the floor and a copy of Harold Robbins's *The Carpetbaggers* resting on a toilet roll. One bedroom was empty except for a few cardboard boxes filled with magazines – mostly soft porn – and second-hand paperbacks, and the other, Charlie's, revealed only an unmade bed and a few clothes.

Downstairs, in one of the sideboard drawers, Banks found the only items of interest: the title deed to the house, Charlie's driving licence, a chequebook and a bankbook that indicated Charlie had made five cash deposits of £200 each over the past month, in addition to what seemed to be his regular pay cheque. A thousand quid. Interesting, Banks thought. That would at least account for the new TV and DVD set-up. What had the crooked little devil been up to? And had it got him killed?

Wednesday morning dawned every bit as dismal as Tuesday. It was still dark when Banks drove into Eastvale, sipping hot black coffee from a specially designed carrying mug on the way. The other CID officers were already in the office when he got there, and DS Hatchley, in particular, looked downhearted that he had missed the opportunity of a day trip to Leicestershire. Or perhaps he was jealous that Banks had Annie's company. He gave Banks the kind of bitter, defeated look that said rank pulled the birds every time, and what was a poor sergeant to do? If only he knew.

'You'll be driving, I suppose?' Annie said when they got out back to the car park.

That was another thing Banks appreciated about Annie: she was a quick learner with a good memory. It *was* unusual for a DCI to drive his own car. Having a driver was one of the perks of his position, but Banks *liked* to drive, even in this weather. He liked to be in control. Every time he let someone else drive him, no matter how good they were, he felt restless and irritated by any minor mistakes they made, constantly wanting to get his own foot on the clutch or the brake. It seemed much simpler to do the driving himself, so that was what he did. Annie understood that and didn't question his idiosyncrasy.

Banks slipped a tape of Mozart wind quintets in the Cavalier's sound system as he turned out of the car park. 'Mmm, that's nice,' said Annie. 'I like a bit of Mozart.' Then she settled back into the seat and lapsed into silence. It was another thing Banks liked about her, he remembered, the way she seemed so centred and self-contained, the way she could appear comfortable and relaxed in the most awkward positions, at ease with silence. It had also taken him a while to get used to her complete lack of deference to senior ranks, especially *his*, as well as to her rather free and easy style of dress, learned from growing up in an artists' commune surrounded by bearded artistic types such as her painter father, Ray Cabbot. Today she was wearing red winkle-picker boots that came up just above her ankles, black jeans and a Fair Isle sweater under her loose suede jacket. Rather conservative for Annie.

'How are you liking it at Eastvale?' Banks asked as they joined the stream of traffic on the A1.

'Hard to say yet. I've hardly got my feet under the desk.'

'What about the travelling?'

'Takes me about three-quarters of an hour each way. That's not bad.' She glanced sideways at him. 'It's about the same for you, as I remember.'

'True. Have you thought of selling the Harkside house?'

'I've thought of it, but I don't think I will. Not just yet. Wait and see what happens.'

Banks remembered Annie's tiny cramped cottage at the centre of a labyrinth of narrow, winding streets in the village of Harkside. He remembered his first visit there, when she had asked him on impulse for dinner and cooked a vegetarian pasta dish as they drank wine and listened to Emmylou Harris, remembered standing in the backyard for an after-dinner smoke, putting his arm around her shoulders and feeling the thin bra strap. Despite all the warning signs . . . he also remembered kissing the little rose tattoo just above her breast, their bodies, sweaty and tired, the unfamiliar street sounds the following morning.

He negotiated his way from the A1 to the M1. Lorries churned up oily rain that coated his windscreen before the wipers could get through it; there were more long delays at roadwork signs where nobody was working; a maniac in a red BMW flashed his lights about a foot from his rear end and then, when Banks changed lanes to accommodate him, zoomed off at well over a ton.

'What did you find out about Charlie?' he asked Annie when he had got into the rhythm of motorway driving.

Annie's eyes were closed. She didn't open them. 'Not much. Probably not more than you know already.'

'Tell me anyway.'

'He was born Charles Douglas Courage in February 1946—'

'You don't have to go that far back.'

'I find it helps. It makes him one of the generation born immediately after the war, when the men came home randy and ready to get on with their lives. He'd have been ten in 1956, too young for Elvis, perhaps, but twenty in 1966, and probably just raring for the all the sex, drugs and rock and roll you lot enjoyed in your youth. Maybe that was where he got his start in crime.'

Banks risked a glance away from the road at her. She still had her eyes closed, but there was a little smile on her face. 'Charlie wasn't into dealing drugs,' he said.

'Maybe it was the rock and roll, then. He was first arrested for distribution of stolen goods in August 1968 – to wit, long-playing records. *Sgt. Pepper's Lonely Hearts Club Band*, to be exact, stolen directly from a factory just outside Manchester.'

'A music lover, our Charlie,' he said. 'Carry on.'

'After that comes a string of minor offences – shoplifting, theft of a car stereo – then, in 1988, he was arrested for theft of livestock. To be exact, seventeen sheep from a farm out Relton way. Did eighteen months.'

'Conclusion?'

'He's a thief. He'll steal anything, even if it walks on four legs.'

'And since then?'

'He appears to have gone straight. Helped Eastvale police out on a number of occasions, mostly minor stuff he found out about through his old contacts.'

'Got a list?'

'DC Templeton's working on it.'

'Okay,' said Banks. 'What next?'

'A number of odd jobs, most recently working as a night-watchman at the Daleview Business Park. Been there since September.'

'Hmm. They must be a trusting lot at Daleview,' said Banks. 'I think one of us might pay them a visit tomorrow. Anything else?'

'That's about it. Single. Never married. Mother and father deceased. No brothers or sisters. Funny, isn't it?'

'What is?'

Annie stirred in the car seat to face him. 'A small-time villain like Charlie Courage getting murdered so far from home.'

'We don't know where he was murdered yet.'

'An inspired guess. You don't shoot someone in the chest with a shotgun and then drive him around bleeding in a car for three hours, do you?'

'Not without making a mess, you don't. You know, it strikes me that Charlie might have been taken on the long ride.'

'The long ride?'

Banks glanced at her. She looked puzzled. 'Never heard of the long ride?'

Annie shook her head. 'Can't say as I have.'

'Just a minute . . .' A slow-moving local delivery van in front of them was sending up so much spray that the windscreen wipers couldn't keep up with it. Carefully, Banks changed lanes and overtook it. 'The long ride,' he said, once he could see again. 'Let's say you've upset someone nasty – you've had your fingers in the till, or you've been telling tales out of school – and he's decided he has to do away with you, right?'

'Okay.'

'He's got a number of options, all with their own pros and cons, and this is one of them. What he does – or rather, what his hired hands do – is they pick you up and take you for a ride. A long ride. It's got two main functions. The first is that it confuses the local police by taking the crime away from the patch that gave rise to it. Follow?'

'And the second? Let me guess.'

'Go on.'

'To scare the shit out of him.'

'Right. Let's say you're driven from Eastvale to Market Harborough. You know exactly what's going to happen at the end of the journey. They make sure you have no doubt about that whatsoever, that there's going to be no reprieve, no commuting of the death sentence, so you've got three hours or thereabouts to contemplate your life and its imminent and inevitable end. An end you can also expect to be painful and brutal.'

'Cruel bastards.'

'It's a cruel world,' said Banks. 'Anyway, from their perspective, it acts as a deterrent to other would-be thieves or snitches. And, remember, it's not as if we're dealing with lily-whites here. The victim is usually a small-time villain who's done something to upset a more powerful villain.'

'Charlie Courage, small-time villain. Fits him to a T.'

'Exactly.'

'Except that he was supposed to be going straight, and there aren't any major crime bosses in Eastvale.'

'Maybe he wasn't going as straight as we thought. Maybe he was just avoiding drawing our attention. And they don't have to be that big. I'm not talking about the Mafia or the Triads here. There are plenty of minor villains who think life is pretty cheap. Maybe Charlie fell foul of one of them. Think about it. Charlie worked as a nightwatchman. He put a thousand quid in the bank – above and beyond his wages – over the past month. What does that tell you, Annie?'

'That he was either selling information, blackmailing someone or he was being paid off to look the other way.'

'Right. And he must have been playing way out of his

league. Maybe we'll get a better idea when we talk to the manager at Daleview tomorrow. Nearly there now.'

Banks negotiated his way around Leicester towards Market Harborough, about thirteen miles south. When they got to the high street there, it was almost noon, and it took Banks another ten minutes to find the police station.

Before they got out of the car, Banks turned to Annie. 'Are we going to be okay?' he asked.

'What do you mean?'

'You know what I mean. This. Working together.'

She flashed him a smile. 'Well, we seem to be doing all right so far, don't we?' she said, and slipped out of the car.

DI Collaton turned out to be a big bear of a man with thinning grey hair, a red face and a slow, country manner. A year or so away from retirement, Banks guessed. No wonder he didn't want to get involved in a murder inquiry. He looked at his watch and said, 'Have you two eaten at all?'

They shook their heads.

He grabbed his raincoat from the stand in the corner of his office. 'I know a place.'

They followed him to a small pub about two streets away. Judging by the smiles and hellos exchanged, Collaton was well known there. He led them to a corner table, which gave a little privacy, then offered the first round of drinks. Annie asked for a tomato juice, though Banks knew she enjoyed beer. He had a pint of the local best bitter. A fire burnt in the hearth and Christmas decorations festooned the walls and ceiling. Apart from the buzz of conversation around the bar, the place was quiet, which was the way Banks liked his pubs. As was Annie's habit in pubs, she seemed to mould herself to the hard chair and stretch her legs out, crossing them at the ankles. DI Collaton raised his eyebrows at her red winkle-pickers, but said nothing.

After Banks had ordered game pie, on Collaton's recommendation, and Annie, being a vegetarian, went for the Ploughman's Lunch, he lit what he realized with some surprise was his first cigarette of the day.

'We don't get a lot of murders down here,' said Collaton after his first sip.

That didn't surprise Banks. From what he had seen, he supposed Market Harborough to be a bit smaller than Eastvale – maybe seventeen or eighteen thousand people – and Charlie Courage was Eastvale's first murder victim of the entire year so far. In December, no less. 'Any idea why they might have chosen your patch?' he asked.

Collaton shook his head. 'Not really. It's handy for the M1,' he said, 'but a bit off the beaten track. If they were taking him somewhere, and he got troublesome . . .'

'Any witnesses?'

'Nobody saw or heard a thing. It's out Husbands Bosworth way, towards the motorway, and at this time of year there's nobody around. More in summer, tourist season, like.'

Banks nodded. Same as Eastvale. 'Any physical evidence?'

'Tyre tracks. That's about all.'

'Anything interesting or unusual on his person?'

'Just the usual. Except his wallet was missing.'

'I doubt robbery was the motive,' Banks mused. 'Maybe a London mugger might blow away someone with a shotgun, but not in some leafy Midlands lane.'

'My thoughts exactly,' said Collaton. 'I thought maybe they'd taken it to help keep his identity unknown a bit longer. Maybe they didn't know he'd got form and we'd find out that way.'

'Possibly.'

'Had he been up to anything lately?'

'We don't know yet,' said Banks. 'Rumour has it he's been going straight. Had a job as a nightwatchman. We know he made five cash deposits of two hundred quid each over the past month, though, and I doubt that he came by the money honestly.'

Their food arrived. Collaton was right about the game pie. Annie nibbled at her cheese and pickled onion. Collaton kept looking at her out of the corner of his eye, when he thought no one noticed. At first Banks thought he was simply puzzled by her, as people often were, then he realized the dirty old bugger fancied her. And him old enough to be her father.

Suddenly, Banks felt himself struck almost physically with the memory of Emily Riddle in his hotel room. Not so much by her white and slender nakedness, the spider tattoo or the feel of her body pressing against his as by her torn dress, her fear, the little question mark of blood and Barry Clough. Why on earth hadn't he followed up on that? The next morning he had simply gone out as soon as the shops had opened and, not being skilled at shopping for women's clothing, bought her a track suit because it seemed easiest. Though he had questioned her about the previous night, she had given away nothing, maintaining a surly silence all the way home. Did she even remember how she got to his hotel room and her awkward attempt at seducing him?

When he had driven her home from the station and left her with her parents, she had given him a look he found hard to interpret. Sad, yes, partly, and perhaps also a little let down, defeated, a little hurt, but not completely without affection, a sort of complicit recognition that they had shared something together, been through an adventure. Banks had decided on the way that he had no reason to tell Riddle what happened down there. If Emily wanted to do so, that was fine, but his part of the bargain was over; she was Riddle's problem now.

Still, it had gnawed at him over the past few weeks – Clough especially. Perhaps, if he had time over the next couple of days, he could make a few discreet enquiries of old friends in the Met, see if Clough had form, find out what his particular line of work was. Dirty Dick Burgess ought to know; he had been working with one of the top-level Criminal Intelligence departments for a while now. But Riddle had asked Banks to be discreet, and sometimes, when you set things in motion, you couldn't always stop them as easily as you wanted to, and you didn't know in which direction they would spin. That was Banks's problem, as Riddle had told him more than once: he had never learned when to leave well alone.

'Sir?'

Banks snapped back from a long distance when he felt Annie's elbow in his ribs. 'Sorry. Miles away.'

'DI Collaton asked if we wanted to have a look at the scene after lunch.'

Banks looked at Collaton, who showed concern in his eyes, whether for Banks's health or the lapse in attention wasn't clear. 'Yes,' he said, pushing his empty plate aside. 'Yes, by all means let's go have a look at poor old Charlie's final resting place.'

After viewing the spot where Charlie Courage's body had been discovered, just off a muddy track in some woods near Husbands Bosworth, they attended the post-mortem in Market Harborough hospital.

Courage's body had already been photographed, fingerprinted, weighed, measured and X-rayed the previous day. Now, the pathologist, Dr Lindsey, and his assistants worked methodically and patiently through a routine they must have carried out many times. Lindsey began with a close external examination, paying special attention to the gunshot pattern.

'Definitely a shotgun wound,' he said. 'Twelve-bore, by the look of it. Range about two or three yards.' He pointed out the central entrance opening over the heart and the numerous single small holes around it from the scattered shot. 'Any closer and it would have been practically circular. Much farther away and the shot would have spread out more into smaller groups. There's still some wadding embedded in the wounds, too. Look.' He held up a piece. 'Depends whether they used a sawn-off, of course, as the shot patterns don't hold as far. Even so, it was pretty close range. And judging by the angle of the main wounds, it looks as if either his killer was very tall or the victim was on his knees at the time.'

Banks guessed that if he was right in assuming Charlie had been taken for the long ride, then his killer would have used a sawn-off shotgun. The legal length for shotgun barrels was twenty-four inches, not including the stock, and no villain would walk or drive around with something that big.

'Then there's this bruising,' Dr Lindsey went on, pointing out the discoloration around Courage's stomach and kidneys. 'It looks as if he was beaten either with fists or some hard object before he was killed. Enough to make him piss blood for a week at least.'

'Perhaps somebody wanted him to tell them something?' Collaton said.

'From what I knew of Charlie, he'd give up his grand-mother if you so much as waved your fist in his face. They might have wanted him to tell them something, but my bet is that he did, and then they carried on beating him up just for the fun of it.'

Next, Dr Lindsey began his dissection with the Y-incision. He took blood samples, then removed and inspected the inner organs, working from the trachea, oesophagus and what was left of the heart, down to the bladder and spleen.

As all this was going on, Banks kept a close eye on Annie. He didn't know how good she was at post-mortems on fairly fresh corpses, as the last one they had been to was of a skeleton disinterred after fifty years. Though she paled a little when Dr Lindsey opened up the body cavity and swallowed rather loudly as he squished out the various organs as if he were shelling oysters, she stood her ground.

Until, that is, the power saw started ripping into the front quadrant of the skull. At that, Annie swayed, put her hand to her mouth and, making a gurgling sound, dashed out of the room. Dr Lindsey rolled his eyes and Collaton glanced at Banks, who just shrugged.

Dr Lindsey pulled out the brain, looked it over, tossed it from hand to hand as if it were a grapefruit, then put it aside for weighing and sectioning.

'Well,' he said, 'until we get the tests back on the blood and tissue samples, we won't know whether he was poisoned before he was shot. I doubt it, myself. Judging by the blood, I'd say the gunshot wound was the cause of death. It blew his heart open. And going by the lividity, I'd also say he was killed at the same spot he was found.'

'Did you determine time of death?' Banks asked, though he knew it was the question all pathologists hated the most.

Dr Lindsey frowned and searched through a pile of notes on the lab bench. 'I made some rough calculations at the scene. Only rough, of course. I've got them somewhere. Now, where . . . ah here it is. Rigor, temperature . . . allowing for the chilly weather and the rain . . . he was found on Tuesday, that's yesterday, at about four p.m., and I surmised he'd been dead at least twenty-four hours, perhaps longer.'

Charlie had been seen by his neighbour on Sunday afternoon at around two o'clock, and if he had been killed sometime on Monday afternoon, that left over twenty-four hours, the last twenty-four hours of his life, unaccounted for. When they got back to Eastvale, Banks would have to initiate some house-to-house inquiries in the neighbourhood, find out if anyone had seen Charlie later than Sunday lunchtime, and if anyone had seen him *with* anyone. He hadn't got to the lane near Husbands Bosworth in his own car, and he certainly hadn't walked there. The fresh tyre tracks that Collaton's men had found most likely belonged to the car that had taken him there, as the lane was an out-of-the-way place. Depending on how good the impressions were, it might be possible to match them up with a particular car – if, of course, they found the car, and if the tyres hadn't been changed.

They had learned just about all they could from Dr Lindsey for the moment, and Banks thanked him for his prompt post-mortem and left with Collaton, looking out for Annie as he walked along the corridors.

They found her standing out in the misty, grey afternoon taking deep breaths. When she saw them, she looked away and ran her hand over her chestnut hair. 'Christ. I'm sorry. I feel such an idiot.'

'It's all right,' said Banks. 'Don't worry about it.'

'It's not that I haven't been to one before.' She pulled a face. 'I was okay, honest I was, until . . . It was the smell, the saw burning the bone, and the noise it made. I couldn't . . . I'm sorry. I feel like such a fool.'

It was the first time Banks had seen any real break in Annie's on-the-job composure. 'I told you,' he said. 'Don't worry about it. Are you up to going home?'

She nodded. He imagined it would be a quiet journey. Annie was clearly pissed off at herself for showing signs of weakness.

Banks looked at Collaton. The indulgent expression on his face indicated he would probably have forgiven Annie *anything*.

It was late when Banks finally got home, after calling in at the station to issue some actions for the following morning. The traffic on the M1 was murder, especially around Sheffield, and patches of dense fog on the A1 meant they had to move at a crawl, keeping in view the rear lights of the lorry in front of them. Banks was reminded of the time when he was lost in the fog, heading for a friend's house, and had blindly followed the car in front right into a private drive. He had been damned embarrassed when the irate driver came to ask him what the hell he thought he was doing.

Annie recovered from her little spell of embarrassment a lot quicker than Banks expected. He had to remind himself that this wasn't Susan Gay, and that Annie didn't worry so much about appearing weak or incompetent; she simply got on with her work and her life.

The fog in the dale slowed him down most on the last leg of his journey. Wraiths of grey mist nuzzled up the daleside and swirled on the road before him. The road ran several feet up the hillside from the valley bottom, where the River Swain meandered through the Leas, and most of the fog had settled low. Banks knew the road well enough not to take too many foolish risks.

Back at the cottage, he found two messages waiting. The first was from Tracy, asking him for ideas about what she should buy her mother for Christmas. A wedding dress, perhaps? Banks thought. But he wouldn't say that to Tracy.

The next caller didn't identify herself, but he knew immediately who she was: 'Hello, it's me. Look, I'm sorry I haven't been in touch . . . it was probably very rude of me . . . I mean, I never really thanked you and all, did I, you know, for what you did for me? I suppose I was pretty fucked up.' There, she broke off and Banks could hear her suck on a cigarette and blow out the smoke. He thought he could hear background noise, too. 'Anyway, you must let me buy you lunch at least. Hey, look, I'll be over in Eastvale tomorrow, so why don't you meet me at the Black Bull on York Road over from Castle Hill, say about one o'clock? Is that all right?' There was a silence on the line, as if she was actually expecting an answer. Then she sighed. 'Okay, then, hope to see you tomorrow. And I'm sorry. Really, I am. Ciao.'

Banks remembered the last time he had seen Emily, at the door of the old mill house, in the pink track suit he had bought for her on Oxford Street, an outfit she obviously loathed, giving him that enigmatic look as he delivered her to her parents. He remembered Jimmy Riddle's clipped thanks and Rosalind's cool silence. It was all unspoken, but he had sensed Riddle's awkward, hidden love for his daughter and Rosalind's distance.

So Emily Riddle wanted to thank him. Should he go? Yes, he thought, reaching for the bottle of Laphroaig; hell, yes, he would go.

6

The Black Bull was a young people's pub at night, with live music and a steady supply of illegal drugs, mostly Ecstasy and crystal meth. It had been targeted by the Eastvale police's 'Operation Pubwatch' on more than one occasion, never without a few arrests being made. At lunchtime, though, it had a totally different character, and most of the customers worked in the various offices and shops along York Road. The only music issued quietly from the jukebox, and the only drugs being consumed were nicotine and alcohol, with a little caffeine for those who preferred tea or coffee with their pie and chips.

When Banks arrived spot on one o'clock, Emily was nowhere in sight. He bought himself a pint and found a table near the window. The road outside was busy, and the traffic splashed up dirty water from the roadside puddles.

As he was studying the blackboard and trying to decide between Bar BQ Chicken and Thai Red Curry, Emily breezed in, out of breath, the way Jenny Fuller always seemed to do, as if it had been a great effort getting there only fifteen minutes late. She plonked her bulging handbag on the chair besides Banks, gave him an impish grin and made for the bar. When she came back, she was carrying one of those strange cocktails that young drinkers, especially female, seem to think are really interesting: in this case, Kahlua and Coke. She must have charmed the landlord into believing she was old enough to drink, Banks thought, though in all honesty she did look well over eighteen. She had a cigarette in her mouth almost before she sat down, a manoeuvre Banks was surprised she could make given that her slightly flared blue jeans looked painted on. Still, it was a testament to Emily's natural style that she didn't look in the least bit tarty, and she had chosen to wear no make-up at all. Not that she needed any. Once she had lit her cigarette and had taken a sip of her drink, she shuffled off her mid-length jacket to reveal a black silk blouse. After she had tidied her hair, she seemed ready to talk, but she kept on fidgeting.

There were moments when Banks looked at her and saw a sophisticated young woman looking back, wise enough in the ways of the world to exploit them for her own ends. Other times, he saw a gauche, nervous teenager, unable to look an adult in the eye. She was still too close to her childhood to recognize its value. When you were Emily's age, Banks remembered, all you wanted to do was enter that magical world of privilege and freedom you saw all around you – adulthood. Hence the smoking, the drinking, the sex. You didn't realize until much, much later – too late, some might say – that the privileges and freedoms you coveted came with a very high price tag indeed.

'Have you decided yet?' she asked.

'Decided what?'

'What you're having for lunch. It's my treat. I told you on the phone.'

'You don't have to do that.'

'I know. Daddy probably paid you well already for bringing me home. But I want to.'

'I'll have the Thai Red Curry, then.' Banks didn't usually go for exotic food in pubs, but the Bull had a good lunchtime reputation. 'And he didn't pay me anything.'

She raised a neatly plucked eyebrow.

'Just so you know.'

Emily paused, then said, 'All right.' She gestured for the woman delivering food at the next table to come over and

118

started to give her order. The woman frowned, told her to order it herself at the bar, then stalked off.

'Get her,' said Emily, pulling a face. Kid again.

Banks scraped his chair against the stone floor. 'I'll go.' He didn't want her to have to go through the agony of getting up and sitting down again; wearing those jeans, she might rupture her spleen or her bladder.

'No.' She jumped to her feet with surprising agility. 'I told you I'd get it.'

Banks watched her walk to the bar, taller than ever in her platform heels, and noticed all the men's eyes were on her body. There wasn't one of them who wouldn't do *anything* for her. Or to her. The women, however, turned up their noses in distaste and cast disapproving frowns in Banks's direction. What the hell, Banks asked himself, was he doing sitting in a pub with the chief constable's daughter, who was definitely breaking one law by drinking under age – if you could call Kahlua and Coke a real drink – and God knows how many other laws simply by the way she looked? It was fortunate that none of the men could be arrested for their fantasies. Not yet.

'Done.' Emily sat again and plucked her cigarette out of the ashtray. 'At least they'll bring it to the bloody table. You don't have to get up and fetch it yourself. Honestly, the service industry in this country.'

Banks wondered how many other countries she had experienced and realized it was probably more than his own daughter had. Chief constables were always getting junkets to America, Belgium, South Africa or Peru. He wondered if the service in Peru was better than that in Yorkshire. Probably.

'What are you having?' he asked.

'Me? Nothing. I don't eat lunch.'

'Nor dinner either, by the look of you.'

'Now, now. Remember, you didn't disapprove of "the look of me" too much in that hotel room.'

So she did remember. Banks felt himself blush, and it got

all the worse when he saw Emily was laughing at him. 'Look—' he said, but she waved him down.

'Don't worry. I haven't told Daddy.' She pouted and wiggled her shoulders. 'Besides, it's the waif look. Most older men like it. Don't you?'

'What about boys your own age?'

She snorted. 'They're so immature. Oh, they're all right for dancing and buying you drinks and stuff, but that's about all. All most of them can talk about is football and sex.' She licked her cherry lips. 'I prefer older men.'

Banks swallowed. He could see where that came from: a father who was never there, someone she desperately wanted to love and be loved by. 'Like Barry Clough?' he said.

A shadow crossed her fine porcelain features. 'That's one of the things I wanted to talk to you about,' she said. Then her face brightened into a smile. 'But first I really do want to thank you. I mean it. I know I wasn't very nice at the time, but I appreciate what you did, taking care of me like that. I was really fucked up. Big time.'

'Do you remember much about it?'

'In the hotel room? Yes. Until I fell asleep. You were the perfect gentleman. And the next morning you went and bought me a track suit. A pink one. It was ugly, but that was sweet of you. I'm sorry I wasn't very friendly on the way home, but I was really down.'

'Thai curry?'

The woman held out a dish of steaming curry. Banks admitted to ownership, and she set it down, narrowly avoiding spilling it on the table, gave Emily a hard glare and walked off.

'What *is* her problem?' Emily said. 'I mean, *really*! The stupid cow.'

'She doesn't like you,' said Banks. 'She doesn't like the way you treated her, and I'd guess she doesn't like your looks much, either.'

'What the fuck do I care if she likes my looks?'

'You asked. I'm simply telling you.'

'Anyway, what's she supposed to be here for if not to serve people food? It's not as if she's not getting paid or anything.'

'Look,' said Banks. 'I'm not going to argue. It's not her job to take orders, and you've got a pretty snotty attitude, when it comes right down to it.' Banks dipped into his curry. It was good and hot.

Emily glared at him for a few seconds, sulking, then started fidgeting with the large ring on her right index finger. 'Stupid old bitch,' she muttered.

Banks ignored her and tucked in, easing the heat with an occasional swig of beer. He finished the pint quicker than he had intended to and, before he could stop her, Emily had jumped to her feet and bought him another one. It was the barmaid who served her this time, not the landlord, and Banks noticed them talking, Emily taking something out of her handbag and showing it to her.

'What was all that about?' he asked when she came back.

'Nothing,' she said, putting the drinks down. 'Christ, this place is in the fucking Dark Ages.'

'What do you mean?'

'I only asked for a TVR, didn't I, and do you think the sad bitch behind the bar had any idea what I was talking about?'

'I can't say I have any idea what you're talking about, either.'

Emily looked at him as if he came from another planet. 'Well, I had to explain it to *her*, too. It's tequila, vodka and Red Bull. Great stuff, gives you a real alcohol high without all that slurring and stumbling. Me and . . . well, you know who . . . we used to drink it in the Cicada Dust in Clerkenwell.'

'And?'

She pulled a face. 'What do *you* think?'

'They didn't have it?'

'Of course they didn't.'

'So what did you settle for?'

'A Snowball.'

Banks had heard of that one: advocaat and lemonade. He had thought it long out of fashion. He remembered that his mother sometimes used to drink a Snowball at Christmas when he was a kid. Just the one, usually, as she was never much of a drinker. 'Mmm, it's good.' Emily held out the glass. 'Want a sip?'

'No, thanks. Have you been in touch with any of the crowd down there? Ruth?'

Emily shook her head. 'Not much.'

'Craig said Barry's minders beat him up outside a pub in Soho while you looked on laughing.'

'The lying bastard.'

'It didn't happen?'

'Oh, it happened, but not the way he told it.'

'You tell me, then.'

'It was in Clerkenwell, outside Barry's club. Craig found out about the place and he started hanging around there, pretending to be taking photographs. He was obsessed. He just wouldn't let go. I told him to stay away, but he wouldn't listen. He even started coming in, but Barry had him barred. When he came up to me, it was the last straw. I wouldn't have let them hit him like that if I could have stopped them, but it all happened so quickly. It was his own fault, really.'

'He said he didn't know where you lived.'

'He didn't. I told Ruth to make sure she didn't tell him. He knew about the club from before, though, from the party.'

'Which party?'

'The one where I met Barry. At some promoter's house. Ruth took us. She knows people in the music scene and all that.'

'Craig was there, too?'

'Yes. That's how he knew Barry owned a club in Clerkenwell. I started seeing Barry after that night and a week or so later I left Craig. He was just getting to be too much.'

'I see. And were you laughing when they beat him up?'

'I wasn't laughing. I was crying. The fool.'

'Why would he lie to me?'

'The truth would hardly make him look good, would it? Craig might seem so nice and well balanced on the surface, but he's got a mean streak, too, you know.'

'Did he ever hit you?'

'No. He knew I wouldn't stand for that. It was just . . . oh, you know, if I came home late or something, he'd always be waiting up and go on at me, calling me a slut and a whore and stuff. It was mean. Nasty. Then he was all pathetic the next morning, telling me he loved me and buying me presents and all that when all he really wanted was to get into my knickers.'

'I still don't understand why he would lie to me. He believed I was your father. Surely he must know I'd find out the truth when I found you?'

Emily laughed. 'Silly. It's the last thing I'd tell my father. Think about it.'

Banks did. She was right. 'But you're telling *me*.'

'That's different. You're not my father. You're not like him at all. You're . . .'

'I'm what?'

'Well, you're more like a friend. Cute, too.'

'I'm flattered, Emily, but you'd better not tell your father that.'

She giggled and put her hand to her mouth, as if embarrassed to catch herself out in a juvenile act. 'You're right about that.'

'Have you heard from Craig at all since you've been back in Yorkshire?'

'No. I've not seen or heard from him since that night outside the club.'

'What about Ruth?'

'I've talked to her a couple of times on the phone. But I

123

didn't give her much cause to like me, did I? I think she fancied Craig and I took him away from her.'

'It was as much his choice. Besides, she'll get over it.'

'Yeah . . . well . . . Ruth's got enough problems without me adding to them.'

'What do you mean?'

'Nothing. She's just a bit fucked up. Couldn't you tell?'

'She did seem strange.' Not stranger than Emily herself, though, Banks thought. He pushed his empty plate aside and lit a cigarette. It wasn't as if there were anything to be gained by trying to act as a positive, non-smoking role model to Emily. 'Are you going to tell me what happened in London that night?' he asked. 'Before you arrived at the hotel.'

Emily licked at the rim of her glass. 'I've been thinking about it.'

'And?'

She looked around, then leaned forward conspiratorially. 'I've decided I will.'

Banks could smell the advocaat on her breath. He leaned back. 'I'm all ears.'

Annie had not been completely honest with Banks, she admitted to herself the next afternoon as she drove out to the Daleview Business Park to meet Charlie Courage's boss at SecuTec, Ian Bennett. As usual, when she found it difficult to talk about something, she had been flip, all style and no substance. Working out of Eastvale, with Banks, bothered her more than she had been able to tell him. It wasn't that she couldn't separate her job from her personal life – she felt she could do the job perfectly well, no matter who she worked with – but so much proximity to Banks might weaken her resolve to end their relationship. After all, she had given him up not because she didn't feel anything for him, but because she found herself feeling too much too soon, and because he brought too many complications from his previous relationship with him, a marriage of over twenty years. Working with him again, she had to admit to herself that she still fancied him.

To hell with it, she told herself, sneaking a quick glance at the map on the car seat beside her. Almost there. She would just do her bloody job and let the rest take care of itself. One thing her brief romance with Banks *had* done was renew her faith in the job, make her think about *why* she had become a policewoman in the first place. Now she had a better sense of herself, more confidence, and she was damn well going for inspector. Not that the job was everything, mind you – she wasn't going to make *that* mistake and end up a dried-up old spinster with no life other than work – but she *was* willing to commit herself as much as it took. And because her work life was going to be hard, she wanted to keep her personal life simple. With Banks in her bed, it wouldn't be.

The black wrought-iron railings to her left bore a large painted sign saying DALEVIEW BUSINESS PARK, along with a list of businesses located there. Annie turned through the gates, which were probably intended more for decoration than security, she thought, and looked for the SecuTec office.

The business park consisted of a large, one-storey red-brick building, built in the shape of a pentagon and divided into a number of units, each with its own logo, and some with showcase windows and parking spots for two or three cars out front. Though it wasn't a shopping precinct as such, the pottery shop and the needlecraft centre had outlets there, along with a stair-lift company, a furniture workshop and an Aga centre. The other units were taken up by offices: a company that rented holiday cottages, for example, and a mail-order exercise-video distribution company, Annie noticed. She wondered if that were some sort of euphemism for what they *really* sold. If it was a front for a porn operation, then it might be connected with Charlie Courage's murder.

Ian Bennett opened the office door for her before she even reached it.

'DS Cabbot,' she said, fishing for her warrant card.

'It's all right,' said Bennett, smiling. 'I believe you. Come on in.'

She followed him into the small office.

'So this is what the well-dressed young policewoman is wearing these days,' he said, looking her up and down.

Under her navy blue raincoat, which hung open, she was wearing boots, black tights, a short denim skirt and a white sweater, none of which she felt was particularly weird. What did he expect? A uniform? A twinset and pearls?

Bennett was younger than she had expected from the voice on the telephone, probably about her age, early thirties, with thick curly dark hair and more of a tan than you can get hanging around Yorkshire in winter. He looked as if he played sports to keep in shape, something that involved a lot of running around, such as tennis or squash, and while his salary probably didn't stretch as far as Armani, he was wearing designer casuals that must have set him back a bob or two. A mobile phone bulged ostentatiously from the pocket of his zip-up suede jacket. Annie guessed that the BMW she had parked next to was probably his.

'So this is what the well-dressed young yuppie-on-the-go is wearing to impress the girls these days,' she countered, aware as soon as she had done so that it wasn't the best way to start an interview. Big problem, Annie: you've never been able to suffer fools gladly, which gives you at least one thing in common with Alan Banks. *Stop thinking about him.*

SecuTec had only a small office at Daleview, where Charlie Courage had spent his nights on guard duty. Annie glanced around and saw that he'd had a small television for company, along with facilities for making tea and a microwave oven for heating up his midnight snack. The office was too small for the two of them, and it smelt of warm plastic. Annie sat on what would have been Charlie's desk and Ian Bennett leaned against the opposite wall by a company calendar. Like so many of those things, it showed a buxom, skinny-waisted smiling blonde in a bikini. She was holding a spanner.

Bennett flushed at her insult. 'I suppose I deserved that,' he said, running his hand over his hair. 'I always say something silly when I meet an attractive woman. Sorry. Can we start again?'

Annie gave him a low-wattage smile, the kind she reserved for the masses. 'Best all round,' she said.

Bennett cleared his throat. 'I'm afraid I can't tell you very much,' he began. 'I didn't know Mr Courage well.'

'When did he last work?'

'Sunday night. He was on the four-to-midnight shift.'

'Are you certain? Did you see him?'

'No, but he logged in. I mean, he has to log in with us so we know someone's there.'

'How does he do this?'

Bennett pointed at the desk beside her. 'Computer.'

'Could someone else have done it? Pretended to be him?'

'I suppose it's possible. But they'd have to know his user name and his password.'

'I see. Was this the shift he always worked?'

'No. Other days he worked from midnight till eight in the morning.'

'Was he the only nightwatchman?'

'No. It works like this. On the days the units are open, we have the other security guard, Colin Finch, work four to midnight and Mr Courage work midnight till eight, when the units start opening in the morning. Then, when we get to Sunday, they alternate. Colin does four to midnight Saturday, Charlie does midnight to eight. Then Colin does eight to four, and so on.'

'I see,' said Annie, who remembered the horrors of shift work very well indeed. Most of the time she hadn't known whether she was coming or going. 'So Colin Finch would have seen Mr Courage when they changed shifts at four on Sunday?'

'Yes. I should think so.'

'Can you give me his address?'

'Of course.' Bennett fiddled with the computer and gave Annie a Ripon address. 'He'll be in at four today, though, if you're still around.'

Annie looked at her watch. It was half past two. 'Did you know that Mr Courage had a criminal record?'

The question seemed to embarrass Bennett. 'He had? Er, actually, no, we didn't know.'

'Surely a security firm like yours runs checks on potential employees?'

'Normally we do. Yes, of course. But this one . . . well . . . it seems he slipped between the cracks.'

' "Slipped between the cracks"?'

'Yes.'

'I see.' Annie made a note in her brand-new notebook. What she actually wrote was, 'Don't forget to pick up something for dinner at Marks & Sparks', but Bennett wasn't to know that. 'Have there been any incidents at the park over the past few months, since Mr Courage started working here?'

'No. Nothing at all. As far as SecuTec is concerned, Mr Courage seemed to be doing his job well.'

'Nothing gone missing?'

'Nothing.'

'The other tenants, are they all satisfied?'

'Yes. As I said, we've had no problems, no complaints at all. I don't suppose it's something you police ever consider, but have you thought at all that Mr Courage might indeed have gone straight, as they say? I mean, just because a man makes a couple of mistakes, it doesn't mean he's marked for ever, does it?'

Annie sighed. This wasn't going to work, she could tell. 'Mr Bennett,' she said, 'why don't you leave the recidivism versus rehabilitation argument to people who know what they're talking about and just answer my questions?'

He smiled. 'I thought that's what I was doing. I mean, I've told you there were no problems. I was only suggesting that it might indicate Mr Courage had changed his ways. You do believe that criminals can change their ways, don't you, Detective Constable Cabbot?'

'It's detective *sergeant*,' Annie corrected him, adding a silent 'pillock' under her breath. 'And I'm merely suggesting that we'll get you back in your Beemer and on your way to your next meeting much faster if you simply answer my questions.'

Bennett fiddled with his mobile, as if hoping it would ring. 'Carry on,' he said, with a drawn-out, long-suffering sigh.

Annie smiled to herself. He would no doubt tell his guests at tonight's dinner party or whatever about his brush with police brutality. 'What exactly were his duties?' she asked.

'He was supposed to walk around the park, check doors and everything once an hour. To be honest, though, it wasn't much of a job; there wasn't a lot for him to do.'

'I shouldn't think so with all these modern security gizmos. Why bother hiring a nightwatchman at all, then?'

'It was a matter of appearances, really. The tenants like it. Believe it or not, no matter how many sophisticated alarm systems you put in place, people always feel a bit more confident if there's a human being around.'

'That's comforting,' said Annie. 'I don't suppose I need to worry about Robocop much any more.'

'Sorry?'

'A joke. Never mind. Carry on.'

'Oh, I see. A copper with a sense of humour. Anyway, having someone on the premises discourages vandals, too.'

'What about a dog?'

'They can be effective, but you can't just leave them alone. Besides, there's the whole problem of lawsuits if they actually bite anyone.'

'How did Mr Courage get the job?'

'He applied through normal channels. I must say, he *seemed* credible enough.'

'The mark of a master criminal.'

'You're joking again?' Bennett smiled.

Annie didn't smile back. 'Mr Courage was paid by cheque, am I correct?'

'Actually, no. His wages were paid directly into his bank account.'

'Were there ever any cash bonuses?'

Bennett frowned. 'Cash bonuses? I don't know what you mean.'

'Cash in hand.'

'Certainly not. That's not SecuTec's policy.'

'And no money has ever been reported missing by any of the businesses operating out of this park during the period of Mr Courage's employment as nightwatchman?'

'No.'

Annie closed her notebook. 'Very well, Mr Bennett,' she said. 'You can go now. We might need to get in touch again later.'

'Fine. Feel free to do whatever you need here, but please remember to lock up when you leave.'

Bennett practically ran out of the office. Annie stood in the doorway and watched him reverse the BMW, then take off in what would have been a cloud of dust had the ground not been so wet. As it was, one of the puddles he hit sent a sheet of water over a woman just walking into the needlework-centre shop a few units down. She looked down at her soaked raincoat and tights and glared after the car, shaking her fist.

She shouldn't have been quite so sharp with Bennett, Annie thought, as she watched him clear the gates and turn right onto the main road. He was a smug pillock, true enough, but she'd had to deal with plenty of those in her time, and she hadn't usually resorted to bullying. He looked like the kind who'd put in a complaint, too. Would that have any effect on her attempt to make inspector? She doubted it. But she also made a mental note to watch herself and be a lot more compassionate towards fools and pillocks.

Now, she thought, it was simply a matter of deciding whether to go right or left and spend an hour or so talking to the people who operated the businesses at Daleview. They would probably know a lot more about its day-to-day operations than Mr Ian bloody Bennett. After that, with any luck, Colin Finch would have reported for duty.

'Barry was very angry after you left,' Emily said, toying with, rather than smoking, another cigarette. 'I've never seen him so angry. When he gets angry, he goes all cold. He doesn't go red in the face and shout or anything, like Dad, he just gets this fixed sort of smile and does everything in a very slow, careful sort of way, like straightening the cushions on the settee or lighting a cigarette. And he talks very quietly. It's frightening.'

'Do you know why he was angry?'

'Because you came asking questions. He doesn't like anyone asking questions, especially strangers.'

'What did he do to you?'

'Barry? He didn't do anything. I'm telling you. He was angry in that cold way he had. He just told me to get ready for the party, then we did another couple of lines of coke and off we went.'

'What kind of party was it?'

'The usual sort. Music-business people, a few minor bands, groupies, along with a few young entrepreneurs, other club owners. The kind of people Barry collects. There was a bonfire and fireworks outside. But we mostly stayed indoors.'

'Drugs?'

She laughed. 'Oh, yes. Of course. Always drugs.'

'Does Barry deal?'

'No. He just buys.'

'Go on.'

Emily paused. For all her bravado, Banks could tell she had difficulty talking about it. 'Barry was weird all evening. I tried to just . . . you know . . . stay away from him until his mood had passed, keep my distance, talk to some of the guys in the bands and stuff, but he kept appearing, smiling in that cold way of his, putting his arm around me, touching me . . . sometimes even squeezing . . . hurting me . . .' She drank some of her Snowball, grimaced and said, 'I don't think I like this, after all. Would you get me a lager and lime or something like that? I'm thirsty.'

'I'm not buying you an alcoholic drink, Emily. You're under age.'

'Don't be a spoilsport. I'm already drinking one, aren't I?'

'You're right. I probably shouldn't even be sitting with you. But I am. If you want me to get you a drink you'll get a lemonade or a Coke.'

'I won't tell you the rest of my story.'

'Doesn't matter.'

'Bastard. And I thought you were supposed to be my friend.'

Banks said nothing. Emily sashayed to the bar, drawing all the male eyes again. Banks sipped some beer and lit his second cigarette. He was definitely going to make some inquiries into Mr Barry Clough and his 'business' activities over the next few days.

Emily came back with a pint of lager and lime and spilled some as she set it triumphantly on the table. For a while, she didn't say anything, then she took a long swig, paused and said, 'It was pretty late. I don't know. Two or three in the morning. Everyone was really wasted. I was feeling weird, like someone had put something in my drink. It might have been one of those date-rape drugs I've read about, but I'd had so much other stuff I didn't fall asleep. I just felt strange. Floating. Anyway, Barry took me aside and said there was something he wanted me to do for him.' As she spoke, she looked into her

132

drink and the fingers of her right hand rubbed at the table's surface. Banks noticed the chewed nails. 'He took me upstairs towards one of the bedrooms. I thought he wanted a blow job or something. He sometimes did. I didn't really want to, I was feeling so spaced out, but . . . if it would get him off my back for a while . . . Anyway, it wasn't that. He opened the bedroom door and there was Andy inside. Anyway, he was stark naked and he . . . I mean, we'd all been taking V and E, so he was, you know, it was . . .'

'V and E?'

She looked at him as if he were an idiot. 'Viagra and Ecstasy. Anyway, like I said, he was . . . like he had a lamp-post between his legs. Barry just gave me a push forward and told me to be nice to him, then I heard the door shut. Anyway, when Barry pushed me I fell on the bed and Andy started pulling at my clothes, rubbing against me. It was gross. I might have been stoned, and I'll admit I've not always been a good girl, but this was seriously out of line. I mean, it ought to be *my* choice who I have sex with, not someone else's, oughtn't it? And it wasn't even him so much. I mean, he was a pathetic creep, but the thought that Barry had *given* me to him as a sort of punishment for you coming and asking questions . . . I don't know. It just made me sick, that's all.'

She paused to drink some lager and lime. Banks felt his anger rise along with the guilt; it was his arrival that had caused the problems for Emily. He told himself that, no matter what, with someone like Clough she would have got to that point eventually anyway, but it didn't help right then. He also remembered the night, not so long ago, in a London bistro, when Annie Cabbot had told him about her sexual humiliation at the hands of some CID colleagues. 'Who was this Andy? Did you know him?'

'Like I said, I'd seen him around. He's one of Barry's gofers. At least I've heard Barry telling him off and ordering him to do stuff sometimes. Takes the piss out of him something terrible, too. Andy has a stutter, see. I mean, that was one of the most humiliating things about it. Like, Barry had *given me to one of his employees*. To someone he thought was a bit of a joke. It made me feel worthless. Like shit.'

'What was his full name?'

'Andrew Handley. But everyone calls him Andy Pandy. Anyway, you know the rest. Or most of it.'

'How did you get away?'

'We struggled. He wasn't really expecting any resistance, so I just kneed him in the balls and he hit me and let go. The door wasn't locked. I ran out, downstairs and out of the house without looking back. I was only worried that Barry might be lurking around at the bottom of the stairs or something and that he'd stop me, but I didn't see him. I was lucky. We were near Victoria Station, so I ran to the taxi rank and the only place I could think of to go was your hotel. And that's it. The sad story of Barry and Emily. Or Barry and Louisa.'

'Did he ever mistreat you before that?'

'No. But I never gave him cause to.'

'What do you mean?'

Emily thought for a moment, then said, 'With Craig, it was easy. He was jealous, maybe a bit too much, and it made him a bit crazy. With Barry, it's different. He's possessive, not jealous. He expects loyalty. You know that there are certain lines you're not supposed to cross. I'm not a fool. I might not know exactly what he's into, but I know it's probably illegal. And I know he hurts people. I saw him hurt Craig.'

'Was that part of the appeal?'

'What? That he hurts people?'

'That he's a criminal, whereas your father's a policeman. After all, they're about the same age.'

Emily snorted. 'That sounds just like something my father would say. Do you all take the same course in pop psychology?'

'There is a kind of logic in it.'

'It's not that at all. Barry's appeal is that he's exciting to be with, he gives great parties, has great drugs and people respect him.'

'Fear him, you mean.'

'Whatever. If fear's the only way you can get respect, what's wrong with that? Nobody disses Barry.'

'Why aren't you still with him, then?'

She started rubbing at the table again. 'I told you.'

A confused kid. Banks had to stop himself from leaning forward and putting his hand over hers. It would have simply been a paternal gesture on his part, though he was aware that neither Emily nor the others in the pub would view it that way. He also noted that in her entire list of Barry Clough's attributes, Emily had not mentioned sex, that he was great in bed. Sex was probably a matter of power for Clough. Banks didn't doubt for a moment that Clough used Emily sexually – she had already said as much – but to her, he guessed, it was more a matter of the price to be paid for the high life than a joy to be shared. And the fact that she priced herself so low was a matter for concern.

'Are you afraid of him, Emily?'

'Course not. It's just . . .'

'What?'

She frowned. 'He's very possessive, like I said. Barry doesn't like to lose his prized possessions.'

An hour later, Annie was wet and miserable and none the wiser. She had gone to each of the units on the estate, talked to managers and workers and discovered absolutely nothing. If anything dodgy had been going on at the Daleview Business Park, it had been kept a very close secret.

It was with a great sense of relief, then, that she approached the last but one business on her list. Banks had called for a late-afternoon meeting to pool their findings and, after that, Annie had visions of a long hot bath, some microwaveable

Marks & Sparks concoction, and an evening alone to do as much or as little as she wished.

The needlework centre was warm and dry, smelling of scented candles, predominantly rose and lemon. It was the kind of place that seemed made of nooks and crannies, all filled with such essentials as pin boxes, thread, étuis, stitch-layers, needle threaders, working frames, stitch-count converters and a thousand other more esoteric items. Finished tapestries hung on the walls. More of a showroom than a shop, it had no counter, but there was a comfortable-looking three-piece suite where clients could sit and discuss their requirements.

A young woman came out of the office in the back, the same woman Bennett had splashed in his hasty getaway. Annie introduced herself.

The woman held out her hand. 'My name's Natalie,' she said. 'Welcome to my empire, for what it's worth. I can't tell you anything, but I've just put the kettle on, if you want to stay out of the rain for a few moments.'

'Please,' said Annie. 'I could murder a cuppa right now.' If accepting free cups of tea counted as corruption, there wouldn't be a copper in the whole of England not up on charges.

'Won't be a minute.' Natalie walked back into the office.

Annie was examining the needlecraft kits and wondered if they would be relaxing or frustrating to do. She had a sudden memory of her mother sitting cross-legged on the floor, her long hair all over the place, wearing one of her flowing velvety creations covered in beadwork and embroidery. She was working on a sampler of a local village scene. It was an odd image, as Annie had never thought of her mother doing needlecraft before, though she knew she made her own clothes, and they were always beautifully embroidered. She would have to phone and ask her father. Maybe some of the samplers were down at the commune near St Ives, and she could take one as a memento. Her mother had died when she was only five. In her imagination, as Annie watched, her mother looked up and smiled at her. Annie felt suddenly sad, and then Natalie returned with the tea.

It must have shown.

'What is it?' Natalie asked. 'You look as if you've seen a ghost, love.'

'Oh, nothing. Memories, that's all.'

Natalie looked around her showroom as if trying to search for the offending object. Annie decided it was time to get on track. 'Thanks for the tea,' she said, taking a sip. 'I know you said you couldn't tell me anything, but I suppose you've heard what happened to Mr Courage?'

'Oh, yes. Word gets around here pretty quickly. After all, most of us have been here since the place opened, so we're used to each other. Shall we sit down?' She gestured to the three-piece suite and Annie sat in the armchair. She felt so weary she wondered whether she would ever be able to get out of it again.

'Did you know him at all?' she asked.

'No. But I know he hadn't been here very long.'

'Since September.'

'Was it? If you say so. Anyway, Mr Bennett brought him around and introduced him to everyone just before he started, so we'd recognize him, know who to call if there were any problems, but other than that I never even saw him again. You see, I'm usually gone by five o'clock most days, except Thursday and Friday, when I stay open till seven. At least I will until after Christmas, then there's not much point until the weather starts getting better. You'd be surprised how many tourists we get just dropping by in spring and summer, but most of my trade comes from regular customers. This is a very specialized business. They know what they want and they know I have it for them. They usually telephone first, of course. Oh, listen to me rattling on. But I did warn you I didn't know anything.'

Annie smiled and sipped some more tea. 'It's all right,' she said. 'Gives me a chance to warm up and drink my tea. So far everyone I've spoken to says there have been no incidents at the park, not even petty theft. Is that right?'

'Well, I can't speak for everyone, but I've had a bit of shoplifting here once in a while. Nothing serious, you understand, but irritating, petty stuff. Thread, packets of needles, that sort of thing.'

'Kids?'

'I doubt it. We don't get a lot of kids here. Needlecraft's hardly the in thing with the younger generation these days.'

'I doubt that it ever was.'

'Still, it's a living. Anyway, I suppose shoplifting's the kind of thing you have to expect in a place like this, but as I said, it's nothing serious.'

'There are some pretty organized gangs of shoplifters. Keep your eyes open. If it gets serious, let us know.'

Natalie nodded.

Annie shifted in her chair. 'Much as I'd love to, I'm afraid I can't sit here all day,' she said, with a quick glance through the window. It was still pouring down outside. She looked at the list Ian Bennett had given her and got to her feet. 'One more to go.'

Natalie frowned. 'Not if you went clockwise from the SecuTec office; there isn't anyone else.'

Annie glanced at the list. 'What do you mean? I've got something called PKF Computer Systems listed here, right next door to you.'

'The computer people? They're gone.'

'When did they move out?'

'Over the weekend. I don't suppose Mr Bennett has got around to updating the list yet.'

'How many people worked there?'

'Only two regulars, as far as I could tell. It's one of the smaller units.'

'Do you know their names?'

'Sorry. I hardly saw them. They weren't the most sociable types.'

'What about people coming and going?'

'Just delivery vans. The usual stuff.'

'Okay. Thank you very much for your time, Natalie. And for the tea.'

'My pleasure. It livens up a dull afternoon.'

Annie left the needlecraft centre and walked to the next unit. If there had been a sign over the door, none hung there now. Instead of a plate-glass window, as in some of the showrooms, the empty PKF unit had three smaller windows at the front. Annie peeped through one of them, and as far as she could make out the inside was empty, completely cleared out. That was all it took to trigger the little alarm bell in her copper's mind. Charlie Courage, last seen alive by a neighbour on Sunday afternoon, apparently worked the four-to-midnight shift that evening and was found dead on Tuesday nearly two hundred miles away. He had received five cash payments of two hundred quid each over the past month. And now this computer company had done a bunk over the weekend.

It certainly ought to be worth a quick look around their deserted premises, and by the time she had finished, Annie thought, Colin Finch would probably be in the SecuTec office. She should just have time to talk to him before heading back to the station for the meeting.

'Don't think I want you acting like some sort of avenging angel,' Emily said. 'You've already done your knight-in-shining-armour bit, thank you very much.'

'Why are you telling me all this, then?'

'Because you asked. And because I owe you an explanation. That's all.'

'You admitted you're frightened of Clough.'

'That was silly of me.' She gave a slight shudder. 'It was

just, you know, talking about it, remembering how he was that night. And I . . .'

'What?'

'It's nothing.'

'Go on.'

'Oh, just that I thought I saw Jamie in the Swainsdale Centre.' She laughed, put her forefinger to her head and twisted it back and forth. 'Me being crazy again. Paranoid Emily, that's what they'll be calling me.' Her nail was chewed almost to the quick.

'Jamie who?'

'Jamie Gilbert. He's one of Barry's closest employees. Barry talks and Jamie jumps. I don't like him. He's good-looking, but he's mean. He gives me the creeps.'

'When was this?'

'A couple of days ago. Monday, I think. But it can't have been him. I must have been seeing things. Barry doesn't even know who I really am or where I live, does he? Remember Louisa Gamine?'

'How could I forget?' Banks wasn't certain that a man like Barry Clough lacked the resources to find out what he wanted about anyone. 'Be careful, though. If you think you see him or Clough around here again, make sure you tell me. Okay?'

'I can take care of myself.'

'Emily, promise you'll tell me if you think you see either of them again.'

Emily waved her hand. 'All right. All right. Don't get your underpants in a twist about it.'

'You never did tell me what business Clough's in.'

'That's because I don't know.'

'Are you certain he's not a drug dealer?'

'No. I mean, I don't think so. Like I said, he's always got drugs around. He knows people, does people favours and things, maybe gets them some stuff, but he's not a dealer. I'm sure of that.'

'How does he make his money?'

'I told you, I don't know. He never talked about it to me. As far as Barry is concerned, women are purely for recreation, not business. There's the club, I suppose, for a start. That takes up a fair bit of his time. And I think maybe he manages some bands and does some concert promotion. He's got business interests all over the country. He was always off here and there. Leeds. Dover. Manchester. Bristol. Sometimes he took me with him, but to be honest it was pretty boring waiting for him in some hotel room or walking the streets of some dingy little dump in the rain. Once he even asked me if I wanted to come here with him.'

'Here? The Black Bull?'

'Eastvale, silly. Can you imagine it? Me and Barry walking around Eastvale? I mean, my mother *works* here.' She slapped the table and made the glasses wobble. 'I don't want to talk about him any more. It's over. Barry will move on to his next little girl and I'll get on with my life.'

'How are things at home?'

She pulled a face. 'Just what you'd expect.'

'What's that?'

'Boring. They just want me to keep quiet and stay out of the way. Mother pretty much ignores me. Dad has his political cronies over most of the time. You should see the way some of them look at me. But he doesn't notice. He's too busy planning his future.'

'And what about you? What do you want to do?'

Emily brightened and took a long swig of her lager and lime. 'I've been thinking I might like to go to university after all.'

'Don't you have to do your A levels first?'

'Of course. But I can do that at a sixth-form college. I could even do them at home if I want to. It's not as if they're hard or anything.'

'Ah,' said Banks, who had found even his O levels hard. 'And where would you go to university?'

'Oxford or Cambridge, of course.'

'Of course.'

Her eyes narrowed. 'Are you taking the piss?'

'Farthest thing from my mind.'

'Right. Yeah . . . well . . . anyway, I also thought I wouldn't mind going to university in America. Harvard or Stanford or somewhere like that. Not Bryn Mawr. It sounds like that nasty little Welsh town we lived in for a while when I was a kid. And not that one in Poughkeepsie, either. That sounds like somewhere you keep pigs.'

'What would you study?'

'I'm not sure yet. Maybe languages. Or acting. I was always good in school plays. But there's plenty of time to think about all that.'

'Yes, there is.' Banks paused and fiddled for another cigarette. Emily lit it for him with a gold lighter. 'I don't want to sound like your father,' he went on, 'but this drugs thing . . .'

'I can take them or leave them.'

'You sure?'

'Sure. I never did much anyway. Just a bit of coke, crystal meth, V and E.'

'Viagra and Ecstasy?'

'You remember.'

'You took that?'

'Yeah.'

'But Viagra's . . . I mean, what does it do? For a woman?'

She came up with a wicked grin and tapped his arm. 'Well, it doesn't exactly give me a hard-on, but it does make fucking really good. Mostly, it gives you a real rush, sort of like speed.'

'I see. And you've had no problems giving up all this stuff?'

'I'm not an *addict*, if that's what you're getting at. I can stop any time I want.'

'I'm not suggesting that you're an addict, just that it can be difficult without outside help.'

'I'm not going on one of those stupid programmes with all those losers, if that's what you mean. No way.' She pouted and looked away.

Banks held his hands up. 'Fine. Fine. All I'm saying is that if you find you *need* any help . . . Well, I know you can hardly go to your father. That's all.'

Emily stared at him for a while, as if digesting and translating what he had said. 'Thanks,' she said finally, not meeting his eyes, and managed a small smile. 'You know why my dad hates you?'

Startled, Banks almost choked on his drink. When he had regained some of his composure, he suggested, 'Personality clash?'

'Because he envies you. That's why.'

'Envies me?'

'It's true. I can tell. I've heard him going on to Mother. Do you know, he thinks you've been having it off with some Pakistani tart in Leeds?'

'She's not Pakistani, she's from Bangladesh. She's not a tart. And we've never had it off.'

'Whatever. And the music. That drives him crazy.'

'But why?'

'Don't you know?'

'I wouldn't be asking if I did.'

'It's because you've got a life. You have a woman on the side, you listen to opera or whatever, *and* you get the job done, you get results. You also do it the way you want. Dad's by the book. Always has been.'

'But he's one of the youngest chief constables we've ever had. Why on earth should *he* be jealous of *my* achievements?'

'You still don't get it, do you?'

'Obviously not.'

'He's envious. You're everything he'd like to be, but can't. He's locked himself on a course he couldn't change even if he wanted to. He's sacrificed everything to get where he's got. Believe me, I should know. I'm one of the things he's sacrificed. All he's got is his ambition. He doesn't have time to listen to music, be with his family, have another woman, read a book. It's like he's made a pact with the devil and he's handed over all his time in exchange for earthly power and position. And there's something else. He can handle the politics, pass exams and courses by the cartload, manage, administrate better than just about anyone else on the force, but there's one thing he could never do worth a damn.'

'What's that?'

'He couldn't detect his way out of a paper bag.'

'Why should that matter?'

'Because that's why he joined up in the first place.'

'How do you know?'

'I don't. I'm only guessing. But I saw his old books once, when we were staying at my grandparents' house in Worthing. They're all, like, sixties paperback editions and stuff, with his name written inside them, all very neatly. A lot of those Penguins with the green covers. Detective stories. Sherlock Holmes. Agatha Christie. Ngaio Marsh. All that boring old crap. And I looked in some of them. Do you know what he's done? He's made his own notes in the margins, about who he thinks did it, what the clues mean. I even read one of them while we were there. He couldn't have been more wrong.'

Banks felt queasy. There was something obscene about this intimate look into Riddle's childhood dreams that made him uncomfortable. 'Where did *you* learn pop psychology?' he said, trying to brush the whole thing off.

Emily smiled. 'There is a kind of logic to it. Think about it. Look, it's been great seeing you, but I really have to be going. I have to meet someone at three. Then I'm off clubbing tonight.' She gathered her handbag, more the size of a small rucksack, really, patted her hair and stood up. 'Maybe we can do this again?'

'I'd like that,' Banks said. 'But it's on my terms next time, or not at all.'

'Your terms?'

'No booze.'

She stuck her tongue out at him. 'Spoilsport. Bye.' Then she picked up her jacket, turned with a flourish and strutted out of the pub. The men all watched her go with hangdog expressions, some of them brought crudely back to reality by harsh remarks from their wives sitting next to them. One woman gave Banks a particularly malevolent look, the kind she probably reserved for child molesters.

After Emily had gone, Banks spent a few moments thinking over what she had said. Self-analysis had not been a habit of his, and it was something he had only really indulged in since the split with Sandra, since his move to the cottage, even. There he had spent many a late evening watching the sunset over the flagstone roofs of Helmthorpe as shadows gathered on the distant valley sides, and probing himself, his motives, what made him the man he was, why he had made the mistakes he had made. There he was, a man in his forties taking stock of his life and finding out it wasn't at all what he thought it had been.

So Riddle hated him because he was a natural detective and because he appeared to have a life, including this illusory mistress. Some of Riddle's envy, then, if that was what it was, was based on error. What could be more pathetic than envying a man the life you only *imagine* he has? It was just a precocious teenager's analysis, of course, but perhaps it wasn't too far from the mark. After all, it wasn't as if Riddle had ever given Banks a chance, right from the start. Still, he thought, knocking back the last of his pint, that wasn't his problem any more. With Riddle in his corner, things were bound to change for the better. As he pulled up his collar and left the pub, he was aware of the women's eyes burning holes in the back of his raincoat.

7

DS Jim Hatchley was the last to arrive at the scheduled meeting that Thursday afternoon, rolling in a little after quarter past five smelling of ale and tobacco and looking as if he'd been dragged through a hedge backwards. Banks, Annie Cabbot and DCs Rickerd, Jackman and Templeton were already gathered in the 'boardroom', so called because of its panels, wainscoting and oil portraits of dead mill owners. A thin patina of dust from the renovations had even reached as far as the long banqueting table, usually so highly polished you could see your reflection in it.

'Sorry, sir,' muttered Hatchley, taking his seat.

Banks turned to Annie Cabbot, who had just started an account of her afternoon at the Daleview Business Park. 'Go on, DS Cabbot,' he said. 'Now that we're all here.'

'Well, sir, there's not a great deal to add. Charlie turned up for work on Sunday afternoon, as usual, logged in, and he went home at midnight. His replacement for the midnight-to-eight shift, Colin Finch, says he actually saw him at four and at midnight, so we know he was still alive when he left the park.'

'Did this Finch have anything more to tell us?' Banks asked.

'Said he hardly knew Charlie. They were ships that passed in the night. His words, not mine. And he'd no sense of anything dodgy going on at Daleview. Nobody else I spoke to there admits to knowing Charlie, either – not surprising, when you consider he was usually at work when the rest had gone home – and there had been no incidents reported at the park, so he didn't even have very much to do.'

'Could his death be unrelated to his work, then?' Banks asked.

'It's possible,' Annie said, glancing at Hatchley. 'After all, he did have form. Mixed with some pretty rough company in his time. But there *was* one odd thing.'

'Yes?'

She took an envelope out of her briefcase and set it on the table. 'One of the companies operating out of Daleview – PKF Computer Systems – cleared out lock, stock and barrel on Sunday evening.'

'Moonlight flit?'

'No, sir. All above board, according to Colin Finch. Just very short notice. They were gone by midnight, when he started his shift.'

'Couldn't pay their bills?'

'They weren't owing when they left, but I should imagine a cash-flow problem might be at the back of it all.'

'Likely,' said Banks. 'But they did nothing wrong?'

'No. Interesting timing, though, wouldn't you say?'

'I would.' PKF had cleared off during Charlie Courage's final evening shift. Banks didn't like coincidences any more than any other copper worth his salt. 'Go on.'

'Anyway, Ian Bennett had given me *carte blanche* and the keys were all there in Mr Courage's old office, so I had a quick shufti around the PKF unit.'

'Find anything?'

'Clean as a whistle. They'd obviously taken care to make sure they left nothing behind. Except this. I found it lodged behind the radiator. It must have fallen there.' She held the envelope and tipped it. A cracked plastic case about five by five and a half inches fell onto the polished table's surface.

'A CD case,' said Banks. 'I suppose you'd expect to find

something like that if they were in the computer business. Software and all that.'

'Yes,' said Annie. 'It probably means nothing. In fact, the whole PKF thing's probably nothing, but I handled it carefully just in case. We might want to check with fingerprints.'

'You think there's something dodgy about PKF?'

Annie leaned back in her chair. She even looked comfortable in the notoriously hard and bum-unfriendly boardroom chair, thought Banks. 'I don't know, sir. It's just the timing, them leaving the same weekend Courage disappeared. It might be worth looking into the company, see who they are, what they do. It might help explain Charlie's sudden riches.'

Banks nodded. 'Right you are. You can get stuck into that tomorrow. And it wouldn't do any harm to get in touch with Vic Manson about those prints, either. If someone working at PKF turns up in our records, as well as Charlie . . .' He glanced over at the three DCs at the far end of the table. They had been on a house-to-house to find out if anyone had seen Charlie Courage after Sunday lunchtime. 'Anything on the victim's movements?'

Winsome Jackman spoke first. 'A neighbour saw him going to work late on Sunday afternoon, sir, and the man across the street saw him taking his milk in at about eight o'clock on Monday morning.'

'Anyone else?'

Winsome shook her head. Kevin Templeton said, 'The woman at number forty-two, Mrs Finlay, noticed something. She says she thought she saw Charlie get into a car with a couple of men later on Monday morning.'

'Description?'

'Nothing very useful, sir.' Templeton doodled in the dust on the table as he spoke. 'One was medium height, the other was a bit taller. They wore jeans and leather jackets – brown or black. The taller one, he was going bald; the other had short fair hair. She said she didn't get a good look and wasn't really paying attention. I asked her if she thought Mr Courage was being forced into the car in any way, and she told me she didn't get that impression, but she could have been wrong.'

Banks sighed. It was typical of most witness statements. Of course, if you didn't know you were witnessing anything momentous, such as a man's final journey, you didn't pay that much attention. Most people don't see much on the peripheries; they're more concerned about where they're going, what they're doing and thinking. 'What about the car?'

'Light coloured. Maybe white. That was the best she could say. Nothing fancy, but new-looking, with a nice shiny finish.'

'Okay,' said Banks. 'Time? Did we fare any better there?'

'A little bit, sir,' said Templeton. 'She said it must have been not long after ten o'clock, because she had just started listening to *Woman's Hour*, and that starts at ten.'

'Interesting.'

'Maybe the trip was pre-arranged?' Annie suggested. 'It could have been something he was looking forward to. Maybe he thought he was going somewhere nice, getting some more money?'

'Could be.' Banks turned to Hatchley. 'What did your afternoon in the fleshpots of Eastvale turn up, Jim?'

Hatchley scratched the side of his bulbous nose. 'Charlie was up to something dodgy, I can tell you that much.'

'Go on.'

Hatchley got his notebook out. Workmen started hammering somewhere in the extension. Hatchley raised his voice. 'According to Len Jackson, one of his old colleagues, Charlie was on to a nice little earner, and it wasn't his job at Daleview, either.'

'Was it connected with that?'

'Charlie didn't say. He was pretty vague about it all. What he did say, though, was that he was already bringing in a bit of extra and pretty soon he'd be in for a much larger slice of the pie. What he was getting now was peanuts to what he'd have soon.'

'Interesting. But he didn't say what pie?'

'No, sir. Charlie was pretty cagey about it, apparently. He wanted his old mates to know he was doing well, but not how he was doing it. Scared of the competition, I suppose.'

'Okay,' said Banks. 'Well, at least that tells us we're on the right track. All we need to know now is what he was into and who was running it. Makes it sound easy, doesn't it?' He shook his head. 'Charlie, Charlie, you should've stayed on the straight and narrow this time.'

'He never was big time, wasn't Charlie,' added Hatchley. 'He must have got in way over his head, not known who he was dealing with.'

Banks nodded. 'Okay, that's it for now,' he said.

Back in his office, with his door tightly shut to keep the noise out, Banks phoned DI Collaton down in Market Harborough to give him an update, more out of professional courtesy than anything else, as there wasn't much to report. After that, he decided to call it a day. He tidied his desk and locked up, then headed for the door. Annie Cabbot was a flight ahead of him on her way down the stairs. She turned at the sound of his footsteps. 'Oh, it's you. Off home?'

'Unless you'd like to go for a quick drink or something?'

'I don't think so,' she said. 'That bloody rain's soaked right into my bones. All I want is to pick up something for dinner, then a long hot bath and a good book to curl up with.'

'Some other time?'

She smiled and pushed open the door. 'Yes. Some other time.'

Maybe she should have accepted Banks's offer of a drink, Annie thought, as she crossed the market square. It wouldn't have done any harm, just a quick drink and a chat. She didn't want to seem to be always giving him the brush-off, and it wasn't as if the men were exactly queuing up to take her out. But things were still a little sensitive, and her inner voice told her to back off, so she did. Not that she always did what her inner voice told her to; if she had done that she would never have got in trouble in her life, and what a boring old time that would have been. But this time, she listened; at least for now.

Though she could still smell it in the air, the rain had stopped and the evening had turned quite mild. Coloured lights hung across Market Street and around the cross, and the shoppers were out in force. She was lucky that most of the shops were staying open late until Christmas, or she'd have nothing but a couple of mouldy old carrots and potatoes for dinner. There was the Indian shop on Gallows View that was always open, but they didn't have much selection; besides, that was too far away in the wrong direction. What she wanted was something easy, something she could boil in the bag or stick in the oven for half an hour, no fuss.

In the end, it was a toss-up between vegetarian lasagne and Indonesian curry. The lasagne won, mostly because she had a bottle of Sainsbury's Chianti at home that would complement it nicely. She also needed eggs, milk, cereal and bread for breakfast.

As she wandered the busy aisles casting her eyes over the myriad varieties of meals specially prepared for those who dined alone, she remembered a book she had read many years ago – something her father had given her – that explained the underhand strategies supermarkets use to make you buy things you don't want. The lighting, for a start, and the soft, hypnotic music. At this time of year, of course, it was all Christmas music played in a cheery, sugary sort of style. Annie sometimes thought that if she heard one more 'fa-la-la-la-la' she would scream. The manufacturers also used certain colours in packaging their products, and there was something about bright things being placed at eye level that just made you reach out and grab them. She couldn't remember all the details, but the book had made an impression on her, and she always felt manipulated when she left a supermarket with more than she had intended to buy. Which she always did. It was the chocolate ice cream this time; it had hardly been at eye level, nor was the package of a colour that made you reach for it, but even stuck away in the freezer it had seemed to be screaming, 'Buy me! Buy me!' and now it nestled in her basket as she waited in the queue to pay.

Maybe if she had been at Eastvale a couple of months, she thought, then she might have taken Banks up on his offer. It was just too soon: too soon after their affair, and too soon after her transfer. If truth be told, she still didn't trust herself with him, either. A couple of drinks might loosen her inhibitions a bit too much, as they almost had the last time she'd been out with him. Then where would she be? It had been all right sleeping with Banks when she worked out of Harkside and he worked out of Eastvale, but if they were both in the same station, it could be awkward.

Suddenly Annie saw someone she knew, someone she had never expected to see again, not here, not anywhere. And someone she had never wanted to set eyes on again. He was walking into the wines and spirits section. As far as she could tell, he hadn't seen her. What the hell was he doing here? Annie felt her skin turn clammy and her heart start to pound.

'That'll be five pounds seventy-two, please, love,' said the plump, smiling woman at the checkout desk. Annie fiddled around in her purse and found a five-pound note and four twenty-pence pieces, which she promptly dropped from her shaking hands all over the floor. She picked them up and handed them to the woman.

'What's up, love? You look as if you've seen a ghost.'

'Something like that,' Annie muttered, hurriedly putting away her purse and heading out with her groceries. She risked one quick glance over her shoulder. He was standing by the bargain reds section scanning the labels and prices. She was still certain that he hadn't seen her.

She burst out onto York Road and took a gulp of fresh air. Her heart was still beating fast and she felt herself shaking inside. It was Wayne Dalton; she was sure of it. Detective Inspector Wayne Dalton. One of the two men who had held her down while a third had raped her more than two years ago.

Banks knew he shouldn't have asked Annie out like that, on impulse, and he hoped he hadn't put her off for good. He didn't want to appear to be pestering her, especially as they worked together and he was, technically, her boss. Not that Annie would ever accuse him of sexual harassment, but . . .

As it happened, his evening turned out to be just what he needed. He made a cheese and onion sandwich for tea and ate it while he read the paper in the kitchen. His son, Brian, phoned at about nine o'clock, excited about the CD. On a whim, Banks asked if he had ever heard of Barry Clough. He hadn't, but said he'd ask around among his colleagues in the business. He also reminded Banks that punk had been a long time ago, as if Banks needed reminding of that.

After lunch with Emily Riddle, Banks also felt the need to talk to Tracy. It would help balance his sanity. After listening to Emily for more than an hour, he had come away with a very warped idea about teenage girls. He needed to know they weren't all like her, especially his own daughter.

Amidst all the craziness, though, and after all she'd been through, Emily still seemed to have a cool head on her shoulders, if her talk about getting her A levels and going to university was to be believed. Like Banks, Tracy had had to work hard to get where she was. She was a bright girl, but not one of those who don't have to apply themselves. The harder she worked, the higher her marks. Emily seemed to think her progress in the world was simply a matter of choice, of deciding what to do and then having it fall into her lap. Perhaps it was for her. Now that he had got a little beyond first impressions, Banks couldn't help but like Emily, but she was the kind of girl he fretted about, and the kind who constantly exasperated him. He almost felt sorry for Jimmy Riddle.

Tracy didn't answer. Out with Damon, no doubt. He left her a message, nothing urgent, just to call if she didn't get in too late.

For a change from peat, Banks lit a log fire in the hearth, though it wasn't a particularly cold evening, and sat down in the old armchair he had picked up at a local estate auction. The blue walls that he had worried might feel cold in winter had turned out just fine, he thought, as he watched the shadows cast by the flames flicker over them. Knotty wood spat and crackled in the fireplace, taking Banks back to his childhood, when the coal they used sometimes hissed and spat. There was no other source of heat in the house, so it was his father's job in winter to get up while it was still dark and light the fire. Usually, when Banks came down for his jam and bread before school, there was a good blaze going, and it had taken most of the chill off the cool damp night air. The years in between, in various London flats and the Eastvale semi, he hadn't had a coal or log fire, only gas or electric, so it was a luxury he was availing himself of a lot this winter.

He put the first CD of Miles Davis's Carnegie Hall concert on, the one with Gil Evans and his orchestra, picked up the latest Kate Atkinson novel, which lay face down on the chair arm about half read, and lit a cigarette. Though he had intended an early night, he found himself enjoying both the music and the book so much that he put another log on the fire and slipped in the second CD. It was a quarter past eleven, and he had set the book aside for a few moments to listen to the live version of the adagio from Rodrigo's *Concierto de Aranjuez*, when the telephone rang.

Thinking it might be Tracy, he turned down the stereo and snatched up the phone. The first thing that assaulted his ears was loud music in the background. He couldn't make out exactly what it was, but it sounded like some sort of post-rave-techno-dance mix. The next thing to assail him was the squeaky voice of DC Rickerd shouting over the music.

'Sir?'

'Yes,' sighed Banks. 'What is it?'

'Sorry to bother you, sir, but I'm on duty tonight.'

'I know that. What is it? Will you get to the point? And do you have to shout so loud?'

'Well, I'm at the Bar None, sir. It's pretty noisy here.'

The Bar None was one of Eastvale's most popular night-clubs for the young crowd. Situated under the shops across the market square from the police station, it usually opened up an hour or so before pub closing time and attracted those kids who were too pissed to drive to Leeds or Manchester, where there were far better clubs. 'Look,' said Banks, 'if there's been a fight or something, I don't want to know.'

'No, sir, it's nothing like that.'

'Well?' Banks lost Rickerd's next words to a surge in the background noise. 'Can you get them to turn the music down?' he yelled.

'It's a suspicious death,' Rickerd said.

'How suspicious?'

'Well, she's dead, sir. I'm pretty sure of that. Inspector Jessup agrees with me, sir. And the blokes from the ambulance. It looks as if somebody beat her up pretty badly.'

If Chris Jessup, inspector in the uniformed branch, thought it was serious enough to call Banks in, then it probably was. 'Who is the victim?' he asked.

'You'd better get down here, sir . . .' Here he became inaudible again. ' . . . can't handle . . . myself.'

'How many of you are there?'

'Inspector Jessup and me and three PCs, sir.'

'That should be enough. I'm sure Inspector Jessup knows exactly what to do. Help him make sure no one leaves and secure the scene. We don't want anyone else tramping about near the body until I get there, including the ambulance crew. Understand?'

'Yes, sir.'

'Better put a call through to Dr Burns, too. It'll take him a while to get there.' Banks was about to ask Rickerd to send for the SOCO unit, but decided to wait until he could assess the scene himself. No sense spending the taxpayers' money until he knew exactly what he was dealing with. 'Have you got the victim's name?'

'Yes, sir. She had a driving licence and one of those proof-of-age cards some of the clubs give out to kids. It's got her photo on it.'

'Good work. What's her name, Rickerd?'

'It's Walker, sir. Ruth Walker.'

'Shit,' said Banks. 'I'll be right there.'

Could it be the same Ruth Walker Banks had talked to in London? If so, what the hell was she doing in an Eastvale nightclub, unless she had come up from London to go clubbing with Emily Riddle? And if Ruth were dead, then Banks wouldn't be at all surprised if Emily was in trouble, too.

Banks picked up his cigarettes and grabbed his leather jacket off the hook at the back of the door. Before he left, he went back to the phone. It was a snap decision between Jim Hatchley, who lived in Eastvale, and Annie Cabbot, who had as long a drive as Banks. Annie won, hands down. He would have been a liar if he had denied any personal preference for Annie's charms over Jim Hatchley's ugly mug, but he didn't do it from entirely selfish motives. Annie was new to Eastvale, and she needed all the experience she could get; she was ambitious, whereas Hatchley was content to remain a DS for the rest of his days; Annie would welcome the opportunity, whereas Hatchley would grumble at being dragged out of bed in the middle of the night; Hatchley had his wife and baby to consider, while Annie lived alone.

There you go rationalizing, Banks thought, as he dialled her number. He could justify calling her until the cows came home if he had to, but what it came down to was that he still fancied her and he thought, with Sandra announcing she wanted to divorce and remarry, that he might be able to get over the stumbling blocks that had derailed him and Annie in the first place and rekindle what they once had.

But even that desire took second place to his concern about Ruth Walker and Emily Riddle.

Annie drove home like a bat out of hell, and when she got to her tiny terraced cottage, she locked, bolted and chained the door, then checked the back and all the windows. Only when she was certain that everything was as secure as it could be did she pour herself a large glass of wine and sit down.

Her hand was still shaking, she noticed, as she took a gulp. And she thought she'd got over her experience. The counselling had helped at first, but when the counsellor said she could do no more, it had been Annie's own inner strength that pulled her through. Through meditation, yoga and diet, she had slowly healed herself. The country seclusion had helped, too: leaving a big city force for a peaceful backwater like Harkside.

She still had dreams in which she experienced the fear, claustrophobia and powerlessness she had felt during the assault and woke up sweating and screaming, and she still had dark moods in which she felt worthless and tainted. But not so often. And she could handle them now; she knew where they came from and could almost stand outside looking down on them, separating herself from the bad feelings, isolating them as you would a tumour. She had even got so far, after two years, as allowing herself that romantic and sexual involvement with Banks, which had been extremely satisfying, not least because it pleased her to find she was still capable of it. What had ended that was nothing at all to do with her rape experience; it was plain, old-fashioned fear of involvement, of emotional entanglement, something that had always been a part of her.

What the hell was Wayne Dalton doing in Eastvale? That was what she wanted to know. Was he on a case? Had he been reassigned to Eastvale Divisional HQ? She didn't think she could handle working with him, not after what happened. The last she had heard he had transferred to the Met. Surely he couldn't be seeking her out? Coming to torment her? True, she had complained to their chief super the following morning, but there was no evidence; it was simply her word against the three of them. The chief super knew that something had gone on, and he also knew it was something he didn't want aired in *his* station, thank you very much, so Annie got shipped out sharpish and the three men, after being rapped on the knuckles, were encouraged to transfer at their leisure.

Later, in her bath, Annie remembered Wayne Dalton's flushed and sweating face as he held her, the little ginger hairs up his nose as he stood over her, waiting his turn. A turn that never came. She remembered walking the streets for hours after her escape, languishing in her bath, just like now, listening to the radio, the sounds of normal life, and scrubbing their filth from her body. Something she shouldn't have done. Something she, in her turn, had advised rape victims *not* to do. But it was far easier to say 'do as I say, not as I do'. At the time, she hadn't thought, had only wanted an escape, a way of undoing what had been done, of going back in time to a day when it had never happened. Foolish, perhaps, but perfectly reasonable, she thought.

And she was still in her bath, on her third glass of wine, when, close to twenty past eleven, her telephone rang.

It was five to twelve when Banks, who had driven well over the speed limit the whole way, parked in the market square next to the ambulance and headed for the club door. DC Rickerd had got a uniformed constable to guard the entrance, Banks was pleased to see, and had even put blue-and-white police tape across the doorway. As he headed down the stone steps, he was also pleased to hear that the music had been silenced and the only sounds drifting up were the murmured conversations of detained clubbers grumbling at the tables.

'Over here, sir.'

The only lights on were the coloured disco lights that whirled over the dance floor, eerie without the accompaniment of music and gyrating bodies. Banks could make out Rickerd and Jessup standing by the door to the ladies' toilet with the ambulance crew, a couple of uniformed officers and a young man. Before he could get there, someone tugged at his sleeve.

'Excuse me, are you in authority?'

'Looks that way,' said Banks. The speaker, wearing jeans and a white shirt, was probably in his early twenties, skinny, with bright eyes and dilated pupils. It wasn't particularly hot in the Bar None, but a sheen of sweat covered his face.

'Why are you keeping us here? It's been nearly an hour now. You can't just keep us here.'

'It's my understanding that there's been a serious crime, sir,' said Banks. 'Until we get things sorted, I'm afraid none of you is going anywhere.' He noticed the boy was still holding his sleeve and plucked it away.

'But this is outrageous. I want to go home.'

Banks leaned forward, close enough to smell the beer and fish and chips on his breath. 'Look, sonny,' he whispered, 'go sit down with your mates and be quiet. One more word out of you and I'll have the Drugs Squad down on you like a ton of bricks. Understand?'

The boy looked as if he were going to protest further, but thought better of it and swayed over to the table where his friends sat. Banks continued on his way to meet Rickerd and Jessup. One of the ambulance crew looked at him and shook his head slowly. Annie Cabbot hadn't arrived yet. She had sounded edgy when he'd called and he had wondered if he had woken her. She said not.

'In here, sir,' said a whey-faced Rickerd, pointing into the ladies'. 'It's not very pretty.' Someone had placed more tape at the entrance, effectively creating an inner crime scene. That was often useful, as you could afford to let some people into the first scene and lead them to think they were privileged, but you kept the real crime scene uncontaminated.

'Who's he?' Banks gestured towards the young man beside Rickerd.

'He found her, sir.'

'Okay. Keep an eye on him. I'll talk to him later. Did you call Dr Burns?'

'Yes, sir. He said he'd get here as soon as he could.'

Banks turned to Inspector Jessup. 'What happened, Chris?'

'Call came in at six minutes past eleven. That lad you just noticed. Name's Darren Hirst. It seems he was with the victim. She went to the toilet and didn't come out. He got worried, went in for a butcher's and called us.'

Banks slipped on his latex gloves and stepped under the tape.

The ladies' toilet was small, given the size of the club. White tile, three stalls, two sinks under a long mirror. The ubiquitous condom machine hung on the wall, the kind that sells all sorts of flavours and colours – Lager & Lime, Rhubarb & Custard, Curry & Chips. The stalls had flimsy wooden doors. 'Cindy Sucks Black Cock' was scrawled in lipstick across the front of one of them.

'It's this one, sir,' said Rickerd, pointing to the end stall.

'Was it locked?'

'Yes, sir.'

'How did you open it?'

Rickerd took off his glasses and wiped them with a white handkerchief. It was a habit Banks had noticed before. 'From the next stall, sir. I stood on the toilet seat, leaned over with a stick and slipped the bolt. It was easy enough. We're bloody lucky the door opens outwards.'

'A locked-toilet mystery, then,' Banks muttered, thinking Rickerd had shown more initiative than he would have expected.

'I didn't disturb anything any more than necessary, sir. Just to establish who she was and that she was dead. Inspector Jessup supervised, and the others made sure no one left.'

'That's all right. You did well.' He pulled the door slowly towards him with his fingertips, anxious not to mess up an already messy scene.

'You won't believe this, sir.' Rickerd said. 'I've never seen anything like it.'

Neither had Banks.

The girl's body was wedged crabwise from wall to wall, her back arched about two feet over the toilet, knees jammed against one wall and her shoulders pushed up hard against the other, her neck bent at an awkward angle. A trickle of blood had run from her nose and there were contusions on her face and head. Broken mirror glass and white powder lay scattered on the floor amid the spilled contents of her handbag. Banks knew that the eyes of the dead have no expression, but hers seemed full of terror and agony, as if she had looked the Grim Reaper right in the eye. Her face was dark, suffused with blood, and the corners of her mouth were turned up in a parody of a grin.

But the worst thing about it all, the thing that caused Banks's blood to scream in his ears and his knees to turn watery and bring him so close to falling down that he had to grab onto the door jamb to stay on his feet, was that the body wasn't Ruth Walker's at all; it was Emily Riddle's.

8

'Alan?' The voice seemed to reach Banks's ears from a great distance. 'Alan? So now you're hanging around ladies' toilets.'

Banks felt someone touch his sleeve, and he turned to see Annie Cabbot standing in the doorway. Never had he seen a more welcome sight. He wanted to fall forward into her arms, have her stroke his head and kiss his face and tell him everything was all right, he'd just had a bad dream, that's all, and it would all be gone in the morning.

'Alan, you're pale as ashes. Are you all right?'

Banks moved away from the doorway to let Annie have a look. 'I've got a daughter not much older than her,' he said.

Annie frowned and edged forward. Banks watched her and noticed the way her eyeballs flicked around, taking in all the details: the body's unusual position, the broken mirror, the white powder, the spilled cosmetics, the contusions. Some of the buttons on Emily's black silk blouse had popped, and the dark spider tattoo was visible against the pale skin below her navel ring. Annie touched nothing but seemed to absorb everything. And when she had finished, even *she* was pale.

'I see what you mean,' she said when they had both gone to stand outside the toilet again. 'Poor cow. What do you think happened?'

'It *looks* as if someone got in there with her and beat the living shit out of her, but that doesn't make sense.'

'No,' said Annie. 'There's hardly enough room for one, let alone space to swing a few punches.'

'And the stall was locked,' Banks added. 'I suppose she could have been beaten elsewhere, then crawled inside and locked it herself before she died, maybe in a vain attempt to keep her attacker out . . .' He shrugged. It seemed a pretty thin thesis. Even if she had locked herself in there to escape a beating, how had she ended up arched crabwise over the toilet? It was the most unusual body position Banks had ever seen, and though he had a glimmer of an idea about what might have caused it, he needed the expert knowledge of a doctor. 'We'll have to wait for the doc. Ah, speak of the devil.'

Dr Burns walked across the dance floor and greeted them. 'Where is she?' he asked.

Banks pointed towards the ladies'. 'Try not to disturb things too much. We haven't got photographs yet.'

'I'll do my best.' Burns passed under the tape.

'Call the SOCOs and the photographer,' Banks said to Annie. He gestured towards Rickerd and lowered his voice. 'DC Rickerd phoned me, and I wanted to be certain we really had a crime on our hands before making a hue and cry.'

'What about the people in the club?'

'Nobody leaves. Including the bar staff. Chris Jessup's lads have instructions to keep them all where they are. There's no telling how many left between the boyfriend's phone call and Jessup's arrival, though.'

'It's still early for this kind of place,' said Annie. 'People would be more likely to be arriving than leaving.'

'Unless they'd just killed someone. Ask one of the uniforms to take everyone's name and address.'

Annie turned to go.

Banks called after her. 'And Annie?'

'Yes?'

'Be prepared for one of the biggest shitstorms that's ever come your way as a copper.'

'Why?'

'Because the victim's Emily Riddle, the chief constable's daughter.'

'Jesus Christ,' said Annie.

'Exactly.'

Annie went off to attend to her duties while Banks collared Darren Hirst, the boy who had found the body. He seemed still in shock, trembling, tears in his eyes. Banks could understand that, having seen Emily's body himself. He had seen many forms of death in his years as a policeman, and though he never quite got inured to it, he certainly had an advantage over the boy. Leaving a uniformed constable guarding the entrance to the toilet, Banks led Darren to an empty table. The club's manager hovered nearby, clearly wanting to know what was going on but not daring to ask. Banks waved him over.

'What time did you open tonight?' he asked.

'Ten o'clock. It starts slow. We don't usually get much of a crowd until after eleven.'

'Has this place got surveillance cameras?'

'On order.'

'Great. Bar still open?'

'The other policeman said I shouldn't serve any more drinks,' he said.

'Quite right, too,' said Banks, 'but this lad's had a bit of a shock and I can't say I've had a pleasant surprise, either, so bring us a couple of double brandies, will you?'

'I thought you weren't supposed to drink on duty.'

'Just bring the drinks.'

'All right, mate. No need to get shirty.' The manager strode off. When he came back, he plonked the drinks down on the table. The measures looked small, but Banks paid him anyway.

'When can I go home?' the man asked. 'Only if we're not serving drinks, we're not making any money, see, and there's not a lot of point staying open.'

'You're not open,' said Banks. 'And if I get much more of that crap out of you, you won't be opening again in the foreseeable future. There's a dead girl in your toilets, in case you hadn't heard.'

'Fucking drug addicts,' he muttered as he stalked away.

'All right, Darren,' said Banks when the manager was out of earshot. 'Like to tell me what happened?' He lit a cigarette. Darren refused his offer of one. The brandy was poor quality, but its bite put a bit of warmth back in Banks's veins.

'She said she wasn't feeling well,' Darren began, after a sip of brandy. A little colour crept back into his cheeks.

'Back up a bit,' said Banks. 'How well did you know her? Was she your girlfriend?'

'No, nothing like that. I mean, I know her, like, in the group. We were just friends, that's all. We all hang out together. She's a bit weird and wild, is Emily, but she can be a lot of fun. We started in the Cross Keys, down Castle Hill.'

'I know it.'

'After that we just walked around town a bit and dropped in for a quick drink at the Queen's Arms. Then we came here.' He pointed to a group of shell-shocked kids at a table across the room. 'The others are over there.'

'What time did you meet in the Cross Keys?'

'About half past six, seven o'clock.'

'Do you remember what time Emily got there?'

'She was the last to arrive. Must've been about seven, maybe a few minutes later.'

So that left Emily four hours unaccounted for between the three o'clock appointment she had mentioned to Banks and meeting her friends in the Cross Keys.

'How did she seem?'

'Fine.'

'Normal?'

'For Emily.'

'And what time did you come here?'

'About half ten. It was pretty quiet. Like the barman says,

it doesn't usually get going till half past eleven or so. But they serve drinks, and there's music, so you can dance.'

'How many people would you say were here?'

'Not a lot. They kept coming in, like, but it wasn't that busy.'

'More than now?'

Darren looked around. 'No, about this many.'

'What happened next?'

'We got some drinks in, then Emily went to the toilet. We were dancing after that, I remember, then she said she wasn't feeling very well.'

'What did she say was wrong with her?'

Darren shook his head. 'Just that she didn't feel well. She said she was getting a stiff neck.' He rubbed his own neck and looked at Banks. 'Was it drugs? It was drugs, wasn't it?'

'Why do you ask that?'

'Just the way she was behaving. You know, like she was flying up there in her own world. Like I said, she's pretty wild.'

'How well did you know Emily, Darren?'

'I told you, hardly at all. When she was home from school for the holidays she'd hang out with me and Rick and Jackie and Tina over there. That's all. I was never her boyfriend or anything. She wasn't interested in me like that. We just danced sometimes, went out with the gang. Had fun.' He ran his hand over his greasy dark hair.

'Did you ever supply her with drugs, Darren?'

'Me? Never. I don't touch them.'

There was something in his tone that made Banks believe him. For the moment. 'Okay. So she felt poorly. What happened next?'

'She said she thought she might need some more medicine.'

'What did she mean by that?'

'More drugs, I assumed. Whatever she was taking.'

'Go on.'

'So she went back to the toilet.'

'How long after her first visit?'

'Dunno. Fifteen, twenty minutes, maybe.'

Banks looked up and saw Peter Darby, the photographer, come in with his battered Pentax hanging around his neck. Banks pointed towards the toilets where the uniformed policeman still stood on guard, and Darby nodded as he headed towards the tape. Annie dropped by the table and told him the SOCOs were on their way. Banks asked her to take statements from Darren and Emily's friends across the room. He drank down the rest of his brandy and asked, 'What happened next?'

'She was a long time. I started to get worried, especially with her saying she wasn't feeling well.'

'When you say a long time, just how long do you mean?'

'I don't know. Ten minutes. Quarter of an hour. Maybe longer. You don't expect someone to stay in the toilet that long if they're all right. I thought maybe she was being sick. She'd been drinking steadily most of the evening, a really weird mix of stuff, and she didn't eat anything in the Cross Keys.'

Or at lunchtime in the Black Bull, Banks remembered, where she had also been drinking some odd concoctions. 'Were many people going in and out of the ladies' toilet during that time?'

'I never really looked. But the place wasn't that busy, so maybe not.'

'You didn't ask anyone to check on her? Jackie or Tina?'

'Tina went in after about five minutes and came right back out. She said Emily was making funny sounds, as if she was being sick or something, and she wouldn't open the door of the stall.'

'Wouldn't or couldn't?'

Darren shrugged.

'What did you do then?'

'I thought about it for a bit, then I decided to go in and see what was up.'

'When was this?'

'Must've been about five or ten minutes later, when she still hadn't come out.'

'Had others been in and out in the meantime?'

'Like I said, I didn't keep an eye on the place all the time, but I saw a couple of girls come and go.'

'Are they still here?'

Darren pointed out two girls at separate tables. 'Okay,' said Banks, 'we'll talk to them later. They didn't say if anything was wrong, though?'

'No. Just Tina thought she was being sick.'

'So you went in the ladies' yourself?'

'Eventually, yes. I was worried. I mean, I'd been dancing with her. I felt she was sort of . . .'

'Your responsibility?'

'In a way. Yes.'

'Even though she wasn't your girlfriend?'

'She was still a friend.'

'What did you find in there?'

Darren looked away and turned pale again. 'You know. You've seen it. God, it was horrible. It's like she wasn't even human.'

'I'm sorry to put you through it, Darren, but it could be important. Describe to me what you found. Was anyone else in there at the time?'

'No.'

'Was the stall door locked?'

'Yes.'

'So how did you know there was something wrong?'

'First I called her name and she didn't answer. Then I just, like, listened at the door and I couldn't hear anything. No sounds of her being sick or even breathing. I got really scared then.'

'So what did you do?'

'I went into the next stall and climbed on the toilet. The

walls don't come right up to the ceiling, so you can lean over and look down. That's when I saw her. She was looking up at me . . . all bruised and twisted . . . and her eyes . . .' He put his head in his hands and started to sob.

Banks touched his shoulder. 'It's all right, Darren. Go ahead and cry.'

Darren let his tears run their course, then wiped his eyes with his sleeve and looked up. 'Who could *do* something like that?'

'We don't know. We don't know *how*, either. Apart from the two girls you mentioned, did you see anyone else go in the toilet while Emily was in there sick?'

'No. But I told you I wasn't looking all the time.'

'You must have been looking quite often, though, if you were worried. You must have been keeping an eye on the door to see if Emily came out again.'

'I suppose so. But I didn't notice anyone else, no.'

'See any men go in?'

'No.'

'Did anyone come in and out while you were there checking on her?'

'No. Look, *I* didn't do this. You're not—'

'Nobody's suggesting that, Darren. I'm just trying to get everything clear, that's all. When you saw her, did you know that she was dead?'

'I couldn't *know*. I mean, I didn't take her pulse or anything. I didn't touch her. But her eyes were open, staring, and her neck was in a weird position, as if someone had broken it or something. And I couldn't see any signs of life.'

'What did you do?'

'I went to the manager and he phoned the police.'

'Did anyone else enter the toilet before Inspector Jessup and DC Rickerd arrived?'

'I don't think so. The manager had a quick look – I was with him the whole time – then he phoned the police and the ambulance. He stayed by the door until the policemen arrived, and he wouldn't let anyone in. He made a couple of girls use the men's toilet. They complained. I remember that. But the police were quick.'

'They didn't have far to come. Did anyone leave the club?'

'A couple of people might have left. But mostly people were arriving. It was still early. And I wasn't really paying attention. I was just worried about Emily, and afterwards I was sort of in shock. The music kept going for quite a long time after . . . after I found her. People were still dancing. Even after the police came. They didn't really know anything serious had happened.'

'Okay, Darren, nearly finished. You're doing really well. Did anything at all odd happen during the evening, either here or when you were at the Cross Keys or the Queen's Arms, that gave you cause for concern about Emily?'

'No. Nothing I can think of.'

'She seemed in good spirits?'

'Yeah.'

'She didn't get into an argument with anyone?'

'No.'

'Did she make any telephone calls?'

'Not that I remember. Everything was fine.'

'Did she mention drugs at all?'

'No.'

'Did you get the impression she was on drugs before you got here?'

'She might have been a bit high when she arrived at the Cross Keys.'

'At seven?'

'Yes. I mean, she wasn't out of it or anything, just a bit giddy. But it wore off.'

That was probably when she got the drugs, Banks thought: between leaving him in the Black Bull and arriving at the Cross Keys four hours later. She'd been smoking grass or snorting coke with someone in the meantime. Christ, *why* hadn't he asked her where she was going? Would she have told him, anyway? 'Did you see her talking to anyone in here before she went to the toilet?' he asked.

'Only us. I mean, we got a table together. We didn't know anyone else here. I went to get the drinks in.'

'Could she have bought the drugs from someone here?'

'I suppose she could've done, but I didn't see her.'

'Inside the toilets, maybe?'

'It's possible.'

'What about the Cross Keys?' The Cross Keys wasn't exactly a Mecca to drugs in the way the Black Bull was, but it wasn't innocent either. 'Did you see her talking to any strangers there?'

'No. I don't think so.'

'Did she disappear for any length of time?'

'No.'

'Okay, Darren. You'll have to give a formal statement later, but it's nothing to worry about.'

'Can I go now?'

'I'm afraid not.'

'Can I sit with my friends?'

'Of course.'

'Is it okay if I use my mobile? I'd like to call my mum and dad, tell them . . . you know, I might be late.'

'Sorry, Darren,' said Banks. 'Not yet. If you really need to let them know, just tell one of the uniformed officers and he'll see to it for you. Go sit with your friends now.'

Darren slouched off to the table and Banks got up and turned to see Dr Burns coming out of the toilet. Peter Darby's camera flashed in the open door behind him.

'So what is it?' Banks asked Dr Burns when they found a table at which they couldn't be overheard. He had his own suspicions, though he had never seen an actual case before, but he wanted Dr Burns to get there first. It was partly a matter of not wanting to look like an idiot, not jumping to conclusions. After all, she *could* have been beaten to death.

'I'm not certain yet,' said Burns, shaking his head.

'But your immediate impression. I'll bet you've got a pretty good idea.'

Burns grimaced. 'We doctors don't like giving our immediate impressions.'

'Was she beaten up?'

'I very much doubt it.'

'The bruising?'

'At a guess I'd say that happened from her head banging into the walls during the convulsions. Hang on a minute; are you all right?'

'I'm fine.' Banks fumbled for another cigarette to take the taste of bile out of his mouth. 'What do you mean, convulsions?'

'As I said, I don't think anyone attacked her. She was alone in there. You noticed the white powder and the broken mirror.'

Banks nodded.

'Cocaine, most likely.'

'Are you saying she died of a cocaine overdose?'

'I never said that.'

'But it's possible?'

Burns paused. 'Hmm. Possible. A cocaine overdose *can* cause spasms and convulsions in extreme cases.'

'But?'

'It would have to be extremely pure. As I said, it's possible, but it's not the most likely explanation.'

'What is, then?'

'How long has she been dead?'

'They called the police at six minutes after eleven, so it must have happened a bit before then. I got here at ten to twelve.'

Burns looked at his watch. 'And it's twenty past now. That means she can't have been dead much more than, say, an hour and a half. Yet rigor's complete. That's highly unusual. I assume you also noticed the stiffness?'

'Yes. So what do you think killed her?'

'At a guess, and it's just a guess until we get toxicology results, I'd say it was strychnine poisoning.'

'It crossed my mind, too, though I'm far from being an expert. I've never actually seen a case before. I've only read about it in textbooks,' said Banks.

'Me, too. It's really quite rare these days. But that would cause the convulsions. She'd have been thrashing herself about the tiny stall quite enough to cause the bruises and contusions you saw on her body. Her back was also arched in a way indicative of final strychnine spasms – it's called *opisthotonos* – and you must have noticed the way the facial muscles were twisted in a sort of extreme grimace, or grin – *risus sardonicus* – and the darkness of the face, the wild, staring eyes?'

The images were impossible to forget, and Banks knew he would have nightmares about them for years, the way he still had about the disembowelled Soho prostitute, Dawn Wadley.

'I'm hesitant to commit myself without a full tox check, but that won't take long. It's one of the easiest poisonous substances to test for. I've never investigated a death by strychnine before, but that's what it looks like to me. Only my immediate impressions, mind you. I also touched a little of the powder to my tongue. Along with the numbness caused by the cocaine, there's a bitter taste, associated with strychnine.'

'What killed her? Heart?'

'She'd have died of asphyxiation, most likely, or maybe just sheer exhaustion from the convulsions. Her neck may be broken too, but you'll have to wait for the post-mortem to confirm that. Not pretty, whichever way you look at it.'

'No. Deliberate, though?'

'Oh, I would think so, wouldn't you? And I'd pretty much rule out suicide, for a start. Even if she did want to kill herself, strychnine is hardly the drug of choice. I've never heard of a case. Besides, from what I can tell, it was mixed with cocaine. That means she was looking for a good time, not for death.'

'Any chance it could just be a bad batch?'

'There's always a chance of that. Dealers use all kinds of weird substances to step on the drugs they sell, including strychnine. But not usually enough to kill a person.'

'How much would that be?'

'It varies. Doses as low as five milligrams can kill, especially if they're absorbed directly into the bloodstream and bypass the digestive system. We'll soon find out if it was a bad batch, anyway.'

'You mean we'll have a whole spate of them?'

'It's possible.'

'God forbid,' said Banks.

'It depends on a number of factors. As I said, a fatal dose can vary widely. What killed this girl might not kill just anyone. She was pretty thin, and it doesn't look as if she ate much. Somebody with more body weight, someone more solid, more robust . . . who can say? But we'll hear about it if it happens.'

Banks remembered how Emily hadn't eaten lunch. Darren said she hadn't eaten dinner, either. 'But if she inhaled it, the stomach contents wouldn't matter.'

'Not as much as if she'd ingested it, no. But general health and stomach contents are all factors we have to take into account.'

'And if it's not a bad batch, then someone had it in for her specifically.'

'That just about sums it up. Either way you look at it, somebody killed her. But that's your realm, isn't it? Ah, here come the cosmonauts.'

Banks looked up and saw the SOCOs entering in their white boiler suits.

'I'll arrange for the mortuary wagon,' said Dr Burns. 'I'd better tell them they'll probably need a crowbar to prise her out of there. And I'll get in touch with Dr Glendenning first thing in the morning. Knowing him, he'll have her opened up by lunchtime.' He stood, but paused a moment before leaving. 'Did you know her, Alan? You seem to be taking this very much to heart.'

'I knew her slightly,' said Banks. 'I might as well tell you now. You'll find out soon enough. She's the chief constable's daughter.'

Dr Burns's reaction was exactly the same as Annie's.

'And, Doc?'

'Yes?'

'Let's keep this under our hats for the time being, shall we? The strychnine.'

'My lips are sealed.' Dr Burns turned and left.

For a moment, Banks stood alone watching the spinning disco lights and listening to mumbled conversations around him. Peter Darby came out of the toilet and said he'd got what he wanted. The SOCOs were in there taking the place apart, collecting samples for analysis. Banks didn't envy them the task of working in a toilet; you never knew what you might catch. Vic Manson would soon be dusting for prints, of which he'd probably find as many as the SOCOs would pubic hairs, and before long the mortuary wagon would come and whisk Emily Riddle's body off to the basement of Eastvale Infirmary.

All so bloody predictable, routines Banks had been part of time and time again. But this time he wanted to cry. Cry and get rat-arsed. He couldn't help but remember Emily's excited talk about her future that lunchtime, about how she didn't fancy Poughkeepsie or Bryn Mawr because of the sound of their names. He remembered the time she turned up at the hotel in London, passing herself off as his daughter, how her dress slid to the ground and he saw her white and naked. Remembered her stoned, adolescent attempt at seducing him. God, if only she knew how close she'd come. Then the way she curled up in the foetal position like a little child on the bed, her thumb in her mouth, the blanket covering her, while he sat in the armchair smoking and listening to Dawn Upshaw sing about sleep and the way the windows rattled and the winter sun rose and tried to claw its way through the grey, greasy clouds.

Dead.

And perhaps because of him, because he had respected his vow of discretion and done nothing, despite all his misgivings.

Annie came over from the table where she had been talking to Emily's friends. Banks told her what Dr Burns had said about strychnine. Annie whistled. 'Learn anything over there?' he asked.

'Not a lot. They say she seemed a bit high when she arrived at the Cross Keys, and they're certain she took something here the first time she went to the toilet.'

'Same as Darren says. Can't have been the same batch, though, can it?'

'I suppose not. Do you believe them?'

'For the most part. Maybe we'll lean on them a bit harder tomorrow. What it looks like is that the first lot she snorted made her feel ill shortly afterwards, so she went back for more and the convulsions hit.'

'So what now?'

'We can start by searching everyone on the premises. They're all suspects at the moment, including the bar staff. Can you get that organized?'

'Of course. I very much doubt we'd have any problems arguing reasonable suspicion, do you?'

'I doubt it.' PACE rules stated that you had to have 'reasonable suspicion' before searching people, and if you searched them somewhere other than at a police station without first arresting them, you had to have reasonable grounds for assuming they might be a danger to themselves or others. With the chief constable's daughter lying dead of possible strychnine poisoning only a few yards away, Banks didn't think they'd have much trouble arguing their case. 'Take it easy, though. If anyone kicks up a fuss, take them over to the station and have the custody officer deal with them. I want this done by the book. You'd better let Detective Superintendent Gristhorpe know, too.'

'Will do.'

'I also want all the known coke dealers in the area brought in for questioning. And we'll need to activate the incident room over at the station.' He looked at his watch. 'We might not be able to get everything in order until morning – especially as far as the civilian staff are concerned – but in the meantime we'll need an office manager.'

'DC Rickerd?'

Banks looked at Rickerd, who was taking a statement at the other side of the club. 'Good idea,' he said. 'Let him show his mettle.'

While Rickerd demonstrated only minimal detective skills, he had an almost obsessive interest in details and the minutiae of organization: exactly what a good office manager needed, as it was his job to supervise the recording and tracking of all information retrieved both from a crime scene and during an investigation.

If truth be told, you needed more than a skill for organization, but Rickerd would do. Maybe he would find his true *métier*. Banks always knew that having a trainspotter in the department would come in useful one day. Rickerd was just the kind to carry around that little book full of printed train numbers and draw a neat line with pen and ruler through each one he actually saw. He was too young for the steam trains, though. When Banks was a kid, there were still a few of them in service, many with exotic names like *The Flying Scotsman*, sleek, streamlined beauties. Many of Banks's friends had been trainspotters, but standing on a windy station platform all day and noting down numbers to cross off later in a little book had never appealed to him. These days, with all the diesels looking like clones of one another, there didn't seem to be much point in trainspotting any more.

Banks called Rickerd over and explained what he wanted him to do. Rickerd went off looking pleased with himself to be given such responsibility. Then Banks lit a cigarette and leaned against a pillar. 'I'd better go and tell her parents,' he sighed.

'One of the uniforms can do that.' Annie put her hand on his arm in a curiously intimate gesture. 'To be quite honest, Alan, you look all in. Maybe you should let me take you home.'

Wouldn't that be nice? Banks thought. Home. Annie. Maybe even bed. The adagio from *Concierto de Aranjuez* drifting up from downstairs. The clock put back so that none of this had ever happened. 'No,' he said. 'I've got to tell them myself. I owe them that much.'

Annie frowned. 'I don't understand. What do you owe them?'

Banks smiled. 'I'll tell you all about it later.' Then he walked up the stairs to the deserted market square.

Banks felt sick and heavy with dread as he approached the Riddles' house close to one thirty that morning. The Old Mill stood in almost complete darkness behind the privet hedge, but a glimmer of light showed through the curtains of one of the ground-floor rooms, and Banks wondered if it had been left on as a means of discouraging burglars. He knew it hadn't when he saw the curtain twitch at the sound of his car on the gravel drive. He should have known Jimmy Riddle would be up working well after midnight. Hard work and long hours were what had got him where he was in the first place.

When he turned the engine off, he could hear the old mill-race running down the garden. He hardly had time to knock before a hall light came on and the door opened. Riddle stood there in an Oxford shirt and grey chinos; it was the first time Banks had seen him in casual dress.

'Banks? I thought that was your car. What on earth . . .?'

But his voice trailed off as recognition that something was seriously wrong crept into his features. Whether he'd been a good one or not, Riddle had been a copper for long enough to know that the call in the middle of night was hardly a social one; he knew enough to read the expression on Banks's face.

'Maybe we could sit down, have a drink,' Banks said, as Riddle stood aside to let him in.

'Tell me first,' said Riddle, leaning back on the door after he closed it.

Banks couldn't look him in the eye. 'I'm sorry, sir,' he said. The honorific sounded odd even as he spoke the word; he had never called Riddle 'sir' before, except in a sarcastic tone.

'It's Emily, isn't it?'

Banks nodded.

'My God.'

'Sir.' Banks took Riddle's elbow and guided him into the living room. Riddle collapsed into an armchair and Banks found the cocktail cabinet. He poured them both a stiff whisky; he was beyond worrying about drink-driving at that point. Riddle held the glass but didn't drink from it right away.

'She's dead, isn't she?' he said.

'I'm afraid so.'

'What happened? How?'

'We're not sure yet, sir.'

'Was there an accident? A car crash?'

'No. It was nothing like that.'

'Out with it, man. This is my daughter we're talking about.'

'I know that, sir. That's why I'm trying to tread softly.'

'Too late for that, Banks. What was it? Drugs?'

'Partly.'

'What do you mean, "partly"? Either it was or it wasn't. Tell me what happened to her!'

Banks paused. It was a terrible thing to tell a dead girl's father how painfully she had died, but he reminded himself that Riddle was also chief constable, a professional, and he would find out soon enough, anyway. Best he find out now. 'We're keeping this strictly confidential for the time being, but Dr Burns thinks it might have been cocaine spiked with strychnine.'

Riddle jerked forward and spilled some whisky on his trousers. He didn't even bother to wipe it off. '*Strychnine!* My God, how . . .? I don't understand.'

'She was taking cocaine at a nightclub in Eastvale,' Banks said. 'The Bar None. You might have heard of it?'

Riddle shook his head.

'Anyway, if the doctor is right, somebody must have put strychnine in her cocaine.'

'Christ, Banks, do you realize what you're saying?'

'I do, sir. I'm saying that, in all likelihood, your daughter was murdered.'

'Is this some sort of sick joke?'

'Believe me, I wish it were.'

Riddle ran his hand over his shiny bald skull, a gesture Banks had often thought ridiculous in the past; now it reeked of despair. He drank some of his whisky before asking the hopeless question everyone asks in his situation: 'You're sure there's no mistake?'

'No mistake, sir. I saw her myself. I know it's no consolation, but it must have been very fast,' Banks lied. 'She can't have suffered very much.'

'Rubbish. I'm not an idiot, Banks. I've studied the textbook. I *know* what strychnine does. She'd have gone into convulsions, bent her spine. She'd have—'

'Don't,' Banks said. 'There's no sense torturing yourself.'

'*Who?*' Riddle asked. 'Who would want to do something like that to Emily?'

'Have you noticed anything strange while she's been here?'

'No.'

'What about today, the last few days? Any changes in her behaviour?'

'No. Look, you went to London, Banks. You found her. What about the people she was hanging around with down there? This Clough character. Do you think he could have had something to do with it?'

Banks paused. Barry Clough had been the first to come to his mind when Dr Burns had told him about the poisoned cocaine. He also remembered how Emily had told him that Clough hated to lose his prize possessions. 'That's a distinct possibility,' he said.

Riddle plucked at the creases of his trousers, then he let out a long sigh. 'You'll do what you have to do, Banks. I know that. Wherever it leads you.'

'Yes, sir. Is there . . .?'

'What?'

'Anything you want to tell me?'

Riddle paused. He seemed to think hard for a few moments, then he shook his head. 'I'm sorry. I can't help you. It's out of my hands now.' He knocked back the rest of the whisky. 'I'll go to the mortuary and identify her.'

'It'll wait till morning.'

Riddle got up and started pacing the room. 'But I must do *something*. I can't just . . . I mean, Christ, man, you've just told me my daughter's been murdered. *Poisoned*. What do you expect me to do! Sit down and cry? Take a bloody sleeping pill? I'm a policeman, Banks. I have to do something.'

'Everything possible is being done,' said Banks. 'I think you'd be best off spending the time with your wife and son.'

'Don't soft-soap me, Banks. My God, just wait till the press gets hold of this.'

Here we go again, thought Banks: his bloody *reputation*. It was only out of respect for Riddle's bereavement that Banks said mildly, 'They hadn't got a whiff when I left the scene, but I don't suppose it'll take them long. The place will be swarming with them come morning. We want to try and keep the strychnine aspect quiet.'

Riddle seemed to collapse in on himself, all his energy gone. He looked tired. 'I'll wake up Ros and tell her. I appreciate your coming, Banks. I mean personally, you know, not sending someone else. The best thing you can do is get back to the scene and stay on top of things. I'll be depending on you, and for once I don't care how many bloody corners you cut or whose feet you tread on.'

'Yes, sir.' Riddle was right; probably the best thing Banks could do right now was throw himself into the investigation. Besides, people need to be alone with their grief. 'I'll need to talk to you both at some point,' he said. 'Tomorrow?'

'Of course.'

They heard a sound from the doorway and turned. Benjamin Riddle stood there in his pyjamas clutching a battered teddy bear. He rubbed his eyes. 'I heard voices, Daddy. I was scared. What is it? Is something wrong?'

9

It was still dark when Banks drove to Eastvale the following morning, and a thin mist nuzzled in the dips and hollows of the road and clung to the buildings, the cobbles and the ancient cross in the market square. It was that time of morning when lights were coming on in the small offices above the shops, some of which were already open, and the mist diffused their light like thin gauze. The air was mild and clammy.

Across the square, the Bar None was still taped off, and a uniformed officer stood on guard. After leaving Riddle's house the previous night, Banks had returned to the club to find the SOCOs still at work and Annie taking statements. Detective Superintendent Gristhorpe had also driven in all the way from Lyndgarth.

Banks had hung around for a while, talking the scene over with Gristhorpe, but there was nothing more he could do there. When the media people started pestering him for comments, he drove home and spent a couple of sleepless hours on the sofa thinking about Emily Riddle's terrible death before heading right back to the station. He tried to keep at bay the feelings of guilt that were crowding at the edge of his mind like circling sharks. He succeeded only partially, and that was because he had a job to do, something to focus on and exclude the rest. The problem was that the bad feelings would continue to accumulate even when he wasn't looking, and the day would come when there were so many of them he could no longer ignore them. By then, he knew from experience, it was usually too late to end up feeling good about himself. For the time being, though, he couldn't afford the self-indulgence of guilt.

The renovators hadn't turned up yet, so things were quiet in the extension. Banks went to his office, read his copies of last night's reports and made some notes on his own impressions. He did this, as most good coppers did, for himself, not for the files; they were very personal impressions, and sometimes they could lead somewhere, often not. Whatever else they were, they were no substitute for facts or evidence. He included in his notes, for example, his sense that Darren Hirst was telling the truth and a gut feeling that Emily had got the drugs somewhere other than the Cross Keys or the Bar None. Already, he noted from the reports, a couple of very sleepy local dealers were cooling their heels in the detention cells in the basement of the station. More would soon follow.

By the time the sun was sniffing its nose at the cloudy horizon, the station was humming with activity. The incident room was quickly taking on form and function, and DC Rickerd had been up all night getting it organized. Computer links had been set up and phone lines activated, and civilian staff were drifting in for data-input, logging and recording duties. By the time Banks felt the need for his breakfast coffee, ACC McLaughlin had arrived from county headquarters at Newby Wiske, outside Northallerton. He set up camp in the board-room, and fifteen or twenty minutes later Banks was summoned in.

McLaughlin, Annie Cabbot and Detective Superintendent Gristhorpe were waiting for him. Banks greeted them and sat down. Annie looked tired, and he imagined she had got as little sleep as he had. She also seemed nervous, which was unusual for her.

'Red Ron' McLaughlin was about fifty, tall and slim, with short, thinning grey hair combed forward, and a small grey moustache. He wore silver-rimmed glasses, which balanced on the tip of his nose, and he had a habit of peering over them at whoever he was speaking to. His eyes were the same shade of grey as his hair.

'Ah, DCI Banks,' he said, then he shuffled some papers and looked over his glasses. 'Right. I'll get straight down to brass tacks. I had a meeting with Chief Constable Riddle this morning – in fact he came to see me – and he was most emphatic that he wanted you to head the investigation into his daughter's death. What do you think of that?'

'I *had* hoped for the case,' said Banks, 'but in all honesty I never expected to be given it.'

'Why not?'

'Because I knew the deceased, sir. Only vaguely, but I knew her. And her family. I assumed we'd have to bring in someone from outside.'

'That would be normal procedure.' McLaughlin scratched his earlobe. 'The chief constable did explain your involvement,' he went on. 'Apparently, he asked you to go to London and find his daughter, which you did. Is that correct?'

'Yes, sir.'

'And you then accompanied her back home?'

'Yes, sir.' Banks felt Annie staring at him but didn't turn to meet her look.

'I hardly think that disqualifies you from acting as Senior Investigating Officer. Do you?'

Banks thought for a moment. He would have to tell Red Ron about the lunch. Someone was bound to come forward about that, and it wouldn't take long now that Emily's murder had featured on the breakfast news. Enough people in the Black Bull had noticed them, and probably at least one or two of them knew who Banks was.

On the other hand, if he told McLaughlin *everything*, he'd be off the case for certain, no matter what Riddle wanted. It was a delicate balancing act. There was also a risk that someone from the Hotel Fifty-Five in London would see Emily's photo in the papers and come forward, although Banks thought that had been long enough ago, and Emily had looked sufficiently different that night, dressed up for the party, her hair piled on top of her head, that it was probably very unlikely.

Still, if Banks accepted the post as SIO, he would be in the best position possible to head off any trouble at the pass. He also knew far more about Emily's life in London than anyone else up here, which gave him an advantage when it came to tracking down possible leads. It was bloody unethical, he knew that, probably more unethical than anything he'd done before. After all, one of Riddle's bugbears had been that Banks too often acted as a maverick. But, Banks guessed, that was why Riddle had asked him to go to London, and that was why he now wanted him to head the investigation. Riddle had said as much last night.

'No, sir,' Banks answered finally. 'I'd like to take the case.' He was aware as he spoke the words that he might well be digging his own grave. The last thing he needed to do was give the new ACC a reason for hating his guts right off the bat. But it couldn't be helped. Emily came first here; he owed her that much at least. He had said he only knew her vaguely. It wasn't a lie, but like many unsatisfactory truths, it left too much out. How could Banks describe the bond he had felt with Emily? It wasn't entirely paternal, but it wasn't simple friendship either.

'As you all know, I'm new to this job and this region,' McLaughlin explained. 'I've done my homework, studied the turf, but I can't hope to be up to scratch this soon. According to Mr Riddle, you're the best man for the job. Detective Superintendent Gristhorpe here agrees, and nothing I've seen in your file contradicts that.'

That was a surprise to Banks; he thought Riddle had weighed his file down with negative reports. But McLaughlin frowned and continued, 'I'm not saying there aren't a few black marks against you, Banks. You've made some mistakes I'd like you to avoid making under my command, but your case results speak for themselves. All indications are that you're the best detective we have in the county, and if I stand for anything, it's for using the abilities of my men to their fullest. There's going to be a lot of changes around here with the new organization, and I'm hoping you can play a big part in them. Is that clear?'

'Yes, sir.'

'That's settled then,' said McLaughlin. 'You'll act as SIO on the Emily Riddle case. I take it you'll have no objection to acting as Deputy Investigating Officer, DS Cabbot?'

'No, sir,' said Annie. 'Thank you.'

McLaughlin turned to Gristhorpe. 'And you'll liaise with me at Regional Headquarters, Superintendent. Okay?'

Gristhorpe nodded.

'What about HOLMES?' McLaughlin asked.

HOLMES, acronym of the Home Office Large Major Enquiry System, was a computer database system developed since the Yorkshire Ripper investigation. Everything would be entered there, from witness statements to SOCO reports. It would all be indexed and cross-indexed so that nothing got lost in the mass of disparate paperwork the way the Ripper's identification had. 'I think we should activate it now,' said Banks. 'Given the seriousness of the case. I'll put DC Jackman on it. She's a trained operator.'

'Very well.' McLaughlin looked from Banks to Annie. 'By the way, Dr Glendenning has offered to conduct the post-mortem early this afternoon, so don't eat a heavy lunch. I think you should both be there. I'll also get some more DCs assigned as soon as possible,' McLaughlin went on. 'There'll probably be a lot of legwork on this. I understand you already have a murder investigation on the go. Can you handle this one, too?'

'I think so, sir.' Banks remembered often having several serious cases on the go when he worked for the Met. 'Officially, the Charlie Courage murder is still DI Collaton's case. Leicestershire Constabulary. DS Cabbot did some of the preliminary interviews, but I can put DS Hatchley on it.'

McLaughlin paused and made a steeple of his hands and looked over his glasses. 'We don't want to appear as if we're playing favourites, ladies and gentlemen,' he said, 'but there's no denying we're giving this case a very high priority indeed. Have you any thoughts so far, DCI Banks?'

'It's too early to say, sir. I'd like to have another talk with the family, maybe later today.'

'Chief Constable Riddle said something about her hanging around with some unsavoury types in London. Anything in that?'

'It's possible,' said Banks. 'There was one in particular, name of Barry Clough. I'll be having a very close look at him.'

'Any other developments? DS Cabbot?'

'We searched the people in the club last night, sir,' Annie said, 'but we didn't find anything except a few tabs of Ecstasy, a bit of marijuana and the odd amphetamine pill or two.'

'All according to PACE, I hope?'

'Yes, sir. Two people resisted and I had them taken over to the station. They were cautioned by the custody officer before being strip-searched. They were both carrying drugs in sufficient quantities for resale. One had crystal meth, the other what appears to be cocaine.'

'Any connection with Ms Riddle's death?'

'As far as we could tell, sir, it wasn't cut with strychnine, but we're holding him while it goes to the lab for tox testing.'

McLaughlin jotted something on his pad. 'What about CCTV?' he asked. 'Was the club covered?'

'Unfortunately,' said Banks, 'the Bar None hasn't had any cameras installed yet, but we might get something from ours.'

The installation of closed circuit television cameras in the market square had been a thorny issue around the division that summer, when Eastvale had experienced a public-order problem caused by drunken louts gathering around the market cross after closing time. Fights broke out between rival gangs, often in town from villages in the Dale, or between locals and squaddies from the nearby army base. In one case an elderly female tourist was hit by flying glass and had to have sixteen stitches in her face.

Knaresborough, Ripon, and Harrogate and Leeds had installed CCTV in their city centres and upped their arrest rates considerably, but at first Jimmy Riddle had pooh-poohed the idea of doing the same in Eastvale, arguing that it would take them over budget and that it wasn't necessary because the police station itself was located on one side of the market square, and all any officer had to do was look out of the window.

After considerable debate, and mostly because he was impressed by the rise in Ripon's arrest rate, Riddle had relented and four cameras were installed on an experimental basis. They fed directly into a small communications room set up on the ground floor of Eastvale Divisional HQ, where the tapes were routinely scanned for the faces of familiar troublemakers and any signs of criminal activity. Banks thought it all smacked a bit too much of Big Brother, but was willing to admit that in a case like this the tapes might be of some value.

'They'll at least tell us if anyone left after Emily and her friends arrived at the club,' he went on. 'Darren Hirst was too upset and confused to be certain last night.'

'Good idea,' McLaughlin said. 'Any point staging a reconstruction?'

Banks took a deep breath. Now was the time. 'I don't think so, sir. I had a brief lunch with Emily yesterday. She wanted to thank me for persuading her to return home, and she also expressed some concern about this Clough character.'

'Go on,' said McLaughlin, without expression.

Banks felt Annie's eyes boring into the side of his head again. Even Gristhorpe was frowning. 'She left the Black Bull to meet someone, or so she said, at three o'clock. We don't know where she was between then and when she met her friends in the Cross Keys around seven. Darren said he thought she was a little high when she arrived at the Cross Keys, so I would guess that she'd been taking drugs with someone, perhaps the person who gave her the poisoned cocaine. After that, they were together as a group all evening. I think we'd have more to gain from a concentrated media campaign. Posters, television, newspapers.'

'I'm concerned about this lunch you had with the victim,' said McLaughlin.

'There was nothing to it, sir. We were in public view the entire time, and I remained there after Emily left. I think she was genuinely worried about Clough. She didn't feel she could talk to her father, but she wanted me to know.'

'Why you?'

'Because I'd met him when I was searching for her. She knew I'd understand what she was talking about.'

'Nasty piece of work, then?'

'Very, sir.'

'Did she give you any idea of where she was going or who she was meeting?'

'No, sir. I wish she had.' Banks wished he had even *asked* her.

'What did she talk about?'

'As I said, she was grateful to me for persuading her to go home. She talked about her future. She wanted to take her A levels and go to university in America.'

'And she expressed concern about Clough?'

'Yes, sir.'

'Did she say he'd been in touch with her, threatened her or anything like that?'

'She said he hadn't contacted her, but she seemed worried. She said he didn't like to lose his prize possessions. And she thought she saw one of his employees in the Swainsdale Centre.'

'Do you think she knew something was going to happen to her, that she was in fear for her life?'

'I wouldn't push it that far, sir.'

'Even so,' said McLaughlin, 'she was a member of the public expressing concern over a dangerous situation she had got herself into and asking for police help. Wasn't she?'

'Yes, sir,' said Banks, relieved that McLaughlin had seen fit to throw him a lifebelt. Banks didn't see any point in telling him that Emily had been drinking under age in his presence, or that they had spent half a night alone together in a London hotel room.

'Good. I'll leave you to fill out the appropriate paperwork to that effect, then, so we can put it on file in case of any problems. I should imagine you were busy at the time and simply postponed the paperwork?'

'Yes, sir.'

'Perfectly understandable. And you don't need me to tell you that quick, positive results on this would be beneficial all around.'

'No, sir.'

With that, ACC Ron McLaughlin left the boardroom.

'You may leave, too, DS Cabbot,' said Gristhorpe. 'Alan, I'd like a word.'

Annie left, flashing Banks a tight, pissed-off look. Banks and Gristhorpe looked at one another. 'Terrible business,' said Gristhorpe. 'No matter what you thought of Jimmy Riddle.'

'It is, sir.'

'This lunch, Alan? It only happened the once, just the way you say it did?'

'Yes, sir.'

Gristhorpe grunted. He was looking old, Banks thought – his unruly hair, if anything, greyer lately, dark bags under his eyes, his normally ruddy, pockmarked complexion paler than usual. He also seemed to have lost weight; his tweed jacket looked baggy on him. Still, Banks reminded himself, Gristhorpe had been up pretty much all night, and he wasn't getting any younger.

'She was a good lass,' Banks said. Then he shook his head. 'No. What am I saying? That's not true. She was what you'd call a wild child. She was exasperating, a pain in the arse, and she no doubt ran Jimmy Riddle ragged.'

'But you liked her?'

'Couldn't help but. She was confused, a bit crazy maybe, rebellious.'

'A bit like you when you were a lad?' said Gristhorpe with a smile.

'Perish the thought. No. She was exactly the sort of girl I hoped Tracy wouldn't turn into, and thank the Lord she didn't. Maybe it was easy to admire the spirit in her because I wasn't her father, and she wasn't really my problem. But she was more confused than bad, and I think she'd have turned out all right, given the chance. She was just too advanced for her years. I want the bastard who did this to her, sir. Maybe more than I've ever wanted any bastard before in my career.'

'Be careful, Alan.' Gristhorpe leaned forward and rested his arms on the table. 'You know as well as I do that you wouldn't be anywhere near this case if it weren't for Jimmy Riddle. But if you screw up just once because it's too personal for you, I'll be down on you like the proverbial ton of bricks. Which is probably nothing to what ACC McLaughlin will do. Got it?'

'Got it,' said Banks. 'Don't worry. I'll play it by the book.'

Gristhorpe leaned back and smiled at him. 'Nay, Alan,' he said. 'You wouldn't want to do that. What'd be the point of having you on the case, then? All I'm saying is don't let anger and a desire for revenge cloud your judgement. Look clearly at the evidence, the facts, before you make any moves. Don't go off half-cocked the way you've done in the past.'

'I'll try not to,' said Banks.

'You do that.'

Someone knocked at the door and Gristhorpe called out for him to come in. It was one of the uniformed officers from downstairs. 'A DI Wayne Dalton, Northumbria CID, to see DCI Banks, sir.'

Banks raised his eyebrows and looked at Gristhorpe. 'Okay,' he said, glancing at his watch. 'Give him a cup of coffee and sit him in my office. I can spare him a few minutes.'

Banks wasn't the only one who had spent a restless night; Annie Cabbot had also lain awake during the hour or two she had spent in bed shortly before dawn, her nerve ends jumping at every little sound. She had tried to tell herself not to be so weak. After all, she had prevented Dalton from raping her two years ago, so why should she be worried about him now? Her martial arts training might be a bit rusty, but she could defend herself well enough if it came to that.

The problem was that reason has no foothold at four or five in the morning; at those hours, reason sleeps and the mind breeds monsters: monsters of fear, of paranoia. And so she had tossed and turned, her mind's eye flashing on images of Dalton's sweat-glossed face and hate-filled eyes, and of Emily Riddle dead, her skinny frame wedged in a toilet cubicle at the Bar None nightclub, her eyes wide open in terror and facial muscles contorted into a grimace.

Now, however, as she came out of the meeting and headed for her office in what little light of day there was, she realized that she wasn't physically afraid of Dalton. She had always known he was the type who could only act violently as part of a gang. His appearance had shaken her, that was all, stirred up memories of that night she would rather forget. The only problem was that she didn't know quite what to do, if anything, about him.

She thought of telling Banks but dismissed the idea quickly. If truth be told, she was pissed off at him. Why hadn't he told her about his relationship with the victim last night? There had been plenty of time. It would have made her feel more like a

DIO and less like a bloody idiot this morning when the ACC brought the matter up.

In a way, she regretted now that she had even told Banks about the rape in the first place, but such intimacy as they had had breeds foolish confessions; she had certainly never told anyone else, not even her father. And now that she was actually working with Banks, even though she still fancied him, she was going to try to keep things on a professional footing. Her career was moving in the right direction again, and she didn't want to mess things up. ACC McLaughlin had given her a great chance by making her DIO. The last thing she wanted to do was go crying to the boss. No, Dalton was *her* problem, and she would deal with him one way or another.

Banks found DI Dalton standing in his office facing the wall, styrofoam cup of coffee in his hand, looking at the Dalesman calendar. December showed a snow-and-ice-covered Goredale Scar, near Malham. Dalton turned as Banks entered. He was about six feet tall and skinny as a rake, with pale, watery blue eyes and a long, thin face with a rather hangdog expression under his head of sparse ginger hair. Banks put his age at around forty. He was wearing a lightweight brown suit, white shirt and tie. A little blood from a shaving cut had dried near the cleft of his chin.

He stuck his hand out. 'DI Wayne Dalton. I seem to have come in the middle of a flap.'

'Haven't you heard?'

'Heard what?'

'The chief constable's daughter was killed last night.'

Dalton rolled his eyes and whistled. 'I'd hate to be the bastard who did that, when you catch him.'

'We will. Sit down. What brings you this far south?'

'It's probably a waste of time,' said Dalton, sitting opposite Banks, 'but it looks like one of our cases stretches down to your turf.'

'Wouldn't be the first time. We've quickly become a very small island indeed.'

'You can say that again. Anyway, late Sunday night – actually, early Monday morning – about twelve thirty, to be as precise as we can be at this point – a white van was hijacked on the B6348 between the A1 and the village of Chatton. The contents were stolen and the driver's still in a coma.'

'What's his name?'

'Jonathan Fearn.'

Banks tapped his pencil on his desk. 'Never heard of him.'

'No reason you should have. He lived here, though.' Dalton consulted his notebook. 'Twenty-six Darlington Road.'

'I know it,' said Banks, making a note. 'We'll look into him. Any form?'

'No. What's interesting, though, is that it turns out this white van was leased by a company called PKF Computer Systems, and—'

'Hang on a minute. Did you say PKF?'

'That's right. Starting to make sense?'

'Not much, but go on.'

'Anyway, we ran a check on PKF and, to cut a long story short, it doesn't exist.'

'What do you mean?'

'Exactly what I say. PKF Computer Systems is not registered as an operating business.'

'That means someone made up the name . . .'

' . . . printed some letterhead paper, got a phone line installed, opened a bank account . . . exactly. A dummy company.'

'Any idea who?'

'That's where I was hoping you might be able to help. We traced PKF to the Daleview Business Park, just outside Eastvale, and we confirmed that the van must have been on its way to a new trading estate near Wooler. At least PKF had rented premises there starting that Monday morning.'

'Let me get this straight,' said Banks. 'PKF, which doesn't exist, moves lock, stock and barrel from the Daleview Business Park, where they haven't been operating more than two or three months, on Sunday night and heads up the A1 towards another business park near Tyneside, where they've also rented premises. A few miles short of their destination, the van's hijacked and its contents removed. Right?'

'So far.'

'On Tuesday,' Banks continued, 'the nightwatchman of the Daleview Business Park was found dead in some woods near Market Harborough, Leicestershire. Shotgun wound.'

'Execution?'

'Looks that way. We think he was killed Monday afternoon.'

'Connection?'

'I'd say so, wouldn't you? Especially when it turns out our nightwatchman had been putting away another two hundred quid a week over and above his wages.'

'And PKF is a phony.'

'Exactly.'

'Any idea what that van might have been carrying?' Dalton asked.

'The only thing my DS found when she checked out the PKF unit at Daleview was an empty case for a compact disc.'

'Compact discs? First time I've ever heard of a CD hijack.'

'We don't know that that's the reason. All I'm saying is that we found a CD case at PKF, which fits with their working in the computer business. Maybe it was computer equipment the thieves were after?'

'Could be. That stuff can be valuable.'

'Any leads at all?'

Dalton shook his head. 'We've been keeping an eye on the unit they rented near Wooler, but no one's shown up yet. Given what's happened, we don't expect them to now. It was late, on a quiet road, so there were no witnesses. They left the van in a lay-by. As I said, the driver's still in a coma and fingerprints will be working to sort out their findings till kingdom come. You and I both know that anyone doing a professional job like this would be wearing gloves, anyway. This was the only lead we got – PKF and the Daleview Business Park.'

'Okay,' said Banks, standing. 'We'll keep in touch on this one.'

'Mind if I stick around a day or two, have a look at the business park, poke about?'

'Be my guest.' Banks pulled his pad towards him. 'The way things are right now we can use all the help we can get. You could also get in touch with DI Collaton at Market Harborough. It looks as if this is all connected. Where are you staying?'

'Fox and Hounds, on North Market Street. Got in yesterday evening. Nice little place.'

'I know it,' said Banks. 'Let us know if you find anything.'

'Will do.' Dalton touched the tips of his fingers in a friendly salute, then left the office.

Banks walked over to the window and looked out on the cobbled market square. The gold hands against the blue front of the church clock stood at quarter past ten. The morning mist had disappeared and it was as light now as it was likely to be all day. He saw DI Dalton walk across the square, pause and linger a moment at the taped-off, guarded entrance of the Bar None, then turn left on York Road towards the bus station and the Swainsdale Centre.

It was difficult for Banks to drum up much enthusiasm for the Charlie Courage investigation since Emily's murder, but he knew he had to keep on top of it. He also knew that they should have checked into PKF the way Dalton had. Any further signs that he was dragging his feet, and Red Ron would, quite rightly, have him on the carpet. Emily was a priority, yes, but that didn't mean poor Charlie counted for nothing. Maybe Dalton would come up with something useful. Banks would put him in touch with Hatchley, and with Annie, so she could share what she'd discovered at Daleview.

Looking at the weak grey light that seemed to cling to everything, bleeding the townscape of all colour, Banks wished he could escape to somewhere warm and sunny for a couple of weeks, find a nice spot on the beach and read novels and biographies and listen to the waves all day. Normally he didn't like that kind of holiday, preferring to explore a foreign city on foot, but there was something about the long, dark Yorkshire winters that made him yearn for the Canaries or the Azores. Or Montego Bay. If he could afford it, though, he thought he would like to go to Mexico for a while, see some Mayan ruins. But that was out of the question, especially with the mortgage on the cottage and Tracy at university.

Besides, Banks thought, opening the window a few inches and lighting a cigarette, he couldn't desert Emily now. He was responsible for what had happened to her, at least in part. There was no escaping that. If he hadn't gone down to London and stirred things up with Clough, then it was unlikely that she would have come back home and ended up dead in a crummy Eastvale nightclub. She had gone the way of Graham Marshall, of Jem and of Phil Simpkins, and he couldn't, wouldn't, just let it go; he *had* to do something.

'Let it roll, Ned,' said Banks. He was in the CCTV viewing room downstairs along with DCs Winsome Jackman and Kevin Templeton, Annie Cabbot and their civilian video technician, Ned Parker.

The screen showed the market square from the police station, including the edge of the Queen's Arms to the right, the church front to the left and all the shops, pubs and offices directly opposite, including the entrance to the Bar None. The picture was grainy black and white, with a slight fish-eye effect, and the glare of the Christmas lights caused one or two problems with the contrast, but it was still possible to make out figures coming and going. Whether they would be able to identify someone coming out of the Bar None from this tape alone, Banks was doubtful.

The time appeared in an on-screen display at the bottom right-hand side, and, starting at 10.00, Parker advanced it quickly so that the people crossing the market square looked like extras in a Keystone Kops chase. Sometime around twenty-five past, Banks noticed a group of people enter the screen from the right, the exit of the Queen's Arms, and told Parker to slow down to normal speed. He then watched Emily walk across the market square. She seemed a little unsteady on the cobbles as she crossed the square, which didn't surprise him, considering the platform heels she was wearing and the amount she had had to drink that day.

When she got to the market cross, she turned to face the police station and did a little dance, and when she finished, she bowed with a flourish to the camera, but before walking away she gave it the finger, just one, in the American style, then she turned and swung her hips exaggeratedly as she walked on to the nightclub. The others laughed. Banks himself smiled as he watched her, almost forgetting for a moment that this was a little cheeky gesture that would never be repeated.

Banks watched them enter the club and asked Parker to keep it running at normal speed as he watched others follow. As far as he could make out, there was no suspicious activity in the market square. No little packages of white powder exchanging hands. As he watched, he realized how much he wanted to be watching what was happening *inside* the club, but there were no cameras there.

At 10.47, two people walked out of the club and headed down York Road. Banks couldn't make out their features, but it looked like a boy in jeans and a short leather jacket and a girl in a long overcoat and a floppy hat. He asked Parker to freeze the frame, but it didn't help much.

After that, another three couples went in, but no one came

out. When DC Rickerd and Inspector Jessup entered the frame, Banks told Parker to turn the machine off.

It was beginning to look very much as if Emily had scored her coke long before she went to the Bar None, as Banks had guessed, and that would make it all the more difficult to find out who had supplied her with the lethal concoction.

'Okay,' Banks said, standing up and stretching. 'That's all your entertainment for today. Winsome, bring in Darren Hirst, would you? Maybe he can help us with the two who left.'

'Friendly, sir?'

'Friendly. He's not a suspect, just helping us with our inquiries.'

Winsome smiled at the hackneyed phrase. 'Will do, sir.'

'Kevin, I'd like you to work with Ned here and see if you can get a decent image of those two who left. Something we can show around.'

'Okay, Guv.'

'And Kevin?'

'Guv?'

'Please don't call me "Guv". It makes me feel as if I'm on television.'

Templeton grinned. 'Right you are, *sir.*'

Then Banks looked at his watch and turned to Annie. 'We'd better go,' he said. 'We've got an appointment with Dr Glendenning in a few minutes.'

Banks drove out to the Old Mill after Emily Riddle's post-mortem, Fauré's Requiem playing on the stereo. He still felt angry and nauseated at what he had just seen. It wasn't the first young girl he had watched Dr Glendenning open up on the slab, but it was the first whose vitality he had known, whose fears and dreams had been shared with him, and watching Dr Glendenning calmly bisecting the black spider tattoo with his scalpel as he made his incision had almost sent Banks the way Annie went down in Market Harborough. Annie had been fine this time, though. Quiet and tense, but fine, even when the saw ripped into the bone of Emily's skull.

Dr Glendenning had confirmed Dr Burns's original determination that strychnine, mixed in a high ratio with pharmaceutical cocaine, had caused Emily's death. Glendenning had performed the simple toxicology test for strychnine himself, dissolving some of the suspect crystals in sulphuric acid and touching the edge of the solution with a crystal of potassium chromate. It turned purple, then crimson, then all colour faded. Proof positive. Further tox tests would be done at Wetherby, but for now, this was enough. So far, all the media knew was that she had died of a suspected drug overdose, but it wouldn't be long before some bright spark of a reporter sniffed out the truth. Sometimes the press seemed even more resourceful than the police.

As it turned out, Emily's neck wasn't broken; she had died of asphyxiation. Other than the fact that she was dead, Glendenning had also told Banks, she was in extremely good health. The drugs and drink and cigarettes clearly hadn't had time to take their toll on her.

The Old Mill stood at the end of a cul-de-sac, like Banks's more humble abode, so the uniformed officers on guard could stand well over a hundred yards away, where the lane turned off the main road, and keep reporters away without even being seen by the Riddles. Banks showed his warrant card and the officer on duty waved him through. Rosalind answered the door and led him through to the same room where he had given Riddle the news. She was dressed in black and her eyes looked dark with lack of sleep. Banks guessed that Riddle must have woken her as soon as he had left last night. They wouldn't have had any sleep since then.

'Banks.' Riddle got slowly to his feet when Banks entered the room. He was dressed in the same clothes he had been wearing last night, a little more the worse for wear. He looked haggard, and there was a listlessness and a defeated air about

201

his movements that Banks had never seen him exhibit before. He had always been energetic and abrupt. Perhaps he had taken a tranquillizer, or perhaps this was the toll recent events had taken on his system. Whichever it was, the man looked as if he could use a doctor as well as a good night's sleep. 'Any news?' he asked, without much hope in his voice.

'Nothing yet, I'm afraid.' Banks didn't want to mention the post-mortem, though he knew Riddle would be aware that it had been conducted. He only hoped the CC had enough common sense not to bring something like that up in front of his wife.

'Confirmed cause of death?' he asked.

'It's what we thought.'

Rosalind put her hand to her throat. 'Strychnine. I've read about that.'

Banks glanced at Riddle. 'You've told her . . .?'

'Ros understands she's to talk to no one about the cause of death. I don't suppose it'll be a secret for long, though?'

'I doubt it,' said Banks. 'Not now the post-mortem's over. Glendenning's sound as a bell, but there's always someone there who lets the cat out of the bag. Mrs Riddle,' he said, perching on the edge of his armchair, 'I need to ask you some questions. I'll try to make it as painless for you as possible.'

'I understand. Jerry explained it to me.'

'Good. Emily had been back from London about a month. During that time, had she given you any cause for concern?'

'No,' said Rosalind. 'In fact, she'd been extremely well behaved. For Emily.'

'Meaning?'

'Meaning, Chief Inspector, that if she wanted to stay out all night at a rave, she would. Emily always was a wilful child, as I'm sure you're aware, difficult to control. But I saw no evidence of drug use, and she was generally polite and good-natured in her dealings with me.'

'I gather that wasn't always the case?'

'It was not.'

'Had she been out a lot since her return?'

'Not much. Last night was only the second or third time.'

'When was the previous time?'

'The night before. Wednesday. She went to the pictures with some friends; that new cinema complex in Eastvale. And a week or so ago she went to a birthday party in Richmond. She was home shortly after midnight both times.'

'What did she do with her time?'

'Believe it or not, she stayed in and read a lot. Watched videos. She also made inquiries about getting into a sixth-form college. I think she was finally deciding to take life a bit more seriously.'

'Did she ever confide in you about any problems she might be having? Boys, or anything like that?'

'That wasn't Emily's way,' said Rosalind. 'She was always secretive, even when she was little. She liked a sense of mystery.'

'What about boyfriends?'

'I don't think there was anyone special. She hung around with a group of people.'

'It must have been difficult for her to make friends locally, with being at school down south so much of the time.'

'It was. And as you probably know yourself, the locals aren't always that welcoming to southerners, even these days. But when she was home for the holidays she'd meet people. I don't know. She didn't seem to have any real trouble making friends. She was outgoing enough. And of course, she still knew people from when she was at St Mary's School here. That was only two years ago.'

'What about Darren Hirst? Did she ever mention him?'

'Yes. In fact, it was *his* birthday party she went to last week. But he wasn't her boyfriend; he was just part of the group she hung out with. The lad with the car. They came to the house to pick her up on Wednesday – Darren and a girl, Nina or Tina or something – and they certainly seemed pleasant enough, although I didn't approve of her hanging around with people who were, for the most part, three or four years older than she was. I knew she went to pubs and could get served easily enough, and I didn't like it. I told her often enough, but she just accused me of going on at her, and in the end I gave up.'

'Did she ever mention someone called Andrew Handley?'

'No.'

'Andy Pandy?'

'Is this some sort of joke? Who's he?'

'It's not a joke. That's his nickname. He's a colleague of the man Emily was living with in London.'

'Never heard of him,' said Rosalind. She reached forward, grabbed a tissue from the box on the table and sniffled into it. 'I'm sorry,' she mumbled. 'Please excuse me.'

Riddle moved over to her and touched her shoulder hesitantly, without much warmth, it seemed. In response, Rosalind's body stiffened, and she turned away. Banks thought he glimpsed something in her eyes as she turned – fear or confusion, perhaps. Did she suspect her husband of being involved in Emily's death? Or was he protecting her? Whatever it was, there was something desperately out of kilter with the Riddle family.

'Did Emily speak to you of her plans for the future, Mrs Riddle?' Banks asked, switching the direction of the interview to something he thought might be a little easier for her to deal with.

'Only that she wanted to do her A levels and go to university,' said Rosalind, still dabbing her eyes with the tissue. 'Preferably in America. I think she wanted to get as far away from here and from us as she could.'

Out of sight, out of mind, thought Banks. And less likely to damage Riddle's fledgeling political career, if that wasn't already damaged beyond repair. He remembered on his first visit, when the Riddles asked him to go to London and find Emily, how he had got the impression that Rosalind hadn't particularly wanted her to come back home. He got the same impression now. 'And you approved?'

'Of course I did. It's better than her running off to London and living with some . . . I don't know . . . some drug dealer.'

'We don't know that he was a drug dealer,' said Banks. 'In fact, Emily swore he wasn't, and I'm inclined to believe her.'

'Well, Emily always could twist men around her little finger.'

'Not Clough. She met her match there.'

'Do you really think he could be responsible?' asked Riddle.

'Oh, yes. The impression I got is that he's a dangerous man and he doesn't like to be crossed.'

'But why would he want to harm her? He had no real motive.'

'I don't know,' said Banks. 'All I can say is that I've met him and I'm convinced he's into something. Perhaps he did it out of sheer maliciousness, because he didn't like to be crossed. Or perhaps he thought she knew too much about his business interests. Did she ever talk about him to you?'

'No. What are you doing about him?' Riddle asked.

'I'm going to London first thing tomorrow. Before that, I just want to find out if there are any more leads I should be following up here.' Banks paused. 'Look, I had lunch with Emily the day she died and—'

'You did what?'

'She phoned and asked me to lunch, said she'd be in Eastvale. She wanted to thank me.'

'She never told us,' said Riddle, looking at Rosalind, who frowned.

'Well, your wife did say she was secretive. And given that, my next question is probably a waste of time, but when she left, she said she was going to meet someone else. Did she say anything to either of you about meeting someone in Eastvale that afternoon?'

They both shook their heads. 'What did she say to you?' Rosalind asked. 'Did she tell you anything?'

'About what?'

'I don't know. Anything that might help explain what happened.'

'Only that she thought she'd seen one of Clough's men in Eastvale. I gather she didn't mention that to you?'

'No,' said Rosalind.

'When did you last see her yesterday?'

'We didn't,' Riddle answered. 'Both Ros and I had gone to work long before she got up that morning, and when we got back she was out.'

'So the last time you saw her was Wednesday?'

'Yes.'

'Did she phone anyone or get any phone calls?'

'Not that I know of,' said Riddle. 'Ros?'

Rosalind shook her head.

'Did she spend much time on the telephone while she was up here?'

'Not a lot, no.'

'Do I have your permission to ask British Telecom for a record of your telephone calls since Emily came home?'

'Of course,' said Riddle. 'I'll see to it myself.'

'That's all right, sir. I'll put DC Templeton on it. Did she have any visitors from London, make any trips back down there?'

'Not that we know of, no,' said Riddle.

'Are you both sure there's no one else you can think of who I should be looking closely at for this?'

'No,' said Riddle, after a moment's pause for thought. 'Not up here. As Ros said, she hung around with a group. They were probably with her at the club. You can talk to them and ascertain whether you think any of them had anything to do with it.'

'We've already talked to them, but we'll follow up on that.

I must say, on first impressions I don't think any of them are responsible. Do you know where she got her drugs?'

It was Rosalind who answered. 'I told you. I don't think she was taking drugs since she came back.'

'Are you certain?'

'Not completely. But . . . I . . .' She glanced at her husband and blushed before she went on. 'I searched her room once. And once or twice I looked in her handbag. I found nothing.'

'Well, she was definitely taking cocaine the night she died,' said Banks.

'Maybe it was her first time since London?'

'When you searched her handbag, Mrs Riddle, did you come across a driving licence and a proof-of-age card?'

Rosalind looked puzzled. 'A driving licence? Good Lord, no. Emily was too young to drive. Besides, I didn't look in her purse.'

'I'm not saying she did actually drive a car, but when she was found, the officer at the scene found a driving licence in her handbag and thought it was hers. He also found one of those cards clubs issue as proof of age, though they're nothing of the kind. That's why there was some confusion over identity at first.'

'It doesn't mean anything to me,' said Rosalind. 'I don't understand.'

'What about the name Ruth Walker?'

Banks saw a strange look flash across Rosalind's eyes, perhaps the surprise of recognition, but it was gone so fast that he didn't trust his own judgement. She pressed her lips tight together. 'No.'

'She was another friend of Emily's in London. Apparently this Ruth met her in the street and took her in when she first arrived. You didn't know about that?'

'No.'

'What about Craig Newton? Ring any bells?'

'Who was he?'

'Her first boyfriend in London. There was a bit of trouble between him and Clough. He seemed a decent enough lad when I talked to him, but he might have been jealous, and he might have held a grudge against Emily for ditching him. She told me he'd been following her around and pestering her.' Banks stood up. 'Clearly I'm going to find more answers down there. For the moment, though, are you certain neither of you can think of anyone who would want to harm Emily?'

They both shook their heads.

Banks looked at Riddle. 'You're a policeman, sir,' he said. 'Can you think of anyone who might have a grudge against you?'

'Oh, come on, Banks. You know I've hardly been fighting in the trenches for years. That's not a chief constable's job.'

'Even so . . .'

'No, I can't think of anyone offhand.'

'Would you check through your previous arrests, no matter how old? Just for form's sake.'

'Of course.' Riddle saw Banks to the door. 'You'll keep in touch, won't you?' he said, grasping Banks's arm tightly. 'I've been advised to stay away from the office for the time being, so I'm taking a leave of absence. But I'm sure I could be more effective there. Anyway, the moment you know, I want to know. Understand? The moment.'

Banks nodded and Riddle released his grip.

Back at the incident room, Banks discovered that Darren Hirst had been and gone. DC Jackman had interviewed him and said he had been unable to shed any light on the couple who had left the Bar None at 10.47. He hadn't even remembered seeing them in the first place. Now it was a matter of getting the rather blurred and grainy image that Ned Parker had pulled from the CCTV video copied up and shown around. It was possible that someone might have remembered seeing them in the pubs around the market square. It would probably come to nothing, but then most police work did.

He also found out that three people who had been in the Black Bull yesterday lunchtime had phoned in and said they had seen the victim with an older man. One person had positively identified the man as 'that detective who was on telly about that there reservoir business in t'summer'. Just as well he'd told the ACC and the Riddles.

Banks walked into the CID office. Down the corridor, it sounded as if someone were going at the floor with a pneumatic drill. He shut the door behind him and leaned against the wall. Hatchley and Annie Cabbot were at their desks. Annie gave him a dirty look, and Hatchley said he had been out investigating an alien abduction.

Banks smiled. 'Come again? Since when have you been working on the *X Files*, Jim?'

'It's true,' said Hatchley. 'Honest to God.' He chuckled; it sounded as if he was coughing up a big one. 'Toy shop down on Elmet Street,' he went on. 'They put out an inflatable little green man to advertise a new line of toys and somebody nicked it. Some kid, probably. Still, it's an alien abduction.'

Banks laughed. 'There's one for the books. Ever hear of a fellow called Jonathan Fearn?' he asked.

'Rings a bell.' Hatchley scratched his ear. 'If I'm thinking of the right one, he's an unemployed yobbo, not above a bit of dodgy dealing every now and then. We've had our eyes on him as driver on a couple of warehouse robberies over the years.'

'But he's got no form?'

Hatchley shrugged. 'Just lucky. Some are. It won't last.'

'His luck's already run out. He's in hospital in Newcastle, in a coma.'

Hatchley whistled. 'Bloody hell. What happened?'

Banks told him as much as he knew. 'Do you know of any connection between this Fearn character and Charlie Courage?'

'Could be,' Hatchley said. 'I mean, they hung out in the same pubs and neither of them was beyond a bit of thievery every now and then. They sound like two peas from the same pod to me.'

'Thanks, Jim,' said Banks. 'Poke around a bit, will you? See if you can find a connection.'

Hatchley, always happy to be sent off to do his work in pubs, beamed. 'My pleasure.'

'There's a DI Dalton around the place somewhere. Down from Northumbria, staying at the Fox and Hounds. He might be able to help. Liaise with him on this one.'

'Will do.'

Annie followed Banks out of the office and caught up with him in the corridor. 'A word?'

'Of course,' said Banks. 'Not here, though. This noise is driving me crazy. Queen's Arms?'

'Fine with me.'

Banks and Annie walked across Market Street to the Queen's Arms.

'I want to know just what the hell you think you've been playing at,' Annie said when they had got drinks and sat down in a quiet corner. She spoke softly, but there was anger in her voice, and she sat stiffly in her chair.

'What do you mean?'

'You know damn well what I mean. What went on you between you and the victim?'

'Emily Riddle?'

'Who else?'

Banks sighed. 'I'm sorry it happened the way it did, Annie, sorry if I embarrassed you in any way. I would have told you, honestly. I just hadn't found the right time.'

'You could have told me last night at the scene.'

'No, I couldn't. There was too much else going on, too

much to do, too much to organize. And I was bloody upset by what I saw – all right?'

'No, it's not all right. You made me feel like a complete bloody idiot this morning. I've been working on the case as long as you, and here you are coming up with a suspect I've never even heard of. Not to mention having lunch with the victim on the day she died.'

'Look, I've said I'm sorry. What else can I say?'

Annie shook her head. 'It's not on, Alan. If I'm supposed to be your DIO, I'm not supposed to be the last bloody person on earth who hears about important developments.'

'It wasn't an important development. It had already happened.'

'Stop splitting hairs. You named a suspect. You had a prior relationship with the victim. You should have told me. It could have a bearing on the investigation.'

'It *does* have a bearing on the investigation. And I *will* tell you if you'll let me.'

'Better late than never.'

Banks told her about London, about GlamourPuss, Clough, Ruth Walker and Craig Newton – everything except the night in the hotel room – and about what he and Emily had discussed over lunch the previous day. When he had finished, Annie seemed to relax in her chair the way she normally did.

'I wasn't keeping it from you, Annie,' he said. 'It was just bad timing, that's all. Honestly.'

'And that's all there is to it?'

'That's all. Scout's honour.'

Annie managed a smile. 'Next time anything like that happens, tell me up front, okay?'

'Okay. Forgive me?'

'I'm working on it. What next?'

'I'm going down to London tomorrow to do a bit of checking up.'

'And me?'

'I want you to take care of things at this end. I'll only be gone for the weekend, most likely, but there's a lot to do. Get posters made up, contact the local TV news people and see if you can get an appeal out for information on anyone who saw her between the time she left the Black Bull just before three and the time she met her friends in the Cross Keys at seven. And stress the fact that even though she was technically only sixteen, she looked older. Men will certainly remember if they saw her. Check local buses and taxis. Get DC Templeton to organize a house-to-house of the area around the Black Bull. Maybe we'll even get reinforcements. Who knows? We might get lucky. Maybe someone saw Clough handing over a gram of coke to her.'

'Okay.'

'And there's another thing.'

'What's that?'

'I had a visit from a DI Dalton this morning. Northumbria CID. It's about the Charlie Courage business. Seems there's some connection with a hijacked van up north. Seeing as you did the preliminary interviews at Daleview, I'd like you to have a quick chat with him before you hand over the file to DS Hatchley. He might be able to help us. He's staying at the Fox and Hounds. You never know. Maybe if you're lucky he'll even buy you a pint.'

That evening at home, Banks tossed a few clothes into his overnight bag, followed by Evelyn Waugh's *The Ordeal of Gilbert Pinfold* and his Renee Fleming and Captain Beefheart tapes. He would have to buy a portable CD player, he decided; it was becoming too time-consuming and expensive to tape everything, and CD timings were getting more difficult to match with tape lengths.

When he had finished packing, he phoned Brian, who answered on the third ring.

'Hi, Dad. How's it going?'

'Fine. Look, I'm going to be down your way again this weekend. Any chance of your being around? I'll be pretty busy, but I'm sure we can fit in lunch or something.'

'Sorry,' said Brian. 'We've got some gigs in Southampton.'

'Ah, well, you can't blame a father for trying. One of these days, maybe. Take care, and I hope you're a big success.'

'Thanks. Oh, Dad?'

'Yes?'

'You remember that bloke you were asking about a while back, the ex-roadie?'

'Barry Clough?'

'That's him.'

'What about him?'

'Nothing, really, but I was talking to one of the producers at the recording studio, name of Terry King; old geezer like you, been around a long time, since punk. You know; the Sex Pistols, the Clash, that sort of thing? Surely you must remember those days?'

'Brian,' said Banks, smiling to himself, 'I even remember Elvis. Now cut the ageism and get to the point.'

'It's nothing, really. Just that he remembered Clough. Called himself something else, then, one of those silly punk names like Sid Vicious – Terry couldn't remember exactly what it was – but it was him, all right. Apparently he got fired from his roadie job.'

'What for?'

'Bootlegging live concerts. Not just the band he worked with, but all the big names.'

'I see.' Banks remembered the booming business in bootleg LPs in the seventies. First Bob Dylan, Jimi Hendrix, the Doors and other popular bands were all bootlegged, and none of them made a penny from the illegal sales. The same thing also happened later with some of the punk bands. Not that any of them needed the money, and most of them were too stoned

213

to notice, but that wasn't the point. Clough's employers *had* noticed and given him the push.

'Like I said, it's not much. But he says he's heard this Clough bloke is a gangster now. A tough guy. Be careful, Dad.'

'I will. I'm not exactly a five-stone weakling myself, you know.'

'Right. Oh, and there's one more thing.'

'Yes?'

'There's this car a mate of mine's selling. Only three years old, got its MOT and everything. I got another—'

'Brian, what do you want?'

'Well, I've got the asking price down a couple of hundred from what it was, but I was wondering, you know, if you could see your way to helping me out?'

'What? Me help out my rich and famous rock-star son?'

Brian laughed. 'Give us a break.'

'How much do you need?'

'Three hundred quid would do nicely. I'll let you have it back when I *am* rich and famous.'

'All right.'

'You're sure?'

'That's what I said, isn't it?'

'That's great! Thanks, Dad. Thanks a lot. I mean it.'

'You're welcome. Talk to you later.'

Banks hung up. Three hundred quid he could ill afford. Still, he would come up with it somehow. After all, he had saved a bundle by missing out on Paris, and he had given Tracy a bit of spending money that weekend. He remembered how much he had wanted a car when he was young; the kids with cars seemed to get all the girls. He had finally bought a rusty old VW Beetle when he was at college in London. It lasted him the length of his course there, then clapped out on the North Circular one cold, rainy Sunday in January, and he hadn't got another one until he and Sandra were married. Yes, he'd find a way to help Brian out.

Next, Banks tried Tracy's number and was surprised when she answered right away: 'Dad! I've been wanting to talk to you. I just heard about Mr Riddle's daughter on the news. Are you all right? I know you didn't get along with him, but . . . Did you know her?'

'Yes,' said Banks. Then he told Tracy the bare details about going to London to find Emily instead of going with her to Paris that weekend.

'Oh, Dad. Don't feel guilty for doing someone a favour. I was disappointed at first, but Damon and I had the most wonderful time.'

I'll bet you did, thought Banks, biting his tongue.

Tracy went on. 'All I heard was that she died after taking an overdose of cocaine in the Bar None, and they're all saying she lived a pretty wild life. Is it something to do with what happened in London?'

'I don't know,' said Banks. 'Maybe.'

'That's terrible. Was it deliberate?'

'Could have been.'

'Do you have any idea who . . .? No, I know I shouldn't ask.'

'It's all right, love. We don't at the moment. A few leads to follow, that's all. I'm going back to London tomorrow. I just wanted to talk to you first, see if you were still on for Christmas.'

'Of course. I wouldn't miss it for the world.'

'Good.'

'She was only sixteen, wasn't she?'

'That's right.'

Tracy paused. 'Look, Dad . . . I just want you to know . . . I mean, I know you worry about me sometimes. I know you and Mum worried about me when we were all together, but you didn't really need to. I'm . . . I mean, I never did anything like that.'

'I know you didn't.'

'No, Dad. You don't *know*. You can't *know*. Even if you knew what signs to look for, you weren't there. I don't mean to be nasty about it. I know about the demands of your job and all, and I know you loved us, but you just *weren't there*. Anyway, I'm telling you the truth. I know you think I've always been little Miss Goody Two-shoes, but it's not true. I did try smoking some marijuana once, but I didn't like the way it made me feel. And once a girl gave me some Ecstasy at a dance. I didn't like that, either. It made my heart beat too fast and all I did was sweat and feel frightened. I suppose you could say I'm a failure as far as drugs are concerned.'

'I'm glad to hear it.' Banks wanted to ask if she'd been sexually active at fourteen, too, but he didn't think it would be a fair question to put to his daughter. She would tell him what she wanted when she wanted to.

'Anyway,' Tracy went on, 'I'm sure you're very busy. And I'm sure if anyone's going to catch him, it'll be you.'

Banks laughed. 'I appreciate your confidence in me. Take care, love. Talk to you soon.'

'Bye, Dad.'

Banks hung up the phone gently and let the silence enfold him again. He always had that same empty, lonely feeling after he'd spoken to someone he loved over the telephone, as if the silence had somehow become charged with that person's absence. He shook it off. It was a mild enough night outside and he still had time to go to his little balcony by the falls for a cigarette and a finger or two of Laphroaig.

10

'Barry Clough,' said Detective Superintendent Richard 'Dirty Dick' Burgess, chewing on a piece of particularly tough steak. 'Now there's an interesting bloke.'

It was Saturday lunchtime, and Banks and Burgess were sitting in a pub just off Oxford Street, the air around them laced with smoke and conversation. It was a mild day, much warmer than the last time Banks had been to London in early November. The pub was crowded with Christmas shoppers taking a break, and one brave couple actually sat at a table outside. Burgess was drinking lager and lime, but Banks had only coffee with his chicken-in-a-basket. He had a busy day ahead and needed to stay alert.

He had phoned Burgess before leaving Eastvale that morning. If anyone could uncover information on Clough, it was Dirty Dick Burgess. He had recently got himself into a bit of trouble for dragging his feet over the investigation into the murder of a black youth. As a result, he'd been shunted off to the National Criminal Intelligence Service, where he couldn't do so much harm. It didn't seem to bother Burgess that he had been identified as a racist; he took it all in his stride with his usual lack of concern.

The two had known each other for years, and while they had tentatively come to enjoy each other's company, their relationship remained mostly confrontational. Banks especially didn't share Burgess's strong right-wing leanings, nor did he concur with his racist and sexist opinions. In his turn, Burgess had called Banks a 'pinko'. About the only thing they had in common was that both were from working-class backgrounds. Burgess, though, unlike Banks, was the Margaret Thatcher kind of working-class lad who had come to the fore in the eighties; someone who had triumphed over a deprived background, then devoted himself to the pursuit of material benefits, and felt no sympathy or solidarity with any of his class who couldn't or wouldn't follow suit.

Banks, or so he hoped, retained some compassion for his fellow man, especially the downtrodden, and occasionally even the criminal. It was difficult to maintain such a view, being a copper all those years, but he had sworn to himself not long after finding Dawn Wadley's dismembered body in a Soho alley that as soon as he stopped caring, he would quit. He had thought that his move from the Met to the softer patch of Eastvale would have made life easier, but somehow, without the sheer volume of human misery that had been his lot in the city, every case seemed to take more of a toll on him. It was similar to the way people found it hard to respond to the deaths of millions of foreigners in a flood or an earthquake, but fell to pieces when a kindly old neighbour was run over.

'Any man's death diminishes me, because I am involved in Mankind,' as John Donne had said, and Banks knew exactly what he meant.

The odd thing about working day-in, day-out against murderers, pimps, drug dealers, muggers and the rest was that you could distance yourself. Partly you did it by developing a dark sense of humour, telling tasteless jokes at crime scenes, getting pissed with the lads after attending a post-mortem, and partly you just built a wall around your feelings. But in Eastvale, where he had more time to devote himself to important cases – especially murders – his defences had been slowly eroded until he was nothing but a bundle of raw nerve ends. Each case took a little bit more of his soul, or so he felt.

Banks remembered some of the victims, especially the

young ones – Deborah Harrison, Sally Lumb, Caroline Hartley. He had come to know and care about all these victims. Even Gloria Shackleton, murdered long before Banks had been born, had come to obsess him only a few months ago. And now Emily Riddle. It didn't matter what anyone said about not becoming personally involved with cases, Banks thought. You *had* to be personally involved; there had to be something more at stake than mere crime statistics.

'Problem is,' Burgess went on, 'we don't really know enough about him.'

'Any form?'

Burgess sniffed. 'Minor drug bust in seventy-four. Half a pound of Nepalese black. Said it was for his own consumption. Well, I believed him – I could go through that much in a week easily – but the magistrates didn't. They gave him eighteen months, out in nine.'

'Is he still dealing?'

'Not that we know of. If he is, he's not in the premier league.' Burgess pushed his plate away. 'Too bloody tough for my teeth,' he said. Apart from his crooked and stained teeth, Banks noticed, Burgess seemed in better shape than the last time they had met. He had even lost a little weight. He still had his greying hair tied in a ponytail, which irritated Banks, who thought that middle-aged men with ponytails looked like prize wankers, and his grey eyes were as sharp, as cynical and as world-weary as ever.

The last time they had met, Banks remembered, was in Amsterdam over a year ago, when Burgess had got pissed and fallen in a canal. Banks had helped him out and taken him back to the hotel, and the last he had seen of him, Burgess was trailing dirty canal water across the lobby, his shoes squelching as he went, head held high, trying to walk in a straight line, with dignity. He had been wearing the same scuffed leather jacket he was wearing today.

'How does he pay for that bloody great villa of his?' Banks asked.

'Which one?'

'Little Venice. You mean he's got more than one?'

'Sure. There's two that we know of. The one in Little Venice and one outside Arenys de Mar, in Spain.'

'So where does his money come from?'

'He's a gangster.'

'So I've heard. I didn't know they were back in fashion.'

'They never really went away. They just adapted, changed names, switched rackets.'

'What sort of a gangster is Clough, then?'

Burgess lit one of his small cigars before answering. 'First off,' he said, 'he's got a legitimate front. He owns a very successful bar in Clerkenwell. Popular with the City boys. Gets some good bands, serves first-class food and booze. You know the type of place: "How about a little coke and crème caramel to end the perfect evening, darling?" Then they go off home for the perfect shag. We know he's into all sorts of things, but we've never been able to get him on anything. He runs things, delegates, doesn't get his hands dirty. Basically, he bankrolls dodgy or downright criminal operations and rakes in a big cut. As far as we know, he made a pile of money managing and promoting bands in the music business years ago and invested it in a life of crime.'

'Bootlegging.'

'What?'

'That's how he made his pile,' Banks explained. 'Making bootleg recordings of live concerts, getting them pressed and selling them.'

Burgess narrowed his eyes. 'You seem to know a lot about him. Sure you want me to go on?'

Banks smiled. 'It's a matter of making a little go a long way. That's *all* I know. Anyway, it looks as if it paid off.'

'Big time.'

'What kinds of things is he interested in now, if it's not drugs?'

'All sorts. I'll give him his due; he's innovative. Prefers newer, safer rackets to the old true, tested and tried. That's why I don't see him dealing drugs. Taking them, yes, but not dealing them. Not his style. You won't find him running girls or protection rackets, either. Not Barry Clough. Guns, though, now there's another matter. Remember that business with the reactivated firearms a year or so back? Up around your neck of the woods, wasn't it?'

'Thirsk,' said Banks. 'Yes, I remember.' Undercover policemen posing as London gangsters had arrested four men on charges of conspiracy to transfer firearms and ammunition, and for selling prohibited weapons. Since the stricter gun laws introduced after the Dunblane school massacre, firearms had become harder to get because the risk attached to possessing or selling them was far greater. That also put their price up. To fill the gap, workshops like the one near Thirsk sprang up. It took about two hours to reactivate an Uzi that had been disabled for legal sale to a collector, and you could sell it for about £1,250. Tanfoglio pistols went for about a grand apiece. Discount for bulk. Needless to say, the weapons were especially popular with drug gangs.

'We thought we had Clough on that but we couldn't prove he was involved.'

'What made you think he was?'

'Circumstantial evidence. Titbits from informers. He'd made a couple of trips to the area shortly prior to the arrests. One of the men arrested had been observed visiting Clough's house. He was a collector of disabled firearms himself. He had connections in both the drugs and firearms worlds. That sort of thing.'

Banks nodded. He knew what Burgess meant. You could know it in your bones that a man was guilty of something, but if you couldn't get enough evidence to interest the Crown

Prosecution Service, then you might as well forget it. And the CPS was notoriously difficult to interest in anything other than a dead cert. He also remembered the guns in the case on Clough's wall. Still, not evidence.

'What happened?'

'We leaned on him a bit. Not me personally, you understand, but we leaned. I think he shied away from that line of business, at least for a while. Besides, I think he found out that it's not as lucrative as he'd hoped. Reactivating guns is more trouble than it's worth, when you get right down to it. And it's not as if they aren't still being smuggled in by the cartload. Christ, I know where you could buy an Uzi for fifty quid not twenty minutes from here.'

'And after that?'

'We suspect, and you know what I mean when I stress that it's just a suspicion, don't you?' Burgess flicked some ash and winked at Banks. 'We *suspect* that, for one thing, he's behind one of the big smuggling operations. Booze and fags. High profit, low risk. You might not know this, Banks, but I've done some work with Customs and Excise, and about eight per cent of cigarettes and five per cent of beer consumed in this country are smuggled. Have you any idea what sort of profits we're talking about here?'

'Given the amount people smoke and drink, I should imagine it's pretty huge.'

'Understatement.' Burgess pointed his cigar at Banks. 'A player like Clough might employ fifty people to get the stuff from warehouses in Europe to his retail outlets over here. Once they get it through customs at Dover, they go to distribution centres – industrial estates, business parks and the like – then their fleet of salesmen pick up their supplies and sell to the retailers. Shops, pubs, clubs, factories. Even schools. Christ, we've even got fucking pet shops and ice-cream vans selling smuggled booze.'

'And Clough's in it that big?'

'So we *suspect*. I mean, it's not as if he drives any of the freighters himself, or drops off a carton or two at the local chippie. Whenever Clough comes back from a month at his villa in Spain you can be damn certain he's clean as a surgeon's scalpel. It really pisses me off, Banks, that when a law-abiding citizen such as me drinks his smuggled French lager there's probably a share of the profits going to a gangster like Clough.'

'So what have you got on him?'

'Precious little, again. Mostly circumstantial. Earlier this year customs stopped a lorry at Dover and found seven million cigarettes. Seven fucking million. Would've netted a profit of about half a million quid on the black market – and don't ask me how much that is in euros. Clough's name came up in the investigation.'

'And what else is he into?'

Burgess flicked some more ash on the floor. 'Like I said, we don't know the full extent of his operations. He's cagey. Has a knack of staying one step ahead, partly because he contracts out and partly because he operates outside London, setting up little workshops like that one near Thirsk and then moving on before anyone's figured out what he's doing. He uses phony companies, gets others to front for him, so his name never appears on any of the paperwork.'

Something in what Burgess had said rang a bell for Banks. It was a very faint one, a very poor connection, but it wasn't an impossible one. 'Ever heard of PKF Computer Systems?' he asked.

Burgess shook his head.

'Bloke called Courage? Charlie Courage?'

'No.'

'Jonathan Fearn?'

'Nope. I can look them up if you like.'

'Doesn't matter,' said Banks. 'One's dead and the other's in a coma. Would murder be Clough's style at all?'

'I'd say a man who does as high a volume of crime as he

does has to maintain a certain level of threat, wouldn't you? And if he does that, he has to make good on it once in a while or nobody's intimidated. He has to keep his workers in line. Nothing like a nice little murder for keeping the lads focused.' He slurped down some lager and lime. 'Two weeks after Clough's name came up in connection with that seized shipment, two known baddies got shot in Dover city centre. No connection proven, of course, but they were business rivals. It's a fucking war zone down there.'

Banks pushed aside the rest of his chicken, which was too dry, and lit a cigarette. He fancied a pint but held off. If he was going to see Barry Clough tonight, as he planned, then he'd need to be sharp, especially after what Burgess had said. 'What about women?' he asked.

Burgess frowned. 'What do you mean?'

'From what I can gather, Clough's a bit of a ladies' man.'

'So I've heard. And apparently he likes them young.'

'Has he ever been suspected of hurting or killing a woman?'

'Nope. Doesn't mean he hasn't done it and got away with it, though. Like I said, Clough's good at staying ahead of the game. The thing is, with someone like him, people don't like to come forward and make themselves known, if you catch my drift.'

'Right.' Banks sipped some black coffee. It tasted bitter, as if it had been left on the burner too long. Still, it beat instant. 'Heard of Andrew Handley?'

'Andy Pandy? Sure. He's one of Clough's chief gofers.'

'Dangerous?'

'Could be.'

'Anything on him hurting women?'

'Not that I know of. Is this about Jimmy Riddle's daughter?'

'Yes,' said Banks. Emily Riddle's murder was all over the newspapers that morning. As Banks had guessed, it hadn't taken the press long to ferret out that she had died of cocaine laced with strychnine, and that was far bigger news than another boring drug overdose.

'You're SIO on that?'

'Yes.'

Burgess clapped his hands together and showered ash on the remains of his steak. 'Well, bugger me!'

'No thanks. Not right after lunch,' said Banks. 'What's so strange about that?'

'Last I heard, Jimmy Riddle had you suspended. I had to pull your chestnuts out of the fire.'

'It was you who put them in there in the first place with all that cloak-and-dagger bollocks,' said Banks. 'But thanks all the same.'

'Ungrateful cunt. Think nothing of it. Now he's got you working on his daughter's case. What's the connection? Why you?'

Banks told him about finding Emily in London.

'Why'd you do that? To get Riddle off your back?'

'Partly, I suppose. At least in the first place. But most of all I think it was the challenge. I'd been on desk duties again for a couple of months after the Hobb's End fiasco, and it was real work again. It was also a bit of a rush going off alone, working outside the rules.'

Burgess grinned. 'Ah, Banks, you're just like me when you get right down to it, aren't you? Crack a few skulls?'

'I didn't need to.'

'Did you fuck her? The kid?'

'For Christ's sake,' said Banks, his teeth clenching. 'She was sixteen years old.'

'So. What's wrong with that? It's legal. Tasty, too, I'll bet.'

It was at times like this Banks wanted to throttle Burgess. Instead, he just shook his head and ignored the comment.

Burgess laughed. 'Typical. Knight in bloody shining armour, aren't you, Banks?'

That was what Emily had called him in the Black Bull, Banks remembered. 'Not a very successful one,' he said.

Burgess took a long drag on his cigar. He inhaled, Banks noticed. 'She was sixteen going on thirty, from what I've heard on the grapevine.'

'What have you heard?'

'Just that she was a crazy kid, bit of an embarrassment to the old man.'

'That's true enough.'

'So he wanted you to head off any trouble at the pass?'

'Something like that.'

'Any ideas?'

'I'd have to put Barry Clough very high on my list.'

'That why you're here? To rattle his cage?'

'It *had* crossed my mind. I'm thinking of paying him a visit tonight.'

Burgess stubbed out his cigar and raised his eyebrows. 'Are you indeed? Fancy some company?'

It was a different bridge, but almost a repeat of his previous trip, Banks thought, as he walked across Vauxhall Bridge on his way to visit Kennington. He looked at his watch: almost three. Ruth had been at home last time; he just hoped she had a Saturday routine she stuck to.

As it turned out, he needn't have worried. Ruth answered the intercom at the first press of the button and buzzed him up.

'You again,' she said, after letting him into the room. 'What is it this time?'

Banks showed her his warrant card. 'I've come about Emily.'

A look of triumph shone in her eyes. 'I knew there was something fishy about you! I told you, didn't I, last time you were here. A copper.'

'Ruth, I was here unofficially last time. I apologize for

pretending to be Emily's father – not that you believed me anyway – but it seemed to be the best way to get the job done.'

'End justifies the means? Typical police mentality, that is.'

'So you knew her real name?'

'What?'

'You didn't seem at all surprised when I called her Emily just now.'

'Well, that's the name they used in the papers yesterday.'

'But you already knew that, didn't you?'

'Yeah, I knew her real name. She told me. So what? I respected her right not to want to use it. If she wanted to call herself Louisa Gamine, it was fine with me.'

'Can I sit down?'

'Go ahead.'

Banks sat. Ruth didn't offer him tea this time. She didn't sit down herself, but lit a cigarette and paced. She seemed edgy, nervous. Banks noticed that she had changed her hair colour; instead of black it was blonde, still cropped to within half an inch of her skull. It didn't look a hell of a lot better and only served to highlight the pastiness of her features. She was wearing baggy jeans with a hole in one knee and a sort of shapeless blue thing, like an artist's smock: the kind of thing you wear when you're by yourself around the house and you think nobody's going to see you. Ruth didn't seem unduly concerned about her appearance, though; she didn't excuse herself to change or apply make-up. Banks gave her credit for that. The music was playing just a little too loud: Lauryn Hill, by the sound of it, singing about her latest misadventures.

'Why don't you sit down and talk to me?' Banks asked.

Ruth glared at him. 'I don't like being lied to. I told you last time. People always seem to think they can just walk right over me.'

'Once again, I apologize.'

Ruth stood a moment glaring at him through narrowed

eyes, then she turned the music down, sat opposite him and crossed her legs. 'All right. I'm sitting. Happy now?'

'It's a start. You know what happened?'

'I told you. I read about it in the paper, and saw it on telly.' Then her hard edges seemed to soften for a moment. 'It's terrible. Poor Emily. I couldn't believe it.'

'I'm sorry. I know you were a friend of hers.'

'Was it . . . I mean . . . were you there? Did you see her?'

'I was at the scene,' said Banks, 'and yes, I saw her.'

'What did she look like? I don't know much about strychnine, but . . . was it, you know, really horrible?'

'I really don't think that's a good idea—'

'Was it quick?'

'Not quick enough.'

'So she suffered?'

'She suffered.'

Ruth looked away, sniffled and reached for a tissue from the low table beside her. 'Sorry,' she said. 'It's not like me.'

'I just want to ask you a few questions, Ruth, then I'll go. Okay?'

Ruth blew her nose, then nodded. 'I don't see how I can help you, though.'

'You'd be surprised. Did you speak to Emily after she left London?'

'Only on the phone a couple of times. I think when she split up with this Barry she felt a bit guilty about neglecting me. Not that I cared, mind you. It was *her* life. And people always do. Neglect me, that is.'

'When was the last time you talked?'

'A week, maybe two weeks before . . . you know.'

'Was there anything on her mind?'

'What do you mean?'

'Did she confide any of her fears in you?'

'Only about that psycho she'd been living with.'

'Barry Clough?'

'Yeah, him.'

'What did she say about him?'

'She didn't give me any gory details, but she said he'd turned out to be a real waste of space, and she sounded worried he was going to come after her. Did she steal some money from him?'

'Why do you ask that?'

Ruth shrugged. 'Dunno. He's rich. It's the sort of thing she'd do.'

'Did she ever steal from you?'

'Not that I know of.' Ruth managed a quick smile. 'Mind you, I can't say I've much worth stealing. Someone ripped the silver spoon out of my mouth at a pretty early age. I've always had to work hard just to make ends meet.'

'When did you miss your driving licence, Ruth?'

'My licence? How did you know about that? It was ages ago.'

'How long?'

'Five, six months?'

'While Emily was here?'

'Yes, just after, but . . . you don't mean . . . Emily?'

'When the report came to me over the phone, the first officer on the scene told me the victim was Ruth Walker. He'd read the name off her driving licence.'

'Bloody hell. So that's what happened. I just thought I'd lost it. I do lose things. Especially bits of paper.'

'What did you do?'

'Applied for a new one. The new kind with the photo on it. But what possible use could the old one be to Emily?'

'I think she used it to help her get one of those proof-of-age cards the clubs give out. She wouldn't have had much difficulty from what I've heard. They practically give them to pretty young girls, whether they've got any proof in the first place or not. The card has her photo on it, but your name and, I assume, your date of birth. Twenty-third of February, 1977.'

'Bloody hell.' Ruth shook her head. 'I knew nothing about it.'

'And maybe she also wanted to drive a car.'

'She was too young to learn.'

'That doesn't always stop people.'

'I suppose not.'

'Some of the most skilled car thieves I've met have been between ten and thirteen.'

'You'd know about that.'

'What did she say about Barry Clough?'

'Just that she thought she'd pissed him off big time when she left without saying goodbye, and he wasn't the kind of man just to let it go by.'

'Did she sound scared?'

'Not really scared. Bit nervous, maybe, in a giggly sort of way. She could put a brave face on things, could Louisa. Emily.'

'When did she tell you her real name?'

'Shortly after she came to stay with me. She asked me not to tell anyone, that she wanted to be called Louisa, so I respected her wishes.'

'Did you tell Clough what her real name was?'

Ruth jerked forward. 'Give me a break! Why would I do something like that?'

'Only asking. So you didn't?'

'No fucking way.'

'Has he been in touch with you at all, asking about her?'

'No. I haven't seen anything of him at all.'

'What about Craig? Did you tell him?'

'No, but he might have known. She might have told him herself.'

'But you didn't?'

'I didn't tell anyone. I can keep a secret.'

Banks lit a cigarette and leaned back in the armchair. 'How have you been, Ruth?'

She frowned. 'What do you mean?'

'Just a simple question. Healthy? Happy?'

'I'm doing all right. As well as can be expected. Why do you want to know?'

'How's work?'

'Fine.'

'What exactly is it that you do?'

'Computers. It's pretty boring stuff.'

'But steady? Well paid?'

'It's steady. That's about the best you can say.'

'Do you own a car?'

Ruth got up and Banks followed her to the window. 'There,' she said pointing, 'that clapped-out cream Fiesta down there.'

Banks smiled. 'I had one like that a few years back,' he said. 'Cortina, actually. Nobody believed I could possibly be driving such a thing. They'd stopped making them years ago. But it was a good car, while it lasted.'

'Well,' said Ruth, folding her arms at the window. 'It'll have to last me a few years longer, that's for sure.'

They sat down again. 'Been on any trips lately?' Banks asked.

'Nope.'

'Seeing anyone?'

'What's it to you?'

'Just being friendly.'

'Well, you don't have to be. Remember, you're a copper and I'm a suspect.'

'Suspect? What makes you think that?'

A nasty smile twisted Ruth's features. 'Because I know you coppers. You wouldn't be here otherwise, asking all sorts of questions. No matter. I didn't do it. You can't blame me.'

'I'm not trying to. How do you know coppers, Ruth? Ever been arrested?'

'No. I read the papers, though, watch the news. I know what racist, sexist bastards you are.'

Banks laughed. 'You must be thinking of Dirty Dick.'

'What?'

'Never mind. Seeing as how you think you're a suspect, though, you might as well tell me where you were on Thursday.'

'I was here. At home.'

'Not at work?'

'I had a cold. Still have. I was off Thursday and Friday. Does that mean I've got no alibi?'

'But you haven't been on any trips recently?'

'No. I told you. I haven't been anywhere. And for your information, no, I'm not screwing anyone, either. You've got to be careful these days. It's a lot different from when *you* were young, you know. We've got AIDS to think about. The worst you had to worry about was crabs or a dose of clap. Either way, it wasn't going to kill you.'

Banks smiled. 'I suppose you're right. Did you go up to visit Emily in Yorkshire over the past month?'

'No.'

'Why not?'

'Too busy at work. Besides, she never asked me.' Ruth snorted. 'I can see why now.'

'Why?'

'It said in the paper that her father's a chief constable and her mother's a solicitor. They don't sound exactly the sort of people she'd want to introduce someone like me to.'

'Oh, I don't know,' said Banks. 'You shouldn't be too hard on yourself.'

Ruth flushed. 'I know what I am.'

'Do you know Emily's mother at all? Rosalind?'

'No. Why should I?'

'Just wondering.'

'Like I said, she'd hardly take me home to meet her mum and dad.'

'I suppose not. So you never spoke with her?'

'She answered the phone a couple of times when I called.'

'So the two of you *have* spoken?'

'Only to say hello, like, and ask for Emily.'

'Rosalind didn't ask you any questions?'

'No. Just my name, that's all.'

'And you told her?'

'Why wouldn't I? What is this? Are you trying to make out her mother killed her now?'

'I hardly think so. Just trying to get things clear, that's all. Have you seen anything of Craig?'

Ruth made herself more comfortable in the armchair, sitting with her legs curled under. 'As a matter of fact, he phoned me after he heard about Emily on the news yesterday morning. We had lunch together. He had to come into town.'

'What for? To pay a call at GlamourPuss?'

'How would I know? He didn't say.'

'How did he seem?'

'Fine, I guess. I mean, we were both upset. Emily breezed in and out of both our lives. But if you've met her, then you'd know she certainly leaves an impression. The thought of somebody doing that to her . . . it's too much to bear. You *are* certain it wasn't just an accident, aren't you? An overdose?'

'We're certain.'

'Like I said, we were . . . you know, we couldn't believe it. What about her father?'

'What about him?'

'Do you think he might have done it? I mean, she used to go on about how horrible he was, and if anyone can get hold of drugs and poisons, it's the police.'

'Remember, he's the one who wanted her back.'

'Yes,' said Ruth, leaning forward and lowering her voice to a whisper. 'You told me that. But *why* did he want her back? Have you ever thought about that?'

Though it was Saturday, there was no time off for Eastvale CID that weekend. It would cost a fortune in overtime, but ACC

McLaughlin and Superintendent Gristhorpe would hardly hesitate to approve the budget; there would be no stinting on this case. If Annie hadn't seen the body for herself, she might have felt a little uncomfortable about the favouritism of it all, but having seen it, she knew that even if the victim had been a pox-ridden whore she would have been working on the case today, and working for nothing if she had to.

And Banks, the SIO, was down in London. Which left Annie in charge. She understood that he had to go and follow the leads he already knew about, but it left her with an unbearably heavy load, especially after so little sleep, and she couldn't help but still feel irritated with him. After their little talk the previous day, she had softened towards him, but she still couldn't help but feel that he was holding something back. She didn't know why or what it was about – something to do with Emily's sojourn in London, she suspected – but it gave her the feeling that he knew something she didn't. And she didn't like that.

Already that morning she had called in at the incident room and found it the usual hive of activity. Winsome was sitting at the computer looking flustered as the pile of green sheets for entry into HOLMES rose quickly beside her, and Gavin Rickerd looked as if he had found his true calling in life making sure every scrap of information was neatly logged and numbered. He also looked as if he hadn't slept since the murder.

After that, Annie had organized the investigation into Emily's whereabouts between three and seven. She had ordered the posters the previous day and they were waiting when she got in. Banks had given her the photo he wanted used, and Annie thought it made Emily look a bit slutty. He said that was how people would remember her, and there was no point asking her parents for the sort of sanitized school photo or studio portrait they were likely to have. He also insisted that her description stressed that she looked older than her sixteen years.

The photo came above the question, 'HAVE YOU SEEN THIS GIRL?' and that in turn was followed by the description, the hours they were interested in, and a telephone number to contact. She had sent out half a dozen uniformed officers to fix them to hoardings and telegraph poles along all the main streets and in as many shop windows as they could manage. After that, the officers were engaged in conducting a house-to-house in central Eastvale and the area around the Black Bull. Despite the stolen driving licence, Emily didn't drive or have access to a car, as far as anyone knew, so the odds were that she had stayed in town. She could have taken a bus or a train, of course, so both stations were being thoroughly covered. There was every chance that a bus driver, fellow passenger or ticket inspector would remember her if she had travelled anywhere in the missing four hours.

Annie herself was set to go on the evening news, she remembered, with a little twinge of fear. She didn't like television, wasn't comfortable with it at all; no matter how serious and public-spirited your appearance was, you knew you were only there to make the presenter look good. But that was one little prejudice she would have to swallow if she were to get the appeal for information across.

It was close to lunchtime, Annie's first real chance that day to sit down at her own desk and do a bit of detective work, with Kevin Templeton making phone calls in the background. Though it was a long shot, she thought she should check and see if there were any other crimes with similar MOs, using cocaine laced with strychnine as a murder weapon. The PHOENIX system, set up by the National Criminal Records Office, offered her nothing. But then there was every chance this killer hadn't ever been convicted.

CATCHEM offered a few more options. Essentially, you could enter the victim details, stressing the salient features of the crime, and the system presented you with a potential scale of probability in several categories. After a little tinkering, Annie discovered that it was not necessarily likely that Emily knew her killer and that the killer might well be someone who felt slighted by society and had sadistic tendencies.

So much for computers.

She was just about to go to lunch when DS Hatchley came in. Annie was one of the few women in Eastvale Divisional HQ, or Western Divisional HQ, as it was now officially known, who didn't particularly mind Sergeant Hatchley. She thought he was all show, all Yorkshire bluff. She knew he wasn't soft underneath it all – Hatchley could be a hard man – but she didn't think he was as daft as he painted himself, either, or as prejudiced as he pretended to be. Some men, she had come to realize over the years, act the way they think they're supposed to act, especially in institutions such as the police and armed forces, while inside they might be desperate to be someone different, to be what they really *feel* they are. But they deny it. It is a kind of protective coloration. Hatchley was no pussy cat, but she thought he had a depth of understanding and sympathy that he didn't know quite what to do with. Marriage and fatherhood, too, had knocked off a few of the rough edges, or so she had heard.

Of course, despite Banks's little crack the previous day, Annie *hadn't* tracked down Dalton at the Fox and Hounds, and she felt a little guilty about palming Hatchley off on him. But not that guilty. Hatchley's eyes had certainly lit up at the prospect of a pint. Annie knew that if Dalton stayed around much longer, it was only a matter of time before they bumped into one another. He might even walk into the CID office this very moment, and then there would be no avoiding him. She didn't want to meet him, didn't want to talk to him, but she wasn't scared of him, and she was damned if she was going to go around the place trying to avoid him any more.

Hatchley said hello and grumbled about his aching feet.

'Where've you been?' Annie asked, feeling conciliatory after asking the favour of him. 'Not another alien abduction?'

'No such luck. Charlie bloody Courage. You know, some people just don't seem to care how much inconvenience they cause by getting themselves murdered.'

Annie smiled. 'Daleview again?'

'Aye. And about as much use as the time you were there.'

'Nobody saw the van?'

'On a Sunday night about ten o'clock? Nobody there.'

'Except Charlie.'

'Except the PKF people, who we're trying to find, Charlie himself, and Jonathan Fearn, the van driver, who's still in a coma in Newcastle.'

'Best way to be, in Newcastle,' said Annie.

'Nay, lass, it's not such a bad place. Some grand pubs there. Anyway, according to my sources, Charlie *did* know Jonathan Fearn, so we've got a connection there, however tenuous. Peas in a pod.'

'Maybe Courage lined up the job for him, thought he was doing him a favour?'

'Could be.'

'What did you find out from this DI . . . what's his name?'

'Dalton. DI Wayne Dalton. Seems a nice enough sort of bloke. You ask me, though, he's down on a weekend break.'

'In December?'

'Why not? The weather's not so bad. He's a bit of a rambler, apparently. Talking about going walking up Reeth way on Sunday morning. Says if he gets a nine o'clock start, he'll just about be ready to enjoy a pint and roast beef dinner at the Bridge in Grinton by twelve. The Bridge does a lovely roast beef and Yorkshire pud. Nice pint, too. Not that you'd catch me walking, mind you.'

Looking at him, Annie could believe it. Hatchley was about six foot two, with fine fair hair starting to thin a bit on top, the 'roast beef' complexion of someone with blood-pressure problems and about thirty or forty pounds excess baggage.

Her thoughts drifted to what he had said. Maybe that was

the answer. If Dalton were indeed planning a walk on Sunday, the odds were that there wouldn't be many people around. The middle of nowhere might be the best place to confront him. The idea excited her. It would mean making herself scarce on Sunday morning, but she thought she could probably manage that if she had everything in order by then. After all, with Banks away, she was in charge, so nobody was going to question her if she was out of the station for a few hours.

Dare she do it? What would she say if she stepped out in front of him on a deserted footpath? What would he do? Would he get physical, perhaps even try to get rid of her permanently? Having seen him again, Annie didn't think she need worry on that score.

But perhaps, when it came down to it, what worried her more than what he might do to her in a lonely place was what *she* might do to *him*.

The lights were blazing in Barry Clough's Little Venice villa when Banks and Burgess arrived shortly after eight that Saturday evening. Someone had even rigged up some Christmas lights on the façade of the house and put up a big tree in the garden.

'Bit early for a party, isn't it?' said Burgess, glancing at his watch.

'It's never too early for this lot,' said Banks. 'Their whole life is one long party.'

'Now, now, Banks. Isn't envy one of the seven deadly sins? Thou must not covet thy neighbour's arse, and all that.'

The iron gates were open, but a minder stood at the front door asking for invitations. He wasn't one of the two Banks had seen on his previous visit. Maybe Clough went through minders the way some people went through chauffeurs or maids. Hard to get good staff these days. Banks and Burgess showed him their warrant cards, but he clearly wasn't programmed to deal with anything like that. The way he screwed up his face in concentration as he looked at them, Banks wondered if he even got past the photographs.

'These mean we get in free,' said Burgess.

'I'll have to check with the boss. Wait here.'

The minder opened the door to go inside, and before he could close it, Burgess had followed him, with Banks not far behind. Banks realized he had to remember who he was with, what a loose cannon Burgess could be, and how he'd have to be on his toes. Still, he had invited the bastard, and it was good to have company you could depend on if the shit hit the fan. Burgess wasn't one to shirk trouble, no matter what form it came in.

There were people all over the place. All sorts of people. Young, old, tough-looking, arty-farty, well-dressed, scruffy, black, white – you name it. Music blasted through speakers that seemed to be positioned, discreetly out of sight, just about everywhere. Cream's 'Tales of Brave Ulysses', Banks noticed. How retro. Still, Clough would have been in his mid-twenties when he was a roadie for the punk band, which meant he had been in his teens when Cream came along, pretty much the same age as Banks. The air reeked of marijuana smoke.

The minder, who had noticed his mistake, elbowed his way roughly through the crowd in the hall, upsetting one or two less-than-sober guests whose drinks he spilled, and returned before the song finished with Barry Clough in tow.

The man himself.

'Did we come at a bad time, Barry?' Burgess asked.

After the initial cold anger had flitted across his chiselled features, Clough smiled with all the warmth of a piranha, clapped his hands and rubbed them together. 'Not at all. Not at all.' The black T-shirt he was wearing stretched tight over his biceps, and other muscles bulged at the chest and shoulders. All he needed for the complete look was a cigarette packet shoved up the sleeve. He wore no jewellery this time, and he was wearing his greying hair loose, tucked behind his ears on each side and hanging down to his shoulders. Banks was glad of that; he didn't think he could handle matching ponytails. The loose hair made Clough look younger and softened his appearance a little, but there was still no mistaking the icy menace in his eyes and the feral threat in his sharply angled features.

'Tales of Brave Ulysses' segued into 'swlabr'. Someone bumped into Banks from behind and muttered an apology. He turned and saw it was an attractive young girl, not much older than Emily had been. He vaguely recognized her from somewhere, but before he could remember, she had disappeared into the crowd.

'Is there somewhere quiet we can talk?' Banks asked Clough.

Clough appeared to consider the question for a moment, head cocked to one side, as if it were *his* decision, a not-so-subtle way of gaining a psychological edge in an interview. It was wasted on Banks. He jerked his head towards the stairs. 'Up there, for example,' he said.

Finally, Clough gave a minuscule nod and led them up the stairs. The first room they went into turned out to be occupied by a couple squirming and moaning on a pile of the guests' coats.

'It's unhygienic, that,' said Burgess. 'I go to a party, you know, I don't expect to go home with my raincoat covered in other people's love juices.'

Clough twisted one corner of his tight lips into what passed for a smile. 'They'll be too fucking stoned to notice,' he said, then he turned to Banks. 'You're not Drugs Squad, are you?'

Banks shook his head.

'It's just that there are a lot of important people here. Even a few coppers. Anything like that would be terribly messy. It would make the Stones' drugs bust look like a vicarage tea party.'

'I remember that one,' said Burgess. 'I wasn't there, but I always wanted to meet the young lady with the Mars bar.' A skinny young girl with a joint in her hand walked past them in the hall. 'In fact,' Burgess went on, grabbing the joint from her, 'some of us coppers quite enjoy a little recreational marijuana every now and then.' He took a deep toke, held the smoke a while, then let it out slowly. 'Paki black? Not bad.' Then he dropped the joint on the carpet and trod on it. 'Sorry, Banks,' he said when he'd done. 'Forgot you might have wanted a toke. On the other hand, you don't strike me as the toking type.'

'That's all right,' said Banks, who actually wouldn't have minded trying the stuff again on another occasion. But he was keeping his mind clear for Emily. Instead, he lit a cigarette.

'I see,' said Clough, staring down at the burnt spot on the carpet. He looked at Burgess. 'You're the bad cop and he's the good cop, right?'

'You don't know the half of it.'

A muscular young man with bleached-blond hair came up to them as they walked along the upstairs hall. 'Everything all right?' he asked Clough. 'Only I didn't think Mr Burgess here was on the invitation list.'

'Yeah, everything's fine and dandy. Maybe we should remember to add him in future. Seems like the life and soul of the party type to me.'

'Who's that?' Banks asked Burgess.

'Jamie Gilbert. Nasty little psycho. He's Barry's chief enforcer.'

Gilbert walked away laughing and Clough turned to them. 'Jamie's my *administrative assistant*,' he said.

'Well, that covers a multitude of sins,' Burgess shot back.

They finally found an empty room on the top floor. Completely empty. No furniture. White walls. White floorboards.

'Is this the best you can do?' said Banks.

Clough shrugged. 'Take it or leave it.'

At least it was protected for the most part from the music downstairs, and there was a light. Trying to conduct an interview while sitting on the floor wouldn't be very dignified, so they all chose to stand and lean against walls. It gave a strange sort of three-sided edge to the conversation.

Clough folded his arms and leaned back. 'So, what's it all about, then?'

'Don't tell me you don't know,' said Banks.

'Humour me. Last time I saw you, you were a friend of Emily's father.'

'I thought she was called Louisa.'

'No, you didn't. You knew what her name was. I only found out from the papers.'

'So you do know what happened?'

'I know she's dead, yes. Nothing to do with me.'

'Well, excuse us for thinking you're a good bet,' Burgess cut in. He had agreed to let Banks do most of the interviewing, but Banks knew he would be impossible to shut up completely. Clough stared at Burgess as if he was a piece of dog shit on his shoe. He didn't know that Burgess thrived on looks like that; they only made him better at his job.

Banks could make out the faint sounds of 'White Room' coming from downstairs. A 'best of' album, then, and not *Disraeli Gears*, as he had originally thought. The song was strangely appropriate, Banks thought, looking around. He wasn't sure what he expected from this interview. Certainly not for Clough to confess. If anything, he wanted to go away with the certainty that he had the right man in his sights, a gut feeling, if that was the best he could come up with, then begin the slow painstaking grind towards finding enough evidence to prove it, knowing that was only the beginning of the struggle.

Between the Crown Prosecution Service's reluctance to prosecute anyone, and the expensive barristers to whom Clough no doubt had access, there was every possibility that the man could get away with murder. Then what? Private vengeance?

Would Riddle do it himself or try to hire Banks to kill Clough the way he had used him to find Emily? Christ, though, you had to draw the line somewhere, and Banks thought he drew his at murder, no matter how despicable the victim. He wasn't too sure about Burgess, though; sometimes his cynical grey eyes took on the look of a killer.

'What we'd expect you to say,' Banks went on, 'but let's back up a little, first. How did you feel when Emily left you?'

'What do you mean, left me? I threw her out.'

'Not what I heard.'

'You heard wrong.'

'Okay.' Banks held his hand up. 'I can tell you're sensitive about it, so let's carry on. That final night, at the party, you pushed her into a room with Andrew Handley, right?'

'I pushed her nowhere. She was so stoned she could hardly walk. She stumbled in there herself.'

'But you don't deny she ended up in a room with Handley?'

'Why should I?'

'And that he tried to rape her?'

'Rape's a bit strong for what happened there.'

'*Attempted* rape, then? I don't think so.'

'Call it what you like. It was nothing to do with me. If Andy wanted to try it on with the little slut, that was his business.'

'And Emily escaped, ran away?'

'When did she tell you all . . . wait a minute.' Clough put one hand to the side of his head and made an expression of mock thinking. 'Wait a minute. I get it. After she left the party, she ran to you. Right? She knew where you were staying. She spent the night with you. That's why you're so upset. Tell me, Chief Inspector Banks, did you like it? Did you like that wet, scaly little tongue of hers licking your—'

Clough didn't finish the sentence because, as Banks struggled with the desire to lash out, Burgess beat him to it and gave Clough a backhander that sent him staggering towards the other wall. Typical Burgess, that; it was all right for him to tease Banks about sleeping with Emily, but not anyone else. Clough looked ready to fight back, muscles twitching, wiping a little thread of blood from the side of his mouth and giving Burgess one of those looks. But he regained his composure. And to give him his due, Banks thought, he didn't make any noise about lawsuits or revenge.

He stuck his tongue out and licked the blood from the corner of his mouth. 'Sorry,' he said, taking up his position against the wall again. 'I got a little carried away then. Very rude of me to speak ill of the dead like that. I apologize.'

Banks relaxed and offered him a cigarette. 'Apology accepted.'

Clough took it, and lit it with his own lighter. 'Thanks. Forgot mine downstairs. I was in the kitchen enjoying a nice glass of Château Margaux when you two arrived.'

'We'll make sure you get back to your wine before it turns to vinegar, Mr Clough,' said Banks. 'But no more flights of fancy, okay? Just answer the questions.'

'Yes, officer.' Clough smiled and cracked the crust of blood, sending another thin stream down his chin. He wiped it off with the back of his hand and went on smoking, blood staining the filter of his cigarette.

'After Emily left, did you check up on her, find out who she was, where she lived?'

'Why would I do that? I'd finished with her. She wasn't worth the effort.'

'So you didn't?'

'No.'

'Did you know who she was?'

'Not until I read it in the papers. Sleeping with a chief constable's daughter, eh?' He laughed. 'Wonder what my associates would say.'

'Your associates being criminals?'

'Now that's close to slander, that is.'

'Sue me.'

'Not worth the effort.'

'Not much is worth the effort with you, is it, Barry?'

'What can I say? Life goes on. Seize the moment. Live for the present.'

Banks looked at Burgess. 'And I never used to believe it when they said drugs could do you permanent damage.'

Burgess laughed.

'Where'd you get the strychnine, Barry?' Banks asked.

'The what?'

'You heard.'

'Never touch the stuff. I've heard it's bad for your health.'

Banks sighed. 'Is Andrew Handley here tonight? I wouldn't mind a word with him.'

'I'll bet you wouldn't. Unfortunately, no, he's not. In fact, he's no longer in my employ.'

'You fired him?'

'Let's say we came to a parting of the ways.'

'Have you got his address?'

'We weren't that close. It was only business.'

'Ever heard of PKF Computer Systems?'

'What?'

Was there just a slight flicker of recognition there? Clough off guard for a moment, letting it through? Banks knew he could easily be imagining it, but he thought his internal antennae had detected something. It wasn't as far-fetched as he had originally thought when Burgess told him about Clough's business practices. Move into a business park, do whatever crooked little thing it is you do and then, before anyone twigs on to it, move somewhere else. Which is where the white van rented by PKF, which didn't exist, was going when it was hijacked. The driver still in a coma. There were plenty of business parks and trading estates in the country, most of them fairly remote. They were good places to operate from. And Emily had said something about Clough visiting Eastvale. She had also thought she saw Jamie Gilbert there. Could there be a motive for killing her in that? Something she knew about Clough's business operations? She had a photographic memory, like her mother, Banks remembered.

'PKF,' Banks repeated.

'No, never heard of it. Why, should I have?'

'Charlie Courage?'

'I'm sure I'd remember someone with a name like that.'

'But you don't.'

'No.'

Banks could sense Burgess getting impatient across from him. Maybe he had a point; they seemed to be getting nowhere fast. 'Where were you last Thursday afternoon?' he asked.

'Why? Is that when it happened?'

'Just answer the fucking question.' Burgess did his world-weary voice.

Clough didn't even look at him. 'I was out of the country.'

'All day?'

'All week, actually. In Spain.'

'Nice for you. Sure you didn't nip up to Yorkshire for an hour or two?'

'Why would I want to do something like that? The weather's far better in Spain.'

'Weekend in the country, perhaps? Get your own back on Emily? After all, you don't like losing your prized possessions, do you?'

Clough laughed. 'If she told you that, then she had a pretty inflated opinion of herself.'

'A little overproof coke, Barry? Make her suffer?'

'You're mad.' Clough pushed himself away from the wall. 'Look, I've been patient with you, but this is absurd. Time for you to go wherever coppers crawl after dark and time for me to get back to my fun and games. Any more talking and my lawyer will be present.'

'Here, is he?'

Clough grinned. 'As a matter of fact, he is.' Then he opened the door and gestured for them to leave. They stood their ground a moment, then, there being no point staying any longer, Banks gave Burgess the nod, and they left. As Burgess was passing Clough on the way out, Banks heard Clough whisper, 'And don't think I'll forget what you did back there. I'll crush you for that, little man. I own people more important than you.'

Burgess gave a mock shudder. 'Ooh! I'm quaking in my boots.'

Then they pushed their way through the stream of people coming up and down the stairs, edged through the hall and said goodnight to the minder, who grunted. While they were still in his earshot, Banks said, 'Maybe we *should* call in the Drugs Squad, after all.'

The bouncer disappeared inside the house like a shot.

'Party-pooper,' said Burgess. 'Besides, they're probably already in there.'

They walked out of the gates and headed towards the canal. 'It was an interesting evening, though,' said Burgess. 'Very interesting indeed. Thanks for inviting me. I enjoyed myself.'

'My pleasure.'

'And, I must say, Banks. You surprise me.'

'What are you talking about?'

'Oh, listen to him. So modest. So naïve. The girl, Banks. The girl in the hotel room. You're the quiet one, aren't you? But you've got hidden depths. My admiration for you has just grown by leaps and bounds. I didn't realize how close to the mark I was.'

Banks gritted his teeth. They were near the Regent's Canal now, which gave Little Venice its name. For Banks, at that moment, it evoked fond memories not of Venice but of Amsterdam, and of Burgess flailing around cursing in the filthy water. Down the steps and a little push, a tiny trip. But no. That would be just *too* childish.

'Nothing happened,' Banks said.

'Like I said, leaps and bounds,' Burgess repeated, clapping his arm around Banks's shoulder. 'And, now, my old cock sparrow, the night is still young, I suggest we head for the nearest pub and get shit-faced. What do you say, Banks?'

Annie didn't stop to consider the folly of her actions – or their possible consequences – until she was following Wayne Dalton up Skelgate Lane, a narrow walled path to the north just before Reeth school.

An hour or so earlier, after asking Winsome Jackman and Kevin Templeton to cover for her, she had parked across North Market Street from the Fox and Hounds, then followed Dalton down to the market square, where he had parked his car. After that, she followed him to Reeth, about a half-hour drive away, and the rest was easy.

Though it was a perfect day for walking, there were few other cars parked on the cobbles outside the shops and none on the green itself. Annie saw a number of people who looked as if they were dressed for rambling. A few clouds marred the blue winter sky, blocking the sun occasionally as they floated by, but it was quite mild and there was very little wind.

Skelgate Lane was overgrown, stony and muddy in places after the recent rains. While Annie had put on suitable walking shoes, there were times, as she squelched through the unavoidable mud, when she thought her red wellies would have been more appropriate.

What the hell did she think she was doing anyway? she asked herself after the first half mile. The investigation into Emily Riddle's murder, of which she was DIO, was going full steam, still in its crucial early stages, and here she was leaving two DCs in charge while she took time out to settle old scores, or tilt at windmills. Her behaviour offended even her own sense of professionalism, but when it came right down to it, her profession was the reason she was doing it. The situation with Dalton was something she had to get resolved quickly, because it had become too much of a distraction.

She had dressed like an anonymous rambler, in a charcoal anorak, black jeans tucked into her grey woollen socks, sturdy walking shoes, hat and an ash stick. She wasn't carrying a rucksack, nor did a plastic folder of Ordnance Survey maps hang around her neck. Instead, she carried a small book of local walks, and when she stopped for a moment to refer to it, she saw where Dalton was likely to be going. It was five and a half miles of relatively easy walking, taking them along the daleside above the River Swale, then down and back along the river to Grinton, arriving there around lunchtime. She looked for a good vantage point where she might confront him and decided that it would be best to wait until they had doubled back over the swing bridge near Reeth. Then they would be near the old Corpse Way to Grinton.

She had two choices: either walk down to the swing bridge and wait a couple of hours for him to come by, or follow him at a safe distance. She decided on the latter course, partly because there were a number of possible diversions from the route. The Dales were criss-crossed by hundreds of footpaths, signposted or not, going off in every direction, not all of them listed in guidebooks. He could, for example, turn off by Calver Hill into Arkengarthdale for a different walk, or continue along the high dale to Gunnerside, though then it would take him much longer to get back to Grinton – more like for dinnertime rather than lunch.

Besides, even if she were only ten yards from him, he would never recognize her, not with the hat and the anorak, and not when he wasn't expecting to see her.

Annie had always marvelled at how, even in summer, you could walk for miles in the Dales and hardly see another soul.

In winter you were even less likely to bump into someone. Along the tops, after emerging from Skelgate Lane into open moorland, she passed a small group of ramblers, probably a club, going the other way. Everyone politely said good morning as they passed by. After that, she couldn't see a soul except Dalton, a good half mile or more ahead, wearing a distinctive red anorak. It certainly made him easy to keep in her sights.

The guidebook advised her to pause and enjoy views of Fremington Edge back in the east and Harkerside on the opposite side of the valley, but though she glanced occasionally at the cloud shadows drifting over the greenish-brown hillsides, with their distinctive patterns of drystone walls – one field shaped like a milk jug, another like a teacup – Annie was in no mood for sightseeing.

Still, up here on the heights looking down on the valley below reminded her of cliff walks around St Ives with her father when she was younger. How he used to point out examples of interesting perspectives, shapes, textures and colours in the landscape, how he was always stopping to sketch frantically in the book he carried with him, eyes and brain tuned to his fingers. At moments like those she might as well not have been there; she didn't exist.

All that was missing today was the crashing of the waves and the screeching of gulls. Instead, hares hopped through the spent heather, and grouse broke cover. The weather turned nasty for a few minutes along the daleside, with a brisk west wind whipping up and at one point blowing a brief hailstorm at her. She had to lean forward into the wind to make progress, looking up occasionally to see the red anorak in the distance.

By the time she came to the steep descent into the village of Healaugh, the wind and hail had all gone, and as she walked through the quiet streets she could almost believe it was summer. A man in a white coat stood selling meat and veg-etables to villagers from the back of a small van. Everyone paused and looked at her as she walked past. None of them smiled or said anything; they just stared. It was an odd feeling. They didn't exactly seem unfriendly, but aloof, a little mournful even, as if they were telling her that their world was not hers and never would be, that she was merely passing through it and she should keep going.

She did.

Shortly beyond the village, which was the turning point in the walk, the path led her through a field down to the riverside. She could see Dalton's red anorak ahead appearing and disappearing between the bare alders that lined the Swale. Empty brown seed cones still clung to many of the branches, making the trees look chocolate brown.

The closer she got, the more nervous and confused Annie became. She still wasn't physically afraid of him, but Dalton's arrival in Eastvale, and the memories it stirred, had played havoc with her usually calm emotional centre. For one thing, she didn't know what to say to him. What *did* you say to a man who had been a willing accessory to your rape, a man who would have raped you himself if you hadn't managed to wriggle free from his grasp and escape? How would he react? Perhaps, she began to think, this wasn't such a good idea after all. It would be easy enough just to turn left at the swing bridge and walk up to Reeth, where her car was parked on the cobbles by the green, and forget the whole thing, get back to work.

But she kept on going.

It was only a small bridge. At that point, the river meandered through meadowland where cows grazed. It was, however, a genuine swing bridge and Annie experienced a frisson of fear as she walked the wooden planks and felt it sway. While not exactly phobic, she had always been a little nervous of bridges, though she didn't know why.

Dalton had paused by the riverbank on the other side, about a hundred yards or so ahead, and he appeared to be watching her approach. Feeling a little dizzy, Annie stayed on the bridge and pretended to admire the view, waiting for him to carry on. But he didn't. He stayed where he was and kept on looking at her. Her heart was in her mouth. Did he recognize her? Had he known she was following him all along?

There was only one thing to do if she wasn't going to run. She walked through the gate at the far end of the bridge and along the grassy path to where he stood. All the way he kept looking at her, but she still didn't sense any recognition on his part. Her fear was quickly turning into anger. How *dare* he not recognize her after what he had done? She tried to take long deep breaths to keep herself calm and centred. They helped a little.

Finally, about five or six yards away from Dalton, she stopped and took off her hat, letting her wavy chestnut hair fall free to her shoulders. She saw the recognition now. He hadn't known who she was before, she could tell, but he did now. She even heard the sharp intake of his breath.

'You,' he said.

'Hello, Wayne,' she said. 'Yes, it's me. Nice to see you again.'

Banks awoke from a disturbing dream at about eight o'clock on Sunday morning. He had been walking in an unfamiliar landscape, which kept switching between rural and urban settings. There was a river somewhere, or perhaps a canal. Whatever it was, there was a sense in the dream that it was never far away. It was always raining and always twilight no matter where he was or how long he seemed to walk. Other people drifted by like shadows, but nobody he knew. He had the feeling that he was supposed to be following someone, but he didn't know who or why.

Suddenly he found himself on a green iron bridge, and a man was walking just in front of him. At that point, Banks felt panic gather, felt as if he couldn't breathe and wanted to wake up and break out of it. The man turned. He wasn't a monster, though, just a perfectly ordinary-looking man.

'I know you've been looking for me,' he said to Banks, smiling. 'My name's Graham Marshall. I was in the army. Then I had my hair cut. Now I'm in the rain. Emily's with me, too, but she can't appear to you right now.' Then he went on to tell a garbled life story of which Banks could remember nothing when he woke in a cold sweat to church bells ringing in the distance.

It was still dark outside, so Banks turned on the bedside light. He was in a small hotel near King's Cross, not the place he had stayed with Annie and Emily. Somehow, going back there hadn't seemed like a good idea.

When he had taken stock of himself, he realized with relief that he felt only mildly hung over. That was, he remembered, because he had declined the invitation to repair to Burgess's flat and drink whisky all night. Surely he wasn't getting wiser in his old age? Anyway, he was glad that all they'd done was visit a few pubs and down a few pints. It must have been a dull evening for Burgess, though; they hadn't got into any fights or picked up any women. Mostly, Burgess had talked about Clough, and Banks got the impression that even if he didn't manage to pin Emily's murder on Clough himself, the man's days of freedom were limited.

The only problem with Clough as a suspect, thought Banks, was that he stood to gain nothing by Emily's death. Still, there was always the chance that she had stolen from him, as Ruth Walker had suggested, or that she knew too much about his business activities, though Banks thought she would have told him if that were the case. It was also possible that Clough only *thought* she knew something she didn't. This was assuming, of course, that the whole matter was one of logic and profit. What if it wasn't? Clough was certainly capable of killing, and if Emily had humiliated him in any way, then he was probably capable of killing her out of sheer malice.

Banks got up and poured himself a glass of water. The beer and the dream had left him with a dry mouth. As he showered in the tiny stall, he put the Graham Marshall dream out of his mind and found himself thinking again of what Ruth had said, how her words had cast suspicion even on Riddle himself, someone Banks had completely overlooked as a suspect.

He found it hard to take it seriously that a man like Jimmy Riddle would deliberately give his daughter cocaine laced with strychnine, even if for some obscure reason he did want her dead. And her death had done nothing to free Riddle of the shame of her exploits; in fact, it had quite the opposite effect, and already the tabloids were raking up stories of the chief constable's daughter and her wild life. That wouldn't do his budding political career any good at all, or his standing in the force, either.

Then there was Rosalind Riddle. Banks had had a strange feeling about her right from the start, when Riddle first asked him to go to London and find Emily. Rosalind hadn't appeared to want Emily back home for some reason. More recently, Rosalind had denied ever hearing of Ruth Walker, yet Ruth said she had spoken to her on the telephone on several occasions. That probably meant nothing, Banks realized, merely a lapse of memory, a misheard name over a poor connection, but Rosalind's role in all this still nagged away at the back of his mind. She was holding something back; of that he was certain. Whether it was important to the investigation or not, he couldn't say. All families have secrets that can fester away behind their protective walls.

Banks decided for the moment to concentrate on the line of inquiry he was pursuing in London, where Emily had done most of her drug-taking and mixed with a rough crowd: primarily Clough, of course, who lied about everything; then Ruth Walker, who remained a bit of an enigma to him, yet seemed a woman embittered far beyond her years; and finally Craig Newton, hurt ex-boyfriend-turned-stalker, and one-time amateur porn photographer, whom Banks was going to visit again that day.

After a quick breakfast of coffee and toast and a short walk around St Pancras Gardens to clear his head, Banks felt ready to face the day. He was only about half a mile away from Euston, so he walked through the quiet streets of Somers Town to Eversholt Street. The train service to Milton Keynes was frequent, even on Sunday, and he only had to wait twenty minutes for an InterCity.

Watching the urban sprawl of London give way to prime commuter territory set amidst rolling fields and grazing cows, Banks wrote up his notes on the previous evening's talk with Barry Clough. Sometimes he took notes at the time, especially of important details, but that hadn't seemed appropriate standing in the white room with Clough and Burgess. Fortunately, though his memory was average in most respects, he had excellent audio recall and could remember a conversation practically verbatim for at least a couple of days.

He also thought about the coming interview with Craig Newton and tried to come up with a strategy. It was official business this time, not private-eye work for Jimmy Riddle. Approaching Craig Newton and getting any sort of trust out of him would be a delicate and difficult matter after all the lies he had told on his last visit. It had been the same with Ruth Walker, and Craig Newton struck him as a far more sensitive person than Ruth. On the other hand, Craig had lied to Banks, too.

Though it was his first visit in daylight, he still saw nothing of Milton Keynes on the taxi ride to Newton's house, except a few glimpses of concrete and glass. Perhaps that was all there was to see.

Craig Newton was at home, and though he seemed puzzled to see Banks again, he invited him into the house. It hadn't changed much since the last visit, still very much the bachelor house, with little piles of newspapers and magazines here and there and coffee rings on the low table.

'I'm sorry,' said Craig. 'You know . . . about your daughter. I read about it in the newspaper.'

Banks felt like an utter shit. Craig seemed the trusting sort, and here he was, letting him down. Still, a hard lesson in the reality of deception probably wouldn't do the kid any harm in the long run. Having been a policeman for years, Banks had long since stopped trying to make everybody *like* him. He still felt like an utter shit as he pulled out his warrant card, though.

Craig gaped at him. 'But . . . you said . . .? I don't understand.'

'It's simple, Craig,' said Banks, sitting down. 'I lied. Emily's father wanted me to find her, and it seemed a good idea to pretend that I was him instead of trying to explain myself. You can understand that, can't you?'

'I suppose so, but . . .'

'It was a simple strategy. Anyone would have more sympathy for the girl's father than for a policeman.'

'So you lied?'

'Yes.'

He seemed to draw in on himself. 'What do you want this time?'

'More information. I'm not the only one who lied, am I, Craig?'

'You talked to Louisa?'

'You must have known I would.'

'What did she say about me?'

'That you were bothering her, following her, stalking her.'

'I'd never have done her any harm. I was just . . . I . . .'

'What, Craig?'

'I loved her. Can't you understand that?'

'It didn't give you the right to follow her around and scare her when she didn't want to see you.'

'*Scare* her? That's a laugh. She hardly noticed me.'

'Clough did, though, didn't he?'

'Who?'

'Oh, come on, Craig. You knew his name, didn't you? You just didn't want me to talk to him about your stalking Emily.'

Craig rubbed his nose. 'The bastard.'

'Never a truer word. Anyway, let's leave that behind us for the moment, shall we?'

'Fine with me. Her real name is Emily. Is that right?'

Banks nodded.

'And Gamine?'

'A joke. It's an anagram of enigma, which is a sort of riddle. Emily Louise Riddle was her real name, and her father's my boss.'

'I see. You probably didn't have much choice, then. I suppose I shouldn't have believed you in the first place, should I? I feel like a real idiot now.'

'No need to. What reason could you possibly have had to think I was lying?'

'None. But still . . . I had my suspicions. I told you. I thought there was something funny about you, the way you kept asking questions.'

Banks smiled. 'Yes, I remember. So credit yourself with that and let's move on.'

'I can't see there's anything I could possibly tell you that's of any use. The papers said she took some poisoned cocaine in a club, is that right?'

'That's right. Did you ever supply Emily with cocaine, Craig?'

'No. I'm not a dealer. I never have been.'

'A user?'

'I've snorted it on occasion. Not for a long time, though.'

'She must have got it from somewhere.'

'Ask her new boyfriend.'

'I doubt that was the first time she took it.'

'Well, ask Ruth's friends, then. It certainly wasn't me.'

'What do you mean, "Ruth's friends"?'

'Just that they're more into drugs than I am, that's all.'

'Selling?'

'No. Just recreational. The music scene. Clubbing. That sort of thing.'

'What about strychnine?'

'What about it?'

'Ever have cause to use it in your line of work?'

'I'm not a bloody rat-catcher, you know.'

'I mean photography.'

'No.'

'Where were you last Thursday?'

Craig frowned. 'Thursday? I don't remember. I could check . . . just a minute. That might have been the day . . .' He got up and pulled a pocket diary from his jacket out in the hall. When he opened it to the right date, he looked relieved. 'Yes, that was the day. I was in Buckingham doing some publicity shots for the university.'

'Anyone see you?'

'The person who was putting the promotional brochure together. A lecturer from the law department. Canadian bloke. I can give you his name.'

'Please.'

Craig gave it.

'How long were you with him?'

'For an hour or so in the morning.'

'And then?'

'Then I walked around and took the photos.'

'So you were pretty much on your own the rest of the day?'

'Yes, but people must have seen me. Am I a suspect?'

'What do you think? Emily finished with you, and you stalked her. It wouldn't be the first time that sort of thing's led to murder. Obviously, if you've got an alibi I can cross you straight off my list. Makes life easier, that's all.'

But Craig Newton didn't have an alibi. He could easily have driven from Buckingham to Eastvale in about three hours.

Banks had thought about the timing and decided that, while there was no telling exactly *when* Emily had been given the poison that killed her, the odds were that she wouldn't have left a stash of coke sitting around for too long without snorting any. There was also the fact that she was back living at home, and she wouldn't dare do it around her parents. It wouldn't be much fun at home alone, anyway, even if they were out. Coke was a social drug, and most likely she would have saved it for a party, or a night out clubbing. It made most sense, then, that whoever had given her the stuff had given it to her on Thursday afternoon, after first giving her a sample of perfectly good, uncontaminated cocaine. That would explain why she turned up a bit high at the Cross Keys.

'I didn't kill her. I told you: I loved her.'

'Craig, if you'd been in this business as long as I have, you'd realize that love is one of the strongest motives.'

'It might be in the twisted world you live in, but pardon me if I haven't had the chance to become that cynical. I loved her. I wouldn't have harmed her.'

'Probably not,' said Banks. 'What kind of car do you drive?'

'Nissan.'

'Colour?'

'White. I suppose you want the number too?'

'Please.'

Craig told him. It meant nothing yet, but if they came across someone who had seen Emily getting into a car, then it could be of value. 'You should be going after that boyfriend of hers, you know,' he went on. 'Instead of harassing innocent people like me.'

'So you keep saying. Believe me, Craig, he's never far from my thoughts. And I'm not harassing you. You'd know it if I was.'

'Why don't you arrest him?'

'No evidence. You overestimate our powers. We can't just go around arresting people without any evidence.' Actually, he could, but Craig wasn't to know that, and he couldn't be bothered to explain the difference between 'arrest' and 'charge'. 'Look, Craig, I realize you're not enjoying this, but I didn't enjoy seeing Emily's body, either.'

'Was it . . .? I mean . . . I've heard about what strychnine does.'

'Did you ever contact Emily after she'd gone home?'

'I didn't even know she'd gone home. You never told me whether you'd found her or not, or whether she'd agreed to go back. To be honest, if I didn't read the papers pretty thoroughly, I wouldn't even have known she was dead. I recognized the photo, but not her name.'

'I understand you were in London yesterday?'

'That's right.'

'Any particular reason?'

'I don't see what it's got to do with you, but I had two business appointments – they are listed here in my appointment book, so you can check them if you want – and I also wanted to have a look at some new photographic equipment. The high street here may be quaint, but you must have noticed that it's hardly chock-a-block with camera shops.'

'And you had a drink with Ruth Walker?'

'Again, that's right.'

'She had a cold, didn't she?'

'She was sniffling a bit, yeah. So what?'

'What did you talk about?'

'We were both stunned to hear of Louisa's death. I suppose we wanted to mourn her together for a while, toast our memories of her. She'd been important to both of us, after all.'

'Could Ruth have been jealous of you and Emily?'

'I can't see why. It's not as if Ruth and me were ever lovers or anything.'

'But she might have wanted it that way.'

'She never said anything. Like I told you before, Ruth and

me were just good friends. There was nothing . . . you know . . . like that between us.'

'At least not in *your* mind.'

'It's the only one I can speak for.'

'Perhaps she wanted there to be something?'

Craig shrugged. 'I didn't fancy her in that way, and I'm pretty sure she knew it. Besides, what you're suggesting is absurd. If Ruth had to be jealous of anyone, it should have been the new boyfriend. He took Louisa completely away from both of us.'

'Jealousy's rarely rational, Craig. Emily breezed in and out of your lives and tossed you both aside. At least that's how Ruth put it. How did you feel about that?'

'Ruth can be a bit melodramatic when the mood takes her. How did I feel? You know damn well how I felt. I told you last time you were here, when you were pretending to be her father. I was devastated. Hurt. Heartbroken. But I got over it.'

'Only after you'd followed her around for a while.'

'Yeah, well, I'm not proud of that. I wasn't thinking clearly.'

'Maybe you weren't thinking clearly when you killed her?'

'That's absurd. No matter how cynical you are, I loved her and I would never have hurt her.'

'So you said. Are you sure?'

'Of course I'm sure. Look, are you suggesting I killed her over three months after she dumped me?'

'People have been known to brood for longer. Especially stalkers.'

'Well, I didn't. And I'm getting sick of this. I don't want to answer any more questions.' He stood up. 'And if you want anything more out of me, you'll have to arrest me.'

Banks sighed. 'I don't want to do that, Craig. Really, I don't. Too much paperwork.'

'Then you'd better leave. I've had enough.'

'I suppose I had,' said Banks, who had asked almost all the

questions he wanted. 'But there is one small thing you might be able to help me with.'

Craig looked at him through narrowed eyes. 'Go on.'

'Last time I came to see you, you told me that when you saw Emily with her boyfriend in London, you were taking candid pictures in the street, right?'

'Yes.'

'Were you really taking pictures or just pretending for the sake of cover?'

'I took some candids. Yes.'

'Do you still have the photos from that day?'

'Yes.'

'Do you have one of Clough?'

'I think so, yes. Why?'

'I know you're pissed off at me, Craig, but would you do me a favour and make me a copy?'

'I could do that. Again, though, why? Oh, I see. You want to show it around up north, don't you? Find out if anyone saw him up there. I suppose he's got a watertight alibi, hasn't he?'

'Something like that,' said Banks. 'Believe me, it would be a great help.'

'At least you're thinking in the right direction again,' said Craig. 'I can probably get some prints to you by tomorrow.'

'What about now?'

'Now?'

'Sooner the better.'

'But I'd have to get set up. I mean . . . it'd take a bit of time.'

'I can come back.' Banks looked at his watch. Lunchtime. 'How about I pop down to the nearest pub and have some lunch while you do the prints, then I'll come back and pick them up.'

Craig sighed. 'Anything to get you off my back. Try the Plough, down by the roundabout, end of the high street. And you don't need to come back. I'll drop them off there. Half an hour to an hour, say?'

'I'll be there,' said Banks.

'Will you do me a favour in exchange?'

'Depends.'

'When's the funeral going to be?'

'That depends on when the coroner releases the body.'

'Will you let me know? Her parents don't know me, so they won't invite me, but I'd like . . . you know . . . at least to be there.'

'Don't worry, Craig. I'll let you know.'

'Thanks. Now, I suppose I'd better get up to the dark-room.'

Of all the different ways that Annie had tried to imagine this moment turning out – confronting her rapist – the one thing that had never occurred to her was that it would end with a sense of anticlimax, of disappointment.

But disappointment was exactly what she felt as she stood in front of Wayne Dalton on the banks of the River Swale, with a steaming cow-pat between them. Indifference, even.

Her heart was still pounding, but more from the anti-cipation and the long walk than from the actual encounter, and he looked like a guilty schoolboy caught masturbating in the toilets. But instead of the monster she had created in her mind, what stood before her was all too human. Dalton wasn't frightening; he was pathetic.

For a few moments they just stared at one another. Neither spoke. Annie felt herself calming down, becoming centred. Her heart returned to its normal rhythm; she was in control.

Finally, Dalton broke the silence. 'What are you doing here?'

'I work here. Eastvale. I followed you.'

'My God. I never knew . . . What do you want?'

'I don't know,' Annie replied honestly. 'I thought I wanted

revenge, but now I'm here it doesn't seem important any more.'

'If it's any consolation,' said Dalton, avoiding her eyes, 'there's not a day gone by when I haven't regretted that night.'

'Regretted that you didn't get to finish what you started?'

'That's not what I mean. We were insane, Annie. I don't know what happened. The drink. The herd mentality.' He shook his head.

'I know. I was there.' Calm as she was inside, Annie felt tears prickling her eyes, and she hated the idea of crying in front of Dalton. 'You know, I've dreamed of this moment, of meeting one of you alone like this, of crushing you. Now we're here, though, it really doesn't matter.'

'It does matter, Annie. It matters to me.'

'What do you mean? And don't you *dare* call me Annie.'

'Sorry. The guilt. That's what I'm talking about. What I have to live with, day in, day out.'

Annie couldn't stop herself from laughing. 'Oh, Wayne,' she said, 'that's a good one. That's a *really* good one. Are you asking *me* for forgiveness?'

'I don't know what I'm asking for. Just for some . . . some sort of end, some resolution.'

'I see. You want closure, is that it? Popular term, these days, especially with victims. Everyone wants the bad guys put away. Gives them a sense of closure. Are you a victim here, Wayne, is that it?' Annie felt herself getting angry as she spoke, the indifference resolving itself into something else, into something harder. Two ramblers approached slowly from the woods beyond the river meadows.

'That's not what I meant,' said Dalton.

'Then tell me exactly what you did mean, Wayne, because from where I'm standing *you*'re the bad guy.'

'Look, I know what we did was wrong, and I know that being drunk, being part of a group is no excuse. But I'm not that kind of person. It's the first, the *only* time I've ever done anything like that.'

'So you're telling me that because you're not a serial rapist you're really an okay guy when it comes right down to it? Is that it? You just made one silly little mistake one night when you and your pals had had a bit too much to drink and there was this young bird just *asking for it*.' She could tell her voice was rising as she spoke but she couldn't help herself. She was losing it. She struggled for control again.

'Christ, that's not what I'm saying. You're twisting my words.'

'Oh, *pardon me*,' said Annie, shaking her head. 'I don't know what's worse, a contrite rapist or an unrepentant one.'

'Don't get it all out of proportion. *I* didn't rape you.'

'No. You didn't get your chance, did you? But you held me, you helped rip off my panties, and you stood there and enjoyed it while your friend raped me. I saw your face, Wayne. Remember? I know how you felt. You were just waiting for your turn, weren't you, like a little kid waiting for his go on the swings. And you would have done it, if you'd got the chance. In my mind that doesn't make you any different from the others. You're just as bad as the others.'

Dalton sighed and looked at the ground. Annie glared at him as the ramblers passed by. They said hello, but neither Annie nor Dalton answered.

'So what do you want from me?' he asked.

'What do I want? I'd like to see you off the job, for a start. In jail would be even better. But I don't suppose that's going to happen, is it? Would I settle for an apology instead? I don't think so.'

'What more can I do?'

'You can admit what happened. You can go back down there, go see the chief super again and tell him you lied, tell him the three of you got carried away and you raped me. That I did nothing to lead you on or encourage you or make you think I was going to let the three of you fuck me senseless. That's what you can do.'

Dalton shook his head. All the colour had drained from his face. 'I can't do that. You know I can't.'

Annie looked at him. She felt her eyes burning again. 'Then the only thing you can do is fuck off, fuck off right out of my life and don't ever come near me again.'

Then she turned and crossed the swaying bridge back to Reeth, the tears like fire as they coursed down her cheeks, not turning to see Dalton staring pathetically after her.

12

Banks came out of the meeting early Monday afternoon with only a little more information than he went in with. A weekend of showing Emily's photograph around town and making house-to-house inquiries had turned up several people who thought they had seen her in various Eastvale shopping areas on Thursday afternoon, always alone, but only one witness who thought she had seen her with anyone else. Unfortunately, the witness was about as useful as most; all she had seen was Emily getting into a car outside the Red Lion Hotel at the big York Road roundabout. She thought the time was about three o'clock. None of the bar staff at the Red Lion had seen Emily, and Banks was certain they would remember if they had.

When it came to the make of car, they all looked the same to the witness. All she could say was that it was light in colour. She also hadn't noticed anything in the least bit odd about what she saw; the girl had seemed to know the driver and smiled as she got in, as if, perhaps, she had been waiting for the lift. No, she hadn't really got a glimpse of the driver at all, except that maybe he or she was fair-haired.

So, if their witness were to be believed, Emily had got into a light-coloured car with someone she probably knew and trusted around the time of the meeting she had mentioned at lunch. She had left the Black Bull shortly before half past two. DC Templeton had checked the bus timetable and discovered that she must have taken the quarter to three to get there on time.

If – and it was a big *if* – their witness was right, then the sighting raised several interesting points. Banks walked over to his office window and lit an illicit cigarette. The day was over-cast but balmy for the time of year. A crew of council workers were putting up the Christmas tree in the market square, watched by a group of children and their teacher. The high-pitched whine of some sort of electric drill came from the extension down the corridor. It reminded Banks of the den-tist's, and he gave a little shudder.

In the first place, Banks thought, why was Emily meeting someone on the edge of town rather than in another pub or in the Swainsdale Centre? Especially if this someone had a car and could easily drive into the town centre. Answer: because she was meeting someone who intended to kill her and who had insisted on the arrangement because he or she didn't want to be seen with Emily. Any secrecy could easily be explained by the fact that drugs were being sold.

Objection: if this person wanted to kill Emily, why not drive her into the country and do it at leisure, then bury her body where it would never be found?

That raised the whole issue of the *way* she was killed. Poison, so the cliché goes, is a woman's weapon. In this case, if Emily's killer hadn't been in the Bar None at the time of her death, then the murder had also occurred at some distance from the killer. That suggested someone who wanted to get rid of her but didn't have any particular *emotional* stake in seeing her die. On the other hand, the use of strychnine as a method implied someone who wanted Emily to suffer an agon-izing and dramatic death. There are far easier and less painful ways of getting rid of a pest. The murder had elements of both calculation in its premeditation and extreme sadism in its method, a profile which might easily fit Barry Clough, the gangster who didn't like to lose his prized possessions. But would Clough drive all the way from London simply to give Emily some poisoned cocaine because she had insulted his macho vanity? He had said he was in Spain at the time, and Banks was having that checked. It wouldn't be easy, given how lax border crossings were these days, but they could tackle the airlines first, and then find out if any of his neighbours in Spain had seen him.

Also, while strychnine wasn't as difficult to get hold of as some poisons, it wasn't exactly on sale in the local chemist's shop. Banks had looked it up. Strychnine, derived originally from the seeds of the nux vomica tree, which grows mainly in India, was used mostly as a rodenticide. It had some medical uses – vets used it as a mild stimulant, for example, and it was sometimes used in research, to cause convulsions in experiments for anti-seizure drugs, and in the treatment of alcoholism. None of Banks's suspects was a doctor or a nurse, and strychnine wasn't issued on prescription, so the medical side could be ruled out. Craig Newton was a photographer, and they sometimes had access to unusual chemicals, though not, as far as Banks could remember, strychnine. Barry Clough could no doubt get hold of anything he wanted.

Then there was Andrew Handley to consider: 'Andy Pandy', Clough's gofer, the one he had 'given' Emily to the night she fled to Banks's hotel. Such rejection could have driven Handley to revenge, if he were that kind of person. Burgess had said he would put some men on trying to track down Handley, so maybe they would get a chance to ask him soon.

But would Emily have *smiled* as she got in his car with either Clough or Handley? Christ, why hadn't Emily told Banks who she was going to meet? Why hadn't he asked her? He rested his forehead against the cool glass and felt the vein throb in his temple.

It was no good, Banks decided; he needed far more information before he could even speculate about what had happened. He had found nothing of use in the contents of her handbag, once they had been gathered up and bagged. Nothing but the usual: cigarettes, tampons, electronic organizer, keys, a purse with £16.53 in it, make-up, a crumpled film magazine, an old family photograph – probably the one Ruth Walker had mentioned – Ruth's driving licence, which she hadn't even really needed any more, and the fake proof-of-age card.

The SOCOs had turned up nothing of interest from the ladies' toilet in the Bar None, except for any number of unidentified pubic hairs, and there were no prints except Emily's on the plastic bag in which the cocaine and strychnine had been kept. There were hundreds of prints around the stall – which testified to the frequency with which the owners thought it necessary to clean the toilets – but Banks suspected they would come to nothing. He was convinced that the killer, whoever it was, hadn't been in the Bar None toilets either with or without Emily, and had not even been in the club at the time of her death – had probably never been there. This was murder from a distance, perhaps even death by proxy, which made it all the more bloody difficult to solve.

DC Templeton had come up with a lead on the couple seen leaving the Bar None at 10.47. A barmaid at the Jolly Roger pub, a popular place for the student crowd on Market Street, seemed to remember them being in the pub earlier that evening. She had seen them before, she said, but didn't know their names; she only recognized the way they were dressed and thought they were students at the college, like most of her customers.

Next, Banks turned his mind to Charlie Courage's murder and felt a singular lack of progress there, too. Charlie's murderer had been at the scene, of course, but Charlie himself had been far from home, in the middle of nowhere. The only solid piece of evidence was the tyre track, and that would be no use at all unless a corresponding car could be found. He decided to phone DI Collaton later in the day and see if anything had turned up at the Market Harborough end. Maybe he could have a word with DI Dalton, too, see if he had come up with anything more on PKF Computer Systems.

Banks stubbed out his cigarette in his waste bin, making sure it was completely dead, and tried to clear the air as best he could by opening the window and waving a file folder about.

When someone knocked at the door and walked in, he felt guilty, like the time his mother noticed cigarette ash on the window ledge of his room and stopped his pocket money. But it was only Annie Cabbot. He had asked her to drop by as soon as she had finished handing out actions to the newly drafted DCs that Red Ron McLaughlin had promised.

She looked particularly good this morning, Banks thought, her shiny chestnut hair falling in waves over her shoulders, her almond eyes serious and alert, though showing just a hint of wariness. She was wearing a loose white shirt and black jeans, which tapered to an end just above her ankles, around one of which she wore a thin gold chain.

'Annie. Sit down.'

Annie sat and crossed her legs. She twitched her nose. 'You've been smoking in here again.'

'*Mea culpa.*'

She smiled. 'What did you want to see me about?'

'In the first place, I'd like you to go over to the office at the bus station, see if you can find out who was driving the quarter to three bus to York, the one that stops at the roundabout.'

Annie made a note.

'Have a chat with him. See if he remembers Emily being on the bus and getting into a light-coloured car near the Red Lion. You might also see if he can give you any leads as to his other passengers. Someone might have noticed something.'

'Okay.'

'And have a chat with the barmaid at the Jolly Roger, see if she can come up with anyone who might know where this couple lives, who they are. It's probably a dead end, but we have to check it out.'

Annie made a note. 'Okay. Anything else?'

Banks paused. 'This is a bit awkward, Annie. I don't want you to get the impression that this is in any way personal, but it's just that since we started this investigation, I don't feel I've had your full co-operation.'

Annie's smile froze. 'What do you mean?'

'I mean it feels like there's a part of you not here – you've been distracted – and I'd like to know why.'

Annie shifted in her chair. 'That's ridiculous.'

'Not from where I'm sitting.'

'Look, what is this? Am I on the carpet, or something? Are you going to give me a bollocking?'

'I just want to know what's going on, if there's something I can help with.'

'Nothing's going on. At least not with me.'

'What's that supposed to mean?'

'Do I have to spell it out for you?'

'Try.'

'All right.' Annie leaned forward. 'You said this wasn't personal, but I think it is. I think you're behaving this way because of what happened with us, because I broke off our relationship. You can't handle working with me.'

Banks sighed. 'Annie, this is a murder case. A sixteen-year-old girl, who also happens to be our chief constable's daughter, was poisoned in a nightclub. I would have hoped I wouldn't have to remind you of that. Until we find out who did it, this is a twenty-four-hour-a-day, seven-day-a-week job for us, and if you're not up to it for one reason or another, I want to know now. Are you in or out?'

'You're blowing this out of all proportion. I'm on the job. I might not be obsessed with the case, but I'm on the job.'

'Are you implying I *am* obsessed?'

'I'm not implying anything, but if the cap fits . . . What I *will* say is that it's a damn sight more personal for you than it is for me. I didn't go to London to track her down, or have lunch with her on the day she died. You did.'

'That's neither here nor there. We're talking about your commitment to the case. What about Sunday?'

'What do you mean?'

'Sunday morning, when I called in for an update. You were out of contact all morning, and DC Jackman sounded decidedly cagey.'

'I'm hardly responsible for DC Jackman's telephone manner.' Annie stood up, flushed, put her palms on his desk and leaned forward, jutting her chin out. 'Look, I took some personal time. All right? Are you going to put me on report? Because if you are, just do it and cut the fucking lecture, will you. I've had enough of this.'

With anyone else, Banks would have hit the roof, but he was used to Annie's insubordinate manner. It was one of the things that had intrigued him about her in the first place, though he still couldn't be sure whether he liked it or not. At the moment, he didn't. 'The last thing I want to do is put you on report,' he said. 'Not with your inspector's boards coming up. I would hope you'd know that. That's why I'm talking to you privately. I don't want this to go any further. I'll tell you something, though: if you keep on behaving like this whenever anyone questions your actions, you'll never make inspector.'

'Is that a threat?'

'Don't be absurd. Look, Annie, sit down. Please.'

Annie held out for a while, glaring, then she sat.

'Can't you see I'm trying to help you out here?' said Banks. 'If there's a problem, something personal, something to do with your family, I don't know, then maybe we can work it out. I'm not here to supervise you twenty-four hours a day.'

'You could have fooled me.'

'But I need to be able to trust you, to leave you alone to get on with the job.'

'Then why don't you?'

'Because I don't think that's what you've been doing.'

'I trusted you, and look what I found out.'

Banks sighed. 'I've explained that.'

'And I've explained what I was doing.'

'Not to my satisfaction, you haven't, and I don't have to remind you that I'm SIO on this one. It's my head on the block. So if there's a problem, if it's something I can help you with, then spit it out, tell me what it is, and I will. No matter what you believe, I'm not after doing you any harm because of what did or didn't happen between us. Not everything is as personal as you think it is. Credit me with a bit more professionalism than that.'

'Professionalism? Is that what this is all about?'

'Annie, there's something wrong. Let me help you.'

She gave a sharp jerk of her head and got to her feet again. 'No.'

At that moment, DI Dalton popped his head around the door.

'What is it?' Banks asked, annoyed at the interruption. Dalton looked at Banks, then at Annie, and an expression of panic crossed his features.

'What is it, DI Dalton?'

Dalton looked at them both again and seemed to compose himself. 'I thought you might like to know that the van driver died early this morning. Jonathan Fearn. Never regained consciousness.'

'Shit,' said Banks, tapping his pen on the desk. 'Okay, Wayne, thanks for letting me know.'

Dalton glanced at his watch. 'I'll be off back to Newcastle now.'

'Keep in touch.'

'Will do.'

Dalton and Annie looked at one another for a split second before he left, and Banks saw right away that there was something between them, some spark, some secret. It hit him smack in the middle of the chest like a hammer blow. *Dalton?* So *that* was what she had been up to. It fitted; her odd behaviour coincided exactly with his arrival in Eastvale. Annie and Dalton had something going. Banks felt icy worms wriggle their way up inside his spine.

Annie stood for a few seconds, her eyes bright, glaring at Banks defiantly, then, with an expression of disgust, she turned on her heels, strode out of his office and slammed the door so hard that his filing cabinet rattled.

Sometimes trying to get a lead was like pulling teeth, Annie reflected. The bus driver had been easy enough to find – in fact he had been eating a late breakfast in the station café before his first scheduled trip of the day – but he had been no help at all. All he'd been able to tell her was that he remembered Emily getting off at the roundabout, but there had been far too much traffic to deal with for him to notice anything more. The bus had been mostly empty, and he didn't know who any of the other passengers were. He could, however, state with some certainty that Emily was the only person to get off at that stop.

Disappointed, Annie headed for the Jolly Roger, still fuming from her run-in with Banks. After her confrontation with Dalton, she had actually felt better, more confident, ready to get on with the job without distractions. She might even have told Banks *why* she had been distracted in the first place if he hadn't taken such a high-handed attitude.

The bloody nerve of him, having her on the carpet like that. He *knew* she hated that sort of thing. Annie had never been able to handle authority well, which can be something of a liability in the police force, but most of the time she could pay lip-service when required. Not with Banks, though. This time, he had hit her where it really hurt: her professionalism. And the fact that he was partly right hurt even more. She would show him, though. She wasn't going to wallow in self-pity; she was going to get back on the damn horse and ride again.

Annie paused briefly at the market square to watch the awestruck expressions on the children's faces as they gathered around the Christmas tree. It took her back to her own child-hood in St Ives. There had been few, if any, practising Christians down at the commune where she had grown up. Most of the people who passed through had no religion at all, other than art, and those who did subscribe tended towards the more esoteric kinds, such as Zen Buddhism and Taoism, the ones without God, where you could ponder the meaning of nothing-ness and the sound of one hand clapping. Annie herself, with her meditation and yoga, came closer to Buddhism than any-thing else, though she never professed to *be* a Buddhist. She wasn't detached enough, for a start; she knew that desire caused suffering, but still she desired.

Christian or not, every Christmas had been a festive time for Annie and the other kids there. There were always some other children around, though most of them never stayed long, and she got used to her friends moving away, being dependent on herself, not on others. But at Christmas, someone always came up with a tree, and someone else scrounged around for some tinsel and decorations, and Annie always got Christmas presents, even if many of them were just sketches and small hand-carved sculptures from whoever was living there at the time. She still had most of them, and some were worth a bit now – not that she would ever sell them. Christmas was as much a tradition at the commune as anywhere else, and it always brought back memories of her mother. She still had a photograph of her mother holding her up to look at the tree decorations. She must have been two or three years old, and though she couldn't remember the moment itself, the photo-graph always brought back waves of nostalgia and loss.

Shrugging off the past, she walked on to the Jolly Roger.

Eastvale didn't have a large student population, and the college itself was an ugly mess of red-brick and concrete boxes on the southern fringes of the town, surrounded by marshland and a couple of industrial estates. Nobody wanted to live out there, even if there had been anywhere to live. Most of the students lived closer to the town centre, and there were enough of them to turn at least one pub into the typical student hangout, and the 'Roger', as they called it, was the one.

On first impressions, Annie thought, the Jolly Roger was no different from any other Victorian-style pub in the touristy neighbourhood around King Street behind the police station, but when she looked around inside, she noticed it was more run-down, and there was an odd selection of music on the jukebox, including far more angry, alternative stuff than pleasant pop and big-name bands. The clientele at that time in the afternoon consisted mostly of students who had finished early or had been there since lunchtime. They sat in small groups, smoking, chatting and drinking. Some favoured the scruffy, Marxist look of old, while others cultivated a more clean-cut Tony Blair style, but they all seemed to mix cheerfully together. One or two loners in thick glasses sat at tables reading as they slowly sipped their pints.

Annie went up to the bar and pulled out the fuzzy image taken from the CCTV video.

'I've been told you might know this couple,' she said to the young man behind the bar, who looked like a student himself. 'One of our lads had a word yesterday.'

'Not me, love,' he said. 'I wasn't on yesterday. That'll be Kath over there.' He pointed to a petite blonde busy pulling a pint and chatting to another girl across the bar. Annie walked over and showed her the photo.

'Any more thoughts on who this might be?' she asked, after introducing herself.

'I've given it a bit of thought,' said Kath, 'but I can't say as I have. I know I've seen them here, but I just can't place them.'

'Let's have a look, Kath,' said the girl. She didn't look old enough to be drinking, but Annie wasn't there to enforce the licensing laws. She was dressed all in black, including lace-trimmed gloves, with orange hair and a pale, pixieish face.

She looked at Annie. 'If that's all right with you?' she added.

'That's fine,' said Annie. 'We need all the help we can get.'

'I'm Sam. Short for Samantha.'

Annie didn't think it was short for Samuel, but you never knew. 'Pleased to meet you, Sam.'

'Lousy picture,' Sam commented. 'That from the Big Brother video?'

'Yes,' said Annie, 'it's from the CCTV cameras in the market square.'

'Talk about an invasion of privacy,' the girl began. 'You know—'

'I'd like to spend some time arguing the pros and cons of city-centre CCTV with you, Sam,' said Annie sweetly. 'Really I would, but a young girl, probably no older than you, was murdered in the Bar None last week, and we're trying to find out who killed her.'

'Yeah, I heard,' said Sam, looking away. 'It's a fucking shame a woman can't go anywhere by herself these days.'

'Any idea who they are?'

'Course I have.'

'Will you tell me?'

'Did they do it?'

'I very much doubt it. But they might have seen something.'

'It's Alex and Carly. Alex Pender and Carly Grant. Carly and I do art together.'

'Know where they live?'

'They've got a flat together on Sebastopol Avenue, you know, one of those big old Victorian terraces. Landlords divide them up into poky flats and rent them out for a fortune. Talk about exploitation.'

'Do you know the number?'

Sam told her.

*

Knowing now the reasons for Annie's erratic behaviour didn't make Banks feel any better. In fact, as the afternoon wore on, it made him feel worse. When she had stormed out of his office, he had stood for a moment to let it sink in, then felt the bile rise and burn in his throat. He might not be sleeping with Annie any more, but the thought of her being with Dalton hurt. He had been through the same thing with Sandra. For months after she left, when he knew she had moved in with Sean, the intolerable images crowded his mind, and during the long nights of drinking alone with random phrases from bitter Bob Dylan love songs echoing around his mind, the jealousy burnt like acid on his soul.

Perhaps it wasn't even jealousy, but envy; he couldn't have Annie, but he couldn't bear thinking about Dalton having her. Whatever it was, it hurt, and Banks had to make an effort to put it out of his mind for the time being and get on with the job.

First, he sent DC Templeton off to get copies made of the photo of Clough he had got from Craig Newton. It was a good shot, candid or not, and Craig had cropped it so that it showed only Clough in full, mean face. When that was done, he would send a team out to check every hotel and guest house in the area to see if Clough had been staying there recently. He would also have Jim Hatchley and Winsome Jackman show it around Daleview and Charlie Courage's neighbourhood. In the meantime, information had started trickling in now the working week had begun again.

He didn't learn much from the Riddles' phone records. British Telecom's Investigations Department had furnished DC Templeton with a list of numbers called on the Riddles' house telephone for the last month, and a subscriber check had supplied the names and addresses. Most seemed to be political cronies of Jimmy Riddle, or calls to Rosalind's law office. Someone, Emily presumably, had phoned Ruth Walker's number twice, but not within ten days of her death. There were no calls either to Craig Newton, Andrew Handley or Barry Clough. The only other calls Emily seemed to have made had been to Darren Hirst and to a sixth-form college in Scarborough. Banks thought it might be a good idea to get hold of Craig's and Clough's records, and do a cross-reference. It would take time, but it might throw up a lead of some sort. Oddly enough, Banks couldn't find the call that Emily had made to him the day before she died. Then he remembered the background noise and realized she must have used a public telephone.

Now that Jonathan Fearn was dead, Banks also had another murder on his plate, or manslaughter at least. Strictly speaking, it was DI Dalton's case, the way Charlie Courage's murder was Collaton's, but there was a strong Eastvale connection, the Daleview Business Park and PKF Computer Systems being at the heart of both. Banks was just about to check if anything was happening in the incident room when his phone rang. It was Vic Manson, the fingerprints expert.

'It's about that CD case you had sent over,' Manson said.

'Find anything?'

'Some very clear prints. I've checked the national index and, lo and behold, they belong to a bloke called Gregory Manners.'

'Who the hell's he when he's at home?'

'You may well ask. He's been a naughty boy, though. Did six months a couple of years back for attempting to defraud Customs and Excise.'

'What?'

'Smuggling, to you and me.'

'Well, well, well.'

'Ring any bells?'

'So loud they're deafening me. Thanks, Vic. Thanks a lot.'

'No problem.'

The minute Banks got off the phone with Manson he

called Dirty Dick Burgess at the National Criminal Intelligence Service.

'Banks. Solved your murder yet?'

'Murders. And no, I haven't.'

'How can I help?'

'I've got a few loose strands that seem to be coming together. Remember that PKF business I asked you about?'

'Something to do with computers, wasn't it?'

'That's right. Charlie Courage, nightwatchman and one-time con, gets murdered the day after a van clears out PKF's Daleview offices, heading for another business park up Tyneside way. Over the past four weeks he's made five two-hundred-pound cash deposits at his bank. With me so far?'

'Hanging on your every word.'

'The van itself gets hijacked north of Newcastle and the entire contents disappear. The driver, Jonathan Fearn, who, by the way is a known associate of Courage's, has just died of injuries received.'

'Another murder, then.'

'Looks that way. But let me finish. PKF is a phony company and we can't trace anyone involved in it. The only bit of evidence we've got is a CD case.'

'That's hardly evidence, is it?' Burgess commented. 'Stands to reason there'll be CD cases around computer people.'

'That's not all. I've just found out that the prints on this case are those of one Gregory Manners, late of Her Majesty's first-class hotel in Preston. Manners did six months for smuggling a lorry-load of cigarettes through Dover. Or trying to. When questioned he said—'

'—he was working alone, and nobody was able to prove any different. All right, you've got a point. As a matter of fact, I do remember that one. It was one of Customs and Excise's few successes that year.'

'Let me guess who was behind it: Barry Clough?'

'The man himself. Seems he's everywhere we look, isn't he?'

'He certainly is. This Manners connection links him directly to PKF, whatever it was up to, and by extension to the murders of Charlie Courage and Jonathan Fearn.'

'Still like him for the girl's murder, too?'

'Very much. But we don't have enough to bring him in yet. You told me yourself how slippery he is.'

'As a jellied eel. You know what I'm thinking, Banks?'

'What?'

'This hijack you told me about. It sounds very much as if someone ripped Barry Clough off.'

'Indeed it does.'

'And we know Barry doesn't like that. Barry throws tantrums when people upset him.'

'Enough for two people to end up dead?'

'I'd say so.'

'So maybe Courage was on Clough's payroll, then he decided to work his own scam, selling information about when PKF was moving and where they were going. He'd hardly have looked the other way during a robbery at Daleview because it would have seemed far too obvious.'

'A hijacked van's pretty obvious, too, if you ask me,' said Burgess.

'Charlie wasn't *that* bright.'

'Obviously not. Anyway, it all sounds possible. It must have been valuable merchandise, though, to make it worth the risk.'

'There wasn't much risk to speak of, believe me. Not up there at that time on a Sunday night.'

'Ah, the provinces. They never cease to amaze me. Ever wondered where the stuff's got to?'

'Yes,' said Banks. 'Whatever it was, I'm assuming it's either been sold or it's in someone's lock-up waiting to cool down. I'm trying to run a check on other business parks around the country, see if there've been any more PKF-type scams lately, but that'll take for ever.'

'What do you want me to do?'

'Can you fax me what you've got on Gregory Manners, for a start?'

'Sure.'

'And have you got any photos of Andrew Handley and Jamie Gilbert on file?'

'Indeed we have.'

'Could you fax them up here, too? It might not be a bad idea to have someone show them around Daleview and Charlie Courage's neighbourhood along with Clough's.'

'Okay.'

'Thanks. And will you keep a close eye on Clough?'

'It's being done as we speak.'

'Because I'll be wanting to talk to him again soon, if anything breaks, and this time I think we'll have him up here.'

'Oh, he'll like that.'

'I'll bet. Anyway, thanks. I'll be in touch.'

'My pleasure. By the way, there's nothing on Andy Pandy yet. It seems that when he wants to hide, he stays hidden. The lads are still on it, though. I'll keep you informed.'

'Thanks.'

Banks hung up the phone and tried to piece together what he'd got. Not much, really, just a lot of vague suspicions as far as both cases were concerned. There was still something missing; the magnet, the one piece that would arrange the chaotic jumble of iron filings into a discernible pattern. Until he had that, he would get nowhere. He had a feeling that part of the answer, at least, lay with PKF and whatever it had been doing. At least he could have Gregory Manners brought in and find out what he had to say about the operation.

Annie found a place to park outside number 37 Sebastopol

Avenue, walked up the front steps and rang the doorbell to flat four.

Luck was still with her; they were in.

The flat was quite nicely done up, Annie thought, when they let her in and offered her a cup of tea. The furniture looked used, probably parental donations, but it was serviceable and comfortable. The small living room was clean and uncluttered, and the only decoration was a poster of a Modigliani nude over the tiled mantelpiece. Annie recognized it from one of her father's books; he had always been a big fan of Modigliani, and of nudes. Under the window was a desk with a PC, and a mini stereo unit stood in a cabinet along with stacks of compact discs. There was no television.

'What are you studying?' Annie asked as Alex brought the tea.

'Physics.'

'Beyond my ken, I'm afraid.' She nodded towards the painting. 'Someone likes art, though, I see.'

'That's me,' said Carly. 'I'm studying art history.' She was a slight girl with dyed black hair, a ring through the far edge of her left eyebrow and another through the centre of her lower lip, which gave her voice a curious lisp.

They talked about art for a while, then when they both seemed relaxed, Annie got down to business. It wasn't as if she was there to interrogate them, but people often got nervous around the police, the way Annie did around gynaecologists.

'Have you any idea why I'm here?' she asked.

They shook their heads.

'I found someone in the Jolly Roger who told me where you lived. Why haven't you come forward before now? You must know of all the appeals for information we've had out.'

'Information about what?' Alex asked, a puzzled expression on his face. He was good-looking enough, in a boyish sort of way, though his hair looked as if it needed a wash and he had an Adam's apple the size of a gobstopper. Could do with a shave, too, Annie thought, or was she just getting conservative in her old age? There was a time, she reminded herself, when she hadn't minded a little stubble on a man. She had even worn a stud through her nose. It wasn't that long ago, either.

'About the murder,' she went on. 'Emily Riddle's murder. Surely you know it happened at the Bar None shortly after you left on Thursday night?'

Alex and Carly looked blank. 'No.'

'It was in all the papers. On telly. Everyone's talking about it.'

'We don't have a TV set and, well, to be honest,' Alex said, 'we haven't looked at a paper in days. Too busy at college.'

Seems like it, Annie thought. 'But haven't you heard anyone talking about it?'

'I've heard people talking about a drug overdose,' Carly said. 'But I didn't make the connection. I didn't pay much attention. It's so negative. I never read about things like that. It upsets my balance. Why are you here?'

'Why did you leave the club so early?'

They looked at one another, then Carly lisped, 'We didn't like the music.'

'That's it?'

'It's enough, isn't it. I mean, you wouldn't like to have to listen to that crap all night, would you?'

Annie smiled. She certainly wouldn't. 'So why go in the first place?'

'We didn't know what sort of music they played,' Alex answered. 'Someone at college said it was a pretty good place to have a few drinks and dance and, you know . . . unwind.'

'And buy drugs?'

Carly reddened. 'We don't do drugs.'

'Is that why you went? To buy drugs? And when you'd bought them you left.'

'She said we don't do drugs and we don't,' said Alex. 'Why can't you just believe us? Not every young person's some sort of drug addict, you know. I knew the cops were prejudiced against blacks and gays, but I didn't think they were prejudiced against the young in general.'

Annie sighed. She'd heard it all before. 'I'd love to believe you, Alex,' she said. 'In a perfect world, maybe. But a girl died a very nasty death after taking some adulterated cocaine in the Bar None not more than half an hour after you left and, as yet, we don't know when she got it or where she got it from. If you can give me any help at all, then surely that gives me the right to come here and ask you a few simple questions, doesn't it?'

'It still doesn't give you the right to accuse us of being druggies,' said Alex.

'Oh, for crying out loud! Grow up, Alex. If I were accusing the two of you of being junkies, you'd be down in the cells now waiting for your legal aid solicitor.'

'But you said—'

'Let's move on, shall we?'

They both sulked for a moment, then nodded.

'What kind of music do you like?'

Alex shrugged. 'All sorts, really. Just not that techno-rave-disco crap they play at the Bar None. It gives me a headache.'

Annie got up and wandered over to look at their CD collection to see for herself. Hole, Nirvana, the Dancing Pigs, even an old Van Morrison. There was quite a variety, but certainly no dance music. One odd thing she noticed was that some of the CDs had no covers, only typed labels stuck on the cases identifying the contents. When she looked more closely, she also saw that the CDs themselves didn't all have record company logos. She glanced at the desk and saw a couple of popular computer software programmes and games there. Again, there was no form of official identification.

'Where did you get these?' she asked, noticing that Carly had reddened when she picked up one of the cases.

'Shop.'

'What shop?'

'Computer shop.'

'Come on, Carly. You think I'm stupid just because I'm an old fogey? Is that it? You didn't buy this in any legitimate computer shop. It's a knock-off, like the music CDs. Where did you buy them?'

'It's not illegal.'

'We won't go into the ins and outs of breach of copyright just now. I just want to know where you bought them.'

After letting the silence stretch for almost a minute, Alex answered. 'Bloke in the used bookshop down by the castle sells them.'

'Castle Hill Books?'

'That's the one.'

Annie made a note. It probably wasn't important, and it wasn't her case, but she couldn't dismiss the connection she felt with the empty CD case she had found at PFK. She would pass the information on to Sergeant Hatchley.

'Are you going to arrest us?' Carly asked.

'No. I'm not going to arrest you. But I do want you to answer a few more questions. Okay?'

'Okay.'

'While you were in the club, did you notice anyone selling drugs or behaving suspiciously?'

'There weren't many people in the place,' Carly said. 'Everyone was just getting in drinks or sitting down.'

'A few people were dancing,' Alex added. 'But things hadn't really got going by then.'

'Did you notice this girl?'

Annie showed them a picture of Emily.

'I think that's the girl who came in with some friends just after us,' Carly said. 'At least it looks like her.'

'About five foot six, taller in her platforms. Flared jeans.'

'That's the one,' Carly said. 'No, I didn't see her doing anything odd at all. They sat down. Someone went for drinks.

I think she was dancing at one point. I don't know. I wasn't really paying attention. The music was already driving me crazy.'

'You didn't notice her talk to anyone outside her immediate group?'

'No.'

'Did you see her go to the toilet?'

'We weren't watching people coming and going from the toilets.'

'So you didn't notice her go?'

'No.'

'All right. Did you recognize her? Have you ever seen her before?'

'No,' Alex answered, with a sly glance at Carly. 'And I think I'd remember.'

Carly threw a cushion at him. He laughed.

'She was too young for you, Alex,' said Annie. 'And by all accounts you'd have been far too young for her.' She thought again of Banks and his lunch with Emily the day she died. Was there any more to it than that? She still got the impression he was holding back, hiding something.

Things were going nowhere fast with Carly and Alex, so she decided to wrap up the interview and call it a day. 'Okay,' she said, standing up and stretching her back. 'If either of you remembers anything about that evening, no matter how insignificant it might seem to you, give me a ring at this number.' She handed her card to Carly who put it on the computer desk, then left the flat, ready to head home. It had been a rough day. Maybe she could treat herself to a book and a long hot bath and put Banks and Dalton out of her mind.

13

The postman came before Banks set off for work on Wednesday morning, and in addition to the usual bills and another letter from Sandra's lawyer, which Banks put aside for later, he also brought with him a small oblong package. Noting the return address, Banks ripped open the padded envelope and held in his hand his son's first officially recorded compact disc, *Blue Rain*, along with a thank-you note for the three-hundred-pound cheque Banks had sent him, and which had cut severely into his Laphroaig budget.

There was a photograph of the band on the cover, Brian at the centre in a practised, cool sort of slouch, torn jeans, T-shirt, a lock of hair practically covering one eye. Andy, Jamisse and Ali flanked him. It was a poor-quality photograph, Banks noticed – Sandra certainly wouldn't approve – and looked more like a grainy black-and-white photocopy of a colour original. Banks didn't much like the band's name, either; Jimson Weed sounded far too sixtyish and druggie, but what did he know?

The music was what counted, and Banks was pleased to see that they had recorded their cover version of Dylan's 'Love Minus Zero / No Limit', a song he had been surprised to hear them play on the only occasion he had seen them perform live. The rest of the songs were all originals, with Brian and Jamisse sharing most of the writing credits, apart from an old Mississippi John Hurt number, 'Avalon Blues'. They weren't a blues band, but blues was an underlying influence on their music, sometimes overlaid with rock, folk and hip-hop elements: the

Grateful Dead meet Snoop Doggy Dogg. Banks was also absurdly pleased to see that in the liner notes Brian had credited him with nurturing an interest in music. Hadn't mentioned that his dad was a copper, though; that wouldn't go down too well in the music business.

He didn't have time to listen to the CD before heading off to the office. If he expected his team to put in a full day on Emily's murder, then he had to set an example. Thoughts of work soon led into thoughts of Annie, who had contributed towards yet another sleepless night. He couldn't understand what she saw in Dalton, who seemed such a dull, unprepossessing type to Banks. Not particularly good-looking, either. But, as he well knew, there was neither rhyme nor reason in matters of sex and love.

He just wished he could get the images of them out of his mind. Last night he had tossed and turned, unable to stop himself from imagining them making love in all sorts of positions, Dalton pleasing her far more than he had ever done, making her cry out in ecstasy as she climaxed, riding him wildly. The morning, dark and wet as it was, brought a respite from the images, but not from the feelings that had generated them. Working with her was turning out to be far more difficult than he had imagined it would be. Maybe she was right, and he just couldn't hack it.

As he turned towards the town centre and slowed in the knot of traffic on North Market Street, which was just opening up for the day, he wondered if everyone suffered from jealousy as much as he did. It had always been that way for him; jealousy had wrecked his relationship with the first girl he had ever slept with.

Her name was Kay Summerville, and she lived on the same Peterborough estate as he did. For weeks he had lusted after her as he watched her walk by in her jeans and yellow jacket, long blonde hair trailing halfway down her back. She seemed unobtainable, ethereal, like most of the women he lusted after,

but he was surprised when one day, walking back from the
newsagent's over the road with her, he plucked up the courage
to ask her out, and she said yes.

Everything went well until Kay left school and got an office
job in town. She made new friends, started going for drinks
with the crowd regularly after work on a Friday. Banks was still
at school, having stayed on for his A levels, and a schoolboy
had far less appeal than these slightly older, better dressed,
more sophisticated men of the world at the office. They had
more money to flash around and, even more important, some
of them had cars. Kay insisted there was no hanky-panky going
on, but Banks became tortured with jealousy, wracked by
imagined infidelities, and in the end, Kay walked away. She
couldn't stand his constant harping on who she was seeing and
what she was doing, she said, and the way he got stroppy if she
ever so much as *looked at* another man.

Shortly after, Banks moved to London and went to college
there. A year or two and several casual relationships later, he
met Sandra. After a rocky few months at the start, when
he realized he wanted her so much he couldn't bear the thought
of anyone else being with her, he saw that if he played his cards
right, nobody else but him was going to be, and for the next
twenty years or so he had very few problems with jealousy.
Then she left him and Sean came on the scene, or vice versa.
Now this with Annie. He was beginning to feel like a sex-
obsessed, acne-plagued teenager again, and he didn't like it at
all.

Though he couldn't play it, Banks had Brian's CD on the
passenger seat beside him, feeling pride every time he managed
to break off his miserable thoughts and look down to see his
son's face on the cover. The marriage might have ended badly,
but at least it had produced Brian and Tracy, Banks told himself,
and the world was a better place for having them in it. He
picked up the CD and dashed through the rain with it into the

station. Once in his office, he set it on his desk, hoping that anyone who dropped by would ask about it.

Because Tuesday had been a day of paperwork, phonework and legwork, Banks was expecting that some of it would pay off today. Teams of uniformed and plain-clothes officers had been sent out with photos of Gregory Manners, Andrew Handley, Jamie Gilbert and Barry Clough. If any of those four had been up to no good in the Eastvale area over the past month or so, then someone would recognize them. Also, as he had looked at the cover of the Jimson Weed CD and thought about some of the things he had discovered lately, a number of disparate strands had started to come together, and he made an appointment to have lunch at half past one in the Queen's Arms with Granville Baird, of North Yorkshire Trading Standards.

Annie was surprised to find herself feeling so good on Wednesday morning, the best she'd felt in a long time. She had awakened after a long, deep and dreamless sleep feeling that old calm, had done her meditation and yoga and seemed to be getting back in the groove. Agitated voices still muttered in the distance of her mind and talons raked at the raw edges of her emotions, but even so, she felt much better. All would be well.

She wondered if it was anything to do with Dalton having gone back to Newcastle, and decided that was only partly it. Certainly it was a blessing not to have him around the place, constantly reminding her, whether he intended to or not, of that terrible night two years ago. In a way, though, she had exorcized all that by confronting him by the swing bridge. Anyway, she didn't intend to dwell on why she was feeling so good. One thing she had learned from her meditation was that sometimes it's best to let go, simply to accept the feelings you have and ride with them.

Banks had been cool and distant towards her since their

blow-up on Monday afternoon, and, while a little warmth wouldn't go amiss, that suited her perfectly well at the moment, because all she wanted to do was get on with the job.

And early that Wednesday afternoon, she was doing exactly that, heading for Scarlea House. The manager there had said he recognized Barry Clough's photograph when one of the DCs turned up on the doorstep showing it around.

It was a dull afternoon, and Annie needed to turn her headlights on. The heavy grey cloud was so low it seemed to rest on top of Fremlington Hill, a high limestone scar which curved like bared teeth around the junction of Swainsdale and the smaller Arkbeckdale, which ran north-west.

She drove through sleepy Lyndgarth, with its village green, its chapel, church and three pubs. Smoke drifted from the chimneys and lost itself in the clouds like her thoughts when she meditated. She passed through the remote hamlet of Longbridge, a name most found funny as it had the smallest, shortest bridge in the Dale. She remembered it was supposed to be famous because someone drove over it in the opening credits of a television programme, but that had been before her time up north. Not a soul stirred; the hamlet looked deserted, its shop closed, rough stone cottages shut up. Only a glimmer of light from the pub showed that anyone lived there at all. It was an eerie feeling, especially in the half-light. Annie felt that if she got out of her car and walked around she would find everything in order – meals on the table, today's newspapers lying open, kettles boiling on the cookers – and nobody there, like on the *Marie Celeste.*

Scarlea House loomed ahead, a huge, dark Gothic limestone pile. None of the windows seemed to have any curtains. It stood on a slight rise at the end of a broad gravel drive, and in the weak light, against the backdrop of the rising, dull-green daleside, it looked like a vampire's castle from an old horror film. All that was needed to complete the effect was a few flickers of lightning and the distant rumble of thunder. But when Annie pulled up outside and turned off her engine, everything was silent apart from the occasional bird call and the burbling of the River Arkbeck on its way to join the Swain along the valley bottom.

Christ, Annie, she thought, you're about to enter one of the most upmarket shooting lodges in the Dales and just look at you; you're a mess. She hadn't dressed for upmarket when she climbed into her jeans and flung on a red roll-neck jumper that morning. Even less so when she picked up her denim jacket on her way out. They'll just have to take me as they find me, she told herself, opening the heavy front door and walking over to the reception area.

The ceiling in the hall was taller than her entire cottage, and, if it wasn't quite the Sistine Chapel, it was certainly ornate, complete with gilded panels and a chandelier. The walls were all dark wood wainscoting, and here and there hung overlarge oil paintings of men with bulbous noses wearing their collars too tight, faces the colour and texture of rare roast beef, like Jim Hatchley's – the kind of paintings that her father called 'optical egotism'. They paid the rent, though. If a local artist got one of those self-styled bigwigs to commission such a portrait, it would probably keep him in paint and canvas for a few years. Even her father knew the value of that.

'Can I help you, miss?'

An elegant silver-haired man in a black suit came forward to greet her. Annie's first impression was that he looked like an undertaker.

'Actually,' she said, feeling a bit snotty and more than a trifle intimidated by her surroundings, 'it's not miss, it's Detective Sergeant Cabbot.'

'Ah, yes, Sergeant, we've been expecting you. My name's Lacey. George Lacey. General Manager. Please, come this way.'

He gestured towards a door with his name on it, and, when they went inside, Annie saw it was a modern office, complete with fax machine, computer, laser printer, the works. She would never have expected it from the old-fashioned décor, but the paying guests would be well-off businessmen, and they would demand all the modern conveniences of the electronic age as well as the primitive excitement of blood lust. And why not? They could afford it all.

Annie sat in a swivel chair and took out her notebook. 'I don't know if I can tell you any more than I told the other officer,' Lacey said, making a steeple of his hands on the desk. He had prissy sort of lips, Annie noticed, shaped in a cupid's bow and far too red. They irritated her when he talked. She tried to keep her eyes on the knot of his regimental tie.

'I'm just here to confirm that it really was the man in the photograph who stayed here.' She laid her copy of Clough's photo on the desk in front of him. 'This man.'

Lacey nodded. 'Mr Clough. Yes. That was, indeed, him.'

'Has he been here before?'

'Mr Clough is a frequent guest during the season.'

'Can you tell me the dates he was here?'

'Just a moment.' Lacey tapped a few keys on the computer and frowned at the screen. 'He stayed here from Saturday, the fifth of December, until Thursday the tenth.'

'It's a bit late in the year for a holiday in the Dales, isn't it?'

'This is a *shooting* lodge, Sergeant. People do not come here for holidays. They come here to shoot grouse. This was the last weekend of the season and we were full to capacity.'

'What about now?'

'Not quite so busy. It comes and goes.'

'But you stay open all winter, even though the grouse season is over?'

'Oh, yes. We're generally booked up over Christmas and New Year, of course. The rest of the time it's . . . well, quieter, though we get a number of foreign guests. Our restaurant has an international reputation. One often has to make dinner reservations weeks in advance.'

'It must be an expensive operation to run.'

'Quite.' Lacey looked at her as if the mere mention of money were vulgar.

'Was Mr Clough alone while he was here?'

'Mr Clough, as usual, came with his personal assistant and a small group of colleagues. The season is very much a social event.'

'His personal assistant?'

'A Mr Gilbert. Jamie Gilbert.'

'Ah, yes. Of course.' Banks had told her, when she had forced his confession about the lunch with Emily, that Emily had imagined she saw Jamie Gilbert in Eastvale the Monday of the week she died. Maybe she hadn't imagined it after all. It was also interesting that Clough had arrived in Yorkshire only a day or two before Charlie Courage's murder and left the day of Emily's, which meant that he had certainly been in a position to supply her with the strychnine-laced cocaine.

'Do you know what time Mr Clough left on the tenth?' she asked.

'Not exactly. Usually our guests depart after breakfast. I'd say between nine and ten o'clock perhaps.'

'Is there anything else you can tell me about his stay, his comings and goings?'

'I'm afraid not. I am not employed to spy on our guests.'

'Is there anyone who might be able to tell me?'

Lacey looked at his watch and curled his lip. 'Mr Ferguson, perhaps. He's the barman. As such, he spends far more time close to the guests in social situations. He might be able to tell you more.'

'Okay,' said Annie. 'Where is he?'

'He won't be in until later this afternoon. Around five o'clock. If you'd care to come back then . . .?'

'Fine.' Annie thought of asking for Ferguson's home address and calling on him there, but decided she could wait. Banks was at lunch with someone from Trading Standards and

Annie knew that he would want to be here if she took this line of inquiry any further. She could phone him on her mobile and arrange to meet back at Scarlea at five. In the meantime she would head out to Barnard Castle and investigate a reported sighting of Emily Riddle there the afternoon before she died.

The news about Clough was exciting, though. It was the only positive lead they had on him since Gregory Manners's fingerprints on the CD case linked him to PKF, and it was the first real lead they'd had linking Clough with Yorkshire and catching him out in a lie. Yes, Banks would certainly want to be in on this.

Banks had first met Granville Baird two years ago, when North Yorkshire Trading Standards had asked for police assistance after one of their investigators had been threatened with violence. Since then, they had worked together when their duties overlapped and had even met socially now and then for a game of darts in the Queen's Arms. They weren't close friends but they were about the same age, and Granville, like Banks, was a jazz fan and a keen opera-goer.

They chatted about Opera North's season for a while, then, jumbo Yorkshire pudding on order and a pint of Theakston's bitter in front of him, the buzz of lunchtime conversation all around, Banks lit a cigarette and asked Granville, 'Know anything about pirating compact discs?'

Granville raised an eyebrow. 'Does that mean you're in the market for something? The "Ring Cycle" perhaps?'

'No. Though now you come to mention it, I wouldn't mind the complete Duke Ellington centenary set, all twenty-four, if you can run some off for me.'

'Wish I could afford it. Does this mean that the police are actually looking at doing something about pirating at last?'

'Apart from copyright infringement, which is hardly a police matter, I wasn't aware that any laws were being broken. If you expect us to come charging in to Bill Gates's rescue every time someone pirates a copy of Windows, then you've got a very funny idea of what our job really is.'

Granville laughed. 'You're behind the times, Alan. It's big business these days. If it were simply a matter of copying Windows or the latest Michael Jackson CD for a friend, nobody would bat an eyelid, but we're talking big operations here. Big money, too.'

'That's exactly what I'm interested in,' said Banks. 'How big?'

'The last raid we carried out netted about a quarter of a million quid's worth of stuff.'

Banks whistled. 'That big?'

'Tip of the iceberg.'

'So it would be a lucrative business for organized crime, would it?'

'Especially as you lot don't even seem to think it's a crime.'

'Point taken. Look, we've got a case on right now – it started with a murder – and I've been putting two and two together and coming up with a pirating business. I don't know how big yet. In fact, we don't know much at all.' Brian's CD had been the final piece in the puzzle. Seeing its amateurishly produced cover, Banks had thought of the CD case Annie had found at PKF, the CDs she saw at Alex and Carly's flat, about Gregory Manners's fingerprints, Barry Clough's dismissal as a roadie for bootlegging live recordings, and the van worth hijacking, the driver worth killing. They still hadn't found the van contents yet, but Banks would bet a pound to a penny they consisted of equipment for copying CDs, along with any stock and blank discs that happened to have been there. What Banks needed to know from Granville Baird was whether there was enough profit in the pirating business to make it of interest to Clough, the way smuggling was.

'What *do* you know?' Granville asked.

'A phony company leases small units in rural business parks, operates for a while, then moves on. Make any sense?'

Granville nodded. 'I've heard rumours of such a set-up, yes. And if you had two or three of these operations running at once, around the country, you could be turning over a million or two a year, or more, easy. If you had the proper equipment, of course.'

'Definitely worth his while, then?'

'Whose while?'

'We're not sure yet. This is just speculation. What sort of things would they pirate?'

'Everything they can get their dirty little hands on. Music, software programs, games, you name it. For the moment, by far the biggest profits are in games. Sony PlayStation stuff, that sort of thing. Everyone's kid wants the latest computer game, right? We've even found pirated stuff on sale that isn't on the market yet. Some of the *Star Wars* tie-in games came over from America before the film even came out here.'

'What about pirated movies?'

'There's a lot of that, but most of it's done in the Far East.'

'How do they get the originals? Insiders?'

'Mostly, yes. As far as the movies are concerned, though, sometimes all they have for a master is a hand-held video of the film being shown at a theatre full of people. I've seen some of the stuff and it's awful. When it comes to the computer programs and games, though, it's easy enough for some employee to sneak a disc out, and if he can make a couple of hundred quid from it, all the better. There even used to be a private website where, for a membership fee, you got offered a variety of pirated stuff to download, but that's defunct. Mind you, it's very much a matter of *caveat emptor*. Some of it's a rip-off. We found a lot of games among the last haul that couldn't be played without complicated by-passes of internal security systems.'

'The manufacturers are wising up, then?'

'Slowly.'

Their food came, and they paused to eat. Banks took a bite

of his Yorkshire pudding filled with roast beef and gravy and washed it down with some beer. He looked at Granville, who was drinking mineral water and nibbling at a salad. 'What's up? On a diet?'

Granville frowned. 'Annual check-up last month. Doc says my cholesterol's too high, so I've got to cut out booze and fatty foods.'

Banks was surprised. Granville looked healthy enough, played squash and was hardly any heavier than Banks was. 'Sorry to hear that.'

'No sweat. You just go right on enjoying yourself until it's your turn.'

Banks, who felt he had led a charmed life thus far, despite the bad diet, the cigarettes and the ale, nodded. 'It'll be either that or the prostate, I know. What about distribution?'

'Wherever you can shift it. I've even heard stories of the local ice-cream van selling PlayStation games to kids. Gives a whole new meaning to Mr Softee.'

Banks laughed. That made a lot of sense, he thought as he ate. Clough could use the same distribution network he had set up for the smuggled cigarettes and alcohol – small shop-keepers like Castle Hill Books, to whom DC Winsome Jackman should be talking this afternoon, market stallholders, pubs, clubs, factories. After all, the customers would often be the same people, none of whom thought they were really doing anything wrong in buying the odd packet of smuggled fags or a pirated computer game for their kid's birthday. Half the cops in the country were smoking contraband cigarettes and drinking smuggled lager. Banks even knew a DI with West Yorkshire who drove to Calais every few weeks and filled up his trunk with booze and cigarettes. He made enough selling them at the station to cover the expenses of his trip and keep himself in the necessities till the next time.

So, why not? people thought. Big deal. They were getting a bargain, Bill Gates already had too much money, and the tax on booze and fags was extortionate. Now the EU had also cut out duty-free purchases among its members. In a way, Banks agreed, the consumers had a point – except that now people like Barry Clough were getting rich from them.

He tried to work out how events might have occurred. Clough's men pay off Charlie Courage, whose ability to sniff out wrongdoing and try for a slice of the pie was legendary, then Charlie sells them out to a rival, who hijacks the van and steals the equipment and stock of pirated CDs to set up somewhere on his own. Only it goes wrong. Clough's men torture Charlie. Does he give up the hijacker? You bet he does. And what happens to both of them?

'It makes sense,' he said to Granville. 'Especially if there's the kind of money in it you're saying there is.'

'Take my word for it. There is. And if your man's really organized, he'll have multi-disc-copying writers so he can churn them out by the dozen.'

'That'd be an expensive piece of equipment, I should imagine?'

'Indeed it would. An investment of thousands.'

That answered one question that had been puzzling Banks. If the PKF van had been carrying a few pirated discs, it would have hardly been worth hijacking, not to mention killing Jonathan Fearn. But if it had been carrying industrial standard multi-disc-copying equipment, that was another matter entirely. 'A very healthy return, I'd imagine, though, if you've got the start-up capital,' Banks said.

'Indeed.'

And Clough certainly had the capital to invest. From his gun-restoring racket, the music business, his club, his smuggling operations and whatever other dirty little scams he was involved in, he had plenty of money. The problem was how to prove his involvement. It was as Burgess had said about Clough's smuggling activities: there was plenty of ground for suspicion, but scant evidence of actual guilt. Everything was done through minions and intermediaries, people like Gregory Manners, Jamie Gilbert and Andy Pandy; Clough never got his own hands dirty. His only contact with anything but the profits was entirely circumstantial.

Or was it? Had Emily Riddle posed some sort of threat to him? Did she have knowledge he considered dangerous? Clough didn't like to lose, didn't like people walking out on him, especially if they took something with them, be that money or knowledge.

It was beginning to seem entirely possible to Banks that the two cases were connected, and that Emily Riddle might have been killed by the same person and for the same reason as Charlie Courage. But who was it? Which of his minions had Clough used? Andy Pandy, who already had a grudge against Emily, the kind of grudge you develop from a hard kick in the balls? Jamie Gilbert, who Burgess had referred to as a psycho? Or someone else, someone they hadn't encountered yet? Gregory Manners might be able to help them, if they could find him.

Banks finished his Yorkshire and lit another cigarette. He had about a third of a pint left, and he decided not to have another one. 'You said you'd heard rumours about a big local operation,' he said. 'Anything in them?'

'There's always something, don't you think? No smoke without fire, as they say. It's mostly a matter of finding a lot more pirated goods flooding the markets around North Yorkshire, which reeks of the kind of organization you've just been talking about. You say they've moved on?'

'Their van was heading for another business park near Wooler, in Northumbria, when it was hijacked. Everything disappeared, and the driver was in a coma for a few days before he died. No prints at the scene. Nothing. All we have is a CD case from PKF's Daleview operation which bears the finger-prints of one Gregory Manners, convicted for smuggling, and a known associate of our Mr Big.'

'That's the thing,' said Baird, leaning forward. 'They're getting into these new areas, the big guys, like cigarette smuggling and pirating games. There's a pile of money to be made if you do it right, and the risks are far less than dealing in drugs. Besides, drugs are cheaper than they've ever been these days. With smuggling and pirating, you just sit back and rake in the profits. That's what we've been trying to tell you lot for ages. And the more you squeeze the drug dealers, the more they're likely to find more creative ways of making their fortunes.'

Banks looked at his watch. Just gone half past two. Time to check on what was happening in the incident room, then ACC McLaughlin and Detective Superintendent Gristhorpe would be waiting for an update. 'I've got to go now, Granville,' he said, 'but could you do me a favour and keep your eyes and ears open?'

'My pleasure.' Granville paused, then said, 'I heard about Jimmy Riddle's daughter. Terrible business.'

'Yes, it is,' Banks agreed.

'Your case?'

'For my sins.'

'Anything in those rumours in the papers? Sex and drugs?'

'You know what it's like, Granville,' said Banks, stubbing out his cigarette and getting up to leave. 'There's always something in it, isn't there? No smoke without fire.'

Annie's news about Clough being seen in the area around the time of both murders gave Banks that tingle of excitement he hadn't felt in a while as he headed for Scarlea House late that afternoon, taking the unfenced high roads, where the only things that slowed him down were wandering sheep. He put Richard and Linda Thompson's *Shoot Out the Lights* on the car stereo and turned it up a bit louder than usual.

Annie's purple Astra was parked outside Scarlea, and she was waiting in the lobby when Banks arrived. Gerald Ferguson had reported for work ten minutes ago, according to George Lacey. He pointed the way, and Banks and Annie walked down the gloomy hall to the double doors at the far end.

'Anything on that sighting in Barnard Castle?' Banks asked.

Annie shook her head. 'False alarm. Witness was an elderly woman and she admitted all teenagers looked alike to her. Soon as I showed her the photo again she began to have doubts.'

Banks pushed open the heavy doors – it took more strength than he expected – and they entered the magnificently appointed dining room. Once a banquet hall, he guessed, it had a number of large windows looking out over the valley bottom to the steep dalesides criss-crossed with drystone walls. It was too dark to see anything now, of course, but breakfasting grouse shooters could no doubt look at the view and anticipate the joys of the coming day's slaughter as they ate their eggs Benedict or juice and cereal.

There would probably have been one large central banquet table before the place had been turned into an upmarket restaurant, Banks thought, but now there were a number of tables scattered about the room, each covered by a spotless heavy linen tablecloth. At the far end were more doors, probably to the kitchen, and a long bar took up one wall, all dark polished wood and brass, the rows of bottles gleaming on shelves in front of the mirror at the back. Banks had never seen so many single malt whiskies in one place before. Most of them he had never even heard of.

A man in a burgundy jacket stood with his back to them fiddling with the optic on the gin bottle when Banks went over and introduced himself and Annie.

'Charmed to meet you,' the man said, glancing back at them. 'I'm Gerald Ferguson, and this bloody thing is a pain in the arse, excuse my French, love. I've told them to buy a new one but they're too bloody tight-fisted. The hell with it.' He left the optic and leaned on the bar to face them. 'What can I do for you?'

He was a little round man of about fifty, with a red face, mutton chop sideboards and a soup-strainer moustache. His jacket tugged a bit at the gold buttons around his chest and stomach, and Banks thought one deep breath would pop them. 'We were hoping you might be able to help us with some information about a guest, Mr Ferguson,' he said.

'Gerald. Please.' He looked around then put his finger to the side of his nose. 'Fancy a wee dram?'

Banks and Annie sat on the high bar stools. 'We wouldn't want to get you into any trouble,' said Banks.

Gerald waved his hand and looked towards the door they had entered by. His fingers were surprisingly long and tapered, Banks thought, the nails neatly clipped and shiny. Perhaps he played piano as a hobby. 'What he doesn't know won't harm him. What's your poison?'

It was an unfortunate turn of phrase, Banks thought, as he scanned the row of bottles and settled on the cask-strength Port Ellen.

'Detective Sergeant Cabbot?'

'Nothing for me, thank you.'

'You certain?'

'Certain.'

Gerald shrugged. 'Up to you.' He poured two glasses of Port Ellen, very generous measures, Banks thought, set one in front of himself and another in front of Banks. '*Slainte*,' he said, and knocked it back in one.

'*Slainte*,' said Banks, and took a little sip. Heaven. He set the glass down. 'It's a guest called Clough we're interested in. Barry Clough. Apparently he's a regular in grouse season.'

'Aye, he's that, all right.'

Banks caught the tone of disapproval in his voice. 'You don't like him?'

'I didn't say that, did I?' said Ferguson, pouring himself another Port Ellen. Banks guessed it wasn't his first and wouldn't be his last one of the day, either. At least this time he sipped it slowly.

'Tell us what you do think of him, then.'

'He's a thug in fancy dress. And as for that factotum of his—'

'Jamie Gilbert?'

'If that's his name. The one with the queer hair.'

'That's him. Go on.'

Ferguson took another sip of whisky and lowered his voice. 'This place used to have a bit of class, do you know that? I've worked here going on twenty-five years and I've seen them all come and go. We've had MPs – a prime minister and an American president once – judges, foreign dignitaries, businessmen from the City, and some of them might have been stingy bastards, but they all had one thing in common: they were gentlemen.'

'And now?'

Ferguson snorted. 'Now? I wouldn't give you twopence for the crowd we get these days.' He glanced over at the doors again. 'Not since he came.'

'Mr Lacey?'

'Mr George bloody Lacey, General Manager. Him and his new ideas. Modernization, for crying out loud.' He pointed towards the windows. 'What do you need modernization for when you've got the best bloody view in the world and all nature on your doorstep? Tell me the answer to that, if you can.'

Banks, who knew a rhetorical question when he heard one, gave a sympathetic nod.

'Since he came,' Ferguson went on, 'we've had nothing but bloody pop stars, actors, television personalities, whiz-kids from the stock market. Christ, we've even had bloody women. Sorry love, no offence intended, but grouse shooting never used to be much of a woman's sport.' He knocked back another mouthful of Port Ellen.

Annie smiled, but Banks had seen that one before; she didn't mean it. Ferguson had better watch out.

'Half of them don't even know one end of a shotgun from t'other,' Ferguson went on. 'It's a wonder we don't have more accidents, I tell you. But they've got plenty of money to throw about. Oh, aye. Take a bloke like that there Clough. Thinks if he tosses you a few bob at the start of the evening you're at his beck and call for the rest of the night. Pillock. And Mary, she's one of the lasses that clean the rooms. Nice lass, but a couple of bob short of a pound, if you know what I mean. The stories she's told me about some of the things she's found.'

'Like what?' Banks asked.

Ferguson thrust his face forward and whispered. 'Syringes, for a start.'

'In Clough's room?'

'No. That were one of the pop stars. Stayed here a week and never once came out of his room. I ask you. Money to throw away, that lot.'

'Back to Barry Clough, Mr Ferguson.'

Ferguson laughed and scratched his head. 'Aye. Sorry. I do run off at the mouth sometimes, don't I? You got me started on one of my little hobby horses.'

'That's fine,' said Banks, 'but can you tell us any more about Barry Clough?'

'What sort of things would you be wanting to know?'

'Did you see much of him while he was here?'

'Aye. I was on the bar every night – I get help when we're busy, like. Mandy, one of the local girls from Longbridge – and Clough was always here for drinks before dinner, and most times he ate here, too.' Ferguson looked around and leaned forward conspiratorially. 'They say the food's spectacular here, but if you ask me there's nowt edible. Foreign muck, for the most part.'

'But Mr Clough enjoyed it?'

'He did. And he knew what wines to order with what

308

courses – we've got a wine waiter, *sommelier*, as he likes to call himself, the stuck-up bugger – from his Châteauneuf-du-bloody-Pape to his Sauternes and his vintage port. See, he's got all the trappings, the expensive clothes – Armani, Paul Smith – all the top-quality shooting gear and what have you, and he thinks he's got style, but you can tell he's common as muck underneath it all. Must've read a bluffer's guide, but he couldn't fool me. There's one thing you can't fake: class. Like I said, a thug. Why? What's he done?'

'We don't know that he's done anything yet.'

'I'll bet you suspect him of something, though, don't you? Stands to reason. You mark my words, bloke like him, he's bound to have done something. Bound to.'

'Did you talk to him much?'

'Like I said, he came on like he thought he was a gentleman, but he couldn't pull it off. For a start, a real gentleman wouldn't pass the time of day talking to the likes of me. He might make a friendly comment on the weather or the quality of that day's shooting, but that's as far as he'd go. There are clear lines. This Clough, though, chatty as anything, propping up the bar, drinking his bloody Cosmopolitans and smoking his Cuban cigars. And that bloody ponytail.'

'What did he talk about?'

'Nothing much, when all's said and done. Football. Seems he's an Arsenal supporter. I'm a Newcastle man, myself. Goes on about his villa in Spain, about going to parties with all these bloody celebrities. As if I give a toss.'

'Did he ever talk about his business?'

'Not that I recall. What is it?'

'That's what we'd like to know.'

'Well, I won't say some people don't sometimes let something slip, you know. Comes with the job. I've actually managed one or two good investments over the years based on things I've heard on this job, but don't tell anyone that. I'm paid to stand behind this bar all bloody night and sometimes people, they look on you as a sort of father confessor, not that I'm Catholic or anything. Straight C of E.'

'Not Clough, though?'

'No. That's why I can hardly remember a word he said.'

'Was he with a party?'

'Yes. About five or six of them.'

'Who?'

'They were a mixed bunch. There was that pretty young pop singer whose picture you see all over the place these days, the one where she's wearing hardly more than a pair of gold silk knickers. Amanda Khan, she's called. Touch of the tarbrush. Lovely skin, though.'

Banks had seen the image in question; it was on the cover of her new CD and also graced posters in HMV and Virgin Records. She looked about as old as Emily Riddle.

'Couldn't even *hold* a bloody gun, her, let alone shoot one. Still, I must say she seemed a nice enough lass, especially for a pop singer. Polite. And far too nice, not to mention too *young*, for the likes of Clough.'

'Was she with him?'

'What do you mean? Were they sleeping together?'

'Yes.'

'I don't know. Whatever they get up to when the bar closes is none of my business.'

'Did you get the impression that they were sleeping together?'

'Well, they did seem a bit close, and I did see him touch her every now and then. You know, put an arm around her, pat her bum, that sort of thing. More as if she were a possession he kept wanting to touch than anything else.'

That sounded like Clough, Banks thought. It hadn't taken him long to get another girl. 'Who else?'

Ferguson scratched his head again. Banks took another sip of the fiery malt. 'I didn't recognize any of the others. I'm sure our Mr Lacey will let you have a look at the registration book, or bloody diskette or whatever he calls it now. Used to have a nice big black leather-bound book. Must've been worth a bob or two. But now it's all bloody computer disks and websites. I ask you. *Websites*.'

Banks slipped the photograph of Emily Riddle out of his briefcase. 'Did he ever meet this girl?'

Some of the colour left Ferguson's face. 'So that's what it's all about, is it? I know who she is, poor lass. I read about her in the papers. You think he did it? Clough?'

'We don't know,' said Banks. 'That's why we're asking these questions.'

'I can't give him an alibi,' said Ferguson. 'Like I said, I saw him most evenings, but never during the day. He could have slipped out any time, really.'

'An alibi's not much use in a case like this,' Banks said. 'At the moment it's enough to know that he was in the area at the time.'

'Oh, he was in the area, all right.'

'Did you see him meet anyone outside his party?'

'Only the once.'

'When was this?'

'I can't recall if it was Sunday or Monday. I think it must have been Sunday. That was the day we had the saddle of lamb. Would have been nice, too, if it hadn't been for all them fancy herbs and sauces cook sloshes over everything he makes. Another drink?'

'No thanks.'

'Sure you won't have a drop, Miss?'

'No, thanks, Mr Ferguson.'

'Gerald. I told you, it's Gerald.'

Annie smiled that non-smile again. 'No, Gerald.'

He beamed at her. 'That's better.'

'This person Clough met,' Banks said. 'Man or a woman?'

'Man. You know, there was something familiar about him, but I just can't put my finger on it right now.'

311

'A media personality?'

'I don't think so. But I've seen him in the papers.'

'What did he look like?'

'About six foot something. Bit dour-looking, as if he'd just been sucking on a lemon. Didn't seem at all comfortable to be there. Only drank mineral water. Kept looking around.'

'Could you tell if they'd met before?'

'Hard to say, really. If I had to guess, I'd say it was their first meeting. I don't know why, but there you are. What you lot would call a hunch.'

'Did you hear any of what they said?'

'No. I was here, behind the bar, and they had a window table.'

'Did they seem friendly?'

'As a matter of fact, no, they didn't. The bloke got up and left before his main course arrived.'

'Were they arguing?'

'If they were, they were doing it quietly. He was certainly red in the face when he left, I can tell you that.'

'Clough?'

'No, the other fellow. Clough was as cool as a cucumber.'

'Anything else you can tell me about this man?'

'Bald as a coot, heavy eyebrows. There was something else familiar about him, too, about his bearing, as if maybe he was a military man or something. No . . . there's still something missing.'

'A uniform, perhaps?' Banks suggested, feeling the tingle at the bottom of his spine. 'A police uniform?'

Ferguson's eyes opened wide. 'By George, I think you've got it. He was wearing a suit that night, but if you picture him in a uniform . . . You're right. I've seen him on telly opening farm shows and spouting about crime figures being down. Mr Riddle, that's who it was, now I think back. Your own chief constable. I wonder what all that was about.'

Great, thought Banks, with that sinking feeling. Just what we need. He had sensed something odd about Riddle the night he went to break the news of Emily's murder. Riddle had mentioned Clough immediately, though Banks had never told him the man's name, and he was damn sure Emily hadn't.

'Thank you, Mr Ferguson,' he said, slugging back the last millimetre of Port Ellen. 'Thank you very much. We might need to talk to you again, if that's all right?'

'You know where I am. We'll try the Caol Ila twenty-two-year-old next time you drop by. Lovely drop of malt. It'll knock your socks off.'

Banks felt as if his socks had been knocked off already as he walked out into the evening darkness. Neither he nor Annie could think of anything to say. He felt tired. His brain couldn't even grapple with the consequences of what Gerald Ferguson had just told him about Chief Constable Riddle dining with Barry Clough. There was too much to take in. But he couldn't let it lie; he had to confront Riddle, and the sooner the better.

Banks still felt tired when he pulled up yet again in front of the Old Mill that night. Annie had seemed annoyed at the station when he told her he wanted to confront Riddle alone with Ferguson's story, but she hadn't argued. Riddle *was* chief constable, after all, and Banks didn't want to give the appearance of a formal interrogation, the way it would appear if two detectives turned up on his doorstep. He wanted an honest explanation, though he had his own ideas about what had transpired, and he believed that Riddle would give him one. It was a job he would have gladly delegated if he thought that was at all possible, but it wasn't. He was still SIO, and if anyone was going to face Chief Constable Riddle with this new development, then it had to be Banks.

Riddle himself answered the door and invited Banks in.

'Ros is out, I'm afraid,' he said. 'She's visiting Charlotte King, our neighbour. Benjamin's in bed.'

They walked through to the large living room and sat

down. Riddle didn't offer anything in the way of refreshments, which was fine; Banks didn't want anything. He blamed the small whisky he'd had at Scarlea for his tiredness. 'How's he taking everything?' he asked. 'Benjamin.'

'He doesn't know what's happened. He knows that his sister has gone to live with Jesus, and he misses her terribly. He keeps asking if it's something to do with the funny pictures of her in the computer.'

'What do you tell him?'

'That it's not. To forget about that. But it seems he can't. We're going to send him to stay with his grandparents – Ros's mother and father down in Barnstaple – after the funeral. He's always got along well with them and we think a change of scene will do him good.'

'When's the funeral?'

'Tomorrow morning. The coroner released the body as quickly as she could.' He paused. 'Will you be there?'

'If I wouldn't be intruding.'

'For better or for worse, you're part of this.'

Banks wished to hell he weren't, but Riddle was right. 'I'll be there,' he said.

'Good.'

'And your wife? How's Mrs Riddle doing?'

'She's bearing up. Ros is strong. She'll survive. Anyway, you're not here to make small talk about my family, Banks. What is it? Have there been any developments?'

Banks paused. 'Yes,' he said finally. 'As a matter of fact there have.'

'Out with it, then.'

'You're not going to like it.'

'More bad news?' Banks noticed a quick flash of fear in Riddle's eyes, something he had never seen there before. Riddle averted his gaze. 'Anyway, it doesn't matter whether I like it or not,' he said. 'Things have gone too far for that. Two months ago, I wouldn't have even imagined having you in my house, let alone inviting you to my daughter's funeral. It doesn't mean I've changed my mind about you, Banks, just that circumstances have changed.'

'I've been useful to you.'

'And haven't I fulfilled my part of the bargain?'

'What were you doing having dinner with Barry Clough at Scarlea House on Sunday, December the sixth?'

Riddle paused before answering. 'I was hoping you wouldn't find out about that,' he said. 'Too much to hope for, I suppose.'

'You should have known.'

'Yes, well . . . Anyway, I didn't have dinner with him. I left before things went that far.'

'Don't split hairs. You met him. Why?'

'Because he asked me to.'

'When?'

'Two days earlier.'

'Friday?'

'Yes. He telephoned me at the station and said he was coming up to Yorkshire for the end of the grouse season the next day, that he'd like to meet me to talk about Emily. That's all he would tell me on the telephone.'

'He called her Emily?'

'Yes.'

'Not Louisa?'

'No.'

'So he'd found out who she was?'

'Oh, he'd found out all right. Starting with her conversation with you in his living room.'

'Bugged?'

'Of course. That's what he told me, anyway.'

'What did he want with you?'

'What do you think?'

'Blackmail?'

'In a nutshell. I've come across his kind before, Banks.

They collect people they think they might be able to use at some point.'

'Tell me about your conversation.'

Riddle scowled. 'You're enjoying this, aren't you?'

'What do mean?'

'Putting me on the receiving end. Isn't this what you've always dreamed about?'

'You overestimate your importance to me,' said Banks, 'and to be perfectly honest, the answer's no, I'm not enjoying it. I haven't enjoyed any of this. Not breaking the news to you about Emily's death, not questioning you and your wife about her movements, and certainly not this. I've had the feeling that one or both of you has been lying or concealing things right from the start, and now I have some concrete evidence of it. I still wish I could simply wash my hands of the lot of you, but I can't. I've got my job to do, and, believe it or not, I feel that I owe your daughter something.'

'Why? What did she ever do for you?'

'Nothing. That's not it at all.'

'What is, then?'

'You wouldn't understand. Let's just get back to that Sunday dinner at Scarlea, shall we? What did Clough want to talk to you about?'

'What do you think? He'd discovered that I'm chief constable and that I was contemplating entering politics. The idea of having such an influential person in his pocket appealed to him.'

'What did he say?'

'He said that he knew Emily in London – as Louisa Gamine, of course – that they had lived together for two or three months and that he had compromising photographs and all sorts of interesting stories he could give to the newspapers about her, things that would spoil my chances of election, should I ever get that far, and things that would even call into doubt my fitness to stay on as chief constable, should I not. He made a few obscene comments about her, and he also indicated that he could probably persuade her to go back with him any time he wanted. He seemed to believe that all he would have to do was whistle.'

'What did you say to him?'

'I told him to sod off. What do you think?'

'What did he say to that?'

'He said he could perfectly understand my reaction and that he'd give me a couple of weeks to think it over, then get in touch again.'

'Is that when you got up and walked away?'

'Yes.'

'Did you hear anything else from him after that?'

'No. It's only been a week and a half.'

'No threats or anything?'

'Nothing. And I don't expect to.'

'Why not?'

'Well, he's hardly going to draw attention to himself by making good on his blackmail threat to me now, is he? Not after the murder.'

'You don't think the murder was a sort of warning for you, a signal?'

'Don't be absurd. Things were delicately balanced. Clough had everything to lose by harming Emily and everything to gain by keeping her alive. He's not a stupid man, Banks. What do you imagine he'd guess my reaction to be if I thought for a moment that he'd murdered my daughter? It just doesn't make sense.'

'I wouldn't be too sure about that.' Banks really wanted a cigarette, but he knew he couldn't have one, not in Riddle's house. 'You must have known we'd find out sooner or later,' he said. 'Why on earth didn't you tell me?'

'It was a calculated risk. Why should I tell you? It was my personal business. My problem. It's up to me to deal with it.'

'This wasn't a personal problem. It stopped being that the

minute someone *murdered* Emily, for Christ's sake. Maybe Clough. You were withholding evidence.'

'What evidence?'

'That he was in the area around the time of her death, for a start. He could have easily given her the drugs.'

'I've tried not to interfere with the investigation in any way. I would like to have steered you away from Clough as a suspect, but I obviously couldn't do that without raising suspicion.' Riddle leaned forward and rested his hands on his knees. 'Think about it for a minute, Banks, before you go off half-cocked on this. What possible reason could Clough have for wanting to kill Emily when she represented his hold over me?'

'She didn't need to be alive for him to make good on his threat.'

'But it wasn't just the threat of revelations he made, remember. He also said he could take her back with him whenever he wanted. He knew I wouldn't be able to bear the thought of her being with him. You should have told me, Banks. When you brought her back. You should have told us the sort of trouble she'd been getting herself into. You blame me for withholding evidence, but neither of you said a word about what Emily had been up to in London.'

Banks sighed. 'What good would it have done?' Though maybe he should have, he thought miserably. He had believed that in keeping quiet he was saving the Riddles from unnecessary pain, and saving Emily perhaps from their disciplinarian backlash. But look what had happened. Emily was dead and Jimmy Riddle was in deep trouble himself. Trouble from which he might never fully recover. Banks remembered what Emily had told him about Riddle being a poor detective, always coming up with the wrong killer in the crime novels he read as an adolescent. He could believe it. 'It's no use blaming me,' he went on. 'Believe me, there are times I wish I'd done things differently. But you. You're a professional copper. You're a bloody chief constable, for crying out loud. I can't believe you'd be so stupid and stubborn and proud not to tell me that a man I've been seriously suspecting as your daughter's killer actually approached you as a blackmail target only four days before she was murdered.'

Riddle's expression hardened. 'I told you. It was a private matter. It has nothing to do with Emily's death. He had no motive for killing her. Don't you think that if I really believed Clough had killed Emily I'd have throttled him with my bare hands by now? You might not understand this, Banks, but I loved my daughter.'

'Who can really know with someone like Clough?' Banks argued. 'Perhaps from a business standpoint he would be better off with Emily alive, but he's also a violent man, from what I've heard, and a possessive one. He doesn't like people walking out on him. Maybe that's why he killed her. Besides, I don't believe she would have gone back to him that easily. She was frightened of him.'

'Well, that might be one good reason for going back to him, mightn't it? Men like him might have a certain fascination for girls like . . . like Emily.'

'What do you mean?'

'Precocious, mischievous, rebellious. She's always been like that. You know that she and I didn't get on, no matter how much I cared about her. It always came out wrong. And Clough. He's about my age, but he's a criminal. Policeman – criminal. Don't you see that she was doing this to hurt me?'

'If she'd wanted to hurt you, she'd have made sure you knew about it.'

Riddle just shook his head.

'Did Clough say anything about his business interests at this dinner?'

'No.'

'Did he mention PKF Computer Systems?'

'No.'

'Charlie Courage? Gregory Manners? Jamie Gilbert?'

'No. I've told you what he said. Don't you think that if he'd told me anything incriminating I would have passed it along to you?'

'After what I've just heard, I don't know about that.'

'There was *nothing*, Banks. Just his not-so-subtle blackmail hints.'

'But he was here, in the Eastvale area, when both Charlie Courage and your daughter were killed. Doesn't that make you stop and think?'

'The first thing it makes me think is that he can't have been responsible for the murders. He's not so stupid as to be on the doorstep when they went down.'

'Stop defending him. For crying out loud, anyone would think you had . . .'

'What?'

'Never mind.'

'What are you going to do about it?'

Banks shook his head. 'I don't know.'

'Whatever it is, please have the decency to wait until after the funeral, would you?'

Banks said he would, but his mind was elsewhere, with what he had left unsaid. He could think of only one good reason why Riddle would be so unprofessional as to conceal the details about his secret meeting with Clough: that he was at least considering capitulating to Clough's request. Which brought Banks to consider an even greater problem. With Emily's death, clearly a large part of Clough's hold over Riddle had been extinguished. If Clough hadn't killed her, then who *did* want Emily Riddle dead, and why?

14

A lot of people, Banks mused, thought that the police attended the funerals of murder victims in the hope of finding the killer there. They didn't. That only happened in books and on television. On the other hand, given that a victim's close relatives were likely to be at the funeral, and given that by far the largest percentage of murders were committed by close family members, then the odds were pretty good that the murderer *would* be at the funeral.

Not this one, though. Barry Clough wasn't there, for a start, and he was the closest they had to a suspect so far, even though Riddle was probably right about Emily being of far more value to him alive. Was Banks wearing blinkers when it came to Clough, or was he going off half-cocked, as Gristhorpe and Riddle had warned him against doing? He didn't think so. He knew it didn't make sense for Clough to kill Emily just after he had used her to attempt to blackmail her father, but he was sure there must be something he was missing, some angle he hadn't considered yet. The only thing he *had* thought of, but didn't really believe in, was that Clough was some sort of psychopath and simply hadn't been able to stop himself. If that had been the case, he would have made damn sure he was there to watch and participate in Emily's murder.

Craig Newton and Ruth Walker had travelled up together; they stood looking puzzled and miserable in the rain as the vicar intoned the Twenty-third Psalm. Banks caught their eyes; Craig gave him a curt nod and Ruth gave him a dirty look.

'The Lord is my shepherd; I shall not want. He maketh me to lie down in green pastures: he leadeth me beside the still waters.' There was nothing green about the Dales pastures that morning; everything, from sky to houses to the unevenly shaped fields and drystone walls, was a dull slate-grey or mud-brown. Nor was there anything still about the River Swain, which tumbled over a series of small waterfalls beside the grave-yard and, along with the wind screaming through the gaps in the drystone wall like a Stockhausen composition, almost drowned out the vicar's words. The wind also drove the rain hard across the churchyard, and the mourners seemed to draw as deeply into their heavy overcoats, gloves and hats as they could.

At least the vicar was using the old version, Banks noticed. 'The Lord is my shepherd; therefore can I lack nothing' had about as much resonance as 'as in a mirror, dimly', he thought. Not that he went to Church very often, but like many people, he remembered the powerful church language of his youth and anything less fell far short. He hadn't known what half of it meant, either then or now, but it never seemed to matter; religion, he thought, was mostly a matter of mumbo-jumbo, anyway. Chants, mantras, whatever. Comforting mumbo-jumbo, in this case, though nobody was fooled. Rosalind Riddle dabbed at her eyes with a white hanky every now and then, Benjamin stood next to her looking confused, and her husband looked as if he had been up all night staring the Grim Reaper himself in the face.

When Riddle caught Banks's eye briefly on the way out to the graveside, he looked away guiltily. And well he might, thought Banks, who still felt a residue of anger towards him for stalling the investigation. He had realized after his interview with Riddle the previous day, though, that he had also been guilty of hiding too many things; he hadn't told Annie about the lunch with Emily at first, and he still hadn't told her about the night in the hotel room. With any luck now, she wouldn't find out about that. Of course, he could rationalize his own shortcomings a lot more easily than he could Riddle's, but he could at least *understand* why Riddle might not like to admit to him that he had kept a dinner engagement with his daughter's lover, a man who also happened to have a criminal reputation. Would Riddle have capitulated with whatever Clough wanted from him in order to protect himself and Emily? What kind of man was he when it came to the crunch? He would never have the chance to find out now. Virtue can't prove itself until it's tested.

'Yea, though I walk through the valley of the shadow of death . . .' *The valley of the shadow of death* was a phrase that had always moved Banks, sent a shiver up his spine, though he would have been hard-pressed to explain what it meant to him. It was one phrase they hadn't got rid of in the new translation, too. He thought of poor Graham Marshall all those years ago, walking through the valley of the shadow of death. They had never found his body, so he never had a funeral like Emily. There had been some sort of memorial service at school, Banks remembered, or a remembrance service, he wasn't sure which. The headmaster had recited the Twenty-third Psalm. So much death. Sometimes his head seemed full of the voices of the dead and he felt he had so much blood on his hands.

Banks found himself wishing the funeral would soon be over. It wasn't only the weather, the rain dripping down the back of his neck and the wet, cold wind that cut right through three layers of clothing to the bone, but the sight of the coffin perched at the graveside ready to be lowered, knowing that Emily was in there, the once vital, mischievous spirit who had once curled up and slept like a little child with her thumb in her mouth in a hotel room, with him sitting in the chair listening to Dawn Upshaw's song about sleep. *Cold, cold is the grave*, line from an old folk ballad, passed through his mind. The grave looked cold indeed, but the only one not feeling it now was Emily.

When it was over, the body lowered into its final resting place, people started drifting towards the car park. Ruth and Craig approached the Riddles. The chief constable seemed oblivious to them, and Craig hung back. Ruth said something to Rosalind, something that looked deeply earnest. Rosalind uttered a few words and touched her arm. Then Rosalind saw Banks alone and walked over to him with an elderly couple in tow.

'My mother and father,' she said, introducing them.

Banks shook their hands and offered his condolences.

'Are you coming to the house?' Rosalind asked.

'No,' he said. 'I'm afraid I can't. Too much work.' He could probably have spared half an hour or so, but the truth was that he didn't fancy making small talk with the Riddle family. 'What did Ruth want?' he asked.

'Oh, so that's who it is,' said Rosalind. 'I wondered. She said she was a friend of Emily's and wondered if she might have some sort of keepsake.'

'And?'

'I suggested she drop by the house and I'd see what I could do. Why?'

'No reason. The boy with her's Craig Newton. Emily's ex-boyfriend.'

'Is he a suspect?'

'Technically, yes. He pestered her after they split up, and he doesn't have an alibi.'

'But realistically?'

Banks shook his head. 'I don't think so.'

Rosalind glanced over at the two of them. 'Then I suppose I should invite them both back to the house, shouldn't I?'

'They've come a long way.'

'How did they know it was today?'

'I phoned Craig last night. The last time I interviewed him he said he'd like to be there, and I could see no reason why not. He must have contacted Ruth.'

Rosalind shook Banks's hand and walked over with her mother and father towards Ruth's car. Banks also saw Darren Hirst and the others who had been in the Bar None with Emily on the night of her death, Tina and Jackie. They all looked shell-shocked. Darren nodded and walked by. That reminded Banks of a glimmer of an idea he'd had, something he wanted to ask Darren. Not now, though; it would keep. Leave the poor lad to his grief for a while.

Back at the office, before Banks could even get his overcoat off and sit down, DS Hatchley knocked on his door and entered.

'How's it going, Jim?' Banks asked.

'Fine. The funeral?'

'What you'd expect.'

Hatchley shut the door behind him and sat down. He was the opposite of Annie when it came to looking comfortable, always perched at the edge of the chair, squirming as if something sharp were digging into his arse. He took his cigarettes out and glanced at Banks for permission. Banks got up and opened the window, despite the cold, and both of them lit up.

'It's about Castle Hill Books,' said Hatchley. 'I sent young Lose Some out there yesterday afternoon and she came back with an interesting haul.'

'Go on.'

'The owner's a slimy little sod called Stan Fish. He's been selling porn on the side for years. Anyway, it turns out he's got a whole cupboardful of pirated computer software, games and music CDs. He says he got them from a chap he knows only as Greg. This Greg comes around every couple of weeks in a white van with a selection. So Lose Some whips out her picture of Gregory Manners, and Bob's your uncle.'

'Good,' said Banks. 'That'll give us a bit of extra ammunition.' He looked at his watch. 'Manners is on his way here as we speak.'

'Lose Some also brought in a few samples of the goods,'

Hatchley went on. 'Vic Manson's checking them for prints now. I'll get him to put a rush on it. If he can match them with Manners's . . .'

'It still doesn't give us much, though,' said Banks. 'Even if we can do Manners for pirating and distributing copyrighted software, it's hardly a serious charge.'

'It might give you a handle on this other villain you're after, though.'

'Barry Clough?'

'Aye.' Hatchley stubbed out his cigarette. 'Yon Lose Some has also been showing Manners's picture around Daleview and a couple of people recognized him.'

'Nobody's seen Clough, Andy Pandy or Jamie Gilbert around there, though?'

'Not yet, but we're still asking.' Hatchley got up to leave. Before he could go, the door opened and Detective Superintendent Gristhorpe barged in brandishing one of the more notorious London tabloids. Gristhorpe sniffed the air, scowled at both of them, then said, 'Seen the papers this morning, Alan?'

Banks looked at the newspaper. 'Even if I'd had time,' he said, 'it wouldn't have been that one.'

A smile split Gristhorpe's ruddy, pockmarked face. 'Wouldn't be my first choice either,' he said. 'More the sort of thing you'd be reading, eh, Sergeant Hatchley?'

'If I'd time, sir,' muttered Hatchley, edging his way out of the office, winking at Banks as he shut the door behind him.

Gristhorpe dropped the tabloid on Banks's desk. 'You'd better have a gander, Alan,' he said. 'It looks as if I'm going to be on damage control for the rest of the day.' Then he left as abruptly as he'd entered.

The front-page colour photo in itself was almost enough to give Banks a heart attack. There were two photos, actually: one of Barry Clough leaving a Soho restaurant, thrusting his palm towards the cameraman, and one of Jimmy Riddle leaving police headquarters. The way the photos were arranged together made it look as if the two men were meeting face to face. Centred below them was a photograph of Emily. It was a good one, professional, and it featured her 'sophisticated' heroin-chic look. She had her blonde hair piled up in an expensive mess and wore a strapless black evening gown. Not the same dress she'd been wearing the night of the hotel room, but a similar one. Banks had seen the picture before, or one very much like it, in Craig Newton's house. Could Craig have sold it to the newspapers? Was he still that bitter over his split-up with Emily? More likely, Banks thought, that Barry Clough had got hold of some copies when Emily was living with him and that this was his response to Emily's death and Riddle's silence.

The headline screamed up at him: CHIEF CONSTABLE'S DAUGHTER MURDER CASE: WHAT ARE THEY HIDING? The story went on to tell of Emily's association with 'well-known club owner and man-about-town Barry Clough', a man 'the same age as her senior policeman father'. After a couple of not-so-subtle indications that 'well-known club owner and man-about-town' was shorthand for gangster, there were a couple of morally high-handed digressions of the 'Do you know what your daughter's doing and who she's with tonight?' sort before the reporter got to the real nitty-gritty: speculation about Clough expanding his 'business empire' up north, and about him and Riddle being involved in some sort of crooked partnership. Emily's role in all this was left to the readers to guess.

The article had obviously been vetted by the paper's solicitors, and it stopped just short of libel. For example, never at any point did the reporter state that Riddle and Clough *had* met and talked, or that Riddle had known about Emily's relationship with Clough – the reporter clearly hadn't found out about Scarlea House yet – but the whole thing was a masterpiece of innuendo, and the implications in themselves were damaging enough. Banks could only imagine how Riddle's political cronies would react to it.

Banks also realized that the damage wouldn't stop with the political set either; this sort of thing could also easily make Riddle a pariah on the job. Whether there was anything in them or not, such rumours could effectively end his police career. Already Banks suspected there were mutterings at high levels about a chief constable so careless as to let his own daughter get murdered while snorting cocaine in a nightclub. Not to mention the rumours of sex that went with it all. One way or another, as a politician or as a high-ranking copper, Banks imagined that Jimmy Riddle's tenuous reign had come to an end. Humpty-Dumpty.

What surprised Banks was that he felt sorry for the poor bastard.

And what about Rosalind and Benjamin? What would all this do to them?

Banks still remembered Ruth Walker's final question to him only last Saturday: *why* did Emily's father want her back, when he hadn't appeared to care about her before? Banks had thought about that a lot since. At first he had suspected Riddle wanted her back to avoid more damage to his career and, to credit him with some fatherly feelings, because he was worried about her after he saw the photos on the porno website. Perhaps he was wrong about that. At some point in the investigation, the Riddles themselves had joined the group of suspects in Banks's mind.

The big problem with Jimmy Riddle as a suspect was that, whichever way you looked at it, Emily's murder only made things *worse* for him. Sure, her continuing existence had always held out the risk of scandal, but her death *guaranteed* it. On the other hand, given the pressure that Riddle might have been under since Clough's approach at Scarlea, something could have snapped in him.

And what about Rosalind? She hadn't particularly wanted

Emily back at home. She had made that clear from the start. What if she had a good reason for it, and Emily had become, somehow, a threat to her? But how? Why? It still didn't feel right, especially given the method, but perhaps it was time to start pushing the grieving parents a bit harder.

A knock at his door jolted him out of his musings. It was DC Templeton.

'Yes, Kev?'

'Thought you'd like to know, sir, uniformed just brought Gregory Manners in. He's waiting in interview room three.'

'Thanks, I'll be right there. Ask DS Hatchley to sit in, too, will you?'

'Will do, sir.'

'By the way, where'd they find him?'

'Strangest place you could imagine.'

'Oh? And where's that?'

DC Templeton grinned. 'At home, sir. Nice little flat out Thirsk way.'

Banks grinned back. 'Oh, and Kev, there's one more thing I'd like you to do.'

Gregory Manners was a smoothie, right from his carefully combed, impossibly brown hair to the soles of his Italian loafers. He was good-looking in a way, and Banks could see that he might appeal to a certain kind of woman.

The interview room was a dingy, airless sort of place with whitewashed walls, a tiny wire-mesh window and metal table and chairs bolted to the floor. The old blue ashtray, stolen from the Queen's Arms, was gone now that smoking had been banned from the building, but the air still seemed to smell of stale smoke, sweat and fear. Manners sat there coolly, legs crossed, idly staring into space. When Banks and Hatchley entered, he asked why he had been brought there.

Banks ignored him and checked the tapes in the recording machine. Hatchley sat impassive as Buddha, and almost as fat.

The tapes worked. Banks went through the time, date and place routine, naming those present in the room, then he turned to Manners and said, 'You're here to help us with our inquiries, Mr Manners.'

'What inquiries?'

'Things will become clear as we move along.'

Manners leaned forward and rested his arms on the table. 'Should I have my lawyer present?'

'I understand you put in a call to your solicitor before you left home.'

'Before I was brought here, yes. And all I got was his answering machine.'

'They're busy people. You left a message?'

'I told him to get up here sharpish.'

'In the meantime, you've been offered the services of a duty solicitor?'

'Some wet-behind-the-ears little pillock who can't get a proper job?'

'And you've declined?'

'Yes.'

'In that case, Mr Manners, let's proceed with the interview. Just for the record, you haven't been charged with anything yet so there's no need to get overexcited. I'm sure your own solicitor will get here as soon as he possibly can, but in the meantime let's just have a little chat, all right?'

Manners narrowed his eyes but sat back in his chair and relaxed, crossing his legs again. 'What do you want to know? I've done nothing wrong.'

'I'm sure you haven't.' Banks took the CD case that Annie had found at PKF out of its envelope and pushed it over the rickety metal table to Manners. 'Know what this is?'

Manners looked at it. 'It's a CD box.'

'Good. Maybe you can tell me what your fingerprints are doing on this particular CD box?'

'I suppose I must have touched it.'

'Yes,' said Banks. 'Indeed, you must have touched it. Can you tell me what you were doing at the Daleview Business Park?'

'Daleview? Working. Why?'

'I don't know, Gregory. That's why I'm asking you.'

'Well, that's what I was doing. Working. I don't understand this. I haven't done anything illegal. Why are you questioning me?'

'We want to know about the operations of PKF Computer Systems.'

'What about it?'

'Is that who you worked for at Daleview?'

'Yes. But I still don't understand what you're getting at.'

'And what if I told you that it's a dummy company? That it doesn't exist?'

'Then I'd be very surprised indeed.'

'Who set it up?'

'What?'

'PKF.'

'I did, of course. The whole thing's me. Just me. Look, there must be some mistake.'

'There's no mistake.'

'A mistake with the paperwork. I was sure I did it right.'

'There is no paperwork, Gregory. Bugger all. PKF doesn't exist.'

'Well, if it doesn't exist, then I can hardly know anything about it, can I? So why don't I just leave now?'

'Sit down!' Hatchley slammed his ham-sized fist on the table and the noise made Manners jump.

'Hey,' said Manners. 'There's no need for that. That's intimidation.'

'Any more of this bollocks, and I'll show you what intimidation is,' growled Hatchley.

'I'm sure if you just answer my questions as clearly and

331

fully as you can, DS Hatchley will listen as eagerly as I will, won't you, Sergeant?'

'Aye,' said Hatchley, 'soon as he stops trying to feed us this crap.'

Manners swallowed. 'Look, what do you want to know? I'm sorry if I ballsed up the paperwork. Is it a criminal offence?'

'Probably,' said Banks, 'but we'll worry about that later. What did you do at PKF?'

'Developed, produced and marketed a commercial database program.'

'Called?'

'PKF.'

'You invented this?'

'I did.'

'You worked alone?'

'For the most part.'

'It sounds like a lot of work for one person.'

'I've never been afraid of hard work. On occasion, I hired casual labour to help with distribution and such things.'

'People like Jonathan Fearn?'

Manners frowned. 'The name doesn't ring a bell, but I might have, yes.'

Banks took the photographs of Andrew Handley, Jamie Gilbert and Barry Clough out of his file folder and slid them across to Manners. 'Ever seen any of *these* men?'

'No.'

Banks tapped the picture of Clough. 'This one in particular,' he said. 'Go on, have a good look. Think about it.'

'I told you. No.'

'Didn't you do six months for smuggling offences down south not long ago?'

'I just happened to get caught doing something people get away with every day.'

'You must be a heavy smoker and drinker, then.'

'I don't smoke.'

'So you were going to sell the goods you smuggled?'

'Of course I was going to sell them. People go over to Calais and load up their cars every bloody weekend, for crying out loud. What's this got to do with anything?'

Banks tapped Clough's photo again. 'We have information that leads us to believe this man was behind both the smuggling operation *and* whatever PKF was up to.'

'Then your information is wrong. I've never seen him in my life. Or the other two. I *imported* the stuff myself, and I also ran PKF. Which wasn't up to anything, by the way. Maybe I got the paperwork wrong, maybe I just forgot to make everything all official, but if that's why I'm here, just charge me and get it over with. You know I'll be walking out the minute my lawyer gets here.'

'Who said anything about charging you?'

'I can't understand why else you had me brought all this way.'

'What's happened to PKF?'

'I'm sure you know already,' said Manners. 'The van was hijacked on its way to our new businesses premises in Northumbria and everything was stolen. There *is* no PKF any more.'

'And the driver was killed.'

'Yes. Very unfortunate, that.'

'A Mr Fearn. Jonathan Fearn.'

'Yes, well, as I said, I'm sorry, but I don't remember his name. I simply hired him to do the job.'

'Where did you find him?'

'Mr Courage, the nightwatchman at Daleview, recommended him.'

'Ah, yes,' said Banks, shuffling some papers in his folder. 'Charlie Courage. Small-time villain. Must have got in over his head.'

Manners frowned. 'Come again?'

'Funny you should mention Mr Courage, Greg. He also

met with an unfortunate accident, shortly after Mr Fearn. He found himself at the wrong end of a shotgun.'

'Yes, I read about that in the paper,' said Manners. 'It was a terrible shock. He seemed a decent enough bloke.'

'He was a crook, but you know all about that. Let's move on.'

'By all means.' Manners shifted in his chair and rearranged his legs.

'Do you believe in coincidences?'

'They happen all the time.'

'And do you believe that the van getting hijacked, Jonathan Fearn dying of injuries received, and Charlie Courage being shot just happen to be coincidences?'

'They could be.'

'Why were you leaving Daleview?'

'The rent was too expensive. This new place was cheaper, and the space was better. Bigger.'

'Tell me again what PKF actually did.'

'I manufactured and distributed a database system I invented.'

'Background in computers? College?'

'Self-taught. A lot of people in the business are.'

'To whom did you distribute this software?'

'Retailers.'

'Names?'

'Look, I'm sure I have a list somewhere. What is this all about?'

The knock came at the door, as arranged, and it couldn't have been better timed. Banks announced DC Templeton's arrival and paused the tape. 'What is it, Kev?'

'Thought you might be interested in this, sir,' said Templeton, glancing at Manners as he spoke. 'It's just come in from fingerprints. Those CD cases.'

'Ah, yes,' said Banks. 'Let's have a look, shall we?' He opened the file. Templeton left the office. Banks pored over the file frowning for a while, showed the papers to Hatchley, then he set the tapes going again.

'This is interesting,' he said to Manners.

'What is it?'

'Fingerprint results. Another CD case.'

'But I don't understand. You've already found my prints on the case. I've explained that to you already.'

'But this is different, see, Greg,' said Banks. 'This is another CD case entirely.'

'Well, I'm sure I've touched more than one.'

'Yes, but it's where we found it and what it contained that interests me.'

Manners seemed to turn a little pale. 'I don't . . . where *did* you find it?'

'Shop called Castle Hill Books. Run by a man called Stan Fish. Ring any bells?'

'He might have been one of my retailers.'

'For your PKF database software?'

'Yes.'

'Then how come this particular CD case contained a brand new Sony PlayStation game?'

'I don't know. Maybe the owner of the shop switched them around.'

'Could be,' said Banks. 'In fact, I'd be inclined to believe that would be exactly the case, except . . .'

'Except what?'

'Except we found your prints on six other CD cases containing the same game, and we have a lot more to test before we're finished. Some of them contain a brand-new music CD by REM. Hardly even in the shops yet. Then there are a few word-processing programmes and so forth. Funny, though, Greg, no PKF database system.'

Manners crossed his arms. 'Right, that's it,' he said. 'I'm not saying another word until my lawyer gets here.'

*

Two hours later, towards the end of the afternoon, Manners was still in custody waiting for his solicitor and Banks was in his office reading through witness statements when his telephone rang.

It was Dirty Dick Burgess calling from London. 'Guess what, Banks.'

'You've been made head of the Race Relations Board?'

'Very funny. No. But Andy Pandy's turned up at last.'

'Has he, indeed?'

'Thought you'd be interested.'

'Any chance of a chat with him in the near future?'

'Not unless you fancy holding a seance. He's dead. Dead as the proverbial doornail, though I never could see how a doornail could be dead as it was never alive in the first place. Anyway, enough philosophical speculation. He's dead.'

'Where?'

'Pretty remote spot on the edge of Exmoor. I tell you, Banks, if it weren't for the anorak brigade and the dog-walkers, bless their souls, we'd never find half the corpses we do.'

'The long ride?'

'Indeed so.'

'Shotgun?'

'Wound to the upper body. Pretty close range. Not much left.'

'Same as Charlie Courage. Any signs of torture?'

'Christ, Banks, there's hardly any signs of the poor bugger's *chest*. What do you expect? Miracles?'

'So what do you think?'

'Pretty obvious, isn't it?'

'Humour me.'

'Andy Pandy's been a naughty boy. He's ripped off Mr Clough. Mr Clough doesn't like being ripped off, so he sends Andy on the long ride. Way I see it.'

'And Charlie Courage?'

'Part of it. Hardly an innocent bystander, from what you told me.'

'He was taking money from Clough, or from Clough's local oppo Gregory Manners, to make sure PKF operated without hassles. Then suddenly, PKF is moving and Charlie's bonuses are gone. I think Charlie knew where PKF was moving to, and when. And I think Andy Pandy came along with a better offer.'

'Why would he do that?'

'Because he's pissed off with Clough for taking him for granted. He wants more respect.' And he's also angry with Clough over the incident with Emily, when she kicked him in the balls, Banks thought.

'Maybe,' said Burgess, sounding unconvinced.

'So he hijacks the van to set up his own business. The van's full of PKF stock, but more important than that, it's also carrying two or three multi-disc-copying machines, very valuable pieces of equipment. He thinks Clough will never guess in a million years that he did it. But Clough's no fool. He sends a couple of goons up to push Charlie around a bit. Now, Charlie might have been a crook, but no one ever said he was a brave man. Charlie rats on Andy Pandy under torture, and they're both history. I wondered why Gregory Manners was still alive.'

'Come again?'

'Manners was in charge of PKF, so he must have been Clough's first suspect. Clough put the frighteners on him and Manners must have convinced him he had nothing to do with the hijack. Maybe Manners told him Andy Pandy had been hanging about asking questions. We'll probably never know for sure now.'

'So what do we do next?'

'We'll keep showing the photographs around Daleview. I've also got Gregory Manners kicking his heels in the cells here waiting for his lawyer, so maybe I'll have another chat with him first.'

'He won't tell you anything. Too shit-scared of Clough.'

'Probably, but I can push him a bit harder. It'd be nice to threaten him with conspiracy to commit murder or something juicy like that. At the moment there's nothing much except pirating software to hold him on, and that'll probably never stick. Minute his lawyer gets here he'll be off.'

'And what's the betting you'll never see him again?'

'I'd put money on it.'

'So where do we go with Andy Pandy?'

'We'll have a hell of a job proving it's anything to do with Clough,' Banks said. 'Anything at the scene?'

'Tyre track.'

Banks thought for a moment, then said, 'I think it's about time we brought Mr Clough up north for a chat. But first, I've got an idea.'

It was late, and Banks was listening to Anne-Sophie Mutter's interpretation of Beethoven's 'Spring' violin sonata and reading a biography of Ian Fleming when he heard a car draw up outside. That was unusual in itself. The dirt lane that ran in front of his cottage ended at the woods about ten yards farther on, where it became a narrow path between the trees and Gratly Beck. Occasionally, tourists would take the wrong road and have to back out, but not at that time of night, or that time of year.

Curious, Banks put down his book, walked over to the window and opened the curtains a few inches. A sporty-looking car, to judge from its shape, had pulled up in front of the cottage and a woman was getting out. He couldn't make out her features, as it was pitch black outside; she was wearing a scarf, and there were no street lamps on the isolated lane. He would soon find out, though, he thought, as she walked to up to his front door and knocked.

When he opened it and saw Rosalind Riddle take off her scarf, he must have looked surprised enough to embarrass her.

'I'm sorry,' she said. 'Have I come at a bad time?'

'No,' said Banks. 'No, not at all.' He stood aside. 'Come in.'

As she passed close to him in the doorway he felt her breast brush lightly against his arm, and he thought he could smell juniper berries on her breath. Gin, most likely. He took her fur coat and hung it in the cupboard by the door. Underneath, she was wearing a simple pastel blue dress; more suitable, Banks thought, for summer than for a miserable winter's night like this one. Still, with a mink on top, you didn't really need anything underneath. He stopped that line of thought before it went any further.

'This is nice,' she said, standing and looking around the small room, with its blue walls and melting-Brie ceiling. Banks had hung a couple of watercolours he had picked up at auctions on the walls, and a blow-up of what he thought the best of Sandra's photographs took pride of place over the mantelpiece. It had been taken, coincidentally, not far away from the cottage where Banks now lived alone, and it showed the view down the daleside to Helmthorpe in late evening, with a red-and-orange sunset sprawled across the sky, smoke drifting from the chimneys, the church with its square tower and odd little turret attached to one corner, the dark graveyard where sheep grazed among the lichen-stained tombstones, and crooked rows of flagstone roofs. He and Sandra might no longer be together, but that didn't mean he rejected her talent. There wasn't much furniture in the room, just a sofa under the window and two matching armchairs arranged at angles to the fireplace, where a couple of lumps of peat burnt and cast shadows on the walls.

'Do you live here alone?' she asked.

'There's hardly room enough for two.'

'I shouldn't have asked. I'm sorry. Of course, I do know something of your circumstances. Your wife . . .'

'Cup of tea or something?'

'Or something. After a day like this one, I need something a bit stronger than tea. Gin and tonic, if you've got it.'

'Coming up.' Banks went into the kitchen and took the gin out of the cupboard where he kept his haphazard selection of spirits – some rum, a little vodka, half a bottle of cognac and the Laphroaig single malt, that smoky Islay, his favourite and a constant drain on his wallet.

'How strange.'

'What?' Banks turned to see that Rosalind had followed him into the kitchen. She was standing at its centre with an odd expression on her face, as if she were listening to a distant voice.

'It feels . . . I don't know . . . sort of haunted, but in a good way.'

Banks was gobsmacked. One of the reasons he had bought the house in the first place was that he had dreamed of the kitchen before he knew it existed – a dream full of warmth and feelings of extreme well-being – so that when he saw it, he knew he had to have it. Luckily the old lady who was selling didn't want it to fall into the hands of an absentee landlord, so she let him have it for the ridiculously low price of £50,000 – a gift when you considered that there were semis and terraced cottages smaller even than this one going for £70,000 and above in some of the more popular Dales villages.

All Banks sensed about the kitchen was that there was definitely some sort of presence, that it was benevolent, and – only God knew why – that it was feminine. He didn't really believe in gods and ghosts, had never thought much about them, being a more practical sort of man, but this was another change that had taken place since Sandra had left. In the end, he accepted, even embraced, whatever the presence was, and came to believe it was some sort of spirit of the house, the way places are said to have spirits. He had read a little about the subject and named his spirit Haltia, after the Finnish, generally believed to be the spirit of the first person to lay claim to a site either by lighting a fire on it, by building a house on it, or even, in some cases, the first person to die there.

Rosalind was the first person other than Banks to feel it. Others had been there – Tracy, Brian, Sandra, Annie, Superintendent Gristhorpe, Jim Hatchley – but none of them had felt the preternatural appeal of the kitchen. Banks felt almost inclined to tell Rosalind about the dream, but he held back for some reason. He hadn't told anyone about it yet for fear of seeming foolish or mad, and there was no point starting now.

'It's a comfortable room to be in,' he said, pouring the drink. 'You should see it when the sun's shining through the windows. Glorious.' That was his favourite time in the kitchen, when the morning sunlight came skipping over Low Fell and sliding down the green daleside, spilling into the kitchen like honey. That wouldn't happen again for a few more months.

'I'd like that,' said Rosalind. Then she looked away and blushed. She had dark semicircles under her eyes, Banks noticed, which made her look mysterious, tragic even, which was hardly surprising given what she had been through this past while. Despite the poor first impression Rosalind had made on him, Banks found himself thinking that she was a woman he would like to have known, perhaps in another time, another life. Also, in another part of his mind, he suspected that she might have had something to do with her daughter's murder.

'Ice? Lemon?'

'Just the tonic water, please.'

Banks handed her the gin and tonic and poured himself a couple of fingers of rapidly dwindling Laphroaig. They went back into the living room. The only light came from the fire and the reading lamp by his armchair. He wondered if he should turn on the overhead light and decided not to. By the look of her as she sat down wearily opposite him, Rosalind Riddle looked glad of the semi-darkness. He turned down the music and lit a cigarette.

'How was the get-together?'

'What you'd expect. You were fortunate you had work to keep you away.'

'I'm not good at those sorts of things. Did you get a chance to talk to Ruth and Craig?'

'A little. You know what those things are like.'

'What was your impression?'

'He seemed a nice-enough boy.'

'He probably is,' Banks said. 'And Ruth?'

'I didn't really get much chance to talk to her. I'm just glad that it's over, that's all.'

'Why did you want to see me? Was there something you wanted to tell me?'

'Tell you? No. What makes you think that?'

'What is it, then?'

She swirled her drink in her glass before answering. 'I'm worried about Jerry. He's taking this all very badly.'

'It's hardly surprising. I mean, after all, your only daughter is dead, murdered. He's bound to take it badly. He's not made of stone. And now this thing in the newspaper.'

'No, it's more than that.'

'What do you mean?'

Rosalind sighed and stretched her legs out, crossing them at the ankles. It was a gesture that reminded Banks of Annie Cabbot.

'All his life,' Rosalind began, 'the only thing that's counted for Jerry is his work. The job. You know what it's like, what the demands are. The sacrifices he's made . . . we've made . . .' She gave a quick shake of her head. 'I'm not saying he doesn't love us, his family, but we've taken the back seat all along. *My* career's taken a back seat, too. We've always had to move where and when Jerry wanted, no matter what I was doing or how well the children were getting on at school. It's been hard, but I accept it. I don't mind. After all, I don't *have* to stay if I don't want to. But the rewards have made it worthwhile. I know you think he's a social climber and maybe he is, but his origins are pretty humble. Like yours, I should imagine.'

Banks smoked and listened. He had never thought about Riddle's origins before but remembered he had vaguely heard something about his coming from a farmworker's family in Suffolk. He got the impression that Rosalind just wanted to talk, and he was quite happy to let her ramble on as long as she liked, though why she had chosen him to unburden herself to was a mystery. Still, it felt good to have an attractive woman in the house – and one who understood the spirit of the place, at that – even if she was Jimmy Riddle's wife; and there was always the possibility that he might learn something relevant to Emily's murder.

'As I said, he's worked hard and we've made a lot of sacrifices. Jerry isn't . . . I mean, he's not the most demonstrative of men. Our marriage . . . He finds it difficult to show emotion.' She smiled. 'I know most men are the same, but he's more so. He loved Emily dearly but he's never been able to express it. He's come across as overprotective, a sort of tyrant who sets the rules and leaves me to enforce them. Which made me a tyrant in my daughter's eyes, too. He was never there when she might have needed him; they never managed to form a strong bond of any kind.'

'Yet he loved her?'

'Yes. Dearly. He doted on her and her achievements as much as he's capable of doting on anyone other than himself.'

'Why are you telling me all this?'

She smiled again. 'I don't know. Maybe because you're a good listener.'

'Go on.'

'There's not much more to tell, really. Because of what's happened, because of the guilt over never having been able to show his feelings, of always trying to control her rather than showing affection, he's coming apart at the seams. He just sits there. Half the time he doesn't even answer when I talk to him. It's as if he's come adrift, got lost in some inner hell and he can't find his way out. After the funeral, it was even worse. I can't talk to him any more, he's shutting me out. Fortunately Benjamin's gone down to Barnstaple with my parents, or I don't know what I'd do. I know I'm not explaining this very well. I'm not very good with words, but I'm worried about him.'

'Is there anything else on his mind?'

'I don't know. Nothing he's told me about, anyway. Isn't it enough?'

'Maybe you should try to get him to seek help? Grief counselling. I'm sure your doctor could recommend the right sort of treatment.'

'I've mentioned it, but it's no good, he won't go.'

'Then I don't know what to suggest.'

'Would *you* talk to him?'

'Me?' Banks almost laughed out loud. 'I can't see that doing him any good. You know he can't stand the sight of me.'

'You might find that he's softened his attitude towards you a bit lately.'

'Since I got Emily to come home?' Banks shook his head. 'I don't think so. He's just sticking to the bargain.' Banks remembered what Emily had told him about Riddle's envy. Deep-rooted feelings like that didn't just disappear after you'd done someone a favour or two. In most cases they intensified because people who didn't like you to start with resented being beholden to you. Besides, Banks had caught Riddle in a lie, too, and that must rankle. He remembered the guilty expression at the funeral.

'But he wanted you in charge of the investigation.'

'That was a purely professional decision.'

'I still wish you'd talk to him.'

'If he doesn't listen to you, he'd hardly listen to me.'

'He might. At least you're a man. He doesn't have a lot of friends.'

'What about his political colleagues? He must have friends there.'

Rosalind sipped some more gin and tonic. 'They're dropping him like a hot potato. It started with Emily's murder, but it's got worse ever since the newspaper article and all those innuendoes. Plenty of phone calls, lots of sympathy, then the old " . . . perhaps it would be best for all of us if . . . for the good of the party". Hypocrites!'

'I'm sorry to hear that.'

'Yes, well, I'm sure it will only contribute more proof to your theory of human nature, especially the human nature of Conservatives.'

Banks said nothing. He looked into the fire and watched the burning peat shift and sigh out a breath of sparks.

'I'm sorry. I shouldn't have said that.' Rosalind laughed harshly. 'I'm talking about me more than about you. I must admit my own view of human nature has taken a bit of a nose-dive over the past few days.'

The music ended and Banks let the silence stretch.

'If you want to put something else on, that's all right,' said Rosalind. 'I like classical music.'

Banks went to the stereo and picked another Beethoven violin sonata, the 'Kreutzer' this time.

'Mmm,' said Rosalind. 'Lovely.'

Banks marvelled at how much she resembled Emily, especially her lips; they were the same full but finely outlined shape and the same natural pinkish-red colour; they even moved in the same way when she spoke. 'I still don't see that there's anything I can do,' said Banks. 'Even if I do talk to him. And I'm not saying I will.'

'You can at least try. If it does no good . . .' Rosalind shrugged.

'What about you?'

'Me? What about me?'

'How are you doing?'

'I'm coping. Surviving. Sometimes I feel as if I'm being pulled apart by millions of little red-hot fish hooks, but other than that, I'm fine.' She smiled. 'Someone has to be. I went back to the office this afternoon, after everyone had gone. I know it sounds odd, but conveyancing helps keep my mind off more serious matters. But Jerry hasn't even got his work now. He's got nothing. He just sits at home all the time brooding. It's frightening watching someone like him unravel. He's always been so strong, so solid.'

How the mighty are fallen, thought Banks, but he didn't voice it because it would have been cruel. Even so, he had thought it, and that made him bad; was he such a rotten person? He understood what Rosalind meant, of course; it is far more terrifying to see someone you have always depended on, your rock, crack apart than it is to watch someone who was fragile to start with have yet another breakdown. Banks had a distant aunt who kept having 'funny turns', as his mother called them, but as she was mentally flimsy to begin with, no one was much surprised. It wasn't that people didn't sympathize or care, just that her 'turns' lacked any sort of tragic dimension.

'All right,' he said. 'I'll try to make time to go over tomorrow and have a talk with him. I can't promise anything, mind you.'

Her face lit up. 'You will? But that's wonderful. That's all I ask.'

How do I let myself get talked into these things? Banks wondered. Do I look like a sucker? First I give up a weekend in Paris with my daughter – abandoning her to the clutches of the monosyllabic Damon – and head off to London to look for

Emily Riddle, now I'm playing visiting shrink to Jimmy Riddle, the man who's done about as much for my career as Margaret Thatcher did for the trade unions.

'While you're here, there are a couple of things I'd like to ask you, if I may.'

'Really?' Rosalind looked away from him and started twisting the wedding ring on her finger. She had finished her drink and let the empty tumbler stand on the arm of the chair.

'Another G and T?'

'No, thanks. I have to drive.' She glanced at her tiny gold wristwatch and sat forward. 'Besides, I really *should* be getting back. I told Jerry I was going for a drive. I don't like to leave him alone for too long at night. It's a bad time for him.'

'I understand,' said Banks. 'I promise I won't keep you more than a couple of minutes more.'

She sat back in the chair but didn't relax. What was she so nervous about? Banks wondered. What was she holding back?

'Ruth Walker told me that you had answered when she phoned to talk to Emily, but you said you'd never heard of her. Why?'

'You surely can't expect me to remember the name of every single person who calls and asks for Emily, can you? Perhaps she never even said what her name was.'

'People usually do, though, don't they? I mean, it's only polite to say who you are.'

'You'd be surprised how many people lack basic politeness. Or maybe you wouldn't. What exactly are you getting at?'

'I don't know. I just get this funny feeling that there's something you're not telling me. Maybe it's to do with Ruth Walker and maybe it's not, but you get very vague every time her name comes up.'

'It must be your imagination.'

'Maybe. I've been told more than once that I've got too much of it for my own good. Your husband's told me often enough.' Banks leaned forward. 'Look, Mrs Riddle, you probably don't think it's very relevant or important, but I've got to warn you that you're making a poor judgement here. The best course of action is to tell me everything you know and let me be the judge. That's my job.'

Rosalind stood up. 'Thanks for the advice. If I did know anything of relevance to your investigation, you can be sure I'd take it, but as I don't . . . Anyway, I really must be going now. Thank you very much for your hospitality. You will call in on Jerry tomorrow?'

'Barring any emergencies, yes, I'll call. Don't tell him, though; he might board up the windows and bar the doors.' Rosalind smiled. It was a sad smile, Banks thought, but nice nonetheless. 'And please think about what I said. If there's anything . . .'

Rosalind nodded quickly and left. Banks stood in the doorway and watched her drive back towards the Helmthorpe road, then he poured another Laphroaig and returned to Anne-Sophie Mutter's Beethoven.

15

Banks and Annie watched Barry Clough walking along the corridor towards them, his police escort following behind, along with another man. Banks noted the Paul Smith suit, the ponytail, the matching gold chain and bracelet, the cocky, confident strut, and thought: *pillock*.

'Sorry to get you out of bed so early, Barry,' he said, opening the door to interview room two, the smallest and smelliest interview room they had. It passed the PACE regulations about the same way Banks's old Cortina had passed its final MOT test: barely.

'You'd better have a damn good reason for dragging me halfway across the country,' Clough said cheerfully. 'One my lawyer will understand.' He gave Annie an appraising look, which she ignored, then turned to the man who had followed him down the corridor.

'Simon Gallagher,' the man said. 'And I'm the lawyer in question.'

And very questionable you look, thought Banks. For once, the client looked better dressed than the lawyer, but Banks was willing to bet that Gallagher's casual elegance cost every bit as much as Clough's Paul Smith, and that it had been thrown together at short notice. He was also willing to bet that, appearances aside, Gallagher was sharp as a tack and very well versed in the intricacies of criminal law. He was in his late twenties, Banks guessed, with a heavy five o'clock shadow, and his dark hair hung in greasy strands over his collar. He also had that edgy, wasted look of someone who stays up too late at too many clubs and takes too many drugs. He sniffed the stale air of the interview room and pulled a face.

Annie turned on the tape recorders and went through the preamble, then she sat beside Banks, a little out of Clough's line of vision. On the periphery, Banks had told her, she could remain unnoticed or distract him with a movement if she wished.

'Can we get on with it?' Gallagher said, glancing at his watch. 'I've got an important appointment back in the City this evening.'

Banks smiled. 'We'll do our best to make sure you don't miss it, Mr Gallagher.' Then he turned to Clough. 'Do you have any idea why we want to talk to you?'

Clough held out his hands, palms open. 'None at all.'

'Okay. Let's start with Emily Riddle. You do admit to knowing her?'

'I knew her as Louisa Gamine. You know that. You came to my house.'

'But you now know that her real name was Emily Louise Riddle?'

'Yes.'

'How did you find out?'

'I told you. I saw it in the papers.'

'Are you sure you didn't know before that?'

'How could I?'

'Perhaps the room in your house, the room in which I talked to her, was wired for sound?'

Clough laughed and glanced over at Simon Gallagher. 'Get that, Simon. That's a laugh, eh? My house bugged.' He looked at Banks again, no longer laughing. 'Now you tell me why I'd want to do something like that?'

'Information?'

'What sort of information?'

'Business information?'

'I don't eavesdrop electronically on my clients or my partners, Chief Inspector. Besides, it's my home we're talking about, not my office.'

'Let's leave that for the moment, then, shall we?' Banks went on. 'What was your relationship with Emily Riddle?'

'Relationship?'

'Yes. You know, the sort of thing human beings have with one another.'

Clough shrugged. 'I fucked her once in a while,' he said. 'She was okay in bed. A hell of a lot better than she was at giving blow jobs.'

'Is that all?'

'What do you mean, is that all?'

'Did you ever do anything else together? Talk, for example?'

'I suppose we must have, though I can't say I remember a word she said.'

'Did you ever tell her anything about your business interests?'

'Certainly not. If you think I'd go around telling some bimbo about my business, you must be crazy.'

'Did she live with you?'

'She lived in the same house.'

'In Little Venice?'

'Yes.'

'Did she live *with* you?'

'We were together some of the time. It's a big house. Sometimes guests come and forget to leave for a long time. You can get lost in there. You should know. You've seen it. Twice.'

'Is this what happened with Emily? She sort of got lost in your big house?'

'I suppose so. I don't remember how she got there.'

'A party?'

'Probably.'

'Did you sleep together?'

'We didn't do much sleeping.'

'Look, Chief Inspector,' Gallagher chipped in, 'this all seems pretty innocuous, as the girl in question was of legal age, but I can't really see where it's getting us.'

'Did Emily Riddle know anything at all about your business dealings, Barry?'

'No. Not unless she spied on me.'

'Is that possible?'

'Anything's possible. I'm careful, but . . .'

'What exactly *is* your business?'

'Bit of this, bit of that.'

'More specifically?'

Clough looked at Gallagher, who nodded.

'I manage a couple of fairly successful rock bands. I own a bar in Clerkenwell. I also promote concerts from time to time. I suppose you could call me a sort of impresario.'

'An impresario.' Banks savoured the word. 'If you say, so, Barry.'

'Has a sort of old-fashioned ring to it, don't you think? "Sunday Night at the London Palladium" and all that.'

'Were you worried that Emily Riddle might have known too much about this impresario business of yours?'

'No. Why would I?'

'You tell me.'

'No.'

'Did she ever indicate that she did? Did she ask you for money, for example?'

'You mean blackmail?'

'Did she?'

'Emily? No. I told you, she was just some young bimbo I used to fuck, that's all.'

'And now she's dead.'

'And now she's dead. Sad, isn't it?'

'Yes,' said Banks, reining in his rising temper. 'It is.'

Clough got to his feet. 'Is that it, then? Can we go now?'

'Sit down, Barry. You'll go when I tell you to go.'

Clough looked at Gallagher, who nodded again.

'Did you see Emily at all after she left London?'

'No. Easy come, easy go.'

'Were you at Scarlea House between December the fifth and December the tenth this year?'

'I can't remember.'

'Oh, come on, Barry. You were there for the grouse shooting. You had your minder Jamie Gilbert with you and a young woman in tow: Amanda Khan, the singer.'

'Oh, yes. I remember now.'

'Last time I asked you, you said you were in Spain at that time.'

'I get confused. I do a lot of travelling. What can I say? But I remember now.'

'You didn't see Emily while you were staying in the area?'

'Why would I? Amanda gives far better head.'

'For old time's sake?'

'Let go and move on. That's my motto.'

'Perhaps to give her a plastic bag of cocaine laced with strychnine?'

'Chief Inspector,' said Gallagher, 'you're treading in dangerous territory here. Be careful.'

'Did you?' Banks asked Clough.

'Now where would I get hold of strychnine?'

'I dare say you'd have your sources. Cocaine wasn't much trouble, was it?'

'You know as well as I do, Chief Inspector, that there's probably enough of that stuff around at any given moment to pay off the national debt. *If* you like that sort of thing. Not for me, of course. But strychnine . . . I wouldn't know where to start.'

'While you were at Scarlea, did you have dinner with Chief Constable Jeremiah Riddle?'

'What if I did?'

'How did you know him?'

'Mutual acquaintance.'

'Bollocks, Barry. When Emily left, with the information you'd overheard from our conversation, you found out who she really was, where she lived. And when you learned that her father was a senior-ranking policeman, you tried to move in and blackmail him.'

'Chief Inspector,' Simon Gallagher broke in, 'I'm going to have to ask you to stop these absurd insinuations. If you want to question my client, go ahead and question him in the prescribed manner.'

'I apologize,' said Banks. 'Why did you have dinner with Chief Constable Riddle?'

'Why don't you ask him?'

'I already have.'

Clough seemed surprised at that, but he soon regained his composure. 'We talked about his daughter. And if he told you anything different, then he's a liar.'

'How did you feel when Emily left you?'

'Come again?'

'You heard what I said.'

'Feel? I didn't feel anything, really. Why would I? I mean she was only—'

'Some bimbo you used to fuck? Yes, yes, so you said before. No need to keep on repeating yourself. But you don't like your bimbos to run out on you, do you? You prefer to give them the boot yourself.'

'That's exactly what happened. She'd served her purpose. It was time to move on. She didn't get the message, so I had to help her along a bit.'

'By trying to toss her into bed with Andrew Handley?'

'Andy Pandy? What's he got to do with this?'

'You do admit to knowing him, then?'

'He works for me from time to time.'

'Not any more, Barry. He's dead.'

'What? Andy? Dead? I don't believe it.'

'He was found shot to death near Exmoor. Know anything about that?'

'Of course I don't. It's . . .'

'Sad?'

'Yeah. Andy was all right.'

'Is that why you pushed Emily into a room with him?'

'I did no such thing. I've told you before. If she went into a room with Andy, she went of her own accord.'

'Sure he didn't get tired of taking your leftovers and decide to strike out for himself?'

'Look, Chief Inspector, my client has answered all these questions before. Unless there's anything new—'

'Gregory Manners,' said Banks.

'Who?' said Clough.

'Gregory Manners. He ran the PKF operation for you at Daleview. Remember, I told you. Their van got hijacked on the way to a new location, and the nightwatchman at Daleview was murdered. Oddly enough, it was the same MO as the Andrew Handley murder.'

'I vaguely remember you going on about that when you came to the house with that other copper. I didn't understand why then, and I don't now.'

'Right. So what about it?'

'What do you mean?'

'Come on, Barry. We found Gregory Manners's fingerprints on a whole stack of bootlegged games and software. That's what you were doing at PKF. A big operation. You had multi-disc-copying machines, and they were in that van. Andy Pandy wanted to break away, didn't he, go into business by himself? So he hatched a plot with the nightwatchman at Daleview. Charlie Courage had already figured out there was something dodgy going on at PKF – Charlie had a nose for that sort of thing – and you were paying him off. Then Andy comes along with a better offer. They arrange it to look like a hijack, but your lads pick up Gregory Manners first, and he tells you he thought there was something fishy going on between Charlie and Andy Pandy. Then you pick up Charlie, and he tells all. So they kill Charlie, and then they kill Andy Pandy. Isn't that how it went?'

Clough turned his head slowly to Gallagher and raised his eyebrows. 'Am I missing something, Simon?' he said. 'I am Barry Clough, aren't I? Mr Banks here seems to have me confused with some criminal named Gregory Manners.'

Gallagher stood up. 'Chief Inspector, you've got an active imagination, I'll say that. But you can't corroborate any of this. You haven't a single shred of evidence connecting my client to either of these men.'

'Mr Manners is still helping us with our inquiries,' Banks lied. 'We have every reason to believe he'll tell us what he knows when he realizes the full extent of the charges that might be brought against him.'

Clough gave Banks a stony gaze. 'So what?' he said.

'What about Andrew Handley?' Banks said to Gallagher. 'Your client has already admitted to knowing him.'

'But that doesn't mean he had anything to do with Mr Handley's unfortunate demise.'

' "Unfortunate demise"?' Banks repeated. 'Andrew Handley's upper body was shredded by a close-range shotgun wound. I'd hardly call that an unfortunate fucking demise.'

'Infelicitous turn of phrase,' muttered Gallagher. 'And there's no need to swear at me.'

'We're all adults here, aren't we? And I'm hardly the first.'

'There's a lady present,' said Clough, grinning at Annie.

'Fuck you,' said Annie.

Gallagher waved his hands in the air. 'All right, all right, ladies and gentlemen, can we all just calm down a minute and get back on track? If there *is* a track.'

'Thank you, Mr Gallagher,' said Banks. 'I believe we were talking about Andrew Handley.'

'All right,' said Clough. 'Yes. I knew him. He worked for me sometimes.'

'Doing what?'

'Managing things. I delegate a lot.'

Banks laughed out loud.

'Chief Inspector!'

'Sorry. Couldn't help it. Delegate. Right. Would you say the two of you were friends?'

'Not really. We might have had a drink together every now and then, talked about business, but other than that, no. I don't know what he got up to.'

'Nor he you?'

'Suppose not.'

'Do you own a shotgun, Barry?'

'Do I look like a fucking farmer?'

'You certainly have plenty of guns at your London house.'

'They're all deactivated and all legal. I'm a collector.'

'So you don't own a shotgun?'

'I've already told you.'

'No, you haven't. You didn't answer my question. Do you own a shotgun?'

'No.'

Banks paused a moment. 'Then what did you use for shooting grouse at Scarlea? A pea-shooter?'

Gallagher put his head in his hands.

'They have guns available for their guests. For hire.'

'Oh, come off it, Barry. Do you expect me to believe that a keen, regular grouse shooter like you doesn't own a shotgun? I find that difficult.'

'Believe what you want.'

'We can check.'

'Okay, okay. So maybe I own a shotgun.'

'Then why didn't you say so?'

'Because the way things are going it looks as if you're

trying to pin a fucking murder on me and my fucking lawyer is—'

'Barry!' said Gallagher. 'Shut up. Just shut up. Okay? Let me take care of it.'

'Lying just makes it worse,' said Banks. He tipped Annie the nod and she officially terminated the taped interview.

'What's going on?' Clough asked. 'Can I go now?'

'Afraid not, Barry,' said Banks. 'We'll be issuing a warrant for your shotgun to be examined by forensic experts in the murders of Andrew Handley and Charles Courage.'

Clough smiled. 'Go ahead. If I did have anything to do with those murders, which I didn't, do you think I'd be stupid enough to use my own shotgun and leave it lying around the house?'

Banks smiled back. 'Probably not,' he said. 'But it doesn't really matter. At least a forensic examination will settle things one way or the other, won't it? We're also looking into some tyre tracks found at the murder scenes. In the meantime you can sample some of our legendary northern hospitality.'

'You mean I can't go?'

Banks shook his head.

'Simon?'

'Your lawyer will tell you we can detain you for twenty-four hours, Barry. Any period of time after that has to be okayed by a more senior officer than me. But if you think that's likely to be a problem, remember that Emily Riddle *was* our chief constable's daughter, you know.'

'He can't do this, can he, Simon?'

'I'm afraid he can,' said Gallagher, staring at Banks. 'But any detention longer than twenty-four hours will come under very severe scrutiny, I can assure you. Now, if you'll excuse me, I'd better cancel my appointment.'

Banks opened the door and asked the uniformed officers to escort Clough to the custody suite in the station's basement. 'You'll be well taken care of, Barry,' Banks said. 'Soon be lunchtime. Beefburger and chips, I think it is today. Sorry there's no Château Margaux to accompany it. You might be able to get a mug of tea. Careful you don't crease your Paul Smith.'

While Banks went to pay another visit to the Riddle house, Annie wandered into the incident room to see what was going on. It was a hive of activity; most of the phone lines were busy and the fax machines were churning stuff out. DC Rickerd held sway over it all, a man who had truly found himself. He blushed when Annie gave him a wink.

Poor Winsome was back at the computer, a stack of green sheets for input and another stack she had already entered.

'How's it going?' Annie asked, picking up the entered stack and idly leafing through it. Just because everything went into HOLMES didn't mean any of it was ever seen again, not unless some sort of link or connection came up, and then you had to be looking for it.

Winsome smiled. 'Okay, I suppose. Sometimes I wish I'd never done that damn course, though.'

'I know what you mean,' said Annie. 'Still, it'll come in useful when you sit your boards.'

'I suppose so.'

Annie was hardly reading the information on the entered sheets, more just letting her gaze slip over them, but something she saw on one of them reached out and smacked her right between the eyes. 'Winsome,' she said, picking it out and putting it on the desk, 'what happened with this?'

Winsome scrutinized the sheet. 'DCI Banks signed it off yesterday,' she said. 'No further action.'

' "No further action",' Annie repeated under her breath.

'Something wrong?'

'No,' said Annie quickly, replacing the sheet in the pile. 'Nothing. Just curious, that's all. See you later.'

Aware of Winsome's puzzled gaze, Annie hurried back to

her office, noticed she had it all to herself, picked up the telephone and dialled an outside line.

'Hotel Fifty-Five,' the answering voice said. 'Can I help you?'

'Mr Poulson?'

'Oh, you want Roger. Just a minute.'

Annie waited a minute and another voice came on the line. 'Roger Poulson here. Can I help you?'

'Detective Sergeant Cabbot, Eastvale CID. I understand you phoned our incident room yesterday with information relating to the death of Emily Riddle?'

'I wouldn't go that far,' Poulson said. 'It was just an odd coincidence, that's all.'

'Tell me about it anyway, Mr Poulson.'

'Well, as I said to the gentleman yesterday—'

'What gentleman?'

'The policeman who called me back yesterday. I didn't catch his name.'

I'll bet you didn't, thought Annie, and we'd have heard no more about it if I hadn't come across the name and number by accident. *Hotel Fifty-Five*. It was where she had stayed with Banks when they visited London in connection with the Gloria Shackleton case. When they were lovers.

'What did he say?' Annie asked.

'He simply took the details and thanked me for calling. To be honest, I didn't expect to hear any more of it. He didn't sound very interested. Why? Has something turned up?'

Annie felt a tightness in her chest. 'No,' she said. 'Nothing like that. It's just down to me to keep the paperwork up to date. You know what it's like.'

'Tell me about it,' said Poulson. 'How can I help you?'

'If you'd just go over the information again briefly . . .?'

'Of course. As I said, it's nothing, really. It was about a month ago, when I was on night duty. I think I saw her, the girl who was killed.'

'Go on.'

'At least, she looked sort of like the girl in the newspaper photo yesterday, with her hair up, a nice evening gown. Mostly it's the eyes and lips, though. I'd almost swear it was her.'

'You say you saw her at the hotel?'

'Yes.'

'Was she a guest?'

'Not exactly.'

'What do you mean?'

'Well, she walked in – I think she'd just got out of a taxi – and said she wanted to see her father.'

'Her father?' Annie was confused. She didn't know that Jimmy Riddle had been down to London looking for his daughter, only Banks. She felt icy water rising fast around her ankles.

'That's right. She said he was staying here. I had no reason not to believe her.'

'Of course not. What did you do?'

'I called his room and told him his daughter was in the lobby, wanting to see him, and she was in a bit of a state. Naturally, he told me to send her up. The thing was, you see, she looked very dishevelled, as if she'd been attacked or involved in some rough stuff. Natural to come to Daddy under such circumstances, even if it was three o'clock in the morning.'

'When you say rough stuff, what exactly do you mean?'

'Nothing really serious, but there was a tear in her dress and a little blood at the corner of her lip.'

'What happened after she'd gone up?'

'Nothing. I mean, I didn't see anything. I was on duty until eight o'clock the next morning, and I didn't see either of them again.'

'So she stayed in his room the rest of the night?'

'Yes.'

The cold water was up to Annie's navel by now and she decided to plunge right in. Sometimes it was the best way. 'What was her father's name?'

'Well, it wasn't Riddle, like it says in the papers. As I said to your colleague yesterday, that's why I thought it was funny. So I looked out the credit-card slip. He's stayed with us here before, I remember. Once with a very attractive young lady. His name is Banks. Alan Banks.'

The shock numbed Annie's blood, even though she had been half expecting it. She thanked Mr Poulson, then hung up in a daze. *Banks.* In a hotel room with Emily Riddle half the night. The *same* hotel he'd taken Annie to. *And he hadn't told her.* This put a new complexion on things.

Banks slipped the tape he had made of Brian's band's CD in the cassette player and reflected on his interview with Clough as he drove out to the Old Mill. Clough was still cooling his heels in the holding cells, but they wouldn't really be able to hold him much after the following morning. Gallagher was right about that. Any infringement of PACE because Clough was a suspect in the murder of the chief constable's daughter would go down very badly and only increase his chances of getting off scot-free. That was how things were now. In the old days, they used to be different, of course, and Banks still wasn't certain which was best. He just hoped to hell that some of the information he was desperate for arrived before the deadline.

The question he always came back to, though, was that if Clough *had* killed Emily, what was his motive? Clough was an astute gangster, surely smart enough not to let an affair with a sixteen-year-old girl ruin what was clearly a charmed and profitable life. Still, Banks thought, remembering the famous gangsters of movieland – James Cagney, Edward G. Robinson – there were plenty of Mob bosses who were also psychopaths and had killed for reasons other than pure business. If Banks were Clough, though, when he found out that Emily had gone and then discovered she was a chief constable's daughter, he would have cut his losses and left well alone. But perhaps that was why Banks *wasn't* Clough.

Had Emily really been doing something foolish, like trying to blackmail Clough? Banks didn't think so. She was a mixed-up kid, but he didn't think she was a blackmailer. He had also got the feeling from talking to her that she was genuinely scared of Clough, and that the more distance there was between them, the better. Besides, her family didn't lack money, and as Riddle had pointed out at the start, they had spoiled her rotten. Even so, the idea of an undisclosed income of her very own might appeal. But would it overcome her fear?

Also, why would Clough wait so long to kill her if he was after revenge for her leaving? It was over a month since Banks had brought Emily back from London. Perhaps it had taken him that long to find out who and where she was. Or perhaps it had taken her that long to start blackmailing him. There had been no telephone calls to Clough on Riddle's phone records, but that didn't necessarily mean Emily hadn't called him from a public box. Something about the sparse phone records nagged at his mind, but he couldn't quite grasp it. Never mind. As his mother always said, if it was that important it would come to the surface soon enough.

He showed his warrant card to the officers at the end of the lane, and they waved him through. A hundred yards farther on, he pulled up on the gravel drive outside the Old Mill and turned off the engine. The rain had stopped but it had swelled the mill-race, which sounded even louder and faster than on his last visit.

This time, Riddle wasn't watching for his arrival. He wondered if Rosalind had told him Banks was coming. He hoped not. He knocked at the door and waited. Nothing. Surely Riddle couldn't have gone back to work already? He knocked again, harder, in case the noise from the stream was covering the sound. Still nothing.

Banks stepped back a few paces from the front door and looked at the front of the house. No windows open. It was a dull afternoon, and someone at home might have put on a light or two, but none showed. Perhaps Riddle had gone out, maybe for a long drive to think things over. Banks felt relief. He had come to fulfil his promise to Rosalind, but it wasn't *his* fault if Riddle wasn't home. What more could he do?

But surely, if Riddle had gone out, the duty officers would have told Banks?

It was then that he became aware of another faint noise beyond the sound of the rushing mill-race. At first, it didn't mean much, but when he realized what it was, it sent a chill through him.

It was coming from the converted barn, and it was the sound of a car engine idling.

Banks dashed towards the barn, doubting his own ears at first, but there was no mistaking the smooth purr of the German engineering. The garage door was closed but not locked. Banks bent and grasped the handle, pulling as he moved back, and the door slid up smoothly and silently on its overhead runners. The stink of exhaust fumes hit him immediately, and he staggered back, digging his hand into his raincoat pocket for a handkerchief. He couldn't find one, but he went in anyway with his forearm over his nose and mouth.

It was dark inside the garage, and Banks couldn't make out very much at first. His eyes adjusted as he moved inside, noticing that rolled-up cloths or towels had been placed against the gap between the floor and the bottom of the garage door. He did the best he could to keep the fumes at bay, covering his mouth and nose with one hand, breathing only as little as necessary. At least now air from outside was displacing the carbon monoxide.

When Banks got to the car, he could see Riddle slumped

across the two front seats. There was no way of knowing yet whether he was dead, so Banks first tried to open a door. They were all locked. He looked around and found a crowbar on one of the shelves. Standing back and swinging it hard, he smashed one of the back windows, reached inside and disengaged the lock mechanism. Then he opened the front door on the driver's side, reached across Riddle and turned off the engine. The fumes were dissipating slowly now the garage doors stood wide open, but Banks was beginning to feel nauseated and dizzy.

He felt for a pulse and found none. Riddle's whole face was as red as his bald head got when he was angry. Cherry red. The hosing he had rigged from the exhaust to the back window was still in place. He had opened the window a crack to admit it and stuffed the opening with oil-stained rags.

Riddle was wearing his uniform, everything polished, shiny and in order, apart from the thin streak of yellowish vomit down his front. Above the dashboard was a sheet of paper with handwriting on it. Leaving it where it was, Banks leaned over and squinted. It was short and to the point:

> The game's over. Please take care of Benjamin and try to ensure that he doesn't think too ill of his father. I'm sorry.
>
> > Jerry

Banks read it again, angry tears pricking at his stinging eyes. You bastard, he thought, *you selfish bastard*. As if his family hadn't suffered enough already.

Groggy and sick, Banks stumbled outside and made it to the mill-race before he emptied out his lunch. He bent over and took handfuls of cold clear water and splashed it over his face, drinking down as much of it as he could manage. He knew that there were two officers only a hundred yards away, but he wasn't sure his legs would carry him that far, so he went back to his car, picked up his mobile and called the station, then he bent forward, put his hands on his knees and took deep breaths as he waited for the circus to begin.

16

Banks spent the evening at home trying to make sense of the day's events. He still felt weak and nauseated, but apart from that, there seemed no serious damage. The ambulance crew had insisted on giving him oxygen and taking him to Eastvale General for a check-up, but the doctor pronounced him fit to go home, with a warning to lay off the ciggies for a while.

From what he had been able to piece together so far, it appeared almost certain that Riddle had committed suicide. They wouldn't know for sure until Dr Glendenning performed the post-mortem, probably tomorrow, but there were no signs of external violence on Riddle's body, the note appeared to be in his handwriting, and the rags and towels used to keep the petrol fumes in the garage had been placed on the *inside* of the door after it had been closed. There were no windows or other means of exit.

Banks would never have pegged Riddle as the suicidal type, but he would be the first to admit that he had no idea if such a type existed. Certainly the murder of his daughter, the destruction of all his political and professional hopes, and the smear campaign started against him in the tabloids would be enough to drive anyone over the edge.

So suicide it might be, Banks thought, but Barry Clough still had a lot to answer for. Clough was enjoying the hospitality of the Eastvale cells that night, while the detectives and forensic experts mobilized by Burgess down south were working overtime following up all the leads they had on the Charlie Courage and Andy Pandy shootings. With any luck by tomorrow, Banks would have something more substantial to confront Clough with in the interview room.

It was nine o'clock when a car pulled up and someone knocked at the door. Puzzled, Banks went to see who it was.

Rosalind Riddle stood there in the cold night air, wearing only a long skirt and sweater. 'Can I come in?' she said. 'It's been a hell of a day.'

Banks could think of no reply to that. He stood aside to let her in and shut the door behind her. She smoothed down her skirt and sat in the armchair by the fire, rubbing her hands together. 'There's a chill in the air,' she said. 'We might get frost tonight.'

'What are you doing here?' Banks asked.

'I've been going insane just sitting around the house. Charlotte came to stay with me for a while but I sent her away. She's nice, but you know, we're not *that* close. It's so empty, and there's nothing to do there. My mind has been running around in circles. I want to talk to you. It seemed . . . I don't know . . . I'm sorry. Perhaps I shouldn't have come.' She moved to stand up.

'No. Sit down. You might as well stop. You're here now. Drink?'

Rosalind paused. 'Are you sure?'

'Yes.'

'All right.' She sat down again. 'Thank you. I wouldn't mind a glass of white wine, if you have any.'

'I'm afraid I've only got red.'

'Okay.'

'It's nothing fancy.'

She smiled. 'Don't worry. I might be a snob about some things, but not about wine.'

'Good.' Banks headed into the kitchen to open the Marks & Sparks Bulgarian Merlot. He poured himself a glass, too. He had a feeling he would need it. After he had handed

Rosalind her drink, Banks sat opposite her. She had clearly made an effort to look her best, applying a little make-up to give some colour to her pallid features; but there was no disguising the bruise-like circles under her eyes, or the rims pink from crying. This was a woman hanging on by her fingernails.

'How are you?' he asked. It sounded like a stupid question after what had happened to her, but he couldn't think of anything else to say.

'I'm . . . I . . . I don't really know. I thought I was coping, but inside . . .' She tapped her chest. 'It all feels so tight and hot inside here. I keep thinking I'm going to explode.' Her eyes brimmed with tears. 'It's quite a thing, you know, losing both your daughter and your husband within a week of one another.' She gave a harsh laugh, then thumped the arm of her chair. 'How *dare* he do this? How *dare* he?'

'What do you mean?'

'He's run away from it all, hasn't he? And where does that leave me? A cold, heartless bitch because *I'm* still alive? Because I didn't care about my daughter's murder enough to kill myself over it?'

'Don't do this, Rosalind,' said Banks, getting up and putting his hands on her shoulders. He could feel the little convulsions as grief and anger surged through her.

After a while, she reached up and gently disengaged his hands. 'I'm all right,' she said, wiping the tears from her eyes. 'I'm sorry for inflicting myself on you, but it's been on my mind all day. Going over and over it again. I can't understand my feelings. I should feel sorrow, loss . . . but all I feel is anger. I *hate* him. I hate him for doing this! And I hate myself for feeling like that.'

Banks could do nothing but sit down helplessly and let her cry again. He remembered his own reaction to finding Riddle's body; there had been a lot of anger in that too, before it gave way to guilt. *The selfish bastard.*

When Rosalind had finished, he said, 'Look, I can't pretend

to know how you feel, but I feel terrible myself. If I'd gone out there sooner I might have saved him.' It sounded even more pathetic than his opening gambit, but he felt he had to get it off his chest.

Rosalind gave him a sharp look. 'You? Don't be silly. Jerry was a very determined man. If he wanted to kill himself, he'd damn well do it, one way or another. There was nothing you could have done except perhaps postpone the inevitable.'

'Even so . . . I keep thinking if only I hadn't put off the visit. If only I hadn't . . . I don't know.'

'Disliked him so much?'

Banks looked away. 'I suppose that's part of it.'

'Don't worry. Jerry wasn't a very likeable man. Even death won't change that. There's no sense in your feeling guilty.'

'I've been thinking about what might have caused him to do it,' Banks said after a short pause. 'I know you said he was depressed over Emily's death and all the fallout that engendered, but somehow, even all that just didn't seem enough in itself.'

'He was upset about those lies in the newspaper.'

Banks paused. He knew he shouldn't be telling Rosalind about her husband's problems with Barry Clough, but he felt she deserved something from him; he also thought it might put Riddle's death in perspective for her a little more clearly. Call it guilt talking. He took a deep breath, then said, 'I was out at a place called Scarlea House yesterday afternoon. Ever heard of it?'

'I've heard of it, yes. It's an upmarket shooting lodge, isn't it?'

'Yes. According to the barman, your husband had dinner with Barry Clough there the Sunday before last.'

Rosalind paled. 'Barry Clough?'

'Yes. The man Emily lived with for a while in London.'

'I remember the name. And you're telling me that Jerry had *dinner* with him?'

'Yes. Are you sure you didn't know?'

'No. Jerry never said anything to me about it. I knew he was out for dinner that night, yes, but I thought it was just one of his political things. I stopped asking him where he went a long time ago. How would a newspaper find out about that anyway, even if it is true?'

'They didn't have to know about that specific meeting,' said Banks. 'Remember, the article never made any direct assertions; it was all innuendo. It's even possible that someone on the staff at Scarlea House – one of the waiters, perhaps – talked to a reporter but refused to be quoted as a source. I don't know. These journalists have their tricks of the trade. The point is that it happened. Did you have any idea at all that your husband had talked to or met Clough?'

'No. Absolutely none.'

Banks believed her. For one thing, Riddle wasn't stupid enough to tell his wife he was having dinner with the man suspected of murdering their daughter. 'Your husband told me that Clough was trying to blackmail him. Using Emily.'

'But Jerry would never agree to anything like that.'

'I think that was his dilemma. That was what tore him apart. Certainly Emily's murder hurt him deeply, but this was what finally pushed him over the edge. There he was, a man of honour, who has to decide whether he wants to fall into the hands of a gangster or have his daughter and, by extension, his entire family, vilified in public.'

'Are you saying that he didn't know whether he would have done what Clough asked or not, and he couldn't face making the decision?'

'Possibly. But going by the tabloid article, it looks as if he had already turned Clough down, or that Clough had lost patience waiting.'

'If Clough was behind it.'

'Who else?'

371

'I don't know.' Rosalind leaned forward. 'But, if all you're saying is true, it doesn't make sense . . .'

'For Clough to kill Emily?'

'No.'

'That's true. That's what your husband said, too, when I asked him about it. Clough had nothing to gain. I still think he's a strong candidate, but I must admit the whole thing's been puzzling me a lot.'

'Who, then?'

'I don't know. I feel as far away from a solution as I ever have.'

'What will you do about Clough?'

'Keep at him. There are other things we want to talk to him about, too. I've got to tell you, though, that I'm not at all hopeful about convicting Clough of anything, no matter what he's done.'

'Why not?'

'A man like him? If he can blackmail a chief constable, imagine what else he's got going, who he might have in his pocket. Besides, he never does anything himself. He delegates, keeps his hands clean. Even if, for some reason we haven't considered, he was responsible for Emily's murder, he'd have got one of his minions like Andrew Handley or Jamie Gilbert to do the dirty work. And he's rich. That means he'll be able to afford the best defence.'

'Sometimes I wish I was in criminal law,' Rosalind said, her eyes burning. 'I'd love to take on his prosecution.'

Banks smiled. 'First we'd have to persuade the CPS it was worth pursuing, and that's a Herculean effort in itself. In the meantime, we've still got a murderer to catch.'

Rosalind sipped some wine. At least she didn't pull a face and spit it out. 'You've probably deduced this already,' she said, 'but our marriage was very much a matter of convenience. He gave me the things I wanted and I didn't embarrass him in public. I like to think I might even have helped him advance. Other than that, we went our separate ways.'

'Affairs?'

'Jerry? I don't think so. For one thing, he didn't have the time. He was married to his work and his political ambitions.' She looked Banks straight in the eye. 'Me? A few. Nothing important. All discreet. None recently.'

They sat quietly for a few seconds. A gust of wind rattled the loose window upstairs. 'You said you wanted to talk to me?' Banks said.

'Oh, it's nothing to do with the murder. I'm sorry. I didn't mean to mislead you in any way. It's just that, well, you think I've been holding something back, not telling you everything.'

Banks nodded. 'Yes. I do think that. I have done from the start.'

'You're right.'

'And now you're going to tell me?'

'No reason not to, now. But first, do you think I might have another glass of wine?'

That evening at home, Annie reheated some vegetable curry and sat in front of the television, hoping the flickering images would take her mind off her problem. No such luck. There seemed to be nothing on but nature programmes, current events or sports, and nothing she watched had the power to absorb or distract her at all. She flipped through her meagre collection and briefly entertained the idea of watching a comfort video, *Doctor Zhivago* or *The Wizard of Oz*, but she even felt too agitated to concentrate on a movie.

Damn Banks, she thought as she washed out her bowl. How could he do this to her? Maybe she *had* let things cool between them romantically, but that gave him no right to treat her like some probationary DC who couldn't be trusted with the full story. She knew that he hadn't been technically wrong in any way, but he *had* been dishonest and cowardly. As SIO,

Banks was quite entitled to follow up a lead and decide whether it required action or not. Obviously, in the case of his night with Emily Riddle, he knew exactly what had occurred, so he knew that no further action was needed.

He must also have known that he was hiding the truth from Annie, though, or he would have told her about that night when he came clean about going to London to find Emily and having lunch with her the day she died. Annie remembered asking him then if that was all he had to tell, and he had said yes. That made him a liar.

So what to do about it? That was the question she agonized over. The way she saw it, she had two choices. She could, of course, simply do nothing, just put in for a transfer and leave the whole mess behind. That had its appeal, certainly, but it left too much up in the air. She had hidden from unpleasant things and turned her back for far too long. Now that her career had actually come to *mean* something to her again after the years of apathetic exile in Harkside, where she had conned herself into thinking everything was well with the world, Annie wanted to set things on the right track. And just how would an abrupt transfer look, with her inspector's boards coming up so soon?

On the other hand, she could confront Banks and find out what he had to say for himself. Maybe she should give him the benefit of the doubt, innocent until proven guilty and all that. After all, it wasn't as if she didn't still have feelings for the bastard.

But she already knew he wasn't innocent, that it was simply a matter of *what* he was guilty of. How much might a run-in with Banks upset her chances of making inspector? She didn't think he was vindictive, didn't think he would deliberately stand in her way, but everything has fallout, especially given the history Banks and Annie had between them.

Giving up on the television, Annie did what she usually did

when she felt agitated; she flung on her fleece-lined jacket and went for a drive. It didn't matter where.

It had turned into a cold night, and she had the heater going full blast. Even so, the car took a while to warm up. The mist was crystallizing on the bare trees, sparkling as her headlights flicked across branches and twigs on her way out of Harkside. Ice-crusted puddles crackled under her wheels.

She crossed the narrow bridge over the River Rowan between the Harksmere and Linwood reservoirs. Harksmere stretched, cold and dark, to the west, and beyond it lay Thornfield Reservoir, where the remains of Hobb's End had once more been covered with water. That was where she had first met Banks, she remembered, towards the end of the hottest, driest summer in years. He had come scrambling down the steep rim looking like a sightseer, and she had stopped him at the bridge. She had been wearing her red wellies and must have looked a sight.

He still didn't know this, but Annie had known who he was the minute she saw him – she had been expecting him – but she wanted a little fun first, so she had challenged him on the pack-horse bridge. She had liked his manner. He hadn't been stuffy or officious with her; he had simply made some reference to Robin Hood and Little John. After that, Annie had to admit that she hadn't resisted him very hard.

And now he was her senior officer, and he had been keeping things from her.

Past the old airbase, Annie took the left fork and headed for the open moorland that stretched for miles on the tops between there and Swainsdale. Up on the unfenced road, the full moon came out from behind the thinning cloud cover, and she could see that the ground all around her was white with rime. It had an eerie beauty that suited her mood well. She could drive for hours through this lunar landscape and her mind would empty of all her problems. She would become nothing but the driver floating through space; the wheel, the car merely extensions of her being, as if she were travelling the astral plane.

Except that Annie now knew where she was going, knew that the road she was on was the one that led over the moors and down through the village of Gratly, where Banks lived.

And she knew that when she got to his drive she would turn into it.

Banks refilled the wineglasses and sat down again. 'Go on,' he said.

Rosalind smiled. 'You might find this hard to believe,' she began, 'but I haven't always been the dull, decent wife of the dull, decent chief constable.'

Banks was startled by her smile. It had so much of Emily in it, that hint of mischief, of *just watch me*. 'That sounds like the beginning of a story,' he said.

'It is.'

'I'm all ears.'

'First, we have to go back a while. My father was a vicar; he's retired now, of course. I grew up in a small village in Kent, an only child, and my childhood was relatively uneventful. I don't mean that it was bad in any way. I did all the normal things kids do. I was happy. It was just unexceptional, dull, even. Like the way Philip Larkin described his in that poem. Then, in the mid-seventies, when I was sixteen, we moved to a parish in Ealing, London. Oh, it was a very nice area – none of that inner-city stuff – and the parishioners were for the most part law-abiding, reasonably affluent citizens.'

'But?'

'But it was near the tube. You can't imagine what wonderful new worlds that opened up to an impressionable sixteen-year-old.'

Banks thought he could. When he moved from Peterborough to Notting Hill at the age of eighteen, his life had changed in many ways. He had met Jem across the hall from his bedsit, for a start, and had lurked at the fringes of the sixties scene – which stretched well into the early seventies – enjoying the music more than the drugs. There was an excitement and vibrancy about the capital that was missing from Peterborough, and would certainly have been missing from a vicarage in Kent.

'Let me guess: the vicar's daughter went a little wild?'

'I was born in 1959. It was November 1975 when we moved to Ealing. While everyone else was listening to Queen, Abba and Hot Chocolate, my friends and I were taking the tube into town to listen to the Sex Pistols. This was right at the start, before anyone really knew anything about them. They'd just played their first gig the day after Bonfire Night at St Martin's College of Art, and one of the girls at my new school was there. She couldn't talk about anything else for weeks. Next time they played, she took me with her. It was fantastic.'

Punk. Banks remembered those days. He was older than Rosalind, though, and identified more closely with sixties music than that of the seventies. When he had lived in London his favourites had been Pink Floyd, Led Zeppelin and the various local blues bands that seemed to form and split up with amazing regularity. Still, he had responded to the angry energy of some punk music – especially the Clash, by far the best of the bunch in his opinion – but not enough to buy any of their records. Also, as he had been a probationary police constable back then, he had experienced the violence of punk first hand, from the other side, and that, too, had put him off.

'Pretty soon,' Rosalind went on, becoming more animated as she relived her memories, 'it was in full swing. The look. The music. The attitude. Everything. My parents didn't know me any more. We saw the Clash, the Damned, the Stranglers, the Jam. You name them. Mostly in small clubs. We pogoed, we hurled ourselves into one another, and we spat at each other. We dyed our hair weird colours. We wore torn clothes, safety pins in our ears and . . .' She paused and pulled up the sleeve of her sweater. Banks could see a number of more or less round white marks, like old scars. 'We stubbed cigarettes out on ourselves.'

Banks raised an eyebrow. 'How on earth did you explain all that to your husband?'

'He was never that curious. I just told him it was an old burn scar.'

'Go on.'

'You can't imagine how exhilarating it was after that stuffy boring childhood in a village in Kent. We went *wild*. Anyway, to cut a long story short, I was just seventeen, and I got pregnant. It doesn't matter who the father was; his name was Mal, and he was long gone before I even knew myself. It happened in someone's poky bedsit after the Pistols did one of their gigs at the 100 Club, the summer of 1976. This is what I could never tell Jerry. He was a terrible prude, as if you didn't know. I don't know if he actually believed I was a virgin when we married, but I'm certain *he* was. If he'd ever found out, well . . . who can say? I kept it from him.'

Banks remembered the 100 Club well. On Oxford Street, it had been part of his patch, and he had been inside the cavernous cellar more than once trying to stop fights and get rid of unruly customers. It turned into a jazz club some years later, he remembered. 'I can understand why you might not have wanted him to know,' he said. 'Even in this day and age, some people are funny about that sort of thing, and it doesn't surprise me that Jimmy – I mean the chief constable – was. But why is that important now?'

'He knew you all called him Jimmy Riddle, you know.'

'He did? He never said anything.'

'He didn't care. Something like that, it didn't bother him, wasn't even of passing interest to him. He was strangely impervious to criticism or having the piss taken. He really didn't have much of a sense of humour, you know. Anyway, I haven't told you the full story yet. You'll see why it's important.' She moved forward in her chair and clasped her hands on her knees. When she spoke, she almost whispered, as if she thought someone were eavesdropping on them. 'My first thought was to have an abortion, but . . . I don't know . . . I didn't really know how to go about it, if you can believe that. A fully fledged punk, pregnant, but I was still a naïve country girl in a lot of ways. Then there was my religious background. When it came down to it, I hadn't the nerve to face it all by myself, and the boy, well, as I said, he was long gone. My father's a good man. He had been preaching grace, mercy and Christian charity all his life.'

'So you went to your parents?'

'Yes.'

'And?'

'They took it well, considering. They were upset, naturally, but they were good to me. They persuaded me to have the baby, of course, as I knew they would. Father doesn't believe in abortion. It's not only Catholics who don't, you know. Anyway, we did it the way they used to do it years ago. A spell with Aunt So-and-So in Tiverton for the last few months, when it started to show, a quick adoption, and it was as if nothing had ever happened. In the meantime, if I happened to get cured of punk, so much the better.'

'Did you?'

'Get cured of punk?'

'Yes.'

'By the time I'd had my baby I was about to sit my A levels. It was 1977. I don't know if you remember, but punk had become very popular and the big bands were being signed up by major labels. The whole scene had got very commercial. Now it seemed that everybody was talking about it, adopting the look. Somehow, it just wasn't the same. They weren't *ours* any more. Besides, I was older and wiser. I was a mother, even if I wasn't a practising one. Yes, I was cured. I spent the summer at home, and in October I went to the University of Bath to study English Literature, became an intellectual snob and switched to new wave, which I'd always secretly preferred, anyway. Elvis Costello, Talking Heads, Roxy Music, Television, Patti Smith. Art-school music. I did one year of English, then changed to law.'

'There's more, isn't there?'

'Yes.'

'The child?'

'As you know, it's perfectly legal now for children to track down their birth parents. I can understand it, but I have to say that in many cases it's the cause of nothing but grief.'

'In your case?'

'She found me easily enough. Late January, it was. The Children Act came into effect in 1975, before she was born, as you probably know. That meant she didn't even have to go for counselling before the Registrar General gave her the information that led her to me. It was always on the cards. She just walked into my office one day. It didn't take her long to work out that I was terrified of her telling my husband. I don't know what would have happened. It was bad enough that he was so prudish and possessive and that I'd kept it from him all those years, but this also happened just as his political ambitions were getting all stirred up, and I wanted to be on that ride, too. I wanted Westminster. Jerry was always big on family values and any hint of a family scandal – *ex-punk wife of chief constable, love child tells all* – well, it would have ruined everything. At least, I believed it would.'

'What did she do?'

'Asked for money.'

'Your own daughter blackmailed you?'

'I wouldn't call it that. She just asked for help now and then.'

'Financial help?'

'Yes. I mean, I *did* owe her, didn't I? Apparently, she hadn't had such a good life with her adoptive parents. They turned out to be unsuitable, she said, though she didn't explain why, and they didn't have much money. Then they died in a fire just after her second year at university, and she was left all alone. She was in her final year when she found me, so every little bit helped. I didn't really mind.'

'Did she ever threaten to tell your husband the truth if you didn't pay up?'

'She . . . she hinted that she might.'

'And you paid for her continuing silence?'

Rosalind averted her eyes. 'Yes.'

'Even after she left university?'

'Yes.'

'That's blackmail,' said Banks. 'Are you going to tell me who she is?'

'Does it matter?'

'It might.'

Rosalind drank some wine, then she said, 'It's Ruth. Ruth Walker.'

Banks almost choked on his drink. 'Ruth Walker is your daughter? Emily's half-sister?'

Rosalind nodded.

'My God, why didn't you tell me this before?'

'I can't see how it could be relevant.'

'That's for me to judge. Did Emily know this?'

'I didn't think so.'

'What do you mean?'

'As far as I knew at the time, they met only once. Ruth used to come to my office in Eastvale. That's where we did all . . . all our business. Believe it or not, I didn't even know her address, where she lived, except she told me she'd grown up in Salford. Once – last Easter, I think it was – Emily was there. She'd come to borrow some money from me to go shopping. Ruth walked in. I introduced my daughter and told her Ruth was here about the new computer system we were thinking of installing. They chatted a bit – about music, what school Emily was at – that sort of thing. Just chit-chat. That was all. Or so I thought.'

'So Emily didn't know *who* Ruth really was?'

'That's what I believed at the time.'

'What changed your mind?'

'After Emily came . . . after you brought Emily back home, the phone rang one day. It was Ruth. I thought she was calling for me. I was angry because I'd specifically told her never to phone the house, but she asked to speak to Emily.'

'And?'

'Afterwards, I asked Emily about it. Then she told me about how Ruth had phoned her a lot at school, how she'd even been down to London once for a weekend and stayed with her. How they were *friends*.'

'So Emily knew that Ruth was her half-sister?'

'Yes.'

'What was her reaction?'

'You knew Emily. She thought it was all rather cool, her mother having a secret past. She promised not to say anything. She was well aware of how her father would react.'

'Did you trust her?'

'For the most part. Emily wasn't malicious, though she could be unpredictable. You know, at her age, I wasn't much different. If we'd been contemporaries, who knows, we might have been friends.'

'I can only imagine the havoc the two of you might have wreaked.'

Rosalind smiled her Emily smile again. 'Yes.'

'Did she know about the blackmail?'

'Good Lord, no. At least, she never said anything about it. And I doubt that's something Ruth would have admitted to her half-sister. Emily was very headstrong and irresponsible, but she was honest at the bottom of it all. I can't see her condoning what Ruth was doing if she knew about it.'

That made sense. But what if Emily had found out on her own? 'Why tell me all this now?' he asked.

Rosalind shrugged. 'A lot of reasons. Jerry's death. Your finding him. Your bringing Emily back. You know, for better or for worse, you've become part of our lives this last month or so. I had to tell *someone* and I couldn't think of anyone else. Isn't that pathetic? Ever since Emily came home, I've been going crazy keeping it to myself, but I couldn't risk telling you then. Not while Jerry was alive. I know you didn't like him, but I know that you policemen stick together. And anything you discover often makes its way into the papers. I'm not saying *you* would have said anything, but . . .'

'Walls have ears?'

'Something like that.'

'And now?'

'It doesn't matter now, does it? Nothing matters now. Apart from my anger, I just feel empty.' She put her glass aside and stood up. 'Now I really must go. I've said what I came to say. Thank you for listening.'

As Annie was about to turn left into Banks's drive just before Gratly Bridge, a car shot out backwards and swung towards her so fast she had to floor the brake pedal to avoid a collision. The other car then set off down the hill towards Helmthorpe.

Heart beating fast, Annie turned left and drove slowly up to Banks's cottage. She could see him silhouetted in the open door, wearing only a shirt and jeans despite the cold.

Annie pulled up in front and got out.

'What the hell are you doing here?' Banks said.

'That's a nice welcome. Can I come in?'

He stood aside. 'You might as well. Everyone else does.'

Annie had come prepared to launch right into him, having pumped herself up on the drive, but the adrenaline surge of her near accident and Banks's offhand manner took some of the wind out of her sails. Inside the cottage, she sat down in the armchair. It was still warm from whoever had just left it.

'And what can I do for you?' Banks said, shutting the door and going over to put more peat on the fire.

'First you can get me a drink.' Annie nodded towards the low table. 'That wine will do just fine.'

Banks went into the kitchen, got another glass and poured her some wine.

'Who was that?' she asked, taking the glass.

'Who?'

'The person who just left like a bat out of hell. The person who damn near backed right into me.'

'Oh, *that* person. Rosalind Riddle.'

'Friend of yours?'

'Work.'

'Work? Oh, well, I can see why you wouldn't want to tell *me* anything about it, then. After all, I'm only your DIO, aren't I?'

'Knock off the sarcasm, Annie. It doesn't suit you. Of course I was going to tell you.'

'Like you tell me everything?'

'Come again?'

'Oh, you know what I mean.'

'Humour me.'

'Rosalind Riddle is work, like her daughter was work, right?'

'I don't get it. What are you implying?'

'I'm not implying anything.' Annie told him about leafing through the green sheets and finding the reference to the Hotel Fifty-Five. 'No further action, or so Winsome told me. So I wondered why I hadn't heard anything about it. I phoned the hotel and, lo and behold, who spent most of a night there together a month ago?'

Banks said nothing; he just gazed sheepishly into the fire.

'What's the matter?' Annie went on. 'Cat got your tongue?'

'I don't see why I should have to explain myself to you.'

'Oh, you don't, don't you? I'll tell you why. Murder. That's why. Emily Riddle was murdered last week, or have you forgotten that?' As she spoke, Annie felt the embers of her anger start to rekindle again. 'Now, after the things I've discovered, I don't think you're fit to be working the case, but I'm your DIO and you owe me at least the *fucking* courtesy of telling me the truth about your relationship with the victim.'

'There *was* no relationship.'

'Liar.'

'Annie, there—'

'Liar.'

'Will you let me talk?'

'If you tell the truth.'

'I *am* telling the truth.'

'Liar.'

'All right. So I *liked* Emily. So what? I don't know why. She was a pain in the arse. But I liked her. That's all. More like a daughter than anything. That's as far as it went. It was my job to find her in London. She got herself into a bit of bother at a party and the only place she knew to come was to the hotel. I'd given her a card with the name written on, so she could contact me if she decided to come home. She was scared and alone and she came there. It's as simple as that.'

'What bother?'

Banks told her about the incident with Andy Pandy at the party.

'And you didn't see fit to share this titbit of information with me, your DIO?' Annie shook her head. 'I can't believe it. What else have you been keeping me in the dark about?'

'Nothing, Annie. Look, I know it was wrong of me, but surely you can see why I was worried how it might appear?'

'How it *might appear*? Emily Riddle turns up at your room at three o'clock in the morning and stays there the rest of the night, and you're worried about how it might appear. Oh, yes, I think I can see why.'

'Surely you can't think . . .?'

'What else am I supposed to think? You tell me. You spend the night in a hotel room with a randy sixteen-year-old slut, and you want me to believe nothing happened? Do you think I was born yesterday?'

'Emily Riddle wasn't a slut.'

'Oh, pardon me! Isn't that grand? Coming to the defence of your poor damsel in distress.'

'Annie, the girl's dead. At least you could show—'

'Show what? Respect?'

'Yes.'

'Were you showing her respect when you slept with her in that hotel room?'

'Annie, I've told you. I *didn't* sleep with her.'

'And I don't believe you. Oh, maybe you only intended to comfort her, give her a little cuddle, tell her everything was all right now, but from what I've heard of her, and from what I know about *men*, I very much doubt it ended there.'

'I never touched her.'

'You should have got her a room of her own.'

'I was going to, but she fell asleep on the bed.'

'Oh, come on.'

'She did. She was stoned. That's exactly what happened.'

'And you? Where were you? I remember those rooms, They're not very big.'

'In the armchair by the window. I sat up for a while listening to some music on the Walkman, then I spent the rest of the night listening to her snoring while I was trying to get to sleep, if you must know.'

Annie said nothing. She was trying to work out whether he was telling the truth or not. She suspected that he probably was, but she was determined not to let him off the hook that easily. However much it hurt or upset Annie, whether Banks had slept with Emily Riddle or not wasn't the real issue, she told herself. He could sleep with whoever he damn well pleased, even if it happened to be a sixteen-year-old girl. Annie had no hold over him. What really mattered was that he had kept important information from her, as he had done before in this investigation, and she was beginning to find it harder and harder to trust him.

'Anyway,' Banks went on, 'you've got a bloody nerve accusing me of screwing up on the job.'

Annie stiffened. 'What do you mean?'

'What about you? Do you really think you've been pulling your weight lately?'

Annie flinched from the accusation. 'I've had a few problems. That's all. I told you. Personal problems.'

'A few problems? Is that what you call sneaking off to sleep with DI Dalton every minute my back was turned? Don't think I didn't notice. I'm not stupid.'

Annie shot forward and slapped him hard across the face. She could tell it hurt him, and he drew back, his cheek reddening. Hot tears brimmed in her eyes.

'I'm sorry,' he said. 'I didn't mean it to sound so harsh. But you've got to admit you were pretty obvious. How do you think I felt?'

Annie could feel the blood roaring through her veins and her heart knocking against her ribs, even louder and faster than when the car almost hit her earlier. She paused for what felt like hours, taking slow, deliberate breaths, trying to calm herself, get rid of the panic and rage that seemed to possess her. When she finally spoke, it was in a voice barely above a whisper. 'You bloody idiot. For your information, DI Dalton was one of the men who raped me. But don't let that bother you. I'll go now.' She started to get up.

'Jesus Christ, Annie! No, don't go. Please don't go.' Banks grasped her wrist. She looked at his hand for a moment, then she sat down again, all the fight gone out of her. Banks refilled her wineglass and his own. 'I don't know what to say,' he said. 'I feel like a fool. Why didn't you *say* something?'

'Like what? Come crying to my boss the first week on the job?'

'Is he the one who actually—'

'One of the others. But that doesn't mean he wouldn't have done it, too, if I'd given him half a chance. As far as I'm concerned they're all three of them equally guilty.'

'But you could have told *me*. You knew that I'd understand.'

'And what would you have done? Gone flexing your macho muscles? Beat him up? Something like that? Had a pissing competition? No, thanks. It was *my* problem. I preferred to handle it myself.'

'Looks like you did a good job.'

'He's still alive, isn't he?'

Banks smiled. 'Annie, you don't have to handle everything in life by yourself.'

'Shows what you know about it. Wasn't anyone around to help when it happened, was there?'

'That doesn't mean there's no one now.'

Annie looked at him and felt herself soften. 'I can't handle this,' she said, shaking her head.

'Annie, I'm sorry. What can I say?'

'It doesn't matter.'

'Yes, it does. I saw the way you and Dalton tensed up when you met and I read it wrongly. I thought there was something between you.'

'There was. Just not what you thought it was.'

'I know that now. And I'm sorry. I should have trusted you.'

Annie made a sound halfway between a sniff and a laugh. 'Like I trusted you?'

'I was jealous. Besides, I didn't give you much reason to trust me, did I? I've handled this all wrong.'

'You can say that again.'

'Annie, I swear on my honour that nothing happened between me and Emily Riddle except she passed out in my room. What was I to do? The next day I bought her some new clothes on Oxford Street and we went home on the train.'

'And you really sat in one of those horrible hotel armchairs listening to your Walkman?'

'Yes. And smoking.'

'And smoking. Of course.'

'Yes.'

'Then you tried to sleep but her snoring kept you awake?'

'Yes. And the wind and rain.'

'And the wind and rain.' He looked so earnest that Annie couldn't help herself; she burst into laughter. The thing was, she could just picture him there doing exactly what he said. He looked hurt. 'I'm sorry, Alan. Really, I am. Nobody could make up a story as silly as that if it didn't really happen.'

Banks frowned. 'So you believe me now?'

'I believe you. I just wish you'd told me earlier. All this deception . . .'

'On both sides.'

'Oh, no. I didn't deceive you. You read the situation wrongly.'

'But you kept something from me.'

'That was private business. It wasn't to do with the case, not like your relationship with Emily Riddle. You really liked her?'

'I don't think I could have stood being around her for very long. She could be quite exhausting. Never stopped talking. And a hell of an attitude. But, yes, I did.'

Annie tilted her head and gave him a crooked grin. 'You're a funny one. You're so straight in some ways, but there's a definite bohemian edge to you.'

'Is that good?'

'It'll do. But I want you to know that I'm still seriously

pissed off at you for not treating me as a professional. You've got a lot of making up to do.'

'Annie, I'm sorry. Really, I am. It's been difficult, given what we had, then me thinking you and Dalton . . . you know. I mean, it's not as if I don't still . . .'

Annie felt her heart give a little somersault. 'Don't still what?'

'Fancy you.' The fire was waning and the air becoming chilly. Banks looked at Annie and she felt the stirrings of her feelings for him that she'd been trying to ignore since they split up. He picked up a lump of peat. 'Are you staying?' he asked. 'Shall I put some more on? It's getting cold.'

Annie gave him a serious look, then bit her lip, stretched out her hand, the same hand she had slapped him with, and said, 'Okay, but we've got a lot of talking to do.'

17

Annie pulled up in the staff car park of the red-brick fire station in Salford just after eleven thirty the next morning, after more than an hour spent crawling along the M62 and getting lost in the centre of Manchester. A lorry had overturned at one of the junctions near Huddersfield, and traffic was backed up as far as the intersection with the M1. The weather hadn't helped either. After last night's heavy frost, the roads were icy despite the brilliant winter sunshine that glinted on windscreens and bonnets.

The fire station stood on an arterial road near the estate of shabby mock-Georgian semis where Ruth Walker had grown up. Banks had told Annie about Ruth being Rosalind Riddle's daughter. Ruth had told a lot of lies, he said, and he thought they should find out more about her background, including the fire in which both her parents had been killed eighteen months ago. It had been easy to track down the address via the Salford Fire Brigade, which was Annie's first port of call. The fire-station chief, George Whitmore, said he would be pleased to talk to her.

The firemen were sitting around playing cards in a large upper room above the gleaming red engines. The place smelled of sweat, aftershave and oil. They were an odd lot, firemen, Annie had always thought. When everything was going well, they had no job to do at all, just the way the police would have nothing to do if people weren't committing crimes. Annie had known one of the local lads back in St Ives who had spent his

391

time at work writing Westerns under a pseudonym, selling about one a month to an American publisher. She had also been out with a fireman who ran a carpet-cleaning business on the side, and one of his friends ran an airport taxi service. They all seemed to have three or four jobs on the go. Of course, fires are as inevitable as crime, and when it came to the crunch, nobody would deny the heroism of firemen if the occasion demanded it. And no matter how politically correct you tried to be about it, no matter how much people talked about recruiting more women to the job, whether you called them Combustion Control Engineers or Flame Suppressant Units, the truth about firemen was summed up in what they always had been and always would be as far as Annie was concerned: *firemen*.

'Mr Whitmore around?' she asked one of the card players.

He gave her the once-over, smiled as if he thought she was sexy and pointed with his thumb. 'Office back there.'

Annie felt his eyes on her behind as she walked away, heard a whisper, then men's laughter. She thought of turning and making some comment about how childish they were but decided they weren't worth the effort.

George Whitmore turned out to be a pleasant man with cropped grey hair, not far from retirement age by the look of him. He had a framed photo of his family, including grand-children, on his desk.

'You're the lass who phoned earlier, are you?' he said, bidding Annie to sit down.

'Yes.'

'Well, I should've told you; you've probably made a long journey for nothing.'

Annie smiled at him. 'I don't mind. It's nice to get out of the office for a while.' She took out her notebook. 'You remember the Walker fire?'

'Yes. I was on the crew back then, before my bad back put me on office duties a year ago.'

'You were at the scene?'

'Yes. It happened, oh, about three or four in the morning, or a bit after. I could look it up if you want the exact time.'

'It doesn't matter for the moment. Just your impressions will do.'

He paused and frowned. 'If you don't mind me asking, love, why do the police want to know about the Walker fire now, after all this time?'

'It's just a background check,' Annie said. 'Routine.'

'Because there was nothing funny about it.'

'I understand there was no police investigation?'

'Not beyond what's required by law and the insurance company. No reason for one.'

'What was the cause of the fire?'

'A smouldering cigarette end down the side of the sofa.'

Another reason smoking's bad for your health, thought Annie. 'And you ruled out arson?'

Whitmore nodded. 'Early on. There were no signs of forced entry, of anything being disturbed, for a start. There was also no evidence of accelerants being used, and, quite honestly, nobody had any reason to harm the Walkers.'

'You knew them?'

'Only in passing. To say hello to. They were active in chapel. Everyone knew that. I'm not a particularly religious sort myself. Nice, God-fearing couple, though, by all accounts. Nice daughter they had, too. Poor lass barely escaped with her life.'

'That'd be Ruth?'

'Aye. They only had the one.'

'So what happened from the moment the alarm went off?'

'They didn't have a smoke detector. If they'd had one, it's likely they wouldn't have died. A neighbour saw the smoke and flames and phoned us. By the time we got there, most of the neighbours were already out in the street. See, a cigarette can smoulder for hours and generate a lot of heat. When it takes hold, it really goes. The fire had taken hold by then, and it took us a good hour or so to put it out completely. At least we managed to stop it spreading.'

'Where was Ruth at this time?'

'They'd taken her to hospital. She jumped out of her bedroom window in the nick of time. Broke her ankle and dislocated her shoulder.'

'Nasty.'

'The ankle was the worst. Bad fracture, apparently. Took her weeks before she could walk again without crutches or a stick. Anyway, it wasn't nearly as nasty as what happened to her mum and dad. She was the lucky one. There'd been a shower earlier in the evening, and the ground was soft, or she might have broken more bones.'

'How did her parents die?'

'Smoke inhalation. That's what the post-mortem showed. Never even had time to get out of bed. Ruth had inhaled some smoke, too, before she jumped, but not enough to do her much harm. A whiff of oxygen and she was right as rain.'

'Why did she have time to escape and her parents didn't?'

Whitmore shrugged. 'Younger, stronger, quicker reflexes. Also, her room was at the front, and the fire was worse farther back. Her parents were probably dead when she jumped.'

'Can you tell me anything else?'

'That's about it, really, love. Told you you'd probably had a wasted journey.'

'Well, you know what it's like,' said Annie. 'Was the house completely destroyed?'

'Pretty much. Inside, at any rate.'

'And now?'

'Oh, someone bought it and had it renovated. To look at it now you'd never know such tragedy happened there.'

Annie stood up. 'Where is it from here, exactly?'

'Carry on along the main road, go left at the next lights and it's the second street on the right.'

'Thanks very much.' Annie left Whitmore's tiny office and walked back past the card players. This time one of them whistled at her. She smiled to herself. It felt quite nice, actually. Thirty-something and she still got whistled at. She'd have to tell Alan about that.

Alan. They had talked most of the night while the peat fire blazed in the hearth and soft jazz played in the background. He told her about Rosalind's visit, about Emily and Ruth, about the guilt he felt on finding Riddle dead in his garage, and she told him about how Dalton's appearance had knocked her out of kilter, brought back feelings she didn't know she still harboured, and how she had confronted him on Sunday morning.

Had it been summer, they would have been up talking until dawn, but because it was December, the only light that shone through the windows at four o'clock in the morning came from a full moon as white as frost. Even then they continued to talk, and the way Annie remembered it, she thought she had probably fallen asleep in mid-sentence.

It wasn't until both had slept for about three hours that they made love – tentatively and tenderly – and in the morning they had to scrape the ice off their car windows and drive like hell to get to work on time.

Now, it seemed to Annie as if there were no more secrets, as if nothing stood between them. She still worried about their working together, especially now that she was stationed at Western Divisional HQ, too; and she could never quite get over her fear of commitment, of rejection. But Banks hadn't asked her for commitment, and if anything, it was *she* who had rejected *him* last time, out of fear of his past impinging on her life.

All she really knew, she decided, was that whatever it was they had, she wanted it. It was time again to take a lesson from her father's synthesis of Eastern philosophy – go with the flow.

Annie smiled as she touched up her make-up using the

rear-view mirror, then she headed off to see if she could discover anything from the Walkers' neighbours.

The atmosphere that had hung over the death scene at the Riddles' garage the previous day seemed to have permeated the entire station, Banks thought as he looked out of his window at the market square. The place had all the atmosphere of an undertaker's. While Riddle might not have been the most loved or admired chief constable they had ever had, he *had* been one of them, and he was dead. It was like losing a member of the family. A distant and austere uncle perhaps, but still a family member. Even Banks felt heavy-hearted as he sipped his bitter black coffee.

The dark mood reminded him of the days after Graham Marshall's disappearance, when everyone in the school seemed to be going around walking on eggs and conversations all seemed to be carried out in whispers. Those days had given Banks his first real taste of guilt, a sense of being responsible for people that was one of the things that spurred him on now in his job. He knew deep down that he was no more responsible for Graham Marshall's disappearance than he was for Phil Simpkins's bleeding to death on the railings, or Jem's overdose of heroin, but he seemed to attract the guilt, draw it to him and wrap it around himself like a comforting mantle.

When he thought of Annie, though, he felt his spirits rise. He knew not to expect too much – she had made that quite clear – but at least they had got beyond the rumours and fears they had been bogged down with in the past week. Banks sensed the possibility of a new, deeper trust. It would have to develop naturally, though; there could be no pushing, not with someone as scared of intimacy as Annie was, or someone as recently battle-scarred as himself. Sandra's asking for a divorce and telling him she wanted to marry Sean might have given him a sense of finality, of liberation, but the old wounds were still there. Which reminded him: he ought to respond to the second solicitor's letter, or Sandra would think he had changed his mind.

Banks could see a knot of reporters outside the station. He looked at his watch: almost opening time. Pretty soon they'd all be ensconced in the Queen's Arms padding out their expense accounts. Riddle's suicide was the kind of thing that got the London dailies this far north. No official statements had been issued yet, and the Riddle house was still under secure guard. Of course, they could have a field day with this one: CHIEF CONSTABLE COMMITS SUICIDE WITH POLICE GUARD ONLY YARDS AWAY. They could spin that to read whichever way they wanted.

Rosalind was going down to stay with her parents in Barnstaple after she had made the funeral arrangements. Then, she had told Banks just before she left the previous evening, she would sell the house and decide what to do next. There was no hurry – she would be well off – but she would move as far away from Yorkshire as possible. Banks felt for her; he had absolutely no conception of how awful it must feel to lose a daughter and a spouse in the space of only a few days. He couldn't even imagine how terrible it would be to lose Brian or Tracy.

Banks's ancient heater hissed and spluttered as he sat down and thought over the previous evening's conversation with Rosalind. One obvious point was that, by telling him what she had, she had inadvertently supplied him with a motive for getting rid of Emily. Or was it inadvertent? He had no doubt that Rosalind could be devious when she wanted to – after all, she *was* a lawyer – but he had no idea why she would want to incriminate herself that way. Put simply, though, if Rosalind wanted to keep Ruth's existence from her husband, and if Emily was a loose cannon on deck, then Rosalind had a motive for getting Emily out of the way.

And, by extension, she had an even better motive for wanting Ruth Walker out of the way, permanently.

Since Riddle's suicide, though, it was all academic. The money, the status, the celebrity, the possibility of a political career – they had all vanished into thin air. Nothing remained for Rosalind except Benjamin and Ruth, and Banks doubted she would have anything more to do with Ruth after all that had happened. It was enough to prove the writer of Ecclesiastes right when he wrote that all is vanity.

Banks couldn't bring himself to believe that Rosalind had actually given her own daughter cocaine laced with strychnine, or that she was right now plotting the demise of her other daughter, but at the same time he had to bear in mind that there was no love lost between any of them and that, once, Rosalind had given her child away to strangers and moved on to the wealth and power and their trappings she seemed to need so much. And when it came right down to it, no matter what Banks's gut instinct told him, we are all capable of murder given the right incentive.

Whichever way he looked at it, Ruth Walker's sudden prominence in the case was a complication he could do without. While Annie dug up information on Ruth's background in Salford, Banks was trying to find out as much as he could about her present life in Kennington while he waited for a call from Burgess. He had already made several phone calls and had two pages of notes.

When his telephone rang, he thought it was Ruth's boss calling him back, but it was the other phone call he'd been waiting for, Burgess's, the one that gave a green light for the second interview with Barry Clough. And not before time, too; they could only hang on to him for another couple of hours at most.

It seemed a pleasant enough neighbourhood, Annie thought, standing by the side of the road looking at the houses. Not at all the sort of place you would expect in Salford, though if she were honest she would have to admit she had never been to

Salford before and had no idea what to expect. Semi-detached houses lined both sides of the quiet road, each with a fair-sized front lawn tucked away behind a privet hedge. The cars parked in the street were not ostentatious, but they weren't clapped-out ten-year-old Fiestas, either. Most of them were Japanese or Korean, and Annie's Astra didn't look too out of place. Crime-wise, she guessed, the biggest problems would be the occasional break-in or car theft.

Number 39 was much like the other houses. As Whitmore had said, there was no indication whatsoever of the tragedy that had taken place there. Annie tried to imagine the flames, the smoke, the screams and neighbours standing out in their slippers and dressing gowns watching, helpless, as Ruth jumped from the upstairs window and her parents suffocated, unable even to get out of their beds.

'Help you, dearie?' Annie turned and saw an elderly woman clutching a carrier bag with arthritis-crippled fingers. 'Only you look like you're lost or something.'

'No,' said Annie, smiling to reassure the woman she wasn't crazy or anything. 'Just lost in thought, maybe.'

'Did you know the Walkers?'

'No.'

'Only you were looking at their house.'

'Yes. I'm a policewoman.' Annie introduced herself.

'Tattersall. Gladys Tattersall,' the woman said. 'Pleased to meet you, I'm sure. Don't tell me you're opening an investigation into the fire after all this time?'

'No. Do you think we should be?'

'Why don't you come inside. I'll put the kettle on. I'm at number thirty-seven here.'

It was the semi adjoining the Walker house. 'It must have been frightening for you,' Annie said as she followed Mrs Tattersall down the path and into the hall.

'I was more frightened during the bombing in the war. Mind you, I was just a lass then. Come in. Sit down.'

Annie entered the living room and sat on a plum velour armchair. A gilt-framed mirror hung over the fireplace and the inevitable television sat on its stand in the corner. At the far end of the room was a dining table with four chairs arranged around it. Mrs Tattersall went into the kitchen and came back. 'Won't be long,' she said, sitting on the sofa. 'You're right, though. It was a frightening night.'

'Was it you who called the fire brigade?'

'No. That was the Hennessy lad over the road. He was coming home late from a club and he saw the flames and smoke. It was him came knocking on our door and told us to get out fast. That's me and my husband, Bernard. He passed away last winter. *Cancer.*'

'I'm sorry to hear it.'

'Oh, it's all right, lass. It was a blessing, really. It was in his lungs, though he was never a smoker. The painkillers weren't doing him much good towards the end.'

Annie paused for a moment. It seemed appropriate after the mention of the late Mr Tattersall. 'Was your house damaged?'

Mrs Tattersall shook her head. 'We were lucky. The walls got a bit warm, I can tell you, but the fire brigade sprayed the exterior with enough water to fill a swimming pool. It was August, you see, warm weather, and we'd left a window open, so a bit of it got inside and did some damage to the walls – peeling paper, stains, that sort of thing. But nothing serious. The insurance paid for it. Perhaps the worst that came out of it for us was having to live here while the people that bought the Walker house after the fire hammered and banged away all hours of the day and night.'

'The renovators?'

'Yes.' The kettle boiled. Mrs Tattersall disappeared for a few minutes and returned with the tea on a tray, which she set down on the low table in front of the electric fire. 'You haven't told me why you're asking,' she said.

'It's just a routine check. Nothing to do with the fire, really. It just seemed like an easy place to start.'

'Routine? That's what you always say on telly.'

Annie laughed. 'It's probably about the only realistic thing about TV coppers, then. It's Ruth we're interested in. The daughter.'

'Is she in any trouble?'

'Not as far as I know. Why do you ask?'

Mrs Tattersall leaned forward and poured. 'Sugar?'

'Just milk, please.'

'You wouldn't be asking about her for the good of your health, would you?'

'It's to do with a friend of hers,' Annie said. Like most police, she was loath to give away the slightest scrap of information.

'I suppose that'll have to do, then,' said Mrs Tattersall, handing Annie the cup and saucer.

'Thank you. Did you know the Walkers well?'

'Pretty well. I mean, as well as you could do.'

'What do you mean?'

'They weren't the most sociable types, weren't the Walkers.'

'Stand-offish? Snobbish?'

'No, not really. I mean, they were polite enough. Polite to a T. And helpful if you needed anything. Lord knows they didn't have much themselves, but they'd give you the shirt off their backs. They just didn't mix.' She paused, then whispered, '*Religious*,' the same way she had whispered *cancer*.

'More than most?'

'I'd say so. Oh, it was nothing strange. None of those weird cults or churches where you can't have blood transfusions or anything. Straight Methodist. But strict observers. Against Sunday shopping, drinking, pop music, that sort of thing.'

'What was Mr Walker's occupation?'

'Wages clerk.'

'Did his wife work?'

'Pauline? Good heavens, no. They were as traditional as you get. She was a housewife.'

'You don't get many of those in this day and age.'

Mrs Tattersall laughed. 'You're telling me you don't, lass. Me, half the time I couldn't wait to get out of the house and to work. Not that I had such a wonderful job, myself. I was only a receptionist at the medical centre down the road. But you get to meet people, chat, find out what's going on in the world. I'd go barmy if I was stuck between four walls day in, day out. Wouldn't you?'

'I would,' said Annie. 'But Mrs Walker didn't seem to mind?'

'She never complained. But it's against their religion, isn't it, complaining?'

'I didn't know that.' Annie would have been the first to admit that she didn't know much about religion except what she had read, and she had read mostly about Buddhism and Taoism. Her father was an atheist, so he hadn't subjected her to Sunday school or any of the usual childhood indoctrination, and the people who came and went in the commune carried with them a variety of ideas about religion and philosophy. Everything was always up for debate, up in the air.

'I mean, if whatever happens to you is God's will, good or bad, then you've no call to be complaining to God about God, if you see what I mean.'

'I think I do.'

'They were just a bit old-fashioned, that's all. People used to laugh behind their backs. Oh, nothing vicious or anything. It was mostly good-humoured. Not that they'd have noticed. That was another thing that wasn't in their religion. Humour. I *did* feel a bit sorry for young Ruth sometimes.'

'Why?'

'Well, there wasn't much *fun* in her life. And young people need fun. Even us old 'uns need a bit of fun from time to time, but when you're young . . .' She sighed. 'Anyway, the Walkers were different from other folk. And they didn't have much money, with only him working.'

'How did they get by?'

'She were a good housekeeper, Pauline, I'll give her that. Good budgeter. But it meant that young Ruth could hardly stay up to date with fashions and whatnot. You'd see her in the same outfit year after year. A nip here and a tuck there. And shoes. Good Lord, she'd be clomping around in the most ugly things you could imagine. Pauline bought her them because they were durable, you see. Sturdy, sensible things with thick soles so they'd last a long time. None of these Nike trainers or Reeboks, like the other kids were wearing. Like it or not, love, fashions are so important to children, especially in their teens.' She laughed. 'I should know; I've brought up two of them.'

'What happened?'

'The usual. The other girls at school laughed at her, called her names, tormented her. Children can be so cruel. And they'd no time for music or telly, either – wouldn't have a record player or a television set in the house – so poor Ruth couldn't join in the conversations with the rest. She didn't know all about the latest hits and the popular television programmes. She was always a bit of a loner. It wasn't as if she was a great beauty, either. She was always a rather pasty-faced, dumpy sort of lass, and that kind are easy to pick on.'

It was starting to sound like a pretty miserable household to grow up in, Annie thought. The artists' colony where she had grown up herself didn't have a television, either, but there was always music – often live – and all sorts of interesting people around. Some nights they would sing songs and recite poems. She could hear them from her bedroom. It was all mumbo-jumbo to her then, of course; none of it rhymed or anything, but they seemed to enjoy themselves. Sometimes, they let her sing for them, too, and if she said so herself, she didn't have a bad voice for traditional folk music.

Still, she thought she could relate to Ruth's feeling of being an outsider. If you're different in any way – no matter whether your family's too strict or too liberal – you get picked on, especially if you aren't up on the latest styles, too. Children *are* cruel; Mrs Tattersall was right about that. Annie could remember some of their cruelties of her own childhood very well indeed.

Once, when she was about thirteen, a gang of classmates had waylaid her in the lane on her way home from school, dragged her into the trees, stripped her and painted flowers all over her body while they made remarks about filthy, drug-taking hippies and flower power. They had then run off with her clothes and left her to make the rest of her way home naked. *Cruel.* You could say that again. Going to school the next day she had found her clothes hanging on a tree by the side of the lane. And that was in 1980, when hippies were history and the sixties was something her classmates could only have read about in books or seen on television documentaries. The people who lived at the commune were artists and writers, free-thinkers, yes, but *hippies*? No. Annie's only sin was to be different, to wear the kind of clothes she wanted to wear (and that her father could afford, artists never having been among the richest members of society). Yes, in an odd way, she could sympathize very easily with Ruth Walker: two sides of the same coin.

'Ruth went off to university, didn't she?'

'Yes. That's what changed everything.'

'What do you mean?'

'Well, they wanted her to go to Manchester, like, and keep on living at home so they could keep an eye on her, but she went to London. They thought university was a den of iniquity, you see, full of sex and drugs, but they also knew you don't get very far in this day and age without a good education. It was a bit of a dilemma for them. Anyway, she got her student grant or loan or whatever they get, so she had a bit of money of her own for the first time, and in the holidays she usually got a job. It gave her her first taste of independence.'

'What did she do with her money?'

'Bought clothes, mostly. You should have seen her when she came back after her first year. Had all the latest styles. Whatever they were wearing at the moment. It all changes far too quickly for me to keep up with it. Anyway, she looked like any other rebellious young lass her age. Had her hair dyed all the colours of the rainbow, rings through her ears and eyebrows. Looked awfully painful. She'd found her brave new world, all right.'

'How did her parents react?'

'I don't know. They never said anything in public. I can't imagine they were pleased, though. I got the feeling they were ashamed of her.'

'Did you hear any rows? Through the walls.'

'They never got angry. Against their religion. I think they pleaded with her and tried to get her to switch to a course in Manchester and come back home, but she'd changed too much by then. It was too late. She'd had her taste of freedom and she wasn't about to give it up. I can't say I blame her.'

'So the matter went unresolved?'

'I suppose so. She spent that summer working at the local supermarket, general floor washer and shelf stacker, that sort of thing. She was a bright lass and a hard worker, and, to do her justice, even when she looked like a tearaway she didn't cause any trouble. She was always polite.'

'So she just looked strange?'

'That's about all. I think she'd reacted against the religion, too. At least she didn't go to chapel with them any more. But kids do that, don't they?'

'They do,' Annie agreed. 'I was talking to one of the firemen, Mr Whitmore, earlier.'

'I know George Whitmore. He was a friend of my

Bernard's. They used to enjoy a game of darts down at the King Billy on a Friday night.'

'He said they didn't see any need to investigate the fire.'

'That's right. I can't see why they would. That's why I was wondering what on earth you were doing here. Nobody would want to hurt the Walkers.'

'Mr Whitmore said it was probably started by a cigarette left smouldering down the side of the sofa.'

'Well, that *was* a bit odd,' said Mrs Tattersall slowly. 'Being religious and all, the way they were, you see, the Walkers didn't smoke or drink.'

'But I'll bet Ruth did,' said Annie.

Clough looked a little the worse for wear after his night in the cells, though the kind of suit he wore hardly showed a wrinkle. He had chosen not to shave, and the stubble, along with the tan and the gold accessories, made him look slightly unreal, like some sort of ageing pop star. His lawyer, Simon Gallagher, however, who had no doubt spent the night in Burgundy House, Eastvale's poshest and priciest hotel, had taken the opportunity to clean himself up a bit, and now looked every inch the high-priced solicitor. He still had the twitchy, perky manner of a habitual cokehead, though, and Banks wondered if he'd snorted a couple of lines before the interview. He didn't say a lot, but he just couldn't sit still.

With Annie in Salford and Winsome back inputting data into HOLMES, Banks got Kevin Templeton to attend the interview with him. After the usual preliminaries, Banks began.

'Hope you had a comfortable night, Barry.'

'You don't give a rat's arse what kind of night I had, so why don't you cut the crap and get to the point.' Clough looked at his watch. 'According to this, my twenty-four hours are up in about one hour and forty-five minutes. That right, Simon?'

Simon Gallagher nodded. Or twitched.

'We aim to please,' said Banks. 'Anyway, I don't know if you've heard, but since we last talked, Chief Constable Riddle has committed suicide.'

'Well, at least that's one thing you can't bang me up for, then, isn't it?'

'Is that all you've got to say about it?'

'What do you expect? I didn't know the man.'

Even people who did know Riddle, Banks thought, might show as little concern as Clough. Banks himself hadn't liked him, and he didn't intend to be hypocritical about it now, but the tragedy and despair of the act pierced his dislike to some extent. Nobody should be reduced to that. 'Were you putting pressure on him, Barry?'

'What do you mean?'

'I think you know what I mean. Putting pressure on him to become your man, to do you the odd favour or two, make sure we looked the other way when you set up your little scams in North Yorkshire.'

'Why would I want to do that?'

'You tell me.'

'I wouldn't.'

'But that's what your meeting was about, wasn't it? That's why he walked out before you really got started, isn't it? What were you using, Barry? Was it Emily? Do you have photographs? Did you threaten him that you could take her back any time you wanted?'

Clough sighed and rolled his eyes at Gallagher.

'I think you've already exhausted this line of questioning,' Gallagher said. 'As you are well aware, my client could have had nothing to do with Mr Riddle's unfortunate death, even if it hadn't been suicide. He has the best of all alibis: he was in your cells.'

'Your client might have been one of the chief factors that drove the chief constable over the edge.'

'You can't prove that,' said Gallagher. 'And even if you

could, it hardly constitutes an indictable offence. Stick to the facts, Chief Inspector. Move on.'

Banks was loath to give up and move on, but Gallagher was probably right. It would take a hell of a lot more than he had to persuade the CPS even to look at the possibility of prosecuting someone for complicity in the suicide of another. If Banks remembered his criminal law correctly, complicity could mean aiding, abetting, counselling or procuring another's suicide, and there was no evidence that Clough, even though he might have been trying to blackmail Riddle, had done any of those things. He was simply the straw that broke the camel's back.

Banks moved on. 'Remember we were talking yesterday about Charlie Courage and Andrew Handley?'

'Vaguely.'

'That both were killed by shotgun blasts, and both were found in rural areas some distance from their homes.'

'I believe I asked what that had to do with me at the time, and now I'm asking again.'

'Just this,' said Banks, pausing and opening the file folder he had brought in with him. 'While you've been enjoying our hospitality downstairs, we've been very busy indeed, and our forensics men have been able to match the tyre tracks at the two scenes.'

'I'm impressed,' said Clough, raising an eyebrow. 'The wonders of modern science.'

'There's even better to come. On further investigation, they were able to match the tracks found at the scene of the two murders to a cream Citroën owned by a Mr Jamie Gilbert. One of your employees, yes?'

'Jamie? You already know that.'

'And it also turns out that one of Charlie Courage's neighbours recognized the photograph of Jamie Gilbert our officer showed her. Jamie was *seen* getting into a car with Charlie Courage around the time he disappeared. Anything to say?'

'They must be mistaken.'

'Who?'

'Your scientists. This witness.'

Banks shook his head. 'Afraid not. Not only do the tyres match, but we were also able to find hair samples and minute traces of blood we believe belong to either Charlie Courage or Andrew Handley in the car. Jamie was careless. He didn't clean it out thoroughly enough. The samples are being checked for DNA now.'

'I don't know what to say,' said Clough. 'I'm shocked. Stunned, even. And I thought I knew Jamie.'

'Evidently not. Anyway, Mr Gilbert is in custody back in London at the moment. He'll no doubt be telling the interviewing officers down there exactly what happened.'

'Jamie won't . . .'

'Jamie won't *what*, Barry?'

Clough smiled. 'I was just about to say that Jamie won't be saying anything. You don't know him as well as I do. He's not the type.'

'But you said just now that you only *thought* you knew him, that you're surprised he's a murderer.'

'An alleged murderer,' Simon Gallagher chipped in.

'My apologies,' Banks went on. 'An alleged murderer.'

'You know what I mean.'

'Do you have any idea *why* Jamie Gilbert would want to kill Charlie Courage and Andrew Handley?'

'None at all.'

'Did he even know Charlie Courage?'

'I don't know who he hangs about with in his spare time.'

'But he works for you.'

'*Worked*. If you think I'm going to keep a murderer in my employ you must think I'm crazy. He's fired as of now.'

'He worked for you at the time of the murders. He was your chief enforcer. And he *did* know Andrew Handley.'

'Jamie was my administrative assistant. I already told you that.'

'What did he administer for you? Punishment?'

'He handled my business affairs.'

'Just exactly what might those be?'

'For Christ's sake!' Clough looked at Gallagher. 'Can't you get him to stop this? It's like an old LP with the bloody needle stuck.'

'Legitimate questions, Barry. Legitimate questions.'

Clough glared at Gallagher, who turned to Banks. 'Get to the point quickly, Chief Inspector. We're all running out of time and patience here.'

'Not me,' said Banks. 'Barry, is it true you were fired as a roadie for bootlegging the band's live performances?'

Clough faltered, clearly not expecting the question. 'What the hell has that got to do with anything?'

'Just answer my question, please.'

'It was years ago. There were no charges or anything.'

'But you do have a history in bootlegging?'

'It was a mistake.'

'Well, pirating is big business these days. Movies, computer software, games. Big business. Maybe not as big here as it is in the Far East or Eastern Europe, but big enough to provide maximum profits for minimum risks. Just the kind of business venture that interests you, isn't it, Barry?'

'Chief Inspector!'

'Sorry, Mr Gallagher. Slip of the tongue.' Banks could see Kevin Templeton trying to stifle a grin. 'You've already admitted you know Gregory Manners, haven't you?' Banks pressed on.

'I've admitted no such thing.'

'Mr Manners has a conviction for smuggling. Customs and Excise had their eyes on him for a while.'

'What's that got to do with me?'

'They had their eyes on you, too.'

'Well, if they'd seen anything they'd have arrested me, wouldn't they?'

'You're obviously a very careful man. It's odd, though, isn't it?'

'What is?'

'So many of your friends and employees being criminals. Jamie Gilbert. Andrew Handley. Gregory Manners. Charlie Courage.'

'I told you, I've never heard of a Gregory Manners or a Charlie Courage.'

'Of course not. My mistake. The others, though.'

'Like I said, it's hardly my responsibility what my employees get up to in their own time. Maybe criminals have more fun.'

'One might be forgiven for assuming that they were merely carrying out your orders.'

'Assume what you want. You can't *prove* anything.'

'I'd say if a man has one criminal employee, that might be carelessness, but *two* . . .?'

'Are we going anywhere with this, Chief Inspector?' Gallagher chipped in. 'Because if we're not, we can stop right here. As they say in the vernacular, shit or get off the pot.'

'And you a well-educated man, Mr Gallagher. Tut-tut. I'm appalled. Wash your mouth out, as my mother would say.'

Clough stood up. 'I've had enough of this.'

'Sit down, Barry,' said Banks.

'You can't make me. I'm free to go whenever—'

'Sit down!'

Clough was so taken aback by Banks's tone that he subsided slowly into his chair again. Gallagher said nothing. He looked as if he badly needed another couple of lines. Banks leaned forward and rested his arms on the table. 'Now, let me tell you what I think happened, Barry. You had a nice little earner going, pirating software and games. You'd rent units in business parks all over the country for a while under phony company names, flood the local markets using the same distribution set-up you'd organized for your smuggling business; then you'd move on, like playing hopscotch, always one step ahead of Trading Standards. Gregory Manners ran the operation in the Daleview Business Park and Andrew Handley oversaw the regional operation; just my guess, of course, but Andy wasn't seen around the place as much as Mr Manners was. Andy Pandy got very pissed off at you, perhaps because you treated him like shit: pushing Emily into the room with him, passing on your leftovers. He decided, in revenge, to rip off the operation. To do this, he enlisted Charlie Courage, nightwatchman and petty criminal. Charlie probably arranged for the move to Northumbria and passed the details on to Andy Pandy, who arranged a hijack, killing the driver, Jonathan Fearn, a local wide boy recruited by Charlie. How am I doing so far?'

Clough sat with his arms folded, a supercilious grin on his face. 'It's fascinating. You should write detective fiction.'

'But you suspect a double-cross. You don't trust what you hear about Charlie Courage. Maybe you don't like strangers being brought in on things. Whatever. You lean on Gregory Manners enough to know it's not him. Which leaves Andy Pandy. Then you have Jamie Gilbert and another minder pick up Charlie and ask him a few questions. The hard way. Charlie never did have much of a stomach for violence, and it doesn't take long before he spills the whole scam. They take him for the long ride and blow him away, then they do the same with Andy Pandy, after they've beaten the whereabouts of the stolen stock and multi-disc-copying machines from him.'

'And where are these machines, then, seeing as you're so clever?'

'Barry,' Gallagher cut in, 'I'd strongly advise—'

Banks waved him down. 'It's all right, Mr Gallagher. I'll answer Barry's question. Andy Pandy had a lock-up in Golders Green, and it was broken into shortly after he disappeared. I think your lads also did that, took back the stolen equipment.

My guess is that you've sold it by now and moved on to something else.'

Clough contemplated his fingernails. 'Like I said, it's a fascinating story. You've missed your vocation. See, Simon, they've got nothing.'

'Remember, Chief Inspector,' said Gallagher, 'time's running out. Shit or get off the pot.'

Banks paused, scribbled a couple of meaningless notes in his file, then got up and said to Kevin Templeton, 'Take Mr Clough downstairs to the custody sergeant, Kevin, and have him charged with conspiracy to commit murder. I'm sure Mr Gallagher will make sure everything's done according to PACE regulations.'

Clough flushed. 'You can't do this. Tell them, Simon. Tell them they can't do this!'

'I'll deal with it, Barry,' said Gallagher. 'Don't worry, I'll have you out in no time.'

'What do you mean, you'll have me out in no time? Out of where?'

'He means out of prison, Barry,' said Banks. 'And if you ask me, I think he's being overly optimistic.'

'If truth be told,' said Banks to Annie over an after-work pint in the Queen's Arms that evening, 'I think it was me being overly optimistic in thinking we can make any charges stick against Clough.'

Annie sipped her pint and settled into her chair. She looked around. The pub was pretty quiet at that time in the evening; most people were at home having dinner and watching the news. Occasionally, a Christmas shopper or two would come in with carrier bags from Marks & Spencer, Tandy or W.H. Smith in the Swainsdale Centre across the square, knock back a quick whisky and head out again. Christmas decorations hung across the ceiling. The pub's dim light glowed in the polished wood and brass, the dimpled, copper-topped tables, the sparkling glasses and the bottles arranged behind the bar. Cyril, the landlord, stood chatting to a regular. The jukebox was mercifully silent and Annie could hear the church choir collecting for a refugee relief fund, singing 'Away in a Manger' under the giant Christmas tree outside. Poor kids, she thought. It was real brass-monkey weather out there; they must be freezing.

'You don't think there's much hope, then?' she asked.

Banks shrugged. 'We'll set up a meeting with Stafford Oakes in the CPS office, but let's just say it's pretty flimsy evidence so far.'

'What about the forensics?'

'I've never put much faith in tyre tracks. Most people don't know Goodyear from Michelin.'

'But the blood?'

'Might be something there, if the lab doesn't "lose" the evidence.'

'What do you mean?'

'Remember that fire at the Wetherby lab a few years ago?'

'Yes.'

'That was started to destroy evidence being kept there. Don't you think someone like Clough is capable of something similar?'

'I hadn't thought of that. What about the witness who saw Jamie Gilbert with Courage?'

'Easy meat.'

'Oh, dear.'

'Indeed. I have a terrible feeling that they'll both walk. Conspiracy's always a bugger to prove. And as for implicating him in Riddle's suicide . . . that was pissing against the wind.'

'It *was* suicide, then?'

'Not much doubt about it. I had a brief word with Dr Glendenning after he did the post-mortem this afternoon. No signs of a struggle, no signs of restraint or drugs in the system. He'll run a full tox check, of course, just to be certain. And the note's been checked by an expert. It's Riddle's handwriting.

No, I think we can be pretty certain that Jimmy Riddle voluntarily sat in his car with the engine running. We can also be damn certain that the business with Emily and the pressure Clough was putting on him were a big part of what drove him to it, but we can't touch Clough for that.'

'He's a slippery bastard, all right.'

'Anyway, I'm getting more and more interested in Ruth Walker.'

'You think she killed Emily?'

'I think she might have. It never really made any sense to me that Clough would have done it, especially after he tried to blackmail Riddle, much as I'd have loved to put him away for it.'

'But Ruth?'

'She certainly had the opportunity, for a start. She was off work, poorly, at the time Emily was killed, or so she says. She could have driven up and back easily.'

'And the means?'

'She said she had a cold, but I think her sniffle might have been caused by something else.'

'Coke?'

'At a guess.'

'What about the strychnine, though?'

'One of the leads I'm following up. As far as I can piece it together, her degree's in computers and information technology. She's very bright, got first-class honours and walked straight from university into a good job. She works for a computer software company. One of the employees told me that they custom-design software systems for business applications.'

'You think she could be connected with Clough's pirating racket?'

'It is a connection that springs immediately to mind, I'll admit, but no. That's not it. This isn't the sort of thing you could profitably pirate. It's tailor-made for very specific business functions.'

'So where does it lead us?'

'This employee I talked to, she thinks that Ruth's working on an inventory control system for a large pharmaceutical company.'

Annie whistled. 'I see.'

'What I'm trying to find out, if I can get hold of the boss there, is whether the job could possibly have given her access to controlled drugs such as strychnine.'

'And if there's any missing?'

'Yes. But it could have been such a small quantity it wouldn't be missed. I don't know how tightly they control these things.'

'Pretty tightly, I'd say. But if Ruth really was working on inventory control . . .'

'She might have access to the inventory. Yes. And she might also have been in a position to falsify data about quantities. We'll just have to wait and see. In the meantime there's another couple of things we need to follow up on.' Banks lit a cigarette. 'Want something to eat?'

Annie shook her head. 'I've got some leftover pasta at home. Pub food's not very appetizing for a vegetarian.'

'They do a nice salad sandwich, I'm told.'

'I know. I've had one. A strip of wilted lettuce and a couple of slices of green tomato. What next?'

'First off, I want you to ask Darren Hirst, the boy who was with Emily the night she died, for access to his mobile phone records. I just realized last night what was bothering me about the Riddles' phone records.'

'What?'

'Emily's call to me the day before she died. It wasn't listed.'

'She could have used a public box.'

'That's what I thought at first, with the background noise and all. But Darren has a mobile and she was out with him and the gang that night. It's my bet she used his phone, and that she also used it to talk to whoever she set up the drug buy with. It's hardly likely she'd risk using her home phone for something like that. What I'd like to know is whether she used Darren's phone to call Ruth close to the time of her murder.'

'That should be easy enough to find out.'

'There's another thing. I also phoned Craig Newton, Emily's ex-boyfriend down in Stony Stratford.'

'And?'

'When I went to talk to him, I remember noticing some photographs of Emily that bore a strong resemblance to the one that appeared in the newspaper yesterday.'

'You think he was behind the story?'

'Craig? No. But he confirmed that Ruth also had prints of the photos because they'd been taken at a party they'd all attended.'

'One of Clough's parties?'

'Not this time, no. Before Clough. The point is, though, that Ruth could have supplied the newspaper with the photograph and the hints about Clough and Jimmy Riddle.'

'But how could she know?'

'I've no idea. It's all speculation so far. She obviously knew about Emily and Clough, probably knew Clough was a bit of a gangster. If she had discovered that Rosalind Riddle was her birth mother and was blackmailing her over it, it's no great leap of imagination to assume that she knew Jimmy Riddle was chief constable.'

'I suppose not. But *why*?'

'To cause trouble for the Riddles. She was already blackmailing Rosalind, remember. Perhaps after Emily's murder Rosalind refused to pay up any more.'

'Are we going to talk to Ruth again soon?'

'Definitely. Up here this time. I'll have her brought up tomorrow. I hope we'll have answers to some of our questions before she arrives. There's one other thing.'

'What's that?'

'We need to talk to the person who saw Emily get into the

car at the Red Lion. So far I've been thinking that a light-coloured car driven by someone with short blond hair probably meant Jamie Gilbert.'

'And now?'

'Ruth Walker. She drives a cream car – I've seen it – and she'd bleached her hair blonde the second time I saw her. Another drink?'

'Better not,' Annie said. 'I've got a long drive home. You should be careful, too.'

'You're going home?'

'Don't look so disappointed. We've got a busy day tomorrow.'

'You're right. But you can't blame me for showing a little disappointment.'

Annie smiled. 'I'd be pissed off if you hadn't. Anyway, after last night I'm worn out. I'm surprised you're not tired, too.'

'It's been a long day. That's true.' Banks swirled the last quarter of his pint around the bottom of the glass. 'Do you think Ruth killed her adoptive parents?'

'Very unlikely. Mind you, I think she was definitely responsible for the cigarette end that started the fire. Her parents didn't smoke or drink. They were good Methodists. Ruth went a bit wild when she got to university. Maybe she'd had a few drinks and didn't put it out properly.'

'It doesn't sound as if she made any attempt to save them.'

'Who knows what happened in there, what she could or couldn't have done? She hurt herself badly getting out.'

'Yes, but she lived. Were post-mortems performed on the parents?'

Annie nodded. 'I checked. No cause for suspicion. In both cases death was due to smoke inhalation. Just as with Chief Constable Riddle, there were no signs that they were restrained in any way, or drugged, and no indication that any obstacles had been placed in the way of their getting out. They were old and slow. That's all there is to it.'

'Makes you wonder, though, doesn't it?'

'About what?'

'Oh, life, the universe, everything.'

Annie slapped his arm, laughed and stood up. 'I'm off before you start getting *really* philosophical. What about you?'

'One more cigarette, then I've got a couple more things to do back at the office.'

'See you tomorrow, then.'

'See you.'

Annie walked out into the cold night air and paused for a while, listening to the choir singing 'Silent Night' through chattering teeth. Then she dropped a few coins in the collection box and hurried off to her car before she changed her mind about Banks' offer.

18

Ruth Walker arrived with her police escort shortly after lunch the following day. Wearing baggy jeans and a shapeless mauve sweatshirt with sleeves that fell long past her hands, she looked both nervous and defiant as she took her seat in the gloomy interview room. She held her head high, but her eyes were all over the place, everywhere but on the person speaking to her. A sprinkling of acne lay over her pale cheeks, and her skin looked pasty and dry.

Unlike Barry Clough, who was now back at his Little Venice villa, Ruth didn't have an expensive lawyer in tow. They had offered to bring in a duty solicitor for her, but she said she didn't need anyone. Banks set the tape recorders going, gave details of the session and began. Annie sat beside him. He had the answers to most of his previous day's questions – including two calls from Darren's mobile, only one of which had been to Banks – in a buff folder on the desk in front of him, and he didn't like the story they told one bit.

'I suppose you know why you're here, don't you, Ruth?' Banks began.

Ruth stared at a squashed fly high on the opposite wall.

'We've been doing a bit of digging.'

'Not really the season for that, is it?' Ruth said.

'This isn't a joking matter,' Banks said. 'So drop it, Ruth. It doesn't suit you.'

'Whatever.'

'You've told me a lot of lies.'

'Lies? Pork pies. They're what I've been living. What else have I got to tell you?'

'It's my job to try and sort out a few truths. Let's start with the fire.'

'What's that got to do with it?'

'With what?'

'With why I'm here.'

'I told you, I'm trying to get at some truths.'

'There was a fire. I woke up and my room was full of smoke. I had to jump out of the window. I broke my ankle really badly. You might have noticed I've still got a limp.'

'What else can you tell us about the fire?'

'What's to tell? It was an accident. I couldn't walk for weeks.'

'What caused the fire?'

'They said it was a cigarette. It can't have been mine. I put it out. I remember.'

'Whose was it then?'

Ruth shrugged. 'Dunno. It wasn't mine.'

'Ruth, it *must* have been your cigarette. Your parents *died* in that fire, and all you can think about is your broken ankle. What's wrong with this picture?'

'You tell me. And they *weren't* my parents. Everyone says I was the lucky one, so I suppose they must be right.'

'Did you *feel* lucky?'

' "Do you feel lucky today, punk?" Sorry. Bad joke again. Blame it on being deprived of humour throughout my childhood and adolescence.'

'Were you deprived of humour?'

'It wasn't part of the deal.'

'What deal?'

'You know. The one where you're not supposed to dance, sing, laugh, cry, love, fuck. The religious deal. I sometimes think the reason they had to adopt a child was that they thought it was a sin to do what they had to do to produce one naturally.'

'How did you feel towards your parents?'

'I told you, they *weren't* my parents. They were my *adoptive* parents. Believe me, it *does* make a difference. Do you know, they never even told me I was adopted?'

'How did you find out?'

'The papers.'

'But surely they must have been destroyed by the fire?'

'They were kept in a safe deposit box at the bank. I only found out after they died and I had to open it. That's where they kept *me*. In a box.'

'But they *were* the parents who brought you up.'

'Oh, yes. Everyone says they were decent, honest, God-fearing folk. Salt of the earth.'

'What do you say?'

'They were stupid imbeciles, too brainwashed to make their own decisions about anything. They were scared of everything except the chapel. Their bodies. The world beyond the street. Their lives. They inflicted all that on me. And more. They made my life miserable, made me a laughing stock at school. I had no friends. I had no one to talk to. They didn't like me hanging around with the other kids. They said God ought to be enough of a friend for anyone. What do you expect me to say about them?'

'Were you glad they died?'

'Yes.' Ruth's left hand shot out of the end of her sleeve and scratched the side of her nose. Her grubby fingernails were bitten to the quick.

'What about your birth mother?'

'Ros? I call her that, you know. It's a bit late to be calling her "Mother", don't you think? And Mrs Riddle seems just a wee bit too formal.'

'How did you find her?'

The edges of Ruth's lips curled in an ugly smirk. 'You ought to know that, if you've done so much digging. My degree's in information technology. You can find out anything these days if you know where to look. The telephone directory is usually pretty reliable, you know. A good place to start. But there's the Internet, too. Lots of information out on that superhighway.'

'Where did you begin?'

'With the Registrar General's office. They'll let you see your original birth certificate if you ask them nicely. From there it's pretty easy.'

'What did the birth certificate tell you?'

'That I was born at 73 Launceston Terrace, Tiverton, on the twenty-third of February, 1977.'

'What else?'

Ruth stared at the walls again, looking bored. 'That my mother was Rosalind Gorwyn and that there was a blank space where my father's name was supposed to be.'

'What did you do next?'

'I went to 73 Launceston Terrace, Tiverton, and found an elderly couple by the name of Gorwyn living there. It's not a very common name, even in Devon. I knew they couldn't be my real parents – they were too old – so I pushed them a bit and found out they were her aunt and uncle and that she had stayed with them while she had the baby. *Me*. Hid away from the world while she gave birth to me.'

'What else did they tell you?'

'That my mother had married a man called Jeremiah Archibald Riddle, an important policeman, that she was a solicitor now, and they lived in North Yorkshire. By then they'd have told me anything to get rid of me. After that it was really easy. A child could have found them.'

'Did you speak to Rosalind's parents at all?'

'Not right at first. But I found out that they'd retired to Barnstaple. He was a vicar. Which probably explains why my mother let me live.'

'What do you mean?' Annie asked.

Ruth looked at her as if seeing her for the first time. She

didn't seem to mind what she saw. 'Well, either way I didn't have much of a chance, did I?' she said. 'She could've just got rid of me, had an abortion. That's what I'd have done in her place. Then I would never have existed at all and none of this would have happened.'

'Or?'

'She could have kept me. Then I'd have been an unwanted baby with a single mother and your chief constable would never have married her. I'd probably have been brought up in some sort of punk commune or something, with people shooting heroin all around my cot, getting high and forgetting me, so I'd have crawled to the edge of the stairs and fallen over and died anyway. So I imagine she thought putting me up for adoption was a better choice for her. Pity it didn't turn out that way for me. I've been told the adoption people are pretty good, very strict in their standards, but some of us slip through the cracks. Like I said, everyone thought the Walkers were the salt of the earth, that they would make wonderful parents, but the Lord hadn't seen fit to bless them with issue. You'd think they'd take that as a sign, wouldn't you?'

Banks and Annie paused to take in what she had said, then Banks picked up the questioning again. 'You went to Rosalind's law office?'

'Yes. I thought it would be best that way. Turned out I was right.' Ruth gave a mean little giggle. 'She was scared shitless I'd say something to her husband. Thought he'd turf her out on her arse if he found out.'

'So you blackmailed her.'

Ruth slammed her fist onto the desk. 'It was only my due! I only asked for my due. I'd had nothing from her in all those years. *Nothing*. And I'd had little but misery from the bloody Walkers. Do you know they once made me wear an old pair of shoes that were so small and tight that my toenails came off and my shoes were full of blood when I got home from school? That was what your bloody salt-of-the-earth Walkers were like.

I had a *right* to something from Ros. She *owed* me. Why should *she* get it all just because she was born a few years later than me, on the right side of the blanket? Answer me that one. It should all have been mine, but she tossed me away. It was only my due.'

The interview room was starting to feel very claustro-phobic. Banks couldn't quite sort out the *she*'s; half the time it seemed as if Ruth was referring to Rosalind, the rest to Emily. 'Were you abused by your adoptive parents, Ruth?'

Ruth gave a harsh laugh. 'Abused? That's a good one. You at least have to *care* about someone to abuse them. No, I wasn't abused, not in the way you mean it. I suppose there's more than one kind of abuse, though. I mean, I'd call being made to wear those shoes until my toes bled abuse. Wouldn't you? Mostly, they were just cold. Ironic they should die by fire, isn't it?'

Again, Banks felt that shiver creep up his spine. He saw Annie frowning. Ruth paid them no attention. 'Did you see Rosalind often?' Banks asked.

'Not that often.'

'When you needed something?'

'I only wanted my due.'

'What about Emily? How did you feel towards her?'

'I'd be a liar if I said I liked her.'

'But you befriended her, took her in. At least I assume that's how it happened and you didn't just meet her by accident near the station. Is that right?'

Ruth nodded. 'When I met her the once in Ros's office, I made a point of finding out where she went to school. She was a boarder, so I phoned her there, and visited her. When she started to trust me, when we began to be friends, she used to call me a lot from school, too. She'd complain about her parents, how strict they were. I had to laugh. I mean, she'd complain to *me* about that. I told her that after she was sixteen she could do what she wanted. It was near the end of the school year and she'd had her birthday, so I said why didn't she come and stay with me in London for a while if she wanted.'

'You mean you lured her to London? You encouraged her to leave home?'

'I think *lured* is too strong a word. I had no trouble getting her there. She was only too pleased to come.'

'But you didn't tell her parents where she was?'

'Why should I? It was her business, and she didn't want them to know.'

'Do you think Rosalind knew?'

'I doubt it. She didn't know how close me and Emily had become. I don't think she even knew where I lived. Didn't bother to ask. That's how interested in me she was after all those years.'

'Did you introduce Emily to Craig Newton?' Banks asked.

Ruth's face clouded. 'I thought he was my friend. I thought he loved me. But he was just like all the rest.'

'Did it hurt you when she took up with Craig?'

Ruth shot him a tortured glance. 'What do you think?'

'Is that why you killed her?'

'I didn't kill her.'

'Come on, Ruth. We've got the evidence. We know. You might as well tell us how it happened. I'm sure there were extenuating circumstances. What about Barry Clough? What part did he play in all this, for example?'

Ruth's eyes narrowed. 'I wondered when you'd get around to him.'

'What do you know about him?'

'Plenty.'

'Like what?'

Ruth paused a minute and rubbed her fist over the top of her thigh as if she had an itch. 'I bet it's something *you* don't know, clever clogs.'

'Maybe it is. Why don't you tell me?'

'They didn't name my father on the birth certificate, as I

told you. But I found out who it was. Barry Clough. My *father*.' Ruth flopped back in her chair and stared at the ceiling. 'I'm tired and I want something to eat. You have to give me something to eat, don't you?'

'I don't know about you, Annie,' Banks said when Ruth was back in her cell eating her canteen burger and chips, 'but I could do with a breath of fresh air.'

'My feelings exactly.'

They left the station and walked across the market square, then they took the narrow, cobbled Castle Wynde past the bare formal gardens down to the riverside. It was a crisp, cold winter day, and their breaths plumed as they walked, crunching over puddles. The hill went steeply down to the river, with small limestone cottages lining both sides, and the cobbles were slippery. Banks could feel the icy wind blowing up from the river. It was just what he needed to get the smell of the interview room out of his system.

'What do you make of all that, then?' Annie asked when they were halfway down.

Banks didn't know what to make of Ruth's bombshell. He didn't even know if it was true; after all, she had told plenty of lies already. But why lie about something like that? 'It raises more questions than it answers,' he said.

'Such as: did anyone else know, and did it have anything to do with Emily's murder?'

'For a start. If Rosalind Riddle knew, she kept it well hidden. I hadn't thought her *that* good an actress.'

'Do you think Ruth killed Emily?'

'If she didn't, she knows what happened, she knows who did. She's a part of it; I'm certain of that.'

They arrived at the river and paused for a while by the waist-high stone wall that ran along its bank. The falls rushed and foamed along the shallows, huge moss-covered slabs of ancient rock jutting out here and there, the result of a geological fault millions of years ago. Banks could feel the icy spray on his cheeks and in his hair. If the cold spell continued for much longer, even the falls would freeze. Above them, the dark mass of the ruined castle keep and towers lay heavy against a pewter sky; it was a black-and-white world, or like the world of a black-and-white photograph with all its subtle variations of grey. Annie slipped her arm in his. It was a good feeling, the only good feeling he'd had that morning.

They walked along the riverside path, past the terraced gardens – no more than a small park dotted with trees – to their left. There weren't many people around, just a young couple walking their Airedale and an old-age pensioner in a flat cap taking his daily constitutional. Banks had often considered buying a flat cap himself. All these years in Yorkshire and he still didn't have one. But he didn't like wearing hats, even in winter.

Across the river, to the right, bare trees lined the opposite bank. Banks could make out the shapes of the large houses facing the Green, beyond which lay the notorious East Side Estate, which pretty much kept the Eastvale police in business year round.

In one of those big houses lived Jenny Fuller, a psychologist Banks had worked with on a number of cases. A friend, too, and a one-time potential lover. Jenny had been polite but cool towards him ever since he stood her up on that date three months ago. It was more than just that, though; it was as if Jenny had put too much of herself on the line, exposed her feelings for him, and the seeming rejection had touched a raw nerve, made her curl in on herself. She was on the rebound from a sour relationship with an American professor at the time, Banks already knew, so she was hurting to start with. He wished he could do something to bridge the distance, rekindle the friendship. It had been important to him over the years.

But there was Annie, too. Banks was no expert, but he knew enough of women to realize that Annie wouldn't appreciate his spending time with someone else other than her, now that he felt free from his marriage.

'Sandra wants a divorce,' he suddenly said to Annie. He felt her arm stiffen in his, but she didn't remove it. First good sign. This was one thing he hadn't told her the other night, one thing he had found too difficult to put into words. It still was, but he knew he would have to try if he and Annie were to go any further. It might put her more at ease or it might scare her off; that was the risk he would have to take.

'I'm sorry,' she said, without looking at him.

'No, I didn't mean it like that. I mean, I'm glad.'

Annie slowed down and turned to face him. 'You're what?'

They started walking again, and he tried to explain to her what he had felt in London, after he first heard the news. He wasn't sure whether he did a good job or not, but Annie nodded here and there and seemed to ponder what he'd said after he finished. Finally, she said, 'That's all right, then.'

'It is?'

'Time to let go.'

Second good sign. 'I suppose so.'

'Does it hurt?'

'Not any more. Oh, there are memories, always will be, and some residual feelings – anger, disappointment, whatever. But no, it doesn't hurt. In fact, I feel better than I have in years.'

'Good.'

'Look, do you fancy coming to the cottage for Christmas dinner? Tracy will be there. Just the three of us.'

'I can't. Really, I'm sorry, Alan, but I *always* go home for Christmas. Ray would never forgive me if I missed it.'

'I understand.'

Annie gave his arm a little squeeze. 'I mean it, Alan. It's not an excuse. I'd love to meet Tracy. Maybe some other time?'

Banks knew she was telling the truth. Annie wasn't a very good liar, as he had discovered. Lying made her all grumpy and withdrawn. 'We'll have a drink together sometime, then,' he said.

'Do you think she'll hate me?'

'Why should she?'

Annie smiled. 'Sometimes you can be pretty damn thick when it comes to women, Alan Banks.'

'I'm not being thick,' Banks said. 'Mothers, daughters, fathers; it can all get pretty complicated. I know that. But Tracy's not a hater. I know my daughter. I wouldn't expect her to rush up to you and hug you – no doubt she'll be a little hesitant, checking you out, as they say – but she's not a hater, and she doesn't see me as the villain in all this. She's got a good head on her shoulders.'

'Unlike Ruth Walker.'

'Indeed. Did you feel the atmosphere in that room?'

Annie nodded.

'I felt something like it before, the times I talked to her in London,' Banks said, 'but it wasn't as powerful. I think it's because she senses she's near the end. She's given up. She's unravelling.'

'You think so?'

'Yes. I think she wants us to know it all now, so we can see her point of view. So we can understand her. Forgive her.'

Annie shook her head. 'I don't think she wants forgiveness, Alan. At least, not the way I'm reading her. I don't think she sees there's anything to forgive.'

'Perhaps not. I should have known.'

'Should have known what?'

'That something was wrong there.'

'But you've only just found out Ruth was Emily's half-sister. How could you have known that?'

'I don't know. I should have dug deeper sooner.'

'Why do you have to take the burden on yourself like this? Why is everything your fault? Why do you think if you only acted differently you could prevent people being killed?'

Banks stopped and looked out over the swirling river; it was the colour of a pint of bitter, an intruder in the black-and-white world. 'Do I?'

'You know you do.'

Banks lit a cigarette. 'It must be something to do with Graham Marshall.'

'Graham Marshall? Who's he?'

'A boy at school. I won't say a friend because I didn't know him very well. He was a quiet kid, bright, shy.'

'What happened?'

'One day he simply disappeared.'

'What happened?'

'Nobody knows. He was never found. Dead or alive.'

'What did the police think?'

'The consensus was that he'd been abducted by a child molester who'd murdered him after he'd had his way. This would probably have been around the time of the Moors Murders, though in a different part of the country, so people were especially sensitive to the disappearance of children.'

'That's sad.' Annie rested her elbows on the wall beside Banks. 'But I still don't see what it's got to do with you.'

'About three or four months before Graham Marshall's disappearance I was playing with some friends down by the river. We were throwing stones in, just having a bit of harmless fun, the way kids do . . .'

As he spoke, Banks remembered the day vividly. It was spitting and the raindrops pitted the murky water. A man approached along the riverbank. All Banks could remember now was that he was tall – but then every adult was tall to him then – and thin, with greasy dark hair and a rough, pockmarked complexion. Banks smiled and politely paused before dropping in a large stone, one he had to hold in both hands, to let the stranger pass by without splashing him.

The next thing he knew, the man had grabbed him by the arms and was pushing him towards the river, the stone forgotten at their feet. He could smell beer on the man's breath, the same smell he remembered from his father, and something else – sweat, a wet-dog smell, body odour, like the smell of his socks after a long rugby game – as he struggled for his life. He called out and looked around for his friends, but they were running down to the gap in the fence where they had got in.

The struggle seemed to go on for ever. Banks managed to wedge his heels at the edge of the riverbank and push back with all his might, but the grass was wet, and the soil under it was fast turning to mud. He didn't think he could keep his grip much longer.

His smallness and wiriness were his only advantages, he knew, and he wriggled as hard as an eel to slip out of the man's strong grasp. He knew that if he didn't escape he would drown. He tried to bite the man's arm, but all he got was a mouthful of vile-tasting cloth, so he gave that up.

The man was breathing hard now, as if the effort was becoming too much for him. Banks drew on his last reserves of energy and wriggled as hard and fast as he could. He managed to get one arm free. The man held him by the other arm and punched him at the side of his right eye. He felt something sharp, like a ring, cut his skin. He flinched with pain and pulled away, succeeding in freeing his other arm. He didn't wait to see if he was being pursued, but ran like the clappers to the hole in the fence.

Only when he caught up with his friends at the edge of the park did he dare risk looking back. Nobody in sight. His friends seemed sheepish as they asked him how he was, but he toughed it out. No problem. Inside, though, he was terribly shaken. They made a pact not to say anything. None of them were supposed to be playing down by the river in the first place. Their parents said it was dangerous. Banks didn't dare tell his parents what had happened, explaining the cut beside his eye by saying he had fallen and cut it on a piece of glass, and he had never relied on anyone to help him out of trouble again in his life.

'I was wrong. I *should* have told my parents, Annie. They would have made me report it to the police, and they might have caught him before he did any more harm. There was a dangerous man out there, and my fear and shame left him free to do as he pleased.'

'You blamed yourself for what happened to Graham Marshall? For the acts of a child molester?'

Banks turned away from the beer-coloured water to face Annie. 'When he went missing, all I could think of was the tall man with the greasy dark hair and the body odour.' Banks shivered. Sometimes he still woke in the night gagging on the taste of the dirty cloth of the man's sleeve, and in the dream, when he looked at the river, it was full of dead boys all floating in the same direction, in perfectly matched rows, and Graham Marshall was the only one he recognized. So much guilt.

'But you don't *know* that it was the same man.'

'Doesn't matter. I still took the guilt on myself. I'd been attacked by an older man, possibly a pervert, and I didn't report it. Then a boy was abducted, possibly by a pervert. Of course I blamed myself. And I certainly couldn't say anything about it later.'

Annie put her hand on his arm. 'So you made a mistake. So you *should* have reported it. You can't spend your life sulking over all the mistakes you've made. You'd never bother getting out of bed in the morning.'

Banks smiled. 'You're right. I try not to let it get me down too much. It's only when something like this happens, something I think I could have prevented.'

Annie started walking again. 'You're not God,' she said over her shoulder. 'You can't change the way things are.'

Banks flicked his cigarette in the river and followed her. Annie was right, he knew; he only wished he could *feel* better about it.

They turned left at the main road by the pre-Roman site, a sort of barrow where ancient graves had been discovered, and then left again, back towards the station, towards whatever other horrors Ruth Walker had in store for them.

Banks started the tape recorders again. 'All right, Ruth,' he said, 'you've had some food and rest. Ready to talk to us again?'

Ruth nodded and retracted her hands deep into the sleeves of her sweatshirt.

'For the record,' Banks said, 'Ms Walker nodded to indicate that she is ready to resume the interview.'

Ruth stared down at her lap.

'Before the break, Ruth, you told us that Barry Clough is your father. I'm sure you know that gives rise to a lot more questions.'

'Go ahead.'

'First of all, is it true?'

'Of course it is. Why should I lie about it?'

'You've lied before. Remember, right at the beginning you told me your life has been a lie?'

'This is true. He's my father. You can check.'

'How did you find out about this if it wasn't on the birth certificate?'

'I talked to Ros's parents.'

'And they told you, just like that?'

'It wasn't as easy as that.'

'How easy was it, then?'

'It was a matter of finding out what name he was using now.'

'What do you mean?'

'All they could tell me was that Ros got herself pregnant by some punk. He hung around with bands, worked as a roadie, played bass a bit, something like that. Ros had told them his name, but he was long gone by the time she even found out she was pregnant. He was in America, they told me. And she didn't want anything to do with him anyway. Neither did her parents. Everybody just did their best to forget him, and it seems as if that was pretty easy.'

'What was his name?'

Ruth laughed. 'You know what they were like back then, all using silly names, thinking they sounded tough? Rat Scabies. Sid Vicious. Johnny Rotten.'

'I remember,' said Banks.

'Well, this bloke was going by the name of Mal Licious. I ask you. *Mal Licious*.'

What an apt name for Barry Clough, Banks thought. 'So nobody knew his real name?'

'Ros's parents and uncle and aunt didn't.'

'Did you ask Rosalind herself?'

'Yes.'

'And?'

'She didn't know, either. Mal Licious was all he went by. She just called him Mal. Seems she hadn't known him that well. I think it was a one-night stand. She didn't really want to talk about it.'

'How *did* you find out, then?'

Ruth shifted in her chair. 'Easy. Information technology. I know a bit about the music scene, I've been to a lot of clubs and raves and stuff, and Craig had a few contacts, he'd taken band photos, that sort of thing. I asked around. It seemed a logical way to start. There was always a chance that this Mal Licious was still on the scene somewhere. A lot of these people never grow up. Look at Rod Stewart, for Christ's sake. Clough was a pretty well-known name on the scene, partly because of his trendy bar and partly because of the bands he promoted. There were still people around who'd known him way back, and someone told me he used to be called Mal Licious. Thought it was a bit of a laugh. Well, there can't have been two of them, can there? Stands to reason.'

Indeed it did, thought Banks. Bright girl. Or woman. A

lot of things were starting to make sense now. 'So none of what happened since Emily went to London was coincidence, then?' he said.

'What do you mean?'

'Emily shacking up with Barry Clough, Clough finding out about Riddle, the article in the newspaper linking them together.'

A look of triumph filled Ruth's eyes. 'No,' she said. 'None of it was coincidence. It was all *me*. I set things in motion. Beyond that, they took on a life of their own. I soon found out that Clough liked young girls, and it wasn't hard to get an invitation to one of his parties. What happened next was up to nature, not me. It really pissed off Craig.'

'Did you ever approach Clough? He's a wealthy man. Wealthier than Rosalind, I should imagine.'

Ruth frowned at him. 'It's not *all* about money, you know. No, I didn't approach him. What was he going to say? Probably didn't even remember Ros's name, let alone that he'd shagged her. They were probably stoned out of their minds.'

'Did you tell Rosalind about Emily and Clough?'

'No.'

'Why on earth not? He was her . . .' Banks had to pause and think for a moment. No matter how terrible it seemed for Rosalind's daughter to be sleeping with a man her mother had slept with, and whose child she had given birth to, Emily wasn't any relation to Clough whatsoever. 'Emily was your half-sister,' was all he could manage.

Ruth smiled. 'Information management. Knowledge is power, as I'm sure you know. If you use it only a little at a time, it can go a long way. I might have had a use for that information eventually. But I was enjoying myself plenty with what I already had. I think if I'd told Ros about them, everything would have come tumbling down, and it wasn't time for that yet.'

You're damn right the whole house of cards would have

come tumbling down, Banks thought. Before he could respond, Annie eased in. 'You said you were enjoying yourself, Ruth. In what way?'

Ruth faced her for a moment before her eyes went off in another direction. 'Why shouldn't I enjoy myself? I've had little enough fun in my life. Why not have a bit for a change?'

'*Fun?*' repeated Annie. 'Ruth, two people have died because of all this. Emily and her father. A family's been torn apart. And you think it's fun?'

'I didn't mean to kill her.'

Annie glanced at Banks and indicated he should pick up the thread. It was the first hint of a confession they'd heard from Ruth so far. Banks didn't want to lose her now, but at the same time he wanted no problems over PACE. 'We're heading into dangerous ground, Ruth,' he said. 'I'm telling you again that you're entitled to have a solicitor present, and I'm asking you if you want us to provide one for you.'

'I've told you before,' Ruth shouted directly into the microphone, 'I don't want any fucking solicitor. Is that clear enough for you?'

'It'll do,' said Banks. 'Let me get this straight, then. You discovered that Barry Clough was your father and you didn't tell either him or Rosalind this. Am I right?'

'Yes.'

'Did you tell Emily?'

'Of course not.'

'But you introduced them at a party.'

'That was all I needed to do.' Ruth's eyes shone. 'That was the beauty of it, you see. I knew Clough liked young girls, and you didn't have to talk to Emily for long before you found out what a twisted little Electra complex she had. She wanted to fuck her daddy. Well, I couldn't arrange that, but at least I could give her a chance to fuck mine. It was perfect.'

'Why?'

'*Because I was the only one who knew the truth.* The joke was on them, on someone else for a change, not on me.'

'What about Barry Clough and Emily's father?'

'That was just a bonus. I know a young reporter. It was a big story, probably made his career. I just gave him one of those photos of Emily all dressed up for a party and I told him that she was fucking Barry Clough and her father was a chief constable. He was off to Yorkshire like a shot. Did the rest of the footwork himself.'

'What about Barry Clough, after Emily had left? Did you tell him who she was, where she lived, who her father was?'

'Yes. I thought it would probably interest him. He struck me as the kind of man who liked to own others. I just thought it would be interesting to put the two of them together when neither of them knew how close they really were.'

'So he doesn't know that you're his daughter or that Emily's your half-sister?'

'Of course not. It wasn't time to go *that* far yet.'

'Again, why?'

'They all thought they were so cool, so beautiful, so powerful, so in control. But all the time it was me pulling the strings. *Me.* They were just running around like headless chickens.'

'And this amused you?'

'Yes. I'm not mad, if that's what you're thinking. I'm not looking to get off on some insanity plea or anything like that. I *would* like a little recognition for all the work I put in, though.'

'What about Emily? You told her she was your half-sister, didn't you?'

'I had to, otherwise she would never have trusted me or come to live with me. She'd have thought I was after her or something. This way it made more sense. It was our little secret.'

Banks paused before going on, knowing he had reached

a crucial stage. 'Ruth, we know you were working for a pharmaceutical company and had access to strychnine. Cocaine's easy enough to get. Did you give Emily the lethal mixture?'

'It wasn't meant to be lethal.'

'What did you intend it to do to her?'

'Give her a scare. Give her the jitters. I didn't mean for it to kill her. Honest. I'm not a murderer.'

'What are you, then?'

Ruth tugged at a frayed edge on her sweatshirt. 'Maybe I've got some problems. People don't like me. But I'm not a murderer.' There were tears in her eyes.

'All right, Ruth. What happened?'

'We'd talked on the telephone a few times and she kept saying she was off the stuff. First, I just wanted to see if I could get her back on again. I mean, people say all sorts of things, don't they, like they've given up smoking, but if you offer them a cigarette, if you put just a little temptation their way . . .'

'And that's what you did?'

'Yes. Dangled a carrot. Well, a gram of coke, actually. She could probably have scored some up here if she'd asked around, but that was a bit too close to her father's territory. I mean, you never know if your dealer is an undercover cop, do you? I even offered to deliver it. Said I had to visit some relatives in Durham and I'd stop by on the way.'

'What did she say?'

'She said she'd ring me back. I knew she was thinking seriously about it. Anyway, the day before I said I was coming up, I was working late . . . she phoned me at work on some lad's mobile and said she was getting bored and she wouldn't mind some for the next day. She was going clubbing with some mates. I knew I could get a couple of days off, say I had a cold or something. Anyway, just after I talked to her and said I'd see her the next day, I had to go into the controlled area to do some product coding, and that's when I got the idea of the strychnine. I didn't know how much to put in. I'd heard they sometimes used it as a base in some street drugs and it makes your jaw and your neck stiff. I just wanted to give her a scare, that's all. It was only a little bit. I didn't think it was enough to kill her, but it might make her twitch a bit in public, maybe even puke and piss herself.'

'That was what you wanted to do to her? Humiliate her in public?'

'It was a start.'

'Even though you wouldn't be there to witness it?'

'But I'd *know*, wouldn't I? Being there would be too dangerous. Don't you see the point? I mean, I didn't actually see her doing it, but I knew she was fucking my father. If you have a bit of imagination you can amuse yourself easily enough.'

'It has to be more than that, Ruth,' Annie chipped in.

Ruth looked away. 'Why?'

'It just does. Why did you hate Emily so much? What did she ever do to you?'

'She had my life, didn't she? What should have been mine.'

'Why did you want her to suffer?'

'Because she had it all. She took Craig from me.'

'Craig was never with you that way,' Banks said, picking up on Annie's rhythm. 'He was never your lover.'

Ruth jutted her chin out. 'That's what *he* says now.'

'Why should he lie?'

'He's against me. She poisoned him against me.'

'That's not enough, Ruth,' Annie chimed in again.

Ruth gave her a sharp glance. 'What do you want? Blood?'

'No. That seems to be what *you* wanted. We want some answers.'

'It was all so bloody easy for her. Everything just fell into her lap. Craig. Barry Clough. My own father, for Christ's sake, was running his hands over her thighs ten minutes after they met.'

'But that was part of your plan, you said,' Annie went on.

'You can't always arrange things so they don't hurt you at least just a little bit. She got everything she wanted, just like that.'

'Then why did she want to run away from home, Ruth?'

'What do you mean?'

'If everything was so perfect in Emily's life, why did she want to run away from her parents?'

'They wouldn't let her do what she wanted. They were strict.'

'Like yours?'

'Nowhere near as bad as mine. You don't know the half of it.'

'Then why didn't you sympathize with her?'

'I did. At first. Then she just . . . she got everything she wanted. Craig started ignoring me. Even Emily deserted me.'

Banks took over again. 'Why did you kill her, Ruth?'

Ruth didn't know who to look at. She looked at the squashed fly again. 'I didn't. I didn't mean to kill her.'

'But you did kill her,' Banks pressed on. 'Why?'

Ruth paused and her face seemed to go through the kind of contortions Emily's must have when the strychnine hit.

'Why did you kill her, Ruth?' Banks persisted, his voice hardly above a whisper. 'Why?'

'Because they took her back!' Ruth blurted out. 'After all that happened. After everything she did to them. She broke their hearts and they took her back. Ros threw me out, but she took her back. They took her back! They took her back!' Ruth started crying, fat tears rolling down her acned cheeks.

There was nothing more to say. Banks called in the uniformed officers to take Ruth back to her cell. Now it was time to charge her and bring in the lawyers.

Banks drove out to the Old Mill that night with a heavy heart. He knew he had to be the one to tell Rosalind what had happened, what Ruth had done, just as he had had to break the news about Emily's murder, but it wasn't a task he cherished.

The lights were on in the front room. He parked out front, glancing towards the garage as he pulled up his collar against the wind and rain, and rang the doorbell.

Rosalind answered and invited him in. She was wearing a short skirt and a cashmere sweater. He followed her into the living room. Her legs looked good, and it didn't seem as if she were wearing any tights. He thought he noticed something different about the smell of the place, but he dismissed it; there were far more serious matters on his mind.

'Drink?' Rosalind asked.

'Small whisky, please.'

'You might as well have a large one. I don't like the stuff, and there's no one else to drink it.'

'I have to drive.'

She raised her eyebrow as she poured. 'Really?'

'Really.' Christ, Banks thought, she was flirting. He would have to tread carefully. He accepted the crystal glass and sat down in the only uncovered armchair. The room was as sterile as ever, and a couple of packing crates sat on the floor. The baby grand was covered by a white sheet, as was most of the other furniture. He took a sip of whisky. It was Glenfiddich, not one of his favourites. At the moment, though, anything would do.

'I was just doing some packing,' Rosalind said. 'Do you know how remarkably little I have to show for all these years?' She poured herself a large gin and tonic, clearly not her first of the evening, pulled a sheet off another armchair and sat down opposite Banks. As she did so, he caught a glimpse of black silk between her legs. He looked away.

'Where are you going?' he asked.

'First?'

'That's a start.'

'I'm going down to Barnstaple after the funeral to be with

Benjamin. We'll be staying with my parents for a while. I can't stand hanging about up here any longer. I feel like some crazy old woman all alone in a Gothic mansion; it's too big. I've even started talking to the furniture and the creaks in the woodwork.'

Banks smiled. 'And then, after Barnstaple?'

'I don't know. I'll have to reinvent myself, won't I? I rather fancy the coast. A little Devon fishing village, for example. I can become the mysterious woman who paces the widow's walk in a long black cloak.'

'That was Lyme Regis,' Banks said. '*The French Lieutenant's Woman.*'

'I know. I saw the film. But this is my version.'

'What about your job?'

'That's not important. It never has been. Jerry's was the only important career in the family, and now that's gone, none of it really matters.'

'And Benjamin?'

'He can walk with me. It would make me more mysterious. I'm sorry, I don't mean to be flippant. It's just . . .' She ran her hand across her brow. 'I've probably had too much to drink.' She frowned. 'Why are you here?'

'I've got something to tell you.'

Her eyes widened. 'Have you caught him? Emily's killer?'

Banks swallowed. This was going to be harder than he had imagined. 'Yes,' he said. 'We've got a confession.'

'Clough?'

That was another bridge he'd have to cross: *Mal Licious.* 'No. Not Clough.' He leaned forward and cupped his drink in both hands, staring into the pale liquid and catching a whiff of it. 'Look, there's no easy way to say this.'

'What?'

'It was Ruth.'

'Ruth? But . . . she can't . . . I mean . . .'

'She confessed. She said she didn't mean to kill Emily, just to give her a scare.'

'Is that true?'

'I honestly don't know. She's contradicted herself quite a bit.'

'*Ruth*.' Rosalind fell silent and Banks let it stretch. Wind lashed the rain against the window panes the way it had the first night he came to the Riddle house. It seemed like years ago.

'Do you want to hear what happened?' Banks asked.

Rosalind looked at him. There was fear in her large blue eyes. 'I suppose I'd better,' she said. 'Look, do smoke if you want to. I know you're a smoker.'

'It's all right.'

'Suit yourself.' Rosalind got up a little unsteadily and pulled a packet of Dunhills and a box of matches from her handbag. She lit up, topped up her gin and tonic and sat down again.

'I didn't think you smoked,' said Banks.

'I didn't. Not for twenty years. But I've started again.'

'Why?'

'Why not?'

Banks lit up too. 'It's bad for you.'

'So's life.'

There was no answer to that. Slowly, Banks told her the whole story of Ruth Walker's twisted, private campaign of hatred and revenge against the Riddle family. First he told her about Ruth's less-than-perfect life with the overzealous Walkers and about the fire that killed them. Then he told her how Ruth had discovered that Barry Clough was her father and how she had hooked him up with Emily out of spite, then put the tabloids on the scent of a scandal. He told her how Ruth arranged to meet Emily and give her the poisoned cocaine, how she didn't even need to be there, that it was enough for her simply to imagine Emily's pain and shame as she humiliated herself. As he spoke, what little colour there had been left

Rosalind Riddle's face and her eyes filled with tears. They didn't fall, just gathered there at the rims, waiting, magnifying her despair. Rosalind left her drink and her cigarette untouched as she listened. A long column of ash fell onto the hardwood floor when a slight tremor passed through her fingers.

When Banks had finished, Rosalind sat in silence for a while, taking it all in, digesting it as best she could, shaking her head slowly as if disagreeing with some inner voice. Then she knocked back the rest of her drink and whispered, 'But why? Why did she do it? Can you answer me that one?'

'She's ill.'

'That's no reason. Why? Why did she do it? Why did she hate us so much? Didn't I do my best for her? I didn't have an abortion. I gave her life. How the hell was I to know her adoptive parents would turn out to be religious fanatics?'

'You weren't.'

'So why does she blame me?'

Ruth's last words still echoed in Banks's mind from that afternoon: *Because they took her back. She broke their hearts and they took her back.* 'Because Ruth sees everything from her own point of view, and only that,' he said. 'All she knows is how things affect *her*, how things hurt *her*, how *she* was deprived. In her way of looking at the world, everything was either done for her or against her. Mostly it was *against* her. She doesn't know any different, doesn't recognize people's normal feelings.'

Rosalind laughed harshly. 'My daughter the psychopath?'

'No. No, I don't think so. Not as simple as that. She enjoyed exercising power over people, inflicting pain, yes, but she didn't have the detachment of a psychopath. She was obsessed, yes, but not psychopathic. And she knows the difference between right and wrong. You'd have to ask a psychiatrist, of course, but that's my opinion.'

Rosalind got up and fixed herself another drink. She offered Banks one, but he refused. He still had a quarter of an inch in the bottom of his glass, and that would do him nicely.

'Will she be put in a mental hospital?' Rosalind asked.

'She'll be sent for psychiatric evaluation, for what it's worth. They'll determine what's best done with her.'

'There'll be a trial? Prison?'

'I'm afraid so.'

Rosalind shook her head. 'Emily's dead. Jerry's dead. Ruth's a murderer. Before Emily died she lived with the man who left me pregnant with Ruth more than twenty years ago. Then I find out that my daughter, my abandoned daughter Ruth, led her into it on purpose, just to humiliate us all in her eyes, so that she could be the only one to know we were all living a lie. Then she killed her. I had two daughters, and one murdered the other. How do you expect me to put all that together? How can I possibly make sense of it all?' She took a long sip of gin and tonic.

Banks shook his head. 'I don't know. In time, perhaps.'

'Remember the first time we met,' Rosalind said, crossing her long legs and leaning back in her chair so that a smooth white stretch of thigh showed. Her voice was a little slurred.

'Yes.'

'I was obnoxious, wasn't I?'

'You were upset.'

'No, that's not it at all. I was obnoxious. Jerry was upset. If anything, I was annoyed, irritated by Emily's irresponsible behaviour, worried what impact it might have on Jerry's political ambitions, on *my* future. I didn't want Emily back. I couldn't handle her.'

'You wanted to protect the world you'd made.'

'And what a world that was. All style and no substance. All glitter and no gold.' She waved her arm in a gesture at the room and spilled some gin and tonic on her skirt. She didn't bother to wipe it off. 'All this. It's strange, but I was thinking about it when you arrived, while I was packing. Funny, it doesn't mean very much now. None of it does. You were right to despise me.'

'I didn't despise you.'

'Yes, you did. Admit it.'

'Maybe I resented you a little.'

'And now?'

'Now?'

'Do you despise me now? Resent me?'

'No.'

'Why not? I'm the same person.'

'No, you're not.'

'How profound. But you're right. I'm not. All the money, the status, the power, the thrill of political ambition, the whiff of Westminster . . . it all used to mean so much. It means nothing now. Less than nothing. Dust.'

'What does have meaning for you now?'

Rosalind paused, sipped some more gin and tonic and stared at him, her eyes slightly unfocused. Outside, the wind continued to howl and rain lashed against the window panes. 'Nothing,' she whispered. 'Not yet. I have to find out. But I won't give up until I do. I'm not like Jerry.' She got unsteadily to her feet. 'Stay and have another drink with me?'

'No. Really. I must be going.'

'Please. Where do you have to go to that's so important? Who do you have to go to?'

She had a point. There was Annie, of course, but he wouldn't be going to Annie so late. Another *small* drink couldn't do any harm. 'All right.'

The drink, when it came, wasn't small, but he didn't have to drink all of it, he told himself.

'I'm sorry there's no music,' Rosalind said. 'We never did have music in the house. I remember your little cottage, how cosy it is with the fire, the music playing. Maybe I'll find somewhere like that.' She looked around bleakly. 'There was nothing like that here.'

Banks wanted to point out the grand piano, but he had a feeling it was just for show. Emily had been forced to take piano lessons, he remembered, because it was part and parcel of the Riddle lifestyle, along with the pony, the proper schools and the rest. Some people managed to be happy with those things for their entire lives, then there were people like Rosalind, who caught Tragedy's wandering eye and got to watch it all come toppling down around them.

'I should never have put her up for adoption.'

'What else could you do?'

'I could have had an abortion, and then Emily's killer would never have been born.'

'If we all knew the consequences of every decision we made, we'd probably never make any,' said Banks. 'Besides, it wasn't your fault that you had to give Ruth up for adoption. Your parents played a part in that. Does that make them responsible for Emily's death, too?' He shook his head. 'It doesn't make any sense, Rosalind. You were young. You couldn't have cared for a child properly, especially without the father's help. You thought she would have a better life. It wasn't your fault that the adoption agency thought they had found Ruth a home with decent people who turned out to be strict religious types. And it wasn't even the Walkers' fault that Ruth turned out the way she did. I'm sure they did their best in many ways. From what I've gathered, they weren't intentionally cruel, just thoughtless and strict and cold. No. You can keep on assigning blame here, there and everywhere, but when it comes right down to it, we're responsible for what we do ourselves.'

Rosalind stubbed out another cigarette and tossed back the rest of her drink. 'Oh, you're right. I know. It'll pass. Everything's just too overwhelming at the moment. I can't seem to take it all in.' She went to refill her glass and bumped her hip against the corner of the cocktail cabinet. Glasses and bottles rattled.

'I'd really better be going,' Banks said. 'It's getting late.'

Rosalind turned and walked towards him, swaying a little. 'No, you can't go yet. I don't want to be alone.'

'I can't help you any more,' said Banks.

Rosalind pouted. 'Please?'

'There's nothing more I can do.'

'There must be. You're a nice man. You've been good to me. You're the only person who has.'

Banks walked towards the front door and opened it. He felt the cold wind around his hands and bare head. Rosalind leaned against the wall, drink in her hand, tears in her eyes.

'I'm sorry,' said Banks, then he pulled the door shut behind him and dashed towards his car. Sorry as he felt for Rosalind Riddle, he didn't want to be part of her life any longer. He wanted to put as much distance between them as possible. Gratly would do for a start, and Barnstaple would be even better.

Before he could get into his car, he heard the crystal tumbler shatter against the door behind him.

Epilogue

Christmas Day

———

Banks woke up early on Christmas morning, and after sitting quietly in the kitchen for a while drinking his tea and enjoying the peace he always felt there, he went into the living room, turned the tree lights on, slipped his *Buena Vista Social Club* CD in the stereo and went back to the kitchen, humming along with 'Chan Chan' as he stood over the large free-range chicken that lay splayed on the chopping block, a copy of *Delia Smith's Christmas* open flat beside it.

He was going to make the traditional pork, sage and onion stuffing, for which he had purchased all the ingredients yesterday. He was shocked to read that Delia said you should make your stuffing on Christmas Eve, but he decided that was perhaps because the enormous turkey she was cooking would probably take all day. He'd be fine. He looked at his watch. Plenty of time.

His back ached because he had had to sleep on the small sofa downstairs. It was a small price to pay for having *both* of his kids with him for Christmas, though.

A couple of days ago, Brian had phoned to say that he had bought the car he'd been after and he had a few days free. He offered to pick up Tracy in Leeds on his way to Gratly if Banks had room for them both. Banks was overjoyed. Of course he had room. He immediately went out and bought more presents: a three-CD history of the Blue Horizon label for Brian, and some of the finest, most expensive make-up brushes he could find for Tracy, along with a few odds and ends to fill out their stockings.

They were both staying until Boxing Day, when Brian would drive Tracy down to London to see her mother and Sean, who were spending Christmas in Dublin. Annie was with her father and the rest of his colony of oddballs in Cornwall, but that was all right. She would be back soon, and they had a date for New Year's Eve.

So this was his imperfect Christmas with his imperfect family, but at least, he reminded himself, he still had a family, despite the damage done over the last year. All Rosalind Riddle had was a young son who would be forever asking where his daddy and his big sister had gone, and a long-abandoned daughter facing charges for murdering her half-sister; though Banks had a feeling that Ruth Walker would probably be committed to a mental hospital rather than sent to prison.

Many times over the past week or so Banks had remembered that expression of despair on Rosalind's face as she sat amidst the packing crates and sheeted furniture listening to him tell her the full story of Ruth's obsession. He also remembered the sound of the crystal glass shattering against the door as he left. It had worried him so much that he had called on Rosalind's closest neighbour, Charlotte King, on his way home, and asked her to keep an eye on Rosalind.

He had also attended Jimmy Riddle's funeral, with full police honours, a week before Christmas. Rosalind had been there, along with Benjamin and her parents, but she had ignored him; another person who had opened up to him too much, like Jenny Fuller, and revealed far too much of the raw, naked self below the surface, then regretted it and turned away.

Afterwards, he heard, they had all gone down to Barnstaple, and the Old Mill was on the market. He wished Rosalind well; God knew, she had suffered enough.

Banks peered at the recipe. He had just mixed the breadcrumbs, sage and onion with the boiling water when his telephone rang. Who the hell could that be at nine o'clock on Christmas morning? he wondered, as he put the bowl aside and went into the living room.

'Merry Crimble, Banks.'

Bloody hell! It was Dirty Dick Burgess. 'Merry Christmas,' Banks said. 'To what do I owe the honour?'

'Got a Christmas present for you.'

'You shouldn't have.'

'*I* didn't.'

'Okay, I give up. What the hell are you talking about?'

'I thought it would come better from me, rather than you reading about it when it's all over the papers or watching it on television.'

'What would?'

'Barry Clough.'

'Barry Clough? What about him?'

'He's dead.'

'Dead?'

'Stop talking like a bloody parrot. Banks. Yes. Dead. D.E.A.D. *Dead.*'

Banks gripped the handset tighter and sat down. 'Tell me what happened.'

As far as Banks knew, after he and Annie had gone to see Stafford Oakes at the CPS office a week or so ago, all charges against Clough had been dropped. It turned out that the tyre match probably wouldn't withstand a close cross-examination, and someone had cocked up on the warrant for the search of Jamie Gilbert's car, rendering all evidence found therein inadmissible. British justice. To add to their troubles, the witness who said she had seen Jamie Gilbert with Charlie Courage had begun having mysterious lapses of memory.

'In the early hours of the morning,' Burgess said, 'Clough was coming out of a nightclub in Arenys de Mar, just up the coast from Barcelona, and somebody shot him. Dead.'

'Who?'

'Girl named Amanda Khan. Supposed to be some kind of pop star – that's why it's going to be a *big* story – but I can't say as I've ever heard of her. Sounds like an A-rab to me.'

'She's half Pakistani,' said Banks. *Amanda Khan*. Clough's new girlfriend. Emily's replacement.

'Whatever. Anyway, it sounds like the classic love triangle from what I've managed to pick up so far. Seems that Clough jilted her for some dago bimbo, and this Amanda was a few stops closer to Barking than he realized. Funny old world, innit?'

'You can say that again.' Banks didn't usually smoke in the mornings, but he reached for his cigarettes.

'What makes it even funnier,' Burgess went on, 'is that she used one of Clough's own guns. Fine irony, that. She was staying at his villa, and apparently he was carrying on with this Dolores Somebody-or-other right under her eyes and trying to palm Amanda off on one of the servants. She picked up one of Clough's guns and waited for them until they came out of the club. Shades of Ruth Ellis.'

'Indeed.' Ruth Ellis was the last woman to be hanged in England; she had shot her lover outside a London pub. 'Was the girl hurt?'

'Winged. One bullet in her upper arm. Flesh wound. Nothing serious. According to my Spanish sources, the Khan woman fired six shots. Two of them hit Clough: one in his ugly mug and one in his miserable bloody heart. Wonder it didn't just bounce off, but he was dead before he hit the ground. Two hit Jamie Gilbert: one in the chest and one in the groin. He's not dead, but they say he'll never be quite the same again and his voice has gone up a few octaves. One shot hit the girl, and the last hit an innocent bystander in the hand, a local teenager. He lost two fingers.'

'So,' said Banks, 'justice of a kind.'

'Best we'll get.'

'Thanks for calling. The girl, how is she?'

'Amanda Khan? Why? Don't tell me you know her, too?'

'No. I was just wondering.'

'As well as anyone in the custody of the Spanish police can expect to be. Bye-bye, Banks. Have a good Christmas.'

'You, too.'

Banks put the phone down slowly. Clough dead. He could only feel a sense of relief that something had finally gone wrong for the bastard. For a while, Clough had seemed able to get away with anything and everything and thumb his nose at the rest of the world while he was doing it. No more. It probably wasn't very Christian to celebrate another man's death, especially on Christmas Day, but Banks would have been a hypocrite if he hadn't admitted to himself that he was glad Clough wouldn't be around to wreak his peculiar brand of havoc on the world any more.

He also imagined the pain and confusion that must have driven Amanda Khan to such an extreme act, how those six shots had probably destroyed her life, too: her future, her career. But if any death was worth celebrating, it was Barry Clough's.

Banks stubbed out the half cigarette that remained, then went back into the kitchen and washed his hands before he started working the sausage meat into the sage-and-onion mixture. He looked at the chicken, not entirely certain which end was which.

Rubén González's delicate, joyous piano playing on 'Pueblos Nuevo' drifted through from the living room. A little sunlight spilled over the long anvil-shaped top of Low Fell into the kitchen and glinted on the copper bottoms of the pans hanging from the wall. Banks heard stirrings from upstairs, old floorboards creaking. Probably Tracy. Brian liked to sleep all morning.

Banks remembered how, when they were kids, they got up before dawn to open their presents. Once, as he had been creeping around their rooms at one o'clock in the morning filling pillowcases with presents, he was certain he had felt Brian's eyes on him, awake to see if there really was a Santa Claus. Neither of them had ever referred to the incident, and Brian had acted as he always did when he opened his presents, but Banks suspected from that Christmas on, his son had lost a little of his innocence.

That was probably how it happened, he mused – innocence was something you lost a bit at a time, over the years; it didn't just happen overnight. But there *were* intense experiences, epiphanies of a kind, that brought about quantum leaps.

Banks remembered standing by the riverbank that day, rain pitting the water, smiling like an idiot, being polite, clutching the big stone to his chest so as not to wet the gentleman passing by. Then the struggle, the hot beery breath, his heels slipping on the muddy bank, the terror, the punch. The world had changed for him that day, and even now, as he leaned against the kitchen counter, he could still taste the dirty, sweaty cloth of the man's sleeve.

He thought of Emily Riddle, of Rosalind, of Ruth Walker and Amanda Khan. When he heard Tracy's footsteps on the staircase, he had a sudden image of Dr Glendenning's scalpel bisecting the spider tattoo on Emily's midriff, and he realized with a shock that the loss of innocence *never* stopped happening, that he was still losing it, that it was like a wound that never healed, and he would probably go on losing it, drop by drop, until the day he died.

AFTERMATH

by Peter Robinson

No. 35 The Hill is about to become infamous.

For when PCs Janet Taylor and Dennis Morrisey arrive there to sort out an alleged domestic dispute they stumble on a truly horrific scene. A scene which leaves one of them dead and one fighting for her life . . .

Inspector Alan Banks, currently Acting Superintendent, has been leading the hunt for a serial killer dubbed the Chameleon. He is immediately called to the house – where, it seems, the Chameleon's identity has finally been revealed.

But this is only the beginning of a shocking investigation that will test everyone to the absolute limit . . .

Aftermath, **the new Inspector Banks mystery, is now available in Macmillan hardback.**

The opening scenes follow here.

Prologue

February 1990

They locked her in the cage when she started to bleed. Tom was already there. He'd been there for three days and had stopped crying now. He was still shivering, though. It was February, there was no heat in the cellar, and both of them were naked. There would be no food, either, she knew, not for a long time, not until her tummy got so hungry it felt as if it were eating her up from the inside.

It wasn't the first time she had been locked in the cage, but this time was different from the others. Before, it had always been because she'd done something wrong or hadn't done what they wanted her to do. This time ... well, it was different, just because of what she was, and she was really scared. They had no use for her now. They wouldn't let her join in their games any more. Maybe they would even sacrifice her on the altar, as they had threatened so often recently.

As soon as they had shut the door at the top of the stairs, the darkness wrapped itself around her like fur. She could feel it rubbing against her skin the way a cat rubs against your legs. She began to shiver. More than anything she hated the cage, more than the blows, more than the humiliations. But she wouldn't cry. She never cried. She didn't know how.

The smell was terrible; they didn't have a toilet to go to, only the bucket in the corner, which they would only be allowed to empty when they were let out. And who knew when that would be?

But worse even than the smell were the little scratching

459

sounds that started when she had been locked up for only a few minutes. Soon, she knew, it would come, the tickle of sharp little feet across her legs or her tummy if she dared lie down. The first time, she had tried to keep moving and making noise all the time to keep them away, but in the end she had become exhausted and fallen asleep, not caring how many there were or what they did. She could tell in the dark, by the way they moved and their weight, whether they were rats or mice. The rats were the worst. One had even bitten her once.

She held Tom and tried to comfort him, making them both a little warmer. If truth be told, she could have done with a little comforting herself, but there was nobody to comfort her. She was the oldest.

She drifted in and out of sleep, becoming oblivious to the mice and rats. She didn't know how long she'd been there before she heard noises upstairs. Different noises. The music had ended a long time ago and everything was silent apart from the scratching and Tom's breathing. She thought she heard a car pull up outside. Voices. Another car. Then she heard someone walking across the floor upstairs. A curse.

Suddenly, all hell broke loose upstairs. It sounded as if someone was battering at the door with a tree trunk, then was a crunching sound and a loud bang as the front door caved in. Tom was awake now, whimpering in her arms.

She heard shouting and what sounded like dozens of pairs of grown-ups' feet running around upstairs. After what seemed like an eternity, she heard someone prise open the lock to the cellar door. A little light spilled in, but not much, and there wasn't a bulb down there. More voices. Then came the lances of bright torch light, coming closer, so close they hurt her eyes and she had to shield them with her hand. Then the beam held her and a strange voice cried. 'Oh God! Oh, my God!'

1

Probationary Police Constable Janet Taylor stood by her patrol car and watched the silver BMW burn, shielding her eyes from its glare, standing upwind of the foul-smelling smoke. Her partner, PC Dennis Morrisey, stood beside her. One or two spectators were peeping out of their bedroom windows, but nobody else seemed very interested. Burning cars weren't exactly a novelty on this estate. Even at four o'clock in the morning.

Orange and red flames, with deep inner hues of blue and green and occasional tentacles of violet, twisted into the darkness, sending up palls of thick black smoke. Even upwind, Janet could smell the burning rubber and plastic. It was giving her a headache, and she knew her uniform and her hair would reek of it for days.

The leading fire-fighter, Gary Cullen, walked over to join them. It was Dennis he spoke to, of course; he always did. They were mates.

'What do you think?'

'Joy-riders.' Dennis nodded towards the car. 'We checked the number plate. Stolen from a nice middle-class residential street in Heaton Moor, Manchester, earlier this evening.'

'Why here, then?'

'Dunno. Could be a connection, a grudge or something. Someone giving a little demonstration of his feelings. Drugs, even. But that's for the lads upstairs to work out. They're the ones paid to have brains. We're done for now. Everything safe?'

'Under control. What if there's a body in the boot?'

Dennis laughed. 'It'll be well done by now, won't it? Hang on a minute, that's our radio, isn't it?'

Janet walked over to the car. 'I'll get it,' she said over her shoulder.

'Control to 354. Come in please, 354. Over.'

Janet picked up the radio. '354 to Control. Over.'

'Domestic dispute reported taking place at number thirty-five, The Hill. Repeat. Three-five. The Hill. Can you respond? Over.'

Christ, thought Janet, a bloody domestic. No copper in her right mind liked domestics, especially at this time in the morning. 'Will do.' She sighed, looking at her watch. 'ETA three minutes.'

She called over to Dennis, who held up his hand and spoke a few more words to Gary Cullen before responding. They were both laughing when Dennis returned to the car.

'Tell him that joke, did you?' Janet asked, settling behind the wheel.

'Which one's that?' Dennis asked, all innocence.

Janet started the car and sped to the main road. 'You know, the one about the blow job."

'I don't know what you're talking about.'

'Only I heard you telling it to that new PC back at the station, the lad who hasn't started shaving yet. You ought to give the poor lad a chance to make his own mind up about women, Den, instead of poisoning his mind right off the bat.'

The centrifugal force almost threw them off the road as Janet took the roundabout at the top of The Hill too fast. Dennis grasped the dashboard and hung on for dear life. 'Jesus Christ. Women drivers. It's only a joke. Have you got no sense of humour?'

Janet smiled to herself as she slowed and kerb-crawled down The Hill looking for number thirty-five.

'Anyway, I'm getting sick of this,' Dennis said.

'Sick of what? My driving?'

'That, too. Mostly, though, it's your constant bitching. It's got so a bloke can't say what's on his mind these days.'

'Not if he's got a mind like a sewer. That's pollution. Anyway, it's changing times, Den. And we have to change with them or we'll end up like the dinosaurs. By the way, about that mole.'

'What mole?'

'You know, the one on your cheek. Next to your nose. The one with all the hairs growing out of it.'

Dennis put his hand up to his cheek. 'What about it?'

'I'd get it seen to quick, if I were you. It looks cancerous to me. Ah, number thirty-five. Here we are.'

She pulled over to the right-hand side of the road and came to a halt a few yards past the house. It was a small detached residence built of redbrick and sandstone, between a plot of allotments and a row of shops. It wasn't much bigger than a cottage, with a slate roof, low-walled garden and a modern garage attached at the right. At the moment, all was quiet.

'There's a light on in the hall,' Janet said. 'Shall we have a dekko?'

Still fingering his mole, Dennis sighed and muttered something she took to be assent. Janet got out of the car first and walked up the path, aware of him dragging his feet behind her. The garden was overgrown and she had to push twigs and shrubbery aside as she walked. A little adrenalin had leaked into her system, put her on super alert, as it always did with domestics. The reason most cops hated them was that you never knew what was going to happen. As likely as not you'd pull the husband off the wife and then the wife would take his side and start bashing you with a rolling pin.

Janet paused by the door. Still all quiet, apart from Dennis's stertorous breathing behind her. It was too early yet for people to be going to work, and most of the late-night revellers had passed out by now. Somewhere in the distance the first birds began to chatter. Sparrows, most likely, Janet thought. Mice with wings.

Seeing no doorbell, Janet knocked on the door.

No response came from inside.

She knocked harder. The hammering seemed to echo up and down the street. Still no response.

Next, Janet went down on her knees and looked through the letterbox. She thought she could make out a figure sprawled on the floor at the bottom of the stairs. A woman's figure. That was probably cause enough for forced entry.

'Let's go in,' she said.

Dennis tried the handle. Locked. Then, gesturing for Janet to stand out of the way, he charged it with his shoulder.

Poor technique, she thought. She'd have reared back and used her foot. But Dennis was a second row rugby forward, she reminded herself, and his shoulders had been pushed up against so many arseholes in their time that they had to be strong.

The door crashed open on first contact and Dennis cannon-balled into the hallway, grabbing hold of the bottom of the banister to stop himself from tripping over the still figure that lay there.

Janet was right behind him, but she had the advantage of walking in at a more dignified pace. She knelt beside the woman on the floor and felt for a pulse. Weak, but steady. One side of her face was bathed in blood.

'My God,' Janet muttered. 'Den? You okay?'

'Fine. You take care of her. I'll have a look around.' Dennis headed upstairs.

For once, Janet didn't mind being told what to do. Nor did she mind that Dennis automatically assumed it was a woman's work to tend the injured while the man went in search of heroic glory. Well, she *minded*, but she felt a real concern for the victim here, so she didn't want to make an issue of it.

Bastard, she thought. Whoever did this. 'It's okay, love,' she said, even though she suspected the woman couldn't hear her. 'We'll get you an ambulance. Just hold on.'

Most of the blood seemed to be coming from one deep cut just above her left ear, Janet noticed, though there was also a little smeared around the nose and lips. Punches, by the looks of it. There were also broken glass and daffodils scattered all around her, along with a damp patch on the carpet. Janet took her personal radio from her belt-hook and called for an ambulance. She was lucky it worked on The Hill; personal UHF radios had much less range than the VHF models fitted in cars, and were notoriously subject to black spots of patchy reception.

Dennis came downstairs shaking his head. 'Bastard's not hiding up there,' he said. He handed Janet a blanket, pillow and towel, nodding to the woman. 'For her.'

Janet eased the pillow under the woman's head, covered her gently with the blanket and applied the towel to the seeping wound on her temple. Well, I never, she thought, full of surprises, our Den. 'Think he's done a runner?' she asked.

'Dunno. I'll have a look in the back. You stay with her till the ambulance arrives.'

Before Janet could say anything, Dennis headed off towards the back of the house. He hadn't been gone more than a minute or so when she heard him call out, 'Janet, come here and have a look at this. Hurry up. It could be important.'

Curious, Janet looked at the injured woman. The bleeding had stopped and there was nothing else she could do. Even so, she was reluctant to leave the poor woman alone.

'Come on,' Dennis called again. 'Hurry up.'

Janet took one last look at the prone figure and walked towards the back of the house. The kitchen was in darkness.

'Down here.'

She couldn't see Dennis, but she knew that his voice came from downstairs. Through an open door to her right, three steps led down to a landing lit by a bare bulb. There was another door, most likely to the garage, she thought, and around the corner were the steps down to the cellar.

Dennis was standing there, near the bottom, in front of a third door. On it was pinned a poster of a naked woman. She lay back on a brass bed with her legs wide open, fingers tugging at the edges of her vagina, smiling down over her large breasts at the viewer, inviting, beckoning him inside. Dennis stood before it, grinning.

'Bastard,' Janet hissed.

'Where's your sense of humour?'

'It's *not* funny.'

'What do you think it means?'

'I don't know.' Janet could see light under the door, faint and flickering, as if from a faulty bulb. She also noticed a peculiar odour. 'What's that smell?' she asked.

'How should I know? Rising damp? Drains?'

But it smelled like decay to Janet. Decay and sandalwood incense. She gave a little shudder.

'Shall we go in?' She was whispering without knowing why.

'I think we'd better.'

Janet walked ahead of him, almost on tiptoe, down the final few steps. The adrenalin was really pumping in her veins now. Slowly, she reached out and tried the door. Locked. She moved aside, and Dennis used his foot this time. The lock splintered, and the door swung open. Dennis stood aside, bowed from the waist in a parody of gentlemanly courtesy, and said, 'Ladies first.'

With Dennis only inches behind her, Janet stepped into the cellar.

She barely had time to register her first impressions of the small room – mirrors, dozens of lit candles surrounding a mattress on the floor, a girl on the mattress, naked and bound, something yellow around her neck, the terrible smell stronger, despite the incense, like blocked drains and rotten meat, crude charcoal drawings on the whitewashed walls – before it happened . . .

THE SUMMER THAT NEVER WAS

For Sheila

Acknowledgments

I would like to thank the following people for reading and commenting on the manuscript in its various stages of completion: Dominick Abel, Robert Barnard, Liz Cowen, Dinah Forbes, Trish Grader, Sheila Halladay, Maria Rejt, Erika Schmid and Anya Serota.

Many people helped with the research and I would like to extend special thanks to the following: Margaret Brown, Clare Ellis, Area Commander Philip Gormley, Jenny Mogford of www.Peterborough.net, Michelle Spring and Detective Inspector Claire Stevens.

The glory dropped from their youth and love,
And both perceived they had dreamed a dream;

Which hovered as dreams do, still above:
But who can take a dream for truth?

Robert Browning, 'The Statue and the Bust'

1

Trevor Dickinson was hung-over and bad-tempered when he turned up for work on Monday morning. His mouth tasted like the bottom of a bird cage, his head was throbbing like the speakers at a heavy metal concert, and his stomach was lurching like a car with a dirty carburettor. He had already drunk half a bottle of Milk of Magnesia and swallowed four extra-strength paracetamol, with no noticeable effect.

When he arrived at the site, Trevor found he had to wait until the police had cleared away the last of the demonstrators before he could start work. There were five left, all sitting cross-legged in the field. *Environmentalists*. One was a little grey-haired old lady. Ought to be ashamed of herself, Trevor thought, a woman of her age squatting down on the grass with a bunch of bloody Marxist homosexual tree-huggers.

He looked around for some clue as to why anyone would want to save those particular few acres. The fields belonged to a farmer who had recently been put out of business by a combination of mad-cow disease and foot and mouth. As far as Trevor knew, there weren't any rare pink-nippled fart warblers that couldn't nest anywhere else in the entire country; nor were there any ivy-leafed lark's turds lurking in the hedgerows. There weren't even any trees, unless you counted the shabby row of poplars that grew between the fields and the A1, stunted and choked from years of exhaust fumes.

The police cleared away the demonstrators – including the old lady – by picking them up bodily and carting them off to a nearby van, then they gave the go-ahead to Trevor and his fellow workers. The weekend's rain had muddied the ground, which made manoeuvring more difficult than usual, but Trevor was a skilled operator, and he soon got his dipper shovel well below the topsoil, hoisting his loads high and dumping them into the waiting lorry. He handled the levers with an innate dexterity, directing the complex system of clutches, gears, shafts and winch drums like a conductor, scooping as much as the power shovel could hold, then straightening it so as not to spill any when he lifted it up and over to the lorry.

Trevor had been at work for well over two hours when he thought he saw something sticking out of the dirt.

Leaning forward from his seat and rubbing condensation from the inside window of the cab, he squinted to see what it was, and when he saw, it took his breath away. He was looking at a human skull, and what was worse was that it seemed to be looking right back at him.

•

Alan Banks didn't feel in the least bit hung-over, but he knew he'd drunk too much ouzo the night before when he saw that he had left the television on. The only channels it received were Greek, and he never watched it when he was sober.

Banks groaned, stretched and made some of the strong Greek coffee he had become so attached to during his first week on the island. While the coffee was brewing, he put on a CD of Mozart's arias, picked up one of last week's newspapers he hadn't read yet, and walked out onto the balcony. Though he had brought his Discman, he felt fortunate that the small timeshare flat had a mini stereo system with a CD player. He had brought a stack of his favourite CDs with him, including Billie Holiday, John Coltrane, Schubert, Walton, the Grateful Dead and Led Zeppelin.

He stood by the iron railings listening to 'Parto, ma tu, ben mio' and looking down at the sea beyond the jumbled terraces of rooftops and walls, a cubist composition of intersecting blue and white planes. The sun was shining in a perfect blue sky, the way it had done every day since he had arrived. He could smell wild lavender and rosemary in the air. A cruise ship had just dropped anchor, and the first launches of the day were carrying their loads of excited camera-bearing tourists to the harbour, gulls squawking in their wake.

Banks went to pour himself some coffee, then came out again and sat down. His white wooden chair scraped against the terracotta tiles, scaring the small lizard-like creature that had been basking in the morning sun.

After looking at the old newspaper and perhaps reading a little more of Homer's *Odyssey*, Banks thought he would walk down to the village for a long lunch, maybe have a glass or two of wine, pick up some fresh bread, olives and goat's cheese, then come back for a nap and a little music, before spending his evening at the taverna on the quayside playing chess with Alexandros, as had been his habit since his second day.

There was nothing much that interested him in the newspapers except the sports and arts pages. Rain had stopped play in the third Test at Old Trafford, which was hardly news, England had won an important World Cup qualifying match, and it wasn't the right day of the week for the book or record reviews. He did, however, notice a brief report on a skeleton uncovered by a construction worker at the site of a new shopping centre by the A1, not far from Peterborough. He only noticed it because he had spent a good part of his early life in Peterborough, and his parents still lived there.

He put the newspaper aside and watched the gulls swoop and circle. They looked as if they were drifting on waves of Mozart's music. Drifting, just like him. He thought back to his second conversation with Alexandros. During their game of chess, Alex had paused, looked seriously at Banks and said, 'You seem like a man with many secrets, Alan, a very sad man. What is it you are running from?'

Banks had thought about that a lot. Was he running? Yes, in a way. Running from a failed marriage and a botched romance, and from a job that had threatened, for the second time in his life, to send him over the edge with its conflicting demands, its proximity to violent death and all that was worst in people. He was seeking a temporary escape, at least.

Or did it go deeper than that? Was he trying to run away from himself, from what he was, or from what he had become? He had sat there pondering the question and answered only, 'I wish I knew,' before making a rash move and putting his queen in jeopardy.

He had managed to avoid affairs of the heart during his brief stay. Andrea, the waitress at Philippe's taverna, flirted with him, but that was all. Occasionally, one of the women from the cruise ships would give him that certain kind of wistful look which led only to one place if you let it, but he hadn't let it. He had also found himself a place where he didn't have to confront crime on a daily basis, more particularly a place where he didn't have to go down into cellars stuffed with the violated bodies of teenage girls, a scene from his last case that still, even here on this peaceful island, haunted his dreams.

So he had achieved his goal, run away from a messy life and found paradise of a kind. Why was it, then, that he still felt so damn restless?

•

Detective Inspector Michelle Hart of the Cambridgeshire Constabulary, Northern Division, entered the forensic anthropology department of the District Hospital. She was looking forward to this morning. Usually at post-mortems she found herself disturbed not so much by the cutting and probing itself as by the contrast between the bright reflective surfaces of utilitarian tile and steel and the messy slosh of stomach contents, the dribbles of blackish blood running into the polished gutters, between the smell of disinfectant and the stench of a punctured bowel. But this morning none of that was going to happen. This morning all that Dr Wendy Cooper, the forensic anthro-pologist, had to examine was bones.

Michelle had worked with her just over a month ago – her first case in her new posting – on some remains that had turned out to be Anglo-Saxon, not unusual in those parts, and they had got on well enough. The only thing she found hard to take was Dr Cooper's predilection for playing country and western music while she worked. She said it helped her to concentrate, but Loretta Lynn had quite the opposite effect on Michelle.

Dr Cooper and her graduate-student assistant, David

Roberts, were bent over the partial skeleton, arranging the small bones of the hands and feet in the correct order. It must be a difficult task, Michelle realized from the one brief anatomy course she had attended: how you told one rib or one knuckle from another was quite beyond her. Dr Cooper seemed to be doing well enough. She was in her early fifties, a rather stout figure with very short grey hair, silver-rimmed glasses and a no-nonsense manner.

'Do you know how many bones there are in a human hand?' Dr Cooper asked without looking away from the skeleton.

'A lot?' Michelle answered.

'Twenty-six,' said Dr Cooper. 'Twenty-six. And awkward little buggers to make out, some of them.'

'Got anything for me yet?' Michelle took out her notebook.

'A little bit. As you can see, we're still trying to put him back together again.'

'Him?'

'Oh, yes. You can take my word for that. The skull and pubis bear it out. Northern European, too, I'd say.' She turned the skull sideways. 'See that straight facial profile, the narrow nasal aperture? All signs. There are others, of course: the high cranium, the eye sockets. But you don't want a lesson in ethnic anthropology, do you?'

'I suppose not,' said Michelle, who actually found the subject quite interesting. Sometimes she thought she might have chosen the wrong career and should instead have become an anthropologist. Or perhaps a doctor. 'Not very tall, though, is he?'

Dr Cooper looked at the bones laid out on the steel trolley. 'Tall enough for his age, I'd say.'

'Don't tell me you know his age.'

'Of course. Only a rough guess, mind you. By measuring the long bones and applying the appropriate formula, and by simple measuring tape here on the table, we've calculated his height at around five foot six. That's somewhere between a hundred and sixty-seven and a hundred and sixty-eight centimetres.'

'A kid, then?'

Dr Cooper nodded and touched the shoulder with her pen. 'The medial clavicular epiphysis – collarbone to you – is the last epiphysis in the body to fuse, normally in the mid-twenties, though it can occur any time between fifteen and thirty-two. His hasn't fused yet. I've also examined the rib ends and vertebrae. In an older person, you'd expect not only signs of wear and tear, but sharper ends and more scalloping on the ribs. His rib ends are flat and smoothly rounded, only slightly undulating, and the vertebrae show no epiphyseal rings at all. Also the fusion of ilium, ischium and pubis is in its early stages. That process usually takes place between the ages of twelve and seventeen.'

'So you're saying he's how old?'

'In my business it doesn't pay to go out on a limb, but I'll say between twelve and fifteen. Allow a couple of years either way as a fair margin of error. The databases we get these figures from aren't always complete and sometimes they're out of date.'

'That's amazing. Anything else?'

'The teeth. Of course, you'll have to bring in the odontologist to examine the roots and check the levels of fluoride, if there is any – it wasn't introduced in toothpaste here until 1959 – but I can tell you three things right now. First off, there are no deciduous teeth left – that's baby teeth – and the second molar has erupted. That means he's aged around twelve, again give or take a couple of years, and I'd hazard a guess, given the other evidence, that he's older rather than younger.'

'And the third thing?'

'A bit less scientific, I'm afraid, but judging by the general state of his teeth and the look of all these metal fillings in the posterior teeth I'd guess vintage school dentist.'

'How long ago was he buried there?'

'Impossible to say. There's no remaining soft tissue or ligaments, the bones are discoloured and there's some flaking, so I'd say more than a decade or two, but beyond that it's anyone's guess until I've done more rigorous tests.'

'Any sign of cause of death?'

'Not yet. I need to get the bones cleaned up. Sometimes you can't see knife marks, for example, because of the encrusted dirt.'

'What about that hole in the skull?'

Dr Cooper ran her finger around the jagged hole. 'Must have occurred during excavation. It's definitely post mortem.'

'How can you tell?'

'If it had happened before death, there'd be signs of healing. This is a clean break.'

'But what if it was the *cause* of death?'

Dr Cooper sighed as if she were talking to a dense undergraduate. Michelle noticed David Roberts grin, and he blushed when he saw her watching him. 'If that were the case,' the doctor went on, 'you'd expect a very different shape. Fresh bones break in a different way from old bones. And look at that.' She pointed to the hole. 'What do you see?'

Michelle peered closely. 'The edges,' she said. 'They're not the same colour as the surrounding bone.'

'Very good. That means it's a recent break. If it had happened around the time of death, you'd expect the edges to have stained the same colour as the rest of the skull, wouldn't you?'

'I suppose so,' said Michelle. 'Simple, isn't it?'

'If you know what you're looking for. There's a fractured humerus, too, right arm, but that's healed, so I'd say it happened while he was alive. And do you see this?' She pointed to the left arm. 'It's slightly longer than his right arm, which may indicate left-handedness. Of course, it could be due to the fracture, but I doubt it. There are differences in the scapulae that also support my hypothesis.'

Michelle made some notes, then turned back to Dr Cooper. 'We know he was most likely buried where he was found,' she said, 'because the remains were about three or four feet underground, but is there any way of knowing whether he died there or was moved there later?'

Dr Cooper shook her head. 'Any evidence of that was destroyed in the same way the skull and some of the other bones were damaged. By the bulldozer.'

'Where's the stuff we found with the body?'

Dr Cooper gestured towards the bench that ran the length of the far wall and turned back to the bones. David Roberts spoke for the first time. He had a habit of keeping his head down when he spoke to Michelle, and of mumbling, so she couldn't always hear what he was saying. He seemed embarrassed in her presence, as if he fancied her. She knew that her combination of blonde hair and green eyes had a captivating effect on some men, but this was ridiculous. Michelle had just turned forty and David couldn't be more than twenty-two.

She followed him over to the bench, where he pointed to a number of barely recognizable objects. 'We can't say for certain that they're his,' he said, 'but all these were gathered within a short radius of the body.' When she looked more closely, Michelle thought she could make out scraps of material, perhaps fragments of clothing, a belt buckle, coins, a penknife, a round-edged triangular shape, shoe leather, lace eyelets, and several round objects. 'What are those?' she asked.

'Marbles.' David rubbed one of them with a cloth and handed it to her.

It felt smooth to Michelle's touch, and inside the heavy glass sphere was a double helix of blue. 'Summer, then,' she said, almost to herself.

'Beg your pardon?'

She looked up at David. 'Oh, sorry. I said summer. Boys usually played marbles in summer. Outdoors, when the weather was good. What about the coins?'

'A few pennies, half a crown, sixpence, a threepenny bit.'

'All old coinage?'

'Before decimalization, at any rate.'

'So that's pre-1971.' She picked up the small triangular object. 'What's this?'

David polished away some of the grime and revealed a tortoiseshell pattern. 'I think it's a plectrum,' he said. 'You know, for a guitar.'

'A musician, then?' Michelle picked up a chain bracelet of some sort, crusted and corroded, with a flat, elongated oval at its centre and something written on it.

Dr Cooper came over. 'Yes, I thought that was interesting,' she said. 'You know what it is?'

'A bracelet of some kind?'

'Yes. I think it's an identity bracelet. They became very popular with teenage boys during the mid-sixties. I remember my brother had one. David was able to clean this one up a bit. All the silver plating's gone, of course, but luckily the engraver's drill went deep into the alloy underneath. You can read part of the name if you look very closely. Here, use this.' She passed Michelle a magnifying glass. Michelle looked through it and was able to make out the faint edges of some of the engraved letters: GR–HA–. That was all.

'Graham, I'd guess,' said Dr Cooper.

Michelle looked at the collection of bones, trying to imagine the warm, living, breathing human being that they had once formed. A boy. '*Graham*,' she whispered. 'Pity he didn't have his last name engraved, too. It'd make our job a lot simpler.'

Dr Cooper put her hands on her ample hips and laughed. 'To be honest, my dear,' she said, 'I don't think you can have it much simpler than this, can you? If I'm right so far, you're looking for a left-handed boy named Graham, aged between say twelve and fifteen, who once broke his upper right arm and went missing at least twenty or thirty years ago, maybe in summer. Oh, and he played marbles and the guitar. Am I forgetting anything? I'll bet there can't be too many matching that description in your files.'

•

Banks walked down the hill and through the village's winding streets at about seven every evening. He loved the quality of the light at that time of day, the way the small white houses with their colourful wooden steps seemed to glow, and the flowers – a profusion of purple, pink and red – seemed incandescent. The scent of gardenia mingled with thyme and oregano. Below him, the wine-dark sea stretched all the way back to the mainland, just as it had done in Homer's day. Although it wasn't exactly *wine* dark, Banks noticed. Not all of it, anyway. Some of the areas closer to land were deep blue or green, and it only darkened to the purple of a young Greek wine much further out.

One or two of the shopkeepers greeted him as he passed. He had been on the island for a little over two weeks now, which was longer than most tourists stayed, and while he wasn't *accepted* his presence was at least acknowledged. It was much the same as in a Yorkshire village, where you remain an incomer until you have wintered out several years. Maybe he *would* stay here that long, learn the language, become a mysterious hermit, merge into the rhythms of island life. He even looked a bit Greek, with his lean frame, closely cropped black hair and tanned skin.

He picked up the two-day-old English newspapers that came on the last boat of the day and carried them with him to Philippe's quayside taverna, where he spent most of his evenings at an outside table overlooking the harbour. He would have an ouzo as an aperitif, make his mind up about what to eat, then drink retsina with dinner. He found that he had come to enjoy the odd, oily taste of the local resinated wine.

Banks lit a cigarette and watched the tourists getting into the launch that would take them back to their cruise ship and the evening's entertainment: probably Cheryl from Cheadle Hulme dancing the dance of the seven veils, or a group of Beatles' imitators from Heckmondwike. Tomorrow they would disembark on a new island, where they would buy overpriced trinkets and take photographs they wouldn't look at more than once. A group of German tourists, who must have been staying overnight at one of the island's few small hotels, took a table at the other side of the patio and ordered beer. They were the only other people sitting outside.

Banks sipped ouzo and nibbled on some olives and dolmades as he settled on fish à la Grecque and a green salad for dinner. The last of the tourists had returned to the cruise ship, and as soon as he had cleared away his stock Alex would come by to play chess. In the meantime, Banks turned to the newspapers.

His attention was caught by an article on the bottom right of the front page, headed, DNA CONFIRMS IDENTITY OF LONG-BURIED BODY. Intrigued, Banks read on:

A week ago the skeleton of a young boy was unearthed by workers digging the foundations of a new shopping centre next to the A1 west of Peterborough, Cambridgeshire. Information discovered at the scene and provided by forensic anthropologist Dr Wendy Cooper led to a very narrow list of possibilities. 'It was almost a gift,' Dr Cooper told our reporter. 'Usually old bones don't tell you so much, but in this case we knew early on that he was a young boy who had broken his right arm once and was most likely left-handed.' An identity bracelet, popular with teenage boys in the mid-sixties, was found near the scene and bore part of a name. Detective Inspector Michelle Hart of the Cambridgeshire Constabulary commented, 'Dr Cooper gave us a lot to work with. It was simply a matter of going through the files, narrowing the possibilities.' When police came up with one strong candidate, Graham Marshall, the boy's parents were approached for DNA samples, and the testing proved positive. 'It's a relief to know they've found our Graham after all these years,' said Mrs Marshall at her home. 'Even though we lived in hope.' Graham Marshall disappeared on Sunday, 22 August 1965, at the age of fourteen while walking his regular newspaper round near his council-estate home in Peterborough. No trace of him has ever been found until now. 'The police at the time exhausted every possible lead,' DI Hart told our reporter, 'but there's always a chance that this discovery will bring new clues.' Asked if there was likely to be a new investigation into the case, DI Hart would only state that, 'Missing persons are never written off until they are found, and if there's the possibility of foul play, then justice must be pursued.' As yet, there are no clear indications of cause of death, though Dr Cooper did point out that the boy could hardly bury himself under three feet of earth.

Banks felt his stomach clench. He put the paper down and stared out to sea, where the setting sun was sprinkling rose dust over the horizon. Everything around him began to shimmer and feel unreal. As if on cue, the tape of Greek music came to 'Zorba's Dance', as it did every night. The taverna, the harbour, the brittle laughter all seemed to vanish into the distance, and there was only Banks with his memories and the stark words in the newspaper.

'Alan? What is it you say: a penny for them?'

Banks looked up and saw the dark, squat figure of Alex standing over him. 'Alex. Sorry. Good to see you. Sit down.'

Alex sat, looking concerned. 'You look as if you've had bad news.'

'You could say that.' Banks lit a cigarette and stared out over the darkening sea. He could smell salt and a whiff of dead fish. Alex gestured to Andrea, and in moments a bottle of ouzo appeared on the table in front of them, along with another plate of olives and dolmades. Philippe lit the lanterns that hung around the outside patio and they swayed in the breeze, casting fleeting shadows over the tables. Alex took out his portable chess set from its leather bag and arranged the pieces.

Banks knew that Alex wouldn't press him. It was one of the things he liked about his new friend. Alex had been born on the island and after university in Athens had travelled the world as an executive for a Greek shipping line, before deciding to pack it all in ten years ago at the age of forty. Now he made a living from tooling leather belts, which he sold to tourists on the quayside. Alex was an extremely cultured man, Banks had soon discovered, with a passion for Greek art and architecture, and his English was almost perfect. He also possessed what seemed to Banks a very deep-rooted sense of himself and a contentment with the simple life which Banks wished he could attain. Of course, he hadn't told Alex what *he* did for a living, merely that he was a civil servant. He had found that telling strangers you met on holiday you were a policeman tended to put them off. Either that or they had a mystery for you to solve, the way people always seem to have strange ailments to ask about when they are introduced to doctors.

'Perhaps it's not a good idea tonight,' Alex said, and Banks noticed he was putting the chess set away. It had always been a mere backdrop to conversation, anyway, as neither man was a skilled player.

'I'm sorry,' said Banks. 'I just don't seem to be in the mood. I'd only lose.'

'You usually do. But it's all right, my friend. Clearly there is something troubling you.' Alex stood to leave, but Banks reached out and touched his arm. Oddly enough, he *wanted* to tell someone. 'No, stay,' he said, pouring them both a generous glass of ouzo. Alex looked at him for a moment with those serious brown eyes and sat down again.

'When I was fourteen,' said Banks, looking out at the lights in the harbour and listening to the stays on the fishing boats rattle, 'a close schoolfriend of mine disappeared. He was never seen again. Nobody ever found out what happened to him. Not a trace.' He smiled and turned to look at Alex. 'It's funny because this music seemed to be playing constantly back then: "Zorba's Dance". It was a big hit in England at the time. Marcello Minerbi. Funny the little things you remember, isn't it?'

Alex nodded. 'Memory is indeed a mysterious process.'

'And often not to be trusted.'

'True, it seems that as things lie there they are . . . strangely metamorphosed.'

'A lovely Greek word, *metamorphosed*.'

'It is. One thinks of Ovid, of course.'

'But it happens to the past, doesn't it? To our memories.'

'Yes.'

'Anyway,' Banks went on, 'there was a general assumption at the time that my friend, Graham was his name, had been abducted by a paedophile – another Greek word, but not so lovely – and done away with.'

'It seems a reasonable assumption, given life in the

cities. But might he not have simply run away from home?'

'That was another theory, but he had no reason to, as far as anyone knew. He was happy enough, and he never talked about running off. Anyway,' Banks went on, 'all attempts to find him failed and he never turned up again. The thing is, about two months earlier I was playing down by the river when a man came and grabbed me and tried to push me in.'

'What happened?'

'I was wiry and slippery enough to wriggle my way free and run off.'

'But you never told the authorities?'

'I never even told my parents.'

'Why not?'

'You know what kids are like, Alex. I wasn't meant to be playing down there, for a start. It was quite a long way from home. I was also playing truant. I was supposed to be at school. And I suppose I blamed myself. I just didn't want to get into trouble.'

Alex poured more ouzo. 'So, when your friend disappeared, you assumed it was the same man?'

'Yes.'

'And you've been carrying the guilt all these years?'

'I suppose so. I never really thought about it, that way, but every once in a while, when I think about it I feel . . . it's like an old wound that never quite heals. I don't know. I think it was partly why I—'

'Why you what?'

'Never mind.'

'Why you became a policeman?'

Banks looked at him in astonishment. 'How did you know?'

Alex was smiling. 'I've met a few in my time. You get to recognize the signs.'

'Like what?'

'Oh, watchfulness, curiosity, a certain way of walking and sitting. Little things.'

Banks laughed. 'By the sound of it, you'd make a pretty good policeman yourself, Alex.'

'Oh, no. I think not.'

'Why?'

'I don't think I could ever be certain that I was on the right side.'

'And are you now?'

'I try to be.'

'So do I,' said Banks.

'I'm sure you are a good policeman. You must remember, though, in Greece . . . well, we've had our share of regimes. But please go on.'

Banks tapped the folded newspaper. 'They've found him,' he said. 'Buried by the roadside about eight miles away from where he disappeared.'

Alex whistled between his teeth.

'They don't know the cause of death yet,' Banks went on, 'but he couldn't have got there by himself.'

'So perhaps the assumptions were right?'

'Yes.'

'And that makes you feel bad all over again, does it?'

'Terrible. What if I was responsible, Alex? What if it *was* the same man? If I'd spoken up—'

'Even if you had reported what happened, it doesn't mean he would have been caught. These men can be very clever, as I'm sure you have learned over the years.' Alex shook his head. 'But I'm not foolish enough to believe that one can talk a man out of his guilt when he's set on feeling it. Do you believe in fate?'

'I don't know.'

'We Greeks are great believers in fate, in destiny.'

'What does it matter, anyway?'

'Because it exonerates you. Don't you see? It's like the Catholic Church absolving you of sin. If it's fate, then you were meant to survive and not tell anyone, and your friend was destined to be abducted and killed and his body discovered many years later.'

'Then I *don't* believe in fate.'

'Well, it was worth a try,' said Alex. 'What are you going to do?'

'I don't know. There's nothing I can do, really, is there? The local police will investigate, and they'll either find out what happened or they won't. My bet is that after all these years they won't.'

Alex said nothing for a moment, just toyed with his ouzo glass, then he took a long sip and sighed.

'What?' said Banks.

'I have a feeling I'm going to miss you, my friend.'

'Why? I'm not going anywhere.'

'You know the Germans occupied this island during the war?'

'Of course,' said Banks, surprised by Alex's abrupt change of subject. 'I've explored the old fortifications. You know I have. We talked about it. It wasn't exactly *The Guns of Navarone*, but I was impressed.'

Alex waved his hand in a dismissive gesture. 'You and I can only imagine what life was like under the Nazi occupation,' he said, 'but my father lived through it. He once told me a story about when he was a boy, not much older than you and your friends were. The German officer in command of the island was called von Braun, and everyone thought he must have been an incompetent bastard to be sent somewhere like this. As you say, my friend, not exactly *The Guns of Navarone*, not exactly the most strategic position in the Mediterranean. Nevertheless, someone had to keep an eye on the populace, and von Braun was the man. It wasn't a very exacting task, and I'm sure the soldiers posted here became very sloppy.

'One day, my father and three of his friends stole a German jeep. The roads are bad, as you can see even now, and they couldn't drive, of course, and knew nothing beyond the rudiments, so they crashed into a boulder after they'd barely gone half a mile. Luckily, they were uninjured and ran away before the soldiers were alerted to what had happened, though apparently one soldier saw them and told von Braun there were four kids.' Alex paused and lit one of his Turkish cigarettes. Banks had once questioned him on the political correctness of a Greek smoking Turkish tobacco, but all he'd said was that it tasted better.

'Anyway,' Alex went on, expelling a plume of smoke, 'whatever the reason, von Braun took it upon himself to seek retribution, make an example, in the same way the Nazis did in many occupied villages. He probably wanted to prove that he wasn't just some soft, incompetent idiot sent to the middle of nowhere to keep him out of harm's way. He rounded up four teenage boys – the same number the soldier had counted – and had them shot just over there.' Alex pointed to where the main street met the quayside. 'Two of them had actually been involved; the other two were innocent. None of them was my father.'

The German tourists laughed at something one of the

women had said and called Andrea to order more beer. They were already pretty drunk in Banks's opinion, and there's not much worse than a drunken German, unless it's a drunken English football fan.

Alex ignored them and went on. 'My father was guilt-stricken for not speaking up, as was his friend, but what could they have done? The Nazis would probably have shot them in addition to the four others they had chosen. It was what the Americans call a no-win situation. He carried that shame and that guilt with him all his life.'

'Is he still alive?'

'He's been dead for years now. But the point is von Braun was one of the minor war criminals tried after the war, and do you know what? My father *went to the trial.* He'd never left the island before in his life, except for one visit to Athens to have his appendix removed, but he *had to go.* To bear witness.'

Banks felt oppressed by Alex's story and the weight of history, felt as if there was nothing he could say that would not be inappropriately light. Finally, he found his voice. 'Are you trying to tell me you think I ought to go back?'

Alex looked at him and smiled sadly. 'I'm not the one who thinks you ought to go back.'

'Ah, shit.' Banks lit a cigarette and tilted the ouzo bottle again. It was nearly empty.

'Am I right?' Alex persisted.

Banks looked out at the sea, dark now, twisting the lights reflected on its shimmering surface, and nodded. There was nothing he could do tonight, of course, but Alex was right; he *would* have to go. He had been carrying his guilty secret around for so long now that it had become a part of him, and he could no more put the discovery of Graham Marshall's bones out of his mind than he could all the other things he had thought he'd left behind: Sandra and her pregnancy, Annie Cabbot, the Job.

He watched a pair of young lovers, arms around one another, stroll along the quayside and felt terribly sad because he knew it was all over now, this brief sojourn in paradise, knew that this would be the last time he and Alex spent a companionable evening together in the Greek warmth, with the waves lapping against the ancient stone quay and the smell of Turkish tobacco and salt and rosemary in the air. He knew that tomorrow he had to go down to the harbour early, take the morning ferry to Piraeus and get on the first flight home. And he wished to hell he didn't.

2

Up in Yorkshire, two days later, the sky was far from cloudless, and the sun was definitely not shining. It had not, in fact, shone since Banks had left for Greece, reflected Detective Inspector Annie Cabbot as she pushed yet another pile of paperwork aside and put her feet up on the desk. It was as if the bugger had gone and taken all the sunshine with him. Nothing but cold rain, grey skies, and more rain. And this was August. Where was summer?

Annie had to admit that she missed Banks. She had ended their romantic relationship, but there was no one else in her life, and she enjoyed his company and his professional insight. In her weaker moments, too, she sometimes wished they had managed to remain lovers, but it wasn't a valid option, given his family baggage and her renewed interest in her career. Too many complications involved in sleeping with the boss. On the plus side, she had found far more time for her painting and had started meditation and yoga again.

Not that she couldn't understand *why* Banks had gone. The poor sod had simply had enough. He needed to recharge his batteries, gird his loins before he entered the fray once more. A month should do it, Assistant Chief Constable Ron McLaughlin had agreed, and Banks had more than enough accrued leave for that. So he had buggered off to Greece, taking the sunshine with him. Lucky sod.

At least Banks's temporary absence meant a quick transfer for Annie from Complaints and Discipline back to CID at the rank of detective inspector, which was what she had been angling for. She didn't have her own office any more, however, only a semi-partitioned corner in the detectives' squad room along with DS Hatchley and six DCs, including Winsome Jackman, Kevin Templeton and Gavin Rickerd, but it was worth the sacrifice to be away from that fat sexist lecher Detective Superintendent Chambers, not to mention a welcome change from the kind of dirty jobs she had been given under his command.

There hadn't been much more crime than sun in the Western Division lately, either, except in Harrogate of all places, where a mysterious epidemic of egg throwing had broken out. Youths seemed to have taken to throwing eggs at passing cars, old folk's windows and even at police stations. But that was Harrogate, not Eastvale. Which was why Annie, bored with looking over reports, mission statements, circulars and cost-cutting proposals, perked her ears up when she heard the tapping of Detective Superintendent Gristhorpe's walking stick approaching the office door. She took her feet off the desk, as much so that Gristhorpe wouldn't notice her red suede ankle boots as anything else, tucked her wavy chestnut hair behind her ears and pretended to be buried deep in paperwork.

Gristhorpe walked over to her desk. He'd lost quite a bit of weight since he shattered his ankle, but he still looked robust enough. Even so, rumour had it that he had been heard to broach the subject of retirement. 'Owt on, Annie?' he asked.

Annie gestured to the papers strewn over her desk. 'Not a lot.'

'Only there's this boy gone missing. Schoolboy, aged fifteen.'

'How long ago?'

'Didn't come home last night.' Gristhorpe put the misper report in front of her. 'Parents have been calling us since yesterday evening.'

Annie raised her eyebrows. 'A bit soon to bring us in on it, isn't it, sir? Kids go missing all the time. Fifteen year olds in particular.'

Gristhorpe scratched his chin. 'Not ones called Luke Armitage, they don't.'

'Luke Armitage? Not . . . '

'Aye. Martin Armitage's son. Stepson, to be accurate.'

'Oh, shit.' Martin Armitage was an ex-football player, who in his time had been one of the major strikers of the Premier League. Since retiring from professional sport, he had become something of a country gentleman. He lived with his wife and stepson Luke in Swainsdale Hall, a magnificent manor house perched on the daleside above Fortford. Armitage was known as a 'Champagne' socialist because he professed to have left-wing leanings, gave to charities, especially those supporting and promoting children's sporting activities, and chose to send his son to Eastvale Comprehensive instead of to a public school.

His wife, Robin Fetherling, had once been a celebrated model, well enough known in her field as Martin Armitage was in his, and her exploits, including drugs, wild parties and stormy public affairs with a variety of rock stars, had provided plenty of fodder twenty years ago or more, when Annie was a teenager. Robin Fetherling and Neil Byrd had been a hot item, the beautiful young couple of the moment, when Annie was at the University of Exeter. She had even listened to Neil Byrd's records in her student flat, but she hadn't heard his name, or his music, in years – hardly surprising, as she had neither the time nor the inclination to keep up with pop music these days. She remembered reading that Robin and Neil had had a baby out of wedlock about fifteen years ago. *Luke.* Then they split up, and Neil Byrd committed suicide while the child was still very young.

'Oh, shit, indeed,' said Gristhorpe. 'I'd not like to think we give better service to the rich and famous than to the poor, Annie, but perhaps you could go and try to set the parents at ease. The kid's probably gone gallivanting off with his mates, run away to London or something, but you know what people's imaginations can get up to.'

'Where did he disappear from, sir?'

'We don't know for certain. He'd been into town yesterday afternoon, and when he didn't come home for tea they started to get worried. At first they thought he might have met up with some mates, but when it got dark and he still wasn't home they started to get worried. By this morning they were frantic, of course. Turns out the lad carried a mobile with him, so they're sure he would have rung if anything came up.'

Annie frowned. 'That *does* sound odd. Have they tried ringing him?'

'No signal. They say his phone's switched off.'

Annie stood up and reached for her umbrella. 'I'll go over there and talk to them now.'

'And Annie?'

'Yes, sir?'

'You hardly need me to tell you this, but try to keep as low a profile as possible. The last thing we want is the local press on the case.'

'Softly, softly, sir.'

Gristhorpe nodded. 'Good.'

Annie walked towards the door.

'Nice boots,' said Gristhorpe from behind her.

•

Banks remembered the days surrounding Graham Marshall's disappearance more clearly than he remembered most days that long ago, he realized, as he closed his eyes and settled back in the airplane seat, though memory, he found, tended to take more of a cavalier view of the past than an accurate one; it conflated, condensed and transposed. It *metamorphosed*, as Alex had said last night.

Weeks, months, years were spread out in his mind's eye, but not necessarily in chronological order. The emotions and incidents might be easy enough to relocate and remember, but sometimes, as in police work, you have to rely on external evidence to reconstruct the true sequence. Whether he had got caught shoplifting in Woolworth's in 1963 or 1965, for example, he couldn't remember, though he recollected with absolute clarity the sense of fear and helplessness in that cramped triangular room under the escalator, the cloying smell of Old Spice aftershave and the way the two dark-suited shop detectives laughed as they pushed him about and made him empty his pockets. But when he thought about it more he remembered it was also the same day he had bought the brand-new *With the Beatles* LP, which was released in late November 1963.

And that was the way it often happened. Remember one small thing – a smell, a piece of music, the weather, a fragment of conversation – then scrutinize it, question it from every angle, and before you know it, there's another piece of information you thought you'd forgotten. And another. It didn't always work, but sometimes when he did this Banks ended up creating a film of his own past, a film which he was both watching and acting in at the same time. He could see what clothes he was wearing, knew what he was feeling, what people were saying, how warm or cold it was. Sometimes the sheer reality of the memory terrified him and he had to snap himself out of it in a cold sweat.

Just over a week after he had returned from a holiday in Blackpool with the Banks family, Graham Marshall had disappeared during his Sunday morning paper round out of Donald Bradford's newsagent's shop across the main road, a round he had been walking for about six months, and one that Banks himself had walked a year or so earlier, when Mr Thackeray owned the shop. At first, of course, nobody knew anything about what had happened apart from Mr and Mrs Marshall and the police.

As Banks leaned back in his seat and closed his eyes, he tried to reconstruct that Sunday. It would have started in the normal way. On weekends, Banks usually stayed in bed until lunchtime, when his mother called him down for the roast. During lunch they would listen to the radio comedies on the Light Programme: *The Navy Lark* and *Round the Horne*, probably repeats because it was summer, until *The Billy Cotton Band Show* drove Banks out of doors to meet up with his friends on the estate.

Sometimes, the five of them – Banks, Graham, Steve Hill, Paul Major and Dave Grenfell – would go to the local park, staking out an area of grass near the playing fields, and listen to Alan Freeman's *Pick of the Pops* on Paul's trannie, watching the girls walk by. Sometimes Steve would get bold and offer one of them a couple of

Woodbines to toss him off, but mostly they just watched and yearned from a distance.

Other Sundays they'd gather at Paul's and play records, which was what they did on the day Graham disappeared, Banks remembered. Paul's was best because he had a new Dansette, which he would bring outside on the steps if the weather was good. They didn't play the music too loudly, so nobody complained. If Paul's mum and dad were out, they'd sneak a cigarette or two as well. That Sunday everyone was there except Graham, and nobody knew why he was missing, unless his parents were keeping him in the house for some reason. They could be strict, Graham's parents, especially his dad. Still, whatever the reason, he wasn't there, and nobody thought too much of it.

There they would be, then, sitting on the steps, wearing their twelve-inch-bottom drainpipe trousers, tight-fitting shirts and winkle-pickers, hair about as long as they could grow it before their parents prescribed a trip to Mad Freddy's, the local barber's. No doubt they played other music, but the highlights of that day, Banks remembered, were Steve's pristine copy of the latest Bob Dylan LP, *Bringing It All Back Home*, and Banks's *Help!*

Along with his fascination for masturbation, Steve Hill had some rather way-out tastes in music. Other kids might like Sandie Shaw, Cliff Richard and Cilla Black, but for Steve it was the Animals, the Who and Bob Dylan. Banks and Graham were with him most of the way, although Banks also enjoyed some of the more traditional pop music, like Dusty Springfield and Gene Pitney, while Dave and Paul were more conservative, sticking with Roy Orbison and Elvis. Of course, everybody hated Val Doonican, Jim Reeves and the Bachelors.

That day, songs like 'Subterranean Homesick Blues' and 'Maggie's Farm' transported Banks to places he didn't know existed, and the mysterious love songs, 'Love Minus Zero/No Limit' and 'She Belongs to Me', lingered with him for days. Though Banks had to admit he didn't understand a word Dylan was singing about, there was something magical about the songs, even vaguely frightening, like a beautiful dream in which someone starts speaking gibberish. But perhaps that was hindsight. This was only the beginning. He didn't become a fully fledged Dylan fan until 'Like a Rolling Stone' knocked him for six a month or two later, and he wouldn't claim, even today, to know what Dylan was singing about half the time.

The girls from down the street walked by at one point, as they always did, very mod in their miniskirts and Mary Quant hairdos, all bobs, fringes and headbands, eye make-up laid on with a trowel, lips pale and pink, noses in the air. They were sixteen, far too old for Banks or his friends, and they all had eighteen-year-old boyfriends with Vespas or Lambrettas.

Dave left early, saying he had to go to his grandparents' house in Ely for tea, though Banks thought it was because Dylan was getting up his nose. Steve headed off a few minutes later, taking his LP with him. Banks couldn't remember the exact time, but he was certain that he and Paul were listening to 'Everyone's Gone to the Moon' when they saw the Ford Zephyr cruising down the street. It couldn't have been the first one, because Graham had been missing since morning, but it was the first one they saw. Paul pointed and started whistling the *Z Cars* theme music. Police cars weren't a novelty on the estate, but they were still rare enough visitors in those days to be noticed. The car stopped at number 58, Graham's house, and two uniformed officers got out and knocked on the door.

Banks remembered watching as Mrs Marshall opened the door, thin cardie wrapped around her, despite the warmth of day, and the two policemen took off their hats and followed her into the house. After that, nothing was ever quite the same on the estate.

Back in the twenty-first century, Banks opened his eyes and rubbed them. The memory had made him even more tired. He'd had a devil of a time getting to Athens the other day, and when he had got there it was only to find that he couldn't get a flight home until the following morning. He'd had to spend the night in a cheap hotel, and he hadn't slept well surrounded by the noise and bustle of a big city, after the peace and quiet of his island retreat.

Now the plane was flying up the Adriatic, between Italy and the former Yugoslavia. Banks was sitting on the left and the sky was so cloudless he fancied he could see all of Italy stretched out below him, greens and blues and earth colours, from the Adriatic to the Mediterranean: mountains, the crater of a volcano, vineyards, the cluster of a village and sprawl of a large city. Soon he would be landing back in Manchester, and soon the quest would begin in earnest. Graham Marshall's bones had been found, and Banks damn well wanted to know how and why they had ended up where they did.

•

Annie turned off the B road between Fortford and Relton onto the gravel drive of Swainsdale Hall. Elm, sycamore and ash dotted the landscape and obscured the view of the hall itself until the last curve, when it was revealed in all its splendour. Built of local limestone and millstone grit in the seventeenth century, the hall was a long, two-storey symmetrical stone building with a central chimneystack and stone-mullioned windows. The Dale's leading family, the Blackwoods, had lived there until they had died out in the way many old aristocratic families had died out: lack of money and no suitable heirs. Though Martin Armitage had bought the place for a song, so the stories went, the cost of upkeep was crippling, and Annie could see as she approached that parts of the flagstone roof were in a state of disrepair.

Annie parked in front of the hall and glanced through the slanting rain over the Dale. It was a magnificent view. Beyond the low hump of the earthworks in the lower field, an ancient Celtic defence against the invading Romans, she could see the entire green valley spread out before her, from the meandering River Swain all the way up the opposite side to the grey limestone scars, which seemed to grin like a skeleton's teeth. The dark, stubby ruins of Devraulx Abbey were visible about halfway up the opposite daleside, as was the village of Lyndgarth with its square church tower and smoke rising from chimneys over roofs darkened by the rain.

A dog barked inside the house as Annie approached the door. More of a cat person herself, she hated the way dogs rushed up when visitors arrived and barked and jumped at you, slobbered and sniffed your crotch, created chaos in the hall while the apologetic owner tried to control the animal's enthusiasm and explain how it really was just very friendly.

This time was no exception. However, the young woman who opened the door got a firm grip on the dog's collar before it could drool on Annie's skirt, and another woman appeared behind her. 'Miata!' she called out. 'Behave! Josie, would you take Miata to the scullery, please?'

'Yes, Ma'am.' Josie disappeared, half-dragging the frustrated Dobermann along with her.

'I'm sorry,' the woman said. 'She gets so excited when we have visitors. She's only being friendly.'

'Miata. Nice name,' said Annie and introduced herself.

'Thank you.' The woman held out her hand. 'I'm Robin Armitage. Please come in.'

Annie followed Robin down the hall and through a door on the right. The room was enormous, reminiscent of an old banqueting hall, with antique furniture scattered around a beautiful central Persian rug, a grand piano, and a stone fireplace bigger than Annie's entire cottage. On the wall over the mantelpiece hung what looked to Annie's trained eye like a genuine Matisse.

The man, who had been staring out of the back window over a lawn the size of a golf course, turned when Annie entered. Like his wife, he looked as if he hadn't slept all night. He introduced himself as Martin Armitage and shook her hand. His grip was firm and brief.

Martin Armitage was over six feet tall, handsome in a rugged, athletic sort of way, with his hair shaved almost to his skull, the way many footballers wore it. He was slim, long-legged and fit, as befitted an ex-sportsman, and even his casual clothes, jeans and a loose hand-knitted sweater, looked as if they cost more than Annie's monthly salary. He glanced down at Annie's boots, and she wished she'd gone for something more conservative that morning. But how was she to know?

'Detective Superintendent Gristhorpe told me about Luke,' Annie said.

'Yes.' Robin Armitage tried to smile, but it came out like the twentieth take of a commercial shoot. 'Look, I'll have Josie bring us some tea. Or coffee, if you'd prefer it?'

'Tea would be fine, thanks,' said Annie, perching carefully on the edge of an antique armchair. One of the most civilized things about being a policewoman, she thought, especially working in plainclothes, was that the people you visited – witnesses, victims and villains alike – invariably offered you some sort of refreshment. Usually tea. It was as English as fish and chips. From what she had read, or seen on television, she couldn't imagine anything like it happening anywhere else in the world. But, for all she knew, perhaps the French offered wine when a gendarme came to call.

'I know how upsetting something like this can be,' Annie began, 'but in ninety-nine per cent of cases there's absolutely nothing to worry about.'

Robin raised a finely plucked eyebrow. 'Do you mean that? You're not just saying it to make us feel better?'

'It's true. You'd be surprised how many mispers we get – sorry, that's police talk for missing persons – and most of them turn up none the worse for wear.'

'*Most* of them?' echoed Martin Armitage.

'I'm just telling you that statistically he's likely—'

'*Statistically?* What kind of—'

'Martin! Calm down. She's only trying to help.' Robin turned to Annie. 'I'm sorry,' she said, 'but neither of us has had much sleep. Luke's never done anything like this before, and we really are quite frantic with worry. Nothing short of seeing Luke back here safe and sound will change that. Please, tell us where you think he is.'

'I wish I could answer that, I really do,' said Annie. She

took out her notebook. 'Can I just get some information from you?'

Martin Armitage ran his hand over his head, sighed and flopped down on the sofa again. 'Yes, of course,' he said. 'And I apologize. My nerves are a bit frazzled, that's all.' When he looked right at her, she could see the concern in his eyes and she could also see the steely gaze of a man who usually got what he wanted. Josie came in with tea, which she served on a silver tray. Annie felt a bit embarrassed, the way she always did around servants.

Martin Armitage's lip curled in a smile, as if he had noticed her discomfort. 'A bit pretentious, isn't it?' he said. 'I suppose you're wondering why a dyed-in-the-wool socialist like me employs a maid? It's not as if I don't know how to make a cup of tea. I grew up with six brothers in a West Yorkshire mining town so small nobody even noticed when Maggie Thatcher wiped it off the face of the earth. Bread and dripping for breakfast, if you were lucky. That sort of thing. Robin here grew up on a small farm in Devon.'

And how many millions of pounds ago was that? Annie wondered, but she wasn't here to discuss their lifestyle. 'It's none of my business,' she said. 'I should imagine you're both very busy; you can use the help.' She paused. 'Just as long as you don't expect me to stick my little finger in the air while I drink my tea.'

Martin managed a weak laugh. 'I always like to dunk digestive biscuits in mine.' Then he leaned forward and became serious again. 'But you're not going to make me feel better by distracting me. What can we do? Where do we look? Where do we begin?'

'We'll do the looking. That's what we're here for. When did you first start to believe something was wrong?'

Martin looked at his wife. 'When was it, love? After tea, early evening?'

Robin nodded. 'He's always home for tea. When he wasn't back by after seven o'clock and we hadn't heard from him, we started to get worried.'

'What did you do?'

'We tried to call him on his mobile,' Martin said.

'And what happened?'

'It was switched off.'

'Then what?'

'Well, about eight o'clock,' Robin said, 'Martin went looking for him.'

'Where did you look, Mr Armitage?'

'I just drove around Eastvale. A bit aimless, really. But I had to do something. Robin stayed at home in case he rang or turned up.'

'How long were you gone?'

'Not long. I was back, oh, around ten.'

Robin nodded in agreement.

'Do you have a recent photograph of Luke?' Annie asked. 'Something we can circulate.'

Robin went over to one of the low polished tables and picked up a package of prints. She thumbed through them and handed one to Annie. 'This was taken at Easter. We took Luke to Paris for the holidays. Will it do?' Annie looked at the photograph. It showed a tall, thin young man, dark hair curling around his ears and brow, who looked older than his fifteen years, even to the point of having the fluffy beginnings of a goatee. He was standing by a grave in an old cemetery looking moody and contemplative, but his face was out of the shadows, and close enough to the camera to be useful for identification purposes.

'He insisted on visiting the Père Lachaise cemetery,' Robin explained. 'That's where all the famous people are buried. Chopin. Balzac. Proust. Edith Piaf. Colette. Luke's standing by Jim Morrison's grave there. Have you heard of Jim Morrison?'

'I've heard of him,' said Annie, who remembered friends of her father's playing loud Doors records even years after Morrison's death. 'Light My Fire' and 'The End' in particular had lodged themselves somewhere in her memories of those days.

'It's funny,' said Robin, 'but most of the people making pilgrimages to that grave weren't even born when he was at the height of his popularity. Even I was just a little girl when the Doors were first big.'

That placed her in her early forties, Annie guessed, and still a striking figure. Robin Armitage's golden tresses hung over her narrow shoulders and shone every bit as much in real life as they did in her magazine adverts for shampoo. Despite signs of strain and worry, hardly a line marred her smooth, pale complexion. Though Robin was shorter than Annie had imagined, her figure looked as slender as it had been in all the posters Annie had ever seen of her, and those lips, which had so tantalizingly sucked the low-fat ice cream off the spoon in a famous television commercial some years ago, were still as full and pink. Even the beauty spot Annie had always imagined was fake was still there at the corner of her mouth, and close up it looked real.

Yes, Robin Armitage looked every bit as good as she had twenty years ago. Annie thought she ought to hate the woman on sight, but she couldn't. It wasn't just because of the missing boy, either, she told herself, but she sensed something very human, very vulnerable, behind the exquisitely packaged model's facade.

'This'll do fine,' said Annie, slipping the photograph into her briefcase. 'I'll get it circulated as soon as I get back. What was he wearing?'

'The usual,' said Robin. 'Black T-shirt and black jeans.'

'You say "the usual". Do you mean he always wears black?'

'It's a phase,' said Martin Armitage. 'Or at least that's what his mother tells me.'

'It is, Martin. You wait; he'll grow out of it. If we ever see him again.'

'Don't worry, Mrs Armitage. He'll turn up. In the meantime, I'd like more information about Luke himself, anything you know about his friends, interests or acquaintances that could help us work out where he may be. First of all, was everything all right between you? Had there been any arguments recently?'

'Not that I can think of,' Robin answered. 'I mean, nothing serious. Everything was fine between us. Luke had everything he wanted.'

'It's been my experience,' said Annie, 'that nobody ever has everything they want, even if someone who loves them very dearly thinks they have. Human needs are so various and so hard to define at times.'

'I didn't only mean material things,' said Robin. 'As a matter of fact, Luke isn't much interested in the things money can buy, except for electronic gadgets and books.' Her long-lashed blue eyes blurred with tears. 'I meant that he has all the love we can give him.'

'I don't doubt it,' said Annie. 'What I was thinking though, was, maybe there was something he wanted to do that you wouldn't let him?'

'Like what?' asked Robin.

'Something you didn't approve of. A pop concert he wanted to go to. Friends you didn't like him being with. That sort of thing.'

'Oh, I see what you mean. But I can't think of anything. Can you, darling?'

Martin Armitage shook his head. 'As parents go, I think we're pretty liberal,' he said. 'We realize kids grow up quickly these days. I grew up quickly myself. And Luke's a smart lad. I can't think of any films I wouldn't want him to see, except for pornography, of course. He's also a quiet, shy sort of boy, not much of a mixer. He keeps to himself.'

'He's very creative,' Robin added. 'He loves to read and he writes stories and poems. When we were in France it was all Rimbaud, Verlaine and Baudelaire.'

Annie had heard of some of those poets through her father, had even read some of them. She thought they were a little advanced for a fifteen-year-old boy, then she remembered that Rimbaud started writing poetry at fifteen and gave it up at nineteen.

'What about girlfriends?' Annie asked.

'He never mentioned anyone,' said Robin.

'He might be embarrassed to tell you,' Annie suggested.

'I'm sure we'd have known.'

Annie changed tack and made a note to look into Luke's love life, or lack of it, later, if necessary. 'I don't know how to put this any more diplomatically,' she said, 'but I understand you're not Luke's biological father, Mr Armitage?'

'True. He's my stepson. But I've always thought of him as my own son. Robin and I have been married ten years now. Luke has our family name.'

'Tell me about Luke's father, Mrs Armitage.'

Robin glanced over at her husband.

'It's all right, darling,' Martin Armitage said. 'It doesn't bother me if you talk about him, though I can't quite see the point of all this.'

Robin turned back to Annie. 'Actually, I'm surprised you don't know already, given the inordinate amount of interest the gutter press took in the whole affair at the time. It's Neil Byrd. I thought most people knew about Neil and me.'

'Oh, I know who he was and what happened. I just don't remember the details. He was a pop singer, wasn't he?'

'A pop singer? He'd have been disgusted to hear himself called that. He thought of himself more as a sort of modern troubadour, more of a poet than anything else.'

From singer-songwriter to footballer, Annie thought, the way Marilyn Monroe went from baseball player to playwright. There was clearly more to Robin Armitage than met the eye. 'Please excuse my ignorance and refresh my memory,' she said.

Robin glanced out of the window, where a large thrush had found a worm on the lawn, then sat down beside her husband. He took her hand as she spoke. 'You're probably thinking it seems like an odd combination,' she said. 'But Neil was the first man not to treat me like a complete moron because of my looks. It's difficult being . . . well, you know, looking like I did. Most men are either too scared to approach you or they think you must be an easy lay. With Neil, it was neither.'

'How long were you together?'

'About five years. Luke was only two when Neil walked out on us. Just like that. No warning. He said he needed his solitude and couldn't afford to be burdened with a family any longer. That's exactly the way he put it: *burdened*.'

'I'm sorry,' said Annie. 'What happened? What about your career?'

'I was twenty-five when we met, and I'd been modelling since I was fourteen. It was hard to get my figure back after Luke, of course, and I was never *quite* the same as before, but I still got work, mostly TV commercials, a small and very forgettable part in a slasher film, part fifteen of some series or other. But why do you need to know all this? It can't have anything to do with Luke's disappearance. Neil's been dead for twelve years.'

'I agree with my wife,' said Martin. 'As I said earlier, I can't see what relevance all this has.'

'I'm just trying to get as much background as I can,' Annie explained. 'You never know what might be important to missing persons, what might trigger them. Does Luke know who his father was?'

'Oh, yes. He doesn't remember Neil, of course, but I told him. I thought it important not to keep secrets from him.'

'How long has he known?'

'I told him when he was twelve.'

'And before that?'

'Martin is the only father he has known.'

So for seven years, Annie calculated, Luke had accepted Martin Armitage as his true father, then his mother had dropped the bombshell about Neil Byrd. 'How did he react to the news?' she asked.

'He was confused, naturally,' said Robin. 'And he asked a lot of questions. But other than that . . . I don't know. He didn't talk about it much afterwards.'

Annie made a couple of notes as she digested this. She thought there must be more to it than Robin let on, but perhaps not. Kids can be surprisingly resilient. And unexpectedly sensitive.

'Do you still have any contact with any of Neil Byrd's friends or relatives?' Annie asked.

'Good Lord, no. Neil's parents both died young – it was one of the things that haunted him – and I don't move in those sort of circles any more.'

'May I see Luke's room?'

'Of course.' Robin led Annie out into the hall, up a flight of worn stone stairs to the upper floor, where she turned to the left and opened the heavy oak door of the second room along.

Annie turned on the bedside light. It took her a few moments to register that the room was black except for the carpeted floor. It faced north, so it didn't get a lot of sun, and even with the bedside light on – there was no ceiling light – it looked gloomy. It was tidier than she had expected, though, and almost spartan in its contents.

Luke, or someone, had painted a solar system and stars on the ceiling. One wall was covered with posters of rock stars and, moving closer, Annie noted the names: Kurt Cobain, Nick Drake, Jeff Buckley, Ian Curtis, Jim Morrison. Most of them were at least vaguely familiar to her, but she thought Banks might know more about them than she did. No sports personalities, she noticed. On the opposite wall, written in silver spray-paint, were the words, 'Le Poëte se fait voyant par un long, immense et raisonné dérèglement de tous les sens.' The words rang a bell, but she couldn't quite place them, and her French wasn't good enough to provide her with a clear translation. 'Do you know what this means?' she asked.

'Sorry,' said Robin. 'I never was any good at French in school.'

Annie copied the words down in her notebook. An electric guitar stood propped against a small amplifier under the mullioned window, a computer sat on a desk, and next to the wardrobe was a mini stereo system and a stack of CDs. She opened the violin case on top of the dresser and saw that it did, indeed, contain a violin.

Annie flipped through the CDs. Most of the bands she'd never heard of, such as Incubus, System of a Down and Slipknot, but she recognized some oldies like Nirvana and REM. There was even some old Bob Dylan. Though Annie knew virtually nothing about the musical tastes of fifteen-year-old boys, she was certain they didn't usually include Bob Dylan.

There was nothing by Neil Byrd. Again, Annie wished Banks were here; he'd be able to read something into all this. The last CD she had bought consisted of chants by Tibetan monks, to help with her yoga and meditation.

Annie glanced at the contents of the bookcase: a lot of novels, including *Sons and Lovers*, *Catcher in the Rye* and *Le Grand Meaulnes*, alongside the more traditional adolescent fare of Philip Pullman and short-story collections by Ray Bradbury and H.P. Lovecraft, a number of poetry anthologies, an oversized book on Pre-Raphaelite art, and that was about it.

Other than that, the room revealed remarkably little. There was no address book, at least none that Annie could find, and not very much of anything except the books, clothes and CDs. Robin told her that Luke carried a battered leather shoulder bag around with him, wouldn't go anywhere without it, and anything important to him would be in there, including his ultra-light laptop.

Annie did find some printed manuscripts in a drawer, short stories and poems, the most recent of which was dated a year ago, and she asked if she could borrow them to look at later. She could tell that Robin wasn't keen, mostly, it seemed, for the sake of Luke's precious privacy, but again a little prodding in the right direction worked wonders. She didn't think the creative work would tell her much, anyway, but it might give her some insight into Luke's character.

There was nothing more to be gained from staying up there and the black walls were beginning to oppress her, so she told Robin she had finished. They went back downstairs, where Martin Armitage was still sitting on the sofa.

'I understand you sent Luke to Eastvale Comprehensive instead of a public school, like Braughtmore,' Annie said.

'We don't believe in public schools,' said Martin, his West Yorkshire accent getting thicker as he spoke. 'They're just breeding grounds for effete civil servants. There's nothing wrong with a comprehensive school education.' Then he paused and smiled. Annie got the impression it was a gesture that had worked for him often with the media, the sudden flow of charm turned on like an electric current. 'Well, maybe there's a lot wrong with it – at least that's what I keep hearing – but it was good enough for me, and it's good enough for most kids. Luke's intelligent and hard working. He'll do fine.'

Judging from her body language – the folded arms and lips pressed together – Annie surmised that Robin didn't agree, that Luke's education had been a matter of some heated discussion.

'Is he happy at school?' she asked.

'He's never complained,' said Martin. 'No more than

any kid would. You know, he doesn't like his geography teacher, doesn't like games, and algebra's too hard. That sort of thing.'

'He's not a sports fan?'

'Unfortunately, no,' said Martin. 'I've tried to get him interested, but . . .' He shrugged.

'What about the other boys at school? Even if he is, as you say, a bit of a loner, he must have *some* contact with his classmates?'

'I suppose so, but I've never seen any evidence of it.'

'He's never brought friends to the house?'

'Never.'

'Or asked permission to visit their houses.'

'No.'

'Does he go out a lot?'

'No more than any other boy his age,' said Martin. 'Maybe even less.'

'We want Luke to have a normal life,' said Robin. 'It's hard knowing what to allow and what not to. It's hard to know how much discipline to apply. If you don't give enough, then the child runs wild, and the parents get the blame. If you keep too strict control, he doesn't develop naturally and he blames you for screwing him up. We do our best to be good parents and strike a fair balance.'

Annie, an outsider herself at school because she was brought up in an artists' commune, the 'hippie chick' to the other kids, understood just how alienated Luke might feel, not through any fault of his parents. For a start, they lived in an out-of-the-way place like Swainsdale Hall, a grand place at that; secondly, they were minor celebrities; and thirdly, he sounded like an introverted personality anyway.

'I'm sure you do,' she said. 'What did he do yesterday?'

'He went into the town centre.'

'How did he get there?'

'Bus. There's a good service, at least until after teatime.'

'Did he have any particular reason to go to Eastvale yesterday?'

'Nothing in particular,' Robin answered. 'He just loves hunting for second-hand books, and he wanted to look at some new computer stuff.'

'That's all?'

'As far as I know. It was nothing out of the ordinary.'

'Has he ever stopped out all night before?'

'No,' said Robin, putting her hand to her throat. 'Never. That's why we're so worried. He wouldn't put us through this unless something . . . something awful's happened.'

She started to cry, and her husband held her, smoothing her silky, spun-gold hair. 'There, there, darling. Don't worry. They'll find him.' All the time his intense eyes were looking right at Annie, as if daring her to disagree. Not that she wanted to. A man used to having his own way. A man of action, too, Annie had no doubt, used to running ahead with the ball and slamming it into the back of the net.

'What about the rest of the family: uncles, aunts, grandparents?' she asked. 'Was he close to anybody in particular?'

'Robin's family's down in Devon,' said Martin. 'My parents are dead, but I've got a married sister living in Dorset and a brother in Cardiff. Of course, we rang everyone we could think of, but nobody's seen him.'

'Did he have any money with him?'

'Not much. A few pounds. Look, Inspector,' he said, 'I do appreciate your questions, but you're on the wrong track. Luke has his mobile. If he wanted to go somewhere or do something that meant he wouldn't be coming home, or that he'd be late, then why wouldn't he give us a buzz?'

'Unless it was something he didn't want you to know about.'

'But he's only *fifteen*,' said Martin. 'What on earth could he be up to that's so secret he wouldn't want his parents to know about it?'

Do you know where your children are? Do you know what your children are doing? It was Annie's experience, both through her own memories and as a policewoman, that there was *no one* more secretive than an adolescent, especially a sensitive, lonely adolescent, but Luke's parents just didn't seem to get this. Hadn't they been through it themselves? Or had so much else happened since their own childhoods that they had forgotten what it was like?

There were any number of reasons why Luke might have thought it necessary to go off for a while without telling his parents – children are often selfish and inconsiderate – but they couldn't seem to think of one. Still, it wasn't the first time Annie had come across such an astonishing gap between parental perception and reality. More often than she would have expected, she had found herself facing the parents of missing children who said they had simply no idea where young Sally could have gone or why she would want to go off anywhere and cause them such pain.

'Have there ever been any threats against you?' she asked.

'No,' said Martin. 'Why do you ask?'

'Celebrities often attract the wrong sort of attention.'

Martin snorted. 'We're hardly Beckham and Posh

Spice. We're not much in the public eye these days. Not for the past five years or so, since we moved here. We both keep a very low profile.'

'Did it cross your mind that someone might have thought Luke was worth kidnapping?' she asked.

'Despite what you think,' Martin said, 'we're actually not all that wealthy.' He gestured around. 'The house, for a start . . . it just eats up money. We'd be very poor marks for a kidnapper, believe me.'

'The kidnapper might not know that.'

Robin and Martin looked at one another. Finally Robin spoke. 'No, I don't think so. As I said, we always wanted Luke to have a normal life, not like mine. We didn't want him surrounded by bodyguards and security. Maybe it was foolish of us, unrealistic, but it's worked until now. Nothing bad ever happened to him.'

'And I'm sure nothing has now,' said Annie. 'Look, I realize it's probably second nature to you, but if anyone from the press comes around asking questions—'

'Don't worry,' said Martin Armitage. 'They'll have me to deal with.'

'Very good, sir. And just to be on the safe side, do you think we could arrange to have any phone calls intercepted?'

'But why?' asked Robin.

'In case of ransom demands.'

She put her hand to her cheek. 'But surely you don't think—'

'It's just a precaution.'

'It's an unlisted number,' Martin said.

'Even so.'

He held Annie's gaze for a few beats before nodding. 'Very well. If you must.'

'Thank you, sir. I'll arrange for the technician to drop by later this morning. Do you have a business office?'

'No,' said Martin. 'Not at the moment.'

'You don't have a business number?'

'No.' He paused, then went on as if he'd sensed an implied slight in Annie's tone or manner. 'Look, I might have been just a football player, but that doesn't mean I'm thick, you know.'

'I didn't—'

'I got my A levels, went to Leeds Polytechnic, as it was back then, and got a business diploma.'

So what did that make him? Annie wondered, unimpressed: the 'thinking woman's crumpet'? 'I didn't mean to imply anything,' she went on. 'I'm simply trying to make sure we've got every eventuality covered.'

'I'm sorry,' Martin said. 'It's been a stressful night. It's just, well, being who we are, Robin and I get that sort of thing a lot. People tend to patronize us.'

'I understand,' said Annie, standing up to leave. 'I won't keep you any longer.' She passed her card over to Robin, who was closer. 'My mobile number's on there, too.' She smiled and added, 'When you can reach it.' Cell-phone coverage was spotty in the Dales, to say the least. 'If you do hear anything at all, you won't hesitate to call me, will you?'

'No,' said Robin. 'Of course not. And if—'

'You'll be the first to hear. Don't worry, we'll be looking for him, I can assure you. We're really very good at this sort of thing.'

'If there's anything I can do—' said Martin.

'Of course.' Annie gave them her best, most confident smile and left, not feeling confident at all.

3

DI Michelle Hart locked up her dark grey Peugeot outside 58 Hazel Crescent and took measure of the neighbourhood. She'd been there twice before: once investigating a string of burglaries and another time because of vandalism. As council estates went these days, the Hazels, as the locals called it, wasn't particularly bad. Built in the early sixties before the 'new town' expansion, its terraces of serviceable brick houses behind low walls and privet hedges were now home to a mixed crowd of unemployed people, teenage mothers, pensioners who couldn't afford to move, and a growing Asian population, mostly from Pakistan or Bangladesh. There were even a few asylum seekers. Like every other estate, the Hazels also had its share of shiftless hooligans who took their greatest pleasure in vandalizing other people's property, stealing cars and spraying graffiti over the walls.

It was still raining, and there was no sign of any gaps in the grey cloud cover. The drab street that curved through the heart of the estate was empty, all the kids indoors playing computer games or surfing the web and their mothers wishing the sun would come out and bring a few moments' peace and quiet.

Michelle knocked on the dark green door. Mrs Marshall, a frail-looking woman, stooped and grey-haired, face lined with care, answered and led her into a small living room and bade her sit on a plum velour armchair.

Michelle had met the Marshalls before, during the identification process, but hadn't yet visited them at home. Everything in the room was so tidy and spotless that she felt a momentary twinge of guilt over her own unwashed breakfast dishes, unmade bed and the dust balls in the corner. Still, who was there to see them but her?

Bill Marshall, incapacitated by a stroke, looked at Michelle, blanket over his knees, walking stick by his side, slack-jawed, a little drool collecting at the corner of his mouth, one half of his face drooping lower than the other, as if it had melted like a Dalí watch. He had been a big man, that much was obvious, but now his body had withered with disease. His eyes were alive, though, the whites a little cloudy, but the grey irises intense and watchful. Michelle said hello to him and thought she saw his head move just a fraction in greeting. Though he couldn't speak, Mrs Marshall had assured Michelle that he could understand everything they said.

Among the framed photographs on the mantelpiece above the electric fire was one of a young boy, aged about thirteen or fourteen, hair in a 'Beatle' cut popular in the early sixties, wearing a black polo neck, standing on a promenade with the sea in the background and a long pier off to one side. He was a good-looking kid, Michelle noticed, perhaps a little feminine, soft and delicate in his features, but he'd probably have grown up to be a real heartbreaker, nonetheless.

Mrs Marshall noticed her looking. 'Yes, that's our Graham. It was taken on the last holiday he had. We couldn't go away that year – Bill had a big job to finish – so the Bankses took him to Blackpool with them. Their lad Alan was a good mate of his. Mr Banks took that photo and gave it to us when they came back.' She paused. 'No more than a week or so later and Graham was gone for ever.'

'He looks like a fine boy,' Michelle said.

Mrs Marshall nodded and sniffed.

'I don't want to bother you for long,' Michelle began, 'but, as you can imagine, finding your son after all this time has come as a bit of a shock to us, too. I need to ask a few more questions, if that's all right?'

'You've got your job to do, love. Don't worry about us. We did our mourning years ago. Most of it, anyhow.' She fingered the collar of her dress. 'Funny, though, how it all just seems like it happened only yesterday, now you've found him.'

'I haven't seen the reports yet, but I understand there was a full investigation in 1965, when Graham first disappeared?'

'Oh, yes. And I can't fault them. They did their best. Searched high and low. Jet Harris himself was in charge, you know. At his wits' end he was when all their efforts turned up nothing. He even came to search our house for clues himself.'

Detective Superintendent John Harris – nicknamed Jet after both his speed and his resemblance to the Shadows' bass guitarist – was still a legend around divisional headquarters. Even Michelle had read the small biographical pamphlet published by one of the local bobbies with a literary bent, and she had been impressed by it, from his lowly birth in the Glasgow slums in 1920, to his Distinguished Conduct Medal with the Royal Marines Commandos in the Second World War, his rise through the ranks to detective chief superintendent, and his legendary retirement party in 1985. His framed photograph hung on the wall near the front entrance, and his hallowed name was mentioned only with suitably hushed awe. Michelle could imagine how his failure to solve the Graham Marshall case must have galled him. Harris had a reputation not only for closing cases quickly, but for hanging on and not letting go until he got a conviction. Since his death from cancer eight years ago, he had become even more revered. 'It'll have been done properly, then,' she said. 'I don't know what to say. Sometimes one just slips through the cracks.'

'Don't apologize, love. I've got no complaints. They turned over every stone they could find, but who'd think to dig there, eight miles away? I mean, they could hardly dig up the whole county, could they?'

'I suppose not,' Michelle agreed.

'And there were those missing kids out Manchester way,' Mrs Marshall went on. 'What they later called the Moors Murders. It wasn't until a couple of months after our Graham disappeared, though, that Brady and Hindley got caught, and then it was all over the news, of course.'

Michelle knew about Ian Brady and Myra Hindley, the Moors Murderers, even though she had been only a child at the time. As with Jack the Ripper, Reginald Christie and the Yorkshire Ripper, the horror of their acts was etched into the consciousness of future generations. She hadn't realized, though, just how closely their crimes were linked chronologically with Graham Marshall's disappearance. It might have been natural for Detective Superintendent Harris at least to assume that Graham's disappearance could somehow be linked with the victims of Brady and Hindley. On the other hand, Peterborough was over a hundred and thirty miles from Manchester, and Brady and Hindley tended to stick to their own neck of the woods.

Before Michelle could formulate her next question,

another woman walked into the room. She bore a strong facial resemblance to the boy in the photograph – the same small, straight nose, oval chin and well-defined cheekbones – only the feminine aspects were even more enhanced in her. She wore her grey-streaked hair long, tied in a pony-tail, and was casually dressed in a dark blue T-shirt and jeans. She was a little too thin for comfort, or perhaps Michelle was jealous, always feeling herself to be five or ten pounds overweight, and the stress of recent events showed in her features, as it did in Mrs Marshall's.

'This is Joan, my daughter,' Mrs Marshall said.

Michelle stood and shook Joan's limp hand.

'She lives in Folkestone, teaches at a comprehensive school there,' Mrs Marshall added with obvious pride. 'She was going on her holidays, but when she heard . . . well, she wanted to be with us.'

'I understand,' said Michelle. 'Were you and Graham close, Joan?'

'As close as any brother and sister with two years between them can be in their teens,' said Joan, with a rueful smile. She sat on the floor in front of the television and crossed her legs. 'Actually, I'm not being fair. Graham wasn't like most other boys his age. He even bought me presents. He didn't tease me or torment me. If anything, he was very protective.'

'From what?'

'Sorry?'

'What did he have to protect you from?'

'Oh, I didn't mean anything in particular. You know, just in general. If anyone tried to bully me or anything like that.'

'Boys?'

'Well, I was only twelve when he disappeared, but yes,

there were a couple of over-amorous local lads he sent packing.'

'Was Graham a tough lad?'

'Not really,' said Mrs Marshall. 'Mind you, he never backed away from a fight. When we moved and he first went to school here, there was a bit of bullying – you know, the way they always like to test the new kid – but in his first week our Graham took on the school bully. He didn't win, but he put up a good fight, blacked an eye and bloodied a nose, so nobody bothered him after that.'

Michelle was wondering how difficult it would be for someone to abduct and murder Graham Marshall if he could put up a good fight. Might it have taken two people? Might he have been drugged or knocked unconscious first? Or was it someone he knew and went with willingly?

'You said you moved up here?' Michelle went on. 'Would that be from the East End?'

'It still shows, does it, after all these years? Once a cockney, always a cockney, I suppose. Not that I'm ashamed of it. Yes, we came from Bethnal Green. We moved around a fair bit because of Bill's work. He's a bricklayer. Or he was. We'd only been here a year or so when it happened. Graham had just finished third form at the local grammar school.'

'But you stayed on after.'

'Yes. There was plenty of work, what with the new town business. Plenty of building. And we like it here. It suits us.'

'Mrs Marshall,' said Michelle, 'I know it's a long time ago, but can you tell me what sort of things Graham was interested in?'

'Interested in? Oh, the usual boys' stuff. Football. Cricket. And pop music. He was pop music crazy. We've still got his old guitar upstairs. Practised chords for hours, he did. Mind you, he read a lot too. Graham was the sort of lad who could amuse himself. He didn't always need someone to entertain him. Loved to read about space. You know, science fiction, rockets to Mars, green-eyed monsters. Space mad, he was.' She looked at the photograph and a faraway expression came over her features. 'Just the day before he . . . well, there was some sort of rocket launch in America, and he was so excited, watching it on telly.'

'Did he have many friends?'

'He made quite a few around here,' Joan answered. She looked at her mother. 'Who was there, Mum?'

'Let me remember. There was the Banks lad, of course, they were very close, and David Grenfell and Paul Major. And Steven Hill. Some others, maybe, but those five all lived on the estate, so they'd walk to school together, play cricket or football on the rec, listen to music together, swap records. That sort of thing. Some of their parents still live here. Those who are still left alive, that is.'

'Was Graham a popular boy?'

'I'd say so, yes,' said Mrs Marshall. 'He had an easy-going nature. I can't see how he could possibly have offended anyone. I'm not saying he was perfect, mind you. He was a normal teenage lad and he had his fair share of high spirits.'

'Was he a bright lad?'

'He did well at school, didn't he, Mum?' said Joan.

'Yes. He'd have got to university easily, just like his sister.'

'What did he want to be when he grew up?'

'An astronaut or a pop star, but I'm sure he would have changed his mind about that. He was good at physics and chemistry. He'd probably have made a good teacher.' She paused. 'What's going to happen now, if you don't mind me asking, Miss Hart? I mean, it was all so long ago. Surely you don't think you can catch whoever did this? Not after all this time.'

'I don't know,' said Michelle. 'I certainly wouldn't want to make any rash promises. But when something like this happens, we do our best to go over the ground again and see if we can find something someone missed the first time around. A fresh pair of eyes. It works sometimes. But if I'm to be completely honest with you, I'd have to say we'll not be giving the case full priority in terms of manpower.'

'Believe me, love, there's plenty of crime going on around here now without you police spending your time digging up the past as well.' She paused. 'It's just that . . . well, I think I *would* like to know, even after all this time. I thought about it a lot the other day, when they came back with the DNA results and said it definitely was our Graham. I thought I'd got resigned that we'd never know, but now, well, I'm not so sure. I mean, if you can just find out what happened to him, and why . . .' She looked at her husband. 'I know he'd like his mind set at ease before . . . well, I'm sure you know what I mean.'

Michelle packed away her notebook in her briefcase. 'Yes, I think I know what you mean,' she said. 'And I promise I'll do my best.'

'There is one question I'd like to ask,' said Mrs Marshall.

'Yes?'

'Well, you know, the way things happened, we never . . . I mean, our Graham never had a proper funeral. Do you think we could do that? You know, the bones . . .'

Michelle thought for a moment. 'We might need them

for a few days longer,' she said, 'for tests and such like. But I don't see why not. Look, I'll talk to the forensic anthropologist. I'm sure she'll do her best to release the remains as soon as possible.'

'You do? Really? Oh, thank you so very much, Miss Hart. You don't know how much it means to us. Do you have any children of your own?'

Michelle felt herself tense up, the way she always did when people asked her that. Finally, she got the words out. 'No. No, I don't.'

Mrs Marshall saw her to the door. 'If there's anything more I can tell you,' she said, 'please don't hesitate to ask.'

'I won't,' said Michelle. 'Thank you.' And she walked down the path in the rain to her car taking deep breaths, shaken, flooded with memories she'd been blocking out, memories of Melissa and of Ted. Now Graham Marshall was more to her than just a pile of bones on a steel table; he was a bright, easy-going lad with a Beatle haircut who wanted to be an astronaut or a pop star. If only she could figure out where to begin.

•

Banks met Annie at the Woolpack, a quiet pub in the tiny village of Maltham, about halfway between Gratly and Harksmere. On his way home from Manchester airport, he had debated whether to call her and he decided in the end it would be a good idea. He wanted to talk to someone about what he had just learned, and Annie was the only person he had told about the incident with the pervert down by the river. It shocked him to realize that he hadn't even told his ex-wife Sandra, though they had been married for over twenty years.

It was drizzling when he pulled up in the market square car park shortly before nine o'clock. Annie's purple Astra was nowhere in sight. He obeyed the sign and stepped on the disinfectant pad before entering the pub. Though there hadn't been an outbreak near Maltham itself, incidences of foot-and-mouth disease had occurred in some of the surrounding areas, and as a consequence strict, sometimes unpopular, measures had been brought in by the Ministry. Many footpaths had been closed and access to the countryside limited. Also, as local farmers used the village pubs and shops, many of the owners had placed disinfectant mats on their doorsteps.

Maltham itself wasn't much of a place, though it did have a fine Norman church, and the Woolpack was one of those pubs that did good business mostly by virtue of its being on a busy road between tourist destinations. That meant most of the trade was transient and during the day, so the few grizzled locals who stood around the bar turned as one and gawped when Banks entered. They did that every time. One of them must have recognized him and said something, because in no time at all they turned back to their pints and ignored him. Banks bought a pint of Black Sheep bitter and a packet of cheese and onion crisps and sat down near the door, as far from the bar as he could get. A couple of the other tables were taken, tourists renting local cottages, by the looks of them. Poor sods, they'd be going out of their minds with no footpaths to walk.

Christ, it was a long way from Greece, Banks thought. Hard to believe that at this time just two nights ago he had been drinking ouzo and nibbling dolmades with Alex in Philippe's taverna. They had drunk well into the small hours, knowing it was to be their last evening together, telling stories and soaking up the scented warmth of the air and the rhythm of the sea lapping at the quayside beside them. In the morning, Banks had looked for Alex by the harbour to say goodbye as he caught the early ferry to Piraeus, but his friend was nowhere to be seen. Probably nursing his hangover, Banks had thought, aware of the pounding in his own head.

The door opened, the men gawped again – with a bit more interest this time – and Annie entered in tight jeans and a light blue sleeveless top, bag slung over her shoulder. She pecked Banks on the cheek and sat down. Smelling her delicate grapefruit-scented shampoo and soap, and aware of the vague outlines of her nipples under the thin cotton, Banks felt a momentary rush of desire for her, but he held himself in check. That part of their relationship was over; they had moved on to something different. Instead, he went back to the bar and bought her a pint.

'Look at that tan,' Annie said when he sat down again, her laugh lines crinkling. 'It's all right for some.'

'I'm sure you'll manage a week in Blackpool before summer's over,' said Banks.

'Dancing to the Wurlitzer in the Tower Ballroom? Donkey rides on the beach in the rain? Candyfloss on the prom and a kiss-me-quick hat? I can hardly wait.' She leaned over and patted his arm. 'It is good to see you again, Alan.'

'You, too.'

'So come on, then. Tell. How was Greece?'

'Magnificent. Magical. Paradisiacal.'

'Then what the bloody hell are you doing back in Yorkshire? You were hardly forthcoming on the phone.'

'Years of practice.'

Annie leaned back in her chair and stretched out her legs the way she did, crossing them at the slender ankles, where the thin gold chain hung, sipped some beer and almost purred. Banks had never met anyone else who could look so comfortable and at home in a hard chair.

'Anyway,' she said, 'you're looking well. Less stressed. Even half a holiday seems to have had some effect.'

Banks considered for a moment and decided that he did feel much better than he had when he left. 'It helped put things in perspective,' he said. 'And you?'

'Swimmingly. Thriving. The job's going well. I'm getting back into yoga and meditation. And I've been doing some painting again.'

'I kept you away from all that?'

Annie laughed. 'Well, it's not as if you twisted my arm, but when you've got as little time as people in our line of work have, then something has to go by the wayside.'

Banks was about to make a sarcastic reference to that something being him this time, but he bit his tongue. He wouldn't have done that two weeks ago. The holiday really must have done him good. 'Well,' he said, 'I'm glad you're happy. I mean it, Annie.'

Annie touched his hand. 'I know you do. Now what brings you back here in such a hurry? I hope it's not serious.'

'It is in a way.' Banks lit a cigarette and went on to explain about the discovery of Graham Marshall's bones.

Annie listened, frowning. When Banks had finished, she said, 'I can understand why you're concerned, but what can you do?'

'I don't know,' Banks said. 'Maybe nothing. If I were the local police, I wouldn't want me sticking my nose in, but when I heard, I just felt . . . I don't know. It was a big part of my adolescence, Annie, Graham just disappearing like that, and I suppose it's a big part of me now, always has been. I can't explain, but there it is. I told you about the man by the river, the one who tried to push me in?'

'Yes.'

'If it was him, then maybe I can help them find him, if he's still alive. I can remember what he looked like. Odds are there could be a photo on file.'

'And if it wasn't him? Is that it? Is this the guilt you talked about before?'

'Partly,' said Banks. 'I *should* have spoken up. But it's more than that. Even if it's nothing to do with the man by the river, *someone* killed Graham and buried his body. Maybe I can remember something, maybe there was something I missed at the time, being just a kid myself. If I can cast my mind back . . . Another?'

Annie looked at her glass. Half full. And she was driving. 'No,' she said. 'Not for me.'

'Don't worry,' said Banks, catching her anxious glance as he went to the bar. 'This'll be my last for the evening.'

'So when are you going down there?' Annie asked when he came back.

'First thing tomorrow morning.'

'And you're going to do what, exactly? Present yourself at the local nick and offer to help them solve their case?'

'Something like that. I haven't thought it out yet. It'll hardly be high priority with the locals. Anyway, surely they'll be interested in someone who was around at the time? They interviewed me back then, you know. I remember it clearly.'

'Well, you said yourself they won't exactly welcome you with open arms, not if you go as a copper trying to tell them how to do their jobs.'

'I'll practise humility.'

Annie laughed. 'You'd better be careful,' she said. 'They might have you down as a suspect.'

'It wouldn't surprise me.'

'Anyway, it's a pity you're not sticking around. We might be able to use your help up here.'

'Oh? What's on?'

'Missing kid.'

'Another?'

'This one disappeared a bit more recently than your friend Graham.'

'Boy or girl?'

'Does it matter?'

'You know it does, Annie. Far more girls are abducted, raped and killed than boys.'

'A boy.'

'How old?'

'Fifteen.'

That was almost Graham's age when he disappeared, Banks thought. 'Then the odds are good he'll turn up none the worse for wear,' he said, though Graham hadn't.

'That's what I told the parents.'

Banks sipped his beer. There were some compensations to being back in Yorkshire, he thought, looking around the quiet, cosy pub, hearing the rain patter on the windows, tasting the Black Sheep and watching Annie shift in her chair as she tried to phrase her concerns.

'He's an odd kid,' she said. 'Bit of a loner. Writes poetry. Doesn't like sports. His room is painted black.'

'What were the circumstances?'

Annie told him. 'And there's another thing.'

'What?'

'He's Luke Armitage.'

'Robin's boy? Neil Byrd's son?'

'Martin Armitage's stepson. Do you know him?'

'Martin Armitage? Hardly. Saw him play once or twice, though. I must say I thought he was overrated. But I've got a couple of CDs by Neil Byrd. They did a compilation three or four years ago, and they've just brought out a collection of out-takes and live performances. He really *was* very good, you know. Did you meet the supermodel?'

'Robin? Yes.'

'Quite the looker, as I remember.'

'Still is,' said Annie, scowling. 'If you like that sort of thing.'

'What sort of thing?'

'Oh, you know . . . skinny, flawless, beautiful.'

Banks grinned. 'So what's the problem?'

'Oh, nothing. It's just me. He'll probably turn up safe and sound.'

'But you're worried?'

'Just a teeny bit.'

'Kidnapping?'

'It crossed my mind, but there's been no ransom demand yet. We searched the house, of course, just in case, but there was no sign he'd been back home.'

'We did talk to the Armitages about security when they first moved to Swainsdale Hall, you know,' Banks said. 'They installed the usual burglar alarms and such, but beyond that they said they just wanted to live a normal life. Nothing much we could do.'

'I suppose not,' Annie agreed. She brought out her notebook and showed Banks the French words she had copied down from Luke's wall. 'Make any sense of this? It's awfully familiar, but I can't put my finger on it.'

Banks frowned as he peered at the text. It looked familiar to him, too, but he couldn't place it, either. 'Le Poëte se fait voyant par un long, immense et raisonné dérèglement de tous les sens.' He tried to decipher it word by word, reaching far back into his memory for his grammar-school French. Hard to believe now that he had been quite good at it at one time, even got a grade two in his O levels. Then he remembered. 'It's Rimbaud, I think. The French poet. Something about the total disordering of all the senses.'

'Of course!' said Annie. 'I could kick myself. Robin Armitage told me Luke was into Rimbaud, Baudelaire and Verlaine and all that stuff. What about these?' She named the subjects of Luke's posters. 'I mean, I've heard of some of them, Nick Drake, for example, and I know Kurt Cobain was in Nirvana and killed himself, but what about the others?'

Banks frowned. 'They're all singers. Ian Curtis used to sing with Joy Division. Jeff Buckley was Tim Buckley's son.'

'Used to? Was? There's an ominous past tense to all this, isn't there?'

'Oh, yes,' said Banks. 'They all either committed suicide or died under mysterious circumstances.'

'Interesting.' Annie's mobile buzzed. Excusing herself, she walked over to the front door before taking it out of her shoulder bag and stepping outside. When she came back two minutes later she looked puzzled.

'Not bad news, I hope?' said Banks.

'No, not at all. Quite the opposite.'

'Do tell.'

'That was Robin. Robin Armitage. Apparently, Luke just rang them.'

'And?'

'He says he just needed some space, that he'll be back home tomorrow.'

'Did he say where he was?'

'Wouldn't tell them.'

'What are you going to do?'

Annie finished her drink. 'I think I'd better go down the station, scale down the manhunt. You know how expensive these things are. I don't want Red Ron on my back for wasting our time and money.'

'Scale down?'

'Yes. Call me overly suspicious, if you like, but I'm not going to call off the search completely until I see Luke Armitage, safe and sound at home, with my own eyes.'

'I wouldn't call that overly suspicious,' said Banks. 'I'd call it very sensible.'

Annie leaned forward and pecked Banks on the cheek again. 'It really is good to see you again, Alan. Stay in touch.'

'I will,' said Banks, and he watched her walk out the door, hint of Body Shop grapefruit soap wafting behind her, the soft pressure of her kiss lingering on his cheek.

4

On the surface, it had seemed a simple enough question to ask: where were the Graham Marshall case files? In reality, it was like searching for the Holy Grail, and it had taken Michelle and her DC, Nat Collins, the best part of two days.

After first trying Bridge Street, in the city centre, which served as Divisional Headquarters until Thorpe Wood opened in 1979, Michelle and DC Collins drove from station to station all across the Northern Division – Bretton, Orton, Werrington, Yaxley, Hampton – discovering that some of them were relatively new, and the premises used in 1965 long since demolished and covered over by new housing estates or shopping centres. What complicated matters even more was that the original forces – Cambridge, Peterborough, Ely and Huntingdon – had amalgamated into the Mid-Anglia Constabulary in 1965, necessitating a major overhaul and restructuring, and had become the present-day Cambridgeshire Constabulary in 1974.

As one helpful duty constable after another suggested possibilities, Michelle had begun to despair of ever finding the old paperwork. About the only bright spot on the horizon was that the weather had improved that morning, and the sun was poking its lazy way through greasy rags of cloud. But that made the air humid, and Michelle was about to throw in the towel around lunchtime. She'd drunk a bit too much wine the previous evening, too – something that was happening rather too often these days – and the fact that she didn't feel a hundred per cent didn't help much either.

When she finally did track the paperwork down, having sent DC Collins to Cambridge to make enquiries there, she could have kicked herself. It was deep in the bowels of Divisional Headquarters, not more than thirty feet or so below her office, and the civilian records clerk, Mrs Metcalfe, proved to be a mine of information and let her sign out a couple of files. Why hadn't Michelle thought to look there in the first place? Easy. She had only been at Thorpe Wood for a short time, and no one had given her the grand tour; she didn't know that the basement was the repository for much of the county force's old paperwork.

The noise level was high in the open-plan squad room, phones ringing, men laughing at dirty jokes, doors opening and closing, but Michelle was able to shut it all out as she put on her reading glasses and opened the first folder, which contained maps and photos of the Hazels estate, along with a summary of any relevant witness statements that helped to pin down Graham's progress on the morning of 22 August 1965.

One useful hand-drawn map showed Graham's paper round in detail, listing all the houses he delivered to and, for good measure, what newspapers they took. The poor lad must have had a hell of a heavy load, as many of the Sunday papers were bulky with magazines and supplements.

At the eastern end of the estate, Wilmer Road separated the Hazels from an area of older houses, soon to be demolished. It was at the T-junction between Wilmer and

Hazel Crescent that Graham had delivered his last news-paper, a *News of the World*, to Mr and Mrs Halloran, who lived in the corner house.

The next delivery was supposed to be to one of the houses across the road, but the Lintons there said they never received their *Observer* that day. Nobody else on the other side of Wilmer Road received a newspaper that morning, either.

The anonymous map-maker had also calculated that it would have been around six-thirty a.m. when Graham, who started at six a.m., got to that part of his round – daylight at that time of year, but still very early in the morning for any sort of traffic, including pedestrian. It was a Sunday, after all, the traditional morning for a lie-in after the excesses of Saturday night, and most of the customers said they were still in bed when their papers arrived.

Michelle looked at the old black-and-white photos. They depicted a very different scene from the one she had visited yesterday, after she had talked to the Marshalls. In 1965, across Wilmer Road, there had been a grim row of old shops, all boarded up and ready for demolition, but today a modern DIY centre stood next to the new estate which had replaced the old houses. The derelict shops looked like just the sort of place a kid might want to explore. Michelle checked the file to see if they had been searched. Of course they had. Dogs brought in, too. Not a trace.

Michelle tucked some strands of blonde hair, which had been tickling her cheek, behind her ears and chewed at the end of her pen as she read over transcripts of the initial interviews. Nearly everything was typed, of course, except some of the documents that were handwritten, and the results looked strange, with the uneven pressure of the keys and the occasional blob of a deformed 'e' or 'g'. Such distinguishing features used to be very handy for identifying which machine a note had been typed on, Michelle reflected, before the anonymity of laser printers. Some of the papers were carbon copies, faint and often hard to read. Occasionally, illegible amendments had been made in pen or pencil between the lines, the original words scratched out. All in all, not a promising start.

Detective Superintendent Benjamin Shaw, now one of the senior officers at Thorpe Wood, was named once or twice as a detective constable on the case. Michelle knew that Shaw had started his career in Peterborough and had recently returned from six years with the Lincolnshire Constabulary, but it still surprised her to see his name in connection with something that happened so long ago. Maybe she should have a word with him, see if he had any theories that hadn't made it into the files.

It seemed that the first person to miss Graham Marshall was his employer, Donald Bradford, owner of the newsagent's shop. Bradford lived some distance away from the shop and employed a local woman to open up, not arriving himself until eight o'clock. According to Bradford's statement, when Graham hadn't returned by eight-fifteen that Sunday, half an hour late for his second round on a neighbouring estate, Bradford drove around the Wilmer Road Estate in search of him. He found nothing. Whatever had happened to Graham, his papers and his canvas bag were missing too. Michelle was willing to bet that some of those scraps of cloth found with the bones came from Graham's newspaper sack.

After that, Donald Bradford called at Graham's house to see if the lad had become ill and hurried home without stopping to report in. He hadn't. Graham's parents, now also worried, searched the estate for their son and found nothing. With news of the Manchester child abductions still fresh in the public eye, both Bradford and the Marshalls were soon concerned enough to call in the police, and a short while after that the official investigation began. Preliminary enquiries were carried out in the immediate area, and Detective Superintendent Harris was put in charge first thing the following day, when still no trace had been found of Graham, and the cumbersome but efficient mechanics of a police investigation groaned into action.

Michelle stretched and tried to work out a crick in her neck without success. It was hot in the office and her tights were killing her. DC Collins, just back from Cambridge, took pity on her and said, 'I'm just off to the canteen, Ma'am. Bring you anything?'

'I'd love a Diet Coke, please,' said Michelle. 'And maybe a slice of chocolate gateau, if they've got any left.' She reached for her handbag.

'It's all right,' said Collins. 'Pay me when I get back.'

Michelle thanked him, adjusted her tights as discreetly as possible below her desk and turned back to the files. As far as she could gather from a cursory glance, there hadn't been any leads at all. Police had interviewed everyone on Graham's round, along with all his friends, family and schoolteachers. None of it led anywhere. Graham was described, among other things, as being bright, cheeky, quiet, polite, rude, sweet-natured, foul-mouthed, talented and secretive. Which pretty much covered every eventuality.

Nobody on Wilmer Road had seen or heard anything unusual that morning – no screams, shouts or sounds of a struggle – though one person said he had heard a car door bang around half-past six. There were no convenient dog-walkers, and even the most devout of church-goers, being for the most part Methodists or low Anglican, were still in the Land of Nod. All the evidence, especially the missing newspaper sack, suggested that Graham had most likely got into a car willingly, with someone he knew, someone local. But who? And why?

DC Collins returned with Michelle's Diet Coke. 'No gateau, I'm afraid,' he said, 'so I brought you a Danish instead.'

'Thanks,' said Michelle, who didn't like Danish but paid him anyway, nibbled at it for a while then dropped the rest in her waste bin and went back to her files. The Coke tin was cold and wet, so she pressed it against her flushed cheek and enjoyed the icy sensation, then she did the same with her other cheek and her forehead.

The police at the time didn't neglect the possibility that Graham might have run away under his own steam, dumping the sack of papers somewhere and heading for the bright lights of London like so many young lads had in the mid-sixties, but they could find nothing at all to support this theory. His home life seemed happy enough, and none of his friends suggested that he was at all interested in running away from home. The sack was never found, either. Even so, missing persons reports went out all over the country, and there were the usual sightings, none of which amounted to anything.

The interviews also turned up nothing, and police checks into the records of several estate dwellers drew a blank. Michelle could read a little excitement between the lines when police discovered that one of the deliveries on Graham's route was to the house of a man who had served time for exposing himself in a local park, but subsequent interviews – no doubt involving some very rough business, knowing police methods of the time and Jet Harris's reputation as a tough guy – led nowhere, and the man was exonerated.

Michelle slipped off her reading glasses and rubbed her tired eyes. At first glance, she had to admit that it seemed very much as if Graham Marshall had disappeared into the void. But she knew one thing that the police hadn't known in 1965. She had seen his bones, and she knew that Graham had been murdered.

•

Annie Cabbot drove out to Swainsdale Hall mid-morning to tie up a few loose ends with the Armitages. The sun had come to the Yorkshire Dales at last, and wraiths of mist rose from the roadsides and the fields that stretched up the dalesides. The grass was bright green after so much rain, and the limestone walls and buildings shone clean grey. The view from the front of Swainsdale Hall was magnificent, and Annie could see plenty of blue sky beyond Fremlington Edge, with only a few light fluffy clouds scudding by on the breeze.

The Armitages must be relieved, Annie thought as she got out of her car. Of course, they would be happier when Luke arrived back home, but at least they knew he was safe.

Josie answered the door and seemed surprised to see her. There was no sign of Miata this time, but Annie could hear the dog barking from the back of the house.

'Sorry I didn't phone ahead,' Annie said. 'Are they in?'

Josie stood aside and let Annie walk through to the same large living room she had been in yesterday. Only

Robin Armitage was there this time, sitting on the sofa and flipping through a copy of *Vogue*. She jumped to her feet when Annie entered and smoothed down her skirt. 'It's you again. What's happened? Is something wrong?'

'Calm down, Mrs Armitage,' said Annie. 'Nothing's happened. I came to see if you're all right.'

'All right? Of course I am. Why shouldn't I be? Luke's coming home.'

'May I sit down?'

'Please.'

Annie sat, but Robin Armitage stayed on her feet, pacing. 'I'd have thought you'd be relieved,' Annie said.

'I am,' said Robin. 'Of course I am. It's just that . . . well, I'll be a lot more settled when Luke's back home again. I'm sure you understand.'

'Have you heard from him again?'

'No. Only the once.'

'And he definitely said he's coming home today?'

'Yes.'

'I'd like to talk to him when he gets back, if that's all right.'

'Certainly. But why?'

'We like to follow up on these matters. Just routine.'

Robin stood up and folded her arms, making it clear that she wanted Annie to leave. 'I'll let you know the minute he's back.'

Annie remained seated. 'Mrs Armitage, you told me yesterday that Luke said he needed some space. Do you know why?'

'Why?'

'Yes. You told me he's a normal teenager, and there's nothing wrong in the family, so why would he run off like that, worry the two of you half to death?'

'I hardly think that's relevant now, do you, Detective Inspector Cabbot?' Annie turned to see Martin Armitage standing in the doorway, briefcase in hand. 'Why are you here? What is it?' Despite his commanding presence, he seemed edgy to Annie, like his wife, shifting his weight from foot to foot as he stood there, as if he had to go to the toilet.

'Nothing,' she said. 'Just a friendly visit.'

'I see. Well, thank you for your efforts and your concern. We really do appreciate it, but I can see no point in your coming and badgering us with more questions now that Luke's safe and sound, can you?'

Interesting choice of words, *badgering*, Annie thought. Most families wouldn't see it that way, not with their son missing.

He glanced at his watch. 'Anyway, I'm afraid I have to hurry off to a business meeting. It's been nice to see you again, Inspector, and thank you again.'

'Yes, thank you,' echoed Robin.

Dismissed. Annie knew when she was beaten. 'I was just leaving,' she said. 'I only wanted to make sure everything was okay. I didn't mean to cause offence.'

'Well, as you can see,' said Martin, 'everything's fine. Luke will be back home this evening, and it will be as if none of this ever happened.'

Annie smiled. 'Well, don't be *too* hard on him.'

Martin managed a tight smile, which didn't reach his eyes. 'I was young once, myself, Detective Inspector Cabbot. I know what it's like.'

'Oh, just one more thing.' Annie paused in the doorway.

'Yes?'

'You said Luke rang you last night.'

'Yes. And immediately afterwards my wife rang you.'

Annie glanced at Robin, then back at Martin. 'Yes, I appreciate that,' she said, 'but I'm wondering why Luke's call wasn't intercepted. After all, the technician had set everything up, and we picked up your wife's call to me.'

'That's easy,' said Martin. 'He called me on my mobile.'

'Did he usually do that?'

'We were supposed to be going out for dinner,' Martin explained. 'As it was, we ended up cancelling, but Luke wasn't to know that.'

'Ah, I see,' said Annie. 'Problem solved. Goodbye, then.'

They both bade her a perfunctory goodbye and she left. At the end of the drive, she turned right, towards Relton, and parked in a lay-by just around the corner from the Armitages' drive, where she took out her mobile and discovered that there was, indeed, a signal in the area. So Martin Armitage hadn't been lying about that. What was it, then, that had given her the unmistakable feeling that something was wrong?

Annie sat for a moment in her car trying to figure out the meaning of the tension she had sensed in the room, not just between her and Robin, but between Robin and Martin. Something was going on; Annie only wished she knew what. Neither Robin nor Martin had behaved like a couple who had just heard that the son whose life they feared for was now safe and would soon be home.

When Martin Armitage's Beemer shot out of the driveway spraying gravel a minute or two later, Annie had an idea. It was rare that she got to think or act spontaneously, as so much police work was governed by procedure, rules and regulations, but Annie was feeling reckless this morning, and the situation called for some initiative on her part.

As far as she knew, Martin Armitage had no idea what make or colour car she drove, so he would hardly be suspicious that a purple Astra was following him at a respectable distance.

•

As Banks drove down the A1 and entered the landscape of bright new shopping centres, electronics warehouses and housing estates that had replaced the old coal mines, pit wheels and slag heaps of West Yorkshire, he thought about the way the country had changed since Graham's disappearance.

1965. Winston Churchill's funeral. The Wilson era. The end of capital punishment. The Kray trial. Carnaby Street. The Moors Murders. The first US space walk. *Help!* Mods and rockers. It was a time of possibility, of hope for the future, the fulcrum of the sixties. Only weeks after Graham disappeared, the sexy, leather-clad Emma Peel debuted in *The Avengers*, Jeremy Sandford's documentary-style TV play about a homeless mother and her children, *Cathy Come Home*, caused a major stir, and the Who were singing about 'My Generation'. Soon, young people were taking to the streets to protest against war, famine and anything else they could think of, shouting 'Make love, not war,' smoking dope and dropping acid. Everything seemed on the verge of blossoming into some new sort of order, and Graham, who had seemed so forward-looking, so *cool* in so many ways, should have been there to see it, but he wasn't.

And what came between then and Blair's Britain? Mostly Margaret Thatcher, who dismantled the country's manufacturing base, emasculated the trades unions, and demoralized the working man, leaving the north, especially, a ghost land of empty factories, thrift shops and decaying council estates, where those growing up had no hope of a job. In their idleness and hopelessness, many turned to crime and vandalism; car theft became commonplace; and the police became the enemy of the people. Today, without doubt, it was a softer, easier, more middle-of-the-road Britain, and a much more American one, with McDonald's, Pizza Huts and shopping malls springing up all over the place. Most people seemed to have what they wanted, but what they wanted was mostly of a material nature – a new car, a DVD player, a pair of Nike trainers – and people were being mugged, even murdered, for their mobile phones.

But were things so very different back in the mid-sixties? Banks asked himself. Wasn't consumerism just as rife back then? That Monday evening in August 1965, when the knock came at their door, the Banks family was settling down to watch *Coronation Street* on their brand-new television set, bought on hire purchase just the previous week. Banks's father was in work then, at the sheet-metal factory, and if anyone had predicted that he would be made redundant seventeen years later, he'd have laughed in their face.

Coronation Street was one of those rituals every Monday and Wednesday when, tea over, dishes washed and put away, homework and odd jobs done, the family sat down to watch television together. So it was an unexpected disruption when someone knocked at the door. No one *ever* did that. As far as the Bankses were concerned, *everyone* on the street – everyone they knew, at any rate – watched *Coronation Street* and would no more think of interrupting than . . . well, Ida Banks was lost for words. Arthur Banks answered the door, prepared to send the commercial traveller and his suitcase of goods packing.

The one thing that entered nobody's mind when he did this, because it was such a disturbance of the normal routine, was that Joey, Banks's pet budgie, was out of his cage, having his evening constitutional, and when Arthur Banks opened the front door to admit the two detectives, he left the living-room door open, too. Joey seized the moment and flew away. No doubt he thought he was flying to the freedom of the open sky, but Banks knew, even at his young age, that such a pretty coloured thing wouldn't survive a day among the winged predators out there. When they realized what had happened, everyone dashed out in the garden looking to see where he had gone, but there wasn't a trace. Joey had vanished, never to return.

More fuss might have been made over Joey's escape had the new visitors not become the centre of everyone's awed attention. They were the first plainclothes policemen ever to enter the Banks household, and even young Banks himself forgot about Joey for the time being. Looking back now, it seemed like some sort of ill omen to him, but at the time he hadn't seen any significance beyond the simple loss of a pet.

Both men wore suits and ties, Banks remembered, but no hats. One of them, the one who did most of the talking, was about the same age as his father, with slicked-back dark hair, a long nose, a general air of benevolence and a twinkle in his eye, the sort of kindly uncle who might slip you half a crown to go to the pictures and wink as he gave it to you. The other one was younger and more nondescript. Banks couldn't remember much about him at all except that he had ginger hair, freckles and sticking-out ears. Banks couldn't remember their names, if he had ever known them.

Banks's father turned off the television set. Nine-year-old Roy just sat and gawped at the men. Neither detective apologized for disturbing the family. They sat, but didn't relax, remaining perched on the edges of their chairs as the kindly uncle asked his questions and the other took notes. Banks couldn't remember the exact wording after so many years, but imagined it went along the following lines.

'You know why we're here, don't you?'

'It's about Graham, isn't it?'

'Yes. You were a friend of his, right?'

'Yes.'

'Do you have any idea where he might have gone?'

'No.'

'When did you see him last?'

'Saturday afternoon.'

'Did he say or do anything unusual?'

'No.'

'What did you do?'

'Went shopping in town.'

'What'd you buy?'

'Just some records.'

'What sort of a mood was Graham in?'

'Just ordinary.'

'Was anything bothering him?'

'He was just like normal.'

'Did he ever talk about running away from home?'

'No.'

'Any idea where he might go if he did run away? Did he talk about any particular places?'

'No. But he was from London. I mean, his parents brought him up from London last year.'

'We know that. We were just wondering if there was anywhere else he talked about.'

'I don't think so.'

'What about secret hiding places?' The detective winked. 'I know all lads have secret places.'

'No.' Banks was unwilling to tell them about the big tree in the park – holly, he thought it was – with prickly leaves and branches right down to the ground. If you made your way through them, you ended up hidden inside, between the thick leaves and the trunk, like being in a teepee. He knew Graham was missing and it was important, but he wasn't going to give away the gang's secrets. He would look in the tree himself later and make sure Graham wasn't there.

'Did Graham have any problems you were aware of? Was he upset about anything?'

'No.'

'School?'

'We're on holiday.'

'I know that, but I mean in general. It was a new school for him, wasn't it? He'd only been there one year. Did he have any problems with the other boys?'

'No, not really. He had a fight with Mick Slack, but he's just a bully. He picks fights with all the new kids.'

'That's all?'

'Yes.'

'Have you seen any strange men hanging around the area lately?'

'No.' Banks probably blushed as he lied. He certainly felt his cheeks burning.

'Nobody?'

'No.'

'Did Graham ever mention anyone bothering him?'

'No.'

'All right then, son, that's it for now. But if you can think of anything at all, you know where the police station is, don't you?'

'Yes.'

'And I'm sorry about your budgie, really I am.'

'Thank you.'

They seemed all set to go then and got to their feet. Just before they left, they asked Roy and Banks's parents a few general questions, and that was it. When they shut the door everyone was quiet. There were still ten minutes of *Coronation Street* left, but nobody thought of switching on the television set again. Banks remembered turning to Joey's empty cage and feeling the tears gather in his eyes.

•

Annie waited until Martin Armitage's Beemer had got a respectable distance ahead, then let a local delivery van get between them before she started to follow. The roads were quiet at that time in the morning – they were quiet most of the time, if truth be told – so she couldn't appear *too* conspicuous. At the village of Relton he turned right and followed the B road that ran about halfway up the valley-side.

They passed through tiny Mortsett, which didn't even have a pub or a general store, and Annie got stuck when the delivery van stopped to make a call at one of the cottages. The road wasn't wide enough for her to pass.

She got out and prepared to show her warrant card and ask the driver to get out of the way – there was a passing area about twenty yards further along – when she noticed

Armitage pull over and halt about half a mile beyond the village. She had a clear view of the open road, so she brought out the binoculars she kept in her glove compartment and watched him.

Armitage got out of the car with his briefcase, looked around and started walking over the grass towards a squat stone shepherd's shelter about eighty yards off the road, up the daleside, and she didn't think he was nervous because he was breaking the government foot-and-mouth regulations.

When he got there he ducked inside the shelter, and when he came out he wasn't carrying his briefcase. Annie watched him walk back to his car. He stumbled once over the uneven ground, then glanced around again and drove off in the direction of Gratly.

'Birds, is it?' a voice asked, disturbing Annie's concentration,

'What?' She turned to face the delivery man, a brash, gel-haired youngster with bad teeth.

'The binoculars,' he said. 'Bird-watching. Can't understand it, myself. Boring. Now, when it comes to the other sort of birds—'

Annie flipped him her warrant card and said, 'Move your van out of the way and let me pass.'

'All right, all right,' he said. 'No need to get shirty. There's no one home, anyway. Never is in this bloody godforsaken hole.'

He drove off and Annie got back into her car. Armitage was long gone by the time she reached the spot where he had stopped, and there were no other cars in sight, save the delivery van fast disappearing ahead.

Annie was the one who felt nervous now. Was someone watching her with binoculars the way she had watched Armitage? She hoped not. If this was what she thought it was, it wouldn't do to reveal police interest. The air was still and mild, and Annie could smell warm grass after rain. Somewhere in the distance a tractor chugged across a field, and sheep baaed from the daleside as she ignored the posted warnings and made her way to the shelter. The place smelled musty and acrid inside. Enough light spilled through the gaps in the drystone for her to see the used condom on the dirt, the empty cigarette packet and crushed lager cans. A local lad's idea of showing his girlfriend a good time, no doubt. She could also see the briefcase, the inexpensive, nylon kind.

Annie picked it up. It felt heavy. She opened the Velcro strips and inside, as she had expected, found stacks of money, mostly ten and twenty pound notes. She had no idea exactly how much there was, but guessed it must be somewhere in the region of ten or fifteen thousand pounds.

She put the briefcase back where it was and returned to her car. She couldn't just sit there by the roadside waiting for something to happen, but she couldn't very well leave the scene either. In the end, she drove back to Mortsett and parked. There was no police station in the tiny hamlet, and she knew it would be no use trying to use her UHF hand radio behind so many hills and at such a distance. Besides, it only had a range of a couple of miles. She was driving her own car, as she often did, and she hadn't got around to having the more powerful VHF radio installed. It hardly seemed necessary, as she wasn't a patrol officer and, more often than not, she simply used the car to drive to work and back, and perhaps to interview witnesses, as she had done that morning. Before she headed out on foot to find a good spot from which to watch the shelter without being seen, Annie picked up her mobile to ring the station and let Detective Superintendent Gristhorpe know what was going on.

And, wouldn't you know it, the damn mobile didn't work. Out of range. Bloody typical. She should have known. She was quite close to Gratly, where Banks lived, and her mobile didn't work there either.

There was an old red telephone box in the village, but the phone had been vandalized, the wires torn from the cash box. *Damn!* Unwilling to take her eyes off the shelter for too long, Annie knocked on some doors, but the van driver had been right; nobody seemed to be home, and the one old lady who did answer said she didn't have a telephone.

Annie cursed under her breath; it looked as if she was on her own for the time being. She couldn't leave the shelter unwatched, and she had no idea how long she would have to stay out there. The sooner she found a good vantage point, the better. Still, she thought, turning towards the hillside, it served her bloody well right for not calling in *before* she followed Armitage. So much for initiative.

5

THE SUMMER THAT NEVER WAS

Nick Lowe's *The Convincer* ended and Banks slipped in David Gray's *White Ladder*. As he approached the turn-off to Peterborough, he wondered what to do first. He had rung his parents to let them know he was coming, of course, so perhaps he should go straight there. On the other hand, he was closer to police HQ, and the sooner he introduced himself to Detective Inspector Michelle Hart, the better. So he headed for the police station in its idyllic setting just off the Nene Parkway, between the nature reserve and the golf course.

In the reception area, he asked to speak to the detective in charge of the Graham Marshall investigation, introducing himself only as Alan Banks, a childhood friend. He didn't want to appear to be pulling rank or even introduce himself as a fellow copper, at least not at first, not until he saw which way the wind was blowing. Besides, just out of curiosity, he wanted to know how they treated an ordinary member of the public who came forward with information. It would do no harm to play a bit of a game.

After he had been waiting about ten minutes, a young woman opened the locked door that led to the main part of the station and beckoned him inside. Conservatively dressed in a navy blue suit, skirt below the knees, and a button-down white blouse, she was petite and slim, with shoulder-length blonde hair parted in the middle and tucked behind her small, delicate ears. She had a jagged fringe that came almost down to her eyes, which were a startling green, a colour Banks remembered seeing somewhere in the sea near Greece. Her mouth was slightly down-turned at the edges, which made her look a bit sad, and she had a small, straight nose. All in all, she was a very attractive woman, Banks thought, but he sensed a severity and a reserve in her – a definite 'No Entry' sign – and there was no mistaking the lines that suffering had etched around her haunting and haunted eyes.

'Mr Banks?' she said, raising her eyebrows.

Banks stood up. 'Yes.'

'I'm Detective Inspector Hart. Please follow me.' She led him to an interview room. It felt very strange being on the receiving end, Banks thought, and he got an inkling of the discomfort some of his interviewees must have felt. He looked around. Though it was a different county, the basics were still the same as in every interview room he had ever seen: table and chairs bolted to the floor, high window covered by a grille, institutional green paint on the walls, and that unforgettable smell of fear.

There was nothing to worry about, of course, but Banks couldn't help feeling just a little nervous as DI Hart put on her silver-rimmed, oval reading glasses and shuffled the papers around in front of her, as he had done many times himself, to draw out the tension and cause anxiety in the person sitting opposite. It touched the raw nerve of his childhood fear of authority, even though he knew he was authority, himself, now. Banks had always been aware of that irony, but a situation like this one really brought it home.

He also felt that DI Hart didn't need to act this way with him, that she was putting on too much of a show. His fault, perhaps, for not saying who he was, but even so, it was a bit heavy-handed to talk to him in an official interview room. He had come in voluntarily and he was neither a witness nor a suspect. She could have found an empty office and sent for coffee. But what would he have done? The same as her, probably; it was the us and them mentality, and in her mind he was a civilian. *Them.*

DI Hart stopped playing with her papers and broke the silence. 'So you say you can help with the Graham Marshall investigation?'

'Perhaps,' said Banks. 'I knew him.'

'Have you any idea at all what might have happened to him?'

'I'm afraid not,' said Banks. He had intended to tell her everything but found it wasn't as easy as that. Not yet. 'We just hung around together.'

'What was he like?'

'Graham? It's hard to say,' said Banks. 'I mean, you don't think about things like that when you're kids, do you?'

'Try now.'

'He was deep, I think. Quiet, at any rate. Most kids joked around, did stupid stuff, but Graham was always more serious, more reserved.' Banks remembered the small, almost secret smile as Graham had watched others act out comic routines – as if he didn't find them funny but knew he had to smile. 'You never felt you were fully privy to what was going on in his mind,' he added.

'You mean he kept secrets?'

'Don't we all?'

'What were his?'

'They wouldn't have been secrets if I knew them, would they? I'm just trying to give you some sense of what he was like. There was a secretive side to his nature.'

'Go on.'

She was becoming edgy, Banks thought. Rough day, probably, and not enough help. 'We did all the usual stuff together: played football and cricket, listened to music, talked about our favourite TV shows.'

'What about girlfriends?'

'Graham was a good-looking kid. The girls liked him, and he liked them, but I don't think he had anyone steady.'

'What kind of mischief did he get up to?'

'Well, I wouldn't want to incriminate myself, but we broke a window or two, did a bit of shoplifting, played truant, and we smoked cigarettes behind the cycle sheds at school. Pretty much normal stuff for teenagers back then. We didn't break into anyone's home, steal cars or mug old ladies.'

'Drugs?'

'This was 1965, for crying out loud.'

'Drugs were around back then.'

'How would you know? You probably weren't even born.'

Michelle reddened. 'I know King Harold got an arrow in his eye at the Battle of Hastings in 1066 and I wasn't born then.'

'Okay. Point taken. But drugs . . .? Not us, at any rate. Cigarettes were about the worst we did back then. Drugs may have been increasingly popular with the younger generation in London, but not with fourteen-year-old kids in a provincial backwater. Look, I should probably have done this before, but . . .' He reached into his inside pocket and took out his warrant card, laying it on the desk in front of her.

Michelle looked at it a minute, picked it up and looked

more closely, then slid it back across the desk to Banks. She took off her reading glasses and set them on the table. 'Prick,' she whispered.

'Come again?'

'You heard me. Why didn't you tell me from the start you were a DCI instead of playing games and stringing me along, making me feel like a complete fool?'

'Because I didn't want to give the impression I was trying to interfere. I'm simply here as someone who knew Graham. Besides, why did you have to come on so heavy-handed? I came here to volunteer information. There was no need to put me in an interview room and use the same tactics you use on a suspect. I'm surprised you didn't leave me here alone to stew for an hour.'

'You're making me wish I had.'

They glared at one another in silence for a few moments, then Banks said, 'Look, I'm sorry. I had no intention of making you feel foolish. And you don't need to. Why should you? It's true that I knew Graham. We were close friends at school. We lived on the same street. But this isn't my case, and I don't want you to think I'm pushing my nose in or anything. That's why I didn't announce myself at first. I'm sorry. You're right. I should have told you I was on the Job right from the start. Okay?'

Michelle gazed at him through narrowed eyes for a while, then twitched the corners of her lips in a brief smile and nodded. 'Your name came up when I was talking to his parents. I would have got in touch eventually.'

'The powers that be not exactly overwhelming you with assistance on this one, then?'

Michelle snorted. 'You could say that. One DC. It's not a high priority case, and I'm the new kid on the block. New *girl*.'

'I know what you mean,' Banks said. He remembered first meeting Annie Cabbot when she was put out to pasture at Harkside and he was in outer Siberia back in Eastvale. That hadn't been a high priority case to start with, either, but it had turned into one. He could sympathize with DI Hart.

'Anyway,' she went on, 'I didn't know you were a copper. I suppose I should call you "sir"? Rank and all?'

'Not necessary. I'm not one to stand on ceremony. Besides, I'm on your patch here. You're the boss. I do have a suggestion, though.'

'Oh?'

Banks looked at his watch. 'It's one o'clock. I drove down from Eastvale this morning without stopping and I haven't had a thing to eat. Why don't we get out of this depressing interview room and talk about Graham over lunch? I'll pay.'

Michelle raised on eyebrow. 'You're asking me out to lunch?'

'To discuss the case. Over lunch. Yes. Dammit, I'm hungry. Know any decent pubs around here?'

She gazed at him again, apparently appraising him for any imminent risk he might pose to her. When she couldn't seem to think of anything, she said, 'Okay. I know a place. Come on. But I'm paying my own way.'

•

What a stupid bloody decision it had been to take to the high ground, Annie Cabbot thought as she trudged illegally up the footpath, trying to avoid the little clusters of sheep droppings that seemed to be everywhere, and failing, as often as not. Her legs ached and she was panting with effort, even though she thought of herself as pretty fit.

She wasn't dressed for a walk in the country, either. Knowing she was visiting the Armitages again that morning, she had dressed in a skirt and blouse. She was even wearing tights. Not to mention the navy pumps that were crippling her. It was a hot day, and she could feel the sweat trickling along every available channel. Stray tresses of hair stuck to her cheeks and forehead.

As she climbed, she kept glancing behind her at the shepherd's shelter, but nobody approached it. She could only hope that she hadn't been spotted, that the kidnapper, if that was what this was all about, wasn't watching her through binoculars from a comfortable distance.

She found a spot she thought would do. It was a gentle dip in the daleside a few yards off the footpath. From there she could lie on her stomach and keep a close eye on the shelter without being seen from below.

Annie felt the warm, damp grass against her body, smelled its sweetness as she lay flat on her stomach, binoculars in hand. It felt good, and she wanted to take off all her clothes, feel the sun and earth on her bare skin, but she told herself not to be such a bloody fool and get on with the job. She compromised by taking off her jacket. The sun beat down on the back of her head and her shoulders. She had no suntan lotion with her, so she put the jacket over the back of her neck, even though it felt too hot. Better than getting sunstroke.

When she had got settled, there she lay. Waiting. Watching. Thoughts drifted through her head the way they did when she settled down to meditation, and she tried to practise the same technique of letting them go without dwelling on them. It started as a sort of free association, then went way beyond: sunlight; warmth;

skin; pigment; her father; Banks; music; Luke Armitage's black room; dead singers; secrets; kidnapping; murder.

Flies buzzed around her, snapping her out of the chain of association. She waved them away. At one point she felt a beetle or some insect creeping down the front of her bra and almost panicked, but she managed to get it off her before it got too far. A couple of curious rabbits approached, twitched their noses and turned away. Annie wondered if she would end up in Wonderland if she followed one.

She took long, deep breaths of grass-scented air. Time passed. An hour. Two. Three. Still nobody came to pick up the briefcase. Of course, the shepherd's shelter was off-limits because of foot and mouth, as was all open country-side, but that hadn't stopped Martin Armitage, and she was certain it wouldn't stop the kidnapper either. In fact, it was probably why the place had been chosen: little chance of anyone passing by. Most people in the area were law-abiding when it came to the restrictions, because they knew how much was at stake, and the tourists were staying away, taking their holidays abroad or in the cities instead. Normally, Annie obeyed the signs, too, but this was an emergency, and she knew she hadn't been anywhere near an infected area in weeks.

She wished she had something to eat and drink. It was long past lunchtime now, and she was starving. The heat was also making her thirsty. And there was something else, she realized, a more pressing urge: she needed to go to the toilet.

Well, she thought, looking around and seeing nothing but sheep in every direction, there's a simple remedy for that. She moved a few yards away from her flattened spot on the ground, checked for nettles and thistles, then took off her tights, squatted and peed. At least a woman could do that during surveillance in the countryside, Annie thought with a smile. It was a bit different if you were sitting cooped up in your car on a city street, as she had found out more than once in the past. Before she had finished, two low-flying jets from a nearby US airbase screamed over, seemingly no more than twenty feet or so from her head. She wondered if the pilots had got a good view. She gave them the finger, the way Americans did.

Back on her stomach, she tried her mobile again on the off-chance that it might just have been local interference before, but still no luck. The moor was a dead zone.

How long should she wait? she wondered. And why hadn't he come? The money was just lying there. What if he didn't come before nightfall and the lovers returned, more important things than foot-and-mouth on their minds? Several thousand quid as well as a quick bonk would be an unexpected bonus for them.

Her stomach rumbling, tongue dry against the roof of her mouth, Annie picked up the binoculars again and trained them on the shelter.

•

Michelle drove Banks to a pub she knew near the A1, wondering more than once on the way why she was doing this. But she knew the answer. She was bored with routine, bored first with tracking down the paperwork, and then bored with reading through it. She needed to get out, blow the cobwebs away, and this was the opportunity to do that and work as well.

She also had to admit that she was intrigued to meet someone who had been a friend of Graham Marshall's, especially as this Banks, despite a touch of grey in his closely cropped black hair, didn't look old enough. He was slim, perhaps stood three or four inches taller than her five foot five, had an angular face with lively blue eyes and a tan. He showed no great clothes sense but was dressed in basic Marks & Sparks casuals – light sports jacket, grey chinos, a blue denim shirt unbuttoned at the collar – and the look suited him. Some men his age only looked good in a business suit, Michelle thought. Anything else made them the male version of mutton dressed up as lamb. But on some older men casual looked natural. It did on Banks.

'Is it to be DI Hart, then?' Banks asked.

Michelle glanced sideways at him. 'I suppose you can call me Michelle, if you want.'

'Michelle it is, then. Nice name.'

Was he *flirting*? 'Come off it,' Michelle said.

'No, seriously. I mean it. No need to blush.'

Angry at herself for letting her embarrassment show, Michelle said, 'Just as long as you don't start singing the old Beatles song.'

'I never sing to a woman I've just met. Besides, I imagine you must have heard it many times.'

Michelle graced him with a smile. 'Too numerous to mention.'

The pub had parking at the back and a big freshly mown lawn with white tables and chairs where they could sit out in the sun. A couple of families were already there, settled in for the afternoon by the look of it, kids running around and playing on the swings and slide the pub provided in a small playground, but Michelle and Banks managed to find a quiet enough spot at the far end near the trees. Michelle watched the children play as Banks went inside to get the drinks. One of them was about six or seven, head covered in lovely golden curls, laughing unselfconsciously as she went higher on the swings. *Melissa*. Michelle felt as if her heart was breaking up inside her chest as she watched. It was a relief when Banks came back with a pint for himself and a shandy for her, and set two menus down on the table.

'What's up?' he asked. 'You look as if you've seen a ghost.'

'Maybe I have,' she said. 'Cheers.' They clinked glasses. Banks was diplomatic, she noted, curious about her mood, but sensitive and considerate enough to leave well enough alone and pretend to be studying the menu. Michelle liked that. She wasn't very hungry, but she ordered a prawn sandwich just to avoid being questioned about her lack of appetite. If truth be told, her stomach still felt sour from last night's wine. Banks was obviously ravenous, as he ordered a huge Yorkshire pudding filled with sausages and gravy.

When their orders were in, they sat back in their chairs and relaxed. They were in the shade of a beech tree, where it was still warm but out of the direct sunlight. Banks drank some beer and lit a cigarette. He looked in good shape, Michelle thought, for someone who smoked, drank and ate huge Yorkshire puddings and sausages. But how long would that last? If he really was Graham Marshall's contemporary, he'd be around fifty now, and wasn't that the age that men started worrying about their arteries and blood pressure, not to mention the prostate? Still, who was she to judge? True, she didn't smoke, but she drank too much and ate far too much junk food.

'So what else can you tell me about Graham Marshall?' she asked.

Banks drew on his cigarette and let the smoke out

slowly. He seemed to be enjoying it, Michelle thought, or was it a strategy he used to gain the upper hand in interviews? They all had some sort of strategy, even Michelle, though she would have been hard-pushed to define what it was. She thought herself quite direct. Finally, he answered, 'We were friends at school, and out of it too. He lived a few doors down the street, and for the year I knew him there was a small gang of us, who were pretty much inseparable.'

'David Grenfell, Paul Major, Steven Hill and you. I've only had time to track down and speak to David and Paul on the phone so far, though neither of them was able to tell me very much. Go on.'

'I haven't see any of them since I left for London when I was eighteen.'

'You only knew Graham for a year?'

'Yes. He was a new kid in our class the September before he disappeared, so it wasn't quite a full year even. His family had moved up from London that July or August, the way quite a lot of people were already doing then. This was before the huge influx; that came later in the sixties and the early seventies, the "new town" expansion. You probably weren't around then.'

'I certainly wasn't here.'

'Where, if you don't mind my asking?'

'I grew up in Hawick, border country. Spent most of my early police career with Greater Manchester, and since then I've been on the move. I've only been here a couple of months. Go on with your story.'

'That explains the accent.' Banks paused to sip beer and smoke again. 'I grew up here, a provincial kid. "Where my childhood was unspent." Graham seemed, I don't know, sort of cool, exotic, different. He was from

London, and that was where it was all happening. When you grow up in the provinces you feel everything's passing you by, happening somewhere else, and London was one of those "in" places back then, like San Francisco.'

'What do you mean by "cool"?'

Banks scratched the scar beside his right eye. Michelle wondered how he'd got it. 'I don't know. Not much fazed him. He never showed much emotion or reaction, and he seemed sort of worldly wise beyond his years. Don't get me wrong, though; Graham had his enthusiasms. He knew a lot about pop music, obscure B-sides and all that. He played guitar quite well. He was crazy about science fiction. And he had a Beatle haircut. My mother wouldn't let me have one. Short back and sides all the way.'

'But he was cool?'

'Yes. I don't know how to define the quality, really. How do you?'

'I think I know what you mean. I had a girlfriend like that. She was just like . . . oh, I don't know . . . someone who made you feel awkward, someone you wanted to emulate, perhaps. I'm not sure I can define it any more clearly.'

'No. Just *cool*, before it was even cool to be cool.'

'His mother said something about bullying.'

'Oh, that was just after he arrived. Mick Slack, the school bully. He had to try it on with everybody. Graham wasn't much of a fighter, but he didn't give up, and Slack never went near him again. Neither did anybody else. It was the only time I ever saw him fight.'

'I know it's hard to remember that far back,' said Michelle, 'but did you notice anything different about him towards the end?'

'No. He seemed much the same as always.'

'He went on holiday with you shortly before he disappeared, so his mother told me.'

'Yes. His parents couldn't go that year, so they let him come with us. It's good to have someone your own age to hang about with when you're away for a couple of weeks. It could get awfully boring with just parents and a younger brother.'

Michelle smiled. 'Younger sister, too. When did you last see Graham?'

'Just the day before he disappeared. Saturday.'

'What did you do?'

Banks gazed away into the trees before answering. 'Do? What we usually did on Saturdays. In the morning we went to the Palace, to the matinee. *Flash Gordon* or *Hopalong Cassidy*, a Three Stooges short.'

'And the afternoon?'

'In town. There was an electrical shop on Bridge Street that used to sell records. Long gone now. Three or four of us would sometimes crowd into one of those booths and smoke ourselves silly listening to the latest singles.'

'And that night?'

'Don't remember. I think I just stayed in watching TV. Saturday nights were good. *Juke Box Jury*, *Dr Who*, *Dixon of Dock Green*. Then there was *The Avengers*, but I don't think it was on that summer. I don't remember it, anyway.'

'Anything odd about the day at all? About Graham?'

'You know, for the life of me I can't remember anything unusual. I'm thinking perhaps I didn't know him very well, after all.'

Michelle was getting the strong impression that Banks *did* know something, that he was holding back. She didn't know why, but she was certain that was the case.

'Number twelve?' A young girl carrying two plates wandered into the garden.

Banks glanced at the number the bartender had given him. 'Over here,' he said.

She delivered the plates. Michelle gazed at her prawn sandwich, wondering if she'd be able to finish it. Banks tucked into his Yorkshire pudding and sausage for a while, then said, 'I used to do Graham's paper round before him, before the shop changed owners. It used to be Thackeray's until old man Thackeray got TB and let the business run into the ground. That's when Bradford bought the shop and built it up again.'

'But you didn't go back?'

'No. I'd got an after-school job at the mushroom farm down past the allotments. Filthy work, but it paid well, at least for back then.'

'Ever have any trouble on the paper round?'

'No. I was thinking about that on my way here, among other things.'

'No strangers ever invited you inside or anything?'

'There was one bloke who always seemed a bit weird at the time, though he was probably harmless.'

'Oh?' Michelle took out her notebook, prawn sandwich still untouched on the plate in front of her, now arousing the interest of a passing bluebottle.

Banks swatted the fly away. 'Better eat it soon,' he said.

'Who was this bloke you were talking about?'

'I can't remember the number, but it was near the end of Hazel Crescent, before you crossed Wilmer Road. Thing was, he was about the only one ever awake at that time, and I got the impression he hadn't even gone to bed. He'd open the door in his pyjamas and ask me to come in for a smoke or drink or whatever, but I always said no.'

'Why?'

Banks shrugged. 'Dunno. Instinct. Something about him. A smell, I don't know. Sometimes when you're a kid you've got a sort of sixth sense for danger. If you're lucky, it stays with you. Anyway, I'd already been well trained not to accept sweets from strange men, so I wasn't going to accept anything else, either.'

'Harry Chatham,' Michelle said.

'What?'

'That'll be Harry Chatham. Body odour, one of his characteristics.'

'You *have* done your homework.'

'He came under suspicion at the time, but he was eventually ruled out. You were right to stay away. He did have a history of exposing himself to young boys. Never went further than that, though.'

'They were sure?'

Michelle nodded. 'He was on holiday in Great Yarmouth. Didn't get back until that Sunday night. Plenty of witnesses. Jet Harris gave him the third degree, I should imagine.'

Banks smiled. '*Jet Harris*. Haven't heard his name in years. You know, when I was a kid growing up around there, it was always, "Better keep your nose clean or Jet Harris will get you and lock you up." We were terrified of him, though none of us had ever met him.'

Michelle laughed. 'It's still pretty much the same today,' she said.

'Surely he must be dead by now?'

'Eight years ago. But the legend lingers on.' She picked up her sandwich and took a bite. It was good. She realized she was hungry after all and had soon devoured the first half. 'Was there anything else?' Michelle asked.

She noticed Banks hesitate again. He had finished his Yorkshire pudding, and he reached for another cigarette. A temporary postponement. Funny, she'd seen the signs before in criminals she'd interviewed. This man definitely had something on his conscience, and he was debating whether to tell her or not. Michelle sensed that she couldn't hurry matters by pushing him, so she let him put the cigarette in his mouth and fiddle with his lighter for a few moments. And she waited.

•

Annie wished she hadn't given up smoking. At least it would have been something to do as she lay on her belly in the wet grass keeping an eye on the distant shepherd's shelter. She glanced at her watch and realized she had been lying there over four hours and nobody had come for the money.

Under her clothes, and the jacket protecting the back of her neck, Annie felt bathed in sweat. All she wanted to do was walk under a nice cool shower and luxuriate there for half an hour. But if she left her spot, what would happen? On the other hand, what would happen if she stayed there?

The kidnapper might turn up, but would Annie go running down the daleside to make an arrest? No, because Luke Armitage certainly wouldn't be with him. Would she have time to get to her car in Mortsett and follow whoever picked up the money? Possibly, but she would have a much better chance if she were already in the car.

In the end, Annie decided that she should go back down to Mortsett, still keeping an eye on the shelter, and keep trying until she found someone home with a telephone, then sit in her car and watch from there until relief came from Eastvale. She felt her bones ache as she stood up and brushed the loose grass from her blouse.

It was a plan, and it beat lying around up here melting in the sun.

•

Now that it was time to confess, Banks was finding it more difficult than he had imagined. He knew he was stalling, playing for time, when what he should do was just come right out with it, but his mouth felt dry and the words stuck in his throat. He sipped some beer. It didn't help much. Sweat tickled the back of his neck and ran down his spine.

'We were playing down by the river,' he said, 'not far from the city centre. It wasn't developed quite as much as it is today, so it was a pretty desolate stretch of water.'

'Who was playing with you?'

'Just Paul and Steve.'

'Go on.'

'It was nothing, really,' Banks said, embarrassed at how slight the events that had haunted him for years now seemed on this bright afternoon sitting under a beech tree with an attractive woman. But there was no backing out now. 'We were throwing stones in the water, skimming, that sort of thing. Then we moved down the riverbank a bit and found some bigger stones and bricks. We started chucking those in to make a big splash. At least I did. Steve and Paul were a bit further down. Anyway, I was holding this big rock to my chest with both hands – it took all my strength – when I noticed this tall, scruffy sort of bloke walking along the riverbank towards me.'

'What did you do?'

'Held on to it,' said Banks. 'So I didn't splash him. Always the polite little bugger, I was. I remember smiling as he got nearer, you know, showing him I was holding off dropping the rock until he was out of range.' Banks paused and drew on his cigarette. 'Next thing I knew,' he went on, 'he'd grabbed hold of me from behind and I'd dropped the rock and splashed us both.'

'What happened? What did he do?'

'We struggled. I thought he was trying to push me in, but I managed to dig in my heels. I might not have been very big, but I was wiry and strong. I think my resistance surprised him. I remember smelling his sweat and I think he'd been drinking. Beer. I remembered smelling it on my father's breath when he came back from the pub sometimes.'

Michelle took her notebook out. 'Can you give me a description?'

'He had a ragged dark beard. His hair was greasy and long, longer than usual back then. It was black. Like Rasputin. And he wore one of those army greatcoats. I remember thinking when I saw him coming that he must be hot in such a heavy overcoat.'

'When was this?'

'Late June. It was a nice day, sort of like today.'

'So what happened?'

'He tried to drag me away, towards the bushes, but I managed to squirm out of his grasp, one arm at any rate, and he swung me around, swore at me and punched me in the face. The momentum broke me loose, so I ran.'

'Where were your friends?'

'Back up by the road by then. A good hundred yards away. Watching.'

'Didn't they help you?'

'They were scared.'

'They didn't call the police?'

'It all happened so fast. When I got free, I ran off and joined them and we never looked back. We decided not to say anything to our parents because we weren't supposed to be playing down by the river in the first place, and we were supposed to be at school. We thought we'd get into trouble.'

'I can imagine you did. What did your parents say about your face?'

'They weren't too pleased. I told them I'd got into a bit of a scrap at school. All in all, I suppose it was a lucky escape. I tried to put it out of my mind, but . . .'

'You couldn't?'

'Off and on. There's been lengthy periods of my life when I haven't thought of it at all.'

'Why do you see a connection with what happened to Graham?'

'It seemed too much of a coincidence, that's all,' said Banks. 'First this pervert trying to push me in the river, dragging me into the bushes, then Graham disappearing like that.'

'Well,' said Michelle, finishing her drink and closing her notebook, 'I'd better go and see if I can find any trace of your mystery man, hadn't I?'

6

Showered and dressed in crisp, clean clothes, Annie presented herself at Detective Superintendent Gristhorpe's office that afternoon, as requested. There was something austere and headmasterly about the room that always intimidated her. Partly, it was to do with the tall bookcases, mostly filled with legal and forensics texts, but dotted here and there with classics such as *Bleak House* and *Anna Karenina*, books Annie had never read, books that mocked her with their oft-mentioned titles and their thickness. And partly it was Gristhorpe's appearance: big, bulky, red-faced, unruly-haired, hook-nosed, pockmarked. Today he wore grey flannel trousers and a tweed jacket with elbow patches. He looked as if he ought to be smoking a pipe, but Annie knew he didn't smoke.

'Right,' said Gristhorpe after he had asked her to sit down. 'Now, tell me what the hell's going on out Mortsett way.'

Annie felt herself flush. 'It was a judgement call, sir.'

Gristhorpe waved his large, hairy hand. 'I'm not questioning your judgement. I want to know what you think is happening.'

Annie relaxed a little and crossed her legs. 'I think Luke Armitage has been kidnapped, sir. Someone communicated a ransom demand to the family last night, and Martin Armitage rang me to cancel the search for Luke.'

'But you didn't?'

'No, sir. Something wasn't right. In my opinion, Luke Armitage wasn't to be considered "found" until I'd seen him with my own eyes and talked to him.'

'Fair enough. What happened next?'

'As you know, sir, I went out to see the family again this morning. I got the distinct impression they didn't want me there, that something was going on.' Annie explained about following Martin Armitage to the drop and being stuck up the hillside watching the shelter by herself for hours, until she went back down to the village and finally found someone at home with a telephone.

'Do you think he saw you? The kidnapper.'

'It's possible,' Annie admitted. 'If he was hiding somewhere nearby and watching through binoculars. It's open country up there. But it's my impression that he'll either wait until nightfall—'

'And risk leaving the money out there all day?'

'It's off the beaten track. And most people follow the government regulations.'

'What else?'

'Pardon, sir.'

'You said "either". To me, that implies an "or". I interrupted you. Go on. What else do you think might have happened?'

'Maybe something has gone wrong, something we don't know about.'

'Like?'

Annie swallowed and looked away. 'Like Luke's dead, sir. It happens sometimes with kidnappings. He tried to escape, struggled too hard . . .'

'But the kidnapper can still collect. Remember, the Armitages can't possibly know their son's dead, if he is, and the money's just sitting there for the taking. If you weren't seen, then only Martin Armitage and the kidnapper know it's there.'

'That's what puzzles me, sir. The money. Obviously a kidnapper who makes a ransom demand is in it for the money, whether the victim lives or dies. Maybe he's just being unduly cautious, waiting for dark, as I suggested earlier.'

'Possibly.' Gristhorpe looked at his watch. 'Who's up there now?'

'DC Templeton, sir.'

'Organize a surveillance rota. I'll ask for permission to plant an electronic tracking device in the briefcase. Someone can put it there under cover of darkness, if the damn thing hasn't been picked up before then.' Gristhorpe grunted. 'Might as well be hanged for a sheep as a lamb. ACC McLaughlin will have my guts for garters.'

'You could always blame me, sir.'

'Aye, you'd like that wouldn't you, Annie, a chance to get bolshie with the bigwigs?'

'Sir—'

'It's all right, lass. I'm only teasing you. Haven't you learned Yorkshire ways yet?'

'Sometimes I despair that I ever will.'

'Give it a few more years. Anyway, that's my job. I can handle the brass.'

'What about the Armitages, sir?'

'I think you'd better pay them another visit, don't you?'

'But what if their place is being watched?'

'The kidnapper doesn't know you.' Gristhorpe smiled. 'And it's not as if you *look* like a plainclothes copper, Annie.'

'And I thought I'd put on my conservative best.'

'All you have to do is wear those red boots again. Are their telephone calls still being intercepted?'

'Yes, sir.'

'Then how the devil . . .?'

'The same thing puzzled me. Martin Armitage said the call from Luke came through on his mobile, so I'm assuming it was the kidnapper's call he was talking about.'

'But why wouldn't he just use the regular land line?'

'Armitage said he and Robin were supposed to go out to dinner that night, so Luke didn't think they'd be home.'

'He believed they would *still* go out to dinner, even after he'd disappeared? And he told his kidnapper this?'

'I know it sounds odd, sir. And in my judgement, Martin Armitage is the last person Luke would call.'

'Ah, I see. Signs of family tension?'

'All under the surface, but definitely there, I'd say. Luke's very much his mother's son, and his biological father's, perhaps. He's creative, artistic, a loner, a dreamer. Martin Armitage is a man of action, a sportsman, bit of a macho tough guy.'

'Go carefully then, Annie. You don't want to disturb a nest of vipers.'

'There might be no choice if I want honest answers to my questions.'

'Then tread softly and carry a big stick.'

'I'll do that.'

'And don't give up on the kid. It's early days yet.'

'Yes, sir,' Annie said, though she wasn't at all certain about that.

•

The old street looked much the same as it had when Banks lived there with his parents between 1962 and 1969

– from 'Love Me Do' to Woodstock – except that everything, the brickwork, the doors, the slate roofs, was just that little bit shabbier, and small satellite dishes had replaced the forest of old television aerials on just about all the houses, including his parents'. That made sense. He couldn't imagine his father living without Sky Sports.

Back in the early sixties the estate was new, and Banks's mother had been thrilled to move from their little back-to-back terraced house with the outside toilet to the new house with 'all mod cons', as they used to say. As far as Banks was concerned, the best 'mod cons' were the indoors WC, a real bathroom to replace the tin tub they had had to fill from a kettle every Friday, and a room of his own. In the old house, he had shared with his brother, Roy, who was five years younger, and like all siblings they fought more than anything else.

The house stood near the western edge of the estate, close to the arterial road, across from an abandoned factory and a row of shops, including the newsagent's. Banks paused for a moment and took in the weathered terraced houses – rows of five, each with a little garden, wooden gate, low wall and privet hedge. Some people had made small improvements, he noticed, and one house had an enclosed porch. The owners must have bought the place when the Conservatives sold off council houses for peanuts in the eighties. Maybe there was even a conservatory around the back, Banks thought, though it would be folly to add an extension made almost entirely of glass on an estate like this.

A knot of kids stood smoking and shoving one another in the middle of the street, some Asian, some white, clocking Banks out of the corners of their eyes. Locals were always suspicious of newcomers, and the kids had no idea who he was, that he had grown up here, too. Some of them were wearing low-slung baggy jeans and hoodies. Mangy dogs wandered up and down the street, barking at everything and nothing, shitting on the pavements, and loud rock music blasted out of an open window several houses east.

Banks opened the gate. He noticed that his mother had planted some colourful flowers and kept the small patch of lawn neatly trimmed. This was the only garden she had ever had, and she always had been proud of her little patch of earth. He walked up the flagstone path and knocked at the door. He saw his mother approach through the frosted-glass pane. She opened the door, rubbed her hands together as if drying them, and gave him a hug. 'Alan,' she said. 'Lovely to see you. Come on in.'

Banks dropped his overnight bag in the hall and followed his mother through to the living room. The wall-paper was a sort of wispy autumn-leaves pattern, the three-piece suite a matching brown velveteen, and there was a sentimental autumnal landscape hanging over the electric fire. He didn't remember this theme from his previous visit, about a year ago, but he couldn't be certain that it hadn't been there, either. So much for the obser-vant detective and the dutiful son.

His father was sitting in his usual armchair, the one with the best straight-on view of the television. He didn't get up, only grunted, 'Son. How you doing?'

'Not bad, Dad. You?'

'Mustn't complain.' Arthur Banks had been suffering from mild angina and an assortment of less specified chronic illnesses for years, ever since he'd been made redundant from the sheet-metal factory, and they seemed to get neither better nor worse as the years went on. He took pills occasionally for the chest pains. Other than that, and the damage booze and fags had wreaked on his liver and lungs over the years, he had always been fit as a fiddle. Short, skinny and hollow-chested, he still had a head of thick dark hair with hardly a trace of grey. He wore it slicked back with lashings of Brylcreem.

Banks's mother, plump and nervy, with pouchy, chipmunk cheeks and a haze of blue-grey hair hovering around her skull, fussed about how thin Banks was looking. 'I don't suppose you've been eating properly since Sandra left, have you?' she said.

'You know how it is,' said Banks. 'I manage to gulp down the occasional Big Mac and fries now and then, if I've got time to spare.'

'Don't be cheeky. Besides, you need *proper* food. In for tea?'

'I suppose so,' Banks said. He hadn't thought about what he was going to do once he actually *got* home. If truth be told, he had imagined that the local police – in the lovely form of DI Michelle Hart – would find his offer of help invaluable and give him an office at Thorpe Wood. But that clearly was not to be. Fair enough, he thought, it's *her* case, after all. 'I'll just take my bag up,' he said, heading for the stairs.

Though Banks hadn't stayed overnight since he had first left for London, somehow he knew that his room would be just as it always had been. And he was right. Almost. It was the same wardrobe, the same small book-case, the same narrow bed he had slept in as a teenager, sneaking his transistor radio under the covers to listen to Radio Luxembourg, or reading a book by the light of a torch. The only thing different was the wallpaper. Gone were the sports-car images of his adolescence, replaced by pink and green stripes. He stood on the threshold for a few moments permitting it all to flow back, allowing the emotion that he felt nudging at the boundaries of his consciousness. It wasn't quite nostalgia, nor was it loss, but something in between.

The view hadn't changed. Banks's bedroom was the only one at the back of the house, next to the WC and bathroom, and it looked out over backyards and an alleyway, beyond which an empty field stretched a hundred yards or so to the next estate. People walked their dogs there, and sometimes the local kids gathered at night.

Banks used to do that, he remembered, with Dave, Paul, Steve and Graham, sharing Woodbines and Park Drives or, if Graham was flush, those long American tipped cigarettes, Peter Stuyvesants or Pall Mall. Later, after Graham had disappeared, Banks had sometimes been there with girlfriends. The field wasn't square and there was a little dog-leg on the other side where, if you were careful, you couldn't be seen from the houses. He remembered well enough those long, raw-lipped snogging sessions, pushed up against the rusty corrugated iron fencing, the fervid struggles with bra hooks, safety pins or whatever other contrivances the local girls so inconsiderately used to keep themselves fastened up.

Banks dropped his bag at the bottom of the bed and stretched. It had been a long drive, and the time spent in the pub garden, the pint he had drunk with DI Hart, all conspired to make him feel tired. He thought of taking a brief nap before tea but decided it would be rude; he could at least go down and talk to his parents as he hadn't been in touch for so long.

First, he unpacked his shirt to hang up in the wardrobe before the creases became too permanent. The other clothes in the wardrobe were unfamiliar, but Banks noticed several cardboard boxes on the floor. He pulled one out and was stunned when he saw it contained his old records: singles, as those were all he could afford back then, when they cost 6/4 and an LP cost 32/6. Of course, he got LPs for Christmas and birthdays, often with record tokens, but they were mostly Beatles and Rolling Stones, and he had taken those to London with him.

The records here represented the beginnings of his musical interests. When he left, he had soon gone on to Cream, Hendrix and Jefferson Airplane, then later discovered jazz and, later still, classical, but these . . . Banks dipped his hand in and lifted out a stack, flipping through them. Here they were in all their glory: Dusty Springfield's 'Goin' Back', The Shadows' 'The Rise & Fall of Flingel Bunt', Cilla Black's 'Anyone Who Had a Heart' and 'Alfie', 'Nutrocker' by B. Bumble and the Stingers, Sandie Shaw's 'Always Something There to Remind Me', 'House of the Rising Sun' by the Animals and 'As Tears Go By' by Marianne Faithfull. There were many more, some he had forgotten, and a few really obscure artists, such as Ral Donner and Kenny Lynch, and cover versions of Del Shannon and Roy Orbison hits made by unnamed performers for Woolworth's cheap Embassy label. What a treasure trove of nostalgia, all the stuff he listened to between the ages of about eleven and sixteen. His old record player was long gone, but his parents had a stereo downstairs, so perhaps he would play a few of the old songs while he was home.

For the moment, he put back the box and pulled out another one, this one full mostly of old toys. There were model aeroplanes – Spitfires, Wellingtons, Junkers and a Messerschmitt with a broken wing – a couple of Dinky toys, a Dan Dare rocket gun, and a small clockwork Dalek that said 'Ex-ter-min-ate! Ex-ter-min-ate!' as it rolled along like an upturned dustbin. There were a few old annuals, too – *The Saint*, *Danger Man* and *The Man From U.N.C.L.E.* – along with what had once been his pride and joy, a pocket-sized Philips transistor radio. Maybe if he put in some new batteries, he could even get it working.

The third box he opened was full of old school reports, magazines, letters and exercise books. He had sometimes wondered over the years what had happened to all this stuff and assumed, if anything, that his parents had chucked it out when they figured he wouldn't need it any more. Not so. It had been hiding away in the wardrobe all this time. There they were: *Beatles Monthly*, *Fabulous*, *Record Song Book* and *The Radio Luxembourg Book of Record Stars*.

Banks pulled out a handful of the small notebooks and found they were his old diaries. Some were plain Letts' diaries, with a little slot for a pencil down the spine, and some were special themed, illustrated ones, such as pop-star, television or sports diaries. The one that was of most immediate interest to him, though, was a *Photoplay* diary with a stiff, laminated cover and a colour photo of Sean Connery and Honor Blackman from 1964's Bond film, *Goldfinger*, on the front. Inside, a photo of a different film star faced each page of dates. The first was Brigitte Bardot, for the week starting Sunday, 27 December 1964, the first full week of his diary for 1965, the year Graham disappeared.

•

Michelle took off her reading glasses and rubbed the bridge of her nose, where she sensed a headache beginning to form between her eyes. She suffered from headaches frequently these days, and while her doctor assured her there was nothing seriously wrong – no brain tumour or neurological disease – and her psychiatrist told her that it was probably just stress and 'coping', she couldn't help but worry.

The air quality in the archives office didn't help either. Instead of signing the heavier boxes out and carrying them up to her office, Michelle had decided she might as well look through the material down there. The reading room was just a glassed-in alcove with a desk and chair. It stood at the entrance to several parallel aisles of old papers, some of which went back to the late nineteenth century. If the environment had been a little more comfortable, she might have considered having a browse around the archives. There was bound to be some fascinating stuff.

For the moment, 1965 would have to do. Michelle wanted to get a general idea of the crimes occurring around the time of Graham's disappearance, to see if she could come up with any links to Banks's mysterious stranger, and Mrs Metcalfe had directed her to the log-books that indexed and recorded all complaints and actions taken, day by day. It made for interesting reading, not all of it relevant to what she was looking for. Many of the calls listed went no further – missing pets, some domestic complaints – but the lists gave her a good impression of what daily life must have been like for a copper back then.

In May, for example, a man had been arrested in connection with an assault on a fourteen-year-old girl, who had accepted a lift with him near the A1, but he bore no resemblance whatsoever to Banks's description of the man by the river. Also in May there had been a major jewellery robbery at a city-centre shop, netting the thieves £18,000. In June a number of youths had gone on the rampage and slashed tyres on about thirty cars in the city centre; in the same month a twenty-one-year-old man had been stabbed outside the Rose and Crown on Bridge Street, after an argument over a girl. In August, two alleged homosexuals had been questioned in connection with lewd goings on at the country mansion of local bigwig, Rupert Mandeville, but the anonymous informant couldn't be located, and all charges had later been dismissed for lack of evidence. Hard to believe that it was a crime to be gay, Michelle thought, but 1965 was back in the dark ages, before homosexuality had been legalized in 1967.

There were certainly plenty of incidents before and after Graham Marshall's disappearance, Michelle was fast discovering, but none of them seemed to have anything remotely to do with Banks's riverbank adventure. She read on. In July police had investigated complaints about a local protection racket modelled on the East London Kray gang's operation, allegedly led by a man called Carlo Fiorino, but no charges were brought.

The more she read, the more Michelle realized what a vast chasm yawned between 1965 and today. She had, in fact, been born in 1961, but she was damned if she was going to admit that to Banks. Her own teenage years had been spent in what Banks would no doubt call a musical wasteland made up of the Bay City Rollers, Elton John and Hot Chocolate, not to mention *Saturday Night Fever* and *Grease*. Punk came along when she was about fifteen, but Michelle was far too conservative to join in with that crowd. If truth be told, the punks scared her with their torn clothes, spiky hair and safety pins in their ears. And the music just sounded like noise to her.

Not that Michelle had had a great deal of time for pop music; she had been a studious child, lamenting that it always seemed to take her so long to finish her homework when others were done and out on the town. Her mother said she was too much of a perfectionist to let something be and have done with it, and perhaps that was true. Painstaking. Perfectionist. These were labels she had come to know and hate from friends, family and the teachers at school. Why not just say pedestrian and plodding and have done with it, if that was what they meant? she sometimes wondered.

She hadn't done brilliantly at school despite all her hard work, but she had managed to pass enough O and A levels to get into a poly – again cramming through all the concerts and parties her fellow students went to – where she had studied business and management techniques before deciding on the police as a career. On those rare occasions when she did have time to go out, late in the seventies, she liked to dance. For that, reggae or two-tone was her music of choice: Bob Marley, the Specials, Madness, UB40.

Michelle had always hated nostalgia snobs, as she called them, and in her experience, the sixties' ones were the worst of the lot. She suspected that Banks was one. To hear them talk, you'd think paradise had been lost or the seventh seal broken now that so many of the great rock icons were dead, geriatric or gaga, and nobody wore beads and kaftans any more, and you'd also think that drug-taking was an innocent way to spend a few hours relaxing, or a means of reaching some exalted spiritual state, instead of a waste of lives and a source of money for evil, unscrupulous dealers.

The archives office was quiet except for the buzzing of the fluorescent light. Silence is a rare thing in a police station, where everyone is pushed together in open-plan offices, but down here Michelle could even hear her watch ticking. After five. Time for a break soon, some fresh air perhaps, and then back down to it.

Reading the crime reports for August, she sensed rather than heard someone approaching the office, and when she looked up, she saw it was Detective Superintendent Benjamin Shaw.

Shaw's bulk filled the doorway and blocked some of the light from coming in. 'What you up to, DI Hart?' he asked.

'Just checking the old logs, sir.'

'I can see that. What for? You won't find anything there, you know. Not after all this time.'

'I was just having a general look around, trying to get some context for the Marshall case. Actually, I was wondering if—'

'*Context*? Is that one of those fancy words they taught you at polytechnic? Bloody time-wasting sounds more like it.'

'Sir—'

'Don't bother to argue, Inspector. You're wasting your time. What do you expect to find in the dusty old files, apart from *context*?'

'I was talking to one of Graham Marshall's friends earlier,' she said. 'He told me he was approached by a strange man on the riverbank about two months before the Marshall boy disappeared. I was just trying to see if any similar incidents were on file.'

Shaw sat on the edge of the desk. It creaked and tilted

a little. Michelle worried that the damn thing would break under his weight. 'And?' he asked. 'I'm curious.'

'Nothing so far, sir. Do you remember anything odd like that?'

Shaw frowned. 'No. But who is this "friend"?'

'He's called Banks, sir. Alan Banks. Actually, it's Detective Chief Inspector Banks.'

'Is it, indeed? Banks? The name sounds vaguely familiar. I take it he didn't report the incident at the time?'

'No, sir. Too scared of what his parents might say.'

'I can imagine. Look, about this Banks chap,' he went on. 'I think I'd like a little word with him. Can you arrange it?'

'I've got his phone number, sir. But . . .' Michelle was about to tell Shaw that it was *her* case and that she didn't appreciate his poaching her interviews, but she decided it wouldn't be diplomatic to alienate one of her senior officers at such an early stage of her career in Peterborough. Besides, he might be helpful, having been involved in the original investigation.

'But what?'

'Nothing, sir.'

'Good.' Shaw stood up. 'We'll have him in, then. Soon as possible.'

•

'I know it must seem odd after all these years,' Banks said, 'but I'm Alan Banks, and I've come to offer my condolences.'

'*Alan Banks*. Well, I never!' The look of suspicion on Mrs Marshall's face was immediately transformed into one of pleasure. She opened the door wide. 'Do come in and make yourself at home.'

It was over thirty-six years since Banks had set foot in the Marshall house, and he had a vague memory that the furniture had been made of much darker wood then, heavier and sturdier. Now the sideboard and television stand looked as if they were made of pine. The three-piece suite seemed much bigger, and a huge television dominated one corner of the room.

Even all those years ago, he remembered, he hadn't been inside Graham's house often. Some parents kept an open house for their children's friends, the way his own did, and Dave's and Paul's, but the Marshalls were always a bit distant, stand-offish. Graham never spoke about his mum and dad much, either, Banks remembered, but that hadn't struck him as at all unusual at the time. Kids don't, except to complain if they're not allowed to do something or are discovered in some deception and have their pocket money stopped. As far as Banks knew, Graham Marshall's home life was every bit as normal as his own.

His mother had told him that Mr Marshall had been disabled by a stroke, so he was prepared for the frail, drooling figure staring up at him from the armchair. Mrs Marshall looked tired and careworn herself, which was hardly surprising, and he wondered how she kept the place so spick and span. Maybe the social helped out, as he doubted she could afford a daily.

'Look, Bill, it's Alan Banks,' said Mrs Marshall. 'You know, one of our Graham's old friends.'

It was hard to read Mr Marshall's expression through the distortions of his face, but his gaze seemed to relax a little when he found out who the visitor was. Banks said hello and sat down. He spotted the old photo of Graham, the one his own father had taken with his Brownie on

Blackpool prom. He had taken one of Banks, too, also wearing a black polo-neck 'Beatle' jumper, but without the matching hairstyle.

Mr Marshall was sitting in the same spot he had always sat in, like Banks's own father. Back then, he had always seemed to be smoking, but now he looked as if he could hardly lift a cigarette to his lips.

'I understand you're an important policeman now,' Mrs Marshall said.

'I don't know about important, but I'm a policeman, yes.'

'You don't have to be so modest. I bump into your mum at the shops from time to time and she's very proud of you.'

That's more than she lets on to me, Banks thought. 'Well,' he said, 'you know what mothers are like.'

'Have you come to help with the investigation?'

'I don't know that I can,' said Banks. 'But if they want any help from me, I'd be happy to give it.'

'She seems very nice. The girl they sent round.'

'I'm sure she'll be just fine.'

'I told her I can't imagine what she can do that Jet Harris and his boys didn't do back then. They were very thorough.'

'I know they were.'

'But he just seemed to have . . . vanished. All these years.'

'I've often thought about him,' Banks said. 'I realize I didn't actually know him for very long, but he was a good friend. I missed him. We all missed him.'

Mrs Marshall sniffed. 'Thank you. He appreciated the way you all accepted him when we were new here. You know how difficult it can be to make friends sometimes.

It's just so hard to believe that he's turned up after all this time.'

'It happens,' said Banks. 'And don't give up on the investigation. There's a lot more science and technology in police work these days. Look how quickly they identified the remains. They couldn't have done that twenty years ago.'

'I just wish I could be of some use,' said Mrs Marshall, 'but I don't remember anything out of the ordinary at all. It just came like a lightning bolt. Out of the blue.'

Banks stood up. 'I know,' he said. 'But if there's anything to be discovered, I'm sure DI Hart will discover it.'

'Are you going already?'

'It's nearly teatime,' Banks said, smiling. 'And my mother would never forgive me if I didn't turn up for tea. She thinks I need fattening up.'

Mrs Marshall smiled. 'Better go then. Mustn't cross your mother. By the way, they can't release the body yet, but Miss Hart said she'd let me know when we can have the funeral. You will come, won't you?'

'Of course,' said Banks. When he looked over to say goodbye to Mr Marshall, he had a sudden flash of the big, muscular man he used to be, the sense of physical menace he had somehow conveyed. Back then, Banks remembered with a shock, he had been *afraid* of Graham's dad. He never had any real reason to feel that way, but he had done.

•

She should have packed it in long ago, Michelle realized, but she was loath to give up without finding at least some trace of Banks's mystery man, if any existed. Besides, the material itself gave her an interesting picture of the times, and she found herself becoming quite fascinated by it all.

1965 hadn't been a bumper crime year for Peterborough, but the fast-growing city had its share of some of the more newsworthy national problems, Michelle was fast discovering. Mods and rockers clashed at some city-centre pubs, cannabis was beginning to insinuate its way into the lifestyles of the young and rebellious – despite what Banks had said – and the pornography trade was blossoming in the shape of tons of German, Danish and Swedish magazines covering every perversion you could imagine and some you couldn't. Why not Norwegian or Finnish, too? Michelle wondered. Weren't they into porn? Burglary and armed robbery were as common as ever, and the only thing that seemed new today was the increase in car theft.

Far fewer people owned cars in 1965, Michelle realized, and that made her think again about Banks's statement. Banks said he had been assaulted by a dirty, scruffy 'Rasputin-like' stranger on the riverside near the city centre. But Graham Marshall had been abducted, along with a heavy canvas bag full of newspapers, two months later, from a council estate several miles away. The MOs were different. It didn't look as if Graham had put up a struggle, for example, which he certainly would have done, as Banks had, if he'd been attacked by this frightening stranger and felt that he had been fighting for his life. Besides, the man who assaulted Banks had been on foot, and Graham hadn't walked all the way to his burial site. It was possible that the mysterious stranger had a car somewhere, but not very likely. Given Banks's description, Michelle would have guessed the man was homeless and poor, perhaps a tramp. *The passing tramp.* Cliché of so many detective stories.

The problem was that she still couldn't see any logical connection between the event Banks had described and the disappearance of Graham Marshall. She thought that Banks's sense of guilt might, over the years, have warped his judgement in the matter. It happened; she'd seen it before. But could it have happened that way? Who was this man?

There was a good chance, Michelle realized, that she might not find out anything about him in the police files. Not everyone had a file, despite what the anti-police groups seemed to think. She might have to dig in the newspaper morgue or perhaps the local mental hospital archives. The man sounded disturbed, and there was a chance he had sought treatment at some time. Of course, there was also every possibility that he wasn't a local. Michelle had no idea where the River Nene started, but she thought it was somewhere down Northampton way, and she knew that it flowed all the way to the Wash. Maybe he was walking the riverbank from town to town.

She flipped through file after file and tossed them aside in frustration. Finally, as her eyes were starting to tire, she struck gold.

7

The Coach and Horses, about a hundred yards along the main road, had changed over the years, Banks noticed, but not as much as some pubs. The large public bar had always housed a diverse group, mixed generations drinking there together, and today it was no different, though the racial mix had changed. Now, among the white faces, there were Pakistanis and Sikhs and, according to Arthur Banks, a group of Kosovan asylum seekers, who lived on the estate, also drank there.

Noisy machines with flashing lights had replaced the old bar-billiards area, the scarred wooden benches had been replaced with padded ones, perhaps the wallpaper had been redone and the light fixtures modernized, but that was about all. The brewery had forked out for this minor facelift sometime in the eighties, Banks's father had told him, hoping to pull in a younger, freer-spending crowd. But it didn't take. The people who drank at the Coach and Horses had, for the most part, been drinking there most of their lives. And their fathers before them. Banks had drunk his first legal pint here, with his father on his eighteenth birthday, though he had been knocking them back with his mates at the Wheatsheaf, about a mile away, since he was sixteen. The last time he had been in the Coach and Horses, he had played one of the earliest pub video games, that silly machine where you bounced the tennis ball back and forth across a green phosphorous screen.

Though there were few young people to be seen there, the Coach and Horses still managed to be a warm and lively place, Banks noticed as he walked in with his father just after eight o'clock that night, his mother's steamed pudding and custard – the *proper* food he was supposed to be eating – still weighing heavily in his stomach. His father had managed the walk without too much puffing and wheezing, which he put down to having stopped smoking two years ago. Banks had tapped his own jacket pocket rather guiltily for his cigarettes as they went out of the door.

This was Arthur Banks's local. He had been coming here almost every day for forty years, and so had his cronies, Harry Finnegan, Jock McFall and Norman Grenfell, Dave's father. Here, Arthur was respected. Here, he could escape the clutches of his ailments and the shame of his redundancy, at least for an hour or two, as he drank, laughed and told lies with the men with whom he felt most comfortable. For the Coach and Horses was, by and large a *men's* pub, despite the occasional couple and groups of women dropping by after work. When Arthur took Ida out for a drink, as he did on Fridays, they went to the Duck and Drake or the Duke of Wellington, where Ida Banks caught up on the local gossip and they took part in trivia quizzes and laughed at people making fools of themselves in the karaoke sessions.

But there was none of that at the Coach and Horses, and the piped sixties' pop music was turned down low enough so that old men could hear each other talk. At the moment, the Kinks were singing 'Waterloo Sunset', one of Banks's favourites. After Banks and his father had settled themselves at the table, pints in front of them and introductions made, Arthur Banks first lamented Jock McFall's absence due to hospitalization for a prostate operation, then Norman Grenfell started the ball rolling.

'We were just saying, before you got here, Alan, what a terrible thing it is about the Marshall boy. I remember you and our David used to play with him.'

'Yes. How is Dave, by the way?'

'He's doing fine,' said Norman. 'He and Ellie still live in Dorchester. The kids have grown up now, of course.'

'They're still together?' Ellie Hatcher was, Banks remembered, Dave's first real girlfriend; they must have started going out together around 1968.

'Some couples stick it out,' muttered Arthur Banks.

Banks ignored the remark and asked Norman to pass on his regards to Dave next time they spoke. Unlike Jock and Harry, Banks remembered, both of whom had worked with Arthur at the sheet-metal factory, Norman had worked in a clothing shop on Midgate, where he could sometimes get his mates a discount on a duffel coat, a pair of jeans or Tuf shoes. Norman drank halves instead of pints and smoked a pipe, which made him different, almost genteel, compared to the rough factory workers. He also had a hobby – he read and collected everything to do with steam trains and had an entire room of his small house devoted to clockwork models – and that set him even further apart from the beer, sport and telly crowd. Yet Norman Grenfell had always been as much a part of the group as Jock or Harry or Arthur himself, though he didn't share that ineffable bond that working men have, of having toiled under the same lousy conditions for the same lousy bosses and faced the same dangers day in, day out, for the same lousy pay. Maybe, Banks wondered, Graham had been a bit like that, too: set apart by his background, by his being a newcomer, by his London *cool*, yet still a part of the gang. The quiet one. The George Harrison of the group.

'Well,' Banks said, raising his glass. 'Here's to Graham. In the long run, I suppose it's best they found him. At least his parents can lay his bones to rest now.'

'True enough,' said Harry.

'Amen,' said Norman.

'Didn't Graham's father used to drink here?' Banks asked.

Arthur Banks laughed. 'He did. He was a rum customer, Bill Marshall. Isn't that right, Harry?'

'A rum customer, indeed. And a couple of bricks short of a full hod, too, if you ask me.'

They all laughed.

'In what way was he rum?' Banks asked.

Harry nudged Banks's father. 'Always the copper, your lad, hey?'

Arthur's brow darkened. Banks knew damn well that his father had never approved of his choice of career, and that no matter how well he did, how successful he was, to his father he would always be a traitor to the working class, who traditionally feared and despised coppers. As far as Arthur Banks was concerned, his son was employed by the middle and upper classes to protect their interests and their property. Never mind that most coppers of Arthur's own generation came from the working classes, unlike today, when many were middle-class university graduates and management types. The two of them had never resolved this problem, and Banks could see even now that his father was bothered by Harry Finnegan's little dig.

'Graham was a friend of mine,' Banks went on quickly to diffuse the tension. 'I was just wondering, that's all.'

'Is that why you're down here?' Norman asked.

'Partly, yes.'

It was the same question Mrs Marshall had asked him. Perhaps people assumed that because he was a policeman, and because he knew Graham, he would be assigned to this particular case. 'I don't know how much I can help,' Banks said, glancing sideways at his father, who was working on his beer. He had never told either of his parents about what had happened down by the river and he wasn't about to do so now. It might come out, of course, if his information led anywhere, and now he had an inkling of what the many witnesses who lied to avoid disclosing a shameful secret had to be anxious about. 'It's just that, well, I've thought about Graham and what happened on and off over the years, and I just thought I ought to come and try to help, that's all.'

'I can understand that,' said Norman, relighting his pipe. 'I think it's been a bit of a shock to the system for all of us, one way or another.'

'You were saying about Graham's father, Dad?'

Arthur Banks glanced at his son. 'Was I?'

'You said he was strange. I didn't know him well. I never really talked to him.'

'Course not,' said Arthur. 'You were just a kid.'

'That's why I'm asking you.'

There was a pause, then Arthur Banks looked over at Harry Finnegan. 'He was shifty, wouldn't you say so, Harry?'

'He was indeed. Always an eye for a fiddle, and not above a bit of strong-arm stuff. I wouldn't have trusted him as far as I could throw him. And he was a big talker, too.'

'What do you mean?' Banks asked.

'Well,' his father said, 'you know the family came up from London?'

'Yes.'

'Bill Marshall worked as a bricklayer and he was a good one, too, but when he'd had a drink or two he'd start letting things slip about some of his other activities in London.'

'I still don't understand.'

'He was a fit bloke, Bill. Strong. Big hands, powerful upper body. Comes from carrying those hods around the building sites.'

'He used to get into fights?'

'You could say that.'

'What your Dad's saying,' explained Harry, leaning forward, 'is that Bill Marshall let slip he used to act as an enforcer for gangsters down the Smoke. Protection rackets, that sort of thing.'

The Smoke? Banks hadn't heard that term for London in years. 'He did?' Banks shook his head. It was hard to imagine the old man in the chair as having been some sort of gang enforcer, but it might help explain the fear Banks remembered feeling in his presence all those years ago, the threat of violence. 'I'd never have—'

'How could you?' his father cut in. 'Like I said, you were just a kid. You couldn't understand things like that.'

The music had changed, Banks noticed. Herb Alpert and his bloody Tijuana Brass, just finishing, thank God. Banks had hated them back then and he hated them now. Next came the Bachelors, 'Marie'. Mum and Dad music. 'Did you tell the police?' he asked.

The men looked at one another, then Arthur looked back at Banks, his lip curling. 'What do *you* think?'

'But he could—'

'Listen. Bill Marshall might have been a big talker, but he had nothing to do with his son's disappearance.'

'How can you know that?'

Arthur Banks snorted. 'You police. All the bloody same, you are. Just because a man might be a bit dodgy in one area, you're ready to fit him up with anything.'

'I've never fitted anyone up in my life,' said Banks.

'What I'm saying is that Bill Marshall might have been a bit of a wild man, but he didn't go around killing young lads, especially not his own son.'

'I didn't say I thought he did it,' Banks said, noticing that the others were watching him and his father now, as if they were the evening's entertainment.

'Then what *did* you mean?'

'Look, Dad,' Banks said, reaching for a cigarette. He had been determined not to smoke in front of his father, mostly because of the old man's health, but not smoking in the Coach and Horses was as pointless as swimming in the no-pissing section of a swimming pool, if such a section were ever to exist. 'If there was any truth in what Bill Marshall said about his criminal background in London, then isn't it possible that something he'd done there came back to haunt him?'

'But nobody hurt *Bill*.'

'Doesn't matter, Dad. These people often have more devious ways of getting back at their enemies. Believe me. I've come across more than a few of them in my time. Did he ever mention any names?'

'What do you mean?'

'I mean in London. The people he worked for. Did he ever mention any names?'

Harry Finnegan gave a nervous laugh. Arthur shot him

a glance and he shut up. 'As a matter of fact,' said Arthur, pausing dramatically, 'he did.'

'Who?'

'The Twins. Reggie and Ronnie Kray.'

'Bloody hell!'

Arthur Banks's eyes shone with triumph. '*Now* do you see why we just thought he had a big mouth on him?'

•

For the second time that day Annie turned up at Swainsdale Hall, only this time she felt the butterflies in the pit of her stomach. People like Martin Armitage were difficult enough to deal with in the first place, and he wouldn't like what she had to say. Still, she thought, for all his tough bluster, he hadn't done much but kick a ball around most of his life. Robin was another matter. Annie sensed that she might feel relieved to have someone else to share her fears with, and that underneath her accommodating exterior and her air of vulnerability, there was a strong woman who was capable of standing up to her husband.

Josie answered the door, as usual, holding a barking Miata by the collar. Annie wanted to talk to Josie and her husband, Calvin, but they could wait. For the moment, the fewer people who knew what was going on the better. Robin and Martin were both out in the garden sitting at a wrought-iron table under a striped umbrella. It was a warm evening, and the back garden faced south, so there was plenty of honey-tinted sunlight and dark shadows cast by tree branches. Annie felt like reaching for her sketch pad. Beyond the high drystone wall that marked the property boundary, the daleside stretched up in a patchwork of uneven fields, green until the sere bareness of the higher slopes, where it rose more steeply to merge into the wild stretch of heather moorland that separated the dales.

Neither Martin nor Robin seemed to be enjoying the beautiful evening or the long, cool drinks that sat in front of them. Both seemed pale, tense and preoccupied, the mobile perched on the table like an unexploded bomb.

'What are you doing here?' Martin Armitage said. 'I told you Luke was on his way home and I'd be in touch when he got here.'

'I take it he's not arrived yet?'

'No.'

'Heard from him again?'

'No.'

Annie sighed and sat down without being invited.

'I didn't ask you to—'

Annie raised her hand to quiet Martin down. 'Look,' she said, 'there's no point pissing about any more. I know what's going on.'

'I don't understand what you mean.'

'Come off it, Mr Armitage. I followed you.'

'You did what?'

'I followed you. After I left this morning I waited in a lay-by and followed you to the shepherd's shelter. What were you doing there?'

'None of your bloody business. Why, what are you going to do? Charge me with disobeying government regulations?'

'Let me tell you what you were doing, Mr Armitage. You were leaving a briefcase full of money. Old bills. Tens and twenties for the most part. Around ten thousand pounds, at a guess, maybe fifteen.'

Armitage was red in the face. Still, Annie pressed on.

'And now let me tell you what happened. They got in touch with you last night on your mobile, said they'd got Luke and you were to hand over the money. You told them you couldn't lay your hands on that much cash until the banks were open, so they gave you until this morning to leave it at the prearranged drop.' Which means they know something about the area, Annie realized, or that they've been watching, scouting for some time. Maybe someone had noticed them. Strangers usually stood out around these parts, especially as the tourist numbers were down. 'How am I doing so far?'

'You've got imagination, I'll certainly give you that.'

'They said no police, which is why my arrival scared the living daylights out of you.'

'I've told you—'

'Martin.' Robin Armitage spoke for the first time, and though her voice was soft and kindly, it was authoritative enough to command her husband's attention. 'Can't you see?' she went on. 'She knows. I must admit that I, for one, feel rather relieved.'

'But he said—'

'They don't know who I am,' said Annie. 'And I'm pretty certain they didn't see me around Mortsett this morning.'

'Pretty certain?'

Annie looked him in the eye. 'I'd be a liar if I said I was a hundred per cent certain.' Birds in the trees filled in the silence that followed, and a light breeze ruffled Annie's hair. She held Martin Armitage's gaze until she saw it waver and finally wane into defeat. His shoulders slumped. Robin leaned over and put her arm around him. 'It's all right, darling,' she said. 'The police will know what to do. They'll be discreet.' Robin looked at Annie as she spoke, as if daring her to disagree. Annie didn't. Martin ran the backs of his hands across his eyes and nodded.

'I'm sorry about what's happened,' Annie said, 'but Mrs Armitage is right.'

'Robin. Please. As we're involved in such an intimate matter, at least you can call me by my first name. My husband, too.'

'Okay. Robin. Look, I have to tell you that I'm not a negotiator. This isn't my area of expertise. We have people specially trained to deal with kidnappers and their demands.'

'But he said no police,' Martin repeated. 'He said if we brought in the police he'd kill Luke.'

'What did you say?'

'I told him I'd already reported Luke missing.'

'And what did he say to that?'

'He was quiet for a moment, as if he was thinking, like.'

'Or consulting with someone else?'

'He could have been, but I didn't hear anyone. Anyway, when he came back on he said that was fine, but to make sure I told you Luke had rung and said that he was coming home. Which I did.'

'It was a man who made the call, then?'

'Yes.'

'What time?'

'About half-past nine. Just before Robin rang you.'

'How much did he ask for?'

'Ten thousand.'

'Accent?'

'None, really.'

'He didn't sound local?'

'He could've been, but he didn't have a strong accent. Sort of bland.'

'And his voice?'

'What do you mean?'

'High or low? Husky, reedy, whatever?'

'Just ordinary. I'm sorry, I'm not good at this sort of thing, especially recognizing voices on the telephone.'

Annie favoured him with a smile. 'Not many people are. Think about it, though. It could be important if there's anything at all you remember about the voice.'

'Yes. I'll think about it.'

'Did he let you speak to Luke?'

'No.'

'Did you ask?'

'Yes, but he said Luke was being kept somewhere else.'

'And he called you on your mobile?'

'Yes.'

'Who knows the number?'

'Family. Close friends. Business colleagues. I suppose it would be easy enough to find out. Luke, of course. He has it programmed into the electronic phone book of his own mobile. At first, I thought it was him because his name was displayed when the call came.'

'So the kidnapper used Luke's mobile to call you?'

'I suppose so. Why does it matter?'

'At least it tells us he's in an area where there's a signal. Or he was when he made the call. Also, if he's used it at other times, we'll be able to get the information from the phone company. It might help us pinpoint him. Of course, it would be better if he left it switched on, but he's not going to make things that easy for us.'

'Tell me,' said Robin, 'in your experience, in how many cases do they . . . how many times do the victims . . .'

'I don't have any statistics offhand,' Annie admitted. 'But if it makes you feel any better, kidnappers are essentially business people. They're in it for the money, not to hurt anyone. There's every chance that this will be resolved and that you'll see Luke back here safe and sound.' Annie could feel her nose growing as she talked. Too much time had passed, she suspected, for a happy ending, though she hoped she was wrong. 'In the meantime, while appearing to go along with his demands and not alarming him in any way, we want to make sure that in addition to getting Luke home safely we take every opportunity to discover the kidnapper's identity and bring him to justice.'

'How can we help?' asked Robin.

'You don't have to do anything,' said Annie. 'You've already played your part. Just leave the rest to us.'

'Maybe you've scared him off,' Martin said. 'Luke should be back by now. It's been hours.'

'Sometimes they wait a long time just to make sure nobody's watching. He's probably waiting till dark.'

'But you can't be certain, can you?' Robin said.

'Nothing's certain in this world, Mrs Armitage.'

'Robin. I told you. Oh, how rude of me!' She got to her feet. 'All this time and I haven't offered you anything to drink.' She was wearing denim shorts, Annie noticed, cut high on her long, smooth legs. There weren't many women who could get away with the bare midriff look at her age, either, Annie thought. She wouldn't even think of it herself, though she was only thirty-four, but what she could see of Robin's stomach looked flat and taut, with a ring of some sort glinting in her navel.

'No,' she said. 'Really. I'm not stopping long.' There wasn't much else Annie could do for Luke except wait, and she had promised herself a nice pint of bitter at the Black Sheep in Relton, where she could sit in peace and mull things over before calling it a day. 'I just want to make certain that you'll report any future communications, if there are any, straight to me. You've got the numbers where I can be reached?'

Both Martin and Robin nodded.

'And, of course, you'll let me know the second Luke turns up.'

'We will,' said Robin. 'I just hope and pray that he does come home soon.'

'Me, too,' said Annie, getting up. 'There's one more thing that puzzles me.'

'What?' asked Robin.

'Last night, when you rang to tell me you'd heard from Luke, you said he would be back tonight.'

'That's what he told Martin. The kidnapper. He said that if we left the money this morning, then Luke would be home unharmed by tonight.'

'And you knew that I wanted to see Luke as soon as he got back, to talk to him?'

'Yes.'

'So how were you going to explain everything?' asked Annie. 'I'm curious.'

Robin looked over at her husband, who answered, 'We were going to persuade Luke to tell you what we said happened in the first place, that he'd run away and phoned us the night before to say he was coming back.'

'Who thought of this?'

'The kidnapper suggested it.'

'Sounds like the perfect crime,' said Annie. 'Only you two, Luke and the kidnapper would ever know that it had been committed, and none of you would be likely to talk.'

Martin looked down at his drink.

'He would have done that?' Annie went on. 'Luke would have lied to the police?'

'He would have done it for me,' said Robin.

Annie looked at her, nodded and left.

•

The Krays, Banks thought as he lay in his narrow bed that night. Reggie and Ronnie. He didn't remember the exact dates, of course, but he had an idea that they were flying high in the mid-sixties, part of the swinging London scene, mixing with celebrities, pop stars and politicians.

It had always intrigued him the way gangsters became celebrities: Al Capone, Lucky Luciano, John Dillinger, Dutch Schultz, Bugsy Malone. Figures of legend. He had known a few of the lesser ones in his time, and they almost always rubbed shoulders with the rich and famous, as if celebrity recognized only itself and was blind to all else – morality, decency, honour – and they never lacked for beautiful women to run around with, the kind who were attracted by danger and the aura of violence. There seemed to be a glamour and mystique attached to making your money out of running prostitutes, supplying drugs and threatening to destroy people's livelihoods if they didn't pay protection, and it was more than likely that most film stars, sports personalities and pop stars were addle-brained enough to fall for it – the glamour of violence. Or was it the violence of glamour?

The Krays were no exception. They knew how to manipulate the media and being photographed with a famous actress, an MP, or a peer of the realm made it less likely that the truth about their real activities would come out. There was a trial in 1965, Banks remembered, and they came out of that more fireproof than they went in.

It was hard to believe that Graham Marshall's dad had anything to do with them, though, and Banks had to admit that his father was probably right; it had just been the beer talking.

Why, though? Why even hint at something like that if there wasn't a scrap of truth in it? Maybe Bill Marshall was a pathological liar. But over his years as a copper Banks had learned that the old cliché 'There's no smoke without fire' had a great deal to recommend it. And there were two other things: the Marshalls came from the East End of London, Kray territory in the mid-sixties, and Banks now remembered feeling afraid around Mr Marshall.

He already knew a bit about the Krays, most of it picked up when he was on the Met years ago, but he could dig deeper. There were plenty of books about them, though he doubted that any mentioned Bill Marshall. If he had done anything for them, it had obviously been low level, going round the customers and exuding physical menace, maybe clobbering the occasional informer or double-dealer in a dark alley.

He would have to tell DI Hart. Michelle. She had left a message with Banks's mother while he was out asking him to drop by Thorpe Wood at nine a.m. the following morning. It was her case, after all. If there was a connection, though, he was surprised that it hadn't come out in the investigation. Usually the parents come under very close scrutiny in missing-child cases, no matter how grief-stricken they appear. Banks had once come across a young couple he had believed to be genuinely grieving the loss of their child, only to find the poor kid strangled for crying too loud and stuffed in the downstairs freezer. No, you couldn't trust surfaces in police work; you had to dig, if only to make certain you weren't having the wool pulled over your eyes.

Banks picked up his old transistor radio. He had bought a battery earlier and wondered if it would still work after all these years. Probably not, but it was worth the price of a battery to find out. He unclipped the back, connected the battery and put the earpiece in his ear. It was just a single unit, like an old hearing aid. No stereo radio back then. When he turned it on, he was thrilled to find that the old trannie actually worked. Banks could hardly believe it. As he tuned the dial, though, he soon began to feel disappointed. The sound quality was poor, but it wasn't only that. The radio received all the local stations, Classic FM and Radios 1, 2, 3, 4 and 5, just like any modern radio, but Banks realized he had been half-expecting to go back in time. The idea that this was a magic radio that still received the Light Programme, Radio Luxembourg and the pirates, Radio Caroline and Radio London, was lodged somewhere in his mind. He had expected to be listening to John Peel's *The Perfumed Garden*, to relive those magical few months in the spring of 1967, when he should have been studying for his O levels but spent half the night with the radio plugged in his ear, hearing Captain Beefheart, the Incredible String Band and Tyrannosaurus Rex for the first time.

Banks switched off the radio and turned to his *Photoplay* diary. At least he had a bedside light in his room now and didn't have to hide under the sheets with a torch. Beside each week was a full-page photograph of an actor or actress popular at the time, usually an actress, or starlet, chosen because of pulchritude rather than acting ability, and more often than not appearing in a risqué pose, bra and panties, the carefully placed bed sheet, the off-the-shoulder strap. He flipped through the pages and there they all were: Natalie Wood, Catherine Deneuve, Martine Beswick, Ursula Andress. Cleavage abounded. 15–21 August were accompanied by a photo of Shirley Eaton in a low-cut dress.

As he flipped through the diary, Banks discovered that he had hardly been voluminous or the least bit analytical; he had simply noted events, adventures and excursions, often in a very cryptic manner. In a way, it was a perfect model for the policeman's notebook he was to keep later. Still, the pages were small, divided into seven sections, with room for a little fact or piece of cinema history at the bottom. If any of the dates happened to be a star's birthday, as many did, a portion of the available space was taken up with that, too. Given the restrictions, he had done a decent enough job, he thought, deciphering the miniature scrawl. He had certainly been to see a lot of films, listing all of them in his diary, along with his terse opinions, which varied from 'Crap' and 'Boring' through 'Okay' to 'Fantastic!' A typical entry might read, 'Went to the Odeon with Dave and Graham to see *Dr Who and the Daleks*. Okay,' 'Played cricket on the rec. Scored 32 not out,' or, 'Rained. Stopped in and read *Casino Royale*. Fantastic!'

He flipped to the Saturday before Graham disappeared, the 21st. 'Went into town with Graham. Bought *Help!* with Uncle Ken's record token.' It was the same LP they had listened to at Paul's the next day. That was all he had written, nothing unusual about Graham's state of mind. On Friday he had watched the Animals, one of his favourite groups, on *Ready, Steady, Go!*

On Sunday he had written, probably while in bed that night, 'Played records at Paul's place. New Bob Dylan LP. Saw police car go to Graham's house.' On Monday, 'Graham's run away from home. Police came. Joey flew away.'

Interesting he should assume that Graham had run away from home. But of course he would at that age. What else? The alternatives would have been too horrific for a fourteen-year-old boy to contemplate. He flipped back to late June, around the time he thought the event on the riverbank had occurred. It was a Tuesday, he noticed. He hadn't written much about it, simply, 'Skived off school and played by river this afternoon. A strange man tried to push me in.'

Tired, Banks put the diary aside, rubbed his eyes and turned out the light. It felt odd to be back in the same bed he had slept in during his teenage years, the same bed where he had had his first sexual experience, with Kay Summerville, while his parents were out visiting his grandparents one Saturday. It hadn't been very good for either Banks or Kay, but they had persevered and got a lot better with practice.

Kay Summerville. He wondered where she was, what she was doing now. Probably married with kids, the same way he had been until recently. She'd been a beauty, though, had Kay: long blonde hair, slender waist, long legs, a mouth like Marianne Faithfull's, firm tits with hard little nipples and hair like spun gold between her legs. Christ, Banks, he told himself, enough with the adolescent fantasies.

He put on his headphones and turned on his portable CD player, listening to Vaughan Williams's second string quartet, and settled back to more pleasant thoughts of Kay

Summerville. But as he approached the edge of sleep his thoughts jumbled, mixing memory with dream. It was cold and dark, and Banks and Graham were walking across a rugby field, goalposts silhouetted by the moon, cracking spider-web patterns in the ice as they walked, their breath misting the air. Banks must have said something about the Krays being arrested – was he interested in criminals, even then? – and Graham just laughed, saying the law could never touch people like them. Banks asked him how he knew, and Graham said he used to live near them. 'They were kings,' he said.

Puzzled by the memory, or dream, Banks turned the bedside light on again and picked up the diary. If what he had just imagined had any basis in reality, then it had happened in winter. He glanced through his entries for January and February 1965: Samantha Eggar, Yvonne Romain, Elke Sommer . . . But no mention of the Krays until 9 March, when he had written, 'Krays went to trial today. Graham laughed and said they'd get off easy.' So Graham *had* mentioned them. It was flimsy, but a start.

He turned off the light again, and this time he drifted off to sleep without further thoughts of either Graham or Kay Summerville.

8

When Banks arrived at Thorpe Wood the following morning and asked to see Detective Inspector Hart, he was surprised when a man came down to greet him. The telephone call that his mother had told him about when he got back from the pub had been from Michelle.

'Mr Banks, or should I say DCI Banks? Come with me please, if you would.' He stood aside and gestured for Banks to enter.

'And you are?'

'Detective Superintendent Shaw. We'll talk in my office.'

Shaw looked familiar, but Banks couldn't place him. It was possible they had met on a course, or even on a case, years ago, and he had forgotten, but he usually had a good memory for faces.

They didn't speak on their way to Shaw's office, and as soon as they got there, Shaw disappeared, saying he'd be back in a couple of minutes. Old copper's trick, Banks knew. And Shaw knew he knew.

There wasn't likely to be anything of interest in the office if Shaw was willing to leave Banks there alone, but he had a poke around nonetheless. Second nature. He wasn't looking for anything in particular, but just looking for the sake of it. The filing cabinets were locked, as were the desk drawers, and the computer required a password. It began to seem very much as if Shaw *expected* Banks to nose about.

There was an interesting framed photograph on the wall, quite a few years old by the look of it, showing a younger Shaw and Jet Harris standing by an unmarked Rover looking for all the world like John Thaw and Dennis Waterman in *The Sweeney*. Or was it Morse and Lewis? Is that how Shaw saw himself, as Sergeant Lewis to Harris's Chief Inspector Morse?

The bookcase held mostly binders and back issues of the *Police Review*. Mixed in were a few legal texts and an American textbook called *Practical Homicide Investigation*. Banks was browsing through this and trying not to look at the gruesome colour illustrations when, after half an hour, Shaw came back, followed by a rather embarrassed-looking DI Michelle Hart.

'Sorry about that,' said Shaw, sitting down opposite Banks. 'Something came up. You know how it is.' Michelle sat to one side looking uncomfortable.

'I know.' Banks put the book aside and reached for a cigarette.

'There's no smoking in here,' said Shaw. 'Not anywhere in the building, not for any of us, these days. Maybe you're a bit behind the times in Yorkshire?'

Banks had known that he probably couldn't smoke, though Shaw had the nicotine-stained fingers of a heavy smoker, and he thought it at least worth a try. Obviously, though, this was going to be played the hard way, even though they had done him the courtesy of conducting the interview in the superintendent's office rather than in a dingy interview room. He didn't feel nervous, just puzzled and pissed off. What was going on?

'So, what can I do for you, Superintendent Shaw?'

'You don't remember me, do you?'

Shaw stared at Banks, and Banks searched through his

store of faces for a match. The ginger hair was thin on top, one long side strand combed over to hide the bald patch, but not fooling anyone, hardly any eyebrows, freckles, pale blue eyes, the face filled out and jowly, the fleshy, red-veined nose of a seasoned drinker. He was familiar, but there was something different about him. Then Banks knew.

'You've had your ears fixed,' he said. 'The wonders of modern medicine.'

Shaw reddened. 'So you *do* remember me.'

'You were the baby DC who came to our house after Graham disappeared.' It was hard to believe, but Shaw would have been about twenty-one at the time, only seven years older than Banks, yet he had seemed an adult, someone from another world.

'Tell me,' said Shaw, leaning forward across the table so Banks could smell the minty breath of a man who drinks his breakfast, 'I've always wondered. Did you ever get your budgie back?'

Banks leaned back in his chair. 'Well, now we've got all the pleasantries out of the way, why don't we get on with it?'

Shaw jerked his head at Michelle, who slid a photograph across the desk to Banks. She looked serious with her reading glasses on. Sexy, too, Banks thought. 'Is this the man?' she asked.

Banks stared at the black and white photo and felt a rush of blood to his brain, ears buzzing and vision clouding. It all flooded back, those few moments of claustrophobia and terror in the stranger's grip, the moments he had thought were his last.

'Are you all right?'

It was Michelle who spoke, a concerned look on her face.

'I'm fine,' he said.

'You look pale. Would you like a drink of water?'

'No, thank you,' said Banks. 'It's him.'

'Are you certain?'

'After all this time I can't be a hundred per cent positive, but I'm as certain as I'll ever be.'

Shaw nodded, and Michelle took the picture back.

'Why?' Banks asked, looking from one to the other. 'Who is it?'

'James Francis McCallum,' Michelle said. 'He went missing from a mental institution near Wisbech on Thursday, the seventeenth of June 1965.'

'That would be about right,' said Banks.

'McCallum hadn't been involved in any violent activity, but the doctors told us that the possibility always existed, and that he might be dangerous.'

'When was he caught?' Banks asked.

Michelle glanced at Shaw before answering. He gave her a curt nod. 'That's just it,' she went on. 'He wasn't. McCallum's body was fished out of the River Nene near Oundle on the first of July.'

Banks felt his mouth open and shut without any sound coming out. 'Dead?' he managed.

'Dead,' echoed Shaw. He tapped his pen on the desk. 'Nearly two months before your friend disappeared. So you see, DCI Banks, you've been labouring under an illusion for all these years. Now, what I'm really interested in is why you lied to me and DI Proctor in the first place.'

Banks felt numb from the shock he had just received. *Dead*. All these years. The guilt. And all for nothing. The man who assaulted him on the riverbank *couldn't* have abducted and killed Graham. He should have felt relieved, but he only felt confused. 'I didn't lie,' he muttered.

'Call it a sin of omission, then. You didn't tell us about McCallum.'

'Doesn't seem as if it would have mattered, does it?'

'Why didn't you tell us?'

'Look, I was just a kid. I hadn't told my parents because I was scared how they'd react. I was upset and ashamed by what happened. Don't ask me why, I don't know, but that's how I felt. Dirty and ashamed, as if it was somehow *my* fault for inviting it.'

'You should have told us. It could have been a lead.'

Banks knew that Shaw was right; he had told reluctant witnesses the same thing himself, time after time. 'Well, I didn't, and it wasn't,' he snapped. 'I'm sorry. Okay?'

But Shaw wasn't going to be so easily put off, Banks could tell. He was enjoying himself, throwing his weight around. It was the bully mentality. To him, Banks was still the fourteen-year-old kid whose budgie had just flown out the door. 'What really happened to your friend?' he asked.

'What do you mean?'

Shaw scratched his chin. 'I remember thinking at the time that you knew something, that you were holding something back. I'd like to have taken you to the station, had you down in the cells for an hour or so, but you were a minor, and Reg Proctor was a bit of a softie, when it came right down to it. What really happened?'

'I don't know. Graham just disappeared.'

'Are you sure you and your mates didn't set on him? Maybe it was an accident, things just went too far?'

'What the hell are you talking about?'

'I'm suggesting that maybe the three of you ganged up on Graham Marshall for some reason and killed him.

These things happen. Then you had to get rid of the body.'

Banks folded his arms. 'And tell me how we did that.'

'I don't know,' Shaw admitted. 'But I don't have to. Maybe you stole a car.'

'None of us could drive.'

'So you say.'

'It wasn't the way it is today, with ten-year-olds behind the wheel.'

'Is that how it happened? A fight broke out and Graham got killed? Maybe fell and smashed his skull, or broke his neck? I'm not saying you *intended* to kill him, but it happened, didn't it? Why don't you come clean with me, Banks? It'll do you good to get it off your chest after all these years.'

'Sir?'

'Shut up, DI Hart. Well, Banks? I'm waiting.'

Banks stood up. 'You'll have a bloody long wait, then. Goodbye.' He walked towards the door. Shaw didn't try to stop him. Just as Banks had turned the handle, he heard the superintendent speak again and turned to face him. Shaw was grinning. 'Only teasing, Banks,' he said. Then his expression became serious. 'My, but you're sensitive. The point I want to make is that you're on *my* turf, and it turns out you can't help us any more now than you could all those years ago. So my advice to you, laddie, is to bugger off back up to Yorkshire, go shag a sheep or two, and forget about Graham Marshall. Leave it to the pros.'

'Bloody good job the pros did last time,' said Banks, leaving and slamming the door behind him, annoyed at himself for losing his temper, but unable to prevent it. Outside the station he kicked a tyre, lit a cigarette and got in his car. Maybe Shaw was right and he should just head back up north. He still had over a week's holiday left and plenty to do around the cottage, whereas there was nothing more he could do down here. Before driving off, he sat for a moment trying to digest what Michelle and Shaw had told him. His guilt over the years had been misplaced, then; McCallum was in no way responsible for Graham's abduction and, by extension, neither was Banks. On the other hand, if he *had* reported the incident, there was a chance that McCallum might have been apprehended and hospitalized instead of drowning. *More guilt, then?*

Banks cast his mind back to that hot June afternoon by the river and asked himself if McCallum would have killed him. The answer, he decided, was yes. So sod the bastard, and sod guilt. McCallum was a dangerous loony and it wasn't Banks's fault he'd fallen in the fucking river and drowned. Good riddance.

Turning up the volume on Cream's 'Crossroads', he sped out of the police car park, daring one of the patrol cars to chase him. Nobody did.

•

They all looked tired, Annie thought, as the Armitage team gathered in the boardroom of Western Area Headquarters late that morning. The boardroom was so called because of its long polished table, high-backed chairs and paintings of nineteenth-century cotton magnates on the walls, red-faced, eyes popping, probably because of the tight collars they were wearing, Annie thought. As works of art, the paintings were negligible, if not execrable, but they lent authority to the room.

Detective Superintendent Gristhorpe sat at the head of the table and poured himself a glass of water. Also present were DCs Templeton, Rickerd and Jackman, and

Detective Sergeant Jim Hatchley, still clearly uneasy with Annie's promotion over him. But as Banks had told Annie more than once, Jim Hatchley was born to be a sergeant, and a damn good one, too. There wasn't much Hatchley didn't know about the shady side of Eastvale. He had a network of informers second only to his network of pub managers and landlords, who all kept an eye on criminal comings and goings for him, and his tiredness was probably due to the fact that his wife had just given birth to their second child a couple of weeks ago. It was the three DCs who had borne the brunt of the previous night's surveillance.

'So we're not much further ahead,' Gristhorpe opened.

'No, sir,' said Annie, who at least had managed her quick pint in Relton, then gone home for a bath and a few hours' sleep before arriving back at the station shortly after dawn. 'Except we've checked with the phone company and got Luke's records. We'll be tracking down all the people he phoned over the last month, though there aren't many. The ransom call to Martin Armitage was the only call made after Luke's disappearance, the only call made that day, and it was local. Wherever Luke is, he's not far away, or he wasn't on Tuesday evening.'

'Anything else?'

'We've got a fair idea of Luke's movements until five-thirty the day he disappeared.'

'Go ahead.'

Annie walked over to the whiteboard and listed the times and places as she mentioned them. She knew the details by heart and didn't need to consult her notebook. 'He arrived at the bus station by the Swainsdale Centre at a quarter to three. The bus driver and several of the passengers remember him. We've been looking at some of the CCTV footage, and he walked around the centre for a while, went into W.H. Smith's, then into HMV, but he didn't appear to buy anything. That takes us up until half-past three. He appeared in that small computer shop on North Market Street at a quarter to four, which is about right, as he was on foot. He stayed there half an hour, trying out some games, then he visited the music shop at the corner of York Road and Barton Place.'

'Did anyone notice anything unusual about his state of mind?' Gristhorpe asked.

'No. Everyone said he just seemed normal. Which, I guess, was pretty weird to start with. I mean, he wasn't exactly a barrel of laughs.'

'And next?'

'The used book shop on the market square.' Annie walked over to the window and pointed. 'That one down there. Norman's.'

'I know it,' said Gristhorpe. 'What did he buy?'

'*Crime and Punishment* and *Portrait of the Artist as a Young Man*.' Right up Gristhorpe's alley, Annie thought.

Gristhorpe whistled. 'Pretty heavy going for a fifteen-year-old. What next?'

'That was it. He walked out of the market square CCTV range at half-past five, and we haven't found anyone who admits to seeing him since. Oh, and he was also seen talking to a group of lads in the square after coming out of the bookshop. It looked as if they were ragging him. One of them took the parcel of books from his hand and they tossed it around to one another while he flailed around trying to get it back.'

'What happened in the end?'

'One of them threw it to him and they went off laughing.'

'Classmates?'

'Yes. We've had a chat with them. At least DC Templeton has.'

'Nothing there, sir,' said Templeton. 'They've all got alibis.'

'Which direction did he walk off in?' Gristhorpe asked.

'Down Market Street. South.'

Gristhorpe scratched his chin and frowned. 'What do you make of it all, Annie?' he asked.

'I don't know, sir. He's been gone three nights now and nobody's seen hide nor hair.'

'What about the Armitages?'

'Nothing.'

'Sure they're telling you the truth?'

'They've no reason to lie now,' Annie said. 'And the kidnapper knows we're treating Luke as a misper. Remember, it was him who suggested that the Armitages get Luke to back up their story.'

'Too late for that, now, isn't it?' said DC Kevin Templeton. 'I mean, wasn't he supposed to come home yesterday?'

'Yes.'

'So what happened?' Gristhorpe asked.

'He's probably dead, sir,' cut in DC Winsome Jackman.

'But why hasn't the kidnapper gone for the money?'

'Because he knows we're watching,' Annie answered. 'It's the only explanation. He must have seen me when I went up to the shelter to check the briefcase.'

Nobody said anything; there was nothing they *could* say. Annie knew they agreed with her and could all sense what she was feeling herself, that gut-wrenching fear that *she* might be responsible for the boy's death, that if she had stuck to rules and procedure, then things might have gone according to plan. To give him his due, though, whatever he thought, Gristhorpe didn't say anything.

'Unless . . .' Annie went on.

'Aye, lass?'

'Well, a couple of things have puzzled me about all this right from the start.'

'I agree that, as kidnappings go, it's hardly conventional,' said Gristhorpe, 'but go on.'

Annie took a sip of water. 'In the first place,' she said, 'why did the kidnapper wait so long before getting in touch with the Armitages and making his demand? Luke disappeared sometime late Monday afternoon or evening, according to what we've managed to find out so far, yet the demand didn't come until after dark on *Tuesday*.'

'Maybe the kidnapper didn't get hold of him until Tuesday,' DC Templeton suggested.

'You mean he really did run away and just happened to get picked up by a kidnapper before he could go back?'

'It's possible, isn't it?'

'Too much of a coincidence, I'd say.'

'Coincidences do happen.'

'Sometimes, maybe.'

'Or the kidnapper might have been keeping an eye on Luke for a while, watching his movements, biding his time.'

'I'll grant you that's more likely,' said Gristhorpe. 'Annie?'

'It still doesn't explain the time delay between Luke not turning up at home Monday night and the ransom demand on Tuesday evening, sir. These people don't usually like to waste time. If they snatched him on Monday, then they'd have rung the Armitages on Monday. Besides, that's only the first thing that bothered me.'

'What's next?' Gristhorpe asked.

'Well, Martin Armitage told me that when he asked to speak to Luke, the kidnapper wouldn't let him, said Luke was somewhere else.'

'So?' said DC Templeton. 'That's perfectly likely, isn't it?'

'But he was calling from Luke's mobile,' Annie pointed out.

'I still don't see your point,' said Templeton. 'Mobiles are mobile. You can take them anywhere. That's what they're for.'

Annie sighed. 'Think about it, Kev. If Luke's being kept somewhere where there isn't a phone, then the kidnapper might have to go to a phone box, and he'd be unlikely to take Luke with him. But the kidnapper was using Luke's mobile, so why isn't he with Luke?'

'Could be where they're keeping the lad is out of cell range,' suggested DC Rickerd.

'Possible,' Annie agreed, remembering her time out of range. 'But isn't it usual for kidnappers to let the people they want the money from speak to their loved ones? Isn't it an incentive to pay? Proof of life?'

'Good point, Annie,' said Gristhorpe. 'So we've got two unusual variations on the formula. First, the time delay, and second, no proof of life. Anything else?'

'Yes,' said Annie. 'The ransom demand.'

'What about it?' asked Gristhorpe.

'It's nowhere near enough.'

'But the Armitages aren't as rich as people think they are,' argued Templeton.

'My point exactly, Kev. So they're struggling to maintain Swainsdale Hall and whatever lifestyle they've become accustomed to. We know that now, since I talked to them, but it wasn't common knowledge. As police, we're privy to a lot of inside information. It's our life-blood. But if you kidnapped the son of a famous ex-model and a famous ex-footballer living in a place like Swains-dale Hall, how much would you *think* they were worth? How much would you ask them for the life of their son? Ten thousand? Twenty thousand? Fifty? I'd go to a hundred, myself, or maybe a quarter of a million. Let them negotiate down a few thousand from there. I certainly wouldn't start at ten.'

'So maybe the kidnapper knew they were on their uppers?' Templeton suggested. 'Maybe it's someone who knows the family?'

'Then why kidnap Luke at all? Why not go for someone who had more money?'

'Maybe that's all they needed. Maybe it's enough.'

'You're clutching at straws, Kev.'

Templeton smiled. 'Just playing devil's advocate, Ma'am, that's all. But if you're right, then perhaps they don't have quite the intelligence we're crediting them with.'

'Okay. Point taken.' Annie looked at Gristhorpe. 'But don't you think it's all a bit puzzling when you add it up, sir?'

Gristhorpe paused and made a steeple of his thick fingers on the desk before answering. 'I do,' he said. 'I can't say I've had to deal with many kidnappings over the course of my career – and for that I thank the Lord, because it's a cowardly crime – but I've dealt with a few, and none of them have been as riddled with anomalies as this one. What are your conclusions, Annie?'

'Either it's an amateur job,' Annie answered. '*Very* amateur, like some junkie who saw the chance to get enough money for his next few fixes and now he's too scared to go through with it.'

'Or?'

'Or it's something else entirely. A set-up, a diversion, the ransom demand merely to deflect us, confuse us, and something else is going on.'

'Like what?' Gristhorpe asked.

'I don't know, sir,' Annie answered. 'All I know is that in either scenario the outcome looks bad for Luke.'

•

It wasn't fair, thought Andrew Naylor, the man from the Ministry, as he drove his government Range Rover over the disinfectant pad at the entrance to the unfenced road above Gratly. He had nothing to do with foot-and-mouth control, yet in the eyes of the locals, all government employees were tarred with the same brush. Everyone knew him in the area, and before the outbreak no one had paid him much mind. Now, though, he was getting sick of the resentful looks he got when he walked into a shop or a pub, the way conversations stopped and whispers began, and the way people sometimes even expressed their anger to his face. In one pub they had been so hostile towards him he thought they were going to beat him up.

It didn't do the slightest bit of good to tell them that he worked for the Department for Environment, Food and Rural Affairs, DEFRA, in the Water and Land Directorate, and that his job was water, because that only made them think of Yorkshire Water – of droughts, leakages, short-ages and restrictions on washing their bloody cars and watering their lawns – and then they got even angrier.

It was part of Andrew's job to collect water samples from local lakes, ponds, tarns and reservoirs, and these were later tested for contaminants at the Central Science Laboratory. Because some of these bodies of water were surrounded by open country, Andrew was one of the few with a special dispensation to visit them, after taking all the proper precautions, of course.

That day, his last call was Hallam Tarn, a godforsaken, hollowed-out bowl of water on the very top of the moor, beyond Tetchley Fell. Legend had it that the place used to be a village once, but the villagers took to Satanic practices, so God smote them with his fist and the tarn was created in place of the village. It was said that on certain days of the year you could see the old houses and streets beneath the water's surface and hear the cries of the villagers. Sometimes, when the light was right and the curlew's cry piped across the desolate moor, Andrew could almost believe it.

Today, though, the sun was shining, and the honeyed air was still and sweet. Summer seemed to have arrived at last, and Andrew couldn't imagine any hint of evil taking place.

The deepest part of the tarn ran closest to the road, and a tall, solid, drystone wall separated it from children and drunks and anyone else foolish enough to wander around up there in the dark. To get access to the water, you had to drive a few yards further on, cross the stile and take a footpath that led to its shallow shore. In the days before the government restrictions it was a popular spot for ramblers and picnickers, but these days it was off-limits, except to people such as Andrew. A government poster nailed to the stile warned people to stay out on penalty of a steep fine.

Before heading out with his dinghy and his sample jar, Andrew sprayed his wellington boots with disinfectant and donned his plastic outerwear. He felt like a spaceman preparing for a walk on the moon. He also felt hot inside the protective clothing, and all he wanted to do was get this over with as soon as possible then head home for a nice long bath and an evening out in Northallerton with Nancy, maybe the pictures, a spot of dinner and a drink after.

Feeling the sweat drip down the back of his neck, he walked along the narrow dirt path the hundred yards or so to the edge of the tarn and squatted by the waterside to fill his sample jar. It was so quiet up there, he could imagine himself the only man left in the world. Because he had to take samples from various depths, he got in the small dinghy and began to row. The tarn wasn't much bigger than a large pond, maybe a couple of hundred yards long and a hundred wide, but it was quite deep in places. Andrew felt a little disquiet at being out there all alone, not another soul in sight, and whenever he looked down into the water, he fancied he could see a roof or a street below. It was an optical illusion, of course, most likely caused by the sun on the water, but it unnerved him nonetheless.

When he neared the wall, he noticed some dark material snagged on the roots of an old tree. The tree was gone, but gnarled roots still jutted out of the bank like arms reaching out of a grave, and there was something about their arched, sinewy shapes that upset Andrew even more. Curious about the material, however, he put his fears aside and rowed closer. Legends and myths couldn't harm him.

When he got near enough, he stretched out his arm and tried to free the material from the root. It was heavier than he thought, and as it jerked free, the dinghy tipped and Andrew, off-balance, fell into the tarn. He was a strong swimmer, so drowning didn't worry him, but what chilled his blood was that the thing he was holding as tightly as a lover in a slow dance was a dead body, and from its ashen face, open dead eyes looked directly into his.

Andrew let go of the burden, mouth full of bile. He struggled back into the dinghy, salvaged his oars and rowed back to shore, where he stopped only long enough to be sick, before squelching back to his van, hoping to God his mobile worked up here. It didn't. Cursing, he threw it on the floor and started the van with shaking hands. As he drove back towards Helmthorpe, he glanced frequently in his rear-view mirror to make sure that no misshapen, supernatural beasts from the depths of the tarn were following him.

•

Banks still felt angry when he pulled up outside his parents' house, brakes squealing, but before he went inside he took several deep breaths and reined in his anger, determined not to let it show. His parents didn't need it; they had problems enough of their own. He found his father in front of the television watching horse racing and his mother in the kitchen fussing over a cake.

'I'm heading home this afternoon,' he said, popping his head around the kitchen door. 'Thanks for letting me stay.'

'There's always a bed for you here,' his mother said. 'You know that, son. Have you finished what you came for?'

'Not really,' said Banks, 'but there's not a lot more I can do.'

'You're a policeman. Surely you can do something to help?'

The way Banks's mother said 'policeman' wasn't quite as vehement as the way his father said it, nor was it as tinged with distaste as the way she used to say it, but it wasn't far off, which was why it had surprised Banks when Mrs Marshall told him his mother was proud of him. Banks's mother had always made it clear that she thought he had sold himself short, that he should have gone into commerce and worked himself up to be managing director of some big international company. It didn't seem to matter how well he did in his job, or how often he was promoted; to his mother, his career choice was undignified, and his achievements always seemed to pale beside those of his stockbroker brother, Roy. Banks had always suspected that Roy was a bit of a shady dealer, a frequent enough occurrence in the world of financial speculation, in his experience, though he would never voice such suspicions to his mother, or indeed to Roy himself. Still, he lived in dread of that telephone call coming from his brother one day: 'Alan, can you help me? I'm in a bit of a fix with the law.'

'It's not my case, Mum,' he said. 'The locals are good. They'll do the best they can.'

'Will you have something to eat with us before you go?'

'Of course. Know what I'd like?'

'What?'

'Fish and chips from over the road,' said Banks. 'I'll get them. My treat.'

'Well, maybe I'll have a fishcake,' said his mother. 'Your dad hasn't eaten from there since it went Chinese, though.'

'Go on, Dad,' said Banks, turning to the living room. 'Or maybe you should stick to your low-fat diet?'

'Bugger low fat,' said Arthur Banks. 'I'll have the

special and chips. Just make sure there's no bloody chop suey or sweet and sour sauce gone anywhere near it.' Banks winked at his mother and walked over to the shop.

The strip of shops across the main road, set back by a stretch of tarmac for customer parking, had gone through dozens of changes over the years. When Banks first moved to the estate, he remembered, there had been the fish and chip shop, a ladies' hairdresser, a butcher's, a greengrocer's and a launderette. Now there was a video rental shop, a takeaway pizza and tandoori place called Caesar's Taj Mahal, a mini-mart and a unisex hair salon. The only constants were the fish and chip shop, which now also sold takeaway Chinese food, too, and the news-agent's, which, according to the signs, was still run by the Walkers, who had taken over from Donald Bradford all those years ago, in 1966. Banks wondered what had become of Bradford. He was said to have been devastated over what had happened to Graham. Had the local police ever followed up on him?

Banks waited to cross the busy road. To the left of the shops stood the remains of the old ball-bearing factory, still untouched for some reason. It could hardly be for historical preservation, as it was a real eyesore. The gates were chained and padlocked shut, and it was surrounded by high wire-mesh fencing with barbed wire on top, the windows beyond covered by rusty grilles. Despite these security precautions, most of the windows were broken anyway, and the front of the blackened brick building was covered in colourful graffiti. Banks remembered when the place was in full production, lorries coming and going, factory whistle blowing and crowds of workers waiting at the bus stop. A lot of them were young women, or girls scarcely out of school – a rough lot, his mother called them – and Banks often used to time his visits to the shops to coincide with the whistle going and the factory gates opening because he lusted after some of the girls.

There was one girl in particular, he remembered, who used to stand at the bus stop smoking, a faraway look in her eyes, scarf done up like a turban on her head. Even her serviceable work clothes couldn't disguise the curves, and she had pale smooth skin and looked a bit like Julie Christie in *Billy Liar*. When Banks used to walk as casually as possible past the bus stop, he remembered as he stood in the fish and chip shop queue, the other girls used to tease him with lewd comments and make him blush.

'Hey, Mandy,' one of them would call out. 'Here comes that lad again. I think he fancies you.'

They would all howl with laughter, Mandy would tell them to shut up and Banks would blush. Once, Mandy tousled his hair and gave him a cigarette. He smoked it over a week, taking a few drags at a time, then nicking it to save for later. In the end it tasted like something he might have picked up from the gutter, but he finished it anyway. After that, Mandy would sometimes smile when he passed by. She had a nice smile. Sometimes strands of hair escaped from under her turban and curled over her cheek, and other times she might have a smudge of oil or dirt on her face. She must have been about eighteen. Four years' age difference. Far from an impossible gap when you get older, but wider than the Grand Canyon at that age.

Then, one day, he noticed that she had started wearing an engagement ring, and a few weeks later she no longer stood at the bus stop with the others, and he never saw her again.

Where was Mandy now? he wondered. She'd be in her fifties if she was still alive, older than Kay Summerville. Had she put on a lot of weight? Had her hair turned grey? Did she look old and worn after years of struggle and poverty? Had she stayed married to the same man? Had she won the Lottery and gone to live on the Costa del Sol? Did she ever think of that love-struck adolescent who used to time his visits to the shops so he could see her waiting at the bus stop? He doubted it very much. The lives we leave behind. So many people. Our paths cross for a while, even as fleetingly as his had crossed Mandy's, and we move on. Some encounters are impressed indelibly on our memories; others slip away into the void. Of course Mandy never thought of him; he was a mere passing amusement to her, whereas she fed deeper into his adolescent dreams of sex, and in his memory she would always be standing there with her hip against the bus stop smoking in her turban with a far-away look in her eyes, a loose lock of hair resting softly against her pale cheek, always beautiful and always eighteen.

'Two specials and chips and one fishcake.'

Banks paid for the fish and chips and set off back home carrying the paper bag. No newspaper-wrapped fish and chips any more. Dirty. Not healthy.

'There was a telephone call for you while you were out, Alan,' his mother said when he got back.

'Who was it?'

'Same woman as called last night. Have you got a new girlfriend already?'

Already. Sandra had been gone nearly two years, was pregnant with another man's child and about to marry him. Had Banks got a new girlfriend *already*?

'No, Mum,' he said. 'It's one of the local coppers. You already know that from last night. They let women on the force these days.'

'No need to be cheeky. Eat your fish and chips before they go cold.'

'What did she say?'

'To ring her back when you had a moment. I wrote down the number just in case you'd forgotten it.'

Banks's mother rolled her eyes when he left the table and headed towards the telephone. His father didn't notice; he had his fish and chips on the paper on his lap and was eating them with his fingers, engrossed in the one-thirty from Newmarket, glass of beer balanced precariously on the arm of the chair.

The number scribbled on the pad by the hall telephone wasn't familiar. It certainly wasn't Thorpe Wood. Curious, Banks dialled.

'DI Hart here. Who's speaking?'

'Michelle? It's me. Alan Banks.'

'Ah, DCI Banks.'

'You left a message for me to call. Is this your mobile number?'

'That's right. Look, first off, I'm sorry about Detective Superintendent Shaw this morning.'

'That's all right. Not your fault.'

'I just felt . . . well, anyway, I'm surprised he's taking such an interest. It's not even his case. I had him marked down as just putting in time till his retirement, now he's all over me like a dirty shirt.'

'What did you want to talk to me about?'

'Are you going home?'

'Yes.'

'When?'

'I don't know. This afternoon. This evening. No point hanging around where I'm not wanted.'

'Don't feel sorry for yourself. It doesn't suit you. Only I was wondering if you'd like to meet up for a chat before you go, if you're not in a hurry.'

'Any particular reason?'

'Perhaps because I *didn't* treat you like an undesirable alien, despite your less than polite introduction.'

'Yes, okay. Why not?'

'Shall we say half-past five in Starbucks, Cathedral Square?'

'There's a Starbucks? In Peterborough?'

'Don't sound so surprised. We're very with it these days. There's a McDonald's, too, if you'd prefer?'

'No. Starbucks will do fine. Half-five it is. That'll give me plenty of time to pack and say my goodbyes. See you there.'

●

Annie and Gristhorpe arrived at Hallam Tarn in time to see two police frogmen haul up the body and pull it back to shore with them. Peter Darby, crime scene photographer, sat in a dinghy nearby and videotaped everything. He had already taken several stills and Polaroids of the spot where the body had been first seen by Andrew Naylor. One of the lads at Helmthorpe had found a dry set of clothes for Naylor, and he stood with the small group, chewing his fingernails as the frogmen edged closer to shore.

Once on shore, they laid the body on the grass at the feet of Dr Burns, the police surgeon. Dr Glendenning, the Home Office pathologist, was unavailable that day, as he had been called in to help a colleague with a difficult case in Scarborough. Detective Sergeant Stefan Nowak, crime scene co-ordinator, and his scene of crime officers were on their way.

Well, Annie thought with some relief, at least it wasn't a floater. She had been at the scene of more than one bloated, misshapen lump pulled from the water, and she didn't relish another. But when she saw the face, she would gladly have accepted an anonymous floater any day. The body was Luke Armitage's. No doubt about it. He was wearing the black T-shirt and jeans that Robin had said he had on when he went to Eastvale, and he hadn't been in the water long enough for his features to become unrecognizable, though the skin was white and there were signs of *cutis anserina*, more commonly known as 'gooseflesh'. The once dark curls were straight now and stuck to his head and face like seaweed.

Annie stood aside and let Dr Burns perform his in situ examination. 'This is going to be difficult,' he told Annie. 'In general, bodies decompose twice as fast in air as in water, but there are so many variables to take into account.'

'Any chance he drowned?'

The doctor examined Luke's mouth for signs of foam and his eyes for the telltale petechial haemorrhages associated with asphyxia, of which drowning is a form. He shook his head and turned back to Annie. 'Hard to be certain. We'll have a better idea when Dr Glendenning checks the lungs and runs a diatomic analysis.'

Diatoms, Annie knew from her basic courses in forensic science, were micro-organisms that lived in the water. If you drowned, you breathed in a lot of them with the water and they spread to every nook and cranny of your body, even your bone marrow; if you hadn't drowned but were found dead in water, then a few diatoms might be found, but they would be nowhere near as abundant or widely spread.

Dr Burns turned the body over and pointed to the back of Luke's head. Annie could see the signs of a blow. 'Would that have been enough to cause death?' she asked.

'Hard blow to the cerebellum?' said Dr Burns. 'Certainly.' He began to examine the body in more detail. 'He's cold,' he said, 'and there's no rigor.'

'What does that tell you?'

'Usually a body is cold after eight to ten hours in the water. I'll have to take his temperature to substantiate this, of course, and we'll need to know the temperature of the water, too. As for the rigor, given the obvious effects of water on his skin, it must have come and gone.'

'How long does that take?'

'In water? Anything from two to four days.'

'Not sooner?'

'Not usually, no. Again, though, I'll have to make some temperature checks. It might be summer but we've hardly been enjoying seasonal temperatures of late.'

Two days, Annie thought. It was Thursday afternoon now, and the ransom demand had come two days ago, on Tuesday evening. Was Luke already dead by then? If so, his death was nothing to do with her rash actions. She began to feel a glimmer of hope. If that were the case, then the kidnapper was trying to cash in on Luke's death, which could have come about for other reasons. Curious. She would have to begin casting about for a motive now.

The sound of an approaching van interrupted Annie's stream of thought, and she looked across to the wall to see DS Nowak and his SOCO team jumping the stile one after another, looking like sheep in their white protective clothing. Well, she thought, maybe the experts would be able to tell her a bit more.

•

Banks arrived half an hour early for his meeting with Michelle, parked in the short-stay round the back of the town hall and cut through the arcade to Bridge Street, where he nipped into Waterstone's and bought a book called *The Profession of Violence*, the story of the Kray twins. As he walked up the busy street towards the square, he marvelled at how much the city centre had changed since his day. For a start, it was all pedestrian precinct now, not busy roads the way it had been when he lived there. And it seemed cleaner, the buildings less shabby and grime-coated. It was a sunny afternoon, and tourists wandered in and out of the cathedral grounds into the square to spend a while browsing through the shops. Banks found it all quite pleasant, which didn't square with his memory of being stuck in a dirty, small-minded provincial backwater. Maybe it was he who had changed the most.

He found Starbucks on the corner by the cathedral entrance and sipped a latte grande while he flipped through the book.

Michelle arrived five minutes late, cool and collected, wearing black slacks and a slate-grey jacket over a cream blouse. She went to the counter for a cappuccino then sat down opposite Banks.

'Bit of a shock for you, wasn't it, this morning?' she said.

'I suppose so,' Banks said. 'After all these years . . . I don't know, I suppose I'd allowed myself to believe there had to be a connection. Conned myself.'

'We all do, one way or another.'

'You're too young to be so cynical.'

'And you should be old and wise enough to realize that flattery will get you nowhere. You've got a bit of froth on your lip.'

Before Banks could wipe it away, Michelle reached out her finger and did it for him, her fingertip brushing his lip.

'Thanks,' he said.

Michelle blushed, turned her head away and let out a little giggle. 'I don't know why I did that,' she said. 'My mother used to do it when I drank milkshakes.'

'Haven't had a milkshake in years,' said Banks.

'Me neither. What next?'

'Home. And you?'

'Dunno. The leads are hardly jumping out at me left, right and centre.'

Banks thought for a moment. He hadn't told Shaw about the possible Kray connection because Shaw had behaved like a bastard. Besides, it wasn't his case. There was no reason to keep it from Michelle, though. It probably meant nothing, but at least it would give her something to do, the illusion of progress.

'I've heard rumours that Graham Marshall's dad was connected with the Krays in London just before the family moved up here.'

'Connected? In what way?'

'Strong-arm man. Enforcer. I don't know how true it is – you know how these things can be exaggerated – but it might be worth a bit of delving into.'

'How do you know this?'

Banks touched the side of his nose. 'I've got my sources.'

'And how long have you known?'

'Just found out before I came here.'

'Yeah, and the Pope's Jewish.'

'The point is, what are you going to do about it?'

Michelle moved the froth in her cup around with a spoon. 'I don't suppose it'd do any harm to set a few enquiries in motion. Might even get a trip to London out of it. You sure I won't come out looking like a complete moron?'

'I can't guarantee that. It's always a risk. Better than being the moron who missed the vital clue, though.'

'Thanks. That's *really* encouraging. I don't know very much about the Krays – before my time. I haven't even seen the film. I do remember the big funeral they gave one of them in the East End not so long ago, though.'

'That'd be Reggie. Couple of years ago. The whole East End came out for him. It was the same when Ronnie died in 1995. Very popular among East Enders, the Krays were. Loved their mother. There were three of them, an older brother called Charlie, but Ronnie and Reggie, the twins, are the ones people focus on. They pretty much ran the East End during the fifties and sixties, and a fair bit of the West End, too, till they got put away. Ronnie was the crazy one. Paranoid schizophrenic. He ended up in Broadmoor. Reggie was Category "A" in Parkhurst. I suppose you could say that he was led astray by his more dominant twin brother, if you wanted to be charitable.'

'But what could they have to do with Graham Marshall's disappearance and murder?'

'Probably nothing,' Banks said. 'They didn't operate outside London much, except for maybe a few clubs in cities like Birmingham or Leicester. But if Bill Marshall did work for them, then there's always the chance he left them reason to bear a grudge, and the twins had a long reach.'

'And for that they'd kill his son?'

'I don't know, Michelle. These people have a very warped sense of justice. And, don't forget, Ronnie was crazy. He was a sexual sadist, a serious pervert, among other things. He was the one who walked into the Blind Beggar and shot George Cornell right between the eyes in front of a room full of witnesses. Know what was playing on the jukebox?'

'Tell me.'

'It was the Walker Brothers, "The Sun Ain't Gonna Shine Anymore". And they say the needle got stuck on "anymore" when he was shot.'

'How melodramatic. I don't remember the Walker Brothers.'

'Not many people do. Want me to sing you a couple of verses?'

'I thought you said you never sing to women you've just met?'

'I did?'

'Don't you remember?'

'Nothing slips past you, does it?'

'Not much. I know you read Philip Larkin, too.'

'How?'

'You quoted him.'

'I'm impressed. Anyway, who knows how someone like Ronnie Kray thinks, if "think" is even the right word? He was seeing enemies all around him by then and coming up with more and more dramatic ways of hurting people. He loved to inspire fear and trembling, even in his own men. He was also a homosexual with a taste for teenage boys. They wouldn't have done Graham themselves, of course – they'd have got agoraphobia if they came this far north of London – but they could have sent someone to do it. Anyway, it's not only that.'

'What, then?'

'If Bill Marshall did work as a strong-arm man for the Krays, what was he doing up here? You know as well as I do that people don't just walk away from that line of work. Maybe he got himself fixed up with someone local, a branch manager.'

'So you're saying he might have been up to the same tricks here and that might have had something to do with Graham's death?'

'I'm just saying it's possible, that's all. Worth investigating.'

'There was a reference to a protection racket in the old crime logs,' Michelle said. 'Someone called Carlo Fiorino. Ring any bells?'

'Vaguely,' said Banks. 'Maybe his name was in the papers when I was a kid. Anyway, it's something to think about.'

'So why didn't it come up in the original investigation?'

'Didn't it?' said Banks. 'Dunno. Want another coffee?'

Michelle looked into her empty cup. 'Sure.'

Banks went and got two more coffees, and when he came back Michelle was leafing through the book.

'Borrow it if you want,' he said. 'I just picked it up to see if I could fill in a bit more background.'

'Thanks. I'd like to read it. Did Graham ever mention the Krays to you?'

'Yes, but I'm not sure that he ever said he or his dad knew them. I've also been thinking about the time frame. Graham and his parents came up here around July or August 1964. In July there was a big brouhaha in the press over Ronnie's alleged homosexual relationship with Lord

Boothby, who denied everything and sued the *Sunday Mirror* for libel. Ronnie followed suit, but all he got was an apology. Still, there was an upside in that the press had to lay off the Krays for a while after that. Nobody wanted any more libel suits. One day Ronnie was a thug and a gangster, the next a sporting gentleman. It set the police investigation back, too. Everyone had to walk on eggs around them. Even so, they were arrested the next January for demanding money with menaces. There was no bail and they were tried at the Old Bailey.'

'What happened?'

'They got off. It was a flimsy enough case to start with. There was talk of jury tampering. See, back then, there was no majority verdict like we have today. All twelve had to agree, or there'd be a retrial, which would give the accused even more time to fix things. They dug up some dirt on one of the main prosecution witnesses and that was it, they were free.'

'But how does any of this relate to Graham?'

'I'm not saying it does, only that that was what was happening around 1964 and 1965, the period we're concerned with. The Krays were in the public eye a lot. The libel case and the trial were both big news, and after they got off they were fireproof for a long time. It was the start of their ascendancy as celebrities, the dark side of Swinging London, you might say. Soon they were being photographed with film stars, sporting figures and pop singers: Barbara Windsor, Sonny Liston, Judy Garland, Victor Spinetti – who was in *A Hard Day's Night*, *Help!* and *Magical Mystery Tour*, if you can handle another piece of trivia. In the summer of 1965 they had a fiddle involving selling stolen American securities and bonds for the Mafia, and they were squaring up for a big fight with their rivals, the Richardson gang.' Banks tapped the book. 'It's all in there. I don't know if it means anything. But as your boss made clear this morning, it's none of my business.'

Michelle frowned. 'Yeah, I know. I keep thinking he's looking over my shoulder, even now, in here.'

'I don't want you to get into trouble for talking to me.'

'Don't worry. I wasn't followed. I'm only being paranoid.'

'It doesn't mean you're *not* being followed. Will you keep in touch, let me know if you come up with anything?'

'I shouldn't, but I will.'

'And if there's any way I can help . . .'

'Of course. If you remember anything Graham said or did that might be useful, I'd appreciate knowing.'

'You will. Look, Graham's mother mentioned a funeral, when the remains have been released. Any idea how long that might be?'

'I'm not sure. It shouldn't be long. I'll see how Dr Cooper's doing tomorrow.'

'Would you? Good. I think I'd like to come down for it. Even Shaw can't complain about *that*. Will you let me know?'

'Of course. Can I ask you something?'

'Go ahead.'

'That remark Shaw made about the budgie. What did he mean?'

Banks related the sad story of Joey's flight to freedom and certain death. By the end, Michelle was smiling. 'That's so sad,' she said. 'You must have been heartbroken.'

'I got over it. He wasn't exactly a wonder-budgie. He couldn't even talk. As everyone told me at the time, he wasn't Goldie the Eagle.'

'Goldie the Eagle?'

'Yes. Earlier the same year, 1965, Goldie the Eagle escaped from London Zoo. They got her back a couple of weeks later. It was a big story at the time.'

'But your Joey was never found?'

'No. He had no defences. He must have thought he was home free, but he couldn't survive all the predators out there. He was in way over his plumage. Look,' Banks went on, 'will you answer a question for me?'

Michelle nodded but looked wary and shuffled in her seat.

'Are you married?' Banks asked.

'No,' she said. 'No, I'm not.' And she got up and walked out without even saying goodbye.

Banks was about to go after her when his mobile rang. Cursing, and feeling like a bit of a pillock, the way he always did when it went off in a public place, Banks answered the call.

'Alan? It's Annie. Hope I haven't called at a bad time.'

'No, not at all.'

'Only we could use a bit of extra help, if you've finished your business down there.'

'Pretty much,' said Banks, thinking that his partings with both members of the local constabulary he had met left a lot to be desired. 'What's up?'

'Know that missing kid I told you about?'

'Luke Armitage?'

'That's the one.'

'What about him?'

'It looks as if it's just turned into a murder case.'

'Shit,' said Banks. 'I'm on my way.'

9

'**Strictly speaking**, you know,' said Banks, 'this is your case. It has been from the start. Are you sure you want me muscling in?'

'I wouldn't have rung you if I didn't, would I?' said Annie. 'Besides, you know I'm not that kind of copper.'

'What kind of copper?'

'All territorial and bureaucratic. I don't go in for pissing matches. I'm all for cooperation, me, not competition.'

'Fair enough. Let's chalk my comment down to recent experience.'

'What do you mean?'

Banks told her about Detective Superintendent Shaw.

'Well,' Annie said. 'Don't say I didn't warn you they wouldn't exactly welcome you with open arms.'

'Thanks.'

'My pleasure. Anyway, you can help me just as long as you give me the respect I deserve and don't treat me like a skivvy.'

'Have I ever?'

'This is a pretty good start.'

Banks's car was in the garage for servicing and wouldn't be ready until after lunch, so they had signed out a department car that morning, and Annie was driving, something Banks usually liked to do himself.

'I was thinking I could sort of get to like it,' said Banks. 'There's a lot to be said for having a *chauffeuse*.'

Annie shot him a look. 'Feel like getting out and walking the rest of the way?'

'No thanks.'

'Well, behave yourself. Anyway,' she went on, 'if you want to be all official about it, it's the Big Man's case. He's the SIO, and he's the one who suggested if I asked you nicely you might come back from leave early and give us the benefit of your considerable expertise.'

'The Big Man?'

'Detective Superintendent Gristhorpe.'

'Does he know you call him that?'

Annie grinned. 'You should hear what we call *you* in the squad room.'

'I must say it's great to be home,' said Banks.

Annie glanced sideways at him. 'How did things go, other than your run-in with the local constabulary?'

'All a bit embarrassing, really.' Banks told her about McCallum turning out to be an escaped mental patient who drowned before Graham disappeared.

'I'm so sorry, Alan,' she said, touching his knee. 'After all those years feeling guilty and responsible . . . But you must be relieved, in a way . . . I mean, knowing it couldn't have been him, so it wasn't your fault?'

'I suppose I must. You know, apart from the police down there, you're the only other person I've ever told about what happened by the river that day.'

'You never told Sandra?'

'No.'

'Why?'

'I don't know.'

Banks felt Annie retreat into silence beside him and knew he'd done again exactly the sort of thing that caused her to end their romantic relationship. It was as if she offered him something warm, soft and sensitive, yet the moment he reached out and touched it, she shot back into her hard, impenetrable shell.

Before either of them could think of anything else to say, they arrived at the end of the Armitages' drive, where reporters clamoured around them with pens, microphones and cameras. The officer on duty lifted the tape and let them through.

'Impressive,' said Banks, when the building's solid, symmetrical architecture came into view. 'I've only seen the place from the riverside walk before.'

'Just wait until you meet the beautiful people inside.'

'Go easy, Annie, they've just lost their son.'

Annie sighed. 'I know that. And I will. Okay?'

'Okay.'

'I'm just not looking forward to this.'

'Who dealt with the identification?'

'Winsome did. Last night.'

'So you haven't seen the family since the boy's body was found?'

'No.'

'If you don't think I'm being patronizing, why don't you let me deal with them?'

'Be my guest. Honest. Given my track record with Martin Armitage, I'd be grateful to be an observer this time. Fresh approach and all that.'

'Okay.'

Josie answered the front door almost the moment they rang the bell and led the two of them into the living room, where Banks introduced himself.

'What is it now?' Martin Armitage asked, glaring at Annie. Neither he nor his wife looked as if they had had much sleep, and they probably hadn't.

'A murder investigation,' said Banks. 'Or so it seems. And we need your help.'

'I don't see how we can help any more than we have done already. We cooperated with you, against the kidnapper's wishes, and look what happened.' He glanced towards Annie again, voice rising. 'I hope you realize this is your fault, that Luke's death is *your* responsibility. If you hadn't followed me to the shelter and then come nosing around here, the kidnapper would have picked up the money and Luke would be home safe and sound.'

'Martin,' said Robin Armitage. 'We've been over this again and again. Don't make a scene.'

'Don't make a scene! Good God, woman, this is your son we're talking about. She as good as killed him.'

'Calm down, Mr Armitage,' said Banks. Martin Armitage wasn't quite as tall as Banks had imagined, but he was fit and bursting with energy. Not the kind of man to sit around waiting for results, but one who went out and made the result happen. That was the way he'd played football, too, Banks remembered. Armitage hadn't been content to hang around the goal mouth waiting for a midfielder to feed him the ball; he had created scoring opportunities himself, and the main criticism levelled at him was that he was greedy for the ball, more apt to shoot and miss than pass to someone in a better scoring position. He had also lacked self-control and attracted a high number of red and yellow cards. Banks remembered once seeing him lash out at a member of the other team who had taken the ball from him fairly in the penalty area. He'd given away a penalty over that, and it lost his side the game.

'This is a difficult enough job as it is,' said Banks, 'without you making it worse. I'm sorry for your loss, but it's no good flinging blame about. We don't know how or why Luke died yet. We don't even know where or when. So until we've been able to answer some of those basic questions we're not in a position to jump to conclusions. I suggest you exercise the same restraint.'

'What else would you say?' said Martin. 'You always stick together, you lot.'

'Can we get down to business?'

'Yes, of course,' said Robin, sitting on the sofa in jeans and a pale green blouse, long legs crossed, hands folded on her lap. Without make-up and with her famous gold-blonde hair tied back in a ponytail, she still looked gorgeous, Banks thought, and the crow's feet only enhanced her beauty. She had the classic model's face, high cheekbones, small nose, pointed chin, perfect proportions, but she also had character and individuality in her features.

Banks had once worked on a case for the Met involving a modelling agency and he had been surprised that so many of these women who looked beautiful in magazines and on television lacked something in real life, their features perfect but bland, unformed and unfinished, like a blank canvas or an actor without a role. But Robin Armitage had presence.

'I'm sure you know,' said Banks, 'that Luke's death changes everything. It changes the way we proceed in the investigation, and we're going to have to go over much of the same ground again. This may seem tedious and pointless to you but, believe me, it's necessary. I'm new to the case, but I took the time this morning to familiarize myself with the investigation so far, and I have to say that I've found nothing out of order, nothing I wouldn't have done had I been in charge myself.'

'Like I said,' Martin chipped in, 'you lot stick together. I'll be complaining to the chief constable. He's a personal friend of mine.'

'That's your privilege, but he'll only tell you the same as I'm telling you. If everyone gave in to a kidnapper's demands without informing the police, it would be the most popular crime in the country.'

'But look what happened when we *did* inform the police. Our son is dead.'

'Something went wrong. This was an unusual case from the start; there are a number of inconsistencies.'

'What are you suggesting? That it *wasn't* a straight-forward kidnapping?'

'There was nothing straightforward about it at all, Mr Armitage.'

'I don't understand,' said Robin. 'The phone call . . . the ransom demand . . . they were genuine, surely?'

'Yes,' said Annie, taking a cue from Banks, 'but the ransom demand came an unusually long time after Luke disappeared, the kidnapper didn't let you speak to your son, and the sum he asked for was ridiculously low.'

'I don't know what you're talking about,' said Martin. 'We're not made of money.'

'I know that,' Annie said. 'But how would the kidnapper know? To all intents and purposes footballers and models make millions, and you're living in a mansion.'

Martin frowned. 'I suppose you've got a point. Unless . . .'

'Yes?' Banks picked up the questioning again.

'Unless it was someone close to us.'

'Can you think of anyone?'

'Of course not. I can't imagine any of our friends doing something like this. Are you insane?'

'Mrs Armitage?'

Robin shook her head. 'No.'

'We'll still need a list of people to talk to.'

'I'm not having you going around bullying our friends,' said Martin.

'Don't worry, we'll be discreet. And, don't forget, you're the one who suggested it might be someone close to you. Anyone have a grudge against either of you?'

'A few goalies, I suppose,' said Martin, 'but nothing serious, no.'

'Mrs Armitage?'

'I don't think so. Modelling can be a brutally competitive career, and I'm sure I stood on my share of toes on the catwalk, but nothing so . . . terrible . . . I mean, nothing to make anyone do something like this, especially so long after.'

'If you'd both like to think about it for a while, it would be a great help.'

'You said it was odd that he wouldn't let us talk to Luke,' Robin said.

'It's unusual, yes,' Annie answered.

'Do you think it was because . . . because Luke was already dead?'

'That's possible,' said Annie, 'but we won't know until the pathologist has finished his job.'

'When will that be?'

'Perhaps by this evening or early tomorrow.' Dr Burns, the police surgeon, had been unable to give an accurate estimate of time of death at the scene, so they would have to wait until Dr Glendenning had finished his post-mortem examination of Luke's body. Even then, they had learned not to expect miracles from medical science.

'Can you remember anything else about the caller?' Banks asked Martin Armitage.

'I've told you everything I know. I can't remember any more.'

'The voice definitely wasn't familiar?'

'No one I recognized.'

'And there was only the one call?'

'Yes.'

'Is there anything else you can tell us that might be of help?'

Both Martin and Robin Armitage shook their heads. Banks and Annie got up. 'We'll need to have a look at Luke's room next,' said Banks, 'and then we'd like to talk to your housekeeper and her husband.'

'Josie and Calvin?' said Martin. 'But why?'

'They might be able to help.'

'I can't see how.'

'Were they close to Luke?'

'Not especially. If truth be told, I always got the impression that they thought him a bit of a weirdo. They're wonderful people, salt of the earth, but sort of traditional in their views of people and behaviour.'

'And Luke didn't fit the mould?'

'No. He might as well have come from outer space as far as they're concerned.'

'Was there any animosity?'

'Of course not. They are our employees, after all. What are you suggesting, that they had something to do with this?'

'I'm not suggesting anything, merely asking. Look, Mr Armitage, I can understand your feelings, honestly I can, but you must let us do our jobs the way we see fit. It's not going to help at all if you start challenging every move we make. I promise you we'll be as discreet as we can with all our enquiries. No matter what you think, we don't go around bullying people. But we also don't accept everything at face value. People lie for a variety of reasons, many of them irrelevant to the investigation, but sometimes it's because they did it, and it's for us to sort out the lies from the truth. You've already lied to us once yourself that we know of, when you rang DI Cabbot and told her you'd heard from Luke.'

'I did that to protect Luke.'

'I understand *why* you did it, but it was still a lie. Maybe you can see how complicated our job becomes when you take all the lies into account. The lies of the innocent, especially. As I said, we don't take things, or people, at face value and, like it or not, every murder investigation begins close to home then moves outwards. Now, if you don't mind, we'll take a look at Luke's room.'

•

Michelle had been joking when she told Banks she was getting paranoid, but she was beginning to think that every time she visited the archives, Mrs Metcalfe rang Detective Superintendent Shaw. Here he was again, preceded by the dark chill of his shadow, on the threshold of the tiny room.

'Any progress?' he asked, leaning against the door.

'I'm not sure,' said Michelle. 'I've been going over the old crime reports for 1965 looking for some sort of connection with Graham's disappearance.'

'And have you found any?'

'Not directly, no.'

'I told you you were wasting your time.'

'Maybe not entirely.'

'What do you mean?'

Michelle paused. She had to be careful what she said because she didn't want Shaw to know that Banks had tipped her off to the Kray connection. That would send him into a tantrum she could well do without. 'I was reading over the reports and statements on a protection racket investigation in July 1965, and Graham's dad's name came up.'

'So? Where's the connection?'

'A club on Church Street called Le Phonographe.'

'I remember that place. It was a discotheque.'

Michelle frowned. 'I thought disco was in the seventies, not the sixties.'

'I'm not talking about the music, but the establishment itself. Clubs like Le Phonographe offered memberships and served meals, usually an inedible beefburger, if my memory serves me well, so they could sell alcohol legally after regular closing time. They'd stay open till three in the morning, or so. There'd be music and dancing, too, but it was usually Motown or soul.'

'You sound familiar with the place, sir.'

'I was young once, DI Hart. Besides, Le Phonographe was the sort of place you kept an eye on. It was a villains' club. Owned by a nasty piece of work called Carlo Fiorino. Used to like to pretend he was Mafia, wore the striped, wide-lapel suits, pencil-thin moustache, spats and everything – very Untouchables – but his father was a POW who ended up staying on after the war and marrying a local farm girl out Huntingdon way. Plenty of local villains hung out there, and you could often pick up a tip or two. And I don't mean for the three-thirty at Kempton Park.'

'So it was a criminal hangout?'

'Back then, yes. But petty. People who liked to think they were big players.'

'Including Bill Marshall?'

'Yes.'

'So you knew about Bill Marshall's activities?'

'Of course we did. He was strictly a minor presence. We kept an eye on him. It was routine.'

'What was this Carlo Fiorino's game?'

'Bit of everything. Soon as the new town expansion was well under way he turned Le Phonographe into a more upmarket club, with decent grub, a better dance floor and a casino. He also owned an escort agency. We think he also got into drugs, prostitution and pornography, but he was always clever enough to stay one step ahead, and he played both sides against the middle. Most of the time.'

'What do you mean, sir?'

'Got himself shot in a drug war with the Jamaicans in 1982.'

'But he never did time?'

'Never got charged with anything, far as I remember.'

'Doesn't that strike you as odd, sir?'

'Odd?' Shaw seemed to snap out of his reminiscing mood and become his grumpy old self again. He stuck his face so close to hers that she could smell his tobacco, mint and whisky breath and see the lattice of purple veins throbbing in his bulbous nose. 'I'll tell you what's bloody odd, DI Hart. It's you asking these questions. That's what's odd. None of this can possibly have anything to do with what happened to Graham Marshall, and that's a fact. You're muck-raking. I don't know why, but that's what you're doing.'

'Sir, all I'm doing is trying to get a handle on the circumstances of the boy's disappearance. Looking over the investigation and over other investigations around the same time seems a reasonable way of doing it to me.'

'It's not your brief to look into the Marshall investigation, DI Hart, or any other for that matter. Who do you think you are, Complaints and Discipline? Stick to your job.'

'But, sir, Bill Marshall was one of the men interviewed in connection with this protection racket, all involved with Carlo Fiorino and Le Phonographe. Some of the city centre shopkeepers filed a complaint, and Marshall was one of the people they named.'

'Was he charged?'

'No, sir. Only questioned. One of the original complainants ended up in hospital and the other witnesses backed off, retracted their statements. No further action.'

Shaw smirked. 'Then it's hardly relevant, is it?'

'But doesn't it seem odd to you that no further action was taken? And that when Graham Marshall disappeared, his father never came under close scrutiny, even though he had recently been implicated in a criminal ring?'

'Why should he? Maybe he didn't do it. Did that thought ever enter your head? And even if he was involved in some petty protection racket, it doesn't make him a child killer, does it? Even by your standards that's a long stretch of the imagination.'

'Was Bill Marshall a police informer?'

'He might have let slip the odd snippet of information. That's how we played the game back then. Tit for tat.'

'Is that why he was protected from prosecution?'

'How the hell should I know? If you've read your paperwork, you'll know I wasn't on that case.' He took a deep breath, then seemed to relax and soften his tone.

'Look,' he said, 'policing was different back then. There was more give and take.'

Plenty of *take*, Michelle thought. She'd heard stories of the old days, of departments, of stations and even of whole counties run wild. But she didn't say anything.

'So we bent the rules every now and then,' Shaw continued. 'Grow up. Welcome to the real world.'

Michelle made a mental note about Bill Marshall's possible role as a police informer. If he had informed on criminals here in Peterborough, she could only imagine what the Krays might have done if he'd tried anything like that with them and then disappeared. The South Pole wouldn't have been far enough, let alone Peterborough. 'From what I can piece together,' she went on, 'the Graham Marshall investigation followed one line of enquiry and one only when it became clear that he hadn't run away from home: a sex killing by a passing pervert.'

'Well? What's so odd about that? It's what the evidence pointed to.'

'Just seems a bit of a coincidence, that's all, that some pervert should happen to be driving by a quiet street at that hour in the morning, just as Graham's doing his paper rounds.'

'Wrong place at the wrong time. Happens often enough. Besides, do you think perverts don't know about paper rounds? Don't you think someone could have been watching, studying, stalking the Marshall kid, the way such perverts often do? Or didn't they teach you that at Bramshill?'

'It's possible, sir.'

'You think you can do better than us, do you?' said Shaw, his face turning red again. 'Think you can out-detect Jet Harris?'

'I didn't say that, sir. It's just the advantage of hindsight, that's all. A long perspective.'

'Look, we worked our bollocks off on that case, Jet Harris, Reg Proctor and me, not to mention dozens more DCs and uniforms. Have you any idea what that sort of investigation is like? The scope of it. How wide a net we cast. We were getting a hundred sightings a day from as far afield as Penzance and the Mull of fucking Kintyre. Now you come along with your fancy education and your Bramshill courses and you have the gall to tell me we were wrong.'

Michelle took a deep breath. 'I'm not saying you were wrong, sir. Only you didn't *solve* the case, did you? You didn't even find a body. Look, I know you came up the hard way, and I respect that, but there are advantages to an education.'

'Yes. Accelerated promotion. They let you buggers run before you can toddle.'

'Policing has changed, sir, as you pointed out not so long ago. And crime has changed, too.'

'Sod that for a theory. Don't spout your book learning at me. A criminal's a criminal. Only the coppers have got softer. Especially the ones at the top.'

Michelle sighed. Time to change tack. 'You were a DC on the Graham Marshall investigation, sir. Can *you* tell me anything at all?'

'Look, if I'd known anything we'd have solved the bloody case, wouldn't we, instead of having you point out how stupid we were?'

'I'm not trying to make anyone look stupid.'

'Aren't you? That's how it sounds to me. It's easy to second-guess, given twenty-twenty hindsight. If Bill Marshall had anything to do with his son's disappearance, believe me, we'd have had him. In the first place, he had an alibi—'

'Who, sir?'

'His wife.'

'Not the most reliable of alibis, is it?'

'She'd hardly give him an alibi for doing in her own son now, would she? Tell me even you aren't so twisted as to think Mrs Marshall was involved.'

'We don't know, sir, do we?' But Michelle remembered Mrs Marshall, her sincerity and dignity, the need to bury her son after all these years. Certainly it was possible she was lying. Some criminals are very good actors. But Michelle didn't think so. And she wouldn't be getting any answers out of Bill Marshall. 'Did the Marshalls own a car?'

'Yes, they did. But don't expect me to remember the make and number. Look, Bill Marshall might have been a bit of a Jack the Lad, but he wasn't a child molester.'

'How do you know that was the motive behind Graham's abduction?'

'Have some brains, woman. Why else does a fourteen-year-old boy go missing without a trace? If you ask me, I'd still say he might have been one of Brady and Hindley's, though we could never prove it.'

'But it's way out of their area. A geographical pro-filer—'

'More benefits of a university education. Profilers? Don't make me laugh. I've had enough of this. It's about time you stopped nosing about down here and got back on the bloody job.' And he turned and stalked out.

Michelle noticed that her hand was shaking when he left, and she felt her breath held tight in her chest. She didn't like confrontation with authority; she had always respected her bosses and the police hierarchy in general; an organization like the police couldn't run efficiently without a quasi-military structure, she believed, orders given and obeyed, sometimes without question, if it came right down to it. But Shaw's rage seemed out of proportion to the situation.

She got up and returned the files to their boxes and gathered together her notes. It was well after lunchtime and time for some fresh air, anyway. Perhaps she would make a few phone calls, find someone who'd been on the job during the Kray era and head down to London the next day.

Back in her office, she found a message slip on her desk informing her that Dr Cooper had rung and wanted to know if she would drop by the mortuary sometime that afternoon. No time like the present, she thought, telling DC Collins where she was going and heading out to her car.

•

The search of Luke's room didn't reveal much except a cassette tape marked 'Songs from a Black Room', which Banks, with Robin's permission, slipped in his pocket to listen to later. Luke's desktop computer contained nothing of interest. There was hardly any email, which was only to be expected, and most of the web sites he visited were connected with music. He also did a fair bit of online purchasing, mostly CDs, also to be expected from someone living in so remote a spot.

Banks was surprised at the range of Luke's musical tastes. There was the usual stuff, of course, the CDs Annie had told him about, but also among the grunge, metal, hip-hop and gothic, he had found other oddities, such as Britten's setting of Rimbaud's 'Les Illuminations' and

Miles Davis's *In a Silent Way*. There were also several indie CDs, including, Banks was thrilled to see, his son Brian's band's first recording, *Blue Rain*. Not your usual listening for a fifteen year old. But Banks was coming to believe that Luke Armitage had been a far from typical fifteen year old.

He had also read some of the stories and poems Annie had collected from her previous visit, and in his humble opinion they showed real promise. They didn't tell him anything about what might have happened to Luke, or his feelings about his father or stepfather, but they revealed a young mind preoccupied with death, war, global destruction and social alienation.

Unlike Annie, Banks wasn't surprised by the room's decor. Brian hadn't painted his room black, but he had stuck posters on the walls and surrounded himself with his favourite music. And the guitar, of course, always the guitar. Annie had no children, so Banks could imagine how the black room would seem more outlandish to her. The only thing that disturbed him was Luke's apparent obsession with dead rock stars, and with the absence of anything to do with his famous father, Neil Byrd. Something was definitely out of kilter there.

Brian had gone on to make a career of music, and now his band was on the verge of recording its first CD for a major label. After getting over the initial shock that Brian wasn't going to follow any safe paths in life, Banks had come to feel very proud of him, a leap of faith that his own parents hadn't seemed able to make yet. Banks wondered if Luke had been any good. Maybe the tape would tell him. From what Annie had told him, and from his own first impressions, he doubted that Martin Armitage would have been thrilled by any signs of musical ability in his stepson: physical fitness and sports seemed to be his measures of success.

Josie and Calvin Batty lived in their own small apartment upstairs at the far eastern end of Swainsdale House. There they had a sitting room, bedroom and a small kitchen, in addition to WC and bathroom with a power shower, all modernized by the Armitages, Josie told them as they stood with her in the kitchen while she boiled the kettle for tea. The whole place was brightly decorated in light colours, creams and pale blues, and made the best of the available light.

Josie looked as if she could be quite an attractive young woman if she made the effort, Banks thought. But as it was, her hair seemed lifeless and ill-cut, her clothes rather plain, shapeless and old-fashioned, and her complexion pale and dry. Her husband was short and thickset with dark, gypsyish colouring and heavy eyebrows that met in the middle.

'What exactly are your duties here?' Banks asked the two of them when they were settled in the living room opposite an enormous TV and VCR combination with a tray of tea and chocolate digestives in front of them.

'General, really. I do most of the washing, ironing, cleaning and cooking. Calvin does odd jobs, takes care of the cars and any heavy work, building repairs, garden, that sort of thing.'

'I imagine there must be a lot of that sort of thing,' Banks said, glancing at Calvin. 'A big old house like this.'

'Aye,' Calvin grunted, dunking a biscuit in his tea.

'What about Luke?'

'What about him?' asked Josie.

'Did any of your duties involve taking care of him?'

'Calvin'd give him a lift to school sometimes, or bring

him back if he happened to be in town. I'd make sure he was well fed if sir and madam had to go away for a few days.'

'Did they do that often?'

'Not often, no.'

'When was the last time he was left alone here?'

'Last month. They both went down to London for some fancy gala charity do.'

'What did Luke do when he was left alone in the house?'

'We didn't spy on him,' said Calvin, 'if that's what you're getting at.'

'Not at all,' said Banks. 'But did you ever hear anything? TV? Stereo? Did he ever have his friends over? That sort of thing.'

'Music were loud enough, but he didn't have no friends to ask over, did he?' said Calvin.

'You know that's not true,' said his wife.

'So he did entertain friends?'

'I didn't say that.'

'Did he, Mrs Batty?'

'Not here.'

Banks took a deep breath. 'Where, then?'

She hugged her grey cardie closer to her. 'I shouldn't be telling tales out of school.'

Annie leaned forward and spoke for the first time. 'Mrs Batty, this is a murder investigation. We need your help. We're in the dark here. If you can help throw any light at all on what happened to Luke, please do so. This is way beyond telling tales or keeping promises.'

Josie looked at Banks, uncertain.

'DI Cabbot's right,' he said. 'All bets are off when it's murder. Who was this friend?'

'Just someone I saw him with, that's all.'

'Where?'

'In Eastvale. Swainsdale Centre.'

'When?'

'Recently.'

'Past week or two?'

'A bit longer.'

'A month?'

'Aye, about that.'

'How old? His age? Older? Younger?'

'Older. She wasn't no fifteen year old, I can tell you that.'

'How old?'

'Hard to say when they're that age.'

'What age?'

'Young woman.'

'How young? Late teens, early twenties?'

'Aye, around that.'

'Taller or shorter than him?'

'Shorter. Luke were a big lad for his age. Tall and skinny.'

'What did she look like?'

'Dark.'

'You mean she was black?'

'No, her skin was pale. She just dressed dark, like him. And her hair was dyed black. She had red lipstick on and them studs and chains all over t'place. And she had a tattoo,' she added in a hushed tone, as if saving the greatest sin for last.

Banks glanced at Annie, who, he happened to know from experience, had a butterfly tattoo just above her right breast. Annie gave him a look. 'Where?' she asked Josie.

Josie touched her upper left arm, just below the shoulder. 'There,' she said. 'She was wearing one of them leather waistcoats over a T-shirt.'

'What was the tattoo?' Annie asked her.

'Couldn't tell,' said Josie. 'Too far away. I could just see there was a mark, like.'

This woman shouldn't be too difficult to find if she lived in or near Eastvale, Banks thought. It was hardly Leeds or Manchester when it came to girls in black with studs, chains and tattoos. There was only one club, the Bar None, which catered for such a crowd, and then only two nights a week, the rest of the time being reserved for the techno-dance set. It was possible she was a student at the college, too, he thought. 'Would you mind if we sent a sketch artist over to work on an impression with you this afternoon?' he asked.

'I suppose not,' said Josie. 'If sir and madam don't mind, like. Only I'm supposed to be doing t'upstairs.'

Banks looked at her. 'I don't think Mr and Mrs Armitage will mind,' he said.

'All right, then. But I can't promise owt. Like I said, I didn't get a close look.'

'Can you tell us anything more about her?' Banks asked.

'No. It was just a quick look. I were having a coffee and a KitKat at the food court when I saw them walk by and go into that there big music shop.'

'HMV?'

'That's the one.'

'Did they see you?'

'No.'

'Did you tell anyone you'd seen them?'

'Not my place, is it. Besides . . .'

'Besides what?'

'It was a school day. He should have been in school.'

'What were they doing?'

'Just walking.'

'Close together?'

'They weren't holding hands, if that's what you mean.'

'Were they talking, laughing, arguing?'

'Just walking. I didn't see them so much as look at one another.'

'But you knew they were together? How?'

'You just know, don't you?'

'Had you seen them together before?'

'No. Only the once.'

'And you, Mr Batty?'

'No. Never.'

'Not even when you picked him up from school?'

'She weren't no schoolgirl,' said Josie. 'Not like I ever saw.'

'No,' said Mr Batty.

'What did you talk about when you gave Luke a lift?'

'Nowt, really. He wasn't much of a one for small talk, and we'd nowt in common. I mean, he weren't interested in sport or anything like that. I don't think he watched telly much, either. He'd nothing to talk about.'

Only death and poetry and music, thought Banks. 'So these journeys passed in silence?'

'I usually put the news on the radio.'

'How did he get on with his parents?'

'Wouldn't know,' answered Josie.

'Hear any rows or anything?'

'There's always rows between parents and kids, isn't there?'

'So you did?'

'Nothing out of the ordinary.'

'Who between? Luke and his mother?'

'Nay. Butter wouldn't melt in his mouth as far as she were concerned. Spoiled him rotten.'

'His stepfather, then?'

'Like I said, it were nowt out of t'ordinary.'

'Did you ever hear what was said, what they were arguing about?'

'Walls is too thick around here.'

Banks could believe that. 'Did anything unusual happen lately?'

'What do you mean?' Josie asked.

'Something out of the routine.'

'No.'

'Seen any strangers hanging about?'

'Fewer than normal, since they can't go for their country walks.'

'So you haven't seen anyone?'

'Hanging about? No.'

'Mr Batty?'

'Nobody.'

They were getting no further with the Battys. Banks wasn't certain whether they were holding anything back or not, but he decided he might have another chat with them a little later on. Just as they were leaving, he turned around to Mr Batty and said, 'Ever been arrested, Mr Batty?'

'No.'

'We can easily find out, you know.'

Batty glared at him. 'All right. Once. It were a long time ago.'

'How long?'

'Twelve years. Public nuisance. I were drunk, all right?

I used to drink a lot in those days. Then I met Josie. I don't drink any more.'

'What was all that about?' Annie asked when they were back in the car.

'What?'

'Asking him if he'd been arrested. You know an offence like that is hardly still going to be in the records.'

'Oh, that,' said Banks, buckling up and settling back in the passenger seat while Annie started the ignition. 'I just wanted to see whether he's a good liar or not. People usually lie the first time when you ask them if they've ever been arrested.'

'And?'

'Well, there was a slightly different inflection on that last "no", the lie, but not different enough to convince me he's not a good liar.'

'Bloody hell,' said Annie, heading off down the drive and spraying gravel. 'A proper Sherlock Holmes I've got beside me.'

•

It was only a short drive down Longthorpe Parkway from police headquarters to the District Hospital, and early that Friday afternoon the traffic was light. Instinctively, Michelle found herself checking her rear-view mirror to see if she was being followed. She wasn't.

She parked in the official visitors' area and made her way to pathology. The forensic anthropology department was small, just a couple of offices and one lab, and none of the staff was permanent. Dr Cooper herself lectured in nearby Cambridge, in addition to her practical duties at the hospital. There certainly weren't enough skeletons to justify a full-time forensic anthropology department –

most counties didn't have one at all and had to hire the services of an expert when circumstances demanded – but there had been enough Anglo-Saxon and Viking remains found in East Anglia for a small, part-time department to be thought justified. For the most part, that was Wendy Cooper's main area of interest, too, ancient remains, not skeletons of boys buried in 1965.

'Ah, DI Hart,' Dr Cooper greeted her in her office, standing up and shaking hands. 'Good of you to come.'

'Not at all. You said you had something to tell me?'

'Show you, actually. It's not much, but it might help. Follow me.'

Curious, Michelle followed her into the lab, where Graham Marshall's bones were still laid out on the table and Tammy Wynette was singing 'Stand by Your Man' on Dr Cooper's portable cassette player. Though still a dirty brownish-yellow, like bad teeth, the bones were a hell of a lot cleaner than they had been a few days ago, Michelle noticed. Dr Cooper and her assistant, nowhere in sight at the moment, had clearly been working hard. The body looked asymmetrical, though, Michelle noticed, and wondered what was missing. When she looked more closely, she could see it was the bottom rib on the left side. Hadn't they been able to find it? But no, there it was on the bench Dr Cooper led her towards.

'We couldn't see it before because of the accumulated dirt,' Dr Cooper explained, 'but once we'd cleaned it up, it was plain as daylight. Look.'

Michelle bent closer and looked. She could see a deep, narrow notch in the bone. It was something she had come across before. She looked at Dr Cooper. 'Knife wound?'

'Very good. That's what I'd say.'

'Pre- or post-mortem?'

'Oh, pre. Cuts in green bone are different from cuts made in bones after death, when they're more brittle. This is a clean, smooth cut. Definitely pre-mortem.'

'Cause of death?'

Dr Cooper frowned. 'I can't say that for certain,' she said. 'I mean, there could have been lethal poison in the system, or the victim might have drowned first, but what I can say is that, in my opinion, the wound would have been sufficient to cause death. If you follow the trajectory of the blade to its natural destination, it pierces the heart.'

Michelle paused a moment, looking at the rib in question, to take it all in. 'Front or behind?' she asked.

'Does it matter?'

'If it was done from behind,' Michelle explained, 'it could have been a stranger. If it happened from the front, someone had to get close enough to the boy to do it without his knowing what was going to happen.'

'Yes, I see,' said Dr Cooper. 'Good point. I never have managed to get the hang of thinking the way you police do.'

'Different training.'

'I suppose so.' Dr Cooper picked up the rib. 'Judging from the position of the cut on the bone – see, it's almost on the *inside* – and by the straightness I'd say that it was done from in front, the classic upthrust though the ribcage and into the heart. Harder to be that accurate from behind. Much more awkward, far more likely to be at an angle.'

'So it had to be someone he would let get that close to him without being suspicious.'

'Close enough to pat him on the shoulder, yes. And whoever did it was right handed.'

'What kind of knife?'

'That I can't tell you, except that it was very sharp and the blade wasn't serrated. It's quite a deep cut, as you can see, so there's plenty of scope for analysis and measurement. There's someone I know who can probably tell you the date it was made and the company who made it, an expert. His name's Dr Hilary Wendell. If you like I can try to track him down, get him to have a look.'

'Could you?'

Dr Cooper laughed. 'I said I'd *try*. Hilary's all over the place. And I mean all over. Including the United States, and Eastern Europe. He's very well known. He even spent some time with the forensic teams in Bosnia and Kosovo.'

'You were there, too, weren't you?'

Dr Cooper gave a little shudder. 'Yes. Kosovo.'

'Any idea when the coroner can release the bones for burial?'

'He can release them now as far as I'm concerned. I'd specify burial rather than cremation, though, just in case we need to exhume.'

'I think that's what they have in mind. And some sort of memorial service. It's just that I know the Marshalls are anxious for some sense of closure. I'll give them a ring and say it's okay to go ahead and make arrangements.'

'Funny thing, that, isn't it?' said Dr Cooper. 'Closure. As if burying someone's remains or sending a criminal to jail actually marks the end of the pain.'

'It's very human, though, don't you think?' said Michelle, for whom closure had simply refused to come, despite all the trappings. 'We need ritual, symbols, ceremonies.'

'I suppose we do. What about this, though?' She pointed to the rib on the lab bench. 'It could even end up being evidence in court.'

'Well,' said Michelle, 'I don't suppose the Marshalls will mind if they know Graham's being buried with a rib missing, will they? Especially if it might help lead us to his killer. I'll get their permission, anyway.'

'Fine,' said Dr Cooper. 'I'll talk to the coroner this afternoon and try to track Hilary down in the meantime.'

'Thanks,' said Michelle. She looked again at the bones on the table, laid out in some sort of semblance of a human skeleton, and then glanced back at the single rib on the bench. Strange, she thought. It didn't matter – they were only old bones – but she couldn't help but feel this odd and deep sense of significance, and the words 'Adam's rib' came to mind. Stupid, she told herself. Nobody's going to create a woman out of Graham Marshall's rib; with a bit of luck, Dr Hilary Wendell is going to tell us something about the knife that killed him.

•

A few dark clouds had blown in on a strong wind from the north, and it looked as if rain was about to spoil yet another fine summer's day when Banks drove out in his own car to the crime scene late that afternoon, listening to Luke Armitage's 'Songs from a Black Room'.

There were only five short songs on the tape, and lyrically they were not sophisticated, about what you'd expect for a fifteen year old with a penchant for reading poetry he couldn't understand. There were no settings of Rimbaud or Baudelaire here, only pure, unadulterated adolescent angst: 'Everybody hates me, but I don't care. / I'm safe in my black room, and the fools are out there.' But at least they were Luke's own songs. When Banks was fourteen, he had got together with Graham, Paul and Steve to form a rudimentary rock band, and all they had managed were rough cover versions of Beatles and Stones songs. Not one of them had had the urge or the talent to write original material.

Luke's music was raw and anguished, as if he were reaching, straining, to find the right voice, his own voice. He backed himself on electric guitar, occasionally using special effects, such as fuzz and wah-wah, but mostly sticking to the simple chord progressions Banks remembered from his own stumbling attempts at guitar. The remarkable thing was how much Luke's voice resembled his father's. He had Neil Byrd's broad range, though his voice hadn't deepened enough to handle the lowest notes yet, and he also had his father's timbre, wistful but bored, and even a little angry, edgy.

Only one song stood out, a quiet ballad with a melody Banks recognized vaguely, perhaps an adaptation of an old folk tune. The last piece on the tape, it was a love song of sorts, or a fifteen year old's version of salvation:

> *He shut me out but you took me in.*
> *He's in the dark but you're a bird on the wing.*
> *I couldn't hold you but you chose to stay.*
> *Why do you care? Please don't go away.*

Was it about his mother, Robin? Or was it the girl Josie had seen him with in the Swainsdale Centre? Along with Winsome Jackman and Kevin Templeton, Annie was out showing the artist's impression around the most likely places. Maybe one of them would get lucky.

The SOCOs were still at Hallam Tarn, the road still taped off, as was a local TV van, along with a gaggle of reporters who barely kept their distance. As he pulled up by the side of the road, Banks even noticed a couple of middle-aged ladies in walking gear; sightseers, no doubt.

Stefan Nowak was in charge, looking suave even in his protective clothing.

'Stefan,' Banks greeted him. 'How's it going?'

'We're trying to get everything done before the rain comes,' Stefan said. 'We've found nothing else in the water so far, but the frogmen are still looking.'

Banks looked around. Christ, but it was wild and lonely up there, an open landscape, hardly a tree in sight, with miles of rolling moorland, a mix of yellow gorse, sandy-coloured tufts of grass and black patches where fires had raged earlier that summer. The heather wouldn't bloom for another month or two, but the dark multi-branched stems spread tough and wiry all around, clinging close to the ground. The view was spectacular, even more dramatic under the louring sky. Over in the west, Banks could see as far as the long flat bulk of the three peaks: Ingleborough, Whernside and Pen-y-ghent.

'Anything interesting?' he asked.

'Maybe,' said Stefan. 'We tried to pin down the exact point on the wall where the body had been dropped over, and it matches the spot where these stones stick out here like steps. Makes climbing easy. Good footholds.'

'I see. It would have taken a bit of strength, though, wouldn't it?'

'Oh, I don't know. He might have been a big lad for his age, but he was still only a kid, and pretty skinny.'

'Could one person have done it?'

'Certainly. Anyway, we've been looking for scuff marks. It's also possible that the killer scratched himself climbing up.'

'You've found blood on the wall?'

'Minute traces. But hold your horses, Alan. We don't even know if it's human blood yet.'

Banks watched the SOCOs taking the wall apart stone by stone and packing it in the back of a van. He wondered what Gristhorpe would think of such destruction. Gristhorpe was building a drystone wall at the back of his house as a hobby. It went nowhere and fenced in nothing. Some of these walls had been standing for centuries without any sort of cement holding them together, but they were far more than mere random piles of rocks. Gristhorpe knew all about the techniques and the patience it took to find just the right stone to fit with the others, and here the men were demolishing it. Still, if it could lead them to Luke's killer, Banks thought, that was worth a drystone wall or two. He knew Gristhorpe would agree.

'Any chance of footprints?'

Stefan shook his head. 'If there was any sort of impression in the grass or the dust you can be sure it's gone now. Don't get your hopes up.'

'Do I ever? Tyre tracks?'

'Again, too many, and it's not a good road surface. But we're looking. We've got a botanist coming up from York, too. There may be some unique plant life by the roadside, especially with it being close to a body of water. You never know. If you find someone with a bit of purple-speckled ragwort sticking to the bottom of his shoe, it just might be your man.'

'Wonderful.' Banks walked back to his car.

'Chief Inspector?' It was one of the reporters, a local man Banks recognized.

'What do you want?' he asked. 'We've just told you lot all we know at the press conference.'

'Is it true what we've been hearing?' the reporter asked.

'What have you been hearing?'

'That it was a botched kidnapping.'

'No comment,' said Banks, muttering, 'shit,' under his breath as he got in his car, turned around in the next lay-by and set off home.

After tracking down a retired detective inspector who had worked out of West End Central and persuading him to talk to her in London the following day, Michelle had left the station and stopped off to rent the video of *The Krays* on her way home. She hoped the film would at least give her a general picture of their life and times.

She had been living in her riverside flat on Viersen Platz for two months now, but it still felt temporary, just another place she was passing through. Partly it was because she hadn't unpacked everything – books, dishes, some clothes and other odds and ends – and partly it was the job, of course. Long hours made it difficult to keep house, and most of her meals were eaten on the run.

The flat itself was cosy and pleasant enough. A modern four-storey building, part of the Rivergate Centre, it faced south, overlooking the river, got plenty of light for the potted plants she liked to keep on her small balcony, and was so close to the city centre as to be practically in the shadow of the cathedral. She didn't know why she hadn't settled in more; it was one of the nicest places she had ever lived in, if a bit pricey. But what else did she have to spend her money on? She particularly liked to sit out on the balcony after dark, look at the lights reflected in the slow-moving river and listen to the trains go by. On weekends she could hear blues music from Charters Bar, an old iron barge moored opposite, by Town Bridge; the customers sometimes made a bit too much noise at closing time, but that was only a minor irritant.

Michelle had no friends to invite for dinner, nor the time or inclination to entertain them, so she hadn't even bothered to unpack her best chinaware. She had even let such basics as laundry, dusting and ironing slip, and as a consequence her flat had the air of someone who used to maintain a certain level of tidiness and cleanliness but had let things go. Even the bed was unmade since that morning.

She glanced at the answering machine, but no light flashed. It never did. She wondered why she even bothered to keep the thing. Work, of course. After a quick blitz on the dishes in the sink and a run around with the Hoover, she felt ready to sit down and watch *The Krays*. But she was hungry. As usual there was nothing in the fridge, at least nothing edible, so she went around the corner to the Indian takeaway and got some prawn curry and rice. Sitting with a tray on her lap and a bottle of South African Merlot beside her, she pressed the remote and the video began.

When it had finished, Michelle didn't feel she knew much more about the Kray twins than before it had begun. Yes, theirs was a violent world and you'd better not cross them. Yes, they seemed to have plenty of money and spend most of their time in ritzy clubs. But what exactly did they do? Apart from vague battles with the Maltese and meetings with American gangsters, the exact nature of their businesses was left unexplained. And, as far as the film was concerned, coppers might as well have not even existed.

She turned to the news, still feeling a little queasy from the violence. Or was it from the curry and wine? She didn't really believe that the Krays had anything to do with Graham Marshall's murder, any more than she believed Brady and Hindley had, and she could imagine how Shaw would laugh if he heard her suggest such a thing.

If Bill Marshall had any serious criminal aspirations, they hadn't done him much good. He never got out of the council house, though the Marshalls had bought it for £4,000 in 1984.

Perhaps he swore off crime. Michelle had checked subsequent police records and found no further mention of him, so he had gone either straight or uncaught. She would guess at the former, given his standard of living. Graham's disappearance must have shaken him, then. Maybe he sensed a connection to the world he had been involved in, so he severed all ties. She would have to find time to have an even closer look at the old crime reports, dig out old action books and the notebooks of the detectives involved. But that could wait until after the weekend.

She turned on her computer and tried to put her thoughts and theories into some kind of order, the way she usually did last thing at night, then she played a couple of games of Freecell and lost.

It got dark. Michelle turned off her computer, cleared away the detritus of her lonely dinner, found there wasn't enough wine left in the bottle to be worth saving, so topped up her glass. As it so often did around bedtime, the depression seemed to close in on her like a dense fog. She sipped her wine and listened to rain tapping against her window. God, how she missed Melissa, even after all this time. She missed Ted, too, sometimes, but mostly she missed Melissa.

Her thoughts went back to the day it happened. It was a movie that ran in her mind, as if on a constant loop. She wasn't there – that was a big part of the problem – but she could picture Melissa outside the school gates, her golden curls, little blue dress with the flowers on it, the other kids milling around, vigilant teachers nearby, then Melissa seeing what she thought was her father's car pulling to a stop across the road, though they always picked her up on *her* side. Then she pictured Melissa waving, smiling, and, before anyone could stop her, running right out in front of the speeding lorry.

Before getting into bed, she took Melissa's dress, the same dress she had died in, from her bedside drawer, lay down, held it to her face and cried herself to sleep.

10

As Annie waited outside ACC McLaughlin's office at county headquarters the following morning, having been 'summoned', she felt the same way she had when her geography teacher sent her to the headmaster's office for defacing a school atlas with her own cartographic designs: fantastic sea creatures and warnings that 'Beyond this point be monsters.'

She had little fear of authority, and a person's rank or status was something she rarely considered in her daily dealings, but somehow this summons made her nervous. Not 'Red Ron' himself – he was known to be stern but fair and had a reputation for standing behind his team – but the situation she might find herself in.

It seemed that since she had decided to pursue her career again, she had made nothing but mistakes. First, sliding arse over tit down the side of Harkside reservoir in full view of several of her colleagues and against the orders of the officer in charge; then the debacle of her excessive force investigation of probationary PC Janet Taylor during her brief (but not brief enough) spell with Complaints and Discipline; and now being blamed for the murder of Luke Armitage. Pretty soon everyone would be calling her Fuck-up Annie, if they didn't already. 'Got a case you want fucking up, mate? Give it to Annie Cabbot, she'll see you right.'

So much for a revitalized career. At least she was

determined to go down with her middle finger high in the air.

It wasn't bloody fair, though, Annie thought, as she paced. She was a damn good detective. Everything she had done in all those instances had been right; it was just the spin, the way it all added up, that made her look bad.

Red Ron's secretary opened the door and ushered Annie into the presence. As befitted his rank, ACC McLaughlin had an even bigger office than Detective Superintendent Gristhorpe's and a carpet with much thicker pile. At least he didn't have the books that intimidated her so in Gristhorpe's office.

Red Ron had done a few things to personalize it since he first came to the job about eight months ago: a framed photo of his wife Carol stood on the desk, and a print of Constable's *The Lock* hung on the wall. The glass cabinet was full of trophies and photos of Red Ron with various police athletics teams, from rowing to archery. He looked fit and was rumoured to be in training for a marathon. He was also rumoured to keep a bottle of fine single malt in his bottom drawer, but Annie didn't expect to see much evidence of that.

'DI Cabbot,' he greeted her, glancing over the top of his wire-rimmed glasses. 'Please sit down. I'll be with you in a moment.'

Annie sat. There was something different about him, she thought. Then she realized. Red Ron had shaved off his moustache since she had last seen him. She was surprised to find that he had an upper lip. She always thought men grew moustaches and beards to hide weak jaws and thin lips. He kept his receding silver hair cut short instead of growing one side long and trying to hide a bald centre by combing it over the top of the skull, the way some men did. Annie didn't understand that. What was so wrong with going bald? She thought some bald men were quite sexy. It was one of those ridiculous macho male things, she guessed, like the obsession with penis length. Were all men so bloody insecure? Well, she would never find out because none of them would ever talk about it. Not even Banks, though he did at least try more than most. Perhaps it was something they really *couldn't* do, something they were genetically incapable of, something going back to the caves and the hunt.

Annie brought herself back to the present. The ACC had just finished signing a stack of papers and after he had buzzed his secretary to come and take them away, he leaned back in his chair and linked his hands behind his head. 'I suppose you know why you're here?' he began.

'Yes, sir.'

'The chief constable got in touch with me last night – just as I was settling down to my dinner, by the way – and said he'd had a complaint about you from Martin Armitage. Would you care to explain what happened?'

Annie told him. As she spoke, she could tell he was listening intently, and every now and then he made a jotting on the pad in front of him. Nice fountain pen, she noticed. A maroon Waterman. Sometimes he frowned, but he didn't interrupt her once. When she had finished, he paused for a while, then said, 'Why did you decide to follow Mr Armitage from his house that morning?'

'Because I thought his behaviour was suspicious, sir. And I was looking for a missing boy.'

'A boy he had already told you was due back that very day.'

'Yes, sir.'

'You didn't believe him?'

'I suppose not, sir.'

'Why not?'

Annie went over the Armitages' behaviour on the morning in question, the tension she had felt, the brusqueness of their response to her, the haste with which they wanted rid of her. 'All I can say, sir,' she said, 'is that I found their behaviour to be out of synch with what I'd expect from parents who'd discovered that their son was all right and was coming home.'

'All very speculative on your part, DI Cabbot.'

Annie gripped the arms of the chair hard. 'I used my judgement, sir. And I stand by it.'

'Hmm.' Red Ron took off his glasses and rubbed his eyes. 'It's a bad business,' he said. 'We've had the press all over us, and needless to say they're hot to trot with this idea of a simple kidnapping gone wrong. Add police cockup to that, and they'd like nothing better.'

'With all due respect, sir, it wasn't a simple kidnapping.' Annie gave her reasons why, as she had done before with Gristhorpe and Banks.

Red Ron stroked his chin as he listened, plucking at his upper lip as if he still expected to feel the moustache. When she had finished, he asked, as she had hoped he wouldn't, 'Didn't it cross your mind just for one moment that the kidnapper might have been watching Mr Armitage make the drop?'

'I . . . er . . .'

'You didn't think of it, did you?'

'I wanted to know what he'd left there.'

'DI Cabbot. Use your intelligence. A man's stepson is missing. He's edgy and anxious to be somewhere, annoyed that the police are on his doorstep. You follow him and see him enter a disused shepherd's shelter with a briefcase and come out without it. What do you surmise?'

Annie felt herself flush with anger at the rightness of his logic. 'When you put it like that, sir,' she said through gritted teeth, 'I suppose it's clear he's paying a ransom. But things don't always seem so clear-cut in the field.'

'You've no need to tell me what it's like in the field, DI Cabbot. I might be an administrator now, but I wasn't always behind this desk. I've served my time in the field. I've seen things that would make your hair curl.'

'Then I'm sure you'll understand what I'm saying.' Was that a half-smile Annie spotted fleeting across Red Ron's features? Surely not.

He went on, 'The point remains that you must have known the risk of being seen by the kidnapper was extremely high, especially as you were in open country-side, and that for whatever reason you disregarded that risk and went into the shelter anyway. And now the boy's dead.'

'There's some indication that Luke Armitage might have been killed even *before* his stepfather delivered the money.'

'That would be a piece of luck for you, wouldn't it?'

'That's not fair, sir. I needed to know what was in the briefcase.'

'Why?'

'I needed to be sure. That's all. And it turned out to be a clue of sorts.'

'The low amount? Yes. But how did you know that wasn't just the first instalment?'

'With respect, sir, kidnappers don't usually work on the instalment plan. Not like blackmailers.'

'But how did you know?'

'I didn't *know*, but it seemed a reasonable assumption.'

'You assumed.'

'Yes, sir.'

'Look, DI Cabbot. I'm not going to beat about the bush. I don't like it when members of the public make complaints about officers under my command. I like it even less when a self-important citizen such as Martin Armitage complains to his golf-club crony, the chief constable, who then passes the buck down to me. Do you understand?'

'Yes, sir. You don't like it.'

'Now, while your actions weren't exactly by the book, and while you might have lacked judgement in acting so impulsively, I don't see anything serious enough in what you did to justify punishment.'

Annie began to feel relieved. A bollocking, that was all she was going to get.

'On the other hand . . .'

Annie's spirits sank again.

'We don't have all the facts in yet.'

'Sir?'

'We don't know whether you *were* seen by the kidnapper or not, do we?'

'No, sir.'

'And we don't know exactly *when* Luke Armitage died.'

'Dr Glendenning's doing the post-mortem sometime today, sir.'

'Yes, I know. So what I'm saying is that until we have all the facts I'll postpone judgement. Go back to your duties, Detective Inspector.'

Annie stood up before he changed his mind. 'Yes, sir.'

'And DI Cabbot?'

'Sir?'

'If you're going to keep on using your own car on the job, get a bloody police radio fitted, would you?'

Annie blushed. 'Yes, sir,' she mumbled, and left.

•

Michelle got off the Intercity train at King's Cross at about half-past one that afternoon and walked down the steps to the tube, struck, as she always was, by the sheer hustle and bustle of London, the constant noise and motion. Cathedral Square on a summer holiday weekend with a rock band playing in the market place didn't even come close.

Unlike many of her contemporaries, Michelle had never worked on the Met. She had thought of moving there after Greater Manchester, after Melissa had died and Ted had left, but instead she had moved around a lot over the past five years and taken numerous courses, convincing herself that it was all for the good of her career. She suspected, though, that she had just been running. Somewhere a bit more out of the way had seemed the best option, at least for the time being, another low-profile position. And you didn't get anywhere in today's police force without switching back and forth a lot – from uniform to CID, from county to county. Career detectives like Jet Harris were a thing of the past.

A few ragged junkies sat propped against the walls of the busy underpass, several of them young girls, Michelle noticed, and too far gone even to beg for change. As she passed, one of them started to moan and wail. She had a bottle in her hand and she banged it hard against the wall until it smashed, echoing in the tiled passage and scattering broken glass all over the place. Like everyone else, Michelle hurried on.

The tube was crowded and she had to stand all the way to Tottenham Court Road, where retired Detective Inspector Robert Lancaster had agreed to talk to her over a late lunch on Dean Street. It was raining when she walked out on to Oxford Street. Christ, she thought, *not again*! At this rate, summer would be over before it had begun. Michelle unfurled her umbrella and made her way through the tourists and hustlers. She turned off Oxford Street and crossed Soho Square, then followed Lancaster's directions and found the place easily enough.

Though it was a pub, Michelle was pleased to see that it looked rather more upmarket than some establishments, with its hanging baskets of flowers outside, stained glass and shiny dark woodwork. She had dressed about as casually as she was capable of, in a mid-length skirt, a pink V-neck top and a light wool jacket, but she would still have looked overdressed in a lot of London pubs. This one, however, catered to a business luncheon crowd. It even had a separate restaurant section away from the smoke and video machines, with table service, no less.

Lancaster, recognizable by the carnation he told Michelle he would be wearing in his grey suit, was a dapper man with a full head of silver hair and a sparkle in his eye. Perhaps a bit portly, Michelle noticed as he stood up to greet her, but definitely well-preserved for his age, which she guessed at around seventy. His face had a florid complexion, but he didn't otherwise look like a serious drinker. At least he didn't have that telltale calligraphy of broken red and purple veins just under the surface, like Shaw.

'Mr Lancaster,' she said, sitting down. 'Thank you for agreeing to see me.'

'The pleasure's mine entirely,' he said, traces of a cockney accent still in his voice. 'Ever since my kids flew the coop and my wife died, I'll take any opportunity to get out of the house. Besides, it's not every day I get to come down the West End and have lunch with a pretty girl like yourself.'

Michelle smiled and felt herself blush a little. A *girl*, he'd called her, when she had turned forty last September. For some reason, she didn't feel offended by Lancaster's particular brand of male chauvinism; it had such a quaint, old-fashioned feel to it that it seemed only natural on her part to accept the compliment and thank him with as much grace as possible. She'd soon find out if it got more wearing as their conversation continued.

'I hope you don't mind my choice of eatery.'

Michelle looked around at the tables with their white linen cloths and weighty cutlery, the uniformed waitresses dashing around. 'Not at all,' she said.

He chuckled, a throaty sound. 'You wouldn't believe what this place used to be like. Used to be a real villains' pub back in the early sixties. Upstairs, especially. You'd be amazed at the jobs planned up there, the contracts put out.'

'Not any more, I hope?'

'Oh, no. It's quite respectable now.' He spoke with a tinge of regret in his voice.

A waitress appeared with her order book.

'What would you like to drink?' Lancaster asked.

'Just a fruit juice, please.'

'Orange, grapefruit or pineapple?' the waitress asked.

'Orange is fine.'

'And I'll have another pint of Guinness, please,' Lancaster said. 'Sure you don't want something a bit stronger, love?'

'No, that'll be just fine, thanks.' Truth was, Michelle had felt the effects of last night's bottle of wine that morning, and she had decided to lay off the booze for a day or two. It was still manageable. She never drank during the day, anyway, only in the evening, alone in her flat with the curtains closed and the television on. But if she didn't nip it in the bud, she'd be the next one with broken blood vessels in her nose.

'The food's quite good here,' said Lancaster while the waitress was fetching their drinks. 'I'd stay away from the lamb curry if I were you, though. Last time I touched it I ended up with a case of Delhi belly.'

Michelle had eaten a curry the previous evening, and though it hadn't given her 'Delhi belly', it had made its presence felt during the night. She wanted something plain, something unencumbered with fancy sauces, something *British*.

The waitress returned with her Britvic orange and Lancaster's Guinness and asked them for their orders.

'I'll have the Cumberland sausage and mashed potatoes, please,' Michelle said. And diet be damned, she added under her breath. Lancaster ordered the roast beef.

'Bangers and mash,' he said, beaming, when the waitress had wandered off. 'Wonderful. One doesn't often meet people who go for the more traditional food these days. It's all that nasty foreign muck, isn't it?'

'I don't mind a bit of pasta or a curry now and then,' said Michelle, 'but sometimes you can't beat the traditional English.'

Lancaster paused for a few moments, drumming his

fingers on the table. Michelle could sense him changing gear, from old-fashioned gallant to seasoned street copper, wondering what she was after and whether it could harm him. She could see it in his eyes, their gaze sharpening, becoming more watchful. She wanted to set him at ease but decided it was best to let him lead, see where it went. At first.

'The bloke that put you on to me said you wanted to know about Reggie and Ronnie.'

There, they were out. The dreaded words. Reggie and Ronnie: *the Krays*.

'Sort of,' Michelle said. 'But let me explain.'

Lancaster listened, taking the occasional sip of Guinness, nodding here and there, as Michelle told him about the Marshalls and what had happened to Graham.

'So, you see,' she finished, 'it's not really the twins, or not *just* them, anyway, that I'm interested in.'

'Yes, I see,' said Lancaster, drumming his fingers again. Their food arrived and they both took a few bites before he spoke again. 'How's your sausage?' he asked.

'Fine,' said Michelle, wondering if he was going to be any use at all or if it was going to be one of those pleasant but pointless sessions.

'Good. Good. I knew Billy Marshall and his family,' said Lancaster. Then he stuffed his mouth full of roast beef and mashed potato and looked at Michelle, eyes wide and expressionless as he chewed, watching for her reaction. She was surprised, and she was also pleased that the information Banks had given her led somewhere, although she still had no idea where.

'Billy and I grew up just around the corner from one another. We went to the same schools, played on the same streets. We even used to drink in the same pub,' he went on when he'd washed his food down with Guinness. 'Does that surprise you?'

'A bit, I suppose. Though, I must say, not much about those days surprises me any more.'

Lancaster laughed. 'You're right there, love. Another world. See, you've got to understand where detectives came from, Michelle. Can I call you Michelle?'

'Of course.'

'The first detectives came from the criminal classes. They were equally at home on either side of the law. Jonathan Wild, the famous thief-taker, for example. Half the time he set up the blokes he fingered. Did you know that? They hanged him in the end. And Vidocq, the Froggie? Thief, police informer, master of disguise. Criminal. And back then, the days you're asking about, I think we were a bit closer to our prototypes than the office boys we seem to have in the force today, if you'll pardon my criticism. Now, I'm not saying I was ever a criminal myself, but I lived close enough to the line at times to know what a thin line it is, and I was also close enough to know how they thought. And do you imagine for a moment those on the other side didn't know that, too?'

'You turned a blind eye sometimes?'

'I told you. I went to school with Billy Marshall, grew up the next street over. Only difference was, he was thick as two short planks, but he could fight, and me, well I had the smarts and the stealth, but I wasn't much of a scrapper. Enough to survive. And believe me you had to have that much or you were a goner. Any trouble and I'd talk my way out of it, and if that didn't work I'd leg it. Mostly I'd talk my way out. Is it any wonder we went our different ways? Thing is, it could've gone either way for me. I ran a bit wild when I was kid, got into a scrape or two. I knew exactly where people like Reggie and Ronnie were coming from. We lived in the same poor neighbourhood, in the shadow of the war. I could think like them. I could've easily used my street-smarts for criminal purposes like Reggie and Ronnie or . . .' He let the sentence trail and ate some more roast beef.

'You're saying morality doesn't come into it?' Michelle asked. 'The law? Justice? Honesty?'

'Words, love,' Lancaster said when he'd finished eating. 'Nice words, I'll grant you, but words nonetheless.'

'So how did you choose? Toss a coin?'

Lancaster laughed. ' "Toss a coin." Good one, that. I'll have to remember it.' Then his expression turned more serious. 'No, love. I probably joined for the same reasons you did, same as most people. There wasn't much pay then, but it seemed a decent enough job, maybe even a bit glamorous and exciting. Fabian of the Yard, and all that stuff. I didn't want to be a plod walking the beat – oh, I did it, of course, we all did, had to – but I knew I wanted CID right from the start, and I got it. What I'm saying, love, is that when it came right down to it, when you stood at the bar of your local, or took your usual table in the corner, the one your father had sat at all his life, and when someone like Billy came in, someone you knew was a bit dodgy, well, then it was just a job you did. Everybody knew it. Nothing personal. We mixed, tolerated one another, hoped our paths never crossed in a serious way, a professional way. And remember I was working out of West End Central then. The East End wasn't my manor. I just grew up there, lived there. Of course, we were all aware there was a barrier between us, at least one we'd better not breech in public, so it was all, "Hello, Billy. How's it going? How's the wife and kid? Oh, fine Bob, can't complain. How's things down the nick? Thriving, Billy boy, thriving. Glad to hear it, mate." That sort of thing.'

'I can understand that,' said Michelle, who thought she took policing a bit more seriously and wouldn't be caught dead in the same pub as known villains, unless she was meeting an informant. It was the same thing that Shaw had said. The lines between them and us weren't so clearly drawn as they are today, mostly because many cops and criminals came from the same backgrounds, went to the same schools and drank in the same pubs, as Lancaster had just pointed out, and as long as no innocent bystanders got hurt . . . no harm done. Nothing personal. Different times.

'Just wanted to get it clear,' said Lancaster, 'so you wouldn't go away thinking I was bent or anything.'

'Why would I think that?'

He winked. 'Oh, there were plenty that were. Vice, Obscene Publications, the Sweeney. Oh, yes. It was all just getting going then, sixty-three, sixty-four, sixty-five. There are some naive buggers who look at it as the beginnings of some new age of enlightenment or something. Aquarius, call it what you will. Fucking hippies, with their peace and love and beads and long hair.' He sneered. 'Know what it really was? It was the beginnings of the rise of organized crime in this country. Oh, I'm not saying we hadn't had gangsters before that, but back in the mid-sixties, when Reggie and Ronnie were at their peak, you could have written what your average British copper knew about organized crime on the back of a postage stamp. I kid you not. We knew bugger all. Even "Nipper" Read, the bloke in charge of nailing the twins. Porn was coming in by the lorryload from Denmark, Germany,

Sweden, the Netherlands. Someone had to control distribution, wholesale, resale. Same with drugs. Opening of the floodgates, the mid-sixties. Licence to print money. Maybe the hippies saw a revolution of peace and love in the future, but people like Reggie and Ronnie only saw even more opportunities to make cash, and ultimately all your hippies were just consumers, just another market. Sex, drugs, rock and roll. Your real criminals were rubbing their hands in glee when flower power came along, like kids given the free run of the sweet shop.'

This was all very well, Michelle thought, but a man with a bee in his bonnet, the way Lancaster seemed to have, could be difficult to get information from. Lancaster ordered another Guinness – Michelle asked for coffee – and sat back in his chair. He took a pill from a small silver container and washed it down with stout.

'Blood pressure,' he explained. 'Anyway, I'm sorry, love,' he went on, as if reading her mind. 'I do go on a bit, don't I? One of the few benefits of getting old. You can go on and on and nobody tells you to shut up.'

'Bill Marshall.'

'Yes, Billy Marshall, as he was called back then. I haven't forgotten. Haven't seen or heard of him for years, by the way. Is he still alive?'

'Barely,' said Michelle. 'He's suffered a serious stroke.'

'Poor sod. And the Missis?'

'Coping.'

He nodded. 'Good. She always was a good coper, was Maggie Marshall.'

Maggie. Michelle just realized that she hadn't known Mrs Marshall's first name. 'Did Bill Marshall work for Reggie and Ronnie?' she asked.

'Yes. In a way.'

'What do you mean?'

'A lot of people in the East End worked for Reggie and Ronnie at one time or another. Fit young geezer like Billy, I'd've been surprised if he hadn't. He was a boxer. Amateur, mind you. And so were the Krays. They were into boxing in a big way. They met up at one of the local gyms. Billy did a few odd jobs with them. It paid to have the twins on your side back then, even if you weren't in deep with them. They made very nasty enemies.'

'So I've read.'

Lancaster laughed. 'You don't know the half of it, love.'

'But he wasn't regularly employed, not on their payroll?'

'That's about it. An occasional encouragement to pay up, or deterrent against talking. You know the sort of thing.'

'He told you this?'

Lancaster laughed. 'Come off it, love. It wasn't something you discussed over a game of darts at the local.'

'But you knew?'

'It was my job to know. Keeping tabs. I liked to think I knew what was going on, even outside my manor, and that those who counted knew that I knew.'

'What do you remember about him?'

'Nice enough bloke, if you didn't cross him. Bit of a temper, especially after a jar or two. Like I said, he was strictly low-level muscle, a boxer.'

'He used to boast that he knew Reggie and Ronnie when he was in his cups, after he'd moved up to Peterborough.'

'Typical Billy, that. Didn't have two brain cells to rub together. I'll tell you one thing, though.'

'What's that?'

'You said the kid was stabbed?'

'That's what the pathologist tells me.'

'Billy never went tooled up. He was strictly a fist man. Maybe a cosh or knuckledusters, depending who he was up against, but never a knife or a gun.'

'I didn't really regard Bill Marshall as a serious suspect,' Michelle said, 'but thanks for letting me know. I'm just wondering if or how all this could have had any connection with Graham's death.'

'I can't honestly say I can see one, love.'

'If Billy did something to upset his masters, then surely—'

'If Billy Marshall had done anything to upset Reggie or Ronnie, love, he'd have been the one pushing up daisies, not the kid.'

'They wouldn't have harmed the boy to make a point?'

'Not their way, no. Direct, not subtle. They had their faults, and there wasn't much they wouldn't do if it came right down to it. But if you crossed them, it wasn't your wife or your kid got hurt, it was you.'

'I understand Ronnie was—'

'Yes, he was. And he liked them young. But not that young.'

'Then—'

'They didn't hurt kids. It was a man's world. There was a code. Unwritten. But it was there. And another thing you've got to understand, love, is that Reggie and Ronnie were like Robin Hood, Dick Turpin and Billy the Kid all rolled into one as far as most East Enders were concerned. Even later, you only have to look at their funerals to see that. Fucking royalty. Pardon my French. Folk heroes.'

'And you were the sheriff of Nottingham?'

Lancaster laughed. 'Hardly. I was only a DC, a mere foot soldier. But you get the picture.'

'I think so. And after the day's battles you'd all adjourn to the local and have a jolly old drink together and talk about football.'

Lancaster laughed. 'Something like that. You know, maybe you're right. Maybe it was a bit of a game. When you nicked someone fair and square, there were no hard feelings. When they put one over on you, you just filed it away till next time. If the courts let them off, then you bought them a pint next time they came in the pub.'

'I think Billy Marshall took the game to Peterborough with him. Ever hear of a bloke called Carlo Fiorino?'

Lancaster's bushy eyebrows knitted in a frown. 'Can't say as I have, no. But that's way off my manor. Besides, I've already told you, Billy didn't have the brains to set up an operation. He didn't have the authority, the command, charisma, call it what you will. Billy Marshall was born to follow orders, not give them, let alone decide what they ought to be. Now that lad of his, he was another matter entirely.'

Michelle pricked up her ears. 'Graham? What about him?'

'Young lad with the Beatle cut, right?'

'Sounds like him.'

'If anyone in that family was destined to go far, I'd have said it would've been him.'

'What do you mean? *Graham* was a criminal?'

'No. Well, not apart from a bit of shoplifting, but they all got into that. Me, too, when I was his age. We figured the shops factored the losses into their prices, see, so we were only taking what was rightfully ours anyway. No, it was just that he had brains – though God knows who he got them from – *and* he also was what they call street-smart these days. Never said much, but you could tell he was taking it all in, looking for the main chance.'

'You're saying that *Graham* might have been involved with the Krays?'

'Nah. Oh, he might have run an errand or two for them, but they didn't mess around with twelve-year-old kids. Too much of a liability. Only that he watched and learned. There wasn't much got by him. Sharp as a tack. Billy used to leave him outside the local, sitting in the street playing marbles with the other kids. It was common enough, then. And some pretty shady customers went in there. Believe me, I know. More than once the young lad would get half a crown and a watching brief. "Keep an eye on that car for me, kid," like. Or, "If you see a couple of blokes in suits coming this way, stick your head around the door and give me a shout." No flies on young Graham Marshall, that's for sure. I'm just sorry to hear he came to such an early end, though I can't say as it surprises me that much.'

•

Dr Glendenning was delayed in Scarborough, so the post-mortem had been put off until late in the afternoon. In the meantime, Banks thought his time would be well spent talking to some of Luke's teachers, starting with Gavin Barlow, the head teacher of Eastvale Comprehensive.

Despite the threatening sky and earth damp from an earlier shower, Barlow was weeding the garden of his north Eastvale semi, dressed in torn jeans and a dirty old shirt. A collie with a sleek coat jumped up at Banks as he entered through the garden gate, but Barlow soon brought the dog to heel, and it curled in a corner under the lilac bush and seemed to go to sleep.

'He's old,' Gavin Barlow said, taking off a glove, wiping his hand on his jeans and offering it. Banks shook and introduced himself.

'Yes, I've been expecting a visit,' said Barlow. 'Terrible business. Let's go inside. No, stay, Tristram. Stay!'

Tristram stayed and Banks followed Barlow into the bright, ordered interior of the house. He was clearly interested in antiques, and by the looks of the gleaming sideboard and drinks cabinet, into restoring them, too. 'Can I offer you a beer, or a lager perhaps? Or aren't you supposed to drink on duty? One never knows, watching Morse and the like on telly.'

Banks smiled. 'We're not supposed to,' he said, not that it had ever stopped him. But it was far too early in the day, and he didn't have weeding the garden as an excuse. 'I'd love a coffee, if you've got some.'

'Only instant, I'm afraid.'

'That's fine.'

'Come on through.'

They went into a small but well-arranged kitchen. Whoever had designed the maple cabinets over the slate-grey countertops had decided on following a pattern of horizontal grain rather than vertical, which made the room seem much more spacious. Banks sat at a breakfast nook with a red-and-white checked tablecloth while Barlow made the coffee.

'Daddy, who's this?'

A girl of about sixteen appeared in the doorway, all long blonde hair and bare leg. She reminded Banks a bit of Kay Summerville.

'It's a policeman come to talk about Luke Armitage, Rose. Off you go.'

Rose pouted, then made a theatrical about-turn and sashayed away, wiggling her hips. 'Daughters,' said Barlow. 'Have you any of your own?'

Banks told him about Tracy.

'Tracy Banks. Of course, now I remember her. I just didn't put two and two together when I saw your identification. Tracy. Very bright girl. How is she doing?'

'Fine. She's just finished her second year at Leeds. History.'

'Do give her my best regards when you see her. I can't say I knew her well . . . so many pupils and so little time . . . but I do remember talking to her.'

Gavin Barlow looked a bit like Tony Blair, Banks thought. Definitely more of an educational unit manager than an old-style school headmaster, the way his predecessor Mr Buxton had been. Banks remembered the old fellow who'd been in charge during the Gallows View case, when Banks had first moved up north. Buxton was the last of a dying breed, with his bat-like cape and a well-thumbed copy of Cicero on his desk. Gavin Barlow probably thought 'Latin' referred to a type of dance music, though maybe that was being a bit unfair. At least the radio station he was tuned into was playing Thelonious Monk's 'Epistrophy' at eleven o'clock in the morning – a good sign.

'I'm not sure I can tell you very much about Luke,' said Gavin Barlow, bringing over two mugs of instant coffee and sitting opposite Banks. 'It's usually only the persistent trouble-makers who come to my attention.'

'And Luke wasn't a trouble-maker?'

'Good heavens, no! You'd hardly know he was there if he didn't move once in a while.'

'Any trouble at all?'

'Not really trouble. Nothing his form-tutor couldn't deal with.'

'Tell me.'

'Luke didn't like games, and he once forged a note from his mother excusing him on the grounds of a stomach upset. It was a note the PE teacher remembered seeing a few months earlier, and Luke had traced it out with a new date. Quite a good forgery, really.'

'What happened?'

'Nothing much. Detention, a warning to his mother. Odd, as he wasn't bad at all.'

'Wasn't bad at what?'

'Rugby. Luke was a decent wing three-quarters. Fast and slippery. When he could be bothered playing.'

'But he didn't like games?'

'He had no interest in sports. He'd far rather read, or just sit in a corner and stare out of the window. God only knows what was going on in that head of his half the time.'

'Did Luke have any close friends at school, any other pupils he might have confided in?'

'I really can't say. He always seemed to be a bit of a loner. We encourage group activities, of course, but you can't always . . . I mean you can't *force* people to be sociable, can you?'

Banks opened his briefcase and slipped out the artist's impression of the girl Josie Batty had seen going into HMV with Luke. 'Do you recognize this girl?' he asked, not sure how close a likeness it was.

Barlow squinted at it, then shook his head. 'No,' he said. 'I can't say as I do. I'm not saying we don't have pupils who affect that general look, but not very many, and nobody quite like this.'

'So you've never seen her or anyone like her with Luke?'

'No.'

Banks returned the sketch to his briefcase. 'What about his schoolwork? Did he show any promise?'

'Enormous promise. His work in maths left a lot to be desired, but when it came to English and music he was remarkably gifted.'

'What about the other subjects?'

'Good enough for university, if that's what you mean. Especially languages and social studies. You could tell that even at his early age. Unless . . .'

'What?'

'Well, unless he went off the rails. I've seen it happen before with bright and sensitive pupils. They fall in with the wrong crowd, neglect their work . . . You can guess the rest.'

Banks, who had gone off the rails a bit himself after Graham's disappearance, could. 'Were there any teachers Luke was particularly close to?' he asked. 'Anyone who might be able to tell me a bit more about him?'

'Yes. You might try Ms Anderson. Lauren Anderson. She teaches English and art history. Luke was way ahead of his classmates in his appreciation of literature, and in its composition, and I believe Ms Anderson gave him extra tuition.'

Lauren Anderson's name had come up in the company's records of Luke's cell-phone calls, Banks remembered. 'Is that something the school does often?'

'If the student seems likely to benefit from it, then yes, certainly. You have to understand that we get such a broad range of abilities and interests, and we have to pitch our teaching level just a little above the middle. Too high and you lose most of the class, too low and the brighter students become bored and distracted. But it's not all as bad as they say it is in the newspapers. We're lucky in that we have a lot of passionate and committed teachers at Eastvale Comprehensive. Ms Anderson is one of them. Luke was also taking violin lessons after school.'

'Yes, he had a violin in his bedroom.'

'I told you, he's not your common-or-garden pupil.' Barlow paused for a moment, staring out the window. '*Wasn't*. We'll miss him.'

'Even if you hardly knew he was there?'

'I was probably overstating the case,' Barlow said with a frown. 'Luke had a certain presence. What I meant was that he just didn't make a lot of noise or demand a lot of attention.'

'Who was giving him violin lessons?'

'Our music teacher, Alastair Ford. He's quite a skilled player himself. Plays with a local string quartet. Strictly amateur, of course. You might have heard of them; they're called the Aeolian Quartet. I understand they're very good, though I must admit that my tastes edge more towards Miles than Mahler.'

The Aeolian. Banks had, indeed heard of them. Not only that, but he had *heard* them. The last time was shortly after Christmas, at the community centre with Annie Cabbot. They had played Schubert's 'Death and the Maiden' quartet and made a very good job of it, Banks remembered.

'Is there anything else you can tell me?' he asked, standing to leave.

'I don't think there is,' said Barlow. 'All in all, Luke Armitage was a bit of a dark horse.'

As they walked through to the hall, Banks felt certain

he caught a flurry of blonde hair and long leg ducking through a doorway, but he could have been mistaken. Why would Rose Barlow want to listen in on their conversation, anyway?

•

The rain seemed to have settled in for the day after a short afternoon respite, a constant drizzle from a sky the colour of dirty dishwater, when Annie did the rounds of Luke's final ports of call. She found out nothing from the HMV staff, perhaps because they had such a high turnover and it was a large shop, hard to keep an eye on everyone. No one recognized the sketch. Besides, as one salesperson told her, many of the kids who shopped there looked pretty much the same. Black clothing wasn't exactly unusual as far as HMV's customers were concerned, nor were body piercing or tattoos.

She fared little better at the computer shop on North Market Street. Gerald Kelly, the sole proprietor and staff member, remembered just about all his customers, but he had seen no one resembling the girl in black with Luke, who had always been alone on his visits to the shop.

Annie had just one last call. Norman's Used Books was a dank, cramped space down a flight of stone steps under a bakery, one of several shops that seemed to be set right into the church walls in the market square. The books all smelled of mildew, but you could find the most obscure things sometimes. Annie herself had shopped there once or twice, looking for old art books, and had even found some decent prints among the boxes the owner kept at the back of the shop, though they were sometimes warped and discoloured because of the damp.

The roof was so low and the small room so full of

books – not only in cases against the walls, but piled up haphazardly on tables, ready to teeter over if you so much as breathed on them – that you had to stoop and make your way around the place very carefully. It must have been even harder for Luke, Annie thought, as he was taller and more gangly than her.

The owner himself, Norman Wells, was just a little over five feet, with thin brown hair, a bulbous sort of face and rheumy eyes. Because it was so cold and damp down there, no matter what the weather was like up above, he always wore a moth-eaten grey cardigan, woolly gloves with the fingers cut off and an old Leeds United scarf. He couldn't make much of a living out of the little shop, Annie thought, though she doubted the overheads were very high. Even in the depths of winter a one-element electric fire was the only source of heat.

Norman Wells glanced up from the paperback he was reading and nodded in Annie's direction. He seemed surprised when she showed her warrant card and spoke to him.

'I've seen you before, haven't I?' he said, taking off his reading glasses, which hung on a piece of string around his neck.

'I've been here once or twice.'

'Thought so. I never forget a face. Art, isn't it?'

'Pardon?'

'Your interest. Art.'

'Oh, yes.' Annie showed him a photograph of Luke. 'Remember him?'

Wells looked alarmed. 'Course I do. He's the lad who disappeared, isn't he? One of your lot was around the other day asking about him. I told him all I know.'

'I'm sure you did, Mr Wells,' said Annie, 'but things

have changed. It's a murder investigation now and we have to go over the ground afresh.'

'Murder? That lad?'

'I'm afraid so.'

'Bloody hell. I hadn't heard. Who'd . . . ? He wouldn't say boo to a goose.'

'Did you know him well, then?'

'Well? No, I wouldn't say that. But we talked.'

'What about?'

'Books. He knew a lot more than most kids his age. His reading level was way beyond that of his contemporaries.'

'How do you know?'

'I . . . never mind.'

'Mr Wells?'

'Let's just say I used to be a teacher, that's all. I know about these things, and that lad was bordering on genius.'

'I understand he bought two books from you on his last visit.'

'Yes, like I told the other copper. *Crime and Punishment* and *Portrait of the Artist as a Young Man*.'

'They sound a bit advanced, even for him.'

'Don't you believe it,' Wells protested. 'If I hadn't thought him ready I wouldn't have sold him them. He'd already been through *The Waste Land*, most of Camus and *Dubliners*. I didn't think he was quite ready for *Ulysses* or Pound's *Cantos*, but he could handle the *Portrait*, no problem.'

Annie, who had heard of these books but had read only the Eliot and a few of Joyce's short stories at school, was impressed. So the books she had seen in Luke's room weren't just for show; he really did read and probably even understand them. At fifteen, she'd been reading historical sagas and sword and sorcery series, not

literature with a capital 'L'. That was reserved for school
and was tedious in the extreme, thanks to Mr Bolton, the
English teacher, who made the stuff sound about as
exciting as a wet Sunday in Cleethorpes.

'How often did Luke call by?' she asked.

'About once a month. Or whenever he was out of
something to read.'

'He had the money. Why didn't he go to Waterstone's
and buy them new?'

'Don't ask me. We got chatting the first time he
dropped in—'

'When was that?'

'Maybe eighteen months or so ago. Anyway, as I say,
we got chatting and he came back.' He looked around at
the stained ceilings, flaking plaster and tottering piles of
books and smiled at Annie, showing crooked teeth. 'I
suppose there must have been something he liked about
the place.'

'Must be the service,' Annie said.

Wells laughed. 'I can tell you one thing. He liked those
old Penguin Modern Classics. The ones with the grey
spines, not these modern pale green things. Real paperbacks, not your trade size. And you can't buy those at
Waterstone's. Same with the old Pan covers.'

Something moved in the back of the shop and a pile of
books fell over. Annie thought she glimpsed a tabby cat
slinking away into the deeper shadows.

Wells sighed. 'Familiar's gone and done it again.'

'Familiar?'

'My cat. No bookshop's complete without a cat. After
witch's familiar. See?'

'I suppose so. Did Luke ever come in here with anyone
else?'

'No.'

Annie took her copy of the artist's impression out and set it on the table in front of him. 'What about her?'

Wells leaned forward, put his glasses on again and examined the sketch. 'It *looks* like her,' he said. 'I told you I never forget a face.'

'But you told me Luke never came in with anyone else,' Annie said, feeling a tingle of excitement rise up her spine.

Wells looked at her. 'Who said she was with him? No, she came in with another bloke, same sort of clothing and body piercing.'

'Who are they?'

'I don't know. They must have been a bit short of money, though.'

'Why do you say that?'

'Because they came in with an armful of brand-new books to sell. Stolen, I thought. Plain as day. Stolen books. I don't have any truck with that sort of thing, so I sent them packing.'

11

Before he cut into Luke Armitage's flesh, Dr Glendenning made a thorough examination of the body's exterior. Banks watched as the doctor examined and measured the head wound. Luke's skin was white and showed some wrinkling from exposure to the water, and there was a slight discoloration around the neck.

'Back of the skull splintered into the cerebellum,' the doctor said.

'Enough to kill him?'

'At a guess.' Glendenning bent over and squinted at the wound. 'And it would have bled quite a bit, if that's any use.'

'Could be,' said Banks. 'Blood's a lot harder to clean up than most people think. What about the weapon?'

'Looks like some sort of round-edged object,' the doctor said. 'Smooth sided.'

'Like what?'

'Well, it's not got a very large circumference, so I'd rule out something like a baseball bat. I can't see any traces – wood splinters or anything – so it could have been metal or ceramic. Hard, anyway.'

'A poker, perhaps?'

'Possible. That would fit the dimensions. It's the angle that puzzles me.'

'What about it?'

'See for yourself.'

Banks bent over the wound, which Dr Glendenning's assistant had shaved and cleaned. There was no blood. A few days in the water would see to that. He could see the indentation clearly enough, about the right size for a poker, but the wound was oblique, almost horizontal.

'You'd expect someone swinging a poker to swing downwards from behind, or at least at a forty-five degree angle, so we'd get a more vertical pattern,' Dr Glendenning said. 'But this was inflicted from sideways on, not from in front or behind, by someone a little shorter than the victim, if the angle's to be believed. That means whoever did it was probably standing *beside* him. Unusual angle, as I said.' He lit a cigarette, strictly forbidden in the hospital, but usually overlooked in Glendenning's case. Everyone knew that when you were dealing with the smells of a post-mortem, a ciggie now and then was a great distraction. And Glendenning was more careful these days; he rarely dropped ash in open incisions.

'Maybe the victim was already bent double from a previous blow?' Banks suggested. 'To the stomach, say. Or on his knees, head bent forward.'

'Praying?'

'It wouldn't be the first time,' Banks said, remembering that more than one executed villain had died on his knees praying for his life. But Luke Armitage wasn't a villain, as far as Banks knew.

'Which side did the blow come from?' Banks asked.

'Right side. You can tell by the pattern of indentation.'

'So that would indicate a left-handed attacker?'

'Likely so. But I'm not happy with this, Banks.'

'What do you mean?'

'Well, in the first place, it's hardly a surefire way to kill somebody. Head blows are tricky. You can't count on them, especially just one.'

Banks knew that well enough. On his last case a man had taken seven or eight blows from a side-handled baton and still survived for a couple of days. In a coma, but alive. 'So our killer's an amateur who got lucky.'

'Could be,' said Glendenning. 'We'll know more when I get a look at the brain tissue.'

'But could this blow have been the cause of death?'

'Can't say for certain. It *could* have killed him, but he might have been dead already. You'll have to wait for the full toxicology report to know whether that might have been the case.'

'Not drowned?'

'I don't think so, but let's wait until we get to the lungs.'

Banks watched patiently, if rather queasily, as Dr Glendenning's assistant made the customary Y-shaped incision and peeled back the skin and muscle from the chest wall with a scalpel. The smell of human muscle, rather like raw lamb, Banks had always thought, emanated from the body. Next the assistant pulled the chest flap up over Luke's face and took a bone-cutter to the ribcage, finally peeling off the chest plate and exposing the inner organs. When he had removed these en bloc, he placed them on the dissecting table and reached for his electric saw. Banks knew what was coming next, that unforgettable sound and burnt-bone smell of the skull, so he turned his attention to Dr Glendenning, who was dissecting the organs, paying particular attention to the lungs.

'No water,' he announced. 'Or minimal.'

'Meaning Luke was dead when he went in the water?'

'I'll send the tissues for diatomic analysis, but I don't expect they'll find much.'

The electric saw stopped, and seconds later Banks heard something rather like a combination grating and sucking sound, and he knew it was the top of the skull coming off. The assistant then cut the spinal cord and the tentorium and lifted the brain out. As he carried it to the jar of formalin in which it would hang suspended for a couple of weeks, making it firmer and easier to handle, Dr Glendenning had a quick look.

'Aha,' he said. 'I thought so. Look, Banks, do you see that damage there, to the frontal lobes?'

Banks saw it. And he knew what it meant. '*Contre coup*?'

'Exactly. Which might explain the unusual angle.'

If a blow is delivered while the victim's head is stationary, then the damage is limited to the point of impact – bones splintered into the brain – but if the victim's head is in motion, then the result is a *contre coup* injury: additional damage *opposite* the point of impact. *Contre coup* injuries are almost always the result of a fall.

'Luke *fell*?'

'Or he was pushed,' said Glendenning. 'But as far as I can tell, there are no other injuries, no broken bones. And as I said, if there was bruising, if someone hit him, say, knocked him over, then unless there are any small bones in the cheek broken, we won't be able to tell. We'll be checking, of course.'

'Can you give me any idea about time of death? It's important.'

'Aye, well . . . I've looked over Dr Burns's measurements at the scene. Very meticulous. He'll go far. Rigor's been and gone, which indicates over two days at the temperatures noted.'

'What about the wrinkling and whitening?'

'*Cutis anserina*? Three to five hours. Water preserves, delays putrefaction, so it makes our job a little harder. There's no lividity, and I'm afraid it'll be almost impossible to tell whether there was any other bruising. The water takes care of that.' He paused and frowned. 'But there's the discoloration around the neck.'

'What about it?'

'That indicates the beginnings of putrefaction. In bodies found in water, it always starts at the root of the neck.'

'After how long?'

'That's just it,' Dr Glendenning said, looking at Banks. 'You understand I can't be more specific, I can't give you less than a twelve-hour margin of error, but not until at least three or four days, not at the temperatures Dr Burns recorded.'

Banks made a mental calculation. 'Bloody hell,' he said. 'Even at the outside, that means Luke had to have been killed just after he went missing.'

'Sometime that very night, by my calculations. Taking everything into account, between about eight p.m. and eight a.m.'

And Dr Glendenning's calculations, perhaps because of his insufferable habit of being unwilling to commit himself to a specific time, were usually not far from the truth. In which case, Banks thought, Luke had died before Annie had even paid her *first* visit to Swainsdale Hall, let alone before she had followed Martin Armitage to the site of the drop.

•

Before she went off duty – though such a thing was somewhat of an illusion in the thick of a major murder investigation – Annie had made a few enquiries around the bookshops, asking after the couple who had tried to sell Norman Wells books he believed were stolen, but she drew a blank. Before meeting Banks for a drink at the Queen's Arms, she had also checked recent shoplifting reports but turned up nothing there either. The artist's impression would be in the evening paper, so she would see what happened after that. There was something else she had intended to do, but it was like that name you can't quite remember, the one on the tip of your tongue. If she put it out of her mind, it would come to her eventually.

Banks was already waiting for her at a corner table, and she saw him before he saw her. He looked tired, Annie thought, and distracted, smoking and staring into the distance. She tapped him on the shoulder and asked him if he wanted a refill. He came back from a long way and shook his head. She bought herself a pint of Theakston's bitter and walked over to join him. 'So what was that mysterious message about your wanting to see me?' she asked.

'Nothing mysterious about it at all,' Banks said, brightening up a little. 'I just wanted to deliver a message myself, in person.'

'I'm all ears.'

'It looks as if you're off the hook as far as Luke Armitage's death is concerned.'

Annie felt her eyes open wide. 'I am? How?'

'Dr Glendenning pegs time of death at least three or four days ago.'

'Before—'

'Yes. Before the first kidnap call even came in.'

Annie raised her eyes to the ceiling and clapped her hands. 'Yes!'

Banks smiled at her. 'Thought you'd be pleased.'

'How? He didn't drown, did he?'

Banks sipped some beer. 'No,' he said. 'Pending tox results, it looks as if cause of death was a blow to the cerebellum, quite possibly the result of a fall.'

'A struggle of some sort, then?'

'Exactly what I thought. Perhaps with the kidnapper, very early on. Or whoever he was with.'

'And that person decided to try and collect anyway?'

'Yes. But that's pure speculation.'

'So Luke died somewhere else and was dumped in the tarn?'

'Yes. Probably wherever he was being held – *if* he was being held. Anyway, there'd have been a fair bit of blood, the doc says, so there's every chance of our still finding evidence at the original scene.'

'If we can find the scene.'

'Exactly.'

'So we *are* making progress?'

'Slowly. What about the girl?'

'Nothing yet.' Annie told him about her meeting with Norman Wells.

She noticed Banks was watching her as she spoke. She could almost see his mind moving, making the connections, taking a shortcut here and filing this or that piece of information away for later. 'Whoever they are,' he said when she'd finished, 'if Wells is right and they had been shoplifting, then that tells us they're short of money. Which gives them a motive for demanding a ransom if they were somehow responsible for Luke's death.'

'More speculation?'

'Yes,' Banks admitted. 'Let's assume they got into a fight over something or other and Luke ended up dead. Maybe not intentionally, but dead is dead. They panicked, thought of a suitable spot and drove out and dumped him into Hallam Tarn later that night, under cover of darkness.'

'They'd need a motor, remember, which might be a bit of a problem if they were broke.'

'Maybe they "borrowed" one?'

'We can check car-theft reports for the night in question. No matter how much they covered up the body, there might still be traces of Luke's blood.'

'Good idea. Anyway, they know who Luke's parents are, think they might be able to make a few bob out of them.'

'Which would explain the low demand.'

'Yes. They're not pros. They've no idea how much to ask. And ten grand is a bloody fortune to them.'

'But they were watching Martin Armitage make the drop and they saw me.'

'More than likely. Sorry, Annie. They might not be pros, but they're not stupid. They knew the money was tainted then. They'd already dumped Luke's body, remember, so they must have known it was just a matter of time before someone found it. They could expect the footpath restrictions to work in their favour for a while, but someone was bound to venture over Hallam Tarn eventually.'

Annie paused to digest what Banks had said. She *had* made a mistake, had scared the kidnappers off, but Luke had already been dead by then, so his death wasn't down to her. What else could she have done, anyway? Stayed away from the shepherd's shelter, perhaps. Red Ron was right about that. She had guessed that the briefcase contained money. Did she need to know exactly how much? So she had behaved impulsively, and not for the first time, but it was all salvageable, the case, her career, everything. It could all be redeemed. 'Have you ever thought,' she said, 'that they *might* have planned on kidnapping Luke right from the start? Maybe that was why they befriended him in the first place, and why they had to kill him. Because he knew who they were.'

'Yes,' said Banks. 'But too many things about this seem hurried, spontaneous, ill thought out. No, Annie, I think they just took advantage of an existing situation.'

'So why kill Luke, then?'

'No idea. We'll have to ask them.'

'If we find them.'

'Oh, we'll find them, all right.'

'When the girl sees her picture in the paper she might go to ground, change her appearance.'

'We'll find them. The only thing is . . .' Banks said, letting the words trail off as he reached for another cigarette.

'Yes?'

'That we need to keep an open mind as regards other lines of enquiry.'

'Such as?'

'I'm not sure yet. There might be something even closer to home. I want to talk to a couple of teachers who knew Luke fairly well. Someone should talk to the Battys again, too. Then there's all the people we know he came into contact with the day he disappeared. Put a list together and get DCs Jackman and Templeton to help with it. We've still got a long way to go.'

'Shit,' said Annie, getting to her feet. She had

remembered the task that had been eluding her all evening.

'What?'

'Just something I should have checked out before.' She looked at her watch and waved goodbye. 'Maybe it's not too late. See you later.'

•

Michelle sat back in her seat and watched the fields drift by under a grey sky, rain streaking the dirty window. Every time she took a train she felt as if she was on holiday. This evening the train was full. Sometimes she forgot just how close Peterborough was to London – only eighty miles or so, about a fifty-minute train ride – and how many people made the journey every day. That was, after all, what the new town expansion had been about. Basildon, Bracknell, Hemel Hempstead, Hatfield, Stevenage, Harlow, Crawley, Welwyn Garden City, Milton Keynes, all in a belt around London, even closer than Peterborough, catchment areas for an overflowing capital, where it was fast becoming too expensive for many to live. She hadn't been around back then, of course, but she knew that the population of Peterborough had risen from about 62,000 in 1961 to 134,000 in 1981.

Unable to concentrate on *The Profession of Violence*, which she had to remember to post back to Banks, she thought back to her lunch with ex-Detective Inspector Robert Lancaster. He had quite a few years on Ben Shaw, but they were both very much cut from the same cloth. Oh, no doubt about it, Shaw was ruder, more sarcastic, a far more unpleasant personality, but underneath they were the *same kind of copper*. Not necessarily bent – Michelle took Lancaster's word on that – but not above turning a blind eye if it was to their advantage, and not above fraternizing with villains. As Lancaster had also pointed out, he had grown up shoulder to shoulder with criminals like the Krays and smaller fry like Billy Marshall, and when it came to future career choices it was often very much a matter of there but for the grace of God go I.

It was interesting what he had said about Graham Marshall, she thought. Interesting that he should even remember the boy at all. She had never considered that it might have been Graham's *own* criminal activities that got him killed, and even now she found it hard to swallow. Not that fourteen year olds were immune to criminal activity. Far from it, especially these days. But if Graham Marshall had been involved in something that was likely to get him killed, wouldn't somebody have known and come forward? Surely Jet Harris or Reg Proctor would have picked up the scent?

The real problem, though, was how she could gather any more information about Graham. She could go through the statements again, read the investigating detectives' notebooks and check all the actions allocated, but if none of them focused on Graham himself as a possible line of enquiry, then she would get no further.

The train slowed down for no apparent reason. It was an Intercity, not a local train, so Michelle went to the buffet car and bought herself a coffee. The paper cup was far too hot, even when she used three or four serviettes to hold it. If she took the top off, it would spill when the train started moving again, so she tore a small hole in the plastic top and decided to wait a little while it cooled.

Michelle looked at her watch. After eight o'clock. Getting dark outside. She had spent a couple of hours shopping on Oxford Street after parting with Lancaster, and she felt a little guilty that she had spent over a hundred pounds on a dress. Perhaps she was turning into a shopaholic. Like the drinking, the spending had to stop. She'd never get a chance to wear the damn thing anyway, as it was a party dress, elegant, strapless and stylish, and she never went to any parties. What could she have been thinking of?

When the train started up again half an hour later, with no explanation for the delay, Michelle realized that if Graham had been involved in anything untoward, there was one person who might know something, even if he didn't know he did: *Banks*. And thinking of him made her once again regret the way she had left him at Starbucks the other day. True, she had resented his intrusion into what she regarded as her private life, a life she kept very guarded indeed, but she had perhaps overreacted a tad. After all, he had only asked her if she was married: a perfectly innocent question in its way, and one you might ask a stranger over a coffee. It didn't have to mean anything, but it was such a raw-nerve point with her, such a no-go area, that she had behaved rudely, and now she regretted it. Well, she wasn't married; that was certainly the truth. Melissa had died because she and Ted got their wires crossed. She was on surveillance and thought *he* was picking up their daughter after school; he had an afternoon meeting and thought *she* was going to do it. Possibly no marriage could survive that amount of trauma – the guilt, blame, grief and anger – and theirs hadn't. Almost six months to the day after Melissa's funeral they had agreed to separate, and Michelle had begun her years of wandering from county to county trying to put the past behind her. Succeeding to a large extent, but still haunted, still in some ways maimed by what had happened.

She hadn't had either the time or the inclination for men, and that was another thing about Banks that bothered her. He was the only man, beyond her immediate colleagues on the Job, with whom she had spent any time in years, and she liked him, found him attractive. Michelle knew that she had been nicknamed the 'Ice Queen' at more than one station over the past five years, but it had only amused her because it couldn't be further from the truth. She was, she knew, deep down, a warm and sensual person, as she had been with Ted, though that was a part of her nature she had neglected for a long time, perhaps even suppressed, out of punishment, being more preoccupied with self-blame. She didn't know if Banks was married or not, though she had noticed that he didn't wear a ring. And he *had* asked her if she were married. In addition to being an intrusion, that had seemed like a come-on line at the time, and maybe it was. The problem was that part of her wanted him, against all her common sense and all the barriers she had built inside, and the result flustered and confused her almost beyond bearing. Banks might be one of the few people who could help her reconstruct Graham Marshall's past, but could she bear to face Banks again in the flesh?

She would have no choice, she realized as the train pulled up and she reached for her briefcase. Graham Marshall's memorial service would be taking place in a matter of days, and she had promised to call and let him know about it.

•

It was almost dark when Banks turned into the lane that ran in front of his small cottage, and he was tired. Annie had left by the time he got back to headquarters after finishing his beer, so he stuck around for an hour or so picking away at the pile of paperwork, then decided to call it a day. Whatever it was she was after, she'd tell him after the weekend.

Memories of Luke's post-mortem hovered unpleasantly close to the surface of his consciousness, the way past cases also haunted him. Over the past few months he had dreamed more than once of Emily Riddle and of the partially buried bodies he had seen in a cellar in Leeds, toes poking through the dirt. Was he going to have to add Luke Armitage to his list of nightmare images now? Was there never any end to it?

Someone had parked a car, an ancient clapped-out Fiesta by the looks of it, in front of the cottage. Unable to get past the obstacle, Banks parked behind it and took out his house keys. There was no one inside the car, so it wasn't a pair of lovers seeking seclusion. Maybe someone had dumped it there, he thought, with a flash of irritation. The dirt lane was little more than a cul-de-sac. It dwindled to a riverside footpath when it reached the woods about twenty feet beyond Banks's cottage, and there was no way for a car to get through. Not everyone knew that, of course, and sometimes cars turned down it by mistake. He ought to consider putting up a sign, he thought, though he had always thought it obvious enough that the track was a private drive.

Then he noticed that the living-room light was on and the curtains closed. He knew he hadn't left the light on that morning. It *could* be burglars, he thought, moving carefully, though if it was, they were very incompetent ones, not only parking in a cul-de-sac but not even bothering to turn their car around for a quick getaway. Still, he'd known far stupider criminals, like the would-be bank robber who had filled out the withdrawal slip with his real name before writing on the back: 'Giv me yor munny, I've got a ~~gun~~ nife' and handing it to the teller. He didn't get far.

The car was definitely a Fiesta, with rusted wheel arches. It would be lucky to pass its next MOT without major and expensive work, Banks thought as he gave it the once-over and memorized the number plate. This was no burglar. He tried to remember to whom he had given a key. Not Annie, at least not any more. Certainly not Sandra. And just as he opened the door, it came to him. There was his son Brian stretched out on the sofa with Tim Buckley playing low on the stereo: 'I Never Asked to Be Your Mountain'. When he heard Banks come in, he uncoiled his long length, sat up and rubbed his eyes.

'Oh. Hi, Dad, it's you.'

'Hello, son. Who else were you expecting?'

'Nobody. I was just half-asleep I suppose. Dreaming.'

'Don't you believe in telephones?'

'Sorry. It's been a bit hectic lately. We're doing some gigs around Teesside starting tomorrow night, so I thought I'd, you know, just drop in and say hello. I had a long drive. All the way from south London.'

'It's good to see you.' Banks gestured with his thumb. 'I'm surprised you made it in one piece. Is that pile of junk out there the car you borrowed two hundred quid off me for?'

'Yeah. Why?'

'I hope you didn't pay any more than that for it, that's all.' Banks put his car keys down on the low table, took off his jacket and hung it on a hook behind the door. 'I didn't know you were a Tim Buckley fan,' he said, sitting down in the armchair.

'You'd be surprised. Actually, I'm not, really. Haven't heard him much. Hell of a voice, though. You can hear it in his son's. Jeff's. He did a great version of this song at a memorial concert for his dad. Most of the time he refused to acknowledge Tim, though.'

'How do you know all this?'

'Read a book about them. *Dream Brother*. It's pretty good. I'll lend it you if I can find it.'

'Thanks.' Mention of Tim and Jeff Buckley's relationship reminded Banks of Luke Armitage and the tape he still had in his pocket. Maybe he'd get Brian's opinion. For the moment, though, a stiff drink was in order. A Laphroaig. 'Can I get you anything to drink?' he asked Brian. 'Drop of single malt, perhaps?'

Brian made a face. 'Can't stand the stuff. If you've got any lager, though . . .'

'I think I can manage that.' Banks poured himself the whisky and found a Carlsberg in the back of the fridge. 'Glass?' he called from the kitchen.

'Can's fine,' Brian called back.

If anything, Brian seemed even taller than the last time Banks had seen him, at least five or six inches taller than his own five-foot nine. He had inherited Banks's constitutional thinness, by the looks of him, and wore the usual uniform of torn jeans and a plain T-shirt. He'd had his hair cut. Not just cut, but massacred, even shorter than Banks's own close crop.

'What's with the haircut?' Banks asked him.

'Kept getting in my eyes. So what are you up to these days, Dad? Still solving crime and keeping the world safe for democracy?'

'Less of your lip.' Banks lit a cigarette. Brian gave him a disgusted look. 'I'm trying to stop,' Banks said. 'It's only my fifth all day.' Brian said nothing, merely raised his eye-brows. 'Anyway,' Banks went on. 'Yes, I'm working.'

'Neil Byrd's son, Luke, right? I heard it on the news while I was driving up. Poor sod.'

'Right. Luke Armitage. You're the musician in the family. What do you think of Neil Byrd?'

'He was pretty cool,' said Brian, 'but maybe just a bit too folksy for me. Too much of a romantic, I guess. Like Dylan, he was a lot better when he went electric. Why?'

'I'm just trying to understand Luke's relationship with him, that's all.'

'He didn't have one. Neil Byrd committed suicide when Luke was only three. He was a dreamer, an idealist. The world could never match up to his expectations.'

'If that were a reason for suicide, Brian, there'd be nobody left alive. But it had to have a powerful effect on the boy. Luke had a bunch of posters in his room. Dead rock stars. Seemed obsessed with them. Not his dad, though.'

'Like who?'

'Jim Morrison, Kurt Cobain, Ian Curtis, Nick Drake. You know. The usual suspects.'

'Covers quite a range,' said Brian. 'I'll bet you thought your generation had cornered the market in dying young, didn't you? Jimi, Janis, Jim.' He nodded towards the stereo. 'Present company.'

'I know some of these were more recent.'

'Well, Nick Drake was another one of your lot. And do you know how old I was when Ian Curtis was with Joy Division? I can't have been more than six or seven.'

'But you have *listened* to Joy Division?'

'I've listened, yeah. Too depressing for me. Kurt Cobain and Jeff Buckley are a lot closer to home. But where's all this going?'

'I honestly don't know,' said Banks. 'I'm just trying to get some sort of grip on Luke's life, his state of mind. He was into some very weird stuff for a fifteen year old. And there was nothing in his room connected with his father.'

'Well, he'd feel pissed off, wouldn't he? Wouldn't you? Only stands to reason. Your old man does a bunk when you're just a baby and then offs himself before you can get to know him at all. Hardly makes you feel wanted, does it?'

'Want to listen to some of his songs?'

'Who? Neil Byrd?'

'No. Luke.'

'Sure.'

Banks paused the Tim Buckley CD, put the tape in, and they both sat in silence sipping their drinks and listening.

'He's good,' said Brian, when the tape had finished. 'Very good. I wish I'd been that good at his age. Still raw, but with a bit of hard work and a lot of practice . . .'

'Do you think he had a future in music, then?'

'It's possible. On the other hand, you see plenty of bands with no talent get to the top and some really terrific musicians struggle just to make a living, so who can say? He's got what it takes in its raw form, though. In my humble opinion. Was he with a band?'

'Not that I know of.'

'He'd be a steal for some up-and-coming group. He's got talent, for a start, and they could milk the Neil Byrd connection for all it was worth. Did you notice the voice? The similarities. Like Tim and Jeff.'

'Yes,' said Banks. 'I did.' He started the Tim Buckley

CD again. It was 'Song to the Siren', which always sent shivers up his spine. 'How's the CD going?' he asked.

'Haven't bloody started it yet, have we? Our manager's still haggling over the contracts. Hence that crappy pile of junk you saw outside.'

'I was expecting a Jag or a red sports car.'

'Soon, Dad, soon. By the way, we've changed our name.'

'Why?'

'The manager thought Jimson Weed was a bit too sixties.'

'He's right.'

'Yeah, well, we're the Blue Lamps now.'

'The police.'

'No, that's another band. The Blue Lamps.'

'I was thinking of *Dixon of Dock Green*.'

'Come again?'

'*The Blue Lamp*. It was a film. Fifties. It's where George Dixon made his debut before it became a TV series. A blue lamp used to be a sign of a police station. Still is in some places. I'm not sure you want to be going around associating yourself with that.'

'The stuff you know. Anyway, our manager thinks it's okay, more modern – you know, White Stripes, Blue Lamps – but I'll tell him what you said. Our sound's hardened up a bit too, got a bit more grungy and less slick. I get to play some real down and dirty guitar solos. You must come and hear us again. We've come a long way since that last gig you were at.'

'I'd love to, but I thought you sounded just fine then.'

'Thanks.'

'I saw your grandparents the other day.'

'Yeah? How are they?'

'Same as ever. You should visit them more often.'

'Oh, you know how it is.'

'No. I don't know.'

'They don't like me, Dad. Not since I screwed up my degree and joined the band. Whenever I see them, it's always Tracy's doing this and Tracy's doing that. They don't care how well *I* do.'

'You know that's not true,' said Banks, who suspected it probably was. After all, weren't they the same way with him? It was all Roy, Roy, Roy, no matter what Banks achieved. He'd had a hard enough time reconciling himself to his son's chosen career, just the same way his mother and father had with him. The only difference was that he had come to terms with Brian's choice, whereas his own parents hadn't even come to terms with *his* career, let alone their grandson's. 'Anyway, I'm sure they'd love to see you.'

'Yeah. Okay. I'll try go and see them when I've got time.'

'How's your mother?'

'Fine, I suppose.'

'Seen her lately?'

'Not for a few weeks.'

'How's she doing with the . . . you know . . . It must be due soon.'

'Yeah, I guess so. Look, Dad, is there anything to eat? I haven't had any dinner yet, and I'm starving.'

Banks thought. He'd eaten a prawn sandwich earlier in the Queen's Arms and wasn't particularly hungry. He knew there was nothing substantial in the fridge or the freezer. He looked at his watch. 'There's a Chinese take-away down in Helmthorpe. They should still be open, if you like.'

'Cool,' said Brian, finishing off his lager. 'What are we waiting for?'

Banks sighed and reached for his jacket again. So much for quality time.

•

Michelle could have walked to Rivergate, it wasn't that far, but it wasn't a particularly pleasant walk and the rain was still pouring down, so she decided to treat herself to a taxi from the station.

The first inkling she got that something was wrong in the flat was when she heard the creaking door of her 'Mystery' screen-saver and saw the lights going on and off in the creepy-looking mansion as the full moon slowly crossed the starlit sky. She knew she had turned her computer off after she'd checked her e-mail that morning. She always did; she was compulsive about it. Also, some-one had pulled some of the books out of one of the boxes that she hadn't got round to unpacking. They weren't damaged or anything, just piled up on the floor beside the box.

Michelle jogged the mouse and the computer returned to its regular display. Only it was open at Michelle's file of notes about the Marshall case, and she knew she hadn't opened that since the previous night. There was nothing secret about her speculations, nothing she had thought would even interest anyone else, so she hadn't bothered with password protection. In future she would know better.

With the hairs prickling at the back of her neck, Michelle stood still and strained her ears for any odd sounds in the flat. Nothing except the clock ticking and the humming of the refrigerator. She took her old side-handled baton from her uniform days out of the closet by the door. Gripping that made her feel a little more courageous as she went to explore the rest of the flat.

The kitchen light was on, and a couple of items that she knew she had put back in the fridge that morning – milk, butter, eggs – lay on the countertop. The butter had melted into a shapeless lump and it oozed over her fingers when she picked it up.

Her bathroom cabinet stood open, and the various pills and potions she kept there were not in their usual order. Her bottle of aspirins sat on the edge of the sink, top off and cotton wool missing. Even as the chills went up her spine, Michelle wondered what the hell all this was about. If someone had searched the place, though she couldn't imagine why anyone would want to, then why not just leave it in a mess? Clearly, whoever had done this had done it to scare her – and they were succeeding.

She went into the bedroom cautiously, gripping the side-handled baton more tightly, expecting the worst. Nobody jumped out of the wardrobe at her, but what she saw there made her drop her baton and put her hands to her mouth.

There was no mess. Perhaps some of her drawers weren't completely closed, the way she had left them, but there was no mess. It was much, much worse.

Spread out neatly on the centre of the bed lay Melissa's dress. When Michelle reached out to pick it up, she found it had been cut cleanly into two halves.

Michelle staggered back against the wall, half the dress clutched to her chest, hardly able to believe what was happening. As she did so, her eye caught the writing on the dressing-table mirror: FORGET GRAHAM

MARSHALL, BITCH. REMEMBER MELISSA. YOU COULD
JOIN HER.

Michelle cried out, covered her face with the dress and
slid down the wall to the floor.

12

Norman Wells sat in the interview room with his folded arms resting on the top of his paunch and his lips pressed tight together. If he was scared, he wasn't showing it. But then, he didn't know how much the police already knew about him.

Banks and Annie sat opposite him, files spread out in front of them. Banks felt well rested after a day off. He had stayed up late Saturday night, eating Chinese food and talking with Brian, but on Sunday, after Brian left, he had done nothing but read the papers, go for a walk from Helmthorpe to Rawley Force and back by himself, stopping for a pub lunch and fiddling with the *Sunday Times* crossword on the way. In the evening, he had thought of ringing Michelle Hart in Peterborough but decided against it. They hadn't parted on the best of terms, so let her contact him first, if she wanted to. After a small Laphroaig and a cigarette outside, enjoying the mild evening air around sunset, he had listened to Ian Bostridge's *English Songbook* CD, gone to bed before half-past ten, and slept as soundly as he could remember in a long time.

'Norman,' said Banks. 'You don't mind if I call you Norman, do you?'

'It's my name.'

'Detective Inspector Cabbot here has been doing a bit of digging around in your background, and it turns out you've been a naughty boy, haven't you?'

Wells said nothing. Annie pushed a file towards Banks, and he opened it. 'You used to be a schoolteacher, am I right?'

'You know I did, or you wouldn't have dragged me in here away from my business.'

Banks raised his eyebrows. 'It's my understanding that you came here of your own free will when asked to help us with our enquiries. Am I wrong?'

'Do you think I'm an idiot?'

'I don't follow.'

'And there's no need to play the thickie with me. You know what I mean. If I hadn't come willingly, you'd have found some way to bring me here, whether I wanted to come or not. So just get on with it. It might not seem much to you, but I have a business to run, customers who rely on me.'

'We'll try to see that you get back to your shop as soon as possible, Norman, but first I'd like you to answer a few questions for me. You taught at a private school in Cheltenham, right?'

'Yes.'

'How long ago?'

'I left seven years ago.'

'Why did you leave?'

'I grew tired of teaching.'

Banks glanced at Annie, who frowned, leaned over and pointed at some lines on the typed sheet of paper in front of Banks. 'Norman,' Banks went on, 'I think I ought to inform you that Detective Inspector Cabbot spoke to your old headmaster, Mr Fulwell, earlier this morning. He was reticent to discuss school business at first, but when she informed him that we were conducting a possible murder investigation, he was a little more forthcoming. We know all about you, Norman.'

The moment of truth. Wells seemed to deflate and shrink in his chair. His plump lower lip pushed up and all but obscured the upper, his chin disappeared into his neck and his arms seemed to wrap more tightly around his lower chest. 'What do you want from me?' he whispered.

'The truth.'

'I had a nervous breakdown.'

'What caused it?'

'The pressures of the job. You've no idea what teaching's like.'

'I don't imagine I have,' Banks admitted, thinking that the last thing he'd want to do was stand up in front of thirty or forty scruffy, hormonally challenged teenagers and try to get them interested in Shakespeare or the War of Jenkins's Ear. Anyone with that skill deserved his admiration. And a medal, too, for that matter. 'What particular pressures led you to decide to leave?'

'It was nothing specific. Just a general sort of breakdown.'

'Stop beating about the bush, Norman,' Annie cut in. 'Does the name Steven Farrow mean anything to you?'

Wells paled. 'Nothing happened. I never touched him. False accusations.'

'According to the headmaster, Norman, you were infatuated with this thirteen-year-old boy. So much so that you neglected your duties, became an embarrassment to the school, and on one occasion—'

'Enough!' Wells slammed his fist down on the metal table. 'You're just like everyone else. You poison the truth with your lies. You can't stare beauty in the eye, so you have to destroy it, poison it for everyone else.'

'Steven Farrow, Norman,' Annie repeated. 'Thirteen years old.'

'It was pure. A pure love.' Wells rubbed his teary eyes with his forearm. 'But you wouldn't understand that, would you? To people like you, anything other than a man and a woman is dirty, abnormal, *perverted*.'

'Try us, Norman,' said Banks. 'Give us a chance. You loved him?'

'Steven was beautiful. An angel. All I wanted was to be close to him, to be with him. What could be wrong with that?'

'But you touched him, Norman,' said Annie. 'He told—'

'I never touched him! He was lying. He turned on me. He wanted money. Can you believe it? My little angel wanted *money*. I would have done anything for him, made any sacrifice. But something so vulgar as *money* . . . I blame them, of course, not Steven. They poisoned him against me. They made him turn on me.' Wells wiped his eyes again.

'Who did, Norman?'

'The others. The other boys.'

'What happened?' Banks asked.

'I refused, of course. Steven went to the headmaster and . . . I was asked to leave, no questions asked, no scandal. All for the good of the school, you see. But word got around. On the scrapheap at thirty-eight. One foolish mistake.' He shook his head. 'That boy broke my heart.'

'Surely you couldn't expect them to keep you on?' Banks said. 'In fact, you're bloody lucky they didn't bring in the police. And you know how we feel about paedophiles.'

'I am not a child molester! I would have been content

just . . . just to be with him. Have you ever been in love, Chief Inspector?'

Banks said nothing. He sensed Annie glance at him.

Wells leaned forward and rested his forearms on the table. 'You can't choose the object of your desire. You know you can't. It may be a cliché to say that love is blind, but like many clichés it's not without a grain of truth. I didn't *choose* to love Steven. I simply couldn't help myself.'

Banks had heard this argument before from paedophiles – that they weren't responsible for their desires, that they didn't *choose* to love little boys – and he had at least a modicum of sympathy for their predicament. After all, it wasn't only paedophiles who fell in love with the wrong people. But he didn't feel enough sympathy to condone their actions. 'I'm sure you are aware,' he said, 'that it's illegal for a thirty-eight-year-old man to initiate a sexual relationship with a thirteen-year-old boy, and that it's inappropriate for a teacher to be involved in any way with a pupil, even if that pupil happened to be over the age of consent, which Steven wasn't.'

'There was no sexual relationship. Steven lied. They made him do it. I never touched him.'

'That's as may be,' said Banks. 'You might not have been able to help your feelings, but you could have controlled your actions. I think you know right from wrong.'

'It's all so hypocritical,' Wells said.

'What do you mean?'

'Who says there can be no real love between youth and age? The Greeks didn't think so.'

'Society,' said Banks. 'The law. And it's not the *love* we legislate against. The law's there to protect the innocent and the vulnerable from those predators who should know better.'

'Ha! It shows how little you know. Who do you think was the vulnerable one here, the innocent one? Steven Farrow? Do you think just because a boy is of a certain tender age that he is incapable of manipulating his elders, incapable of blackmail? That's very naive of you, if you don't mind my saying so.'

'Luke Armitage,' Annie cut in.

Wells leaned back and licked his lips. He was sweating profusely, Banks noticed, and starting to smell sour and rank. 'I wondered when we'd be getting around to him.'

'That's why you're here, Norman. Did you think it was about Steven Farrow?'

'I'd no idea what it would be about. I haven't done anything wrong.'

'The Farrow affair's all water under the bridge. Hushed up. No charges, no serious damage done.'

'Except to me.'

'You were among the last people to see Luke Armitage on the day he disappeared, Norman,' Annie went on. 'When we found out about your past, wasn't it only natural that we should want to talk to you about him?'

'I know nothing about what happened to him.'

'But you were friends with him, weren't you?'

'Acquaintances. He was a customer. We talked about books sometimes. That's all.'

'He was an attractive boy, wasn't he, Norman? Like Steven Farrow. Did he remind you of Steven?'

Wells sighed. 'The boy left my shop. I never saw him again.'

'Are you certain?' Banks asked. 'Are you sure he didn't come back, or you didn't meet him somewhere else? Your house, perhaps?'

'I never saw him again. Why would he come to my house?'

'I don't know,' said Banks. 'You tell me.'

'He didn't.'

'Never?'

'Never.'

'Did he come back to the shop? Did something happen there? Something bad. Did you kill him and then move him after dark? Maybe it was a terrible accident. I can't believe you meant to kill him. Not if you loved him.'

'I didn't *love* him. Society has seen to it that I'm quite incapable of loving anyone ever again. No matter what you think of me, I am not a fool. I *do* know wrong from right, Chief Inspector, whether I agree with the definition or not. I am capable of self-control. I am an emotional eunuch. I know that society regards my urges as evil and sinful, and I have no desire to spend the rest of my days in jail. Believe me, the prison of my own making is bad enough.'

'I suppose the money was an afterthought, was it?' Banks went on. 'But why not? Why not make a little money out of what you'd done? I mean, you could do with it, couldn't you? Look at the dump you spend your days in. A crappy used-book business in a dank, cold dungeon can't be making much money, can it? An extra ten thousand quid would have set you up nicely. Not too greedy. Just enough.'

Wells had tears in his eyes again, and he was shaking his head slowly from side to side. 'It's all I've got,' he said, his voice catching in his throat, his whole body starting to shake now. 'My books. My cat. They're all I've got. Can't you see that, man?' He pushed his florid, bulbous face towards Banks and banged his fist to his heart. 'There's nothing else left here for me. Have you no humanity?'

'But it's still not very much, is it?' Banks pressed on.

Wells looked him in the eye and regained some of his composure. 'Who are you to say that? Who are you to pronounce judgement on a man's life? Do you think I don't know I'm ugly? Do you think I don't notice the way people look at me? Do you think I don't know I'm the object of laughter and derision? Do you think I have no feelings? Every day I sit down there in my dank, cold dungeon, as you so cruelly refer to it, like some sort of pariah, some deformed monster in his lair, some . . . some *Quasimodo*, and I contemplate my sins, my desires, my dreams of love and beauty and purity deemed ugly and evil by a hypocritical world. All I have is my books, and the unconditional love of one of God's creatures. How *dare* you judge me?'

'No matter what you feel,' said Banks, 'society has to protect its children, and for that we need laws. They may seem arbitrary to you. Sometimes they seem arbitrary to me. I mean, fifteen, sixteen, seventeen, eighteen? Fourteen? Where do you draw the line? Who knows, Norman, maybe one day we'll be as enlightened as you'd like us to be and lower the age of consent to thirteen, but until then we have to have those lines, or all becomes chaos.' He was thinking of Graham Marshall as well as Luke Armitage as he spoke. Society hadn't done a very good job of protecting either of them.

'I have done nothing wrong,' said Wells, crossing his arms again.

The problem was, as Banks and Annie had already discussed, that the closed-circuit television cameras corroborated Wells's story. Luke Armitage had entered Norman's Used Books at two minutes to five and left – alone – at five twenty-four.

'What time did you close that day?' Banks asked.

'Half-past five, as usual.'

'And what did you do?'

'I went home.'

'Number 57 Arden Terrace?'

'Yes.'

'That's off Market Street, isn't it?'

'Close, yes.'

'Do you live alone?'

'Yes.'

'Do you own a car?'

'A second-hand Renault.'

'Good enough to get you out to Hallam Tarn and back?'

Wells hung his head in his hands. 'I've told you. I did nothing. I haven't been near Hallam Tarn in months. Certainly not since the foot-and-mouth outbreak.'

Banks could smell his sweat even more strongly now, sharp and acrid, like an animal secretion. 'What did you do after you went home?'

'Had my tea. Leftover chicken casserole, if you're interested. Watched television. Read for a while, then went to sleep.'

'What time?'

'I'd say I was in bed by half-past ten.'

'Alone?'

Wells just glared at Banks.

'You didn't go out again that evening?'

'Where would I go?'

'Pub? Pictures?'

'I don't drink and I don't socialize. I prefer my own

company. And I happen to believe that there hasn't been a decent picture made in the last forty years.'

'Did Luke Armitage visit your house at any time that evening?'

'No.'

'Has Luke Armitage ever visited your house?'

'No.'

'He's never even stepped inside your front door, not just for a moment?'

'I talk to him in the shop sometimes. That's all. He doesn't even know where I live.'

'Did you ever give him a lift anywhere?'

'No. How could I do that? I walk to and from the shop every day. It's not far, and it's good exercise. Besides, you know what parking's like around the market square.'

'So Luke has never been in your car?'

'Never.'

'In that case,' said Banks, 'I'm sure you won't mind if our forensic experts have a close look at your house and your car. We'd also like to take a DNA sample, just for comparison.'

Wells stuck his chin out. 'What if I *do* mind?'

'We'll keep you here until we get a search warrant. Remember, Norman, I wouldn't like to say judges are swayed by such things, but Luke Armitage came from a wealthy and well-respected family, while you're a disgraced schoolteacher eking out a living in a dingy used bookshop. And that shop was the last place we know Luke visited before he disappeared.'

Wells hung his head. 'Fine,' he said. 'Go ahead. Do what you will. I don't care any more.'

●

After a sleepless night on Saturday, Michelle had spent Sunday getting over the shock of what had happened in her flat and trying to rein in her emotional response in favour of more analytical thought.

She hadn't got very far.

That someone had gained entry and arranged things in order to frighten her was obvious enough. Why was another matter entirely. That the interloper knew about Melissa surprised her, though she supposed people could find out anything about her if they really wanted to. But, given that he knew, it would have been evident when he searched her bedside drawers that the little dress was Melissa's, and that its desecration would cause her a great deal of anguish. In other words, it had been a cold, calculated assault.

The flats were supposed to be secure, but Michelle had been a copper long enough to know that a talented burglar could get around almost anything. Though it went against every grain in Michelle's nature not to report the break-in to the police, in the end she decided against it. Mostly this was because Graham Marshall's name had been written in her own red lipstick on the dressing-table mirror. The intrusion was meant to frighten her off the case, and the only people who knew she was working on it, apart from the Marshalls themselves, were other police officers, or people connected with them, like Dr Cooper. True, Michelle's name had been in the papers once or twice when the bones had first been found, so technically everyone in the entire country could know she was on the case, but she felt the answers lay a lot closer to home.

The question was, 'Was she going to be frightened off the case?' The answer was, 'No.'

At least there hadn't been much cleaning up to do.

Michelle had, however, dumped the entire contents of her bathroom cabinet and would have to contact her doctor for new prescriptions. She had also dumped the contents of the fridge, which hadn't been a big job at all. More important, she had found a locksmith in the *Yellow Pages* and arranged to have a chain and an extra deadbolt lock put on her door.

As a result of her weekend experience, Michelle felt drained and edgy on Monday morning and found herself looking at everyone in Divisional Headquarters differently, as if they knew something she didn't, as if they were pointing at her and talking about her. It was a frightening feeling, and every time she caught someone's eye she looked away. Creeping paranoia, she told herself, and tried to shake it off.

First, she had a brief meeting with DC Collins, who told her he was getting nowhere checking the old perv reports. Most of the people the police had interviewed at the time were either dead or in jail, and those who weren't had nothing new to add. She phoned Dr Cooper, who still hadn't located her knife expert, Hilary Wendell, yet, then she went down to the archives to check out the old notebooks and action allocations.

These days, since the Police and Criminal Evidence Act, there were very strict rules regarding police notebooks. You couldn't leave blank pages, for example. Each page was numbered, and if you missed one by mistake you had to draw a line through it and write 'omitted in error'. Entries had to be preceded by date and time, underlined, and at the end of each day the officer had to draw a continuous line below the final entry. Most of this was to prevent officers from 'verballing' suspects – attributing to them words they hadn't used, confessions they hadn't made – and to avoid any sort of revisions after the fact. Notes were made on the spot, often quickly, and accuracy was important because the notebooks might need to be used in court.

An officer's notebooks could be invaluable when trying to reconstruct the pattern of an investigation, as could the action allocations, records made of all the instructions issued to investigating officers by the senior investigating officer. For example, if DC Higginbottom was asked to go and interview Joe Smith's neighbour, that order, or 'action', would be recorded in the actions allocation book, and his record of the interview would be in his notebook. By looking at the actions, you could determine which areas of enquiry had been pursued and which had not, and by reading the notebooks, you could unearth impressions that might not have made it into final statements and formal reports.

Completed notebooks were first handed to a detective inspector, who would look them over and, if everything was acceptable, send them to the records clerk for filing. That meant they piled up over the years. Whoever said we were heading for a paperless world, Michelle thought, as she walked along the rows of shelving stacked to the ceiling with boxes, obviously wasn't a copper.

Mrs Metcalfe showed her where the notebooks were filed, and Michelle went first, by instinct, to Ben Shaw's. But no matter how many times she flipped through the boxes, checked and rechecked the dates, in the end she had to admit that if there had been notebooks covering the period of major activity in the Graham Marshall case, on the day of his disappearance, 22 August 1965, and over the next month or two, then they had vanished.

Michelle found it difficult to decipher Shaw's

handwriting in the notebooks she did find, but she could just about make out that his last entry was on 15 August 1965, when he had been questioning a witness to a post office robbery, and the next one was a new notebook started on 6 October of the same year.

Michelle asked for Mrs Metcalfe's help, but after half an hour even the poor records clerk had to admit defeat. 'I can't imagine where they've got to, love,' she said. 'Except they might have got misfiled by my predecessor, or been lost in one of the moves.'

'Could someone have taken them?' Michelle asked.

'I don't see who. Or why. I mean, it's only people like you who come down here. Other police.'

Exactly what Michelle had been thinking. She could have taken out anything she wanted during her visits and Mrs Metcalfe would have been none the wiser. Which meant that anyone else could too. Someone had gained entry to her flat and tried to scare her off the case, and now she found that nearly two months' worth, a crucial two months' worth, of notebooks had somehow disappeared. Coincidence? Michelle didn't think so.

Half an hour later, when they had run into the same problem with the action allocation book for the Graham Marshall case, Michelle knew in her bones that the actions and the notebooks were gone for ever, destroyed most likely. But why? And by whom? The discovery didn't help her paranoia one bit. She was beginning to feel way out of her depth. What the hell should she do now?

●

After the interview, Banks felt the urge to get out of the station, away from the acrid stink of Norman Wells's sweat, so he decided to head out Lyndgarth way and talk to Luke Armitage's music teacher, Alastair Ford, while Annie continued to supervise the search for Luke's mystery woman.

In Banks's experience, music teachers were an odd lot indeed, partly, no doubt, because of the frustration of trying to instil the beauties of Beethoven and Bach into minds addled with Radiohead and Mercury Rev. Not that Banks had anything against pop music. In his day, the class had kept pestering their music teacher, Mr Watson, to play the Beatles. He relented once, but looked glum the whole time. His feet didn't tap, and his heart wasn't in it. When he played Dvorak's 'New World Symphony' or Tchaikovsky's 'Pathétique', however, it was another matter. He closed his eyes, swayed and conducted, hummed along as the main themes swelled. All the time the kids in the class were laughing at him and reading comics under their desks, but he was oblivious, in a world of his own. One day Mr Watson failed to turn up for class. Rumour had it that he'd suffered a nervous breakdown and was 'resting' in a sanatorium. He never returned to teaching as far as Banks knew.

Yesterday's rain had rinsed the landscape clean and brought out the bright greens of the lower daleside, dotted with purple clover, yellow buttercups and celandines. The limestone scar of Fremlington Edge glowed in the sunlight, and below it the village of Lyndgarth, with its small church and lopsided village green, like a handkerchief flapping in the wind, seemed asleep. Banks consulted his map, found the minor road he was looking for and turned right.

Ford's cottage was about as isolated as Banks's own, and when he parked behind the dark blue Honda, he understood why. It wasn't the 'New World Symphony' but the beautiful 'Recordare' for soprano and mezzo-soprano from Verdi's *Requiem* blasting out of the open windows at full volume. If Banks hadn't been playing the Stones' *Aftermath* CD in the car, he would have heard it a mile away.

It took a bit of hammering at the door, but eventually the music quietened down and it was answered by the man Banks recognized from the Aeolian String Quartet concert. Alastair Ford had a five o'clock shadow, a long, hooked nose and a bright gleam in his eyes. If he had any, his hair would probably have been sticking out in all directions, but he was quite bald. What was it about Luke Armitage? Banks wondered. This was the second person he'd met that day who had spent time with the boy and looked as mad as a hatter. Maybe Luke attracted weirdos. Maybe it was because he was more than a little weird himself. However, Banks determined to keep an open mind. Whether Alastair Ford's eccentricity had a dangerous edge remained to be seen.

'I'm as fond of Verdi as the next man,' said Banks, showing his warrant card, 'but don't you think it's a bit too loud?'

'Oh, don't tell me old Farmer Jones has complained about the music again. He says it curdles his cows' milk. Philistine!'

'I'm not here about the noise, Mr Ford. Might I come in and have a word?'

'Now I'm curious,' said Ford, leading the way inside. His house was clean but lived in, with little piles of sheet music here and there, a violin on a table, and the massive stereo system dominating the living room. 'A policeman who knows his Verdi.'

'I'm no expert,' Banks said, 'but I've recently bought a new recording, so I've listened to it a few times lately.'

'Ah, yes. Renée Fleming and the Kirov. Very nice, but I must admit I'm still rather attached to the von Otter and Gardiner. Anyway, I can't imagine you've come here to discuss old Joe Green with me. What can I do for you?' Ford was birdlike in many ways, especially in his sudden, jerky movements, but when he sat down in the over-stuffed armchair he fell still, fingers linked in his lap. He wasn't relaxed, though. Banks could sense the man's tension and unease, and he wondered what its cause was. Maybe he just didn't like being questioned by the police.

'It's about Luke Armitage,' said Banks. 'I understand you knew him?'

'Ah, poor Luke. A remarkably talented boy. Such a great loss.'

'When did you last see him?'

'Around the end of term.'

'Are you sure you haven't seen him since?'

'I've barely left the cottage since then, except to drive into Lyndgarth for groceries. Alone with my music after a term of teaching those philistines. What bliss!'

'I gather Luke Armitage wasn't a philistine, though?'

'Far from it.'

'You were giving him violin lessons, am I right?'

'Yes.'

'Here or at school?'

'At school. Tuesday evenings. We have a reasonably well-equipped music room there. Mind you, we ought to be grateful for anything these days. They'll spend a fortune on sports equipment, but when it comes to music . . . '

'Did Luke ever talk to you about anything that was on his mind?'

'He didn't talk a lot. Mostly he concentrated on his playing. He had remarkable powers of concentration, unlike so many of today's youth. He wasn't much of a one for small talk. We did chat about music, argued once or twice about pop music, which I gathered he was rather fond of.'

'Never about anything else?'

'Like what?'

'Anything that might have been bothering him, worrying him, anyone he might have been afraid of. That sort of thing.'

'I'm afraid not. Luke was a very private person, and I'm not the prying kind. Truth be told, I'm not very good at helping people with their emotional problems.' He ran his hand over his smooth head and smiled. 'That's why I prefer to live alone.'

'Not married?'

'Was. Many moons ago.'

'What happened.'

'Search me. What usually happens?'

Banks thought of Sandra. *What usually happens?* 'So you just taught him the violin, that's all?'

'Mainly, yes. I mean, he was in my class, too, at school. But I wouldn't say I *knew* him or that we were friends or anything like that. I respected his talent, even if he did dabble in pop music, but that's as far as it went.'

'Did he ever mention his parents?'

'Not to me.'

'What about his biological father? Neil Byrd?'

'Never heard of him.'

Banks looked around the room. 'It's a very isolated cottage you have here, Mr Ford.'

'Is it? Yes, I suppose it is.'

'Isolation suits you?'

'It must do, mustn't it?' Ford's foot started tapping on

the floor, his knee jerking, and not to the rhythm of the now barely audible *Requiem*.

'Do you ever have company?'

'Rarely. I play in a string quartet, and sometimes the other members come out here to rehearse. Other than that, I'm rather given to solitary pursuits. Look, I—'

'No girlfriends?'

'I told you, I'm not good at relationships.'

'Boyfriends?'

Ford raised an eyebrow. 'I'm not good at relationships.'

'Yet you manage the teacher–student relationship.'

'I have a talent for teaching.'

'Do you enjoy it?'

'In a way. Sometimes.'

Banks got up and walked over to the window. There was a fine view of the dale, looking back towards Eastvale in the distance. Banks thought he could just make out the castle on its hill.

'Did Luke Armitage ever come here?' he asked, turning to face Ford.

'No.'

'You're certain?'

'Very few people come here. I would remember. Look, if you want to know about Luke, ask Lauren.'

'Lauren Anderson?'

'Yes. She knew him far better than I did. She's a . . . well, you know, she's the sort of person people talk to, about their problems and stuff.'

'Emotions.'

'Yes.'

'Do you know if Luke was close to anyone else?'

'You could try our headmaster's daughter.'

Banks had a quick flash of that sudden flurry of blonde hair and long leg he had noticed after his conversation with Gavin Barlow. 'Rose Barlow?'

'That's the one. Little minx.'

'Were she and Luke friends?'

'Thick as thieves.'

'When was this?'

'Earlier this year. February or March.'

'Where did you see them together?'

'At school.'

'Nowhere else?'

'I don't go anywhere else. Except here. All I can say is I saw them talking sometimes in the corridors and playground, and they seemed close.'

Banks made a mental note to follow up on Rose Barlow. 'Do you have a mobile phone?' he asked.

'Good Lord, what an odd question!'

'Do you?'

'No. I see no use for one, personally. I barely use the telephone I do have.'

'Where were you last Monday?'

'Here.'

'Were you in Eastvale at all last week?'

'I've already told you. I've hardly left the cottage.'

'What have you been doing?'

'What do you mean?'

'Here. In the cottage. Alone. All this time.'

Ford got to his feet and the birdlike motions started up again. 'Playing music. Listening. Reading. Dabbling in a little composition. Look, really it's none of your business, you know, even if you *are* a policeman. The last time I noticed, we were still living in a free country.'

'It was just a simple question, Mr Ford. No need to get upset.'

Ford's voice took on a piercing edge. 'I'm not getting upset. But you're prying. I hate people prying. I can't tell you anything. Go and talk to Lauren. Leave me alone.'

Banks stared at him for a moment. Ford wouldn't meet his gaze. 'If I find out you've been lying to me, Mr Ford, I'll be back. Do you understand?'

'I'm not lying. I haven't done anything. Leave me alone.'

Before leaving, Banks showed him the artist's impression of the girl Josie Batty had seen with Luke. Ford hardly glanced at the sketch and said he didn't recognize her. He was weird, without a doubt, Banks thought as he started his car, but you couldn't arrest people just for being weird. The volume went way up again, and Banks could hear Verdi's 'Lacrimosa' chasing him all the way to Lyndgarth.

•

'Thank you for seeing to the release, love,' Mrs Marshall said. 'We'll be holding the funeral service at St Peter's the day after tomorrow. Joan's coming back up for it, of course. I must say the vicar's been very good considering none of us were what you'd call regular church-goers. You'll be there?'

'Yes, of course,' said Michelle. 'There's just one thing.'

'What's that, love?'

Michelle told her about the rib they needed for evidence.

Mrs Marshall frowned and thought for a moment. 'I don't think we need worry about a little thing like a missing rib, need we? Especially if it might help you.'

'Thank you,' said Michelle.

'You look tired, love. Is everything all right?'

'Yes. Fine.' Michelle managed to dredge up a weak smile.

'Is there any more news?'

'No, I'm afraid not. Only more questions.'

'I can't understand what else I have to tell you, but please go ahead.'

Michelle leaned back in her chair. This was going to be difficult, she knew. To find out about any mischief Graham might have been up to without suggesting that he got up to mischief – which his mother would never accept – was almost to do the impossible. Still, she could but try. 'Was Graham ever away from home for any periods of time?'

'What do you mean? Did we send him away?'

'No. But you know what kids are like. Sometimes they just like to take off and not tell you where they've been. They worry you sick, but they don't seem to realize it at the time.'

'Oh, I know what you mean. I'm not saying our Graham was any different from other kids that way. He missed his tea from time to time, and once or twice he missed his nine o'clock curfew. And many's the occasion we didn't see hide nor hair of him from dawn till dusk. Not during term-time, mind you. Just weekends and school holidays he could be a bit unreliable.'

'Did you have any idea where he'd been when he turned up late?'

'Playing with his pals. Sometimes he'd have his guitar with him, too. They were practising, see. The group.'

'Where did they do that?'

'David Grenfell's house.'

'Other than group practice, did he ever stay out late on other occasions?'

'Once in a while. He was just a normal boy.'

'How much pocket money did you give him?'

'Five shillings a week. It was all we could afford. But he had his paper round and that made him a bit extra.'

'And you bought all his clothes?'

'Sometimes he'd save up if there was something he really wanted. Like a Beatles jumper. You know, like the one he's wearing in the photo there.'

'So he didn't go short of anything?'

'No. Not so's you'd notice. Why? What are you trying to get at?'

'I'm just trying to get a picture of his activities, Mrs Marshall. It'll help me try to work out what might have happened to him, who might have stopped and picked him up.'

'You think it was somebody he knew?'

'I didn't say that, but it's possible.'

Mrs Marshall fiddled with her necklace. The idea clearly upset her. Whether it was the idea of an acquaintance being responsible, or whether she had suspected such a thing deep down, was impossible to say. 'But we didn't know anybody like that,' she said.

'Like what?'

'A pervert,' she whispered.

'We don't know that it *was* a pervert.'

'I don't understand. That's what the police said. Who else could it be?'

'Jet Harris told you that?'

'Yes.'

'Did anyone ever suggest, at any time, that Graham might have been abducted by someone he knew?'

'Heavens, no! Why would anyone do that?'

'Why indeed?' said Michelle. 'And you know nothing about any unsavoury company Graham might have been keeping – perhaps on the occasions when he stayed out late or was gone all day?'

'No. He was with his friends. I don't understand what you're trying to say.'

'It's all right,' said Michelle. 'I'm not sure that I understand it myself. I suppose all I really want to ask is whether Graham had any friends you disliked, or spent time with anyone you didn't approve of.'

'Oh. No. They were all just regular lads. We knew their mums and dads. They were just like us.'

'No older boys? No one you thought was a bad influence?'

'No.'

'And Graham never seemed to have more money than you expected him to have?'

Mrs Marshall's expression sharpened and Michelle knew she'd gone too far. She also knew that she had touched a raw nerve.

'Are you suggesting our Graham was a thief?'

'Of course not,' Michelle backtracked. 'I just wondered if he maybe did other odd jobs he didn't tell you about, other than the paper round, perhaps when he should have been at school.'

Mrs Marshall still eyed her suspiciously. Bill Marshall seemed to be taking everything in, his beady eyes moving from one to the other as they spoke, but they were the only things moving in his face. If only he could talk, Michelle thought. And then she realized that would be no use. He wouldn't tell her anything.

'I suppose it's just a mark of my frustration with the case,' Michelle admitted. 'After all, it was so long ago.'

'Jet Harris always said it was them Moors Murderers, the ones who were tried the year after. He said we'd all probably have nightmares for the rest of our lives if we ever knew how many young lives they'd taken and where the bodies were buried.'

'He told you that, did he?' said Michelle. How very convenient. She was fast coming to the conclusion – or reaffirming what she had suspected earlier – that Detective Superintendent Harris had run the case with blinkers on, and Mrs Marshall, like so many mothers, hadn't a clue what her son was up to most of the time. She wondered if his father knew. Bill Marshall's lopsided face gave away nothing, but Michelle fancied she could see wariness in his eyes. And something else. She couldn't say with any certainty that it was guilt, but it looked like that to her. Michelle took a deep breath and plunged in.

'I understand your husband used to work for the Kray twins back in London.'

There was a short silence, then Mrs Marshall said, 'Bill didn't *work* for them, as such. He did used to spar with them down the gym. We knew them. Of course we did. We grew up in the same neighbourhood. Everybody knew Reggie and Ronnie. Always polite to me, they were, no matter what anybody says about them, and I've heard some stories as would make your hair curl. But they were basically good lads. People don't like it when others get a bit above their station, you know.'

Michelle could feel her jaw dropping. There was nothing more to be gained here, she realized, and if she was going to solve this case she was going to do so without the family's help, and without Ben Shaw's. And perhaps in peril of her life. *'Remember Melissa. You could join her . . .'* Promising again that she would be at the funeral, Michelle excused herself and hurried off.

•

That evening at home, Banks glanced through the evening paper over a Madras curry he'd bought earlier at Marks & Spencer, slipped Bill Evans's *Paris Concert* into the CD player, poured himself a couple of fingers of Laphroaig and flopped down on the sofa with his 1965 *Photoplay* diary. He thought it was Oscar Wilde who had said, 'I never travel without my diary. One should always have something sensational to read on the train,' but he could have been wrong. It was easy to attribute just about any witty saying to Oscar Wilde or Groucho Marx. Curious, though, he stirred himself and checked *The Oxford Dictionary of Quotations* and found that he was right this time.

Banks's diary was far from sensational. As he flipped the pages once again, glancing at the pretty actresses he hardly remembered – Carol Lynley, Jill St John, Yvette Mimieux – he was struck by how many records he had bought and films he had seen. Until, just a couple of weeks from Graham's disappearance, Banks saw that his diary did, in fact, have its moments, and as he read the trivial or cryptic entries, he was able to fill in the rest with his memory and imagination.

In the first week of August 1965 the Banks family had set off for their annual holidays. There was nothing unusual in that; they went every year at the same time, his father's annual factory shut-down fortnight. What *was* unusual that year was that they went to Blackpool – much further afield than their usual trip to Great Yarmouth or

Skegness – and that they took Graham Marshall with them.

At fourteen, Banks was of an age when he found wandering around a seaside resort with his parents embarrassing, and riding the donkey on the beach or playing with a bucket and spade no longer held any appeal. As Graham's dad had just started on a large building project – his work being far more seasonal than Arthur Banks's – and it didn't look as if the Marshalls would get a holiday that year, financial arrangements were made and Graham was allowed to accompany them.

Visit Blackpool! See the Famous Tower! Hear Reginald Dixon at the Mighty Organ! See the glorious Golden Mile! Go to a star-studded Variety Show on one of the Three Piers! Have hours of Family Fun at the Pleasure Beach!

It might as well have been the moon.

At some ridiculously early hour in the morning, because that was when they always set off on holiday, they would have piled their cases into the back of Arthur Banks's Morris Traveller, a popular sort of estate car with a wood-frame rear, and headed north on their long journey, no doubt arriving tired and cranky, but in good time for tea at Mrs Barraclough's boarding house. Bed, breakfast and evening meal at six o'clock on the dot, and woe betide you if you were late. Mrs Barraclough was a large, forbidding presence, whom Banks remembered even now as dressed in a pinny, standing with her thick legs apart and her arms folded under her massive bosom.

Banks saw that he had recorded the weather every day at the top of his entry, and as holidays went they had done quite well: nine days of at least partial sunshine out of fourteen, and only two and a half complete washouts. On the rainy days Banks and Graham had hung about the amusement arcades on the Golden Mile, he noted, or on one of the piers, and played the one-armed bandits and pinball machines. One rainy Sunday afternoon they spent watching the old war films that always seemed to be showing on rainy Sunday afternoons, patriotic films with titles such as *The Day Will Dawn*, *In Which We Serve* and *Went the Day Well?*

On overcast days they would wander along the prom eating fish and chips from newspapers or boiled shrimps from paper bags and go hunting through the town's few second-hand bookshops, Banks looking for Sexton Blake novelettes (he had bought one called *The Mind Killers*) or Ian Fleming novels, while Graham went after *Famous Monsters* magazines and Isaac Asimov stories.

One night they all went to the Tower Circus, and Banks noted in his diary that he found Charlie Cairoli's act 'very funny'. They also took in a variety show on the North Pier, with Morecambe and Wise providing the comedy and the Hollies the music.

But most evenings after tea they spent watching television in the guests' lounge. The TV was an old model, even for then, with a small screen, Banks remembered, and you turned it on by opening a sprung flap on the top, under which were the volume and contrast controls. Banks hadn't recorded it in his diary, but no doubt there would have been some adult wanting to watch *Sunday Night at the London Palladium* instead of *Perry Mason*, which was only to be expected of adults. Luckily, Roy was sleeping on a camp bed in his parents' room, so Banks and Graham would just go up to their room and read, listen to Radio Luxembourg on their transistors, or pore over the dirty magazines Graham seemed to get hold of in abundance.

Of course, they didn't spend every minute of every day together. Graham had been moody at times, unusually quiet, and looking back Banks suspected he had been preoccupied with some problem or other. At the time, though, he hadn't given it a second thought, had simply gone his own way on occasion.

On his third day, wandering the streets alone looking for somewhere to sit down and have a cigarette, Banks discovered a coffee bar down a flight of stairs off the beaten track. He hadn't thought of this in years, but the stark diary entry brought it back in all its rich detail. He could even hear the hissing of the espresso machine and smell the dark-roasted coffee.

The place had a tropical ambience, with rough stucco walls, potted palms and soft calypso music playing in the background, but it was the girl behind the counter who drew him back there time after time. She was far too old for him, even if he did look older when he smoked and could pass for sixteen and get into 'X' films. Probably over twenty, she would have an older boyfriend with a car and lots of money, a pretty girl like her, but Banks fell for her the way he had fallen for the factory girl, Mandy. Linda was her name.

That Linda was beautiful went without saying. She had long dark hair, sparkling blue eyes, an easy smile and lips he yearned to kiss. What he could see of the rest of her body when she came out from behind the counter was also the stuff that fantasies were made on: like Ursula Andress walking out of the sea in *Dr No*. She was nice to him, too. She talked to him, smiled at him, and one day she even gave him a second cup of espresso for nothing. He loved to watch her working the machines behind the counter, nibbling her lower lip as she frothed the milk.

Once or twice she caught him looking and smiled. He could feel himself blush to the roots of his being and he knew that she knew he was in love with her. This was one secret, and one place, he didn't share with Graham.

As the holiday progressed, Banks and Graham did all the usual things, some with the rest of the family, and some by themselves. When it was warm enough, they spent time lounging with Banks's mother and father on the beach in their swimming trunks among crowds of rough northerners with knotted hankies on their heads. They even went in the sea once or twice, but it was cold, so they didn't stay long. Mostly they just lay there plugged into their radios hoping to hear the Animals singing 'We've Gotta Get Out of This Place' or the Byrds doing 'Mr Tambourine Man', and surreptitiously eyeing the girls in their bathing costumes.

In fact, reading over his diary, not only of the holiday but of the entire year, Banks was amazed at how much of his time was taken up with girls, with thoughts and dreams of sex. His hormones were running his life that year, no doubt about it.

The highlight of the week, though, was the two girls, and that was where Banks's diary approached the sensational. One fine evening Banks and Graham headed down to the Pleasure Beach opposite the South Pier. They took one of the open trams, sitting on the upper deck and thrilling at the lights with the wind in their hair.

The Pleasure Beach was a bustle of colour and sound, from the rattling of the rides to the shrieks and screams of the passengers. As they were walking around trying to decide which ride to go on first, they noticed two girls about their own age who kept looking at them, whispering to one another and giggling, the way girls did. They weren't mods, but wore blouses and skirts of the more conservative length some parents still insisted on.

Eventually, Banks and Graham approached them and, Graham being the silent, moody type, Banks offered them cigarettes and started chatting them up. He couldn't remember what he said, just something to make the girls laugh and think these boys were cool. The way it turned out, this time he linked up with the one he fancied most, though to be honest they were both all right, not like the usual pairing of the good-looking one with the ugly friend.

Tina was short with rather large breasts, a dark complexion and long wavy brown hair. Her friend, Sharon, was a slender blonde. The only flaws Banks noticed were a couple of spots under her make-up and the bubblegum she was chewing. But there was nothing she could do about the spots – he knew, he had a couple of embarrassing ones himself – and she soon took out the gum and threw it away.

They went on the Ghost Train first, and the girls got scared when phosphorescent skeletons jumped out and hung in front of the slow-moving cars. But what made them scream and lean closer into the chests of their companions were the cobwebs that occasionally brushed across their faces in the dark.

After the Ghost Train they were holding hands, and Graham suggested they ride on the Big Dipper, a huge roller-coaster, next. Tina was scared, but the others assured her it would be okay. Graham paid.

That was something Banks remembered as he read through his diary. He lit a cigarette, sipped some Laphroaig and thought about it for a moment as Bill Evans played on. Graham often paid. He always seemed to have plenty of money, always enough, even back in Peterborough, for ten Gold Leaf and a double bill at the Gaumont. Maybe even some Kia-Ora and a choc ice from the woman who came around with the tray during the intermission. Banks never wondered or asked where he got it from at the time; he just assumed that Graham got plenty of pocket money from his dad in addition to his paper-round money. Looking back now, though, it seemed odd that a working-class kid, a bricklayer's son, should always have so much ready cash to spend.

If the Ghost Train had set things up nicely, Banks thought, going back to the memory, the Big Dipper had the girls throwing their arms around Banks and Graham and burying their faces in their shoulders. Banks even stole a quick kiss from Sharon as they rose up towards one of the steepest descents, and she clung to him all the way down, hair streaming, shrieking blue murder.

Flushed and exhilarated, they walked out of the Pleasure Beach on to the prom. The Illuminations didn't start until later in the year, but there were still bracelets and necklaces of lights all over the front, like Christmas decorations, Banks had written in a strangely rare poetic moment, and the trams themselves were lit with bulbs so you could see their outlines coming from miles away.

After only token resistance, the girls agreed to a walk on the beach and the four of them inevitably settled under the South Pier, a well-established 'courting' spot. Banks remembered as he read his vague and brief descriptions, how he lay with Sharon and kissed her, gently at first, then the two of them working their lips harder, trying a little tongue, feeling her body stir under him. He let his imagination go to work on the scanty details he had recorded in his bed back at Mrs Barraclough's that night: 'G and me went with Tina and Sharon <u>under south pier!</u>'

Somehow, he had worked his hand under her blouse and felt her firm little breast. She didn't complain when after a while of that he wriggled under her bra and felt the warm, soft flesh itself, squeezing the nipple between his thumb and forefinger. She took a sharp breath and went back to kissing him with her tongue. He got some of her hair in his mouth. He could smell bubblegum on her breath, mingled with the seaweed and brine of the beach. Trams rolled by above them and waves crashed on the shore. Sometime later, getting brave, he slid his hand down her thigh and put it up inside her skirt. She would only let him touch her over the cloth of her knickers, freezing or firmly pulling his hand away when he tried to go further, but that was the furthest he had ever been before, so it was all right with him. Graham said later that Tina let him go all the way with her, but Banks didn't believe him.

And that was as sensational as it got.

They went out with Sharon and Tina twice more, once to the pictures to see *Help!* and once to the amusement arcades, Graham as usual supplying most of the cash, and their evenings ended the same way. No matter how much Banks tried and hinted, Sharon wouldn't relinquish her treasure. She always stopped him at the threshold. It was a tease balanced only later with the delicious ritual of self-administered relief.

When it was time to leave, they exchanged names and addresses and said they'd write, but Banks never heard from Sharon again. As far as he knew, Graham hadn't heard from Tina before he disappeared, either. Now, looking back, Banks hoped she really *had* let him go all the way with her.

Remembering their holiday had made him also

remember other things, and some of them started to ring alarm bells in his policeman's mind. Quiet at first, then getting louder and louder.

But soon, it wasn't an inner alarm bell, it was the telephone that was ringing. Banks picked it up.

'DCI Banks?' A woman's voice, familiar, strained.

'Yes.'

'It's DI Hart. Michelle.'

'I haven't forgotten your name yet,' Banks said. 'What can I do for you? Any news?'

'Are you busy?'

'Just after you left me in Starbucks a missing persons case turned into a murder, so yes, I am.'

'Look, I'm sorry about that. I mean . . . This is so difficult.'

'Just tell me.'

Michelle paused for so long that Banks was beginning to think she would just hang up. She seemed to be good at putting an abrupt end to conversations. But she didn't. After an eternity she said, 'Today I discovered that Ben Shaw's notebooks and the Graham Marshall actions allocations are missing.'

'Missing?'

'I looked all over the files. I couldn't find them. I got the records clerk to help, too, but even she couldn't find them. There's a gap in the notebooks from 15 August to 6 October 1965.'

Banks whistled between his teeth. 'And the actions?'

'Just for that case. Gone. I don't know . . . I mean, I've never . . . There's something else, too. Something that happened over the weekend. But I don't want to talk about it over the phone.' She gave a nervous laugh. 'I suppose I'm asking you for advice. I don't know what to do.'

'You should tell someone.'

'I'm telling you.'

'I mean someone in your station.'

'That's the problem,' she said. 'I just don't know who I can trust down here. That's why I thought of you. I know you have a personal interest in the case, and it would be helpful for me to have another professional around. One I know I can trust.'

Banks thought it over for a moment. Michelle was right; he did have an interest in the case. And the way it sounded, she was out on a limb by herself down there. 'I'm not sure what I can do to help,' he said, 'but I'll see if I can get away.' As he spoke the words, an image of himself charging down to Peterborough and Michelle on a white steed, wearing armour and carrying a lance, mocked him. 'Any news on the funeral service?'

'Day after tomorrow.'

'I'll get away as soon as I can,' he said. 'Maybe tomorrow. In the meantime, don't say or do anything. Just carry on as normal. Okay?'

'Okay. And Alan?'

'Yes?'

'Thanks. I mean it. I'm in a jam.' She paused, then added, 'And I'm scared.'

'I'll be there.'

After Banks hung up, he refilled his glass, put the second Bill Evans set on and settled down to think over the repercussions of what he had realized earlier that evening, reading his diary, and of what he had just heard from Michelle.

13

Lauren Anderson lived in a small semi not too far from where Banks used to live with Sandra before their separation. He hadn't passed the end of his old street in a long time, and it brought back memories he would rather forget. He felt cheated, somehow. The memories should have been good – he and Sandra *had* had good times together, had been in love for many years – but everything seemed tainted by her betrayal and now by her forthcoming marriage to Sean. And the baby, of course. The baby hurt a lot.

He spoke nothing of his thoughts to Annie, who sat beside him. She didn't even know he used to live there, as he had only met her after he moved to the Gratly cottage. Besides, she had made it clear that she wasn't interested in his old life with Sandra and the kids; that was one of the main things that had come between them and broken up their brief and edgy romance.

It was as fine a summer's day as they had seen in a while. They were in Banks's car this time, the way he preferred it, with the windows open listening to Marianne Faithfull singing 'Summer Nights' on a greatest hits CD. That was back when her voice was rich and smooth, before the booze, drugs and cigarettes had taken their toll, the same way it had happened with Billie Holiday. It was also a hit around the time Graham disappeared and it captured the mood of that sex-preoccupied adolescent summer.

'I can't believe you still listen to this stuff,' said Annie.

'Why not?'

'I don't know. It's just so . . . old.'

'So is Beethoven.'

'Clever clogs. You know what I mean.'

'I used to fancy her like crazy.'

Annie shot him a sidelong glance. 'Marianne Faithfull?'

'Yes. Why not? She used to come on *Ready, Steady, Go!* and *Top of the Pops* every time she had a new record out, and she'd sit on a high stool with her guitar looking just like a schoolgirl. But she'd be wearing a low-cut dress, legs crossed, and that sweet voice would come out, and you'd just want to . . .'

'Go on.'

Banks stopped at a traffic light and smiled at Annie. 'I'm sure you get the picture,' he said. 'She just looked so innocent, so virginal.'

'But if the stories are true, she put herself about quite a bit, didn't she? Far from virginal, I'd say.'

'Maybe that was part of it, too,' Banks agreed. 'You just knew she . . . *did* it. There were stories. Gene Pitney. Mick Jagger. The parties and all that.'

'Saint and Sinner all in one package,' said Annie. 'How perfect for you.'

'Christ, Annie, I was only a kid.'

'Quite a randy one, too, it seems.'

'Well, what did you think about at fourteen?'

'I don't know. Boys, maybe, but not in a sexual way. Having fun. Romance. Clothes. Make-up.'

'Maybe that's why I always fancied older women,' said Banks.

Annie nudged him hard in the ribs.

'Ouch! What did you do that for?'

'You know. Park here. Men,' she said, as Banks parked and they got out of the car. 'When you're young you want older women, and when you're old you want younger women.'

'These days,' said Banks, 'I take whatever I can get.'

'Charming.' Annie pressed the doorbell and a few seconds later saw the shape coming towards them through the frosted glass.

Lauren Anderson was dressed in jeans and a thin V-neck jumper, and she wore no make-up. Younger than Banks had expected, she was willowy, with full lips, a pale oval face and heavy-lidded pale blue eyes, all framed by long auburn hair spilling down over her shoulders. As she stood in the doorway, she wrapped her arms around herself as if she were cold.

'Police,' Banks said, holding out his warrant card. 'May we come in?'

'Of course.' Lauren stood aside.

'In here?' Banks asked, pointing towards what looked like the living room.

'If you like. I'll make some tea, shall I?'

'Lovely,' said Annie, following her into the kitchen.

Banks could hear them talking as he had a quick look around the living room. He was impressed by the two walls of bookshelves groaning under the weight of classics he had meant to read but never got around to. All the Victorians, along with the major Russians and French. A few recent novels: Ian McEwan, Graham Swift, A.S. Byatt. Quite a lot of poetry, too, from Heaney's *Beowulf* translation to the latest issue of *Poetry Review* lying on the low coffee table. There were plays, too: Tennessee Williams, Edward Albee, Tom Stoppard, the Elizabethans and Jacobeans. There was also a section devoted to art and one to classical mythology. Not to mention the rows of literary criticism, from Aristotle's *Poetics* to David Lodge on the vagaries of post-structuralism. Most of the music in the CD rack was classical, favouring Bach, Mozart and Handel.

Banks found a comfortable chair and sat down. In a short while Annie and Lauren came in with the tea. Noting an ashtray on the table and getting a distinct whiff of stale smoke in the air, Banks asked if he might light up. Lauren said sure and accepted one of his Silk Cut. Annie turned up her nose the way only an ex-smoker can do.

'It's a nice place,' Banks said.

'Thank you.'

'Do you live here alone?'

'I do now. I used to share it with one of the other teachers, but she got her own flat a few months ago. I'm not sure, but I think I like it better by myself.'

'I don't blame you,' said Banks. 'Look, the reason we're here is that we heard you used to give Luke Armitage extra tuition in English, and we wondered if you could tell us anything about him.'

'I'm not sure I can tell you anything about him, but, yes, I used to tutor Luke.' Lauren sat on the small sofa with her legs tucked under her, cup held in both hands. She blew on the tea. 'He was so far ahead of the rest of his class he must have been bored silly at school. He was far ahead of me most of the time.' She raised her hand and flicked some troublesome locks of hair out of her face.

'That good?'

'Well, his enthusiasm made up for what he lacked in formal training.'

'I gather he was a talented writer, too.'

'Very. Again, he needed discipline, but he was young, raw. He'd have gone far if . . . if . . .' She held her cup in one hand and rubbed her sleeve across her eyes. 'I'm sorry,' she said. 'I just can't get over it. Luke. Dead. Such a waste.'

Annie passed her a tissue from the box on one of the bookshelves. 'Thank you,' she said, then blew her nose. She shifted on the sofa and Banks noticed her feet were bare and her toenails painted red.

'I know it's hard to accept,' said Banks, 'but I'm sure you can understand why we need to know as much about him as possible.'

'Yes, of course. Though, as I said, I don't see how I can tell you much.'

'Alastair Ford said you're the kind who listens to people's problems.'

She snorted. 'Alastair! He was probably trying to say I'm a prying bitch. Alastair runs a mile if anyone comes within vague hailing distance of whatever warped emotions he might possess.'

Banks had got the same impression himself, though he wouldn't have put it in quite those words. On early impressions, Lauren Anderson was turning out to be perhaps the most *normal* friend Luke had had. But the competition – Ford and Wells – wasn't very stiff.

'Did Luke ever talk about himself?'

'Not much,' said Lauren. 'He could be very closed, could Luke.'

'Sometimes?'

'Sometimes he might let his guard drop a little, yes.'

'And what did he talk about then?'

'Oh, the usual. School. His parents.'

'What did he say about them?'

'He hated school. Not only were most things boring for him, but he didn't like the discipline, the formality.'

Banks thought of the boys who had tormented Luke in the market square. 'What about bullying?'

'Yes, that too. But it wasn't serious. I mean, Luke was never beaten up or anything.'

'What was it, then?'

'Mostly teasing. Name-calling. A bit of jostling. Oh, I'm not saying he wasn't hurt by it. He was very sensitive. But he could handle it, in a way.'

'What do you mean?'

'It didn't really bother him. I mean, he knew the boys who were doing it were morons, that they couldn't help themselves. And he knew they were doing it because he was different.'

'Superior?'

'No, I don't think Luke ever believed himself to be superior to anyone else. He just knew he was different.'

'What did he have to say about his parents?'

Lauren paused for a moment before answering. 'It was very private,' she said.

Annie leaned forward. 'Ms Anderson,' she said. 'Luke's dead.'

'Yes. Yes, I know.'

'And we need to know everything.'

'But you surely can't think his parents had anything to do with his death?'

'What did he say about them?'

Lauren paused, then went on. 'Not much. It was clear he wasn't very happy at home. He said he loved his mother, but he gave the impression that he didn't get along with his stepfather.'

Banks could well imagine it. Martin Armitage was a physical, dominating presence, used to getting his own way, and his interests seemed worlds away from those of his stepson. 'Did you get the impression that his step-father abused him in any way?' he asked.

'Good Lord, no,' said Lauren. 'Nobody ever beat him or abused him in any way. It was just . . . they were so different. They'd nothing in common. I mean, Luke couldn't care less about football, for a start.'

'What was he going to do about his problems?'

'Nothing. What could he do? He was only fifteen. Maybe he'd have left home in a year or so, but we'll never know now, will we? For the time being he had to put up with it.'

'Kids put up with a lot worse,' said Banks.

'Indeed they do. The family was well off and Luke never lacked for material comforts. I'm sure that both his mother and his stepfather loved him very much. He was a sensitive, creative boy with a boorish stepfather and an empty-headed mother.'

Banks wouldn't have said Robin Armitage was empty-headed, but perhaps Lauren was making the sort of assumption people often make about models. 'What about Neil Byrd?' Banks went on. 'Did Luke ever talk about him?'

'Hardly ever. He got very emotional when the subject came up. Angry, even. Luke had a lot of unresolved issues. You just knew to back away.'

'Can you explain?'

Lauren's brow furrowed. 'I think he was angry because he never knew his father. Angry because Neil Byrd abandoned him when he was just a baby and then went and committed suicide. Can you imagine how that would make you feel? You don't even mean enough to your father for him to stay alive and watch you grow up.'

'Was there anything in particular that might have been bothering him recently, anything he might have mentioned to you?'

'No. The last time I saw him, at the end of term, he was excited about the summer holidays. I assigned him some reading.'

'*A Portrait of the Artist as a Young Man* and *Crime and Punishment*?'

Her eyes widened. 'Those were two of the books. How do you know that?'

'It doesn't matter,' said Banks. 'How did you go about tutoring him?'

'Usually I'd assign him some reading, maybe a novel or some poetry, and then we'd meet here and discuss it. Often we'd move out from there and discuss painting, history, Greek and Roman mythology. He was very advanced when it came to understanding literature. And he had an insatiable appetite for it.'

'Advanced enough for Rimbaud, Baudelaire. Verlaine?'

'Rimbaud was a mere boy himself. And young teens are often attracted to Baudelaire.'

'Le Poëte se fait voyant par un long, immense et raisonné dérèglement de tous les sens,' Banks quoted, in an accent he hoped wasn't too incomprehensible. 'Does that mean anything to you?'

'Why, of course. It's Rimbaud's description of the method he used to make himself a *seer*. "A total disordering of all the senses."'

'It was written on Luke's bedroom wall. Did it involve taking drugs?'

'Not that I know of. Not in Luke's case, anyway. It was

about opening oneself to experience of all kinds. To be quite honest, I didn't approve of Luke's fascination with Rimbaud. In so many cases like that it's a fascination with the romantic ideal of the tortured boy-poet, not with the work itself.'

Not wanting to get lost in the realms of literary criticism, Banks moved on. 'You felt very close to Luke, am I right?'

'In a way, I suppose. If you really *could* be close to him. He was slippery, chameleon-like, often moody, quiet and withdrawn. But I liked him and I believed in his talent, if that's what you mean.'

'If Luke had come to you for help, would you have given it?'

'That depends on the circumstances.'

'If he was running away from home, for example.'

'I'd do all I could to discourage him.'

'That sounds like the official line.'

'It's the one I'd follow.'

'You wouldn't harbour him?'

'Of course not.'

'Because we don't know where he went the day he disappeared. Not after about five-thirty, anyway. But he was last seen walking north on Market Street. That would eventually have brought him to your neighbourhood, wouldn't it?'

'Yes, but . . . I mean . . . why would he come here?'

'Maybe he trusted you, needed your help with something.'

'I can't imagine what.'

'When were the two of you next due to meet?'

'Not until next term. I'm going home next week for the rest of the holidays. My father's not been well lately and my mother's finding it hard to cope.'

'I'm sorry to hear that. Where's home?'

'South Wales. Tenby. A sleepy little place, but it's by the sea, lots of cliffs to walk on and think.'

'Are you sure Luke never came to see you the Monday before last?'

'Of course I'm sure. He had no reason to.'

'You were only his tutor, right?'

Lauren stood up and anger flashed in her eyes. 'What do you mean? What are you trying to insinuate?'

Banks held his hand up. 'Whoa. Wait a minute. I was only thinking that he might have considered you as a friend and mentor, someone he could go to if he was in trouble.'

'Well, he didn't. Look, as it happens, I wasn't even home the Monday before last.'

'Where were you?'

'Visiting my brother, Vernon.'

'And where does Vernon live?'

'Harrogate.'

'What time did you leave?'

'About five. Shortly after.'

'And what time did you get back?'

'I didn't. As a matter of fact, I had a bit too much to drink. Too much to risk driving, at any rate. So I slept on Vernon's sofa. I didn't come back here until about lunchtime on Tuesday.'

Banks glanced at Annie, who put her notebook aside and pulled the artist's impression out of her briefcase. 'Have you ever seen this girl, Ms Anderson?' she asked. 'Think carefully.'

Lauren studied the drawing and shook her head. 'No. I've seen the look, but the face isn't familiar.'

'Not someone from school?'

'If she is, I don't recognize her.'

'We think she might have been Luke's girlfriend,' Banks said. 'And we're trying to find her.'

Lauren shot Banks a glance. '*Girlfriend?* But Luke didn't have a girlfriend.'

'How do you know? You said he didn't tell you everything.'

She fingered the collar of her V-neck. 'But . . . but I'd have *known*.'

'I can't see how,' said Banks. 'What about Rose Barlow?'

'What about her?'

'I've heard she and Luke were pretty friendly.'

'Who told you that?'

'Were they?'

'I believe they went out once or twice earlier this year. Rose Barlow isn't anywhere near Luke's league. She's strictly a plodder.'

'So it didn't last.'

'Not to my knowledge. Though, as you pointed out, I wouldn't necessarily be the one to know.'

Banks and Annie stood up to leave. Lauren walked to the door with them.

'Thanks for your time,' Banks said. 'And if you do remember anything else, you'll let us know, won't you?'

'Yes, of course. Anything I can do,' Lauren said. 'I do hope you catch whoever did this. Luke had such a promising future ahead of him.'

'Don't worry,' said Banks, with more confidence than he felt. 'We will.'

●

Ever since she had rung Banks, Michelle had thought of confronting Shaw with what she had discovered. It would have been easy enough for any authorized person to remove the notebooks and actions from their file boxes. Michelle could have done it herself, so who would think to question an officer of Shaw's rank? Certainly not Mrs Metcalfe.

But still she resisted a direct approach. The thing was, she *had* to be certain. Once something like that was out in the open, there was no taking it back. She had been down in the archives again first thing that morning on another fruitless search, which had at least convinced her that the objects she was looking for were missing. And they *should* have been there.

What she needed to do now was think. Think about what it all meant. She couldn't do that in the station with Shaw wandering around the place, so she decided to drive over to the Hazels estate and walk Graham's route again.

She parked in front of the row of shops opposite the estate and stood for a moment enjoying the feel of the sun on her hair. She looked at the newsagent's shop, now run by Mrs Walker. That was where it had all begun. On a whim, Michelle entered the shop and found the sturdy, grey-haired old lady arranging newspapers on the counter.

'Yes, love,' the woman said with a smile. 'What can I do for you?'

'Are you Mrs Walker?'

'Indeed I am.'

'I don't know if you can do anything,' said Michelle, presenting her warrant card, 'but you might have heard we found some bones not long ago and—'

'The lad who used to work here?'

'Yes, that's right.'

'I read about it. Terrible business.'

'It is.'

'But I don't see how I can help you. It was before my time.'

'When did you come here?'

'My husband and I bought the shop in the autumn of 1966.'

'Did you buy it from Mr Bradford, the previous owner?'

'As far as I know we did. The estate agent handled all the details, along with my husband, of course, bless his soul.'

'Mr Walker is deceased?'

'A good ten years now.'

'I'm sorry.'

'No need to be. He went just like that. Never felt a thing. Brain aneurysm. We had a good life together, and I'm well provided for.' She looked around the shop. 'I can't say it's exactly a goldmine, but it's a living. Hard work, too. People say I should retire, sell up, but what would I do with my time?'

'Did you know Graham Marshall at all?'

'No. We moved here from Spalding, so we didn't know anyone at first. We'd been looking for a nice little newsagent's shop and this one came on the market at the right price. Good timing, too, what with the new town development starting in 1967, shortly after we got here.'

'But you did meet Mr Bradford?'

'Oh, yes. He was very helpful during the transition. Showed us the ropes and everything.'

'What was he like?'

'I can't say I knew him well. My husband had most dealings with him. But he seemed all right. Pleasant enough. A bit abrupt, maybe. A bit stiff and military in his bearing. I remember he was something important during the war, a member of some special unit or other in Burma. But he was helpful.'

'Did you hear from him after you took over?'

'No.'

'Did he ever mention Graham?'

'Oh, yes. That's why he left. Partly, at any rate. He said his heart hadn't been in the business since the boy disappeared, so he wanted to move away and try to forget.'

'Do you know where he moved to?'

'The north, or so he said. Carlisle.'

'That's certainly far enough away.'

'Yes.'

'I don't suppose you had a forwarding address, did you?'

'Didn't you know? Mr Bradford died. Killed in a burglary not weeks after he moved. Tragic, it was. In all the local papers at the time.'

'Indeed?' said Michelle, curious. 'No, I didn't know.' It probably wasn't relevant to her enquiry, but it was suspicious. One of the last people to see Graham alive had, himself, been killed.

Michelle thanked Mrs Walker and went back outside. She crossed the road and started walking along Hazel Crescent, the same route Graham would have taken all those years ago. It was an early morning in August 1965, she remembered; the sun was just up, but an overcast sky made it still fairly dark. Everybody was sleeping off Saturday night, and the church-goers were not even up yet. Lights would have been on in one or two windows, perhaps – the insomniacs and chronic early risers – but nobody had seen anything.

She reached Wilmer Road at the far end of the estate. Even now, years later and in mid-morning, there wasn't much traffic, and most of it was for the DIY centre, which hadn't existed back in 1965. Michelle was almost certain that Graham *knew* his attacker and that he got in the car willingly, taking his canvas bag of papers with him. If someone had tried to force him into a car, he would have dropped the papers and struggled, and the abductor was unlikely to stick around and pick them up.

But how could Graham be persuaded to go somewhere without finishing his paper round? A family emergency, perhaps? Michelle didn't think so. His family only lived a few yards away, back on the estate; he could have walked there in less than a minute. There was no doubt that fourteen-year-old kids could act irresponsibly, so maybe he did just that and skived off somewhere for some reason.

As Michelle stood in the street watching the people come and go from the DIY centre, she thought again about the missing notebooks and actions and was struck by a notion so obvious she could have kicked herself for not seeing it earlier.

That the missing notebooks were Detective Superintendent Shaw's disturbed her for a different reason now she realized what she should have seen the moment she discovered they were missing. Shaw was a mere DC, a junior, on the case, so what on earth could he have had to hide? He had no power; he wasn't in charge, and he certainly hadn't assigned the actions. He had simply been along taking notes of Detective Inspector Reg Proctor's interviews; that was all.

Michelle had focused on Shaw mostly because she disliked him and resented the way he had been treating her, but when it came right down to it, the person in charge of the case, the one who might possibly have had the most to hide in the event of a future investigation was not Shaw but that legend of the local constabulary: Detective Superintendent John Harris.

Thinking about Jet Harris, and what he might possibly have had to hide, Michelle walked back to where she had left her car parked in front of the shops. Perhaps she was a little distracted by her thoughts, and perhaps she didn't pay as much attention as she usually did to crossing the road, but on the other hand, perhaps the beige van with the tinted windows really *did* start up as she approached, and perhaps the driver really *did* put his foot on the accelerator when she stepped into the road.

Either way, she saw it coming – fast – and just had time to jump out of the way. The side of the van brushed against her hip as she stumbled and fell face forward onto the warm tarmac, putting out her arms to break her fall. Another car honked and swerved around her and a woman across the street came over to help her to her feet. By the time Michelle realized what was happening, the van was out of sight. One thing she did remember, though: the number plate was so covered in mud it was impossible to read.

'Honestly,' the woman said, helping Michelle to the other side. 'Some drivers. I don't know what the place is coming to, I really don't. Are you all right, love?'

'Yes,' said Michelle, dusting herself off. 'Yes, I'm fine, thanks very much. Just a bit shaken up.' And she was still trembling when she got in her own car. She gripped the steering wheel tightly to steady herself, took several deep breaths and waited until her heart rate slowed to normal before she set off back to the station.

•

'Can you manage by yourself for a day or so?' Banks asked Annie over a lunchtime pint in the Queen's Arms. Like most of the pubs in the area since the outbreak of foot and mouth it was half-empty, and even the jukebox and video machines were mercifully silent. One of the local farmers, who had already had too much to drink, stood at the bar fulminating against the government's mishandling of the outbreak to the landlord, Cyril, who gave a polite grunt of agreement every now and then. Everybody was suffering: not only the farmers, but the pub landlords, bed-and-breakfast owners, local trades-men, butcher, baker and candlestick-maker, old Uncle Tom Cobbleigh and all. And, unlike the farmers, they didn't get any compensation from the government. Only a week or so ago the owner of a walking-gear shop in Helmthorpe had committed suicide because his business had gone down the tubes.

Annie put her glass down. 'Course I can,' she said. 'What's up?'

'It's Graham Marshall's funeral tomorrow. There'll likely be some old friends around. I'd like to go down this evening.'

'No problem. Have you asked the boss?'

'Detective Superintendent Gristhorpe has given me permission to be absent from school for two days. I just wanted to clear it with you before taking off.'

'I've got plenty to keep me occupied. Talking about school, you told me you weren't satisfied with your Alastair Ford interview yesterday.'

Banks lit a cigarette. 'No,' he said. 'No, I'm not. Not at all.'

'So is he a suspect?'

'I don't know. Maybe his coming hot on the heels of

Norman Wells was just a bit too much for me. His house is very isolated, which makes it a good place to keep someone prisoner, or kill someone and dump the body in the middle of the night without any neighbours noticing. But then you could probably get away with murder in the town centre, too, given most people's powers of observation and unwillingness to get involved.'

'Except for the CCTV.'

'And a damn lot of good that's done us. Anyway, Ford is a solitary. He jealously protects his privacy, probably feels superior to people who are content to make small talk and share their opinions. He *may* be homosexual – there was something distinctly odd about the way he responded to my question about boyfriends – but even that doesn't make him a suspect. We don't know the motive for Luke's murder, and according to Dr Glendenning there was no evidence of sexual assault, although a few days in the water might have taken care of any traces of that. You know, Annie, the more I think about it, the more the kidnapping *seems* as if it was just a smokescreen, but oddly enough it might turn out to be the most important thing.'

Annie frowned. 'What do you mean?'

'I mean, why? If somebody just wanted Luke dead, whatever the reason, then why come up with this elaborate and iffy kidnapping scheme and increase the risk of getting caught?'

'Money?'

'Well, yes, but you told me yourself whoever it was set his sights remarkably low. It wasn't a professional job.'

'That did bother me. It's what made me think he *knew* about the Armitages' finances. I mean, they could certainly manage ten grand to get Luke back, but hardly more, at least not at such short notice.'

'But Luke was already dead.'

'Yes. Perhaps he tried to escape.'

'Perhaps. Or maybe we need to look a lot closer to home.'

'The parents?'

'It's possible, isn't it?' Banks said. 'Maybe we've been looking at this all wrong. Maybe Martin Armitage killed Luke and set up the elaborate hoax of a kidnapping just to put us off the scent.'

'Martin?'

'Why not? He was gone for two hours the evening Luke disappeared, according to his statement, just driving around, or so he says. Maybe he found Luke and they had an argument and Luke ended up dead. An accident, even. Excessive roughness. That wouldn't be unusual for Martin Armitage. According to Lauren Anderson and everything you've told me, Luke had a difficult relationship with his stepfather. Armitage is the antithesis of Neil Byrd in many ways. Byrd was sensitive, creative, artistic, and he also had many of the problems that seem to come with that territory: drugs, drink, an addictive personality, need for oblivion, experimentation, self-absorption, mood swings, depression. It can't have been easy being Neil Byrd, as his songs tell us so many times, but he was aiming at some kind of exalted spiritual state, some sort of transcendence, and he believed he caught glimpses of it from time to time. They gave him enough faith to keep going, for a while, at least. I often thought some of the songs were also a cry for help, and Luke's songs echo that in a weird way.'

'And Martin Armitage?'

'Physical, rational, powerful, clean living. Football was his life. It got him out of the slums and made him a national figure. It also made him rich. I dare say he's had his share of ale, but I doubt he tried anything more experimental. I don't think he has the capability to understand or tolerate the artistic temperament his stepson seems to have inherited. Probably the kind who associates artistic interests with homosexuality. I'm sure he tried to be a loving father, treated the lad as his own, but Luke had Neil Byrd's genes.'

'And Robin?'

'Now, there's an interesting one,' Banks said. 'You tell me. You've seen more of her than I have.'

'She clearly had a wild youth. Sex, drugs, rock and roll. Early fame and fortune often seem to send people over the top. But, however she did it, she came through, and with a son. I'd say she's tougher than she looks, and no doubt she loved Luke but had no more idea how to deal with his problems than her husband had. I think boys like Luke invent secret worlds to exclude adults and protect themselves, even from their contemporaries. He probably spent most of his time in his room reading, writing or recording his songs. That black room.'

'Do you think he had ambitions to follow in his father's footsteps?'

'Musically, perhaps. But I think his attitude towards his father was very complex and ambiguous. A mix of admiration and anger at abandonment.'

'None of this seems to transform into a motive, though, does it?' said Banks. He stubbed out his cigarette. 'What about Josie and Calvin Batty?'

'As suspects?'

'In general.'

'Josie is the only person we've talked to so far who says she saw Luke with the tattooed girl.'

'Norman Wells recognized the description.'

'Yes,' Annie pointed out. 'But not in connection with Luke. I'm not saying we stop looking for her, just that we mustn't pin all our hopes on her. We still have to keep an open mind on this one.'

'Agreed.'

'By the way, Winsome ran a check on all cars reported stolen in the Eastvale area the night Luke disappeared. There are two possibilities, one abandoned near Hawes, in Wensleydale, and the other in Richmond.'

'Then we'd better have Stefan's team check them both for any signs of blood.'

Annie made a note. 'Okay.'

The server brought their lunches over: a salad sandwich for Annie and lasagne and chips for Banks. He didn't usually like pub lasagne – it was too soupy – but Cyril's wife Glenys made a good one.

'Talking about cars,' Banks said, after pausing for a few mouthfuls, 'how are forensics coming on with Norman Wells's?'

'Stefan called in a couple of hours ago. Nothing yet. Do you really expect anything?'

'Maybe not. But it's got to be done.'

'Do you think we should have detained him?'

Banks took a sip of beer before answering. 'We've nothing to hold him on,' he said. 'And he does have his business to run. Besides, I don't think Mr Wells is going anywhere.'

'What about Lauren Anderson?'

'Methinks the lady did protest too much.'

'What do you mean?'

'I don't know. Just that her reaction to a simple question seemed extreme.'

'She did sound awfully close to Luke. Emotionally, I mean.'

'But she does have an alibi. Ask Winsome to check with the brother, Vernon, just to be certain, but I can't imagine she'd risk lying about that. And it was a man's voice on the ransom call.'

'I'm not suggesting she *did* it – she certainly seemed genuine in her regard for him – just that she might know more than she's letting on about what Luke was up to.'

'You're right,' said Banks. 'We shouldn't rule her out. Maybe you could get Winsome and young Kevin to run background checks on everyone we know who was connected with Luke, and that includes the Battys, Alastair Ford, Lauren Anderson and the mystery girl, if we ever find her.'

'What about Rose Barlow?'

'I don't know,' Banks said. 'We should have a word with her, though it seems that whatever went on between her and Luke ended months ago.'

'What about forensic checks on Ford's house and the Anderson woman's?'

Banks shook his head. 'We can't afford to be sending expensive forensic teams to everyone's house. With Wells we had good reason – his history, for a start. Besides, we know Luke has been in Lauren Anderson's house.'

'But if there's blood . . .?'

'We still can't justify the expense at this point.'

'And Alastair Ford?'

'Check into his background first. We'll keep that one up our sleeves in case we need it.'

'You'll stay in touch?'

'I'll leave my mobile on all the time. I'm not deserting you, Annie.' Banks still couldn't help feeling a little guilty – and it wasn't because he was leaving the case to Annie, but because he would be seeing Michelle again, and the idea appealed to him.

Annie touched his sleeve. 'I know you're not. Don't think I'm so insensitive as not to know how hard it is for you, them finding Graham Marshall's bones and all.' She grinned. 'You go and pay your respects and have a piss-up with your old mates. You'll have a lot to catch up on. When did you last see them?'

'Not since I went to London, when I was eighteen. We just sort of lost touch.'

'I know what you mean. It happens. I don't know anyone I went to school with any more.'

Banks considered telling Annie about Michelle's phone call but decided against it. Why complicate matters? Annie had enough on her plate. Besides, he wasn't sure there was much he could do about Michelle's concerns. If there had been some sort of cover-up, then it would have to be investigated by an outside force, not some maverick from North Yorkshire. Yet a part of him wanted to get involved, wanted to get to the bottom of Graham's death, as well as Luke's. They were linked in his mind in some odd way. Not technically, of course, but two very different boys from very different times had ended up dead before their time, and both had died violently. Banks wanted to know why, what it was about these two children that had attracted such cruel fates.

14

Early in the afternoon Annie showed the artist's impression of the mystery girl around the Swainsdale Centre and the bus station again. At the end of an hour she was beginning to wonder whether the girl existed, or whether she was just a figment of Josie Batty's puritan imagination.

She walked along York Road enjoying the sunshine, glancing in the shop windows as she walked. A stylish red leather jacket caught her eye in one of the more exclusive clothes shops, but she knew it would be way out of her price range. Even so, she went in and enquired. It was.

The market square was clogged with wandering tourists and cars trying to find parking space. A large group of Japanese, along with their tour guide and translator, stood gazing up at the front of the Norman church, where several sculpted figures of saints were carved in a row high over the doors. Some of the tourists were catching the moment on videotape, though Annie didn't remember the stone saints ever doing the can-can or anything that even remotely involved movement.

One of the cars, she noticed – partly because it screeched straight into a disabled parking space and almost hit a young woman – was Martin Armitage's BMW. What the hell was he doing here? And what the hell was he doing in a disabled parking spot? Maybe she should arrange for him to get towed? But when she saw him jump out of the car, slam the door and head for the shops built into the side of the church, she knew what was going on.

Annie pushed her way through the tourist crowd by the church and got there just in time to see Armitage disappearing down the stairs into Norman's Used Books. *Shit*. She dashed down right behind him, but he already had Wells by the throat and judging by the blood pouring from the little man's nose had punched him at least once. Wells was whimpering and trying to wriggle free. The bookshop was as dank as ever, but the day's heat had permeated enough to make the air humid. Annie felt clammy the moment she entered. Familiar, the cat, was screeching and hissing somewhere in the dark recesses of the cavern.

'Mr Armitage!' Annie called out as she grabbed his arm. 'Martin! Stop it. This won't get you anywhere.'

Armitage shook her off as if she were a troublesome insect. 'This pervert killed my son,' he said. 'If you lot can't do it, I'll get a bloody confession, even if I have to shake it out of him.' As if to prove his point, he started to shake Wells again and slap him back and forth across the face. Blood and saliva dribbled from Wells's slack jaw.

Annie tried to wedge herself between them, knocking over a teetering pile of books as she did so. A cloud of dust rose up and the cat screeched even louder. Armitage was strong. He pushed Annie and she staggered back into a table. It broke and more books slid to the floor. She almost joined them there.

Gathering all her strength, Annie made one more attempt, launching herself towards the struggling men in the cramped space, but Armitage saw her coming and swung his fist beyond Wells's head, connecting directly with Annie's mouth. The blow stunned her and she fell back again, in pain this time, and put her hand to her mouth. It came away covered in blood.

Armitage was still shaking Wells and Annie feared the bookseller was going to choke to death, if he didn't have a heart attack first. Armitage was paying her no mind now, and she managed to edge behind him to the door and dash up the steps. The police station was only yards away, across Market Street, and nobody asked her any questions when she rushed in the front door, blood streaming from her mouth.

Two burly PCs followed her back to the shop, and it took both of them to subdue Armitage, wrecking most of the place in the process. There were old books all over the floor, broken tables and clouds of dust in the air by the time they got the handcuffs on him and marched him outside up the stairs. Wells was bleeding, clutching his chest and looking distinctly unwell. Annie got his arm around her shoulder and helped him stumble up into the fresh air. Hearing the fracas, the Japanese tourists turned away from the church facade and pointed their camcorders at the five of them. Well, Annie thought, digging for a handkerchief deep in her purse, at least we're bloody *moving*.

•

It had been a while since Banks had spent much time in his office, and the *Dalesman* calendar was still open at July's photo of Skidby Windmill on the edge of the Yorkshire Wolds. He had the radio tuned in to Radio 3 and was listening to an orchestral concert of music by Holst, Haydn and Vaughan Williams as he whittled away at the pile of paperwork on his desk. He had just settled

into the *Lento Moderato* of Vaughan Williams's 'Pastoral'
Symphony and yet another memo on cost-effectiveness,
when his phone rang.

'Alan, it's Stefan.'

'Good news, I hope?'

'Depends on how you look at it. Your man Norman
Wells is clean, as far as we can tell. We were pretty
thorough, and I'm sure if there'd been any traces of Luke
Armitage in his car or house we'd have found something.'

'You didn't?'

'Nada.'

'Okay, well I suppose that shows us where *not* to concentrate our attention. Anything positive?'

'The blood on the drystone wall.'

'I remember.'

'There was enough for DNA analysis. It's definitely
human, and it doesn't match the victim's.'

Banks whistled. 'So there's a good chance it could
belong to whoever dropped Luke over the wall?'

'A pretty good chance, yes. But don't get your hopes up
too high. It *could* belong to anyone.'

'But you'll be able to match it with any samples we can
get?'

'Of course.'

'Okay. Thanks, Stefan.'

'My pleasure.'

Banks wondered whom he should ask to provide DNA
samples. Norman Wells, of course, even though the
forensic search of his house had turned up nothing
incriminating. Alastair Ford, perhaps, just because he
lived in a remote cottage and was connected to Luke
though the violin lessons. And because he was weird.
Lauren Anderson, because she gave Luke English tuition

after school hours and seemed to be close to him. Who else? Josie and Calvin Batty, perhaps. And the parents, Martin and Robin. They'd no doubt kick up a holy fuss and run crying to the chief constable, but that couldn't be helped. DNA could be processed in two or three days now, but it was a very expensive proposition. Banks would just have to see how much he could get away with.

Then there was the mystery girl, of course. They would definitely need a sample from her if they ever found her, if she existed.

No sooner had the *Moderato Pesante* begun than his phone rang again. This time it was the duty constable. Someone to see him in connection with Luke Armitage. A young woman.

'Send her up,' said Banks, wondering if *this* could be the mystery woman. She must know that she was wanted by now, and if she did, then her failure to show up was suspicious in itself.

A minute or so later a uniformed constable tapped on Banks's office door and ushered in the girl. Banks recognized Rose Barlow immediately. She strutted into his office all blue-jeaned leg, blonde hair and attitude. Her visit would save him or Annie the trouble of seeking her out.

'I'm Rose,' she said. 'Rose Barlow. You don't remember me, do you?'

'I know who you are,' said Banks. 'What can I do for you?'

Rose carried on snooping around the office, taking books off the shelf and rifling through the pages, putting them back, adjusting the calendar so it was square with the filing cabinet. She wore a short, sleeveless top so that, Banks presumed, the rose tattoo on her upper left arm and the collection of jewellery dangling from her navel showed to best advantage.

'It's more a matter of what *I* can do for *you*,' she said, sitting down and giving him what he was sure she thought of as an enigmatic look. It came across as vacant. She must be a handful for her father, he thought. It seemed so often the case that the daughters of authority figures – vicars, headmasters, chief constables – were the first to rebel, and he could only think himself lucky that Tracy, a mere chief inspector's daughter, seemed to have a good head on her shoulders. She must have got it from her mother, Banks thought, then veered away from thoughts of Sandra, showing now, no doubt, glowing with the joys of coming motherhood. Well, good luck to her and Sean; they'd need it.

'And what can you do for me?' Banks asked, deciding to let her get to her reason for coming before asking questions of his own.

She turned her nose up at the radio. 'What's that?'

'Vaughan Williams.'

'It's boring.'

'Sorry you don't like it. What can you do for me?'

'Do you know who killed Luke?'

'I thought you could do something for me?'

'Spoilsport. Why won't you tell me?'

Banks sighed. 'Rose. Miss Barlow. If we'd found Luke's killer you'd have read about it in the papers by now. Now, tell me what you came to say. I'm busy.'

Rose didn't like that, and Banks realized that letting his impatience show was a mistake. She probably got that sort of response from her father all the time, the way Tracy and Brian had often heard the same thing from Banks. Rose craved attention because she didn't feel she got enough. Banks wondered if his children felt the same way. Did Tracy try so hard and do so well academically because she wanted attention? Did Brian stand up on stage in front of an audience night after night and bare his soul because he craved it, too? And had Luke Armitage craved the same thing? Perhaps. In his children's cases, though, the response to the need was a pretty healthy, creative one. Banks wasn't sure to what lengths Rose Barlow might go to get the attention *she* felt she deserved.

'I'm sorry,' he went on, 'but I'm sure you understand that we're in a hurry to find out who killed Luke, and if you know anything that might help us . . . '

Rose leaned forward, her eyes wide. 'Why? Do you think he's going to kill someone else? Do you think it's a serial killer?'

'We've no reason to think anything of the sort.'

'Then relax, why don't you?'

Banks felt his back teeth grinding as he tried to smile.

'Anyway,' Rose went on, 'I was going to tell you. Have you talked to Miss Anderson yet?'

'Lauren Anderson? Yes.'

A mischievous glint lit Rose's eyes. 'And did she tell you about her and Luke?'

'She told us she gave him extra tuition in English because he was ahead of the rest of the class.'

Rose laughed. '*Extra tuition*. That's a good one. And did she tell you where she gave this tuition?'

'At her house.'

Rose leaned back and folded her arms. 'Exactly.'

'So?'

'Oh, come on. Surely you can't be *that* naive? Do I have to spell it out for you?'

'I'm not sure what you're getting at,' said Banks,

who was perfectly sure but wanted her to get there by herself.

'They were having it off, weren't they?'

'You know that for a fact?'

'Stands to reason.'

'Why?'

'She's nothing but a slut, that Miss Anderson, and a cradle-snatcher.'

'What makes you say that?'

'Well, she didn't give anybody *else* private tuition in her home, did she?'

'I don't know,' said Banks.

'Well she *didn't*.'

'Tell me, Rose,' Banks said, wishing he could have a cigarette, 'what did you think of Luke? You knew him, didn't you?'

'We were in the same class, yes.'

'Did you like him?'

Rose twirled some strands of hair. 'He was all right, I suppose.'

'Pretty cool, huh?'

'*Cool!* More like sad, if you ask me.'

'Why?'

'He never talked to anybody – except high and mighty Miss Anderson, of course. It's like he was better than the rest of us.'

'Maybe he was shy.'

'Just because he had a famous father. Well, I think his father's music sucks, and he couldn't have been much of a father if he went and killed himself, could he? He was nothing but a drug addict.'

Nice line in compassion, Rose, Banks thought, but he didn't bother voicing his opinion. 'So you didn't like Luke?'

'I told you. He was all right. Just a bit weird.'

'But he was pretty good-looking, wasn't he?'

Rose made a face. 'Ugh! I wouldn't have gone out with him if he was the last boy on earth.'

'I don't think you're telling me the truth, Rose, are you?'

'What do you mean?'

'You know very well what I mean. You and Luke. Earlier this year.'

'Who told you that?'

'Never you mind. How far did it go?'

'Go? That's a laugh. It didn't go anywhere.'

'But you wanted it to, didn't you?'

Rose twisted in her chair. 'He thought he was better than the rest of us.'

'So why did you spend time talking to him?'

'I don't know. Just . . . I mean, he was different. The other boys, they only want one thing.'

'And Luke didn't?'

'I never got to find out, did I? We just talked.'

'What about?'

'Music and stuff.'

'You never actually went out together?'

'No. I mean, we went to McDonald's a couple of times after school, but that's all.'

'Rose, do you have any evidence at all to support your accusation that Luke and Lauren Anderson were having an affair?'

'If you mean was I watching at her window, then no. But it's obvious, isn't it? Why else would she spend her spare time with someone like him?'

'But *you* spent time with him.'

'Yeah. Well . . . that was different.'

'Didn't you try to be nice to him, to befriend him, when you talked to him in the hallways and the playground, and when you went to McDonald's with him?'

Rose looked away and continued twirling her hair around her fingers. 'Of course I did.'

'And what happened?'

'Nothing. He just sort of . . . like he got *bored* with me or something. Like I didn't read all those stupid books he was always carrying around, and I didn't listen to the same lousy music. I wasn't good enough for him. He was a snob. Above the rest of us.'

'And because of this you assumed he was having sexual relations with a teacher. That's a bit of a far stretch, isn't it?'

'*You* didn't see them together.'

'Did you see them kissing, touching, holding hands?'

'Of course not. They were too careful to do anything like that in public, weren't they?'

'What then?'

'The way they looked at each other. The way she always left him alone in class. The way they talked. The way he made her laugh.'

'You were just jealous, weren't you, Rose? That's why you're saying all this. Because you couldn't get along with Luke, but Miss Anderson could.'

'I was *not* jealous! Certainly not of that ugly old bitch.'

For a moment, Banks wondered if there was anything in what Rose Barlow was telling him other than sour grapes. It may have been innocent, a true teacher–pupil relationship, but Banks had enough experience to know that anything involving two people of the opposite sex – or the same sex for that matter – in close proximity could turn into something sexual, no matter what the difference in their ages. He had also read about such things in the newspapers. He would keep an open mind and have another talk with Lauren Anderson when he got back from Peterborough, push her a little harder and see if any cracks showed.

'What do you think of Miss Anderson?' he asked Rose.

'She's all right, I suppose.'

'You just called her an ugly old bitch.'

'Well . . . I didn't mean . . . I was angry . . . I mean she's okay as a teacher. All right?'

'Do you get on well with her in class?'

'Okay.'

'So if I ask any of the other pupils in the class they'd tell me that you and Miss Anderson get along just fine?'

Rose reddened. 'She picks on me sometimes. She put me in detention once.'

'What for?'

'Not reading some stupid Shakespeare play. So I was reading a magazine under the desk. So what? I can't be bothered with all that boring *English* stuff.'

'So you had a few run-ins with her?'

'Yes. But that's not why I'm here. That's not why I'm telling you what I know.'

'I'm sure it's not, Rose, but you have to admit it does give you a bit of a motive to cause trouble for Miss Anderson, especially if you also tried to get Luke to be *your* boyfriend.'

Rose jumped to her feet. 'Why are you being so horrible to me? I come here to help you and give you important information and you treat *me* like a criminal. I'm going to tell my *father* about you.'

Banks couldn't help smiling. 'It wouldn't be the first time I've been reported to the head teacher,' he said.

Before Rose could respond, two things happened in quick succession. First, there came an urgent tap at his door and Annie Cabbot walked in, a handkerchief to her mouth covered with what looked like blood. But before Annie could speak, Kevin Templeton poked his head around the door behind her, his gaze resting on Rose for a few seconds too long for her comfort, and said to Banks, 'Sorry to interrupt you, sir, but we think we've got a positive ID on you know who.'

Banks knew who he meant. The mystery girl. So she *did* exist.

'Better than that,' Templeton went on, 'we've got an address.'

•

Michelle discovered from DC Collins that Shaw had gone home after lunch, complaining of a stomach upset. Collins's tone was such as to suggest it might be more a matter of the number of whiskies Shaw had downed at lunch. He had been taking quite a lot of time off lately. At least that left the coast clear for Michelle. She didn't want to see Shaw, especially after what had happened in her flat on Saturday. Sometimes, when she let her guard down, it was him she saw in her imagination, going through her bedside drawers, cutting Melissa's dress in half. It wasn't such a stretch to imagine him driving the beige van that bore down on her as she crossed the road earlier, either; he had been out of the station at the time. And the whiskies? Dutch courage?

It was time to stop idle speculation and follow up on what she had discovered from Mrs Walker. Michelle picked up the telephone and an hour or so later, after a lot of false trails and time wasted on hold, she managed to reach one of the retired Carlisle police officers who had looked into Donald Bradford's death: ex-Detective Sergeant Raymond Scholes, now living out his retirement on the Cumbrian coast.

'I don't know what I can tell you after all this time,' Scholes said. 'Donald Bradford was just unlucky.'

'What happened?'

'Surprised a burglar. Someone broke into his house, and before Bradford could do anything he got beaten so badly he died of his injuries.'

Michelle felt a chill. The same thing might have happened to her on Saturday if she'd been home earlier. 'Ever catch the burglar?' she asked.

'No. He must have taken Bradford by surprise, though.'

'Why do you say that?'

'Because he was a pretty tough customer, himself. *I* wouldn't have fancied tackling him. Way it looks is the burglar must have heard him coming and hid behind the door, then bashed the back of Bradford's head in with a cosh of some kind.'

'You never found a weapon?'

'No.'

'No clues? No prints?'

'Nothing usable.'

'No witnesses?'

'None that we could find.'

'What was taken?'

'Wallet, a few knick-knacks, by the looks of it. Place was a bit of a mess.'

'Did it appear as if someone had been *looking* for something?'

'I never really thought about that. As I say, though, it

was a mess. Turned upside down. Why the sudden interest?'

Michelle told him a little bit about Graham Marshall.

'Yes, I've read about that. Terrible business. I hadn't realized there was a connection.'

'Was Bradford married?'

'No. He lived alone.'

Michelle could sense him pause, as if he was going to add something. 'What?' she asked.

'Oh, it's nothing. Bit of a laugh, really.'

'Tell me anyway.'

'Well, afterwards, you know, we had to have a look around the house and we found . . . well . . . at the time it seemed quite risqué, though by today's standards . . .'

Out with it, man, Michelle found herself thinking. What are you talking about?

'What was it?' she asked.

'Pornographic magazines. A bundle of them. And some blue films. I won't go into detail, but they covered quite a range of perversions.'

Michelle found herself gripping the receiver tighter. 'Including paedophilia?'

'Well, there were some pretty young-looking models involved, I can tell you that. Male and female. Not kiddy porn, though, if that's what you're thinking.'

Michelle supposed there was a distinction to be made. In some ways, once you had pubic hair, breasts and all the rest, you didn't qualify as 'kiddy porn', but you still might only be fourteen years old. Grey area.

'What happened to all this stuff?'

'Destroyed.'

But not before you and your lads had a good look at it, I'll bet, Michelle thought.

'We didn't let anything slip at the time,' he went on, 'because it didn't seem . . . well, the bloke *had* just been killed, after all. There seemed no point in blackening his name with that sort of thing.'

'Understandable,' said Michelle. 'Who claimed the body?'

'Nobody. Mr Bradford had no immediate family. The local authorities took care of everything.'

'Thank you, Mr Scholes,' she said. 'You've been a great help.'

'Think nothing of it.'

Michelle hung up and nibbled the end of her pencil as she thought about what she'd heard. She hadn't come to any conclusions yet, but she had a lot to discuss with Banks when he arrived.

•

PC Flaherty, who had tracked down the mystery girl's address, had been asking around Eastvale College, thinking that a girl who looked like she did must be a student. As it turned out, she wasn't, but her boyfriend was, and one of the people he spoke to remembered seeing her at a college dance. The boyfriend's name was Ryan Milne and the girl was known as Elizabeth Palmer. They lived together in a flat above a hat shop on South Market Street, the direction in which Luke Armitage had been walking when he was last seen.

Annie insisted that she felt well enough to make the call. She was damned, she told Banks, if she was going to be excluded after all the footwork she'd done just because some over-testosteroned lout had punched her in the mouth. It was her pride that hurt more than anything. After she'd cleaned up the wound, it didn't look too bad anyway. Some women, she went on to say, paid a fortune for collagen shots to make themselves look like she did. Banks decided he would make the call with her before setting off for Peterborough. He phoned and arranged to meet Michelle in a city-centre pub at nine o'clock, just to be on the safe side.

Martin Armitage was cooling off in the custody suite and Norman Wells was in Eastvale General Infirmary. No doubt there would be recriminations from Armitage's pal the chief constable, but for the moment he could stay where he was. They could also charge him with assaulting a police officer. After they had visited the mystery girl.

Within twenty minutes of getting the address, Banks and Annie climbed the lino-covered stairs and knocked on the door. The building seemed so silent that Banks couldn't imagine anyone being at home, but only seconds later a young woman opened the door. *The* young woman.

'DCI Banks and DI Cabbot,' Banks said, flashing his card. 'We'd like a word.'

'You'd better come in then.' She stood aside.

One reason why it had taken so long to locate her was obvious to Banks: she didn't look anywhere near as *weird* as the description Josie Batty had given of her, which was hardly surprising when you imagined that most young people probably looked weird to Josie Batty.

The pixyish facial features were right enough, the heart-shaped face, large eyes and small mouth, but that was about all. She was far prettier than Josie Batty had indicated to the police artist, and she had a pale, flawless complexion. She also had the sort of breasts adolescent boys, and many grown men, dream about, and her smooth cleavage was shown to advantage by the laced-up leather waistcoat she wore. The small tattoo on her upper arm was a simple double helix, and there was no sign of body piercing anywhere except the silver spider-web earrings dangling from her ears. Her short black hair was dyed and gelled, but there was nothing weird about that.

The flat was clean and tidy, not a filthy crack house full of sprawled drug-addled kids. It was an old room with a fireplace complete with poker and tongs, which must only have been for show, as a gas fire filled the hearth. Sunlight shone through the half-open window and the sounds and smells of South Market Street drifted up: car exhaust and horns, warm tar, fresh-baked bread, take-away curry and pigeons on the rooftops. Banks and Annie walked around the small room, checking it out, while the girl arranged beanbag cushions for them.

'Elizabeth, is it?' asked Banks.

'I prefer Liz.'

'Okay. Ryan not here?'

'He's got classes.'

'When will he be back?'

'Not till after teatime.'

'What do you do, Liz?'

'I'm a musician.'

'Make a living at it?'

'You know what it's like . . .'

Banks did, having a son in the business. But Brian's success was unusual, and even that hadn't brought in heaps of money. Not even enough for a new car. He moved on. 'You know why we're here, don't you?'

Liz nodded. 'About Luke.'

'You could have come forward and saved us a lot of trouble.'

Liz sat down. 'But I don't know anything.'

'Let us be the judge of that,' said Banks, pausing in his examination of her CD collection. He had noticed a cassette labelled 'Songs from a Black Room' mixed in with a lot of other tapes.

'How was I to know you were looking for me?'

'Don't you read the papers or watch television?' Annie asked.

'Not much. They're boring. Life's too short. Mostly I practise, listen to music or read.'

'What instrument?' Banks asked.

'Keyboards, some woodwinds. Flute, clarinet.'

'Did you study music professionally?'

'No. Just lessons at school.'

'How old are you, Liz?'

'Twenty-one.'

'And Ryan?'

'The same. He's in his last year at college.'

'He a musician, too?'

'Yes.'

'Do you live together?'

'Yes.'

Annie sat down on one of the beanbags, but Banks went to stand by the window, leaning the backs of his thighs against the sill. The room was small and hot and seemed too crowded with three people in it.

'What was your relationship with Luke Armitage?' Annie asked.

'He's . . . he *was* in our band.'

'Along with?'

'Me and Ryan. We don't have a drummer yet.'

'How long have you been together?'

She chewed on her lip and thought for a moment. 'We've only been practising together since earlier this year, after we met Luke. But Ryan and me had been talking about doing something like this for ages.'

'How did you meet Luke?'

'At a concert at the college.'

'What concert?'

'Just a couple of local bands. Back in March.'

'How did Luke get into a college concert?' Banks asked. 'He was only fifteen.'

Liz smiled. 'Not to look at. Or to talk to. Luke was far more mature than his years. You didn't know him.'

'Who was he with?'

'No one. He was by himself, checking out the band.'

'And you just started talking to him?'

'Ryan did, first.'

'And then?'

'Well, we found out he was interested in music, too, looking to get a band together. He had some songs.'

Banks pointed towards the tape. 'Those? "Songs from a Black Room"?'

'No. Those are more recent.'

'How recent?'

'Past month or so.'

'Did you know he was only fifteen?'

'We didn't find out until later.'

'How?'

'He told us.'

'He told you? Just like that?'

'No, not just like that. He had to explain why he couldn't just do what he wanted, you know. He was living with his parents and going to school. He said he was sixteen at first, but then told us later he'd lied because he was worried we'd think he was too young to be in the band.'

'And did you?'

'No way. Not someone with his talent. We might have had a few problems down the line, if things had got that far. Playing licensed premises, you know, stuff like that, but we figured we'd just deal with all that when we got there.'

'What about who his real father was? Did you know that?'

Liz looked away. 'He didn't tell us that until later, either. He didn't seem to want anything to do with Neil Byrd and his legacy.'

'How did you find out?' Banks asked. 'I mean, did Luke just come right out and tell you who his father was?'

'No. No. He didn't like to talk about him. It was something on the radio while he was over here, a review of that new compilation. He got upset about it and then it just sort of slipped out. It made a lot of sense.'

'What do you mean?' Annie asked.

'That voice. His talent. There was *something* about it all that rang a bell.'

'What happened after you knew?'

'What do you mean?'

'Did it make a difference?'

'Not really.'

'Oh, come on, Liz,' said Banks. 'You had Neil Byrd's *son* in your band. You can't expect us to believe that you weren't aware that would make a big difference commercially.'

'Okay,' said Liz. 'Sure, we were all aware of that. But the point is that we weren't *anywhere* commercially at that time. We're still not. We haven't even played in public yet, for crying out loud. And now, without Luke . . . I don't know.'

Banks moved away from the window and sat on a hard-backed chair against the wall. Annie shifted on her beanbag, as if trying to get comfortable. It was the first time he'd seen her look ill at ease in any sort of seat, then he realized she might have hurt herself falling over in the bookshop. She should be at the hospital getting checked out, especially the way on-the-job injury insurance worked these days, but there was no telling her. He didn't blame her; he'd be doing the same himself.

'Who did the singing?' Banks asked.

'Mostly me and Luke.'

'What kind of music do you play?'

'What does it matter?'

'Let's just say I'm interested. Humour me.'

'It's hard to describe,' Liz answered.

'Try.'

She looked at him, as if trying to size up his musical knowledge. 'Well, it's all about the songs, really. We're not trendy and we don't go in for long solos and stuff. It's more . . . have you heard of David Gray?'

'Yes.'

'Beth Orton?'

'Yes.'

If Liz was surprised by Banks's familiarity with contemporary music, she didn't show it. 'Well, we're not *like* them, but that's sort of what we're interested in. Having something to say, and maybe a bit jazzy and bluesy. I play quite a bit of flute as well as organ.'

'Did you know that Luke was taking violin lessons?'

'Yes. That would have been wonderful. We were looking to expand, bring in more musicians, but we were being very careful about it.' She looked Banks in the eye. 'We were serious about making a real go of this, you know,' she said. 'But without selling out or being commercial. We're absolutely gutted by what's happened. Not just as a band, I mean, but personally, too.'

'I understand, and I appreciate that,' said Banks. 'Did you have any other sort of relationship with Luke? Other than musical?'

'What do you mean?'

'Did you sleep with him?'

'With Luke?'

'Why not? He was a good-looking kid.'

'But that's all he was. A kid.'

'You said he was wise beyond his years.'

'I know that, but I'm not a bloody cradle-snatcher. Besides, I'm perfectly happy with Ryan, thank you very much.' Liz's face was red.

'So you were never Luke's girlfriend?'

'No way. I told you. I was with Ryan when we met. It was all about the music.'

'So there's no chance that Ryan caught the two of you in bed together and ended up killing Luke, then deciding he might as well cash in on it?'

'I don't know how you can even suggest something as horrible as that.' Liz seemed close to tears and Banks was starting to feel like a shit. She seemed a good kid. But *seemed* wasn't good enough. He remembered Rose Barlow's visit, as well as her angry exit. Liz was younger than Lauren Anderson, and a far more likely candidate for Luke's bedfellow, in Banks's opinion. He didn't know how strong Liz's relationship with Ryan was, or how open.

'It happens,' Banks said. 'You'd be surprised. Maybe it was an accident, you just couldn't see any other way out.'

'I told you. Nothing like that happened. Luke was in the band, that's all.'

'Did Luke ever confide in you?' Annie asked, easing off the pressure a little. 'You know, tell you what was on his mind, what was worrying him.'

Liz paused, regaining her composure. She seemed to be looking at Annie's swollen red lips, but she didn't ask about them. 'He complained about school a lot,' she said finally.

'Ever say anything about his stepfather?'

'The rugby player?'

'Ex-footballer.'

'Whatever. No, not a lot. I don't think Luke liked him very much.'

'Why do you say that?'

'Nothing in particular. Just the way he talked.'

'Did you ever meet Luke's parents?'

'No. I don't think he even told them about us, about the band.'

'How do you know?'

'Just my impression.'

It was probably true, Banks realized. According to Annie and to his own observations, the Armitages didn't seem to have a clue what Luke was up to half the time. 'Did he seem worried about anything?'

'Like what?'

'Anything at all,' Annie went on. 'Did he mention if any threats had been made against him, for example, or if he thought someone was following him? Anything unusual, out of the ordinary?'

'No, nothing like that. Like I said, he didn't like school and couldn't wait to leave home. I'd say that's pretty normal, wouldn't you?'

Banks smiled. He'd been the same at that age. Later, too. And he had also left home at the first opportunity.

'When did you last see Luke?' Annie asked.

'About a week before he disappeared. Band practice.'

Annie looked around the small room and struggled to her feet. 'Where do you practise?'

'Church basement, down the street. The vicar's pretty broad-minded, a young bloke, and he lets us use their space if we don't make too much noise.'

'And you haven't seen Luke since?'

'No.'

'Has he ever been here?' Banks asked. 'In this flat?'

'Sure. Plenty of times.' Liz stood up, as if she sensed they were leaving.

'Did he ever leave anything here?'

'Like what?'

'Any of his stuff. You know, notebooks, poems, stories, clothes, that sort of thing. We're looking for anything that might help us understand what happened to him.'

'He never left any clothes here,' Liz said coldly, 'but he sometimes left tapes of songs for us, if that's what you mean. And some lyrics, maybe. But . . .'

'Could you collect them all together for us?'

'I suppose so. I mean, I don't know what's here or where everything is. Do you mean right now? Can't you come back later?'

'Now would be best,' said Banks. 'We'll help you look, if you like.'

'No! I mean, no. It's all right. I'll find them.'

'Is there something here you don't want us to see, Liz?'

'No, nothing. There's only a few tapes and some poems, notes for songs. I don't see how they can help you. Look . . . will I get these tapes and things back?'

'Why would you get them back?' Annie asked. 'They were Luke's property, weren't they?'

'Technically, I suppose. But he brought them for us. The band. To share.'

'They'll still most likely go to the family,' Banks told her.

'Luke's family! But they don't care. They can't . . .'

'Can't what, Liz?'

'I was going to say they can't appreciate his talent. They'll just throw them away. How could you let something like that happen?'

'Can't be helped. It's the law.'

Liz shifted from foot to foot, arms folded, as if she needed to go to the toilet. 'Look, couldn't you go away and come back, just for a while, give me just a bit of time to get everything together?'

'We can't do that, Liz. I'm sorry.'

'So you'll just take everything and give it to Luke's parents, just like that? You won't even give me time to make copies.'

'This is a murder investigation,' Annie reminded her.

'But still . . .' Liz sat down, close to tears again. 'It doesn't seem fair. It seems such a waste . . . I don't know. His parents don't care. We were so close.'

'So close to what?'

'To *making* something of ourselves.'

Banks felt sorry for her. He suspected that she wanted to hang on to Luke's tapes and writings for selfish reasons, so that the band could one day ride on Luke's and his father's coat-tails to success. If they couldn't do it with Luke's voice and talent, at least they could try to do it with some of his material. That Luke had been murdered would also, no doubt, help boost the public interest. Banks didn't think particularly ill of Liz for this. He'd probably have wanted the same if he were in her situation and felt passionate about a career in music. He didn't think it lessened her genuine feelings for Luke. But there was something else that bothered him; the way she had reacted when he had offered to help look around. He glanced at Annie. It was one of those rare moments when each knew what the other was thinking.

'Mind if we have a little look around?' Annie asked.

'What? Why? I've told you. I'll give you everything you want.' She got up and went over to the tapes, picking out three. 'These for a start. The writings are in—'

'Why are you so jumpy, Liz?'

'I'm not jumpy.'

'Yes, you are. I think we should have a look around the place.'

'You can't do that. You need a search warrant.'

Banks sighed. *Again.* 'Are you certain you want that?' he asked. 'Because we can get one.'

'Go do it then. Get one.'

Banks looked at Annie. 'DI Cabbot, will you please go—'

Liz looked from one to the other, puzzled. 'Not just *her*. Both of you go.'

'It doesn't work like that,' said Banks. 'One of us has to stay here to make sure you don't interfere with anything. We'd hardly be doing our jobs if we disappeared and let drug dealers flush their stuff down the toilet, would we?'

'I'm not a drug dealer.'

'I'm sure you're not. But there's something you don't want us to find. I'll stay here while DI Cabbot gets the warrant, then she'll come back with four or five constables and we'll tear the place apart.'

Liz turned so pale Banks worried she might faint. He

could tell she was sensitive and he didn't like bullying her, but he didn't like what had happened to Luke, either. 'What's it to be, Liz? Will you give us consent to look around now, or do we do it the hard way?'

Liz looked up at him, big eyes brimming with tears. 'I don't have much choice, do I?'

'There's always a choice.'

'You'd find it anyway. I told Ryan he was stupid to keep it.'

'Find what, Liz?'

'It's in the cupboard by the door, under the sleeping bag.'

Banks and Annie opened the cupboard by the door and moved aside the sleeping bag. Underneath it was a battered leather shoulder bag, exactly the kind that Luke Armitage had been carrying when the bullies taunted him in the market square.

'I think you and Ryan have got quite a bit of explaining to do, don't you?' said Banks.

15

The Bridge Fair came every March. As a young boy, Banks would go with his parents. He remembered sitting on his father's knee in the dodgem car, clinging on for dear life, remembered the feel of the rough nap and the raw-wool smell of his dad's jacket, the sparks flashing off the high poles. He remembered strolling around holding his mother's hand, eating candyfloss or toffee apples while she nibbled at a brandysnap and his father ate a hot dog smothered in fried onions. He would hear his father curse as he tried to throw biased darts at playing cards and his mother laugh as she tried to toss ping-pong balls into goldfish bowls.

But when Banks was fourteen, he wouldn't be seen dead at the fair with his parents; he went with his mates, and Saturday night was the big night.

Why was it, he thought, as he drove past the small roadside fair which had sparked his memory, that they always seemed to be playing old rock-and-roll music at fairgrounds, even in the sixties? Whenever he thought of nights at the fair with Paul, Graham, Steve and Dave, it was always Freddy Cannon's 'Palisades Park' that played in his mind, or Eddie Cochran's 'Summertime Blues' as the waltzers spun and the bright lights blazed in the dark, not the Beatles or the Rolling Stones.

His favourite ride was the caterpillar, but you had to go on that one with a girl. As the train went faster and faster in undulating circles, the canvas cover, like a shop's awning, would slowly unfurl until it covered up the whole ride – hence the name caterpillar – and you were in the dark, riding fast with your girl. On his own, he liked the waltzers and the speedway best, but all rides were better shared with girls when you were fourteen.

For Banks and his friends, the fair began days before it opened. He remembered passing the stretch of common ground with Graham one wet afternoon – it must have been 1965 because that was the only year Graham was around for the spring fair – and watching the brightly coloured lorries roll in, watching the suspicious and unsmiling fairground workers unload sections of track and cars and begin the magical process of fitting the whole thing together. Banks would come back to check the progress, watch the men put the last section of the carousel in place, set up the booths, the stalls and the shies, and sure enough, everything was ready on opening night.

You had to go after dark. There was no point if the brightly coloured lights didn't flash and spin and if the music wasn't loud, if the smell of fried onions and spun sugar didn't waft through the night air to mingle with the discernible whiff of violence. For the fairs were where you went to pick a fight or settle your scores, and you could always see trouble brewing a mile off. First the looks, the whispers, the casual bumps, then someone running, others in pursuit, a scuffle and muffled cries, the fair-ground workers always somehow outside or beyond it all, stepping between the spokes as the waltzers got faster and faster, collecting money, impressing the girls with their dare-devil nonchalance.

And the girls . . . Well, the girls were all on parade at the fair, all bubblegum, miniskirts and eyeshadow. *If you didn't get shagged on Saturday night, you didn't get shagged at all*, as the old rugby song went. Well, Banks didn't get shagged, but he sometimes got kissed. That night it was Sylvia Nixon, a pretty little blonde from the girls' school down the street. They'd been eyeing one another shyly all night, standing up on the boards right beside the rides, watching the riders scream and yell and cling on tight. She was with her quiet friend, June, that was the problem. Which Graham, bless his soul, helped solve. Soon they were off on the caterpillar, and Banks felt that delicious anticipation as the cover started to close over them.

But something odd happened later.

Banks was persuading the girls to come with them to the park the next day if the weather was fine. There were plenty of sheltered, well-hidden areas where you could lie in the grass or stand up against a tree and snog. He was almost there, just overcoming the last, perfunctory shreds of resistance, when Graham said, 'Sorry, I can't go tomorrow.' When Banks asked him why, he just smiled vaguely and answered with his characteristic evasiveness, 'I've got something else to do, that's all.' The girls weren't too thrilled with that, and Banks never got to go out with Sylvia Nixon again.

A fight broke out somewhere near the dodgems, Banks remembered, and a couple of older men broke it up. But his chief memory, apart from kissing Sylvia on the caterpillar and Graham's weak reason for missing the next day's rendezvous, was that Graham paid. Again. He had Benson & Hedges, too: ten of them, king size, in the golden packet.

As Banks turned off the A1 to Peterborough, he racked his brains, trying to remember if he had ever asked Graham where he got his money, but he didn't think he had. Maybe he didn't want to know. Kids are selfish, and as long as they're having a good time they don't feel the need to question where it's coming from, or at whose expense it might be. But there weren't many places a kid Graham's age could get his hands on so much ready cash. The paper round wouldn't cover it, but an occasional dip in the till might. Or perhaps he stole it from his mother's purse?

The trouble was that it didn't seem to matter so much, just as long as Graham had the money. That he was generous went without saying. But what had he done to get it, and where, and *whom*, had he got it from?

Now, Banks also found himself wondering what it was that Graham had to do that Sunday that was so much more important than snogging with Sylvia Nixon's friend June in the park. And he remembered other occasions, too, right up until the day of his disappearance, when Graham simply wasn't there. No reason, no excuse, no explanation.

•

Annie's face was starting to ache when she went to interview Liz Palmer. She'd taken a couple of paracetamol earlier, but the effect was wearing off. She took another two and probed a loose tooth with her tongue. Wonderful. The last thing she needed was a trip to the dentist's. That bastard Armitage. His high-priced lawyer had been down the station like a shot, and as soon as the custody officer had drawn up the papers charging Armitage with criminal assault, he'd been bound over to appear in front of the magistrate the following day and sent off home. Annie would have liked to see him cooling his heels in the custody suite at least overnight, but no such luck. He'd probably walk on the charges, too. People like him usually did.

Because the Luke Armitage murder was a high-profile case, Gristhorpe and DC Winsome Jackman were interviewing Ryan Milne at the same time next door. So far, since they had picked him up at the college, Milne had been about as forthcoming as Liz.

Annie took DC Kevin Templeton with her into Interview Room 2, made sure Liz was clear about her rights and started the tape recorders. As yet, Annie explained, no charges had been brought and nobody was under arrest. She simply wanted an explanation as to how Luke Armitage's shoulder bag had got into Liz's hall cupboard. The bag and its contents were already with forensics.

'You told me you last saw Luke at band practice in the church basement about a week before he disappeared, right?' Annie began.

Liz nodded. She slumped in her chair and worked at a fingernail, looking a lot younger than her twenty-one years.

'Did he have the shoulder bag with him?'

'He always had it with him.'

'Then what was it doing in your cupboard?'

'I've no idea.'

'How long has it been there?'

'Must've been since band practice.'

'He came to the flat first?'

'Yes.'

Annie glanced at Kevin Templeton and sighed. 'Problem is, Liz,' she went on, 'that the market square CCTV cameras caught Luke before he disappeared a week ago last Monday, and he had the bag with him then.'

'It must've been a new one.'

'No,' Annie said. 'It was the same one.' She couldn't be

certain of that, of course – perhaps Luke *had* left his bag at Liz's and bought a new one – but she thought it unlikely Luke would have left all his things there, too. After all, it wasn't the bag itself that counted, but the possessions it contained: his notebook, his laptop computer, portable CD player, tapes and CDs.

Liz frowned. 'Well, I don't see how . . .'

'Me, neither. Unless you're not telling us the truth.'

'Why would I lie?'

'Oh, come off it,' Kevin Templeton butted in. 'Luke's dead. I'd say that's a pretty good reason to lie, wouldn't you?'

Liz jerked forward. '*I* didn't kill him! You can't think I killed him.'

'I don't know what we're supposed to think,' said Annie, spreading her hands. 'But I'm sure you can see our problem. Luke and his bag go missing, then Luke turns up dead, and we find his bag in your cupboard. Bit of a coincidence, don't you think?'

'I've told you, I don't know when he put it there.'

'Where were you that afternoon?'

'What afternoon?'

'The Monday Luke disappeared.'

'I don't know. Home, I suppose.'

'Are you sure he didn't call at the flat, then perhaps forget his bag when he went off somewhere else?' Annie knew she was giving Liz an out, but it seemed the only way to get her talking.

'I didn't see him.'

'Did he have a key?'

'No.'

'So you couldn't have gone out for a minute and he let himself in?'

'I don't see how.'

So much for that line of questioning. 'Liz, you're not making our job any easier. I'll ask you again: how did Luke's bag find its way into your hall cupboard?'

'I told you, I don't know.'

'And I don't believe you.'

'Well, that's your problem.'

'No, Liz. It's *your* problem. And it's going to be a very big one if you don't tell us the truth soon.'

'Maybe it was Ryan,' Kevin Templeton suggested.

Liz looked confused. 'Ryan? What do you mean?'

'Well,' Templeton went on, 'let me tell you what I think happened.' Annie gave him the nod. 'I think Luke went to your flat after he'd been in the market square—'

'No. I told you. He didn't come that day.'

'Let me finish.'

'But it's not true! You're making it up.'

'Be quiet,' Annie said. 'Listen to what DC Templeton has to say.'

Liz flopped back in her chair. 'Whatever.'

'Luke came to your place after he'd been in the market square. It was late afternoon. Ryan was out and the two of you thought you had time for a roll on the bed. He was a good-looking kid, fit, looked older than his age—'

'No! That didn't happen. It wasn't like that!'

'But Ryan came home and caught you at it. The two of them got in a scuffle and one way or another Luke ended up dead. I'm sure Ryan didn't mean to kill him, but you had a body on your hands. What could you do? You waited until dark and then you loaded Luke's body into the car and took it to Hallam Tarn, where Ryan hoisted him up the wall and dropped him over. He should have sunk the way dead bodies do, at least for a while, until they start to decompose and the gases build up and carry them to the surface, but he didn't. His T-shirt snagged on an old tree root. Bad luck. Ryan wasn't to know that. And nobody should have been in a position to find Luke because the whole area was quarantined due to foot-and-mouth restrictions. But a man from the Ministry had to take water samples. Bad luck, again. Ryan wasn't to know that, either.' Templeton smiled, showing his white teeth, and folded his arms. 'How am I doing so far, Liz?'

'It's all lies. Nothing like that happened. You're just making it up to get us in trouble. I've heard about the police doing things like this before.'

'You're already in trouble,' Annie said. 'We're trying to help you out, find an explanation for what happened. Maybe it did happen the way DC Templeton suggested. Maybe it *was* an accident. If it was, we can help. But you *have to tell us the truth*.'

'Look, I don't know how that bag got there,' Liz said. 'We hadn't seen Luke since the last band practice.'

'You're not making it easy for us,' Annie said.

'I can't help it! What do you want me to do? Make something up just to satisfy you?'

'I want the truth.'

'I've told you the truth.'

'You've told us nothing, Liz.'

'Look,' said Templeton, 'we can check, you know. Our forensics people are very good.'

'What do you mean?'

'I mean they'll go through your flat with the proverbial fine-tooth comb, and if there's any evidence of wrong-doing, even a drop of Luke's blood, they'll find it.'

'He's right,' Annie said. 'There's the poker, for a start. I noticed it when we were talking to you. You don't see them very often these days. If there's any trace of Luke's blood or hair on it, we'll find it. And if there are any traces on the carpet, between the floorboards, down the sink, we'll find them.'

Liz crossed her arms and bit her lip. Annie could tell she'd touched a nerve. What was it? The mention of blood? Did Liz know they'd find traces of Luke's blood in the flat? 'What is it, Liz?' she asked. 'Something to tell me?'

Liz shook her head.

'Ryan's being interviewed just next door,' Templeton said. 'I'll bet he's telling them it was all your fault, that you killed Luke and he had to get rid of the body for you.'

'Ryan wouldn't do that.'

'Even if it were true?' Annie asked.

'But it's *not* true. We didn't kill anyone. How many times do I have to tell you?'

'Until we believe you,' Annie said. 'And until you come up with a satisfactory explanation of how Luke's bag got into your cupboard.'

'I don't know.'

'What about the ransom demands?'

'What about them?'

'Whose idea was that? Was it Ryan's? Did he see it as an easy opportunity to make some money now that Luke was dead anyway? Or did he do it to confuse us?'

'I don't know what you're talking about.'

Annie stood up and Templeton followed suit. 'Right,' Annie said, switching off the tapes. 'I'm fed up with this. Have her taken to the custody suite, Kev, and arrange for the taking of intimate samples. Maybe we'll be lucky and get a DNA match with the blood on the wall. And get a search warrant. We'll have forensics in her flat within an hour. Then we'll talk to the super and find out what Ryan had to say for himself.'

'Right, Ma'am,' said Templeton.

And don't bloody call me Ma'am, Annie added under her breath.

Liz stood up. 'You can't do this! You can't keep me here.'

'Just watch us,' said Annie.

•

Banks tapped on his parents' front door and walked in. It was early evening, and he had plenty of time to spare before his nine o'clock meeting with Michelle. His parents had finished washing the dishes and were settling down to watch *Coronation Street*, just as they had all those years ago, the night the police came to call about Graham, the night Joey flew away.

'It's all right, don't get up,' Banks said to his mother. 'I'm not stopping long. I have to go out. I just came by to drop off my overnight bag first.'

'You'll have a cup of tea, though, won't you, dear?' his mother insisted.

'Maybe he wants something stronger,' his father suggested.

'No thanks, Dad,' said Banks. 'Tea will be fine.'

'Up to you,' said Arthur Banks. 'The sun's well over the yardarm. I'll have that bottle of ale while you're up, love.'

Ida Banks disappeared into the kitchen, leaving Banks and his father to their uneasy silence.

'Any progress?' Banks senior finally asked.

'On what?'

'Your old pal. Graham Marshall.'

'Not much,' said Banks.

'That why you're here again?'

'No,' Banks lied. 'It's not my case. It's the funeral tomorrow.'

Arthur Banks nodded.

Banks's mother popped her head around the kitchen door. 'I knew I had something to tell you, Alan. I've got a head like a sieve these days. I was talking to Elsie Grenfell yesterday, and she said her David's coming down for the service tomorrow. And that Major lad's supposed to be here as well. Won't it be exciting, seeing all your old pals again?'

'Yes,' said Banks, smiling to himself. Some things, like the *Coronation Street* ritual – and thank the Lord there was still ten minutes to go before the programme started – never changed. Paul Major had always been 'that Major lad' to Ida Banks, even though she knew full well that his name was Paul. It was meant to indicate that she didn't quite approve of him. Banks couldn't imagine why. Of all of them, Paul Major had been the most goody-goody, the one most likely to become a chartered accountant or a banker.

'What about Steve?' Banks asked. 'Steve Hill?'

'I haven't heard anything about him for years,' Ida Banks said, then disappeared back into the kitchen.

It wasn't surprising. The Hills had moved off the estate many years ago when Steve's dad got transferred to Northumberland. Banks had lost track of them and didn't know where they lived now. He wondered if Steve had even heard about the finding of Graham's bones.

'I don't suppose it came to anything, what we were talking about in the Coach last time you were here?' Arthur Banks said.

'About the Krays and Mr Marshall? Probably not. But it was useful background.'

Arthur Banks coughed. 'Had over half the Metropolitan Police in their pockets, the Krays did, in their time.'

'So I've heard.'

Mrs Banks came through with the tea and her husband's beer on a rose-patterned tray. 'Our Roy phoned this afternoon,' she said, beaming. 'He said to say hello.'

'How is he?' Banks asked.

'Thriving, he said. He's jetting off to America for some business meetings, so he just wanted us to know he'd be away for a few days in case we were worried or anything.'

'Oh, good,' said Banks, who much to his mother's chagrin, he imagined, never jetted anywhere – unless Greece counted. Just like brother Roy to let his mother know what a high-powered life he was leading. He wondered what kind of shady dealings Roy was up to in America. None of his business.

'There was a programme on telly the other night about that police corruption scandal a few years back,' Banks's father said. 'Interesting, some of the things your lot get up to.'

Banks sighed. The defining event of Arthur Banks's life was not the Second World War, which he had missed fighting in by about a year, but the miners' strike of 1984, when Maggie Thatcher broke the unions and brought the workers to their knees. Every night he had been glued to the news and filled with the justified outrage of the working man. Over the years, Banks knew, his father had never been able to dispel the image of policemen in riot gear waving rolls of overtime fivers to taunt the starving miners. Banks had been working undercover in London then, mostly on drugs cases, but he knew that in his father's mind he was one of them. The enemy. Would it never end? He said nothing.

'So where are you going tonight, love?' Ida Banks asked. 'Are you seeing that policewoman again?'

She made it sound like a date. Banks felt a brief wave of guilt for thinking of it that way himself, then he said, 'It's police business.'

'To do with Graham?'

'Yes.'

'I thought you said that wasn't your case,' his father chipped in.

'It's not, but I might be able to help a bit.'

'Helping police with their enquiries?' Arthur Banks chuckled. It turned into a coughing fit until he spat into a handkerchief.

Fortunately, before anyone could say another word, the *Coronation Street* theme music started up and all conversation ceased.

•

It wasn't often that Detective Superintendent Gristhorpe visited the Queen's Arms, but after they had finished the interviews and put Ryan Milne and Liz Palmer under lock and key for the night, he suggested to Annie that they discuss the results over a bite to eat. Hungry and thirsty, Annie thought it a good idea.

Gristhorpe, like a true gentleman, insisted on going to the bar to get their drinks, though Annie would have been happy to go herself. Instead she sat down and made herself comfortable. Gristhorpe still intimidated her a little, though she didn't know why, but she felt easier with him in an environment like the Queen's Arms than in his book-lined office, so she was doubly glad he had suggested the pub. She definitely had a loose tooth, though, so she would have to be careful how she ate.

Gristhorpe returned with a pint of bitter for her and a half of shandy for himself. They glanced over the menu chalked on the blackboard, and Annie went for a vegetarian lasagne, which ought to be easy on her tooth, while Gristhorpe settled on fish and chips. The old man was looking healthier than he had in quite a while, Annie thought. The first few times she had seen him after his accident, he had seemed pale, gaunt and drawn, but now he had a bit more flesh on his bones and a warm glow to his pock-marked face. She supposed that accidents and illness took a lot more out of you the older you got, and that recovery took longer. But how old was he? He couldn't be all that much over sixty.

'How's your mouth feeling?' he asked.

'The pain seems to have gone for now, sir, thanks for asking.'

'You should have gone to the hospital.'

'It was nothing. Just a glancing blow.'

'Even so . . . these things can have complications. How's Wells?'

'Last I heard still in the infirmary. Armitage gave him a real going over.'

'He always was a hot-head, that one. Even as a football player. Now what about the Palmer girl? Anything interesting there?'

Annie recounted what little she had got from Liz Palmer, then Gristhorpe sipped some shandy and told her about Ryan Milne's interview. 'He said he knew nothing about the bag, just like his girlfriend. He told me he was out that day and didn't see Luke at all.'

'Did you believe him, sir?'

'No. Winsome went at him a bit – she's very good in

interviews, that lass, a real tigress – but neither of us could shake him.'

'So what are they hiding?'

'Dunno. Maybe a night in the cells will soften them up a bit.'

'Do you think they did it, sir?'

'Did it?'

'Killed Luke and dumped the body.'

Gristhorpe pursed his lips, then said, 'I don't know, Annie. Milne's got an old banger, so they had the means of transport. Like you, I suggested some sort of romantic angle, something going on between Luke and Liz, but Milne didn't bite, and to be quite honest I didn't notice any signs I'd hit the nail on the head.'

'So you don't think there was any romantic angle?'

'Luke was only fifteen, and Liz Palmer is what?'

'Twenty-one.'

'As I remember, the last thing a twenty-one-year-old woman would want is a fifteen-year-old boyfriend. Now maybe if she were forty-one . . .'

Annie smiled. 'A toyboy?'

'I've heard it called that. But I still think fifteen's too young.'

'I don't know,' said Annie. 'The head teacher's daughter told DCI Banks she thought Luke was having it off with his English teacher, and she's pushing thirty.'

'Lauren Anderson?'

'That's the one.'

'Stranger things have happened. What does Alan think?'

'That little Miss Barlow had reasons of her own for causing trouble for Miss Anderson.' Annie sipped some beer. Nectar. 'But I wouldn't say it's out of the question that

Luke was having relations with someone older than himself. Everything I've heard about him indicates he seemed much older than his age, both physically and mentally.'

'How about emotionally?'

'That I don't know.'

'Well, that's the one that counts,' Gristhorpe mused. 'That's what causes people to get out of their depth. They can understand something intellectually, accomplish something physically, but the emotional aspect can hit them like a sledgehammer if they're not mature enough. Teenagers are particularly vulnerable.'

Annie agreed. She'd had enough experience with troubled teens in her job to know it was true, and Luke Armitage had been a complex personality, a mass of conflicting desires and unresolved problems. Add to that his creativity, his sensitivity, and Luke was probably as volatile to handle as nitroglycerine.

'Does the Anderson woman have a jealous boyfriend?' Gristhorpe asked.

'Not according to Winsome. She did a bit of digging. Only bit of dirt on Ms Anderson is that her brother Vernon's got a record.'

Gristhorpe raised his bushy eyebrows. 'Oh?'

'Nothing really nasty. Just dodgy cheques.'

'I've written a few of those in my time, according to my bank manager. What about the other teacher, Alastair Ford?'

'Kevin Templeton says there are rumours he's gay, but only rumours. As far as anyone *knows* he has no sex life at all.'

'Any evidence that Luke Armitage was gay, too?'

'None. But there's no evidence he was straight, either. Ford has a temper, though, like Armitage, and he's been seeing a psychiatrist for several years now. Definitely the unstable kind.'

'Not to be ruled out, then?'

'No.'

'And Norman Wells?'

'Looking less likely, isn't he?'

When their food arrived, both were hungry enough to stop talking for a while and eat, then Gristhorpe slowed down. 'Any ideas of your own about how Luke's bag ended up where it did, Annie?' he asked.

Annie finished her mouthful of lasagne, then said, 'I think Luke went there after his run-in with the three bullies in the market square. What happened after that, I don't know, but either he died there or something happened that made him run off without his bag, which I don't think he'd do under any normal circumstances.'

'So *something* happened there?'

'Yes. Certainly.'

'What about his mobile?'

'One of those tiny models you can just flip open and shut. Probably couldn't find it among all the stuff if he kept it in his bag, so he carried it in his pocket. Anyway, it hasn't been found yet.'

'Has it been used?'

'Not since the ransom call. Hasn't even been switched on. I checked again with the company.'

'Anything valuable in the bag?'

'Stefan's going through it. From what I saw, though, I don't think so. I mean, the laptop was worth a bob or two, but I don't think theft was the motive here. That is . . .'

'Yes, Annie?'

'Well, there was nothing valuable to you or me, nothing of any real material value, but I got the impression that Liz, at least, is ambitious, and there's a chance they could ride a lot further and a lot faster on Luke Armitage's coat-tails – or rather Neil Byrd's coat-tails.'

'I think I must be a bit of an old fogey,' said Gristhorpe, scratching the side of his hooked nose, 'but I can't say I've ever heard of Neil Byrd. I know who he was to Luke and what happened to him, of course, but that's about as far as it goes.'

'Alan – DCI Banks – knows a lot more about it than I do, sir, but Byrd was quite famous in his time. The record company is still bringing out CDs of previously unreleased stuff, greatest hits and live concerts, so there's still a thriving Neil Byrd industry out there, a dozen years after his death. Luke inherited some of his father's talent, and if Liz and Ryan wanted to milk the connection, I'm sure there are plenty of song ideas and fragments on the laptop and in his notebooks.'

'But he was only a kid, Annie. Surely he can't have had *that* much to say?'

'It's not what you say, sir, it's how you say it. Teenage angst, mostly, from what I've heard. But it's the *name* that's the point. And, not to be too ghoulish about it, the circumstances. Dead son of famous rock suicide. With a promotion like that, the songs wouldn't *need* to be that good. It'd get Liz's band known, get them a name, and that's more than half the battle in the music business.'

'But legally all Luke's stuff belongs to his family now. Wouldn't they sue if these people got as far as making a record of Luke's songs?'

'Maybe, but it'd be too late then, wouldn't it? And you know what they say: no publicity's bad publicity. A lawsuit would only further Liz's and Ryan's career. It's just a thought, sir.'

Gristhorpe finished his last chip and pushed his plate aside, taking a sip of shandy. 'So what you're saying is that, whether the two of them killed Luke or not, they somehow found themselves with a goldmine of material, and they thought they might as well hang on to it until they could use it?'

'As I said, sir, it's only an idea. If they'd been a bit more cautious, they'd have got rid of the bag and we'd be none the wiser.'

'But they never thought we'd search their flat.'

'Why would they? They didn't even know that anyone had seen Luke with Liz.'

'What about the vicar at that church where they practised?'

Annie rolled her eyes. 'Winsome talked to him. Said he's so otherworldly he hadn't a clue who Luke Armitage was or that he'd disappeared.'

'Would Liz and Ryan have killed Luke for his stuff?' he asked.

'I don't think so, sir. That's the problem. Whichever way you look at it, they'd be far better off with Luke alive. *He* would have been the real draw. Without him, well . . . they're simply doing the best they can.'

'So they had nothing to gain by killing him?'

'No. Not unless he was intending to walk out on them, for example, and take all his works with him. One of them could have lost it with him then. Or, as I suggested earlier, unless there was some sort of romantic relationship and Ryan found out.'

'A *crime passionel*? I suppose so. Wouldn't be the first time. We can't discount anything yet. Let's just give them a bit of time, hope forensics turn up something, and have at them again in the morning.'

'Good idea, sir.' Annie finished her pint.

'Annie, before you go . . . ?'

'Sir?'

'I don't mean to pry, but you and Alan . . . ?'

'Just colleagues, sir. And friends.'

Gristhorpe seemed pleased with her answer. 'Aye,' he said. 'Good. Good. Get some sleep, lass. I'll see you bright and early in the morning.'

•

The pub was closer to the riverside than the city centre, though even that wasn't very far. Banks parked by the Rivergate Centre and walked the rest of the way. It was a pleasant evening, not a leaf stirring in the warm air. The sunset painted the sky bright orange and crimson. Banks could see Venus low on the horizon, and the constellations were slowly taking shape overhead. He wished he could recognize them all, but he could only make out Hercules. That made him think of those dreadful spaghetti spectacles he used to love in the early sixties with cheap special effects, Steve Reeves, and a scantily clad Sylva Koscina.

Michelle was five minutes late, and Banks had already settled at a small corner table with a pint of bitter. The lounge was small and smoky, but most of the people stood at the bar, and the video machines were mercifully silent. Piped music played softly, some sort of modern pop stuff Banks didn't recognize. Michelle was wearing tight black trousers and a green blouse tucked in at the waist. She carried a tan suede jacket slung over her shoulder. Banks had never seen her dressed so casually before. Hadn't seen her looking as good, either. She'd had her hair done, he noticed: nothing drastic, just tidied up a bit, the fringe trimmed, highlights renewed. And she wore a little make-up, just enough to accentuate her green eyes and high cheekbones.

She seemed self-conscious about her appearance because she wouldn't meet his eyes at first. Only when he had offered her a drink and she asked for a dry white wine, did she favour him with a look and a shy smile.

'Thanks for coming,' Michelle said, when Banks placed the drink in front of her and sat down.

'My pleasure,' said Banks. 'I'd have come tomorrow for the service, anyway, so another evening doesn't make much difference.'

'I know you're busy.'

'I'm covered. Besides, we had a lucky break just before I set off.' Banks told her about finding Luke Armitage's bag at Liz Palmer's flat.

'Poor kid,' said Michelle. 'He wasn't much older than Graham Marshall, was he?'

'A year or so.'

'Why would anyone want to kill a boy that age? What could he possibly have done?'

'I don't know. I suppose that's why we assume it's a paedophile when the victim's so young. We can easily imagine older people being killed for other motives, for greed or to cover up something, but it's hard with kids. Anyway, it looked like a kidnapping, but I have my doubts. What about you? Any more news?'

Michelle gave him the gist of her conversation with retired DI Robert Lancaster in London, especially his remarks about Graham seeming streetwise beyond his years.

'So your ex-copper thought Graham had a future in crime, did he?' Banks said. 'Interesting, that.'

'Why? Have you remembered something?'

'Nothing, really. Just that Graham never seemed short of money, and I'd no idea where he got it from.'

'There's something else,' Michelle said. She seemed hesitant, Banks thought, unwilling to meet his eyes.

'Yes?'

'Someone was in my flat on Saturday, while I was down in London.'

'Anything taken?'

'Not as far as I can tell, just a few things out of place. But whoever it was had also been having a good look at my computer files.'

Banks got the impression that she wasn't telling him everything, but he didn't pursue it. If there was something she was omitting, it was probably for a good reason, such as personal embarrassment. She'd hardly want to tell him if someone had been going through her undies, would she? 'Anything there?'

'Not much. Personal notes. Speculations.'

'About the case?'

'Some of it.'

'Did you report the break-in?'

'Of course not. Under the circumstances.'

'How did he get in?'

'Finessed the lock somehow.' Michelle smiled. 'Don't worry, I've had it changed. The locksmith assures me the place is as impregnable as a fortress now.'

'Anything else?'

'Maybe.'

'What does that mean?'

'Yesterday, as I was crossing the road near the Hazels estate, I was almost hit by a small van.'

'Almost?'

'Yes, no damage. I couldn't be certain, but I thought it was deliberate.'

'Any idea who?'

'The number plate was obscured.'

'A guess?'

'Well, I hesitate to say it, but after the missing notebooks and actions, my mind can't help but wander towards Shaw. Thing is, I can't bring myself to believe it, that he would do something like that.'

Banks didn't have much of a problem believing it. He'd known bent coppers before, and known them well enough to realize that they were capable of anything when cornered. Many coppers were also as skilled at picking locks as burglars were. But why did Shaw feel cornered? And what was it he'd done? Banks remembered the quiet young man with the freckles, ginger hair and sticking-out ears, rather than the bloated, red-nosed bully Shaw had become. 'Shaw was teamed up with DI Proctor, right?'

'Reg Proctor, yes. He took early retirement in 1975 and then died of liver cancer in 1978. He was only forty-seven.'

'Any rumours, hints of scandal?'

Michelle sipped some wine and shook her head. 'Not that I could uncover. Seems to have had an exemplary career.'

Banks asked Michelle's permission and lit a cigarette. 'Shaw and Proctor were the detectives who came to our house,' he said. 'They were obviously interviewing friends of Graham's and people on the estate. There would no doubt have been other teams assigned other tasks, but for some reason someone wanted rid of *Shaw's* notes. Shaw himself?'

'He was only a DC at the time,' said Michelle.

'Right. What could he have to hide? There must have been something in his notebooks that incriminated someone else. Maybe Harris or Proctor.'

'The notebooks *could* have been missing since Harris retired in 1985,' Michelle said. 'They could also have been taken before Proctor's death in 1978, I suppose.'

'But why? Nobody's had reason to look at them for years. Graham had been missing since 1965. Why mess with the paperwork unless there was some compelling reason? And what could that be except that his body's been found and the case is open again?'

'True enough,' said Michelle.

'The actions would show us how the investigation was managed,' Banks mused. 'Most of them probably came from Jet Harris himself. They'd show the direction the investigation took, or didn't take, the shape of it.'

'We keep getting back to this blinkered approach,' Michelle said. 'DS Shaw even hinted they all knew Brady and Hindley did it.'

'That's a load of bollocks,' said Banks.

'The timing's right.'

'But that's all that's right. You might just as well say Reggie and Ronnie did it.'

'Maybe they did.'

Banks laughed. 'It makes more sense than Brady and Hindley. They operated miles away. No, there's something else going on. Something we can't figure out because there are still too many missing pieces. Another?'

'I'll go.'

Michelle walked to the bar and Banks sat wondering what the hell it was all about. So far, all they had was an investigation that had concentrated on only one possibility – the passing paedophile. Now they had Bill

Marshall's relationship with the Krays and with Carlo Fiorino and Le Phonographe, and the fact that Banks remembered Graham often had money enough to pay for their entertainment. And now the missing records. There were links – Graham, Bill Marshall, Carlo Fiorino – but where did it go after that? And how did Jet Harris fit in? It was possible that he'd been on the take, paid by Fiorino to head off trouble. Jet Harris, bent copper. That would go down well at headquarters. But how did it relate to Graham and his murder?

Michelle came back with the drinks and told him about Donald Bradford's death and the pornography that had been found in his flat. 'There might be no connection,' she said. 'I mean, Bradford could have been the victim of a random break-in, and plenty of people have collections of pornography.'

'True,' Banks said. 'But it's a bit of a coincidence, isn't it?'

'It is indeed.'

'What if Bradford was using the newsagent's shop as an outlet for distributing porn?' Banks suggested.

'And Graham delivered it?'

'Why not? He always seemed to be able to get his hands on it. That's another thing I remember. A bit of Danish submission with your *Sunday Times*, sir? Or how about some Swedish sodomy with your *News of the World*, madam? Gives a whole new meaning to the term Sunday supplement, doesn't it?'

Michelle laughed. 'Maybe he just found out about it.'

'Is that worth killing someone for?'

'Who knows? People have killed for less.'

'But all we're assuming is that Bradford was a minor porn dealer.'

'He had to get it from a wholesaler, didn't he? Maybe Bradford was working for someone with even more at stake?'

'Someone like Carlo Fiorino?' suggested Banks. 'And Harris was on Fiorino's payroll? It's possible, but still speculation. And it doesn't get us a lot further with the missing notebooks.'

'Unless Proctor and Shaw inadvertently hit on the truth during their interviews, and it was recorded in Shaw's notebooks. I don't know how we'd find out, though. It's not as if we can talk to Harris or Proctor.'

'Maybe not,' said Banks. 'But we might be able to do the next best thing. Were they married?'

'Harris was. Not Proctor.'

'Is his wife still alive?'

'As far as I know.'

'Maybe she'll be able to tell us something. Think you can find her?'

'Piece of cake,' said Michelle.

'And let's delve a little deeper into Donald Bradford's domain, including the circumstances of his death.'

'Okay. But what about DS Shaw?'

'Avoid him as best you can.'

'That shouldn't be too difficult these days,' Michelle said. 'He's off sick half the time.'

'The booze?'

'That's what I'd put my money on.'

'Are you going to the funeral tomorrow?'

'Yes.'

'Good.' Banks finished his drink. 'Another?'

Michelle looked at her watch. 'No. Really. I'd better go.'

'Okay. I suppose I should go, too.' Banks smiled. 'I'm sure my mum'll be waiting up for me.'

Michelle laughed. It was a nice sound. Soft, warm, musical. Banks realized he hadn't heard her laugh before. 'Can I give you a lift?' he asked.

'Oh, no. Thank you,' said Michelle, standing up. 'I'm just around the corner.'

'I'll walk with you, then.'

'You don't need to. It's quite safe.'

'I insist. Especially after what you've just told me.'

Michelle said nothing. They walked out into the mild darkness, crossed the road and neared the riverside flats, close to where Banks had parked his car. Michelle had been right; it really was within spitting distance.

'This is right across the river from where they used to have the fair when I was a kid,' he said. 'Funny, but I was just thinking about it as I was driving down.'

'Before my time,' said Michelle.

'Yes.' Banks walked her up to her door.

'Well,' she said, fumbling for her key, giving him a brief smile over her shoulder. 'Goodnight, then.'

'I'll just wait and make sure everything's okay.'

'You mean until you're sure there are no bogeymen waiting for me?'

'Something like that.'

Michelle opened her door, put on the lights and did a quick check while Banks stood in the doorway and glanced around the living room. It seemed a bit barren, no real character, as if Michelle hadn't put her stamp on it yet.

'All clear,' she said, emerging from the bedroom.

'Goodnight, then,' said Banks, trying to hide his disappointment that she didn't even invite him in for a coffee. 'And take care. See you tomorrow.'

'Yes.' She gave him a smile. 'Tomorrow.' Then she closed the door gently behind him, and the sound of the bolt slipping home seemed far louder than it probably was.

•

It was all very well for Gristhorpe to tell Annie to get a good night's sleep, but she couldn't. She had taken more paracetamol and gone to bed early, but the pain had returned to her mouth with a vengeance. Every tooth ached and now two of them felt loose.

The blow from Armitage had shaken her more than she had cared to admit to either Banks or Gristhorpe because it had made her feel the same way she had felt when she was raped nearly three years ago: a powerless victim. She had sworn afterwards that she would never allow herself to feel that way again, but down in the cramped, dank space of Norman Wells's book cellar, she had felt it, the deep, gut-wrenching fear of female powerlessness against male strength and sheer brute force.

Annie got up, went downstairs and poured herself a glass of milk with shaking hands, sitting at the kitchen table in the dark as she sipped it. She remembered the very first time Banks had been to her house. They had sat in the kitchen and eaten dinner together while the light faded. All the while Annie had been wondering what she would do if he made a move. She had impulsively invited him into her home, after all, offering to cook dinner instead of going to a restaurant or a pub, as he had suggested. Had she known right then, when she did that, what was going to happen? She didn't think so.

As the evening wore on, their mood had got more and more mellow, thanks partly to liberal quantities of Chianti. When she had gone outside into the backyard with Banks, who wanted a cigarette, and when he had put his arm around her, she'd felt herself tremble like a teenager as she had blurted out all the reasons about why they *shouldn't* do what they were about to do.

Well, they had done it. And now she had ended the affair. Sometimes she regretted that and wondered why she had done it. Partly it was because of her career, of course. Working in the same station as the DCI you were screwing was bad policy. But maybe that was just an excuse. Besides, it didn't have to be that way. She could have worked in another station, somewhere where the opportunities were just as good, if not better, than at Western Area Headquarters.

It was true that Banks still seemed tied to his past, to his marriage, but she could have handled that. It was also something that would have waned in time. Everyone had emotional baggage, including Annie herself. No, she thought, the reasons for what she did were within herself, not the job, not Banks's past. Intimacy had felt like a threat to her, and the closer she had got to Banks, the more she had felt suffocated and tried to pull away.

Would it be like that with every man she met? Was it to do with the rape? Possibly, she thought. Or at least partly. She wasn't sure she would *ever* completely get over that. What happened that night had certainly damaged her deeply. She didn't think she was beyond repair, just that she had a long way to go. She still had occasional nightmares, and though she had never told Banks this, sex had sometimes been an effort for her, had even hurt at times. Sometimes the simple act of penetration, however consensual and gentle, had brought back the surge of panic and the feeling of sheer *powerlessness* she had first experienced that night. Sex certainly had its dark side, Annie knew. It could be demonic, close to violence, pushing you into dangerous and vaguely imagined desires and dark areas, beyond taboo. It was no wonder, then, she thought, that the idea of sex was so often mentioned in the same breath as violence. Or that sex and death were so intimately linked in the words and works of so many writers and artists.

Annie finished her milk and tried to laugh off her morbid thoughts. Still, they seemed to be the only kind she had at night, alone and unable to sleep. She put the kettle on for tea and went into the living room to browse through her small video collection. In the end she settled on *Doctor Zhivago*, which had always been one of her favourite films, and when the tea was ready she lounged on the sofa in the dark with her steaming mug, legs tucked under her and gave herself up to the haunting theme music and the epic story of love in a time of revolution.

●

Banks walked down the stairs and tried to shake off his sense of disappointment. It was just as well, he told himself; the last thing he needed right now was to make a fool of himself over yet another woman. And Michelle had her own demons, whatever they were. Everyone did, it seemed. You couldn't get to a certain age without attracting a lot of clutter. But why did it always have to get in the way? Why couldn't you just shrug it off and get on with life? Why was misery so easy to embrace and joy so bloody elusive?

Just around the corner from the flats, he stopped to light a cigarette. Before he got his lighter out of his pocket, he felt something thud into him from behind. He staggered forward and turned to face whoever had hit him. He got only a quick glimpse of a pug nose and piggy eyes before a blow to the face upset both his vision and his balance. Another blow knocked him to the ground. Next he felt a sharp pain in his ribs and a kick to his stomach made him retch.

Then he heard a dog barking and a man's voice shouting beyond the walls of pain, felt rather than saw his attacker hesitate and heard him whisper, 'Go back where you came from, or there'll be more of that,' before he ran off into the night.

Banks got to his knees and felt sick, head hanging on his chest. Christ, he was getting too old for this kind of thing. He tried to stand, but his legs still felt too wobbly. Then a hand grasped his elbow and he managed to get to his feet.

'Are you all right, Mister?' Banks swayed and took a couple of deep breaths. That felt a little better. His head was still spinning, but his vision had cleared. A young man stood beside him, Jack Russell terrier on a leash. 'Only I was just taking Pugwash here for a walk and I saw two blokes setting on you.'

'Two? Are you certain?'

'Yes. They ran off towards the city centre.'

'Thank you,' said Banks. 'That was very brave of you. You saved my bacon.'

'Is there anything else I can do? Call you a taxi or something?'

Banks paused to get his thoughts in some sort of order, then he looked towards the flats. 'No,' he said. 'No thanks. I've a friend lives just over there. I'll be fine.'

'If you're certain.'

'Yes. And thanks again. Not many people bother to get involved these days.'

The young man shrugged. 'No problem. Come on,

Pugwash.' And they wandered off, the man casting a couple of backward glances as he went.

Still a bit wobbly, Banks made his way back to Michelle's flat and pressed the intercom. A few moments later her voice crackled into the night air. 'Yes? Who is it?'

'It's me, Alan,' said Banks.

'What is it?'

'I've had a little accident. I wonder if . . .'

But before he could finish Michelle buzzed him in, and he made his way up to her door. She was already standing there, looking concerned, and came forward to help him towards the sofa. Not that it was necessary, but he thought it was a nice gesture.

'What happened?' she asked.

'Someone jumped me. Thank God for dog walkers or I'd probably be in the river by now. Funny, isn't it? I thought I was going to end up in the Nene all those years ago and I almost ended up there tonight.'

'You're rambling,' Michelle said. 'Sit down.'

Banks still felt a bit dizzy and nauseated when he sat down. 'Just give me a few minutes,' he said. 'I'll be fine.'

Michelle handed him a glass. 'Drink,' she said.

He drank. Cognac. A good one, too. As the fiery liquor spread through his limbs he started to feel even better. His mind came into sharper focus, and he was able to assess the damage. Not much, really. His ribs felt tender, but he didn't feel as if anything was broken. He looked up and saw Michelle standing over him.

'How do you feel now?'

'Much better, thank you.' Banks sipped some more cognac. 'Look,' he said, 'I'd better call a taxi. I don't feel very much like driving in this condition, especially not after this.' He held up the glass. Michelle tipped in more from the Courvoisier VSOP bottle, and poured herself a generous measure, too.

'Okay,' she said. 'But you must let me see to your nose first.'

'Nose?' Banks realized his nose and upper lip felt numb. He put his hand up and it came away bloody.

'I don't think it's broken,' Michelle said, leading him towards the bathroom, 'but I'd better clean you up and put something on it before you go. There's a small cut on your lip, too. Whoever hit you must have been wearing a ring or something.'

The bathroom was small, almost too small for two people to stand without touching. Banks stood with the backs of his legs against the toilet bowl as Michelle used a damp facecloth to wipe away the blood then looked in the cabinet and came up with some TCP liquid antiseptic. She put a small swab of cotton wool over the top of the bottle and tipped it up, then carefully applied it to his lip. It stung, and the acrid smell made him gasp. Michelle took the cotton wool away.

'It's all right,' he said.

She dropped one bloodstained swab into the waste bin and prepared another. Banks watched her face close to his, the look of concentration as she applied the cotton wool, tip of her tongue nipped between her teeth. She caught his eye, blushed and looked away. 'What?'

'Nothing,' he said. She was so close he could feel the warmth of her body, smell the cognac on her breath.

'Go on,' she said. 'You were going to say something.'

'It's just like *Chinatown*,' Banks said.

'What do you mean?'

'The film, *Chinatown*. Haven't you seen it?'

'What happens?'

'Jack Nicholson gets his nose cut by Roman Polanski, and Faye Dunaway, well . . . she does what you're doing now.'

'Puts TCP on it?'

'Well, I don't think it was TCP – I don't think they have that in America – but the idea's the same. Anyway, it's a very sexy scene.'

'Sexy?' Michelle paused. Banks could see her flushed skin, feel the heat from her cheeks. The bathroom seemed to be getting smaller.

'Yes,' said Banks.

She dabbed at him again. Her hand was trembling. 'I don't see how putting TCP on a cut could be sexy,' she said. 'I mean, what happens?'

She was so close to him now that he could feel her breast touching ever so lightly against his arm. He could have leaned the top half of his body further back, bent at the knees, but he stood his ground. 'First, they kiss,' he said.

'But wouldn't it hurt?'

'It was just his nose that got cut. Remember?'

'Of course. How silly of me.'

'Michelle?'

'What? What is it?'

Banks took her trembling hand by the wrist and moved it away from his mouth, then he put his other hand under her chin and cupped it gently so she was looking at him, her brilliant green eyes questioning but holding his gaze, not looking away now. He could feel his heart thudding in his chest and his knees wobbling as he pulled her closer to him and felt her yield.

16

'**You were late back last night**,' Banks's mother said, without turning from the kitchen sink. 'Tea's fresh.'

Banks poured himself a cup of tea and added a splash of milk. He had expected this sort of reaction. His mother had probably lain awake until two in the morning listening for him the way she did when he was a teenager. He and Michelle had decided that, for many reasons, it was not a good idea for him to stay with her overnight, but even so Michelle had laughed at the idea of his having to go home to his mother.

Ida Banks turned. 'Alan! What *have* you done to your face?'

'It's nothing,' said Banks.

'But it's all bruised. And your lip's cut. What have you been up to?'

Banks turned away. 'I told you, it's nothing.'

'Were you fighting? Was it some criminal you were arresting? Is that why you were so late? You could have rung.' She gave him a look that spoke volumes about what she thought of his chosen career.

'Something like that,' Banks said. 'I had a bit of business to take care of. Look, I'm sorry I didn't ring, but it was so late. I didn't want to wake you.'

His mother gave him the reproving look she was so good at. 'Son,' she said, 'you ought to know by now that I can't get to sleep until you're home safe and sound.'

'Well, you can't have slept much these past thirty years or so,' Banks said, and immediately regretted it when he saw the other look she was so good at, the suffering martyr, lower lip trembling. He went over and gave her a hug. 'Sorry, Mum,' he said, 'but I'm all right. Really I am.'

His mother sniffed and nodded. 'Well,' she said. 'I suppose you'll be hungry. Bacon and eggs?'

Banks knew from experience that feeding him would help his mother get over her bad night. He wasn't all that hungry, but he couldn't deal with the protests he knew he'd get if all he asked for was cereal. He was also in a hurry. Michelle had suggested he come down to headquarters to search through the mugshots for his attacker. He wasn't certain he could identify the man, though the piggy eyes and pug nose were distinctive enough. Still, Mother comes first; bacon and eggs it had to be. 'If it's no trouble,' he said.

His mother walked over to the fridge. 'It's no trouble.'

'Where's Dad?' he asked, as his mother turned on the cooker.

'Down at the allotment.'

'I didn't know he still went there.'

'It's more of a social thing. He doesn't do much digging or anything these days. Mostly he sits and passes the time of day with his mates. And he has a cigarette or two. He thinks I don't know, but I can smell it on him when he comes home.'

'Well, don't be too hard on him, Mum.'

'I'm not. But it's not only *his* health, is it? What am I supposed to do if he goes and drops dead?'

'He's not going to drop dead.'

'Doctor says he's not supposed to smoke. And you should stop, too, while you're still young.'

Young? It was a long time since Banks had been called young. Or felt young, for that matter. Except perhaps last night, with Michelle. Once she had made her decision, dropped her defences a little, she was a different person, Banks marvelled. It had clearly been a long time since she had been with anyone, so their love-making was slow and tentative at first, but none the worse for that. And once she threw aside her inhibitions she proved to be a warm and generous lover. Michelle had also been gentle because of Banks's cut lip and bruised ribs. He cursed his bad luck, that he had to be injured in combat the first night he got to sleep with her. He also thought it was ironic that such physical injuries were so rare in his line of work, yet both he and Annie had been hurt within hours of one another. Some malevolent force working against them, no doubt.

Banks remembered Michelle's sleepy late-night kiss at the door as he left, her warm body pressed against him. He sipped some tea. 'Is the paper around?' he asked his mother.

'Your dad took it with him.'

'I'll just nip over the road, then.' His father took the *Daily Mail*, anyway, and Banks preferred the *Independent* or the *Guardian*.

'Your bacon and eggs will be ready.'

'Don't worry. I'll be back before they're done.'

Banks's mother sighed, and he headed out. It was warm but cloudy outside, and looking like rain again. That close, sticky muggy weather he hated. As he entered the newsagent's shop, he remembered the way it used to be laid out, the counter in a different place, racks arranged differently. Different magazines and covers back then, too: *Film Show*, *Fabulous*, *Jackie*, *Honey*, *Tit-Bits*, *Annabelle*.

Banks remembered his conversation with Michelle in the pub about Donald Bradford and his collection of porn, and wondered if he really had acted as a distributor. While Banks couldn't imagine Graham slipping a magazine of French *fellatio* between the pages of the *People* and putting it through Number 42's letterbox, he *could* imagine Bradford keeping his stock under the counter or hidden in the back. And maybe Graham had stumbled upon it.

He could remember the first time he had ever seen a pornographic magazine. Not just the ones with naked women in them, like *Playboy*, *Swank* and *Mayfair*, but true porn, magazines that showed people *doing* things.

It was in their den inside the tree and, interestingly enough, the magazines were Graham's. At least, he brought them. Had Banks never wondered at the time where Graham got them from? He didn't know. And if Graham had mentioned it, Banks didn't remember.

It was a warm day, and there were only three of them there, but he wasn't sure whether the third was Dave, Paul or Steve. The branches and leaves came right down to the ground, hard, shiny green leaves with thorns on them, he remembered now, and he could feel himself slipping through the concealed entrance, where the foliage wasn't too dense, the thorns pricking his skin. Once you got inside, the space seemed bigger than it could possibly be, just the way the inside of Dr Who's TARDIS was bigger than the outside. They had plenty of space to sit around and smoke, and enough light got through for them to look at dirty magazines. The smell of the place came back, too, so real he could smell it as he stood waiting to cross the road. Pine needles. Or something similar. And there was a soft beige carpet of them on the ground.

That day Graham had the two magazines stuffed down the front of his shirt and he brought them out with a flourish. He probably said, 'Feast your eyes on this, lads,' but Banks couldn't remember the actual words, and he didn't have time to settle down and try to reconstruct the memory in full. It wasn't important anyway.

What *was* important was that for the next hour or so the three teenagers looked in awe on some of the most amazing, exciting, unbelievable images they had ever seen in their lives, people doing things they had never even dreamed could or *should* be done.

By today's standards, Banks realized, it was pretty mild, but for a fourteen-year-old provincial kid in the summer of 1965 to see colour photos of a woman sucking a man's penis or a man sticking his penis up a woman's arse was shocking in the extreme. There were no animals, Banks remembered, and certainly no children. Mostly he remembered images of impossibly large-breasted women, some of them with semen spurting all over their breasts and faces, and well-endowed men usually on top of them or being ridden by them. Graham wouldn't lend the magazines out, Banks remembered, so the only time they had to look at them was then and there, inside the tree. The titles and text, or what he remembered of them, were in a foreign language. He knew it wasn't German or French because he took those languages at school.

While this didn't become a regular occurrence, Banks did remember a couple of other occasions that summer when Graham brought magazines to the tree. Different ones each time. And then, of course, Graham disappeared and Banks didn't see that kind of porn again until he became a policeman.

So was it a clue or not? As Michelle had said last night,

it hardly seemed something worth murdering over, even back then, but if it was a part of something bigger – the Kray empire, for example – and if Graham had got involved in it way beyond his depth, beyond borrowing a few magazines, then there might be a link to his murder. It was worth looking into, at any rate, if Banks could figure out where to start.

Tapping the newspaper against his thigh, Banks crossed the busy road and hurried back home before his bacon and eggs turned cold. The last thing he needed was to upset his mother again this morning.

•

Despite her late night, Michelle was at her desk long before Detective Superintendent Shaw was likely to see the light of day. If he bothered coming in at all. Maybe he would take another sick day. At any rate, the last thing she wanted was him breathing over her shoulder while Banks was in an interview room looking through the mugshots. There were people around the office, so she and Banks hadn't had a chance to do much more than say a quick hello before they got down to business. She had given him a choice of the computer version or the plain, old-fashioned photo albums, and he had chosen the albums.

She had felt a little shy when he walked in and could still hardly believe that she had gone ahead and slept with him like that, even though she knew she had wanted to. It wasn't as if she had been saving herself or anything, or that she was afraid, or had lost interest in sex, only that she had been far too preoccupied by the aftermath of Melissa's death and the end of her marriage to Ted. You don't get over something like that overnight.

Still, she was surprised at her new-found boldness and blushed even now as she thought about the way it had made her feel. She didn't know what Banks's personal situation was, except that he was going through a divorce. He hadn't talked about his wife, or his children, if he had any. Michelle found herself curious. She hadn't told him about Melissa and Ted either, and she didn't know if she would. Not for a while, anyway. It was just too painful.

The only real drawback was that he was on the Job. But where else was she likely to meet someone? People who form relationships often meet at their places of work. Besides, North Yorkshire was a fair distance from Cambridgeshire, and after they'd got the Graham Marshall case sorted, she doubted they would ever have to work together again. But would they even *see* each other? That was the question. It was a long way to travel. Or perhaps it was foolish of her even to imagine a relationship, or to want one. Maybe it had just been a one-night stand and Banks already had a lover up in Eastvale.

Putting aside her thoughts, and her memories of the previous night, Michelle got down to work. She had a couple of things to do before Graham Marshall's funeral service that afternoon, including tracking down Jet Harris's wife and ringing Dr Cooper. But before she could pick up the telephone, Dr Cooper rang *her*.

'Dr Cooper. I was going to ring you this morning,' said Michelle. 'Any news?'

'Sorry it took me so long to get the information you wanted, but I told you Hilary Wendell's a tough man to track down.'

'You've got something?'

'Hilary has. He won't commit himself to this absolutely, so he'd be very unwilling to testify if it ever came to a court case.'

'It probably won't,' said Michelle, 'but the information might be useful to me.'

'Well, from careful measurement of the nick on the underside of the rib, he's made a few projections and he's pretty certain it's a military knife of some kind. His money's on a Fairbairn–Sykes.'

'What's that?'

'British commando knife. Introduced in 1940. Seven-inch, double-edged blade. Stiletto point.'

'A commando knife?'

'Yes. Is that of any use?'

'It might be,' said Michelle. 'Thanks a lot.'

'You're welcome.'

'And please thank Dr Wendell from me.'

'Will do.'

A *commando knife*. In 1965 the war had only been over for twenty years and plenty of men in their early forties would have fought in it, and had access to such a knife. What worried Michelle most of all, though, was that the only person she *knew* had served as a Royal Marines Commando was Jet Harris; she remembered it from the brief biography she had read when she first came to Thorpe Wood. He had also been awarded a Distinguished Conduct Medal.

The thought of it sent shivers up her spine: Jet Harris, himself, as killer, misdirecting the investigation at every turn, away from Bradford, perhaps because of Fiorino, as Banks had suggested, and away from himself. This was one theory she certainly couldn't go to Shaw with, or to anyone else in the division either. Harris was a local hero and she'd need a hell of a lot of hard evidence if she expected anyone to entertain even the remotest suspicion that Jet Harris was a murderer.

After he'd been in about an hour, Banks poked his head out of the interview-room door, no doubt looking to see if Shaw was around, then carried one of the books over to Michelle.

'I think that's him,' he said.

Michelle looked at the photo. The man was in his late twenties, with medium-length brown hair, badly cut, a stocky build, piggy eyes, and a pug nose. His name was Des Wayman, and according to his record he had been in and out of the courts ever since his days as juvenile car thief, progressing from that to public disorder offences and GBH. His most recent incarceration, a lenient nine months, was for receiving stolen goods, and he had been out just over a year and a half.

'What next?' Banks asked.

'I'll go and have a word with him.'

'Want me to come along?'

'No. I think it would work better if I could question him without you there. After all, it might come to an identity parade. If any charges are brought, I want to make sure this is done right.'

'Fair enough,' said Banks. 'But he looks like a tough customer.' He rubbed his jaw. 'Feels like one, too.'

Michelle tapped her pen against her lips and looked across the office, where DC Collins sat talking on the phone, shirtsleeves rolled up, scribbling on the pad in front of him. She hadn't let him in on her suspicions about Shaw and Harris. Could she trust him? He was almost as new as she was, for a start, and that went in his favour. She had never seen him hanging around with Shaw or with any of the other old brigade, either, another plus. In the end, she decided she *had* to trust someone, and Collins was it.

'I'll take DC Collins,' she said, then lowered her voice. 'Look, there's a couple of things I need to talk to you about, but not here.'

'After the funeral this afternoon?'

'Okay,' said Michelle, jotting Des Wayman's address down in her notebook. 'I should know a bit more about Mr Wayman's activities by then. Oh, and guess where he lives?'

'Where?'

'The Hazels.'

•

Annie pored over Luke Armitage's notebooks and computer files in her office that morning. At least she felt a bit better, despite a poor night's sleep. Eventually, the pain-killers had kicked in and she woke up at half-past seven in the morning, not even having got around to putting in the second *Doctor Zhivago* tape. This morning, though her jaw was still throbbing a bit, it didn't hurt anywhere near as much as it had.

The one thing that intrigued her about Luke's jottings was the increasing eroticism mixed in with the vague classical references to Persephone, Psyche and Ophelia. Then she remembered that Ophelia wasn't a character from classical mythology, but Hamlet's girlfriend, driven mad by his violent rejection of her. She remembered studying the play at school and finding it rather too long and dense for her taste at the time. She had seen several film versions since then, including one with Mel Gibson as Hamlet and another with Marianne Faithfull as Ophelia, and she remembered from somewhere the image of Ophelia floating down a river surrounded by flowers. Did Luke feel guilty about rejecting someone, then? Had he been killed out of revenge, by 'a woman scorned'? And if so, who? Liz Palmer? Lauren Anderson? Rose Barlow?

Of course, the repeated references to 'sweet white breasts', 'pale cheeks' and 'soft white thighs' in Luke's fragments of songs and poems could have been mere adolescent fantasy. Luke certainly had a romantic imagination and, if Banks were to be believed, adolescent boys thought of nothing but sex. But they could also point to the fact that Luke had been involved in a sexual relationship. Liz Palmer looked a likely candidate, despite her denials. Annie also shouldn't forget that according to the head teacher's daughter, Rose Barlow, there might have been something going on between Luke and Lauren Anderson. Rose was unreliable, but it might be worth talking to Lauren again if she got nowhere with Liz and Ryan. Rose had been involved with Luke, in however slight a way, and she had no doubt felt jilted when he spent more time with Liz or Lauren. Or was there someone else Annie was overlooking, some connection she was missing? She felt that she was, but no matter how she tried, the missing link still eluded her.

Her phone rang just as she was turning off Luke's computer.

'Annie, it's Stefan Nowak. Don't get your hopes up too high, but I might have a bit of good news for you.'

'Do tell. I could do with some good news round about now.'

'The lab hasn't finished trying to match your DNA samples with the blood on the drystone wall yet, so I can't tell you about that, but my team *did* find blood at the flat.'

'Liz Palmer's flat?'

'Yes.'

'How much?'

'Only a small amount.'

'Where?'

'Not where you'd expect. Smeared under the bathroom sink.'

'As if someone gripped it while leaning over?'

'Could be, yes. But there are no prints or anything, just a small smear of blood.'

'Is it enough for analysis?'

'Oh, yes. We're working on it now. All the lab has been able to tell me so far is that it matches Luke Armitage's blood type and that it doesn't match the samples we took from Liz Palmer or Ryan Milne.'

'But that's fantastic, Stefan! Don't you see? It puts Luke Armitage bleeding in Liz Palmer's flat.'

'Maybe. But it won't tell you *when*.'

'For the moment, I'll take what I can get. At least that gives me some leverage in the next interview.'

'There's more.'

'What?'

'I've just been talking to Dr Glendenning, and he tells me the tox screen on Luke shows an unusually large amount of diazepam.'

'Diazepam? That's Valium, isn't it?'

'That's one name for it. There are many. But the point is that it was mostly undigested.'

'So he died very soon after taking it, and his system didn't have time to digest it?'

'Yes.'

'But it's not the cause of death?'

'No way.'

'Would it have been enough to kill him?'

'Probably not.'

'Anything else?'

'In the flat? Yes. Drugs. Some marijuana, LSD, Ecstasy.'

'Dealing?'

'No. Not enough. Just for personal use, I'd say. And no diazepam.'

'Thanks, Stefan. Thanks a lot.'

Annie hung up and pondered what she had just heard. Luke had bled in Liz and Ryan's flat, and he had undigested diazepam in his system. Where did he get it? She didn't remember anything about medication in the information they'd gathered on him. She wasn't even sure that doctors prescribed diazepam to someone that young. She should at least check with Robin. Even though Stefan's team hadn't found any in the flat, the first thing to do, Annie thought, getting to her feet and reaching for her jacket, was to find out if either Liz or Ryan had prescriptions for diazepam.

•

According to his file, Des Wayman lived in a two-bedroom council house on Hazel Way, just off the crescent at the Wilmer Road end of the estate. It was mid-morning when Michelle and DC Collins parked outside and walked down the path. The sky was covered in grey cloud and the air was so saturated with moisture it felt like warm drizzle. Michelle's clothes were sticking to her, and DC Collins had taken off his suit jacket and loosened his tie. Even so, there were damp patches under his arms. She was glad Collins was with her. He played second row for the police rugby team, and his solid presence was enough to put anyone off trying anything. As far as Michelle could make out, nobody had followed them, and she hadn't seen any beige vans in the area.

Michelle knocked at the scratched red door of Number 15. The man who opened it seemed surprised to see her. It was Des Wayman, no doubt about it. The pug nose gave him away, and the piggy eyes. He was wearing grubby jeans, with his shirt hanging out.

'Who are you? I thought it was a mate of mine,' he said, with a leer. 'I'm off out. But seeing as you're here, how about coming with us for a drink?'

Michelle showed her warrant card and DC Collins followed suit. The man's expression became wary.

'Mr Wayman?' Michelle said.

'And what if it is?'

'We'd like a word, sir. Mind if we come in?'

'Like I said, I'm just on my way out. Can't we talk down the pub?' He licked his lips and nodded towards the pub at the bottom of the street, the Lord Nelson. Then he looked at Collins. 'And you can leave your chaperon behind.'

'It'd be better here, sir,' Michelle insisted. When Wayman made no move, she walked past him into the house. He stood and looked at her for a moment, then followed her into his living room, DC Collins right behind him.

The place was a tip, to put it mildly. Empty beer cans littered the floor, along with overflowing ashtrays. The heavy curtains were closed, allowing just enough light to illuminate the mess. The medley of smells was hard to define. Accumulated dust, stale beer and smoke, with overtones of used socks and sweat. But there was more: something vaguely sexual that turned Michelle's stomach. She flung the curtains open and opened the window. The latter took a bit of doing, as it hadn't been opened in a long time and had jammed. DC Collins lent a hand, and the two of them finally got it open. The still, humid air outside didn't help much, and the room looked even worse in full light.

'What are you doing?' Wayman protested. 'I value my privacy. I don't want the whole fucking estate looking through my window.'

'We value our health, Mr Wayman,' Michelle said. 'It's already at risk just by being here, but a little fresh air might help.'

'Sarky bitch,' said Wayman, sitting down on a worn and stained sofa. 'Get to the point, then, love.' He picked up a can of beer from the table and ripped the tab. Foam spilled over the top and he licked it off before it fell to the floor.

Michelle looked around and saw no surface she felt comfortable sitting on, so she stood. By the window. 'First off, don't call me "love",' she said, 'and second, you're in a bit of trouble, Des.'

'What's new? You lot are always trying to fit me up.'

'This isn't a fit-up,' said Michelle, aware of DC Collins paying careful attention to her. She hadn't explained much to him in the car; all she had said was not to take notes. He hadn't a clue what this was all about, or how it linked to the Graham Marshall case. 'It's cut and dried.'

Wayman folded his arms. 'So tell me what I'm supposed to have done.'

'Last night at approximately ten fifty-five, you and another man assaulted a man outside a riverside flat.'

'I did no such thing,' said Wayman.

'Des,' Michelle said, leaning forward. 'He saw you. He picked you out of the villains' album.'

That seemed to stop him for a moment. He frowned, and she could almost see the wheels spinning, cogs turning in his addled brain, looking for a way out, an explanation. 'He must be mistaken,' he said. 'His word against mine.'

Michelle laughed. 'Is that the best you can do?'

'His word against mine.'

'Where were you?'

'Matter of fact, I was having a bevvy or two in the Pig and Whistle.'

'Anyone see you?'

'Lots of people. It was very busy.'

'That's not far away from where the attack took place,' said Michelle. 'What time did you leave?'

'Dunno. After closing time.'

'Sure you didn't sneak out a few minutes early and then go back for last orders?'

'And waste good drinking time? Why would I do that?'

'That's what I'm trying to find out.'

'Not me, Miss.'

'Show me your hands, Des.'

Wayman stretched his hands out, palms up.

'Turn them over.'

Wayman did as she asked.

'Where'd you get that skinned knuckle?'

'I don't know,' said Wayman. 'Must have brushed it against the wall or something.'

'And that ring you've got,' Michelle went on. 'Sharp, I'll bet. Sharp enough to cut someone. I bet there'll still be traces of blood on the metal,' she said. 'Enough to identify as your victim's.'

Wayman lit a cigarette and fell silent. Even with the window open the air soon became thick with smoke.

'Right,' said Michelle, 'I'm sick of pissing about. DC Collins, let's take Mr Wayman down the station and organize an identity parade. That should settle things once and for all.'

Collins moved forward.

'Just a minute,' said Wayman. 'I'm not going to no station. I've got an appointment. People are expecting me.'

'In your local. I know. But if you want to enjoy a nice pint this lunchtime, or any lunchtime for the next little while, you'd better tell us what we want to know.'

'But I've already told you. I didn't do anything.'

'And I've told you you were identified. Stop lying, Des. Do yourself a favour. Think about that nice, thirst-quenching pint sitting there on the bar at the Lord Nelson, just waiting for you.' Michelle paused to let the image sink in. She could do with a pint, herself, even though she rarely drank beer. The air was fast becoming unbreathable, and she didn't know if she could stand it much longer. She had one last card to play before she would have to take Wayman in. 'Trouble is, Des,' she said, 'the man you attacked, the man who recognized you . . .'

'Yeah? What about him?'

'He's a copper. He's one of us.'

'Come off it. You're trying it on. Trying to fit me up.'

'No. It's true. What was it you said earlier? His word against yours? Whose word do you think the judge is going to believe, Des?'

'Nobody told me—'

'Told you what?'

'Shut up. I've got to think.'

'You've not got long. Assaulting a police officer. That's a serious charge. You'll go down for a lot longer than nine months on that one.'

Wayman dropped his cigarette stub in the empty beer can, tossed it on the floor and opened another one. His fleshy lips were wet with foam and beer. He reached for another cigarette.

'Please don't light another one of those, Des,' Michelle said.

'What do you mean? Surely it's not got so bad a bloke can't even smoke in his own house these days?'

'When we're gone you can smoke yourself silly,' said Michelle. 'That's if we leave without you. Up to you. There's no smoking in the holding cells any more.'

Wayman laughed. 'You know,' he said, puffing out his chest, 'I'm practically one of you lot, myself. I don't know where you get off coming and pinning this assault on me when it's police business to start with.'

Michelle felt a little shiver up her spine. 'What are you talking about?'

'You know damn well what I'm talking about.' Wayman touched the side of his pug nose. 'I told you, I was on police business. Undercover. Sometimes a little tap on the head and a few words of warning work wonders. It's the way they used to do things in the old days, so I hear. And don't tell me you don't know what I'm talking about. Your boss certainly does.'

'Boss?'

'Yes. The big ugly bloke. *Numero uno*. Detective bloody Superintendent Ben Shaw.'

'*Shaw?*' Michelle had been more than half-suspecting that Shaw was behind the attacks on her and Banks, but found herself stunned to have it confirmed.

Wayman tilted the can and took a long swig, then he wiped his mouth with the back of his hand and grinned. 'Don't look so surprised, love.'

'Superintendent Shaw told you to do this? Wait a minute. Are you telling me you're an undercover police officer following Detective Superintendent Shaw's orders?'

Wayman shrugged, perhaps sensing he'd gone too far. 'Well, maybe I'm not exactly what you'd call an under-cover officer, but I've done your boss a little favour from time to time. You know, like giving him the nod where the stuff from the Curry's warehouse job was stashed. That sort of thing.'

'So you're Shaw's snitch?'

'I've been happy to help out now and then. He'll see me all right. So do us a favour and bugger off, then just maybe I won't tell your boss you've been round upsetting me.'

'Do you own a beige van?' Michelle asked.

'What? I don't own a van at all. Dark blue Corsa, if you must know.'

'Ever done time for burglary?'

'You've read my form. Did you notice anything about burglary?'

Michelle hadn't. So Wayman most likely wasn't respon-sible for the damage to her flat and the attempt on her life. Somehow, she sensed he didn't have the subtlety to do what had been done with the dress, even if his employer had told him about Melissa. He clearly wasn't the only vil-lain on Shaw's payroll. Michelle sensed DC Collins paying rapt attention beside her. She glanced at him and he raised his eyebrows. 'Look,' she said, wishing she could sit down. Her shoes were killing her. But it wasn't worth catching something. 'You're in a lot of trouble, Des. GBH is bad enough in itself, but against a copper, well . . . you don't need me to tell you . . .'

For the first time, Wayman looked worried. 'But I

didn't know he was a copper, did I? Do you think I'd have done something like that if I'd known who he was? You must think I'm crazy.'

'But you did it, didn't you?'

'Where's this going?'

'Up to you, Des.'

'What do you mean?'

Michelle spread her hands. 'I mean it's up to you where it goes from here. It could go to the station, to the lawyers, to court eventually. Or it could end here.'

Wayman swallowed. 'End? How? I mean . . . I don't . . .'

'Do I have to spell it out?'

'You promise?'

'Only if you tell me what I want to know.'

'It goes no further?'

Michelle looked at DC Collins, who looked lost. 'No,' she said. 'This bloke you and your friend assaulted last night, what did Shaw tell you about him?'

'That he was a small-time villain from up north looking to get himself established on our patch.'

'And what did Detective Superintendent Shaw ask you to do?'

'Nip it in the bud.'

'Can you be more specific?'

'Shaw didn't want to know. I mean, he'd just asked me to handle the situation, do something about it. He didn't tell me how, and he didn't want to know.'

'But it usually meant violence?'

'Most people understand a thump on the nose.'

'That's your understanding of the situation?'

'If you like.'

'So that's what you did?'

'Yes.'

'How did you find out he was in town?'

'I've been keeping an eye out. I recognized his car from when he was down here last week.'

'And how did you know where he was that evening?'

'I got a call on my mobile in the Pig and Whistle.'

'From who?'

'Who do you think?'

'Go on.'

'He said our mutual friend was drinking in a pub down the street, and if an opportunity presented itself . . . well, I was to have a quiet word, like.'

'But how did he . . . Never mind.' Michelle realized that Shaw must have been using his whole network of informers to keep an eye on the comings and goings in the Graham Marshall investigation. But why? To hide the truth, that the great local hero Jet Harris was a murderer?

'So what did you do?'

'We waited outside and followed the two of you back to the riverside flats. We were a bit worried because we thought he might be going in to get his end away, like, no disrespect, and we might not get back to the Pig and Whistle till they'd stopped serving, so it was all sweetness and joy when he came straight down those stairs and into the street. We didn't muck about.'

'And the beating was your idea?'

'Like I said, it gets the point across. Anyway, we wouldn't have hurt him too much. We didn't even get a chance to finish. Some interfering bastard walking his dog started making a lot of noise. Not that we couldn't have dealt with him, too, but the bloody dog was waking the whole street up.'

'And that's everything?' Michelle asked.

'Scout's honour.'

'When were you ever a scout?'

'Boys' Brigade, as a matter of fact. What's going to happen now? Remember what you promised.'

Michelle looked at DC Collins. 'What's going to happen now,' she said, 'is that we're going to go away, and you're going to the Lord Nelson to drink yourself into a stupor. And if you ever cross my path again, I'll make sure they put you somewhere that'll make the Middle East look like an alcoholic's paradise. That clear?'

'Yes, ma'am.' But Wayman was smiling. The prospect of a drink in the present, Michelle thought, by far outdid any fears for the future. He wouldn't change.

'Do you think you can tell me what all that was about?' asked DC Collins when they got outside.

Michelle took a deep breath and smiled. 'Yes,' she said. 'Of course, Nat. I'm sorry for keeping you in the dark so long, but I think you'll understand when you hear what I have to say. And I'll tell you over a pie and a pint. My treat.' She looked around. 'But not in the Lord Nelson.'

17

'**Glad you could come**, Alan,' said Mrs Marshall, sticking out her black-gloved hand. 'My, my. You've been in the wars.'

Banks touched his lip. 'It's nothing,' he said.

'I hope you'll come back to the house for drinks and sandwiches.'

They were standing outside the chapel in the light drizzle after Graham's funeral. It had been tasteful enough, as such things went, Banks thought, though there was something odd about a funeral service for someone who has been dead over thirty years. They had the usual readings, including the 23rd Psalm, and Graham's sister gave a short eulogy throughout which she verged on tears.

'Of course,' Banks said, shaking Mrs Marshall's hand. Then he saw Michelle walking down the path under her umbrella. 'Excuse me a moment.'

He hurried along after Michelle. During the service, he had caught her eye once or twice and she had looked away. He wanted to know what was wrong. She had said earlier that she wanted to talk to him. Was it about last night? Was she having regrets? Did she want to tell him she'd made a mistake and didn't want to see him again? 'Michelle?' He put his hand gently on her shoulder.

Michelle turned to face him. When she looked him in the eye, she smiled and lifted the umbrella so it covered his head too. 'Shall we walk a while?'

'Fine,' said Banks. 'Everything okay?'

'Of course it is. Why do you ask?'

So there was nothing wrong. Banks could have kicked himself. He'd got so used to feeling that his every move, every meeting, was so fragile, partly because they *had* been – like walking on eggs – with Annie, that he was turning normal behaviour into perceived slights. They were police officers in public – in a bloody chapel, for crying out loud. What did he expect her to do? Make doe eyes at him? Walk over to his pew and sit on his knee and whisper sweet nothings in his ear?

'This morning, in the station, I wanted to tell you that I enjoyed last night, but I could hardly say that in the cop shop, could I?'

She reached over and touched his sore lip. 'I enjoyed it, too.'

'Are you coming back to the house?'

'No, I don't think so. I don't like that sort of thing.'

'Me neither. I'd better go, though.'

'Of course.'

They walked down one of the narrow gravel paths between graves, carved headstones dark with rain. Yews overhung the path and rain dripped from their leaves onto the umbrella, tapping harder than the drizzle. 'You said you wanted to talk to me.'

'Yes.' Michelle told him about Dr Wendell's tentative identification of the Fairbairn-Sykes commando knife and Harris's wartime record.

Banks whistled between his teeth. 'And you say Jet Harris was a commando?'

'Yes.'

'Bloody hell. That's a real can of worms.' Banks shook his head. 'It's hard to believe that Jet Harris might have killed Graham,' he said. 'It just doesn't make any sense. I mean, what possible motive could he have had?'

'I don't know. Only what we speculated about yesterday, that he was somehow connected with Fiorino and the porn racket and Graham fell foul of them. Even so, it's hard to imagine someone in Harris's position doing a job like that himself. And we don't really have any hard evidence; it's all just circumstantial. Anyway, he's not the only candidate. I remembered Mrs Walker – you know, the woman in the newsagent's – said something about Donald Bradford being in a special unit in Burma. I checked. Turns out it was a commando unit.'

'Bradford, too? That complicates things.'

'Well, at least we know that Bradford had some sort of involvement with pornography. We don't even have any evidence that Harris was bent yet,' said Michelle. 'Only Shaw's behaviour. Which brings me to our interview with Des Wayman.'

'What did he have to say for himself?'

Michelle told him about Wayman's assertion that Shaw was behind last night's attack. 'He'd deny he ever said it if we challenged him, and I'm sure Shaw will deny it, too.'

'But *we* know it's true,' said Banks. 'That gives us an edge. It was a stupid move on Shaw's part. It means he's worried, getting desperate. What about the burglary at your flat and the van that tried to run you down?'

Michelle shook her head. 'Wayman knows nothing about them. Shaw must have got someone else, maybe someone a bit brighter. My impression is that Wayman is okay for the strong-arm stuff but couldn't think his way out of a paper bag.'

'Like Bill Marshall?'

'Yes.'

'You think we should have a chat with Shaw?'

'Soon. It'd be nice to know a bit more about Harris first.'

'I'll call you later.'

'Okay.' Michelle turned and carried on walking down the path.

'Where are you going now?' Banks asked.

She slowed, turned and smiled at him. 'You're a very nosy fellow,' she said. 'And you know what happens to nosy fellows, don't you?' Then she walked on, leaving Banks to gape after her. He could swear he saw her shoulders shaking with laughter.

●

'Okay, Liz, are you going to tell us the truth now?' Annie asked once the interview room was set up and the tapes turned on.

'We didn't do anything wrong, Ryan and me,' Liz said.

'I have to remind you that you're entitled to a lawyer. If you can't afford one we'll get a duty solicitor for you.'

Liz shook her head. 'I don't need a lawyer. That's like admitting I did it.'

'As you like. You know we found drugs in your flat, don't you?'

'There wasn't much. It was only . . . you know, for Ryan and me.'

'It's still a crime.'

'Are you going to arrest us for that?'

'Depends on what you have to tell me. I just want you to know that you're in trouble already. You can make it better by telling me the truth, or you can make it worse by continuing with your lies. What's it to be, Liz?'

'I'm tired.'

'The sooner we're done with this, the sooner you can go home. What's it to be?'

Liz nibbled at her trembling lower lip.

'Maybe it would help,' said Annie, 'if I told you we found traces of Luke's blood under your bathroom sink.'

Liz looked at her, wide-eyed. 'But we didn't kill Luke. Honest we didn't!'

'Tell me what happened. Convince me.'

Liz started crying. Annie passed her some tissues and waited till she calmed down. 'Did Luke call at your flat the day he disappeared?' she asked.

After a long silence, Liz said, 'Yes.'

'Good,' breathed Annie. 'Now we're getting somewhere.'

'But we didn't do him any harm.'

'Okay. We'll get to that. What time did he arrive?'

'Time? I don't know. Early in the evening. Maybe six-ish.'

'So he must have come straight from the market square?'

'I suppose so. I don't know where he'd been. He was a bit upset, I remember, because he said some of the kids from the school had pushed him around in the square, so maybe he *had* come straight from there.'

'What happened in the flat?'

Liz looked down at her chewed fingernails.

'Liz?'

'What?'

'Was Ryan there?'

'Yes.'

'All the time? Even when Luke arrived?'

'Yes.'

So that put paid to Annie's theory that Ryan had

interrupted something between Liz and Luke. 'What did the three of you do?'

Liz paused, then took a deep breath. 'First we had something to eat,' she said. 'It must've been around teatime.'

'Then what?'

'We just talked, went through a few songs.'

'I thought you did your rehearsals in the church basement.'

'We do. But Ryan's got an acoustic guitar. We just played around with a couple of arrangements, that's all.'

'And then?'

Again, Liz fell silent and her eyes filled with tears. She rubbed the back of her hand across her face and said, 'Ryan rolled a joint. Luke . . . he'd . . . like he was a virgin, you know, when it came to drugs. I mean we'd offered to share before but he always said no.'

'Not that night?'

'No. That night he said yes. The first time. It was like he . . . you know . . . *wanted* to lose his virginity. I don't know why. I suppose he just felt it was time.'

'What happened?'

'Nothing much at first. I think he was disappointed. A lot of people are the first time.'

'So what did you do?'

'We smoked some more and it seemed to work. It was pretty strong stuff, opiated hash. He got all giggly at first, then he went sort of introspective.'

'So what went wrong?'

'It was when Ryan put that Neil Byrd CD on. You know, that new compilation, *The Summer that Never Was*.'

'He did *what*?' Annie could imagine what effect something like that might have on Luke if he was under the influence of strong cannabis. Maybe it wasn't a seriously dangerous drug, but it could cause paranoia in people, and it intensified and exaggerated emotions. Annie knew; she'd smoked it more than once in her teenage years. Reining in her temper, she asked, 'How did Luke react to the music?'

'He freaked. He just freaked. Ryan was thinking it would be a neat idea to do a Neil Byrd song, you know, with Luke singing. I mean, it'd get a lot of attention.'

'Didn't you realize how confused Luke was about his real father? Didn't you know he *never* listened to Neil Byrd's music?'

'Yes, but we thought this was a good time to try it,' Liz protested. 'We thought his mind was, you know, open to new things, mellow from the dope, that it was more likely he'd see how *beautiful* his father's work was.'

'When he was disoriented, ultra-sensitive?' Annie shook her head in disbelief. 'You're a lot more stupid than I thought you were. Stupid or so selfish and blinkered it amounts to much the same thing.'

'But that's not fair! We didn't mean any harm.'

'Fine,' said Annie. 'Let's just say you were guilty of poor judgement and move on. What happened next?'

'Nothing at first. It seemed as if Luke was just listening to the song. Ryan was playing the chords along with it, trying a little harmony. All of a sudden Luke just went crazy. He knocked the guitar out of Ryan's hand and went over to the CD player and took the CD out and started trying to break it in two.'

'What did you do?'

'Ryan struggled with him, but Luke was, like, *possessed.*'

'What about the blood?'

'In the end Ryan just punched him. That was where the blood came from. Luke ran into the bathroom. I was just behind him, to see if he was all right. There wasn't much blood, it was only like a nosebleed. Luke looked in the mirror and started going crazy again and banging the mirror with his fists. I tried to calm him down, but he pushed past me and left.'

'And that was it?'

'Yes.'

'Neither of you went after him?'

'No. We figured he just wanted to be by himself.'

'A disturbed fifteen-year-old having a bad drug experience? Oh, come on, Liz. Surely you can't be *that* stupid?'

'Well, *we* were stoned, too. I'm not saying we were, like, the most *rational* we could be. It just seemed . . . I don't know.' She lowered her head and sobbed.

Though she believed Liz's story, Annie found it hard to dredge up any sympathy. Legally, however, any charges that could be brought against them were minor. If reckless negligence could be proven, then they could, at a stretch, be convicted of manslaughter, but even though they had given Luke drugs, Annie reminded herself, she still didn't know how he had died, or why.

'Do you know where he went after he left your flat?' Annie asked.

'No,' said Liz between sobs. 'We never saw him again. I'm sorry. I'm so sorry.'

'Did you or Ryan give Luke any Valium, to calm him down, perhaps?'

Liz frowned and looked at Annie through her tears. 'No. We didn't do stuff like that.'

'So you never had any Valium in the house?'

'No.'

'And there's nothing more you can tell me?'

'I've told you everything.' She looked up at Annie with red eyes. 'Can I go home now? I'm tired.'

Annie stood up and called for a uniformed officer. 'Yes,' she said. 'But don't wander too far. We'll be wanting to talk to you again.'

When Liz had been escorted away, Annie closed the interview-room door behind her and sat down again and held her throbbing head in her hands.

•

'Another drink, Alan?'

Banks's beer glass was half full, and he had just arranged to go out drinking that evening with Dave Grenfell and Paul Major, so he declined Mrs Marshall's offer and ate another potted meat sandwich instead. Besides, the beer was a neighbour's home brew and it tasted like it.

'You know, I'm glad we did this,' Mrs Marshall went on. 'The service. I know it probably seems silly to some people, after all this time, but it means a lot to me.'

'It doesn't seem silly,' said Banks, looking around the room. Most of the guests were family and neighbours, some of whom Banks recognized. Dave's and Paul's parents were there, along with Banks's own. Pachelbel's 'Canon' played in the background. Graham would have hated it, Banks thought. Or probably not. If he'd lived, his tastes would no doubt have changed, as Banks's had. Even so, what he really wanted to listen to was 'Ticket to Ride' or 'Summer Nights' or 'Mr Tambourine Man'.

'I think it meant a lot to all of us,' he said.

'Thank you,' Mrs Marshall said tearfully. 'Are you sure you won't have some more?'

'No, thank you.'

Mrs Marshall wandered off. Banks noticed Bill
Marshall in his armchair by the fireplace, a blanket over
his knees despite the muggy day. The windows were all
open, but it was still too stuffy in the house. Banks saw
Paul talking to a couple he didn't recognize, probably old
neighbours, and Dave was chatting with Graham's sister,
Joan. His own parents were talking to Mr and Mrs
Grenfell. Feeling the call of nature, Banks set his glass
down on the sideboard and went upstairs.

When he had finished in the toilet, he noticed that the
door to Graham's old room was open, and he was
surprised to see that the space-rocket wallpaper he
remembered from years back was still on the walls.
Drawn by the odd sight, he wandered into the small bedroom. Of course, everything else had changed. The bed
had gone, along with the small glass-fronted bookcase
Banks remembered, mostly full of science fiction. The
only familiar object stood in a case leaning against the
wall. Graham's guitar. So they had kept it all these years.

Certain that no one would mind, Banks sat down on a
hard-backed chair and took the guitar out of its case.
Graham had been so proud of it, he remembered. Of
course, he had wanted an electric one, a Rickenbacker
like the one John Lennon played, but he had been chuffed
to death with the second-hand acoustic his parents had
bought him for Christmas 1964.

Banks remembered the fingering, even after so long,
and strummed a C chord. Way out of tune. He grimaced.
Tuning it would be too much of a job for the moment.
He wondered if Mrs Marshall wanted to keep it as a
memento, or if she would consider selling it. If she would,
he'd be glad to buy it from her. He strummed an out-of-

tune G seventh, then moved to put the guitar back in its case. As he did so, he thought he heard something slip around inside it. Gently, he shook the guitar, and there it was again: something scraping inside.

Curious, Banks loosened the strings so that he could slip his hand inside. With a bit of juggling and shaking he managed to grab hold of what felt like a piece of stiff, rolled-up paper. Carefully, he pulled it out, noticing the dried Sellotape Graham had used to stick it to the inside of the guitar. That made it something he had tried to hide.

And when Banks unrolled it, he saw why.

It was a photograph: Graham sprawled on a sheepskin rug in front of a large, ornate fireplace, arms behind him, hands propping him up, legs stretched out in front. He was smiling at the camera in a flirtatious and knowing manner.

And he was absolutely stark naked.

•

Michelle was lucky to find a parking spot about a hundred yards from the former Mrs Harris's pretentious pile of mock Tudor on Long Road, Cambridge, opposite the grounds of Long Road Sixth Form College. It was still drizzling outside, so she took the umbrella from the back of her car.

It hadn't been too hard to track down Jet Harris's ex-wife. The biographical pamphlet told Michelle that her maiden name was Edith Dalton and that she had been married to Harris for twenty-three years, between 1950 and 1973, and that she was ten years his junior. A few discreet enquiries around the office yielded the information that a retired civilian employee, Margery Jenkins, visited her occasionally, and she was happy to give Michelle the address. She also told her that the former Mrs Harris had remarried and was now called Mrs Gifford. Michelle hoped that the nature of her enquiries didn't get back to Shaw before she got the information she needed, whatever that was. She wasn't even sure what Mrs Gifford could, or would, tell her.

A slim, elegantly dressed, grey-haired woman answered the door, and Michelle introduced herself. With a puzzled but interested expression, Mrs Gifford led Michelle to her large living room. There was no clutter, just a white three-piece suite, various antique cabinets stuffed with crystal and a large sideboard against the wall. Mrs Gifford offered nothing in the way of refreshments but sat, legs crossed, and lit a cigarette from a gold lighter. She had a calculating look about her, Michelle noticed, around the eyes, in the eyes themselves, in the strict set of her jaw and sharp angles of her cheeks. She was also very well preserved for her seventy-plus years and had a deep tan, the sort she couldn't have got in England so far this summer.

'The Algarve,' she said, as if she had noticed Michelle looking. 'Got back last week. My husband and I have a nice little villa there. He was a doctor, a plastic surgeon, but he's retired now, of course. Anyway, what can I do for you? It's been a long time since the coppers came to call.'

So Edith Dalton had landed on her feet after twenty-three years of marriage to Jet Harris. 'Just information,' said Michelle. 'You've heard about the Graham Marshall case?'

'Yes. Poor lad.' Mrs Gifford tapped her cigarette against the side of a glass ashtray. 'What about him?'

'Your husband was in charge of that investigation.'

'I remember.'

'Did he ever talk about it, tell you any of his theories?'

'John never talked about his work to me.'

'But something like that? A local boy. Surely you must have been curious?'

'Naturally. But he made a point of not discussing his cases at home.'

'So he didn't have any theories?'

'Not that he shared with me.'

'Do you remember Ben Shaw?'

'Ben? Of course. He worked closely with John.' She smiled. 'Regan and Carter they used to think of themselves. *The Sweeney*. Quite the lads. How is Ben? I haven't seen him for years.'

'What did you think of him?'

Her eyes narrowed. 'As a man or as a copper?'

'Both. Either.'

Mrs Gifford flicked some ash. 'Not much, if truth be told. Ben Shaw rode on John's coat-tails, but he wasn't half the man. Or a quarter the copper.'

'His notebooks covering the Graham Marshall case are missing.'

Mrs Gifford raised a finely pencilled eyebrow. 'Well, things do have a habit of disappearing over time.'

'It just seems a bit of a coincidence.'

'Coincidences do happen.'

'I was just wondering if you knew anything about Shaw, that's all.'

'Like what? Are you asking me if Ben Shaw is bent?'

'Is he?'

'I don't know. John certainly never said anything about it.'

'And he would have known?'

'Oh, yes.' She nodded. 'John would have known. Not much got by him.'

'So you never heard any rumours?'

'No.'

'I understand your husband was a commando during the war.'

'Yes. A real war hero, John was.'

'Do you know if he owned a Fairbairn–Sykes commando knife?'

'Not that I saw.'

'He didn't have any mementos?'

'He gave everything up when he was demobbed. He never talked about those days much. He just wanted to forget. Look, where is all this leading?'

Michelle didn't know how to come straight out with it and ask her if her ex-husband was bent, but she got the impression that Mrs Gifford was a hard one to deceive. 'You lived with Mr Harris for twenty-three years,' she said. 'Why leave after so long?'

Mrs Gifford raised her eyebrows. 'What an odd question. And a rather rude one, if I may say so.'

'I'm sorry, but—'

Mrs Gifford waved her cigarette in the air. 'Yes, yes, you've got your job to do. I know. It doesn't matter now, anyway. I waited until the children left home. It's amazing how much one will put up with for the sake of the children, and for appearances.'

'Put up with?'

'Marriage to John wasn't a bed of roses.'

'But there must have been some compensations.'

Mrs Gifford frowned. 'Compensations?'

'The high life.'

Mrs Gifford laughed. 'The high life? My dear, we lived in that poky little semi in Peterborough almost all our married life. I'd hardly call that the high life.'

'I don't know how to say this diplomatically,' Michelle went on.

'Then bugger diplomacy. I've always been one to face things head on. Come on, out with it.'

'But there seem to be some anomalies in the original investigation into the Graham Marshall disappearance. Things seem to have been steered in one direction, away from other possibilities, and—'

'And my John was the one doing the steering?'

'Well, he was senior investigating officer.'

'And you want to know if he was being paid off?'

'It looks that way. Do you remember Carlo Fiorino?'

'I've heard the name. A long time ago. Wasn't he shot in some drug war?'

'Yes, but before that he pretty much ran crime in the area.'

Mrs Gifford laughed. 'I'm sorry, dear,' she said, 'but the image of some sort of Mafia don running crime in sleepy old Peterborough is . . . well, to say the least, it's *ridiculous*.'

'He wasn't Mafia. Wasn't even Italian. He was the son of a POW and a local girl.'

'Even so, it still sounds absurd.'

'Where there are people, there's crime, Mrs Gifford. And Peterborough was growing fast. The new town expansion. There's nothing anyone likes better than a quickly expanding market. People want to gamble, they want sex, they want to feel safe. If someone supplies them with all these needs, there's quite a tidy profit to be made. And the job's made all the easier if you have a senior policeman in your pocket.' She didn't mean it to come out so bluntly, but she wanted to get Mrs Gifford to take her seriously.

'So you're saying John was on the take?'

'I'm asking you if you noticed anything that might indicate he was receiving extra money, yes.'

'Well, if he was, I never saw any of it. I can tell you that much.'

'So where did it all go? Wine, women and song?'

Mrs Gifford laughed again and stubbed out her cigarette. 'My dear,' she said, 'John was strictly an ale and whisky man. He also had a tin ear, and you can forget the women. I've not told anyone except my present husband this, but I'll tell you now, John Harris was queer as a three-pound note.'

•

'Another round?'

'My shout,' said Banks.

'I'll come with you.' Dave Grenfell got up and accompanied Banks to the bar. For old times' sake, they were in the Wheatsheaf, where the three of them had drunk their very first pints of beer at the age of sixteen. The place had been tarted up over the years, and now it seemed a lot more upmarket than the shabby Victorian backstreet boozer it had been all those years ago. Probably got the lunchtime crowd from the new 'business park' over the road, Banks guessed, though now, early in the evening, it was practically deserted.

Over the first pint, they had caught up with one another to the extent that Banks knew Dave, as his father had said, still worked as a mechanic in a garage in Dorchester and still lived with his first wife, Ellie, whereas Paul was cheerfully unemployed and gay as the day is long. Coming hot on the heels of hearing Mrs Gifford's revelations about Jet Harris over the phone from Michelle, this last discovery shocked Banks only because he had never spotted any signs of it back when they were kids. Not that he would have recognized them. Paul had seemed to leer over the porn just as much as the others, laugh at the jokes about poofs, and Banks was sure he remembered him having a steady girlfriend at one point.

Still, back in 1965 people denied, pretended, tried to 'pass' for straight. Even after legalization, there was so much stigma attached to it, especially on the more macho working-class estates where they had all lived. And in the police force. Banks wondered how hard it had been for Paul to come to terms with himself and come out. Clearly Jet Harris had never been able to do so. And Banks was willing to bet a pound to a penny that *someone* had known about it, and that someone had used the knowledge to advantage. Jet Harris hadn't been bent; he'd been blackmailed.

As Dave prattled on about how gobsmacked *he* was to find out Paul had turned into an 'arse-bandit', Banks's thoughts returned to the photo he had found in Graham's guitar. He hadn't told Mr or Mrs Marshall, hadn't told anyone except Michelle, over his mobile phone when he took the photo up to his room before meeting the others in the Wheatsheaf. What did it mean, and why was it there? Graham must have put it there, Banks assumed, and he had done so because he wanted to hide it. But why did he have it in his possession, why had he posed for it, who took it, and where was it taken? The fireplace looked distinctive enough. Adam, Banks guessed, and you didn't find those just anywhere.

Banks could begin to formulate a few answers to his questions, but he didn't have enough pieces yet to make a complete pattern. Two things he and Michelle had agreed on for certain during their phone conversation: the photo was in some way connected with Graham's murder, and Donald Bradford and Jet Harris were involved in whatever nasty business had been going on. Maybe Carlo Fiorino and Bill Marshall, too. But there were still a few pieces missing.

They carried the drinks back to the table, where Paul sat glancing around the room. 'Remember the old juke-box?' he said.

Banks nodded. The Wheatsheaf used to have a great jukebox for a provincial pub outside the city centre, he remembered, and they spent almost as much money on that as they did on beer. The sixties of familiar, if senti-mental, memory was in full bloom then, when they were sixteen: Procol Harum's 'A Whiter Shade of Pale', the Flowerpot Men singing 'Let's Go to San Francisco', the Beatles' 'Magical Mystery Tour'.

'What do you listen to now, Alan?' Dave asked Banks.

'Bit of everything, I suppose,' Banks said. 'Jazz, classical, some of the old rock stuff. You?'

'Nothing much. I sort of lost interest in music in the seventies, when we had the kids. Never really got it back. Remember Steve, though, the kind of stuff he used to make us listen to on Sunday afternoons? Dylan and all that.'

Banks laughed. 'He was ahead of his time, was Steve. Where the hell is he, anyway? Surely he must have heard, someone must have been in touch with him.'

'Hadn't you heard?' Paul said.

Banks and Dave both stared at him. 'What?'

'Shit. I thought you must know. I'm sorry. Steve's dead.'

Banks felt a shiver up his spine. *The Big Chill.* It was one thing to get to an age when the generation ahead started dying off, but another thing entirely to face the mortality of your own generation. 'What happened?' he asked.

'Lung cancer. About three years ago. I only know 'cos his mum and dad kept in touch with mine, like. Christmas cards, that sort of thing. I hadn't actually seen him for years. Apparently he had a couple of kids, too.'

'Poor sod,' said Dave.

After a brief silence, they raised their glasses and drank a toast to the memory of Steve, early Dylan fan. Then they toasted Graham again. Two down, three to go.

Banks looked closely at each of his old friends and saw that Dave had lost most of his hair and Paul was grey and had put on a lot of weight. He started to feel gloomy, and even the memory of Michelle naked beside him failed to dispel the gloom. His lip burned and his left side ached from where his assailant had kicked him. He felt like getting pissed, but he knew when he felt that way that it never worked. No matter how much he drank he never reached the state of oblivion he aimed for. Even so, he didn't have to watch what he drank. He wasn't driving anywhere that night. He had thought he might try to get in touch with Michelle later, depending on how the evening went, but they hadn't made any firm arrangements. Both needed time to absorb what had happened between them, Banks sensed. That was okay. He didn't feel that she was backing off or anything, no more than he was. Besides, she had a lot to do. Things were moving fast.

Banks looked at his cigarette smouldering in the ashtray and thought of Steve. Lung cancer. Shit. He reached forward and stubbed it out even though it was only half smoked. Maybe it would be his last. That thought made him feel a bit better, yet even that feeling was fast followed by a wave of sheer panic at how unbearable his life would be without cigarettes. The coffee in the morning, a pint of beer in the Queen's Arms, that late evening Laphroaig out by the beck. Impossible. Well, he told himself, let's just take it a day at a time.

Banks's mobile rang, startling him out of his gloomy reverie. 'Sorry,' he said. 'I'd better take it. Might be important.'

He walked out into the street and sheltered from the rain under a shop awning. It was getting dark and there wasn't much traffic about. The road surface glistened in the lights of the occasional car, and puddles reflected the blue neon sign of a video rental shop across the street. 'Alan, it's Annie,' said the voice at the other end.

'Annie? What's happening?'

Annie told Banks about the Liz Palmer interview, and he could sense anger and sadness in her account.

'You think she's telling the truth?'

'Pretty certain,' said Annie. 'The Big Man interviewed Ryan Milne at the same time and the details check out. They haven't been allowed to get together and concoct a story since they've been in custody.'

'Okay,' said Banks. 'So where does that leave us?'

'With a distraught and disoriented Luke Armitage wandering off into the night alone,' Anne said. 'The thoughtless bastards.'

'So where did he go?'

'We don't know. It's back to the drawing board. There's just one thing . . .'

'Yes.'

'The undigested diazepam that Dr Glendenning found in Luke's system.'

'What about it?'

'Well, he didn't get it at Liz and Ryan's flat. Neither of them has a prescription and we didn't find any in our search.'

'They could have got it illegally, along with the cannabis and LSD, then got rid of it.'

'They could have,' said Annie. 'But why lie about it?'

'That I can't answer. What's your theory?'

'Well, if Luke was freaking out the way it seems he was, then someone might have thought it was a good idea to give him some Valium to calm him down.'

'Or to keep him quiet.'

'Possibly.'

'What next?'

'We need to find out where he went. I'm going to talk to Luke's parents again tomorrow. They might be able to help now we know a bit more about his movements. I'll be talking to Lauren Anderson, too, and perhaps Gavin Barlow.'

'Why?'

'Maybe there was still something going on between Luke and Rose, and maybe her father didn't approve.'

'Enough to kill him?'

'Enough to make it physical. We still can't say for certain that anyone *murdered* Luke. Anyway, I'd like to know where they both were the night Luke disappeared. Maybe it was Rose he went to see.'

'Fair enough,' said Banks. 'And don't forget that Martin Armitage was out and about that night, too.'

'Don't worry. I won't.'

'What's happened with him by the way?'

'He appeared before the magistrates this afternoon. He's out on bail till the preliminary hearing.'

'What about Norman Wells?'

'He'll mend. When will you be back?'

'Tomorrow or the day after.'

'Getting anywhere?'

'I think so.'

'And what are you up to tonight?'

'School reunion,' said Banks, walking back to the pub. An approaching car seemed to be going way too fast, and Banks felt a momentary rush of panic. He ducked into a shop doorway. The car sped by him, too close to the kerb, and splashed water from the gutter over his trouser bottoms. He cursed.

'What is it?' Annie asked.

Banks told her, and she laughed. 'Have a good time at your school reunion,' she said.

'I'll tell you all about it when I see you.' He ended the call and returned to his seat. Dave and Paul had been making uneasy small talk in his absence, and Dave seemed glad to see him come back.

'So you're a copper,' said Paul, shaking his head when Banks sat down again. 'I still can't get over it. If I'd had to guess, I'd have said you'd end up a teacher or a newspaper reporter or something like that. But a copper . . .'

Banks smiled. 'Funny how things turn out.'

'Very queer, indeed,' muttered Dave. His voice sounded as if the beer was having an early effect.

Paul gave him a sharp glance, then tapped Banks's arm. 'Hey,' he said, 'you'd have had to arrest me back then, wouldn't you? For being *queer*.'

Banks sensed the tension escalating and moved on to the subject he'd been wanting to talk about from the start: Graham. 'Do either of you remember anything odd happening around the time Graham disappeared?' he asked.

'You're not working on the case, are you?' asked Dave, eager to be given a change of subject.

'No,' said Banks, 'but I'm interested in what happened. I mean, I *am* a copper, and Graham was a mate. Naturally, I'm curious.'

'Did you ever tell them about that bloke by the river?' Paul asked.

'It didn't lead anywhere,' Banks said, explaining. 'Besides, I think it's a lot closer to home.'

'What do you mean?' Paul asked.

Banks didn't want to tell them about the photograph. Apart from Michelle, he didn't want anyone to know about that if he could help it. Maybe he was protecting Graham's memory, but the idea of people seeing him like that was abhorrent to Banks. He also didn't want to tell them about Jet Harris, Shaw and the missing notebooks. 'Do you remember Donald Bradford?' he asked. 'The bloke who ran the newsagent's.'

'Dirty Don?' said Paul. 'Sure. I remember him.'

'Why did you call him Dirty Don?'

'I don't know.' Paul shrugged. 'Maybe he sold dirty magazines. It's just something my dad called him. Don't you remember?'

Banks didn't. But he found it interesting that Paul's dad had known about Bradford's interest in porn. Had his own father known? Had anyone told Proctor and Shaw all those years ago when they came to conduct the interviews? Was that why the notebooks and action allocations had to disappear, so that suspicion wouldn't point towards Bradford? Next to the family, Donald Bradford should have come under the most scrutiny, but he had been virtually ignored. 'Did Graham ever tell you where he got those magazines he used to show us inside the tree?'

'What magazines?' Dave asked.

'Don't you remember?' Paul said. 'I do. Women with bloody great bazookas.' He shuddered. 'Gave me the willies even then.'

'I seem to remember you enjoyed them as much as the rest of us,' said Banks. 'Do you really not remember, Dave?'

'Maybe I'm blanking it out for some reason, but I don't.'

Banks turned to Paul. 'Did he ever tell you where he got them?'

'Not that I remember. Why? Do you think it was Bradford?'

'It's a possibility. A newsagent's shop would be a pretty good outlet for things like that. And Graham always seemed to have money to spare.'

'He once told me he stole it from his mother's purse,' said Dave. 'I remember that.'

'Did you believe him?' Banks asked.

'Saw no reason not to. It shocked me, though, that he'd be so callous about it. I'd never have dared steal from *my* mother's purse. She'd have killed me.' He put his hand to his mouth. 'Oops, sorry about that. Didn't mean it to come out that way.'

'It's all right,' said Banks. 'I very much doubt that Graham's mother killed him for stealing from her purse.' On the other hand, Graham's father, Banks thought, was another matter entirely. 'I think there was more to it than that.'

'What?' Paul asked.

'I don't know. I just think Graham had something going with Donald Bradford, most likely something involving porn. And I think that led to his death.'

'You think Bradford killed him?'

'It's a possibility. Maybe he was helping distribute the stuff, or maybe he found out about it and was blackmailing Bradford. I don't know. All I know is that there's a connection.'

'Graham? Blackmailing?' said Dave. 'Now, hold on a minute, Alan, this is our mate Graham we're talking about. The one whose funeral we just went to. Remember? Stealing a few bob from his mum's purse is one thing, but blackmail . . . ?'

'I don't think things were exactly as we thought they were back then,' said Banks.

'Come again,' said Dave.

'He means none of you knew I was queer, for a start,' said Paul.

Banks looked at him. 'But we didn't, did we? You're right. And I don't think we knew a hell of a lot about Graham, either, mate or not.' He looked at Dave. 'For fuck's sake, Dave, you don't even remember the dirty magazines.'

'Maybe I've got a psychological block.'

'Do you at least remember the tree?' Banks asked.

'Our den? Of course I do. I remember lots of things. Just not looking at those magazines.'

'But you did,' said Paul. 'I remember you once saying pictures like that must have been taken at Randy Mandy's. Don't you remember that?'

'Randy Mandy's?' Banks asked. 'What the hell's that?'

'Don't tell me *you* don't remember, either,' said Paul, exasperated.

'Obviously I don't,' said Banks. 'What does it mean?'

'Randy Mandy's? It was Rupert Mandeville's place, that big house up Market Deeping way. Remember?'

Banks felt a vague recollection at the edge of his consciousness. 'I think I remember.'

'It was just our joke, that's all,' Paul went on. 'We thought they had all sorts of sex orgies there. Like that place where Profumo used to go a couple of years earlier. Remember that? Christine Keeler and Mandy Rice-Davies?'

Banks remembered Christine Keeler and Mandy Rice-Davies. The newspapers had been full of risqué photographs and salacious 'confessions' around the time of the Profumo scandal. But that was in 1963, not 1965.

'I remember now,' said Dave. 'Rupert Mandeville's house. Bloody great country mansion, more like. We used to think it was some sort of den of iniquity back then, somewhere all sorts of naughty things went on. Whenever we came across something dirty we always said it must have come from Randy Mandy's. You must remember, Alan. God knows where we got the idea from, but there was this high wall and a big swimming pool in the garden, and we used to imagine all the girls we fancied swimming naked there.'

'Vaguely,' said Banks, who wondered if there was any truth in this. It was worth checking into, anyway. He'd talk to Michelle, see if she knew anything. 'This Mandeville still around?'

'Wasn't he an MP or something?' said Dave.

'I think so,' Paul said. 'I remember reading about him in the papers a few years ago. I think he's in the House of Lords now.'

'Lord Randy Mandy,' said Dave, and they laughed for old times' sake.

Conversation meandered on for another hour or so and at least one round of double Scotches. Dave seemed to stick at a certain level of drunkenness, one he had achieved early on, and now it was Paul who began to show the effects of alcohol the most, and his manner became more exaggeratedly effeminate as time went on.

Banks could sense Dave getting impatient and embarrassed by the looks they were receiving from some of the other customers. He was finding it harder and harder to imagine that they had all had so much in common once, but then it had been a lot easier and more innocent: you supported the same football team, even if they weren't very good, you liked pop music and lusted after Emma Peel and Marianne Faithfull, and that was enough. It helped if you weren't a swot at school and if you lived on the same estate.

Perhaps the bonds of adolescence weren't any more shallow than those of adulthood, Banks mused, but it had sure as hell been easier to make friends back then. Now, as he looked from one to the other – Paul growing more red-faced and camp, Dave, lips tight, barely able to keep his homophobia in check – Banks decided it was time to leave. They had lived apart for over thirty years and would continue to do so without any sense of loss.

When Banks said he had to go, Dave took his cue, and Paul said he wasn't going to sit there by himself. The rain had stopped and the night smelled fresh. Banks wanted a cigarette but resisted. As they walked the short distance back to the estate, none of them said much, sensing perhaps that tonight marked the end of something. Finally, Banks got to his parents' door, their first stop, and said goodnight. They all made vague lies about keeping in touch and then walked back to their own separate lives.

•

Michelle was eating warmed-up chicken casserole, sipping a glass of sauvignon blanc and watching a television documentary on ocean life when her telephone rang late that evening. She was irritated by the interruption but, thinking it might be Banks, she answered it.

'Hope I didn't disturb you,' Banks said.

'No, not at all,' Michelle lied, putting her half-eaten food aside and turning down the volume with the remote control. 'It's good to hear from you.' And it was.

'Look, it's a bit late, and I've had a few drinks,' he said, 'so I'd probably better not drop by tonight.'

'You men. You take a girl to bed once, and then it's back to your mates and your beer.'

'I didn't say I'd had *too* much to drink,' Banks replied. 'In fact, I think I'll phone for a taxi right now.'

Michelle laughed. 'It's all right. I'm only teasing. Believe me, I could do with an early night. Besides, you'll only get in trouble with your mother. Did you find out anything from your old pals?'

'A bit.' Banks told her about Bradford's 'Dirty Don' epithet and the rumours they used to hear about the Mandeville house.

'I've heard of that place recently,' Michelle said. 'I don't know if Shaw mentioned it, or if I read about it in an old file, but I'll check up on it tomorrow. Who'd have thought it? A house of sin. In Peterborough.'

'Well, I suppose, strictly speaking, it's outside the city limits,' said Banks. 'But going by the photo I found in Graham's guitar and the information you got from Jet Harris's ex-wife, I think we'd better look into anything even remotely linked with illicit sex around the time of Graham's murder, don't you?'

'That's it!' Michelle said. 'The connection.'

'What connection?'

'The Mandeville house. It was something to do with illicit sex. At least it was illicit back then. Homosexuality.

There was a complaint about goings on at the Mandeville house. I read about it in the old logs. No further action taken.'

'Tomorrow might turn into a busy day, then,' said Banks.

'All the more reason to get an early night. Can you stick around to help, or do you have to head back up north?'

'One more day won't do any harm.'

'Good. Why don't you come to dinner tomorrow?'

'Your place?'

'Yes. If I can tempt you away from your mates in the boozer, that is.'

'You don't have to offer dinner to do that.'

'Believe it or not, I'm quite a good cook if I put my mind to it.'

'I don't doubt it for a moment. Just one question.'

'Yes?'

'I thought you told me you hadn't seen *Chinatown*.'

Michelle laughed. 'I remember saying no such thing. Goodnight.' And she hung up, still laughing. She noticed the photo of Ted and Melissa from the corner of her eye and felt a little surge of guilt. But it soon passed, and she felt that unfamiliar lightness again, a buoyancy of spirit. She was tired, but before calling it a night she went into the kitchen, pulled out a box of books and flipped through them before putting them on her shelves. Poetry for the most part. She loved poetry. Including Philip Larkin. Then she hefted out a box full of her best china and kitchen-ware. Looking around at the mostly empty cabinets, she tried to decide where would be the best place for each item.

18

All the way to Swainsdale Hall Annie worried about what she was going to say to the Armitages. Their son had lived a good part of his life unknown to them, mixed with people they didn't know and wouldn't approve of, especially Martin. But don't all kids? Annie had grown up in an artists' commune near St Ives, and some of the people she had mixed with would have made Martin Armitage's hair stand on end. Even so, she hadn't told her father about the wild group she took up with one summer, whose idea of fun was a Saturday afternoon shoplifting expedition in town.

The view over Swainsdale looked gloomy that morning in the low cloud and impending rain, dull gradations of grey and green. Even the patches of yellow rapeseed on the far hillsides looked jaundiced. As Annie rang the doorbell, she felt a surge of anxiety at the thought of seeing Martin Armitage again. It was foolish, she knew; he wasn't going to assault her – not in front of his wife – but she still had an aching jaw, two loose teeth and an upcoming dentist's appointment by which to remember their last meeting.

Josie opened the door and the dog sniffed Annie's crotch as she walked in. Josie collared it and took it away. Only Robin Armitage sat on the large living-room sofa in jeans and a navy blue top, flipping through a copy of *Vogue*. Annie breathed a sigh of relief. Maybe Martin was out. She'd have to talk to him, but a little procrastination wouldn't do any harm. Robin wore no make-up and seemed to have grown older since Luke's death. She looked as if a strong gust of wind would blow her away. She stood up when Annie entered, gave her a thin smile and bade her sit down. She asked Josie to bring in some coffee.

'Is your husband not home?' Annie asked.

'He's in his study. I'll ask Josie to send for him when she brings the coffee. Are you making any progress?'

'Some,' said Annie. 'That's why I wanted to talk to you both again, ask you a few questions.'

'Are you all right? Your mouth still looks bruised.'

Annie put her hand up to her jaw. 'I'm fine.'

'I'm really sorry for what happened. I know Martin is absolutely guilt stricken.' She managed a weak smile. 'It'll take him all his courage to come down and face you again.'

'No hard feelings,' Annie said, which wasn't exactly the truth, but there was no point in taking it out on Robin.

Josie came in with the coffee and digestive biscuits on a tray and Robin asked her to call Mr Armitage down. When he walked into the living room a couple of minutes later, Annie felt a wave of panic. It passed, but it left her heart pounding and her mouth dry. This was ridiculous, she told herself, but her body couldn't help but respond that way to whatever aura of violence Martin Armitage emitted. It just seemed closer to the surface in him than in most people.

Naturally, he was contrite and embarrassed. 'Please accept my apologies,' he said. 'I don't know what came over me. I've never laid a finger on a woman before.' Robin patted his knee.

'It's all right,' said Annie, eager to move on.

'Of course, if there are any medical expenses . . .'

'Don't worry about it.'

'How's Mr Wells?'

Annie had talked with the hospital and discovered that, while Norman Wells's physical injuries were healing well, the psychological damage went a lot deeper. He seemed, they said, to be suffering from depression. He couldn't sleep, but he didn't want to get out of bed, had no interest in food and seemed unconcerned about his future. Hardly surprising, Annie thought, given what the poor sod had been through over the past week or so. And now the newspapers had got hold of the story, there'd be no more bookshop for Wells. Once everyone knew what he had been accused of, nobody would go down there, or if they did it would only be to cause damage. Norman Wells would become a pariah.

'He'll be fine,' Annie said. 'Actually, I have a few more questions for the both of you.'

'I can't imagine what more we can tell you,' said Robin. 'But please go ahead.'

'First of all, do either you or your husband have a prescription for Valium or any other form of diazepam?'

Robin frowned. 'Martin doesn't, but I do. Nerves.'

'Have you noticed any missing lately?'

'No.'

'Would you?'

'Of course.' Robin reached for her handbag on the sofa beside her and took out a small plastic container. 'Here they are,' she said. 'Look. Almost full. Why do you ask?'

Annie looked, then dunked her digestive biscuit in her coffee. Though she had to eat it carefully, avoiding the loose teeth, it tasted good, and it gave her a moment to phrase her response to avoid using images that might upset Robin. 'It's just that the pathologist found traces in Luke's system,' she said – it sounded better than stomach contents. 'We were wondering where he got it from.'

'Luke? Valium? Certainly not from us.'

'And I assume he didn't have a prescription of his own?'

Martin and Robin looked at one another, frowning. 'Of course not,' said Robin. 'Someone else must have given it to him.'

'Is that what killed him?' Martin Armitage asked.

'No,' said Annie. 'It's just another complication I'd like to get out of the way, that's all.'

'I'm sorry we can't help you,' said Robin.

Annie struggled to phrase her next question, too. Talking to these two was like walking on eggs, but it had to be done. 'Mrs Armitage, Robin, you know Luke was confused about his biological father, don't you?'

'Neil? Well, yes, I suppose . . . But, I mean, Luke never knew him.'

'Surely you knew he must have wondered what happened, why his father didn't want him?'

'It wasn't like that. Neil just couldn't cope. He was a child himself in so many ways.'

'And a drug addict.'

'Neil wasn't an addict. He used drugs, but they were just a sort of tool for him, a means to an end.'

Annie didn't bother arguing that that was what they were for most people; it would be easier if she took Neil Byrd's exalted artistic status in her stride, especially when talking to Robin. 'But you knew Luke couldn't listen to his music, didn't you?'

'I never asked him to. I don't listen to it myself any more.'

'Well, he couldn't,' Annie said. 'Any reference to Neil Byrd or his music upset him. Did he ever talk to either of you about any friends of his called Liz and Ryan?'

'Not to me, no,' said Robin. 'Martin?'

Martin Armitage shook his head.

'He was in a band with them. Didn't you know?'

'No,' said Robin. 'He didn't tell us.'

'Why would he keep it from you?'

Robin paused and looked at her husband, who shifted in his seat and spoke. 'Probably because we'd already had arguments about that sort of thing.'

'What sort of thing?'

'I thought Luke was devoting far too much of his time to poetry and music, and that he ought to get more involved in team sports, get more exercise. He was starting to look pasty-faced from spending all his time indoors.'

'How did he react to this?'

Martin looked at Robin, then back at Annie. 'Not well. We had a bit of an argument about it. He insisted he was the best judge of how to spend his time.'

'Why didn't you tell me any of this earlier?'

'Because it didn't seem relevant. It still doesn't.' Martin sat forward and stared at her with that intense, disconcerting look of his. 'Someone kidnapped Luke and murdered him, and all you can do is ask questions about Neil Byrd and my relationship with Luke.'

'I think I'm the best judge of what questions I should be asking, Mr Armitage,' said Annie, aware of her heart pounding again. Surely they could hear it? 'Did you agree with your husband?' she asked Robin.

'Sort of. But I didn't want to stand in the way of Luke's creative development. If I'd known about the band, I would have been concerned. I wouldn't have wanted him getting into that kind of life. Believe me, I've seen it at first-hand. I've been there.'

'So you wouldn't have been thrilled, either, if you'd known that Luke was playing in a group?'

'No.'

'Was drug use a concern?'

'We warned him about drugs, of course, and he swore he didn't take them.'

'He didn't,' Annie said. 'At least not until the day he disappeared.'

Robin's eyes widened. 'What are you saying? You know how he died?'

'No. No, we don't know that yet. All we know is that he was with two friends, that he took some drugs and they played him his father's music. Luke got upset and left. We still don't know where he went after that.'

Robin put her coffee cup down in the saucer. Some of the coffee spilled. She didn't notice. 'I can't believe it,' she said.

'Who are these people?' Martin butted in.

'And what will you do if I tell you, Mr Armitage?' Annie said. 'Go and beat them up?'

Armitage's chin jutted out as he spoke. 'It's no less than they deserve if what you say is true. Giving my son drugs.'

'Mr Armitage,' Annie said. 'What did you do when you went out for two hours the night Luke disappeared?'

'I told you. I just drove around looking for him.'

'Drove where?'

'Eastvale.'

'Any particular areas or streets?'

'I don't remember. I just drove around. Why is it important?'

Annie's chest felt tight, but she forged ahead. 'Did you find him?'

'Of course I didn't. What are you talking about? If I'd found him, he'd be here safe and sound right now, wouldn't he?'

'I've seen a demonstration of your temper, Mr Armitage.' There, it was out. 'I also know from talking to several people that you and your stepson didn't get along very well.'

'What are you suggesting?'

Armitage's tone chilled Annie, but it was too late to stop now. 'That if anything happened that evening. Some sort of . . . accident . . . then it's better to tell me now than have me find out by some other means.'

'Accident? Let me get this straight. Are you asking me if I found Luke, picked him up in my car, then lost my temper and killed him?'

'I'm asking you if you did see him that night, yes, and if anything happened between you that I should know about.'

Armitage shook his head. 'You really are a piece of work, DI Cabbot. First you act rashly and probably cause my son's death, then you accuse *me* of killing him. For your information, I did exactly what I told you. I drove around Eastvale looking for Luke. It was probably pointless, I know, but I had to do something. I needed to act. I couldn't just sit around and wait. I didn't find him. All right?'

'Fine,' said Annie.

'And I resent your accusation.'

'I haven't accused you of anything.'

Martin Armitage stood up. 'It shows how little progress you've made, scraping the bottom of the barrel like this. Will that be all? I'm going back to my study now.'

Annie felt relieved when Armitage had left the room.

'That was cruel,' said Robin. 'Martin loved Luke like his own son, did his best for the boy, even if they didn't always agree. Luke was no angel, you know. He could be difficult.'

'I'm sure he could,' said Annie. 'All teenagers can. And I'm sorry I had to ask those questions. Police work can be uncomfortable at times, but the solution often lies close to home, and we'd be derelict in our duty if we didn't pursue such lines of enquiry. Did you know that Luke had a girlfriend?'

'Certainly not.'

'He never said anything to you?'

'I don't even believe he had a girlfriend.'

'Everyone says he was mature for his age, and he was a good-looking boy, too. Why shouldn't he?'

'He just never . . .'

'It might have been someone he didn't feel he could bring home to meet his parents. Maybe even Liz Palmer, the girl in the group.'

'You think that's why he was killed? Because of this *girl*?'

'We don't know. It's just one possibility we've been looking at. What about Lauren Anderson?'

'Miss Anderson? But she was his English teacher. You can't think . . .'

'I don't know. It's not as if these things don't happen. Rose Barlow?'

'Rose? The headmaster's daughter. Well, she came round to the house once, but it was all perfectly innocent.'

'Rose Barlow came to your house? Why didn't you tell me?'

'But it was ages ago.'

'February? March?'

'Around that time. Yes. How do you know?'

'Because somebody else noticed Luke and Rose were spending time together then, thought maybe they were going out together.'

'I don't think so,' said Robin. 'It was something to do with a school project.'

'Did she visit often?'

'Only the once.'

'And she never came back?'

'No.'

'Did Luke ever talk about her?'

'Except to say that he'd ended up doing most of the project himself, no. Look, I don't understand all this, all your questions. Don't you think he just wandered off and someone kidnapped him?'

'No,' said Annie. 'I don't think that's what happened at all.'

'Then what?'

Annie stood up to leave. 'Give me a little more time,' she said. 'I'm getting there.'

●

Michelle had made three important discoveries before lunch that day and it seemed a nice goal to set oneself. Who was it, she tried to remember, who had made it a point to believe six impossible things before breakfast? Was it Alice in *Through the Looking Glass*?

Well, the things Michelle had discovered were far from impossible. First, she had gone back to the logbook for the summer of 1965 and found the reference to the Mandeville house. On 1 August that year, an anonymous informant had telephoned the station with allegations of under-age sex and homosexuality. The possibility of drug taking was also mentioned. A young DC called Geoff Talbot had gone out to make enquiries and had arrested two men he said he found naked together in a bedroom there. After that, nothing more appeared on the case except a note that all charges were dropped and an official apology issued to Mr Rupert Mandeville, who, she discovered from an Internet search, had served as a Conservative Member of Parliament from 1979 to 1990 and was granted a life peerage in 1994.

It took Michelle a bit longer to track Geoff Talbot down, as he had left the police force in 1970 to work as a consultant with a television company. Eventually, through a patient personnel officer, she managed to find his address in Barnet, a North London suburb. She had rung him and he had agreed to talk to her.

After that, Michelle had enlisted DC Collins's aid and discovered through local land registry records that Donald Bradford's shop had been owned by a company linked to Carlo Fiorino, the late but unlamented local crime kingpin. The company had also owned Le Phonographe discotheque and several other newsagents' shops in the Peterborough area. Ownership of Bradford's shop went to the Walkers when he sold, but many of the other shops remained under Fiorino's control well through the new town expansion and into the seventies.

What it all meant, Michelle wasn't too sure, but it looked very much as if Carlo Fiorino had set up the perfect retail distribution chain for his wholesale porn business, and who knew what else besides? Drugs, perhaps? And maybe even some of those advertising cards in the news-agents' windows weren't quite so innocent after all.

All this she told to Banks as she drove through a steady drizzle down the A1 to Barnet. As they talked, she kept a keen eye on her rear-view mirror. A grey Passat seemed to stay on their tail a bit too long and too close for comfort, but it finally turned off at Welwyn Garden City.

'Bradford must have got Graham involved somehow, through the magazines,' said Banks. 'But it didn't stop there. He must have come to the attention of Fiorino and Mandeville, too. It helps to explain where all that extra money came from.'

'Look, I know he was your friend, Alan, but you have to admit that it looks as if he was up to some unsavoury stuff, as if he got greedy.'

'I admit it,' said Banks. 'The photo must have been Graham's insurance. Evidence. He could use it to black-mail Bradford into paying him more money, only he didn't know what he'd got himself into. Word got back to Fiorino and he signed Graham's death warrant.'

'And who carried it out?'

'Bradford, most likely. He didn't have an alibi. Or Harris. I mean, we can't rule him out completely. Despite what his ex-wife told you, he could have kept the com-mando knife, and if he was being threatened with exposure as a homosexual, he might have been driven to kill. Remember, it wouldn't only have meant his career back then, but jail, and you know how long coppers survive behind bars.'

'Jet Harris searched Graham Marshall's house person-ally just after the boy disappeared,' said Michelle.

'Harris did that? Searched the house? How do you know?'

'Mrs Marshall mentioned it the first time I went to talk to her. I didn't think anything of it at the time, but now . . . a superintendent conducting a routine search?'

'He must have been after the photo.'

'Then why didn't he find it?'

'He obviously didn't look hard enough, did he?' said Banks. 'Adolescents are naturally very secretive. Sometimes, of necessity, they have an uncanny knack for hiding things. And at the time, if that photo had been securely Sellotaped to the inside of Graham's guitar, nobody could know it was there without taking the guitar apart. It was only because the adhesive had dried out and the Sellotape had stiffened over the years that the photo broke free and I found it.'

'I suppose so,' Michelle said. 'But does that make Harris a murderer?'

'I don't know. It's not proof. But he was in it. Deep.'

'I also rang Ray Scholes this morning,' Michelle said. 'Remember, the detective who investigated Donald Bradford's murder?'

'I remember.'

'It turns out there was a Fairbairn-Sykes knife among Bradford's possessions.'

'What happened to it?'

'Forget it. It's long gone. Sold to a dealer. Who knows how many times it's changed hands since then?'

'Pity. But at least we know it was in his possession when he died.'

'You said the photo was evidence,' Michelle said. 'But what of? How?'

'Well, there might have been fingerprints on it, but I think it was more dangerous because people would have known where it was taken. I doubt there are that many Adam fireplaces around, and probably none quite as distinctive as that one. The rug, too.'

'You're thinking of the Mandeville house?'

'Sounds a likely place to me. I'm certain it was all connected: Fiorino's porn business, his escort agency, the Mandeville parties, Graham's murder. I think this is where we turn off.'

Michelle kept going.

'The junction's coming up,' Banks said. 'Here. Move over or you'll miss it. Now!'

Michelle waited and made a last-minute lane change. Horns blared as she sped across two lanes of traffic to the off ramp.

'Jesus Christ!' said Banks. 'You could have got us killed.'

Michelle flashed him a quick grin. 'Oh, don't be such a pussycat. I knew what I was doing. This way we can be certain no one's following us. Where now?'

When his heart rate slowed, Banks picked up the street guide and directed Michelle to the pleasant suburban semi where ex DC Geoff Talbot enjoyed his retirement.

Talbot answered the door and asked them in. Michelle introduced herself and Banks.

'Miserable day, isn't it?' Talbot said. 'One wonders if summer will ever arrive.'

'Too true,' said Banks.

'Coffee? Tea?'

'A cup of tea would be nice,' Michelle said. Banks agreed.

Michelle and Banks followed Talbot into the kitchen,

which turned out to be a bright, high-ceilinged room with a central island surrounded by tall stools.

'We can talk here, if it's all right with you,' Talbot said. 'My wife keeps pestering me for a conservatory, but I don't see the need. On a nice day we can always sit outside.'

Michelle looked out of the window and saw the well-manicured lawn and neat flower beds. Someone in the family was obviously a keen gardener. A copper beech provided some shade. It would indeed have been nice to sit outside, but not in the rain.

'You didn't give me much of an idea what you wanted to talk about over the telephone,' Talbot said, looking over his shoulder as he dropped a couple of teabags into the pot.

'That's because it's still a bit vague,' Michelle said. 'How's your memory?' She and Banks had agreed that, as it was her case and he had no official capacity, she would do most of the questioning.

'Not so bad for an old man.'

Talbot didn't look that old, Michelle thought. He was carrying a few pounds too many and his hair was almost white, but other than that his face was remarkably unlined and his movements smooth and fluid. 'Remember when you served on the Cambridge Constabulary?' she asked.

'Of course. Mid-sixties, that'd be. Peterborough. It was called the Mid-Anglia Constabulary back then. Why?'

'Do you remember a case involving Rupert Mandeville?'

'Do I? How could I forget. That's the reason I left Cambridgeshire. If it comes right down to it, it's the reason I left the force not long after, too.'

'Could you tell us what happened?'

The kettle boiled and Talbot filled the pot with boiling water, then carried it on a tray along with three cups and saucers to the island. 'Nothing happened,' he said. 'That was the problem. I was told to lay off.'

'By whom?'

'The super.'

'Detective Superintendent Harris?'

'Jet Harris. That's the one. Oh, it was all above board. Not enough evidence, my word against theirs, anonymous informant, that sort of thing. You couldn't fault his arguments.'

'Then what?'

Talbot paused. 'It just didn't feel right, that's all. I can't put it any other way than that. There'd been rumours for some time about things going on at the Mandeville house. Procurement, under-age boys, that sort of thing. It was the start of what they called the permissive society, after all. Ever heard of Carlo Fiorino?'

'We have,' said Michelle.

Talbot poured the tea. 'Rumour has it he was the supplier. Anyway, the problem was that Rupert Mandeville was too well connected, and some of the people who attended his parties were in the government, or in other high-level positions. Real Profumo stuff. Of course, I was the naive young copper fresh from probation, proud to be in CID, thinking he could take on the world. Not a care had I for rank or sway. We were all equal in the eyes of God as far as I was concerned, though I wasn't a religious man. Well, I soon learned the error of my ways. Had my eyes opened for me. When the super found out I'd been out there and caused a fuss, he had me in his office and told me in no uncertain terms that Mandeville was off-limits.'

'Did he say why?' Michelle asked.

'He didn't need to. It's not difficult to add up.'

'An operation like that, and one like Fiorino's, would need police protection,' Banks said. 'And Harris was it. Or part of it.'

'Exactly,' said Talbot. 'Oh, he was clever, though. He never admitted it in so many words, and he got me transferred out of the county before my feet even touched the ground. Cumbria. I ask you! Well, I ran into one or two nice little gentleman's agreements between local villains and constabulary up there too, so I called it a day. I mean, I'm no saint, but it just seemed to me that no matter where I went I found corruption. I couldn't fight it. Not from my position. So I resigned from the force. Best move I ever made.'

'And you told no one of your suspicions about Harris?' Michelle asked.

'What was the point? Who'd believe me? Jet Harris was practically a god around the place even then. Besides, there were implied threats of what might happen to me if I didn't do as he said, and some of them were quite physical. I'm not a coward, but I'm no fool either. I cut my losses.'

'Was anyone else involved?'

'Might have been,' said Talbot. 'The chief constable himself might have been a regular at Mandeville's parties, for all I know.'

'But no one you knew of?'

'No. I didn't even *know* about Harris. Like I said, it just felt wrong. I just guessed from his attitude, his wording. It was only him and me in his office. Even by the time I got outside I was thinking I'd been reading too much into it.'

'What happened that day?'

'From the start?'

'Yes.'

'It was a warm Sunday morning, end of July or beginning of August.'

'It was was the first of August,' Michelle said.

'Right. Anyway, I was by myself, not much on, I remember, when the phone call came and the switchboard patched it through to the office.'

'Do you remember anything about the voice?'

Talbot frowned. 'It's so long ago, I don't . . .'

'Man? Woman?'

'It was a woman's voice. I remember that much.'

'Did she sound upset?'

'Yes. That's why I headed out there so impulsively. She said there'd been a party going on since the previous night, and she was convinced that some of the girls and boys were under-age and people were taking drugs. She sounded frightened. She hung up very abruptly, too.'

'So you went?'

'Yes. I logged the details and drove out there like a knight in shining armour. If I'd had half the sense I have now, I'd at least have taken the time to organize a small raiding party, but I didn't. God knows what I thought I was going to do when I got there.'

'Did you meet the woman who'd phoned?'

'Not that I know of. I mean, if she was there she never came forward and admitted she was the one who phoned. But then she wouldn't, would she?'

'Who opened the door?'

'A young man. He just opened it, glanced at my identification and wandered off. He didn't seem interested at all. I thought he was on drugs, but I must admit I didn't know much about them at the time. I'm not even sure we had a drugs squad back then.'

'What did you find inside?'

'It was more like the aftermath of a party, really. Some people were sleeping on the sofa, a couple on the floor . . .'

'How many?'

'Hard to say. Maybe twenty or so.'

'What kind of people?'

'A mix. Young and old. Businessmen. Mods. One or two of the girls looked like swinging London types, mini-skirts and what have you. There was a funny smell, too, I remember. At the time I didn't know what it was, but I smelled it again later. Marijuana.'

'What did you do?'

'To be honest, I felt a bit out of my depth.' He laughed. 'Like Mr Jones in that Bob Dylan song, I didn't really know what was happening. I wasn't even sure if any of it was illegal. I mean, the girls and the men didn't *look* under-age to me, but what did I know? I talked to a few people, took names. A couple of the girls I'd seen before at Le Phonographe. I think they also worked for Fiorino's escort agency.'

'You used your notebook?'

'Yes.'

'What happened to it?'

'Same as usual, I suppose.'

'You also found two men together?'

'Yes. I looked in some of the rooms, and in one bedroom I saw two men in bed together. Naked.'

'Were they doing anything?'

'Not when I opened the door. They were just . . . very close together. I'd never seen anything like that before. I mean, I knew about homosexuality, I wasn't that naive, but I'd never actually seen it.'

'Did either of them look under-age?'

'No. One I pegged at early twenties, the other older, maybe forty. But it didn't matter how old you were back then.'

'So what did you do?'

'I . . . er . . . I arrested them.'

'Did they resist?'

'No. They just laughed, put their clothes on and went back to the station with me.'

'What happened then?'

'Jet Harris was waiting for me. He was furious.'

'He was at the station waiting for you? On a Sunday morning?'

'Yes. I suppose someone from Mandeville's house must have phoned him.'

'Probably dragged him out of church,' Banks said.

'What did he do?' Michelle asked.

'He had a private talk with the two men, let them go and had his little chat with me. That was the end of it. No further action.'

'Just out of interest,' Michelle asked, 'how old was Rupert Mandeville at the time?'

'Quite young. In his thirties. His parents had been killed in a plane crash not too long before, I remember, and he'd inherited a fortune, even after tax. I suppose he was just doing what many young people would have done if they'd gained their freedom and had unlimited funds.'

'Ever hear of Donald Bradford?' Michelle asked.

'The name doesn't ring a bell.'

'Bill Marshall?'

'He was one of Fiorino's musclemen. I ran into him a

couple of times in Le Phonographe. Tough character. Thick as the proverbial pigshit.'

'Thank you, Mr Talbot.'

'You're welcome. Look, I can't see as I've been any help, but . . .'

Banks placed the photograph of Graham Marshall in front of him. 'Do you recognize that boy?'

Talbot paled. 'My God, isn't that the boy who . . . ? His photograph was in the papers only a few weeks ago.'

'Did you see him at the Mandeville house?'

'No . . . I . . . but that's the room. Mandeville's living room. I remember the sheepskin rug and the fireplace. Does that mean what I think it means? That the boy's death is somehow connected with Mandeville and Harris?'

'Somehow,' said Michelle. 'We're just not quite sure how yet.'

Talbot tapped the photo. 'If we'd had something like that back then, we'd have had some evidence,' he said.

'Possibly,' said Banks. 'If it ever saw the light of day.'

They stood up and Talbot showed them to the door. 'You know,' he said, 'I felt at the time that there was more going on than met the eye. I've always wondered what would have happened if I'd pushed it a bit harder, not let go too easily.'

'You'd have probably ended up under a field with Graham Marshall,' said Banks. 'Bye, Mr Talbot. And thank you.'

•

Gavin Barlow was in his study when Annie called, and he invited her to sit with him there while they talked. It was a light, airy room, with plenty of space, and the bookcases didn't feel as overwhelming as the ones in Gristhorpe's office. Barlow pushed his laptop aside on his desk and smiled. 'It might be summer holidays for most,' he said, 'but some of us still have work to do.'

'I won't take up much of your time,' Annie said. 'It's about your daughter.'

'Rose? I'm afraid she's out.'

'Perhaps you can answer my questions, then.'

'I'll try. But look, if Rose is in any sort of trouble . . .'

'What?'

'I don't know. Maybe I should call my solicitor or something.'

'Why would you want to do that?'

'Just tell me what you've come to say.'

'Your daughter came to the station and made some pretty serious allegations about Lauren Anderson and Luke Armitage.'

'She did what?'

'And now it turns out that she was seeing Luke earlier this year. She even visited him at Swainsdale Hall on at least one occasion. Do you know anything about that?'

'Of course. It was a school project the students were asked to partner up on. To promote working together, task sharing. Rose worked with Luke.'

'Her choice or his?'

'I don't know. I should imagine the teacher assigned them.'

'Lauren Anderson?'

'No, actually. It was a science project. It would have been Mr Sawyer.'

'Do you know if Luke and Rose had any sort of romantic involvement?'

'Not as far as I know. Look, Ms Cabbot, I'm not so naive

as to think that teenagers their age don't form liaisons. I've been a head teacher too long to think otherwise. I've even come across my share of teenage pregnancies. But I also know my own daughter, and believe me, I would have known if she'd been seeing Luke Armitage.'

'They were seen talking together in and around the school. Did she ever talk to you about Luke?'

'She might have mentioned him once or twice, yes. It was only natural. I mean, they were in the same class, he was a little odd and something of a minor celebrity. At least his parents are.'

'Was she obsessed with him?'

'Don't be ridiculous!'

'Would you have approved if they had been going out together?'

Barlow pursed his lips. 'I can't say that I would, no.'

'Why not?'

'She's my daughter, for crying out loud. You don't think I'd have wanted her going out with that . . .'

'That what, Mr Barlow?'

'I was going to say that *boy.*'

'Oh, were you?'

'Yes. But I'll admit that, as a father, I thought Luke Armitage just a little too weird for my daughter.'

'How far would you have gone to stop them going out together?'

'Now, hold on a minute. I won't have you—'

'Where were you and Rose the night Luke disappeared? That's a week ago last Monday, in case you don't remember.'

'Here.'

'Both of you?'

'As far as I know. My wife will remember.'

'Why would Rose want to make trouble for Ms Anderson?'

'I don't know.'

'How well does your daughter do at English?'

'It's not her best subject, or her favourite.'

'Was she jealous?'

'Of what?'

'Of the attention Luke got from Lauren Anderson?'

'Why don't you ask Lauren?'

'I will. But I'm asking you first.'

'And I'm telling you I don't know.'

They stared at one another, and Annie tried to weigh up whether he was telling the truth or not. She decided he was holding something back. 'What is it, Mr Barlow?' she asked. 'If it's nothing to do with Luke's death, it will go no further than these walls, I promise.'

Barlow sighed and stared out of the window. The clouds had split in places and shafts of light lanced the distant hills. The laptop hummed on his desk.

'Mr Barlow?'

He turned back to face her, and his facade of benevolent authority had disappeared. In its place was the look of a man with a burden. He stared at her a long time before speaking. 'It was nothing,' he said, finally, his voice little more than a whisper. 'Really. Nothing.'

'Then tell me.'

'Ms Anderson. Lauren. If you've seen her, you must have noticed she's an attractive woman, quite the Pre-Raphaelite beauty,' Barlow said. 'I'm only as human as the next man, but everyone expects me to be above reproach.'

'You're a head teacher,' said Annie. 'You're supposed

to be *responsible*. What happened? Did you have an affair? Did Rose find out?'

'Oh, good lord, no. Nothing like that. I might have flirted a bit, as one does, but Lauren wasn't interested in me. She made that quite clear.'

Annie frowned. 'Then I don't understand.'

A thin smile twisted his lips. 'Don't you? Sometimes things can seem other than they are, and any attempt to explain them away only makes you seem more guilty.'

'Can you elaborate on that?'

'Lauren came to see me in my office shortly after Christmas. A family problem. Her father had been diagnosed with Alzheimer's and she was upset, needed some time off. I put an arm around her, just to comfort her, you understand, and Rose chose that moment to come barging in with some family matter. It's one of the disadvantages of being the head of the school your daughter attends. Rose was usually pretty good about observing the boundaries, but on this occasion . . . Well, she misread the situation and went running off.'

'I see,' said Annie. 'Did she tell your wife?'

'No. No, thank God. I managed to talk to her. I'm not sure she quite believed in my innocence, but she agreed not to say anything.'

'And that's the root of her animosity towards Lauren Anderson?'

'I should imagine so. Maybe she had a crush on Luke Armitage, too, at one time, but believe me, I'd have known if there was more to it than that.'

'Are you sure there's nothing else?'

'Not that I can think of.'

'You *were* attracted to Lauren, though, weren't you? What did you call her? A Pre-Raphaelite beauty?'

'Yes. As I said, I'm only human. And she *is* a very attractive woman. You can't arrest a man for his thoughts. At least not yet. The damn thing is, I'd done nothing wrong, but because I wanted it I felt as guilty as if I had, anyway.' He gave a bitter laugh. 'Funny, isn't it?'

'Yes,' said Annie. 'Very funny.' But her thoughts were elsewhere. Barlow might not have given her the answers she was hoping for, but he had certainly given her plenty to think about.

•

'Well, if it isn't our two lovebirds,' said Ben Shaw, opening the door to Banks and Michelle. 'What the fuck do you two want?'

'A few words,' said Banks.

'And why should I want a few words with you?'

'Des Wayman,' said Michelle.

Shaw squinted at her, then shut the door, slid off the chain and opened it, walking away from them, leaving Banks to shut the door behind them and follow.

The house was far neater than Banks had expected. He had pegged Shaw as an alcoholic living alone, and that usually meant chaos. At least Shaw probably hired a cleaning lady, and his personal habits seemed tidy enough. The only booze in sight was a half-empty bottle of Bell's on the living-room table, a full glass beside it. Shaw sat down and took a slug without offering his guests anything. Well, Banks thought, why should he?

Grieg's *Peer Gynt* Suite was playing on the radio, another surprise for Banks. He wouldn't have guessed Shaw to be a man of classical tastes. Or maybe it didn't matter what was on as long as there was sound.

'So what porkies has Mr Wayman been telling today?'

'Stop pissing around,' said Banks. 'You told Wayman and a mate to work me over and get me out of the picture. It backfired.'

'If he told you that, he's lying.'

'He told me, sir,' said Michelle, 'and, with all due respect, I think he was telling the truth.'

'*All due respect?* You don't know the meaning of the term.' Shaw lit a cigarette and Banks felt a wave of pure need surge inside him. He was already feeling light-headed and edgy from not smoking but this . . . this was ten times worse than he'd imagined. He took a grip. 'Wayman's nothing but criminal scum,' Shaw went on. 'And you'd take his word over mine?'

'That's neither here nor there,' Banks went on. 'DI Hart has done a bit of digging into your Regan and Carter days with Jet Harris, and we were just wondering how much the two of you took in from Carlo Fiorino.'

'You bastard!' Shaw lurched forward to grab Banks's lapel but he was already a bit unsteady with drink, and Banks pushed him back down into his chair. He paled, and a grimace of pain passed over his face.

'What is it?' asked Banks.

'Fuck you.' Shaw coughed and reached for more whisky. 'John Harris was worth ten of you. You're not worth the piss stains in his underwear.'

'Come off it, Shaw, the two of you were as bent as the day is long. He might have had a good excuse for it, but you . . . ? You couldn't remove every scrap of evidence from the archives. All your arrests were for burglary, assault, fraud and the occasional domestic murder. Doesn't that tell you something?'

'What, smart arse?'

'That all the time Carlo Fiorino was running prostitution, escort agencies, illegal gambling, protection, porn and drugs with absolute impunity. Sure, you had him or one of his henchmen brought in once or twice for questioning, just for the sake of appearances, but guess what – either the evidence disappeared or witnesses changed their statements.'

Shaw said nothing, just sipped more whisky.

'Fiorino fed you his opposition,' Banks went on. 'He had eyes and ears out on the street. He knew what jobs were going down. Small fry, or competition. Either way it made you look good and deflected attention from his own operations, which included supplying Rupert Mandeville with as many bodies as he wanted for his "parties", male and female.'

Shaw slammed the tumbler down on the table so hard the whisky slopped over the side. 'All right,' he said. 'You want the truth? I'll tell you. I'm not stupid. I worked with John for too many years not to have my suspicions, but – know what? – I never took a fucking penny in my life. And maybe I blinkered myself, maybe I even protected him, but we did our jobs. We brought down the bad guys. I loved the man. He taught me everything. He even saved my life once. He had charisma, did John. He was the kind of bloke everybody noticed when he walked in the room. He's a fucking hero around these parts, or hadn't you noticed?'

'And that's why you've been doing everything in your power to scupper DI Hart's investigation into Graham Marshall's murder? To protect your old pal's memory. To protect Jet Harris's reputation. To do that you get someone to break into her flat, try to run her down, have me beaten up.'

'What the fuck are you talking about?'

'You know what I'm talking about.'

He looked at Michelle, then back at Banks, a puzzled expression on his face. 'I certainly never had anyone intimidate DI Hart in any way. I wasn't worried about her. It was you I was worried about.'

'Why's that?'

'You're the loose cannon. It was you I needed to keep an eye on. It was different for you. Personal. You knew the victim. I could tell the first time I saw you that you weren't going to let go.' He shook his head and looked at Michelle again. 'No,' he said. 'If anyone had a go at you, DI Hart, it wasn't down to me.'

Banks and Michelle exchanged glances, then Banks moved on. 'Are you asking us to believe that you worked with Harris all those years and you hadn't a clue what he was up to?'

'I'm saying I had my suspicions, but I buried them. For the sake of the force. For John's sake. Listen, squash a bug like Fiorino and another one takes his place. You can no more stop prostitution, porn and drugs than you can stop sex and drinking. They're always going to be there. Policing was different then. Sometimes you had to rub shoulders with some pretty nasty bedfellows to do the job.'

'And what about Graham Marshall?'

Shaw looked surprised. 'What about him?'

'Did you know what really happened to him? Have you been covering that up all these years, too?'

'I don't know what the fuck you're talking about.' Shaw's voice was little more than a whisper now.

'Well, let me tell you a story,' said Banks. 'We can't prove it, but this is what DI Hart and I believe happened.

Donald Bradford most likely killed Graham. He owned the kind of knife that was used and Graham trusted him. All Bradford had to do was drive down Wilmer Road around the time Graham would be heading for the other side and tell him something else had come up, to get in the car. That's why he took his bag of newspapers with him. He thought he would be going back to finish his round later.'

'What possible motive could Bradford have?'

'That's where it gets complicated, and that's where your boss comes in. Donald Bradford distributed pornographic magazines and blue films for Carlo Fiorino. Fiorino had quite a network of newsagents working for him. I'm surprised you didn't know about it, you being a vigilant copper and all.'

'Sod you, Banks.' Shaw scowled and topped up his glass.

'Somehow or other,' Banks went on, 'Graham Marshall became involved in this operation. Maybe he found some of Bradford's stock by accident, showed interest. I don't know. But Graham was a street-smart kid – he grew up around the Krays and their world, and his father was a small-time muscleman – and he had an eye for the main chance. Maybe he worked for Bradford to earn extra money – which he always seemed to have – or maybe he blackmailed him for it. Either way, he was involved.'

'You said yourself you can't prove any of this.'

'Graham came to the attention of one of Fiorino's most influential customers, Rupert Mandeville,' Banks went on. 'I know he posed for some nude photos because I found one at his house. Whether it went any further than that, I don't know, but we can tie him to the Mandeville house, and we know what went on there. Under-age sex, drugs, you name it. Mandeville couldn't afford to come under scrutiny. He was an important person with political goals to pursue. Graham probably asked for more money or he'd tell the police. Mandeville panicked, especially as this came hot on the heels of Geoff Talbot's visit. He got Fiorino to fix it, and Jet Harris scuppered the murder investigation. You knew that, knew there was something wrong, so you've been trying to erase the traces to protect Harris's reputation. How am I doing?'

'You're arguing against your own logic, Banks. What would it matter if he told the police, if we were all as corrupt as you make out? Why go so far as to kill the kid if Bradford thought we could control the outcome anyway?'

Banks looked at Michelle before continuing. 'That puzzled me for a while, too,' he said. 'I can only conclude that he knew which police officer *not* to tell.'

'How do you mean?'

'Graham had definitely been to the Mandeville house. What if he saw someone there? Someone who shouldn't have been there, like a certain detective superintendent?'

'That's absurd. John wasn't like that.'

'Wasn't like what? Mandeville's parties catered to all tastes. According to his wife, John Harris was homo-sexual. We don't know if Mandeville or Fiorino found out and blackmailed him or if they set him up. Maybe that's how he took his pay-offs from Fiorini and Mandeville, in young boys. Or drugs. It doesn't matter. Point is, I think Graham saw him there or knew he was connected in some way and made this clear to Bradford, too, that he'd go elsewhere with his story.'

Shaw turned pale. 'John? *Homosexual?* I don't believe that.'

'One of my old schoolfriends has turned out to be gay,'

said Banks. 'And I didn't know that, either. John Harris had two damn good reasons for keeping it a secret. It was illegal until 1967 and he was a copper. Even today you know how tough it is for coppers to come out. We're all such bloody macho tough guys that gays terrify the crap out of us.'

'Bollocks. This is all pure speculation.'

'Not about John Harris,' Michelle said. 'It's what his ex-wife told me.'

'She's a lying bitch, then. With all due respect.'

'Why would she lie?'

'She hated John.'

'Sounds like she had good reason to,' Banks said. 'But back to Graham. He threatened to tell. I don't know why. It could have been greed, but it could also have been because Mandeville wanted him to do more than pose for photos. I'd like to think that was where Graham drew the line, but we'll probably never know. It also explains why he was preoccupied when we were on holiday in Blackpool just before he disappeared. He must have been worrying about what to do. Anyway, Graham knew he'd better go further afield than the local nick. And he had the photo as evidence, a photo that could incriminate Rupert Mandeville. He compromised the whole operation. Mandeville's *and* Fiorino's. That was why he had to die.'

'So what happened?'

'The order went down to Donald Bradford to get rid of him. Bradford had to be at the shop by eight o'clock, as usual, that morning. That gave him an hour and a half to abduct Graham, kill him and dispose of the body. It takes a while to dig a hole that deep, so my guess is that he planned it in advance, picked the spot and dug the hole.

Either that or he had help and another of Fiorino's henchmen buried the body. Either way, with Harris on the payroll, Bradford could at least be certain that no one was looking too closely at his lack of an alibi.'

'Are you saying that John Harris ordered the boy's death because—'

'I don't know. I don't think so. I'd say it was Fiorino, or Mandeville, but Harris had to know about it in order to misdirect the investigation. And that makes him just as guilty in my book.'

Shaw closed his eyes and shook his head. 'Not John. No. Maybe he didn't always play by the rules, maybe he did turn a blind eye to one or two things, but not murder. Not a dead kid.'

'You have to accept it,' Banks went on. 'It's the only thing that makes sense of later events.'

'What later events?'

'The botched investigation and the missing notebooks and actions. I don't know who got rid of them – you, Harris or Reg Proctor, but one of you did.'

'It wasn't me. All I've done was discourage DI Hart here from digging too deeply into the past.'

'And set Wayman on me.'

'You won't get me to admit to that.'

'It doesn't matter anyway,' said Banks. 'So Harris took them himself when he left. That makes sense. It wasn't his finest hour, and he wouldn't want the evidence hanging around for anyone to see if Graham's body ever did turn up. Insurance. Cast your mind back. You were there in the summer of 1965. You and Reg Proctor covered the estate. What did you find out?'

'Nobody knew anything.'

'I'll bet that's not true,' said Banks. 'I'll bet there were one or two references to "Dirty Don" in your notebooks. One of my old mates remembered referring to him that way. And I'll bet there was a rumour or two about porn.'

'Rumours, maybe,' said Shaw, looking away, 'but that's all they were.'

'How do you know?'

Shaw scowled at him.

'Exactly,' said Banks. 'You only know because Harris told you so. Remember, you were just a young DC back then. You didn't question your superior officers. If anything showed up in your interviews that pointed you in the right direction – Bradford, Fiorino, Mandeville – then Harris ignored it, dismissed it as mere rumour, a dead end. You just skimmed the surface, exactly as he wanted. That's why the action allocations are missing, too. Harris was in charge of the investigation. He'd have issued the actions. And we'd have found out what direction they all pointed in – the passing paedophile theory, later made more credible by Brady and Hindley's arrest – and, what's more important, what they pointed *away* from. The truth.'

'It's still all theory,' said Shaw.

'Yes,' Banks admitted. 'But you know it's true. We've got the photo of Graham, taken at Mandeville's house, Bradford's connection with the porn business and the possible murder weapon, and the missing notebooks. Go ahead, see if it adds up any other way.'

Shaw sighed. 'I just can't believe John would do something like that. I know he gave Fiorino a lot of leeway, but I thought at the time that he got his reward in information. Fair exchange. That's all I was trying to protect. A bit of tit for tat. All those years I knew him . . . and I still can't fucking believe it.'

'Maybe you didn't really know him at all,' said Banks.

'No more than I knew Graham Marshall.'

Shaw looked over at Banks. His eyes were pink and red-rimmed. Then he looked at Michelle. 'What do you think about all this?'

'I think it's true, sir,' Michelle said. 'It's the only explanation that makes sense. You didn't want me to look too closely at the past because you were worried I'd find out something that might tarnish Harris's reputation. You suspected he was bent, you knew he gave Fiorino a wide berth in exchange for information, and something about the Graham Marshall case bothered you. You didn't want it stirring up again because you didn't know what would come to the surface.'

'What next?' Shaw asked.

'There'll have to be a report. I'm not going to bury this. I'll report my findings and any conclusions that can be drawn to the ACC. After that, it's up to him. There might be media interest.'

'And John's memory?'

Michelle shrugged. 'I don't know. If it all comes out, if people believe it, then his reputation will take a bit of a knock.'

'The lad's family?'

'It'll be hard for them, too. But is it any better than not knowing?'

'And me?'

'Maybe it's time to retire,' Banks said. 'You must be long past due.'

Shaw snorted, then coughed. He lit another cigarette and reached for his drink. 'Maybe you're right.' His gaze went from Banks to Michelle and back. 'I should have known it would mean big trouble the minute those bones were found. There wasn't much, you know, in those

notebooks. It was just like what you said. A hint here, a
lead there.'

'But there was enough,' said Banks. 'And, let's face it,
you know as well as I do that in that sort of investigation
you first look close and hard at the immediate family and
circle. If anybody had done that, they'd have found one or
two points of interest, some lines of enquiry that just
weren't followed. You dig deepest close to home. Nobody
bothered. That in itself seems odd enough.'

'Because John steered the investigation?'

'Yes. It must have been a much smaller division back
then, wasn't it? He'd have had close to absolute power
over it.'

Shaw hung his head again. 'Oh, nobody questioned Jet
Harris's judgement, that was for certain.' He looked up.
'I've got cancer,' he said, glancing towards Michelle.
'That's why I've been taking so much time off. Stomach.'
He grimaced. 'There's not much they can do. Anyway,
maybe retirement isn't such a bad idea.' He laughed.
'Enjoy my last few months gardening or stamp collecting
or something peaceful like that.'

Banks didn't know what to say. Michelle said, 'I'm
sorry.'

Shaw looked at her and scowled. 'You've no reason to
be. It won't make a scrap of difference to you whether I
live or die. Come to think of it, your life will be a lot easier
without me.'

'Even so . . .'

Shaw looked at Banks again. 'I wish you'd never come
back down here, Banks,' he said. 'Why couldn't you stay
up in Yorkshire and shag a few sheep?'

'You wouldn't understand.'

'Oh, wouldn't I? Don't you be too sure I'm as corrupt

as you think I am. Now if you're not going to charge me or beat me up, why don't the two of you just bugger off and leave me alone?'

Banks and Michelle looked at one another. There was nothing else to say to Shaw, so they left. Back in the car, Banks turned to Michelle and said, 'Do you believe him?'

'About not being responsible for the burglary and the van?'

'Yes.'

'I think so. He seemed genuinely horrified by the idea. What reason has he to lie about it now?'

'It's a serious crime. That's reason enough. But I think you're right. I don't think he was behind it. He was just doing his best to protect Harris's reputation.'

'Then are you thinking who I'm thinking?'

Banks nodded. 'Rupert Mandeville.'

'Shall we pay him a visit?'

'You want me along?'

Michelle looked at Banks and said, 'Yes. I feel we're getting near the end. Graham Marshall was your friend. You deserve to be there. I'd just like to stop off at the station and check a few things out first.'

'He won't tell us anything, you know.'

Michelle smiled. 'We'll see about that. It certainly won't do any harm to yank his chain a bit.'

19

It didn't take Annie long to drive to Harrogate and find the small terraced house off the Leeds Road. Vernon Anderson answered the door and, looking puzzled, invited her into his spartan living room. She admired the framed Vermeer print over the fireplace and settled down in one of the two armchairs.

'I see you have an eye for a good painting,' Annie said.

'Art appreciation must run in the family,' said Vernon. 'Though I confess I'm not as much of a reader as our Lauren is. I'd rather see a good film any day.'

On the low table under the window a couple of lottery tickets rested on a newspaper open at the racing page, some of the horses with red rings around their names.

'Any luck today?' Annie asked.

'You know what it's like,' Vernon said with an impish grin. 'You win a little, then you lose a little.' He sat on the sofa and crossed his legs.

Vernon Anderson didn't look much like his sister, Annie noted. He had dark hair, short tight curls receding a little at the temples, and he was thickset, with a muscular upper body and rather short legs. With his long lashes, dimples and easy charm, though, she imagined he would be quite successful with the opposite sex. Not that any of those things did much for her. If there was any resemblance, it was in the eyes; Vernon's were the same pale blue as Lauren's. He wore jeans and a T-shirt advertising Guinness. And sandals over white socks.

'What's all this about?'

'I'm looking into the kidnapping and murder of Luke Armitage,' Annie said. 'Your sister was his teacher.'

'Yes, I know. She's very upset about it.'

'Did you ever meet Luke?'

'Me? No. I'd heard of him, of course; of his father, anyway.'

'Martin Armitage?'

'That's right. I've won a few bob on teams he played for over the years.' Vernon grinned.

'But you never met Luke?'

'No.'

'Did your sister tell you much about him?'

'She talked about school sometimes,' Vernon said. 'She might have mentioned him.'

'In what context?'

'As one of her pupils.'

'But not how exceptional he was and that she gave him private tuition?'

'No.' Vernon's eyes narrowed. 'Where are we going here?'

'Lauren said she was visiting you the day Luke disappeared. That'd be a week ago last Monday. Is that true?'

'Yes. Look, I've already been through all this with the other detective, the one who came by a few days ago.'

'I know,' said Annie. 'That was one of the locals helping us out. It's not always possible to get away. I'm sorry to bother you with it, but do you think you could bear to go through it again with me?'

Vernon folded his arms. 'I suppose so. If you think it's necessary.'

'If you don't mind.'

'It's just as I told the chap the other day. We had rather too much to drink and Lauren stayed over.' He patted the sofa. 'It's comfortable enough. Safer than trying to drive.'

'Admirable,' said Annie. People always seemed to make nervous comments about drinking and driving when police officers were around, as if that were the only crime they had time to pursue, all they were interested in. 'Where were you drinking?'

'Where?'

'Which pub?'

'Oh, I see. We didn't go to a pub. She came here for dinner and we had wine.'

'What kind?'

'Just an Australian Chardonnay. On sale at Sainsbury's.'

'Did your sister visit you often?'

'Fairly often. Though I can't see what that's got to do with anything. Our father's ill and mother's not coping too well. We had a lot to talk about.'

'Yes. I know about the Alzheimer's. I'm sorry to hear it.'

Vernon's jaw dropped. 'You know? Lauren told you?'

'It's surprising the information you pick up sometimes in this job. Anyway, I just wanted to make sure I'd got all the times right, for the record, you know. You'd be amazed if you knew how much of our job is just paperwork.'

Vernon smiled. 'Well, as I remember, she arrived at about six o'clock, and that was it. We ate at around half-past seven.'

'What did you cook?'

'Venison in white wine. From Nigella Lawson.'

It didn't sound very appetizing to a vegetarian such as

Annie, but to each his own, she thought. 'And no doubt there was a fair bit of wine to wash it down with?'

'A couple of bottles. That's why Lauren ended up staying. That and the Grand Marnier.'

'Liqueurs, too. You were really pushing the boat out.'

'I'm afraid we both got a bit upset. Over Father. Lauren had paid a brief visit home at half-term and he hadn't recognized her. I know alcohol doesn't help solve problems, but one does tend to reach for it in times of trouble.'

'Of course,' said Annie. 'So you went to bed around what time?'

'Me? I'm not sure. It's a bit of a blur. Probably around midnight.'

'And your sister?'

'I don't know how late she stayed up.'

'But she did stay all night?'

'Of course.'

'How do you know?'

'I remember going to the toilet once. You have to go through the living room. She was asleep on the sofa then.'

'What time was that?'

'I don't know. I didn't look at my watch. Dark, though.'

'But she could have been gone for a few hours and returned, couldn't she?'

'I'd have heard her.'

'Are you certain? If you'd had that much to drink you probably slept quite heavily.'

'Don't forget, we *both* had too much to drink.'

'Did she receive any phone calls during the evening?'

'No.'

'What time did she leave?'

'About eleven o'clock the following morning.'

'It must have been a bit of a rough morning for you at work, after all that drink. Or did you take the day off?'

'I'm presently unemployed, if it's any of your business. And I can handle the drink. I'm not an alcoholic, you know.'

'Of course not.' Annie paused for a moment. 'Did you ever get any hints that Lauren's relationship with Luke might have been a bit more than the normal teacher–pupil one?'

'I certainly did not.'

'She never talked about him in an affectionate way?'

'I've had quite enough of this,' Vernon said. 'It's one thing checking up on times, but quite another to suggest that my sister had some sort of affair with this boy.' He stood up. 'Look, I've told you what you want to know. Now why don't you just go and leave me alone.'

'What's wrong, Mr Anderson?'

'Nothing's wrong.'

'You seem a bit agitated, that's all.'

'Well, wouldn't you feel agitated if someone came into your house and started flinging accusations around?'

'What accusations? I'm simply trying to make certain that your sister didn't see Luke Armitage the night he was killed. Can't you see how important this is, Vernon? If she did see him, he might have told her something. She might have had some idea of where he was going, who he was seeing.'

'I'm sorry. I still can't help. Lauren was here all night.'

Annie sighed. 'All right, then. Just one more thing before I leave you in peace.'

'What?'

'I understand you have a criminal record.'

Vernon reddened. 'I wondered when that would come

out. Look, it was a long time ago. I forged my boss's signature on a cheque. I'm not proud of it. It was a stupid thing to do, okay, but I was desperate. I paid the price.'

'Well, that's all right, then, isn't it,' said Annie, who was thinking it was amazing what people would do when they were desperate. 'Thanks for your time, Mr Anderson.'

Vernon said nothing, just slammed the door behind her. Annie had noticed a bookie's on the main road, just around the corner from Vernon's street. She glanced at her watch. Time for a quick call before it closed. In her experience, bookies' shops were always full of smoke, so she took a deep breath and went inside.

•

If this was the face of evil, then it was remarkably bland, Banks thought as he and Michelle were ushered into Rupert Mandeville's presence by a young man who looked more like a clerk than a butler. In fact, Mandeville reminded Banks of the old prime minister, Edward Heath, who came to lead the party in opposition in 1965. Casually dressed in white cricket trousers, a cream shirt open at the collar, and a mauve V-necked pullover, he had the same slightly startled, slightly befuddled, look about him as Heath, the same silver hair and pinkish skin. Why was it, Banks wondered, that every politician he had ever seen had skin like pink vinyl? Were they born that way?

The sheepskin rug was gone, replaced by a carpet with a complex Middle Eastern design, but the fireplace was the same one as in Graham's photograph. Being in the room where the picture had been taken all those years ago made Banks shiver. What else had happened here? Had Graham been involved in sex acts, too? With Mandeville? He realized that he would probably never know.

Reconstructing the past after so long was as faulty and unreliable a process as memory itself.

At least they now had some idea how Mandeville knew about the progress of Michelle's investigation, even if they couldn't prove anything. According to a local reporter Michelle had rung from the station, Mandeville had spies everywhere; it was how he had managed to survive so long in such a ruthless world as politics. It was also rumoured that he had close contacts within the police force, though no names were mentioned. That must have been how he knew so much about the investigation into Graham's death, and the threat that it was beginning to pose for him.

Mandeville was courtesy personified, pulling out a chair for Michelle and offering refreshments, which they refused. 'It's been many years since I had a visit from the police,' he said. 'How can I help you?'

'Would Geoff Talbot's visit have been the one you're thinking about?' Michelle asked. It was still her case, Banks knew, and he was only present because she had invited him; therefore, she got to ask the questions.

'I can't say I remember the young man's name.'

'You ought at least to remember the month and year: August 1965.'

'So long ago. How time flies.'

'And the reason for the visit.'

'It was a mistake. An apology was offered, and accepted.'

'By Detective Superintendent Harris?'

'Again, I must confess I don't remember the person's name.'

'Take my word for it.'

'Very well. Look, I sense a little hostility in your tone.

Can you please either tell me why you're here or leave?'

'We're here to ask you some questions relating to the Graham Marshall investigation.'

'Oh, yes. That poor boy whose skeleton was uncovered some days ago. Tragic. But I don't see how that has anything to do with me.'

'We're just tying up a few loose ends, that's all.'

'And I'm a loose end. How fascinating!' His glaucous eyes gleamed with mockery.

Banks took the photo from his briefcase and slid it across the table to Mandeville, who looked at it without expression.

'Interesting,' he said. 'But, again . . .'

'Do you recognize the boy?' Michelle asked.

'I'm afraid I don't.'

'Do you recognize the fireplace?'

Mandeville glanced towards his own Adam fireplace and smiled at her. 'I'd be a liar if I said I don't,' he said. 'Though I hardly imagine it's the only one of its kind in existence.'

'I think it's unique enough for our purposes,' Michelle said.

'Photographs can be faked, you know.'

Michelle tapped the photo. 'Are you saying this is a forgery?'

'Of course. Unless someone has been using my house for illicit purposes in my absence.'

'Let's get back to 1965, when this photo was taken, in this room,' Michelle said. 'You were quite famous for your parties, weren't you?'

Mandeville shrugged. 'I was young, wealthy. What else was I to do but share it around a bit? Maybe I was foolish, too.'

'Parties that catered for every taste, including drugs, prostitutes and under-age sex partners, male and female.'

'Don't be absurd.'

'This boy was fourteen when that photo was taken.'

'And he was a friend of mine,' said Banks, catching Mandeville's eye and holding his gaze.

'Then I'm sorry for your loss,' said Mandeville, 'but I still don't see what it has to do with me.'

'You had him killed,' said Michelle.

'I did what? I'd be careful, if I were you, young lady, going around making accusations like that.'

'Or what? You'll have your chauffeur break into my flat again, or try to run me over?'

Mandeville raised his eyebrows. 'I was actually going to warn you about the possibility of slander.'

'I did a bit of homework before I came out here,' Michelle said. 'Checked into the background of your employees. Derek Janson, your chauffeur, served a prison sentence for burglary fifteen years ago. He came to be regarded as somewhat of an expert at picking locks. I'm sure he knows how to drive a van, too.'

'I know about Derek's background,' Mandeville said. 'It's very difficult for ex-convicts to get employment. Surely you can't fault me for doing my little bit for Derek's rehabilitation? I happen to trust him completely.'

'I'm sure you do. When the investigation into Graham Marshall's disappearance was reopened, after we found his remains and discovered that he had been murdered, you did everything in your power to put me off.'

'Why would I want to do that?'

'Because he was using the photo to blackmail you, and you asked Carlo Fiorino to take care of him. You paid Fiorino well for his various services, so he obliged.'

'This is absurd. You have no evidence for any of this.'

'We've got the photograph,' Banks said.

'As I said before, photographs can be faked.'

'They can be authenticated, too,' Banks said.

Mandeville stared at them, assessing the damage. Finally, he stood up, put his hands on the table, palms down and leaned forward. 'Well,' he said, 'that's quite a story the two of you have concocted. It's a pity that none of it will stand up in court, or anywhere else for that matter.'

'Maybe you're right,' Michelle said. 'But you still have to admit that it doesn't look good. Some mud's bound to stick.'

'I'm not without influence, you know.'

'Is that a threat?'

'I don't stoop to threats.'

'No, you get someone else to do that for you.'

'What do you intend to do now?'

'Whatever I can to make sure you pay for what you did. For a start, we'll have a nice chat with Mr Janson.'

Mandeville walked over and leaned against the fireplace, smiling. 'Derek won't tell you anything.'

'You never know. We're not without influence, either, especially with ex-cons. Then there's Geoff Talbot's note-book. Jet Harris didn't bother to remove that from the archives. No reason to. There was no investigation.'

'I don't know what you're talking about.'

'Names,' said Banks. 'Talbot made a note of the names of the people he talked to when he came up here. I'm sure if we dig around a bit, we'll find one or two people who remember the old days: partygoers, perhaps, or club patrons.'

Mandeville's face darkened and he went back to sit at

the table. 'I'm warning you,' he said, 'if you attempt to spread these vicious lies about me, I'll have your jobs.'

But Michelle was already out of the room, striding towards the front door.

Banks took the opportunity of a few seconds alone with Mandeville to lean in close, smile and lower his voice. 'And if DI Hart so much as trips on a banana skin, I'll be right back here to rip out your spine and shove it down your throat. Your lordship.'

He couldn't swear to it, but judging by the change in Mandeville's expression, he thought he had got his point across.

•

It was already the evening of a long day, and the shadows were lengthening when Lauren Anderson led Annie into the book-lined living room. Classical music was playing, a violin concerto, but Annie didn't recognize it. Banks would have done, she thought. Lauren was barefoot, wearing ice-blue jeans and a white sleeveless top. Her shoulders were pale and freckled, like her face. Her mane of auburn hair was fastened behind her head by a leather barrette. 'What do you want?' she asked. 'Have you caught them?'

'I think so. But first sit down and listen to what I have to say. You can correct me if I'm wrong about anything.'

'I don't know what you mean.'

'You will in a minute. Sit down, Lauren.' Annie crossed her legs and leaned back in the armchair. She had worked out how to approach Lauren on the drive back from Harrogate, then made a couple of phone calls and picked up DC Winsome Jackman, whom she had instructed to stay outside in the car for the time being. She didn't expect any trouble, and it would be easier for her to talk to Lauren alone. 'We know where Luke was shortly before he was killed,' she began. 'Did he ever mention a girl called Liz Palmer to you?'

'No. Why?'

'Are you sure? She meant a lot to Luke.'

Lauren shook her head. 'No, that can't be true. I don't believe you.'

'Why not, Lauren? Why can't it be true?'

'Luke . . . he didn't . . . he wasn't like that. He was devoted to art.'

'Oh, come off it, Lauren. He was just a randy adolescent, like any other. This Liz was a bit older than him and she—'

'No! Stop it. I won't listen to this.'

'What's the problem, Lauren?'

'I won't have you tarnishing Luke's memory.'

'Tarnishing? What's so wrong about a fifteen-year-old boy losing his virginity to an older woman? It's a time-honoured tradition, even if it is technically having sex with a minor. Who cares about a few petty rules and regulations? Especially if it's the boy who's under-age and not the woman. At least we know now Luke got to enjoy the pleasures of sex before he died.'

'I don't know why,' Lauren said, looking into Annie's eyes, 'but you're lying to me. There is no "Liz".'

'Yes there is. I can introduce you.'

'No.'

'What is it, Lauren? Jealous?'

'Luke meant a lot to me. You know he did. He was so talented.'

'It was more than that, though, wasn't it?'

'What do you mean?'

'You were lovers, weren't you?'

Lauren hesitated for a moment, then said, 'What if we were? Are you going to arrest me for that?'

'No. I'm going to arrest you for murder.'

Lauren jerked upright. 'You can't be serious.'

'I'm serious all right. You see, Liz and her boyfriend live about five minutes' walk away from here, and Luke was distraught when he left their flat. I asked myself, where would he go? Maybe it took me too long to come up with the right answer, the *only* possible answer, but that was because of the clever smokescreen you put up. The kidnapping. We thought we were looking for a man or someone closer to home. But Luke couldn't have gone home because the last bus had gone and we checked all the taxis. We suspected his music teacher, Alastair Ford, too. But Luke couldn't have gone to his house because it's so remote, and he had no means of getting there. That leaves you, Lauren. Luke didn't have a wide circle of friends and acquaintances. Also, he was very upset. You're the one he talked to about his emotional problems. How long had you been lovers, Lauren?'

Lauren sighed. 'Near the end of term. It just happened. It was so . . . so natural. I wasn't trying to seduce him or anything like that.' Annie could see tears clouding her eyes. 'We were looking at some pictures. Pre-Raphaelites. He remarked on my resemblance to one of the models.'

'Elizabeth Siddal, Dante Gabriel Rossetti's first wife. You do look a lot like her, Lauren. Or a lot like the paintings of her. A typical Pre-Raphaelite beauty, as someone said.'

'You know?'

'I should have made the connection sooner,' Annie said. 'My father's an artist, and I do a bit of painting myself. I've picked up a thing or two over the years.'

'But how could you have known?'

'We found Luke's shoulder bag at the other flat, too. I read over his recent writings and found a lot of classical references I didn't understand. One thing I did understand is that they were of a sexual nature, very intimate, and they stressed a kind of Pre-Raphaelite look. There were also references to Ophelia, but I don't think it was Shakespeare Luke had in mind. It was John Everett Millais. He painted Ophelia and used Elizabeth Siddal as a model. She caught pneumonia lying in a tepid bath every day posing as Ophelia floating down the river. Very romantic. But what I don't understand is why. Why did you do it, Lauren? Why did you kill him? Was he going to leave you?'

'You don't understand anything. I didn't kill him. You've got no proof. I've got an alibi. Talk to Vernon.'

'I've already talked to Vernon,' said Annie, 'and I'd trust him about as far as I could throw him. Your brother lied for you, Lauren. Only natural. But I'm willing to bet that he's the one who helped you get rid of the body. You couldn't have done it all by yourself. And he's the one who hatched the kidnapping scheme. That had all the hallmarks of an afterthought. It wasn't the reason for Luke's disappearance and death. Your brother thought he'd try and cash in on it and he's small-time enough to ask for only ten thousand. Besides, you'd probably talked about Luke and told him the family wasn't quite as wealthy as people assumed. He's a gambler, Lauren. And a loser. He needs the money. I talked to his bookie. Your brother's in debt up to his eyeballs. Did you even know what he'd done after he'd helped you?'

Lauren looked down into her lap. Her fingers were

twined together, grasping so tightly all the knuckles were white. She shook her head. 'I don't believe Vernon would do anything like that.'

'But you must have suspected, after you heard about the kidnap demand?'

'It confused me. I didn't know what was going on. Maybe I had my suspicions, I don't know. I was too upset to think about it.'

'The thing is,' Annie went on, 'that our Scene-of-Crimes Officers found minute traces of blood on the wall where Luke was shoved over into Hallam Tarn. Minute, but enough to provide a DNA profile. I think that profile would match you or your brother. I'm also certain that when our men come in here and go over your place, they'll find traces of Luke's blood. Now that might not be conclusive in itself, as we know Luke was punched in the nose before he came here, but it's all starting to add up, Lauren.'

Lauren looked at Annie, her eyes red-rimmed and almost unbearably sad. 'I didn't kill him,' she said, in a small, distant voice. 'I would never have harmed Luke. I loved him.'

'What happened, Lauren?'

Lauren reached for her cigarettes and lit one. Then she eyed Annie sadly and began her story.

•

'Do you think I might have a word alone with your husband?' Banks asked Mrs Marshall at her house that evening.

'Bill? I don't know what he can tell you,' she said. 'You know he can't talk.'

'There might be one or two little things.' Banks looked

at the invalid who, judging by the hard expression in his eyes, certainly knew he was being talked about. 'Can he write?'

'Yes,' said Mrs Marshall. 'But he can't hold a pencil properly. He can only grasp it in his fist and scribble a few letters.'

'That'll do,' said Banks. 'Can you get me a pad and pencil, if it's no trouble?'

Mrs Marshall brought Banks a lined pad and a pencil from the sideboard drawer.

'Come on,' said Michelle, taking her arm and leading her towards the kitchen. 'Let's go make some tea. I've got a few things to tell you.' Banks and Michelle had agreed on a sanitized version of events to tell Mrs Marshall. If the media dug too deeply and the story hit the news, then she might find out more than she wanted about her son's life and death, but that was for the future. Now, maybe it was enough for Michelle to tell her that Donald Bradford killed Graham because he found out something about Bradford's illegal activities.

When they had gone into the kitchen and closed the door, Banks put the pad and pencil on Bill Marshall's knee and settled in front of him, gazing into the expressionless eyes. 'I think you know why I want to talk to you,' he said.

Bill Marshall made no sign that he understood.

'You used to spar with Reggie and Ronnie Kray in your younger days,' he said. 'Then, when you came up here, you fell in with Carlo Fiorino and did a few strong-arm jobs for him. Am I right? Can you nod or write something down?'

Bill Marshall did nothing.

'Okay, so that's how you want to play it,' Banks said.

'Fine. I'm not saying you had anything to do with Graham's death. You didn't. You'd never have done anything like that. But you knew who did it, didn't you?'

Bill Marshall just stared at Banks.

'See, the trouble with people like you, Bill, is they insist on working outside the law. You've no use for coppers, have you? Never have had, I shouldn't think. Just like my own dad. Want to know what I think happened? Well, I'll tell you anyway. I think Donald Bradford just wasn't cut out to be a killer of young boys. I don't think he had much choice in the matter, though. Fiorino pushed him into it. After all, Graham was *his* responsibility, and Graham was in a position to do a lot of serious damage. There was just too much at stake. Not just the empire as it existed then, but the future. The city was expanding, becoming a new town. Soon it would double in population. What an opportunity for a man like Fiorino. He supplied what people always seem to want, for a good price. Are you with me so far?'

Marshall just glared at Banks. A little drool slid down his stubbly chin.

'Fiorino had no use for the law, either, unless it was in his pay, so he used other people to do his dirty work. Shortly after the killing, Bradford sold up and moved out. Fiorino didn't like that. Didn't like people escaping his control, being out of his line of sight. Especially if they knew as much as Bradford did and were fast becoming unstable and unreliable. Bradford was guilt-ridden by what he had done. Also, I think he took some of Fiorino's goods with him, though that's just a minor matter. What really counted was that Bradford was out of sight and untrustworthy. And he knew too much.'

Marshall still showed no reaction. Banks could hear

muffled voices from the kitchen. 'So what does he do when he has a problem with Bradford? Well, he could pay for a hit, I suppose, and that's one option. But he knows you. That's an easier one. He knows that whatever you do, you'll do it yourself, you won't go running to the police. So he tells you that Bradford killed your son, though not on *his* orders. He convinces you that Bradford was a pervert. He also gives you Bradford's address. Easy. All he had to do next was leave the rest up to you. Am I right so far, Bill?'

Banks could tell by the anger and hatred in Bill Marshall's eyes that he was right. 'You went up to Carlisle, didn't you? Probably told everyone you were looking for work. Then you broke into Donald Bradford's flat and waited for him to come home. You knew Bradford was a tough customer, so you attacked him from behind with a cosh. I don't blame you, Bill. The man murdered your son. I'd want to do the same to anyone who harmed either of my children. But you let your wife suffer all those years. You *knew* Graham was dead and you knew who killed him. Maybe you didn't know where the body was, but I'll bet you could have found out. Instead, you went up there and murdered Bradford and said nothing to your wife or your daughter. All these years they've lived not knowing what happened to Graham. That's unforgivable, Bill.' Banks nodded towards the pad. 'What do you have to say about that? Come on, tell me something.'

Marshall held his gaze for a while, then grasped the pencil, moved his hand with difficulty and scrawled on the pad. When he had done, he handed it to Banks. There were three words in capital letters: FUCK OFF COPPER.

•

'He came to me, like you said,' Lauren Anderson began. 'He was in a terrible state. He was upset because . . . well, you know why. I tried to calm him down and we went to . . . We just lay down on the bed together and I held him. I'd already realized I had to end it. I just hadn't been able to find the courage. But I knew that it couldn't go on. Someone would find out eventually and that would be it. My career, reputation . . . everything. A fifteen-year-old boy and a twenty-nine-year-old woman. Taboo. I thought I'd got him calm enough, so I started talking about it, you know, how we should probably cool things for a while.'

'Did he tell you he'd been smoking cannabis earlier?'

'Cannabis? No. He never told me that. But that must be why he seemed so disoriented and excitable. I'd never seen him like that before. He scared me.'

'How did he react when you told him you wanted to finish the affair?' Annie asked, remembering that it hadn't been too long ago when she had told Banks the same thing.

'He didn't want to accept it. He said he couldn't bear to lose me.' Lauren started crying. 'He said he'd kill himself.'

'What happened next?'

She dabbed her eyes with a tissue. 'He stormed off to the bathroom. I gave him a couple of minutes, then I heard all the things falling out of the cupboard into the sink, glass breaking, so I went after him.'

'Was the bathroom door locked?'

'No.'

'He was after the Valium?'

'You know?'

'We know he took some Valium shortly before he died, yes.'

'I have a prescription. But I suppose you know that, too?'

Annie nodded. 'I checked.'

'He had the bottle open, and he poured some tablets into his hand and swallowed them. I went to him and struggled with him over the bottle. We fought, pulling and pushing each other, and then he went down. Just like that. He was in his socks, and the floor tiles can be slippery. His feet just went from under him and he hit his head on the side of the bath. I did what I could. I tried to revive him, mouth to mouth. I checked for a pulse and listened for his heartbeat, and then I even tried holding a mirror to his mouth. But it was no use. He was dead. So much blood.'

'What did you do then?'

'I didn't know what to do. I panicked. I knew if any of it came out I'd be finished. I didn't know where to turn, so I called Vernon. He said he'd come right away and not to do anything until he got here. The rest you know.'

'What happened to Luke's mobile?'

'It fell out of his pocket in the car. Vernon took it.'

That explained the call to Armitage's mobile. Vernon had looked up Martin's number on Luke's phone. He wasn't to know that Luke would be unlikely to call his stepfather for anything. Vernon could easily have driven up to Eastvale and made the call there to avoid detection. Harrogate wasn't that far away.

'*Did* you know about the ransom demand?'

Lauren shook her head. 'No. I'd never agree to anything like that. And as I said, I was too upset to think about it. If anything, I thought it must be some sort of cruel practical joke. I'm so sorry for what happened.' '

reached out and grasped Annie's wrist. 'You've got to believe me. I'd never have harmed Luke. I loved him. Maybe if I hadn't been so insensitive, so selfish, and not tried to end it when he was so upset, or just held him the way he wanted, it might not have happened. I've relived that moment over and over again ever since it happened. I can't sleep. I don't know how I'm going to go back to work. Nothing seems to matter any more.'

Annie stood up.

'What are you going to do now?'

'I'm going to call in my partner from the car outside, and we're going to make sure you know your rights before we take you to the police station to make a formal statement. We'll also be sending a message to the Harrogate police to pick up your brother.'

'What's going to happen to me?'

'I don't know, Lauren,' Annie said. Again, she was feeling shitty about doing her job. Harden up, she told herself. Maybe Lauren Anderson didn't deliberately kill Luke, but she was at least partly responsible for his death, along with Liz Palmer and Ryan Milne. All adults who should have known better than to tamper with the feelings of a confused and disturbed fifteen year old. All of whom were selfish and used Luke for their own ends. Even if that end, at least in Lauren's case, was love. A romantic imagination and adolescent lust could be a dangerous combination.

But maybe, Annie thought, if she *didn't* feel pity for a woman in Lauren's position, then she would lose some of her humanity. One of the things working with Banks had taught her was how to do the job without becoming callous and cynical, the way she had been going before she met him. Lauren would probably get off quite lightly,

Annie told herself. If Luke had died during a struggle, the object of which was to stop him taking an overdose of Valium, and if Lauren had not known of her brother's botched ransom demand, then she wouldn't get a very stiff sentence.

Lauren would lose her job, though, and, like Norman Wells, she would become a pariah for some – the seductress and corrupter of youth. And the family would suffer – Robin and Martin – as it was all dragged into the open. Because this would be a high-profile trial, no doubt about it. Neil Byrd's son, a famous model and a sports star. Not a chance of escaping the media circus. It was a damn shame they couldn't prosecute Liz and Ryan, Annie thought as she walked Lauren, head hung low, out to the car. They were at least as much to blame for what happened as Lauren was, if not more so. But it wasn't her judgement to make.

•

'Jet Harris *bent*? I can't believe it,' said Arthur Banks in the Coach and Horses early that evening. Banks had dragged him out there to tell him the full story, and they sat over their pints in the dreary, half-empty pub. Banks felt a craving for nicotine rush through his cells like a desperate need for air, but he pushed it aside. One day at a time. One craving at a time. It passed. People said the cravings got less and less powerful as time went on. But others said you were never rid of the habit. He knew people who had started again after they'd been off for ten years. One day at a time.

Arthur Banks stared at his son in disbelief. 'Is this going to come out?' he asked.

'Probably,' said Banks. 'We don't actually hand our

reports to the press, but they have their ways. Depends on the media interest.'

'Oh, there'll be media interest around here, all right. Jet Harris, homo and bent copper.' He eyed Banks warily. 'You sure you're not going to hush it up, then?'

'Dad,' said Banks. 'We don't go in for cover-ups. At least *I* don't, and nor does DI Hart. This investigation has cost her a lot. She's only been at the division a couple of months and here she is, debunking the legend. Imagine how popular that's going to make her around the place.' It had nearly cost Michelle her life, too, Banks thought. She would be safe from now on, he was certain, and not because of his melodramatic threat. Now Mandeville knew there were more people involved, he could hardly scare or kill off everyone. He would just have to take his chances that time had hidden his secrets.

'Why are you telling *me*?' Arthur Banks asked.

Banks sipped some beer. 'Dad, you and mum have never really given me a chance, you know, ever since I joined the force. You've always pointed out the negative side of the job. I just wanted you to know that some of us aren't crooked, that some of us take our work seriously. Even if it never comes out in public, at least *you'll* know the truth, and you'll know *I* told you.'

Arthur Banks paused for a moment, looking his son in the eye, then he said, 'And did you also find out what happened to your friend Graham after all these years?'

'Yes. Well, DI Hart did most of the work. I just filled in the blanks.' Banks leaned forward. 'But yes, Dad, I found out. It's what I do. I don't go around waving rolls of fivers at striking miners, I don't beat up suspects in the cells, I don't botch investigations into murdered black youths, and I don't steal confiscated drugs and sell them back on the street. Mostly, I push paper. Sometimes I catch murderers. Sometimes I fail, but I always do my damnedest.'

'So who did it?'

Banks told him.

'Donald Bradford! You'd have thought that would've been the first place they'd look.'

'That's what made us suspect some sort of mis-direction.'

'And Rupert Mandeville. That'll make a nice headline.'

'If we can pin anything on him. Remember, it was a long time ago, and he's hardly likely to confess.'

'Even so . . . your pal Graham was up to no good, wasn't he?'

'Why do you say that?'

'I don't know. He always seemed a bit shifty to me, that's all. Like his father.'

'Well, Graham wasn't exactly walking the straight and narrow, but that's no excuse for killing him.'

'Course not.' Banks senior fell silent for a moment, contemplating his son through narrowed eyes. Then he let slip a thin smile. 'You've stopped smoking, haven't you?'

'I wasn't going to tell anyone.'

'There's not much you can slip past your own father.'

'Dad, have you been listening to me? All I've been trying to demonstrate to you all these years,' Banks went on, 'is that I've been doing a decent, honest day's work, just like you did.'

'And Jet Harris, local legend, was a bent copper?'

'Yes.'

'And you're going to expose him.'

'Something like that.'

'Well,' said Arthur Banks, rubbing his hands together. 'That's all right, then. You'll be having another pint, I suppose? On me, this time.'

Banks looked at his watch. 'Better make it a half,' he said. 'I've got a date.'

> *Was it the age of my innocence,*
> *Or was it the lost land of Oz?*
> *Was it only a foolish illusion,*
> *The summer that never was?*

> *Did I walk through the fields with the child in my*
>   *arms*
> *And the golden wheat over my head?*
> *Did I feel my heart breaking under the weight?*
> *Was my sweet sleeping boychild a burden, like*
>   *lead?*

> *I remember him crying the day he was born*
> *And his hand like a spider that wouldn't let go*
> *And he wouldn't let go and he wouldn't let go*
> *And the pain tore my heart out and filled me with*
>   *woe.*

> *Can a dreamer take hold of reality*
> *And become a responsible man?*
> *Can a killer become a lover*
> *Or is he forever damned?*

> *You can't follow me where I'm going now*
> *And you can't go to the places I've been*
> *Don't listen to the demons I've listened to*
> *Or look into the darkness I've seen.*

> *There's a field and a boy and the tall golden*
> *   wheat*
> *And eternity held in a day*
> *But it's so hard to hold and it's so hard to reach*
> *And forever rushing away.*
> *Was it the age of my innocence,*
> *Or was it the lost land of Oz?*
> *Was it only a foolish illusion,*
> *The summer that never was?*

Banks lay in bed late that night listening to Neil Byrd's CD on his Walkman after dinner with Michelle and a phone call from Annie. 'The Summer that Never Was' was the first song on the CD, though the liner notes said it was the last song Byrd had recorded, just weeks before his suicide. As Banks listened to the subtle interplay of words and music, all set against acoustic guitar and stand-up bass, with flute and a violin weaving in and out, like Van Morrison's *Astral Weeks*, he felt the despair and defeat of the singer. He didn't understand the song, didn't know what all the tortured phrases meant, only that they were tortured.

Here was a man at the end of his tether. And he was thinking of his child, or of his own childhood. Or both.

Banks couldn't even begin to imagine what this had meant to Luke Armitage when, his mind disoriented with strong cannabis, he had heard it for the first time in Liz and Ryan's flat. Annie was right. How callous could the bastards be? Or stupid. It no doubt never even entered their addled minds what damage they might be doing. All they could think of was opening up Luke's mind to his father's music to further their careers, and everyone knew that drugs opened the doors of perception.

Banks remembered the Rimbaud quote written in silver on Luke's black wall: 'Le Poëte se fait voyant par un long, immense et raisonné dérèglement de tous les sens.'

Well, had Luke become a seer? What had he seen? Was he trying to kill himself with the diazepam, or was he just trying to stop the pain?

In Banks's mind, Luke Armitage and Graham Marshall became one. They might have died in different ways for different reasons – not to mention in different times – but they were just two kids lost in a grown-up world, where needs and emotions were bigger than theirs, stronger and more complex than they could comprehend. Graham had tried to play the big leagues at their own game and lost, while Luke had tried to find love and acceptance in all the wrong places. He had lost, too. Accident though his death was, according to Annie, it was a tragic accident made up of many acts, each one of which was like a door closing behind Luke as he moved towards his fate.

Banks put the CD player on the bedside table, turned over and tried to go to sleep. He didn't think it would be easy. The song had left him with such a feeling of desolation and loneliness that he ached with need for someone to hold and found himself wishing he had stayed at Michelle's after their love-making. He almost took out his mobile and rang her, but it was past two in the morning, way too late. Besides, how would she react if he showed such neediness so early in their relationship? She'd probably run a mile, like Annie. And quite rightly.

He could hear his father snoring in the next room. At least there had been a reconciliation of sorts between the two of them. Though Arthur Banks would never actually admit anything, his attitude had changed since their drink together that evening. Banks could tell that his father had been proud of him for his success in solving Graham's murder – though he insisted Michelle had done most of the work – and for not trying to cover up Jet Harris's role. Proud for perhaps the first time in his life.

How strange it was to be at home in his old bed. As he drifted towards sleep, he imagined his mother calling him for school in the morning: 'Hurry up, Alan, or you'll be late!' In his dream, he fastened his tie as he dashed downstairs for a quick bowl of cornflakes and a glass of milk before picking up his satchel and meeting the others out in the street. But when he walked out of the door, Dave and Paul and Steve and Graham all stood there waiting for him with the bat, the ball and the wickets. The sun shone in a bright blue sky and the air was warm and fragrant. There was no school. They were on holiday. They were going to play cricket on the rec. 'It's summer, you fool,' Graham said, and they all laughed at him. *The summer that never was.*